VOLUME IV

The Temple Buck Quartet: A Rocky Mountain Odyssey 1822-1837

Glory Days Gone Under

One trapper's personal chronicle
of the American Rocky Mountain
fur trade 1833-1837

EDWARD LOUIS HENRY

Christopher Matthews Publishing

www.christophermatthewspub.com
Bozeman, Montana

ALSO BY EDWARD LOUIS HENRY

The Temple Buck Quartet
A Rocky Mountain Odyssey

Volume I: Backbone of the World (1822-1824)
Volume II: Free Men (1824-1826)
Volume III: Shinin' Times! (1828-1833)
Volume IV: Glory Days Gone Under (1833-1837)

* * *

Poredevil's Beaver Tales

Glory Days Gone Under
One trapper's personal chronicle of the American Rocky Mountain fur trade
1833-1837

Copyright © 2014 by Edward Louis Henry

At the specific preference of the author, the publisher allowed this work to remain exactly as the author intended, verbatim, without editorial input.

Editor: Jeremy Soldevilla
Cover design by Armen Kojoyian
Engraving: T.D. Booth, *The Trapper's Last Shot*, ca.1830's, Library of Congress

ISBN: 978-1-938985-19-5

Published by

CHRISTOPHER MATTHEWS PUBLISHING

www.christophermatthewspub.com

Bozeman, Montana

Printed in the United States of America

For Gloria, without whom nothing would have happened, who never faltered in her faith and loving support, and for all the saddle tramps and buckskinners with whom I've been privileged to share a cookfire, swapping lies and sharing friendship, throughout my life.

Glory Days Gone Under

One Trapper's Personal Chronicle
of the American Rocky Mountain Fur Trade
& what cooked it's goose
1833 —1837
by
Temple Buck, Trapper

Euphemius Hobbes, Esq.
Editor

TABLE OF CONTENTS

It is with a certain sense of melancholy that I pen this preface to this final volume that chronicles the exploits and misadventures of Mister Temple Buck and his companions in the American Rocky Mountain fur trade from 1833 to 1837. It has been my dubious privilege to function as editor of three previous manuscripts penned by Mister Buck which describe his experiences in the American fur trade from its beginning in 1822 through the year 1833, published under the titles of *Backbone of the World, Free Men,* and *Shinin' Times!,* and now this fourth and final account, *Glory Days Gone Under,* which concerns the regrettable demise of that admirable adventure in the western wilderness of America. The author declares that no more books will be forthcoming.

My professional association with Mister Buck has often been a difficult and trying one, inasmuch as he has steadfastly refused to accept my guidance and advice in his choice of language, eschewing the cultured vocabulary and phrasing of the best models of contemporary American literature, preferring instead often to employ the common, frequently ribald, ungrammatical vernacular of ill-educated backwoodsmen. Although Mister Buck possesses a remarkable gift for mimicry in reproducing on paper the sounds of common American speech, I must deplore its use in a published work.

Mister Buck has also resisted my attempts to convince him to eliminate his unvarnished descriptions of certain human activity, especially between the sexes, that should never be committed to the printed page. The author insists, however, on "telling it like it is in the mountains" and often reminds me that it is he who controls the purse strings.

I include these remarks here as a warning to the unwary reader and so that I may not be considered guilty of abetting Mister Buck's recklessness in exposing innocent youth to his coarse observations. My literary counsel and attempts to beautify his homespun prose have come to naught. My professional efforts have been confined to matters of grammar and orthography and little else. Mister Temple Buck is solely responsible for the content of this book, as he is for his previous literary attempts.

Now that I have disclaimed any personal and professional responsibility for the content and quality of expression of this work, it is only fair to the author that I express here my reluctant admiration for the honesty of his narrative and the integrity of his descriptions of life and events as they actually occur in the primitive wilderness that has been Mister Buck's home for the past fifteen years. I recommend his books to any gentleman who wishes to acquaint himself with life and circumstances as they truly exist in the Rocky Mountain wilderness.

On the other hand, I caution the reader to exert every effort to prevent Mister Buck's questionable literary efforts from falling beneath the innocent gaze of women of refinement, especially unmarried young women and maiden ladies, whose tender sensibilities are certain to be offended, if not corrupted, by exposure to the author's unrestrained candor.

Euphemius Hobbes, Esq.

Editor

St. Louis, Missouri, 1838

This is the fourth and final volume of my personal account of the American Rocky Mountain fur trade as I saw it and lived it from the first get-go, when we ascended the Missouri River in a clumsy keelboat in 1822 until sensible trappers were forced to admit that beaver will never shine again after the 1837 rendezvous at Horse Creek. Those fifteen years were the most glorious adventure that any men in all of history ever lived and my only regret is that it could not have gone on forever.

Some men still refuse to believe it, naturally, insisting that "Beaver'll shine agin!" and I wish them well. I only wish that they were right.

I have titled this book *Glory Days Gone Under, 1833-1837* because that is what it is about, the last five years of the fur trade as we knew it and lived it and collected the scars to prove it. This is my last book. There will be no more. In completing this long narrative of my experience in the mountains I have fulfilled the promise I made to my mother before her death. My early years in the mountains are described in the first three books I wrote, *Backbone of the World 1822-1824, Free Men 1824-1826,* and *Shinin' Times! 1828-1833.* This one completes my fifteen-year chronicle of the American Rocky Mountain fur trade when it was a vital part of what made America great, before capricious fashion and our own short-sighted greed swept it into the dustbin of history.

I made that promise to my dying mother when I returned to my birthplace—Whynot, Ohio, nigh the Ohio River—after my first five years in the mountains. My schoolmarm mother was interested in everything, especially anything new. She never tired of hearing about my life in the Rockies, constantly coaxing one more story out of me about my fellow trappers, Indians, critters, weather in the mountains, or whatever. It was she, naturally, who taught me to read and write and instilled in me a love of learning. When her illness grew worse and the end was near, she wrung a promise from me that I would write a history of everything I did in the fur trade, a promise which I have done my best to keep. She didn't tell me to publish my scribbling in a book, but I reckon that doing so is further proof that I am keeping my promise to her.

If anybody ever bothers to read what I have written, I daresay it will put a smile on my mother's face, wherever she might be. If not, leastaways I honored my pledge to her.

Temple Buck, Trapper
St. Louis, Missouri, 1838

CHAPTER I
JUMPING OFF

Nothing in this world makes my heart big and enlivens my spirit like the feel of a good horse betwixt my thighs. Well, hardly anything, but such matters would have to wait until we reached our goal in the Shining Mountains, still several weeks off, as our packtrain plodded westwards from Missouri to the once-a-year trappers' rendezvous, its precise location still unknown to us. But wherever it might be, cherished old friends would be amongst the hundreds of trappers and Indians gathered there, especially nigh a score of men in my own trapping bunch, men grown dear to me as blood-kin ever could be, in the decade since we first glimpsed the snowy peaks of the Rocky Mountains, where we have plied the trapper's trade since the first giddyap in 1822. Women, too, the Indian wives of my comrades, and especially my four-year-old daughter Iris, orphaned by the death of my wife Rainbow two years earlier.

"Ye be lookin' proud as Lucifer, Temple Buck, astride that 'ere high-bred Kaintuck hoss o' your'n, lookin' like some ol' rich-as-hell nabob come out'n the East! Damn if ye don't!"

My pleasant thoughts of reunion evaporated, replaced by the homely mug of Black Harris, our seasoned guide and a consummate story-teller of outrageous fibs. "Reckon I do," I replied huffily. "An' you would, too, if ye owned a critter as fine as this'n!"

Harris ran his eyes over my tall sunburnt-black Kentucky-bred gelding, a full sixteen hands, deep of chest and barrel, sleek of hide and muscled like a prizefighter. "Reckon I mought at that," he allowed grudgingly. "Daresay ye paid a purty penny fer 'im, too."

"Reckon I did," I admitted, "but he's worth every copper I had to give for 'im. Besides, cash money ain't worth much where we're headin'."

"Ye allus did have an eye fer good hossflesh, Temple. I'll give ye that." Black returned his gaze to my mount and added admiringly, "'Pears that'n'll carry ye to hell an' back, once he larns his manners—an' in fine style, too." He fell silent for a spell before he asked, "Whatcha aim to call 'im?"

"Coffee," I replied, almost without thinking. Up to then I had simply called him Horse. "It'll do. He's black as sin an' strong as ye could wish for. Coffee it is!"

"It's a good 'un," Harris agreed. "Short an' sweet an' right fer color."

Just then, a call for Harris was relayed back amongst the hostlers leading the pack animals trudging in front of us. Without a word, our pilot touched spur to his mount and loped to the head of the column. I returned to my thoughts.

ȣ   ȣ   ȣ

There had been little time for calm reflection in the weeks before that moment, occupied as I was in getting my outfit together for the long haul to the mountains, equipping myself to resume my life as a trapper of fine furs, mostly beaver destined to become toppers perched upon the noggins of citified fops the world over. I needed just about everything. When I bade farewell to my companions and my daughter the previous fall and made my way to Saint Louis, I had little hope that I would ever see them again. I reckoned that what I thought was a pistol ball lodged nigh my heart would likely put a full stop to my personal paragraph before long, so I gave away everything I owned, except for my weapons, my journals, and a few items of clothing—horses, mules, saddles, traps and tools, books, trade goods, whatever anybody wanted. Which, naturally, was every last scrap. Settlement wares are highly-prized in the wilderness. Nothing goes to waste.

As it turned out, what we thought was a pistol ball was merely a pebble fired off a measly powder charge, hiding under a rib, nowheres near my heart, and handily removed by a first-rate Chinese medico, who patched me up and turned me loose within a week's time, leaving me with not much to do in Saint Louis for the next half-year, until I could return to the mountains with the annual packtrain headed for rendezvous. Which is how I came to write still one more book about my life in the Rocky Mountains as a beaver-trapping mountaineer during the years 1828 to 1832. I called that history *Shinin' Times!*, for those years of the beaver trade were the best we have ever seen, although much else of what happened during that time was far from what a body might have wished for.

My penchant for getting lead-poisoning is mostly responsible for my literary endeavors. I also wrote two other books about my life in the Rocky Mountain fur trade, from its commencement in 1822 up to the year 1826, whilst I was healing up from a charge of goose shot in my legs, which was donated by the man who believed he was my real father, but who meant to kill me anyways. I called those two histories *Backbone of the World* and *Free Men*. You can likely get copies of those books from a scholarly gentleman name of Euphemius Hobbes, who lives in Saint Louis nowadays. I am pretty sure that he still has plenty on hand.

Now it was a warm spring morning in May of 1833 and our caravan, crewed mostly by greenhorn hostlers mounted on ill-trained mules, was moving as briskly as the flock of smelly, bleating, unruly sheep permitted. As usual, a number of woolies and beef cattle were included amongst our menagerie to provide meat until we arrived at buffalo country. Harris hates sheep, but he conceded that our progress couldn't be much more rapid, anyways, until the pack animals were properly trail-broke and his tenderfoot hostlers learned their skills. As it was, loose cinches and ill-fitting harness and top-heavy, poorly-balanced packs of precious trade goods toppling off fractious mules were as much to blame as the mutinous muttons. Even so, the woolies were first into the stew-kettles during the initial stage of our journey.

I had my own hands full with my own critters and the considerable amount of plunder that I was carrying to the mountains. All of my animals were new to me, most of them unused to workaday discipline, certainly strangers to the behavior I demand of my equines. Still, a long journey stretched out before us and wet saddle blankets are the best training tools so far invented. A firm, experienced, understanding hand and a couple months on the trail perform wonders in civilizing critters. A solid seat in the saddle helps, too.

಄   ಄   ಄

The previous fortnight had been hectic, preparing for my return to the mountains. Sound, reliable livestock was my first requirement, so it was with satisfaction that I read a scribbled note from Charlie Bowden, a self-described "'orse-coper, man an' boy," the proprietor of a Saint Louis horse and mule sale yard with whom I had done business five years before. I smiled when I saw that Charlie is just as assiduous in dropping his aitches in his scribbles as he is in his speech. The penciled note read: "guvner ive come by the very orse ye ast me fer long time since. come quick fore sumbuddy snaps im up."

I wasted no time complying with Charlie's summons. For all his hard-fisted horse-trading chicanery, Charlie Bowden is a shrewd judge of horseflesh who knows by now that I won't tolerate inferior critters. Quick as scat, I hustled off to the sale yard.

On the way, I stopped by a tobacconist's shop. As I fumbled in my poke for coins, the proprietor enquired what I thought, so far, of Andy Jackson's second term as America's president. I confessed that I hadn't been aware that the Hero of New Orleans had served a first term, which did nothing to recommend me to that gentleman. He cast a disparaging glance at my britchclout and workaday buckskins, shrugged, and threw my coins into his cashbox. I refrained from explaining that such matters don't matter much at all in the mountains.

When I first caught sight of the tall sunburnt-black running free in one of Charlie's paddocks, I fairly gasped, wondering how Bowden had divined precisely what was in my mind when I described the saddlehorse that I desired. He was everything I had envisioned and more—deep-chested, a short back, big shoulders sloping smoothly into a thick arched neck surmounted by a graceful head and slightly-dished face, prick-eared, with large, kind, wide-set eyes, decent withers neither too high and bony nor mutton-backed, sturdy hindquarters and powerful gaskins, long, strong legs and short stifles for a long stride, sloping pasterns for a comfortable gait, clean-limbed and not a speck of white hair anywheres on his fetlocks, solid black hooves, muscles rippling under his glossy coat.

I fought to keep a straight face whilst the little Cockney horse-trader trotted to my side. "I see ye found 'im, gov'nor, the very 'orse I wrote ye 'bout." Charlie grinned triumphantly, displaying a mouthful of jagged, tobacco-stained teeth. "'E'd be 'ard to miss, that'n, I warrant, a beauty like 'e be, eyen't 'e now? Kentucky's bloody finest 'e be, gov'nor. Bred like a bloody prince, 'e be, from the bone out, 'e be! Ye'll be the envy of ev'ry eye that sets upon ye, ye will! E'll be carryin' ye to the ends o' the earth in grand style, like the bloody Pope o' Rome himself, 'e will!"

Struggling to appear casual, I replied cautiously, "He's worth considerin'." Playing for time to control my enthusiasm, although I knew—and he knew—that Charlie had me in the palm of his money-grubbing hand, I said, "Let's have a look at his mouth."

"'E be five year old, soon comin' six, not a dye more, gov'nor. I warrant ye that on me ol' mum's sainted 'ead, I do. Come. I'll show ye."

Charlie hadn't lied. The horse was an honest six at most, wolf teeth still in place. He stood calmly, trembling only slightly, whilst we peered into his mouth. I knew I was lost, completely at the little Brit's mercy. In an effort to salvage some shreds of dignity and perhaps a few dollars, I said, "I'm needin' a whole new outfit, Charlie. A couple more saddlers and pack mules, too, for headin' back. Hang on to this'n for me and we'll talk price for the lot when ye get 'em together."

Bowden tried but failed to hide his smirk when he replied. "As ye like, gov'nor. Whate'er ye sye."

As I retreated, I recalled the treacherous, boggy, springtime prairieland that I had traveled five years before on my first overland trip to the mountains. I called back over my shoulder, "Whilst you're at it, ye might as well keep an eye out for a couple good saddle mules, as well." Bowden's triumphant cackle rang in my ears when I fled his premises.

~ ~ ~

I returned to my lodgings, or rather, the lavish apartments of my Saint Louis paramour, Lucette Papillon, owner and madam of the city's best-by-far bordello, a genteel establishment that caters to the mostly-French aristocracy and anyone else who is sufficiently well-heeled and good-mannered enough to enjoy her hospitality. Lucette came to my aid eleven years before, when I was but nineteen, a ragged-arse waif from Ohio, penniless and without prospects, beset by a trio of riverboat bullies. She and I have been on-and-off lovers ever since, inseparable whenever chance brings me to Saint Louis from my extended absences in the wilderness, always years at a time, always welcome to her bed and board when I return. I have no idea what she does for companionship when I am gone and I don't wish to be enlightened in that regard.

Lucette is what white folks smugly term an octoroon, of uncertain mostly-French-Creole ancestry. She is blessed with a flawless café-au-lait complexion, a beautiful face and a slim, athletic body that defy the years, hard-headed intelligence, an indomitable spirit and determination, and a mercurial temper redeemed by a wild sense of humor and her loving attentions in the bedchamber. She has always been, at once, my consummate lover, madcap companion, protector and benefactor if required, level-headed counselor, and the most steadfast friend I could ever wish for.

My reception that late forenoon when I entered her opulent apartment gave the lie to the pleasant description I penned in the preceding paragraphs. Lucette was sulking, punctuated by fiery outbursts condemning me for deserting her, followed by pleas that I remain with her, lest I perish at the hands of bloodthirsty *Indiens sauvages,* grey bears, or rattling serpents, likely all three. It was a familiar drama, repeated every time I prepared to depart, since I first declined to be her permanent pampered fancy man, when I volunteered to join Major Andrew Henry's 1822 fur-trapping expedition into the Rocky Mountain wilderness.

I had informed Lucette only that morning that I would soon be quitting Saint Louis and returning to the mountains with Robert Campbell's packtrain. Fortunately Charlie Bowden's note arrived shortly thereafter, which spared me most of her initial explosion, and my high good spirits occasioned by my imminent acquisition of Charlie's magnificent Kentucky thoroughbred armored me now against her tirade. I let her ill-temper run its course and when, at last, she ran out of breath, I seized that opportunity to remind her that not only would she be relieved of my presence, but also that of my Delaware Indian companion Zeetlah, otherwise known as Old Foot. Which helped to brighten Lucette's mood.

Zeetlah is a man of many parts—warrior, hunter, trapper, herbalist and healer, waterman, wilderness guide, sage counselor, to name just a few. The part that gives Lucette the most concern, howsomever, is the part he uses to seduce her chambermaids and possibly some of the perfumed courtesans she employs to entertain her customers. Trappers call him Old Foot, but Zeetlah is ageless. He is not very tall, but he is sturdy and agile, an excellent horseman, and a tireless runner, which accounts for his name in the Lenni-lenapee tongue. Zeetlah means Feet. He is universally curious and possessed of an acerbic wit and wry humor. His weathered, unreadable features, redeemed by twinkling black eyes, belie his athletic body, which more befits a stripling than an elder. And, unlike most Indians in their cups, he is a good-natured drunk.

When it was determined that I must return to the settlements or likely die of my wound in the mountains, Zeetlah, the healer, volunteered to accompany me on the long, difficult, and dangerous journey to Saint Louis. Once there, he first assisted the Chinese surgeon in the operation that restored me to health, then charmed that medical gentleman with his willingness to share his knowledge of herbal medicines.

Now, somewhat relieved of concern for the dubious virtue of her female charges, Lucette softened and put aside her annoyance with me. She smiled and said, as she rose to take my hand, "Eef eet mus' be, I mus' accep'. Come, *cheri*, we mus' make ze mos' of ze time zat we 'ave togezzer, *n'est-ce pas?*"

It was unthinkable not to agree. We spent the afternoon in her bed, rehearsing lessons of love and exploring a few not theretofore recorded in our copybook.

🛶 🛶 🛶

With hardly more than a week to prepare before setting out on my journey, I was anxious to get to my errands—purchasing all the plunder I would need on the trail and in the mountains. I was pretty much starting over from scratch, replacing my entire outfit— livestock, clothing, saddles and harness, and weapons from Jacob Hawken's gunshop, as well as buying gifts for friends. I fidgeted during the long, leisurely breakfast Lucette and I shared each morning. She noted my impatience, but she accepted it with good grace, with hardly a cluck of displeasure, announcing that she, too, needed to be about her duties, which are considerable, conducting the affairs of her large establishment.

I borrowed a horse from Lucette's stable and set off on my rounds. First stop was *The Missouri Republican*, where I delivered the final pages of manuscript for my *Shinin' Times!* history to Mister Euphemius Hobbes, my editor, who promised to return corrected copies within the week. Breathing a silent prayer to I Know Not Whom that the bibulous Mister Hobbes would remain sober until the chore was finished, I continued on my way.

Next I visited M. Pierre Chouteau, Cadet, at *Berthold et Chouteau Cie.*, in order to obtain the large amount of gold and silver coin that I would need for my transactions with Charlie Bowden and the old Spaniard proprietor of the best saddlery in Saint Louis. Paper money is a poor substitute for hard coin when you are haggling. The clink of gold and silver rattled in one's poke is a powerful persuader when you are closing a deal, even in Saint Louis, just as the glitter of a trader's shiny brass tacks will often make a wilderness Indian give up his furs for less than their worth.

Naturally Chouteau called for *café complet* after I was ushered into his office. Whilst we drank strong French chickoried coffee and nibbled flaky *croissants*, I announced my intention to depart soon for the mountains and explained my need for hard cash. Cadet rang for his cashier. "Bot of course, *mon ami*, you weel need many sings for your *voyage aux montagnes* an' your *équipement* for pursuing your *métier*. I am 'appy to learn zat you weel go wiz Robert Campbell an' Moise 'Arris. Zey weel be ze mos' safe *compagnons de voyage pour* zat mos' *difficile et dangereuse voyage*." Then, after an exchange in rapid French with Gaston, his chief clerk and cashier, and some small talk with me, he enquired, "'Ave you given furzzer *considération* to joining my *opérations* wiz *Américain* Fur, Temple?"

This was always a difficult topic for me in my relations with Pierre Chouteau, who has been my friend and benefactor since my earliest days in the fur trade. Thanks to his shrewd judgment and industry and his careful husbanding of the money I have earned by trapping but mostly acquired by fortuitous happenstance, I have become comfortably wealthy during the time that I have known him. I have little regard for money, but I cherish his friendship almost above all things. Chouteau has long encouraged me to join his fur trade operations, but I have been reluctant to renounce my freedom as a Rocky Mountain free trapper, beholden to no man, accountable to nothing, taking my own chances, always at liberty to do precisely as I please.

It is not easy to say no to Pierre Chouteau, Cadet, scion of an old, powerful, aristocratic French Creole mercantile family, every inch a gentleman, slim, hawkishly handsome, well-mannered, always elegantly attired, intelligent and energetic, admired by all who know him well, envied by his competitors in trade. As I sputtered my excuses, he smiled, raised his hand to cut me off, and relieved my embarrassment. Speaking now in French, which he knows that I understand well enough, he said, "I understand your feeling, Temple —perhaps more than you will ever know—your desire to remain free, obliged to no man, willing to pit yourself against all obstacles, to live and do solely as you desire. I admire—even, sometimes, I envy—you for that. I respect your wishes.

"But there will come a time, perhaps not far off, when the life you have known will not be supportable. When that time comes, my offer will stand. You and those companions whom you trust will be welcome to assist my activities in the mountains. Until then, I congratulate you on your freedom. I wish you success in all that you do and safe passage to your beloved mountains."

Greatly relieved, I thanked him for his understanding, which he dismissed with a wave of his hand, repeating that, in many ways, he envies the life I have chosen.

When Gaston, the sallow-faced senior clerk and cashier, returned bearing a heavy leather poke and plumped it upon the table, I protested that the amount of money it contained was far more than I required. Chouteau reassured me, still in French. "It is a small fraction, a mere *bagatelle*, of your holdings here. Take it with you. You will need hard money on your way."

I thanked him again, assured him that I would call on him before I departed Saint Louis, and hurried off.

∾   ∾   ∾

Charlie Bowden wore, in spite of his efforts to conceal it, the look of a hungry parson taking his seat at your Sunday dinner table. He could barely resist rubbing his palms together in anticipation of the pelf that would soon be his. "G'mornin', guv'nor," he greeted me. "I done like ye ast. Brought up me finest saddle 'orses an' me 'andsomest mules fer ridin', as well as them ye'd be usin' jist fer packin' yer plunder, an' all of 'em cheap as dirt in whatcha might be callin' a risin' market 'ere in Sain' Looie. Charlie Bowden's allus lookin' out fer 'is friends, 'e is."

Looking past the little trader, I spied the black gelding, then quickly looked away, lest I lose the composure I needed for the haggling sure to come. As it turned out, Charlie had made easy work of choosing my animals. The stock he trotted out was of superior quality, the horses all young geldings reasonably broken to saddle, free of blemish, and without vice, leastaways as best I could tell right then and there. Our previous dealings had apparently convinced him that I wouldn't tolerate his foisting off defective critters

I chose a stout line-back dun gelding saddler for myself and two sturdy bays for Zeetlah. My Delaware friend would have preferred piebalds—most Indians do—but Charlie possessed no spotted horses at that time.

Bowden disappeared into the barn and soon emerged leading a pair of tall, clean-limbed mules that made me gulp. If I hadn't known better I would have sworn they were the identical saddle mules that I had bought for my friend Micah and myself five years before. Charlie read my mind. "Pratic'ly the syme, guv'nor!" he crowed. "These 'ere two 'ere be arf-brothers out o' the syme two mares an' the syme jack what sired them two ye bought offa me fi' year ago!"

There was no question that the two saddle mules must be mine and selecting four tall, stout-limbed pack mules, three jacks and a jenny, coarse but sound and in good fettle, from the dozen or so specimens that he offered, took hardly any time at all. Riding each of the saddle animals in Bowden's large paddock—including the black, who thrilled me to the marrow, although I fought to conceal it—took up the rest of forenoon. Charlie and I retired to a nearby eating-house for dinner, where we commenced negotiations between mouthfuls, continuing until our plates were empty and the dining room deserted, each of us scribbling and ciphering on paper scraps, pounding the table at times, the little Cockney lamenting loudly the while, "What ye be off'rin' won't let me be sendin' a single blarsted copper to me sainted ol' mum, purely starvin' she be, back in Ol' Blighty, it won't!" We still hadn't come to final terms by time we walked back to his sale yard, although I had managed to pare down his original asking price nearly by half.

Just as we entered the yard, one of Bowden's stablemen turned a handsome critter into one of the paddocks. At first I thought it was another saddle mule, mouse-grey-colored and as tall as a horse. Then I spied what some folks call the Jesus cross, a broad black stripe down his back and a similar stripe across his shoulders. A closer look assured me that he was not a mule but a jackass, a donkey complete with all his equipment. An antic thought struck me then. If I could get that animal to rendezvous, I would gift him to Rainbow's father, Iron Bow, my former father-in-law, who had long-admired our saddle mules. "Tell ye what, Charlie, I'm through hagglin'. Throw in that critter, that big jackass there, and I'll pay your price."

Whilst Charlie ranted and raved and extolled the potential procreative virtues of the young jackass, as yet untried in the breeding pen, I held my tongue. I retreated to a perch upon a paddock rail and occasionally rattled my poke. I learned that the young jack was the direct son of the sire of all of Charlie's fine saddle mules, bred out of a European jenny, and, one day, possibly worth his weight in rubies. Meanwhile the solid clink of gold and the tempting ring of silver coins had my Cockney friend nigh slavering. At last he could stand it no more. We came to terms, although it cost me a couple extra gold pieces.

Dusk was fast approaching by then. Charlie promised to deliver my livestock to Lucette's stables next morning, along with the horse I had borrowed, but there was no doubting that I would ride my sunburnt-black home that evening.

No conquering Roman general ever made a more triumphal progress through the streets of Rome than I did that evening, scattering terrified townsmen willy-nilly as my skittish steed pranced and reared and capered and curvetted along the thoroughfares of Saint Louis.

℞   ℞   ℞

Lucette greeted me at the door of her chambers, smiling but wrinkling her nose at my fragrance. Her maids were already filling the large copper tub with pitchers of steaming water, preparing my bath. "Come, *cheri*, eet ees pas' time for *le souper*, bot firs', your bat', *n'est-ce pas?*" She sniffed elaborately for emphasis.

Odoriferous as I was after my day-long exertions a-horseback, I refused to delay showing off my new horse. Lucette hastily threw a discreet wrapper over her scanty nightclothes and accompanied me to the stables, where she outdid me in her expressions of admiration of the black. Lucette possesses a keen eye for value, no matter the object.

Afterwards, bathed and dressed in fresh clothes, I joined her at table, the two of us chattering in high spirits whilst we consumed a hearty supper of delicious vittles from the *maison's* excellent kitchen. We lingered only briefly over our cognacs, for our mutual good humor demanded a closer union that could be achieved only on the perfumed sheets of her huge canopied bed. There, when I was able to think clearly enough, I marveled at the endless variety of that fascinating female, who never failed to arouse and enchant me with her mischievous wit, her desirable person, and her seemingly infinite carnal invention. We slept only fitfully between encounters, until grey dawn poked past the draperies and we fell into exhausted slumber, limbs entwined, nuzzling, murmuring endearments until we knew no more.

The previous night's good feeling persisted through our substantial breakfast, after which a smiling Lucette shooed me off to pursue my chores, the first of which promised to be an exercise nearly equal to yesterday's jousting with Charlie Bowden.

On my way to the stables, I stopped by Zeetlah's bedchamber, hoping to enlist him in my efforts, but he was absent, possibly still romancing one of his doxies or poking about in a pasture or woodland with the Chinese Doctor Yuan, searching for the healing roots and herbs and funguses they prize.

Bowden had already delivered my critters and Lucette's stablemen had installed them in suitable quarters. I reckoned I would have my hands full with the plunder I expected to purchase, so, instead of the spirited black, I saddled the less excitable lineback dun and haltered two of the packmules before I set out for the lair of the old Spaniard saddler who builds the best horse-clothing in all of Saint Louis and possibly anywheres else.

I discovered the old gentleman seated amidst his leathery wares—high-pommeled Spaniard saddles, packsaddles, headstalls, *alforjas* saddlebags, harness, belts and holsters, and the like, redolent of neatsfoot, gleaming softly in the meager sunshine that penetrated his den. His workmen plied their skills quietly in the adjoining workshop. He himself might have been a product of his own manufacture. His once-fine swarthy features, now wrinkled and lined with age, seemed to be crafted of the finest morocco. Only his bright, inquisitive eyes betrayed the youth that still burned in him.

He didn't rise when I entered, but his *bienvenido* was hearty and sincere and he made it clear that he remembered me and my custom, although half a decade had passed since we had haggled and sipped his fiery *aguardiente* together. Which he insisted we do before we commenced our dealings and frequently thereafter. As I succeeded in letting him know each item I desired, he barked out a command to one or another of his workmen, who came running with the merchandise. I first purchased a handsome high-pommeled Spaniard saddle, complete with trappings, for myself and another for Zeetlah, then nine packsaddles—for I require every saddle animal, even my favorites, to carry a pack when he's not being ridden—then all the headstalls, bits, halters, hobbles, harness, britching, saddlepads, and suchlike required for my numerous equines, which amounted to a formidable heap when I had done.

The total price demanded for the lot was not unreasonable, far less than I expected, but, just the same, in order not to offend the old gentleman's feelings, I haggled with him, albeit half-heartedly, until he finally accepted my money. Whereupon he threw in half-a-dozen grass *reatas* and a pair of saddle holsters for boot and insisted that we drink a final stirrup-cup together whilst his workmen saddled my horse and bundled my purchases onto the packmules.

Still tipsy from the old saddler's *aguardiente*, I shared a hasty dinner with Lucette before I set out for Berthold et Chouteau's mercantile. That afternoon proved to be only the first of four tedious days of picking and choosing what I would carry to the mountains for my own needs, for gifts to my comrades in our trapping bunch and their ever-acquisitive wives and current lights-o'-love, for my former in-laws, Iron Bow and his son Fast Horse, and trade goods for swapping and gifting amongst various Indian bands we could expect to encounter along our way.

Listing here all the plunder that I amassed would be wearisome both for me, even if I could remember it all, and whoever reads this book, so I will mention only the principal kinds of merchandise that Chouteau's counter-jumpers heaped up at my behest. There was much to choose from. The fur trade was booming and so was the Santa Fe market. Years of experience in what was required for trade and survival had taught Saint Louis merchants what to stock. The bins and shelves of Berthold et Chouteau's mercantile bulged and groaned with a cornucopia of goods both essential and what rough trappers and Indians consider to be luxuries.

It was difficult to restrain my greed for ever more plunder. Goods in Saint Louis cost a mere pittance compared with what traders charge in the mountains, often as much as a thousand percent and more over their cost in the settlements. Awls that cost sixty cents the gross in Saint Louis go for a dollar apiece at rendezvous. Money was of little consideration. Le Cadet had assured me that no matter how much I might spend, it would make barely a dent in what he holds for me. I was like a kid in a candy shop. All that kept me from going purely hog-wild was knowing that every jot and tittle needed to be carried two thousand miles through a hostile wilderness.

First, I outfitted myself with half-a-dozen good English Manchester beaver traps—then added another half-dozen for gifts—a broad-brimmed felt hat for me, to ward off rain and hail, several dozen calico shirts, four-point English Witney blankets, woolen *capotes*, knives—tools such as axe- and hammerheads, spades, and shovels, just the heads—aspenwood, plentiful in the Rockies, makes good-enough handles once it seasons—rasps and files, an assortment of nails, screws, and bolts—draw-knives for skinning bark off lodgepoles, gifts for the women of Iron Bow's Flathead band—gunpowder, lead, percussion caps, bird- and buckshot, good English flints, several pounds of iron arrow points, canvas sheeting, picket pins, forty fathoms of stout rope, tallow candles, and other essentials, including razors and soap, a couple thick leather-bound ledgers for the journal I intended to keep, foolscap, pencils, ink blocks, and steel pens. Then I multiplied most of the lot by a half-a-dozen or so for gifting at rendezvous. Naturally I stocked up on such luxuries as coffee, tea, honey, molasses, sugar, flour, dried fruit, beans, peas, corn and such. Tobacco for smoking and chaw is not a luxury for trappers. It is nearly as important as gunpowder. A bushel, then two, of tobacco twisted in yard-long carrots was added to the heap.

I needed trade goods as much for my bunch's own use as for swapping with Indians greedy for white-eyes plunder. My mountain of merchandise grew ever higher with yards of trade woolens, calicos and osnaburg, satins and Chinese silks, ribbon, fancy horse clothing, nests of tin-lined copper kettles, a couple gross of tiny mirrors both for ornaments and vanity, brass tacks and thimbles, packets of vermilion and powdered paint, fishhooks and silk line, half a gross of metal tweezers for tweaking stray hairs off Indian warriors' chins and plucking out ever-present head-lice, dozens of butcher knives, pipe-tomahawks both for persuasion and for smoking, colored beads by the pound, needles and thread, scissors, and fistfuls of ornamental trinkets and gewgaws called foofurraw in the mountains. And that is just a sample of what I accumulated.

Most of what I bought was manufactured in Europe, mostly England and France, for, I am sorry to say, American goods don't measure up to what comes from over the seas. Indians, primitive as they are considered to be, have a shrewd eye for quality and they hold Yankee manufacture in low esteem. It is an unwise trader who hauls inferior goods two thousand miles to the Rockies, only to have them rejected as trash by a painted aborigine with a keen sense of value.

On the fourth day, although I shuddered at the task I had already set myself, I indulged my fancy by purchasing a pair of five-gallon tin kegs shaped to fit on a packhorse. I had one filled with good Kentucky whiskey, the other with fine French cognac. On a whim, I bought a second pair and had them filled with pure grain alcohol. After all, rendezvous comes but once a year.

A sturdy packhorse can carry a load of 300 pounds and a packmule isn't strained under 250 pounds. I prefer mules for packing. Cantankerous as they mostly are, they are more sure-footed and they can get along on measly forage that would starve a horse. As it turned out, I was forced to return to Charlie Bowden to buy still another packmule and to the ancient Spaniard for one more packsaddle and a suit of harness.

‽ ‽ ‽

In the midst of my mercantile spree, I granted myself a half-holiday and rode my new black horse out to the estate of General William Clark to show him off to my old friend Moses Harris, otherwise known as Black, thanks to an exploding gunbarrel that peppered his cheeks and brow with gunpowder, which did nothing to improve his already homely phiz. The general generously allows the trader Bill Sublette and his partners to use some of his barns and paddocks when they are preparing to launch their packtrain to the mountains.

Black whistled softly, admiring my new saddlehorse. "Ye gotcherse'f one helluva critter thar, Temple," he observed after making a thorough inspection of my mount. "Ol' Fitz's goin' to turn green when he spies 'im. That'n's sure as hell a match fer that 'ere Kaintuck hoss Tom brung up last year. Mebbe even better."

"That's the one I had in mind when I told Charlie what I wanted, but I never thought he'd find me one as good as this'n."

"Wal, ye'd best be gittin' 'im ready fer trailin', an' damn quick, too. We been busy as a purty whore on Satiddy night, gittin' set fer jumpin' off fer the mountains. Bobby's itchin' to git on with it an' Billy Sublette's awready headed up the Missourah with his keelboats. Onliest thang holdin' us be a coupl'a greenhorn fops Billy said could come along fer adventurin' an' sich. They ain't showed up yet."

Black saw my look of alarm and held up his hand to stall my protests. "Don'tcha fret none, Temple. I war jist funnin' ye. We cain't git started, nohaow, afore anuther week or so, 'til the prairie dries out some. Jist the same, ye'd best git a move on an' git yerse'f ready to ride afore then, so's ye kin lend me a hand if'n I need ye." He chuckled evilly and added, "Hell! It'll take ye that long to pry that 'ere Injun pard o' your'n offa his whores, won't it?"

I explained that Old Foot was not occupied with whores, but rather with unpaid amateurs who found his dubious charms irresistible. "Wal, thar ain't no accountin' fer wimmen's taste, that's a gawddamn fact," he replied with a laugh. "Hell! Look at me. I ain't no prize, but I do awright."

Harris changed the subject to Bill Sublette's latest adventure. "Ol' Billy an' Bobby Campbell are fixin' to go inter compertishun with Amurrican Fur up aroun' the Yellerstone an' on up to the Falls. Gonna build theirse'fs a dozen or so tradin' forts, like they be tellin' it, an' give ol' Redcoat McKenzie a run fer his money, tradin' fer fur an' robes an' sich wi' Stonies an' Mandans an' Hidatsas an' Crows— even Grovants an' Blackfoots. That's what Billy's doin' right naow, headin' up the Missourah with a coupla keelboats, carryin' all manner o' trade goods an' buildin' supplies an' a passel o' smiths an' carpenters an' sich fer gittin' the job done. Hell! He's even carryin' a sawmill up thar! They like to cleaned Sain' Looie out o' ever' las' saw an' hammer an' nail an' builder thar war hyarabouts."

"Keelboats!" I exclaimed, recalling my own experience in 'twenty-two, rowing, poling, and hauling one of those clumsy arks up the high-running, treacherous Missouri with *cordelle* ropes. Black read my expression of dismay at such a venture, now that steamboats were available.

"Hold on, Temple," Black cut in. "Ye don't s'pose Billy Sublette's one to be overlookin' nuthin' what kin he'p 'im, do ye? Nope. He's draggin' them 'ere keelboats a'hind o' one o' them steamboats—the *Otto*—leastaways as far as Fort Pier. Arter that, they'll hafta go back to the old ways, but from thar, it ain't that fur to the Yellerstone."

I should have known better. Bill Sublette rarely, if ever, misses a trick that will enrich him.

I saw that it was fast approaching noon and I had still much to accomplish that day. I bade Black farewell, promising to "git a move on," as he had advised.

On the way back to town, when I wasn't attending to my untrained horse, I mused over William Sublette's current project. Unlike most trappers, who barely make a living by the hard, dangerous work we do, Billy had become rich in the fur trade. I, too, had acquired wealth during my ten years in the mountains, but in my case it was mostly fool luck and fortuitous happenstance that provided my comfortable financial situation. Sublette, along with Jedediah Smith and Davey Jackson, had been, early on, in 1823, a favorite of General William Ashley, one of the two leaders of our 1822 fur-trapping expedition to the Rockies. Bill worked hard and smart, as the other two did also, until the three of them were able to succeed Ashley as primary suppliers of necessary plunder to trappers, whose year-long efforts, enduring peril and hardship, were in most cases rewarded with just enough profit to buy an outfit for one more year in the mountains and a drunken binge at rendezvous. High prices at the traders' tents keep most mountaineers broke. The golden harvest of beaver fur drains into the pockets of a few hard-nose traders, not the men who wade the icy streams and beaver ponds and daily risk their lives against hostile Indians, grizzly bears and catamounts, and unforgiving weather.

What keeps us there sums up in a single word—freedom. No other men in all of history and long before have ever known the freedom that Rocky Mountain free trappers possess. We are beholden to no man or government or society that whips its citizens into line, either by laws, disapproval of neighbors, or Bible-pounding parsons. If a man has grit and smarts enough to survive the perils and hardships of wilderness life, he can thumb his nose at all authority that seeks to compromise his absolute freedom. True, we depend on traders to provide the essentials of our survival there, but we reward them handsomely for their efforts

Sublette was the businessman of Smith, Jackson & Sublette, hard-fisted and flinty-eyed, single-minded in cold-hearted pursuit of a dollar. Davey Jackson was the efficient, good-natured leader of trapping operations in the mountains and Jed Smith appeared to be mostly concerned with his Bible and seeing what was on the other side of the mountain. He was forever leading his men on wild-goose chases to California and getting most of them killed whilst he was at it. After they got rich enough to sell out to Rocky Mountain Fur, Davey went off to settle in California and Smith got himself killed by Indians in the desert on the way to Santa Fe.

Bill Sublette stayed on in the fur business. He alone owned the sizeable debt owed by the Rocky Mountain Fur Co., a partnership comprised of Tom Fitzpatrick, Jim Bridger, Bill's brother Milton, Henry Fraeb, and Jean Gervais, all of them trusted comrades and good friends to my bunch and me.

Never one to overlook additional profit, Bill squeezed RMF into a deal that made him the sole supplier of merchandise from Saint Louis, at his prices, as well as the only provider of transportation of their furs back to the settlements, also at charges determined by Bill.

Bill Sublette has formed a partnership with Robert Campbell, a good man from a wealthy Philadelphia family. Bobby has come a long way from the sickly kid we first met in 'twenty-four, come to the mountains for his health. Nowadays he is a first-rate mountaineer and an able businessman. It was Bobby's packtrain that I meant to accompany to the Rockies.

Now, riding back to town, I wondered at Sublette's grit in taking on John Jacob Astor's powerful American Fur Company and hard-fisted Kenneth McKenzie, the man who calls himself King of the Missouri, who runs American Fur's Upper Missouri Outfit. It was a conundrum, but if anybody could pull it off, I reckoned Bill Sublette was the one to do it.

Between my buying binges at the mercantile, I paid a farewell visit to the gunshop owned by the Hawken brothers, Jacob and Samuel, who make sturdy, reliable, plumb-shooting percussion rifles, pistols, and fowlers, which are fast replacing flintlocks amongst Rocky Mountain trappers. Naturally, not every trapper trusts those new-fangled weapons and most Indians won't have anything to do with them. They prefer flintlock muskets that require only gunpowder and lead—or maybe a smooth, round pebble when their galena runs out.

Jake Hawken greeted me with a smile and a warm hello when I entered the shop and Brother Sam'l waved from the workroom, where a bevy of workmen were busy assembling a variety of weapons. I had been a steady customer there ever since Jake convinced me that the nuisance of carrying percussion caps in addition to powder and lead is well repaid by the reliability of weapons that will likely shoot in any kind of weather.

"Good to see ye, Temple," Jake said. "Reckon ye be gettin' yourself ready for goin' back to the mountains with Campbell's outfit. He was in here, day before yesterday." Then, genuine interest in his eyes, he asked, "And Micah? He still with ye?"

"Oh, yes," I assured him. "He's flourishing. Best choice he could've made. I doubt he'll ever come back to the settlements. Ye could say he out-Injuns the Injuns, nowadays."

Jake laughed and the smile that followed bespoke profound affection for his one-time helper. Then, professional interest taking over, he asked, "Ye still got your irons? They workin' all right?"

I told him that, yes, my rifle and pistol were still as good as the day I bought them, but that I needed a fowler, inasmuch as I had given away all but those two weapons when I departed the mountains the previous fall.

"I daresay we've got a couple-three fowlers that'll suit your fancy," Jake assured me, stepping to a wall festooned with an armory of rifles, pistols, and shotguns gleaming with whale oil. He was correct in that assumption. I bought the best he had, a double-barreled fowling-piece, light as a feather, beautifully-engraved, and stocked with tiger maple. I didn't need such luxury, but mountaineers love their firearms beyond all common reasoning, living as we do in a hostile wilderness, where plumb-shooting, sure-firing weapons mean the difference between life and death by an enemy or, just as deadly, starvation.

As it turned out, I purchased another heavy-caliber pistol to match the one I already possessed, then four more of common grade for gifts, then four percussion mountain rifles and a common fowler. Whilst Jake was totting up my purchases, I spied a small double-barreled percussion belly gun on one of his counters. It was very well-made and packed a hefty charge that was sure to be lethal at close quarters. I told Jake to include it with the rest.

Fact is, I felt somewhat guilty about that purchase, for that belly gun would replace a similar flintlock that Lucette had given me more than a decade before, a weapon that had nestled against my midriff every day and most nights ever since, a gun that more than once had saved my life in close combat. Practicality struggled with sentiment, but commonsense won out. Henceforth I would carry the much more reliable capgun.

There is no bargaining in the Hawkens' gunshop. Prices are fixed and non-negotiable, which doubtless distresses their French Creole customers. They dearly love to haggle over every item they buy, no matter how measly it might be. After I threw in another gallon of percussion caps, just for luck, and asked that Jake gather up a quantity of assorted gun parts for repairs, I signed the bill and told him to present it to Chouteau's chief clerk when they delivered my purchases to the mercantile.

As you might suppose, the Hawken brothers were beaming even more sunnily by time I departed.

℔ ℔ ℔

The packtrain had traveled several miles on the westward trail through Missouri to Lexington before the cares of the previous fortnight mostly drained away, allowing my spirits to lift as I day-dreamed of reunion with my daughter and my dear friends, once the long, difficult journey that lay ahead was accomplished. Daytimes had been filled with paying my respects to Chouteau and a few others, shouting-matches with Hobbes concerning my manuscript, errands to bookstores and apothecaries, the mercantile, and Doctor Yuan's to obtain a surgical kit and to retrieve the mostly-errant Zeetlah to assist in sorting, time and again, a mountain of plunder into well-balanced packs for the critters, careful not to put all of an item into a single pack, lest we lose all of it if an animal should disappear in a bog or be swept away at a river crossing.

Nights with Lucette were bittersweet with bickering over my faithlessness in deserting her, followed by feverish, frantic lovemaking that left us gasping, sweaty, clinging, murmuring endearments, until we were able to resume our amorous *adieus*.

Now, exhausted though I was by a final sleepless night of fervent farewelling, I gazed cheerfully at the long, disorderly procession that strung out ahead, straggling past the farmfields and pastures that border Saint Louis. Far ahead, leading the van, were Robert Campbell and Black Harris, likely accompanied by Sublette's wealthy guests. Moping at my side was Zeetlah, looking rather the worse for wear after a rowdy night of drunken coupling.

His excesses notwithstanding, a frowzy Zeetlah had appeared at my door at dawn, ready to lend an unsteady hand to loading our pack animals in Lucette's stableyard. Naturally her grooms and stablehands helped to make short work of the chore. Fortunately our parting was brief. Tears glistening in her eyes, Lucette struggled to maintain her composure in the presence of her people. A quick kiss and a squeeze of the hand sufficed. Then my Delaware friend and I clattered out of the courtyard and onto the street, leading our packstring, headed for General Clark's estate, where Campbell had assembled his caravan.

I noticed that Zeetlah's sack of personal plunder, slung atop the pack carried by his saddle mule, bulged rather more fully than I would have supposed. He usually relied on me to supply his wants. It was none of my business, howsomever, so I paid it no nevermind.

❧   ❧   ❧

The first day's hike had been, as is usual, a short one. We were barely out of sight of Saint Louis when Harris called a halt, so that the hostlers could adjust harness, repack loads, and, in some cases, speed back to town to retrieve forgotten items. The company loads were light, for most of the trade goods was being transported to Lexington by Sublette before he continued upriver, but the mules were green as grass. It was amusing to watch both hostlers and plunder bucked sky-high, time and again, during the brief journey that first day and for several thereafter. Our own critters were far from seasoned, but Charlie Bowden's livestock was downright sedate in comparison with Campbell's long-eared rebels. That revolutionary spirit applied only to the hostlers' critters. Bobby and his elegant guests were mounted on well-trained blooded horses from Sublette's own stables.

There was no need to build a cookfire. Lucette had provided a large hamper stuffed with tasty vittles. As expected, Black Harris moseyed by, looking hungry, as usual. Naturally I invited him to join us. Between mouthfuls, he jerked his head towards the men and animals scattered around the pasture, helped himself to another roasted chicken and a slab of Virginia ham, and observed, "Shore war some kind o' circus today, warn't it?"

I allowed that it had indeed been an entertaining spectacle.

"Allus is," he agreed. "But we'll git 'em settled daown, mostly, time we git to Lexin'ton."

"How come you're not supping with Campbell?" I enquired slyly.

Harris snorted. "Reckon ye know why! Bobby don't figger I'd be fittin' comp'ny fer them highfalutin nabobs he's draggin' along thi'shere time! An' I don't mind, neither. The less I have to do with the likes o' that 'ere kind, the better!"

"Oh, I daresay you'll be havin' plenty to do with 'em, before long—savin' their arse from one wreck or another."

Black looked glum. "'Fraid you're right. All but one of 'em, anyways— feller name o' Stewart, a Scotty-Brit sojer-boy what's some kind o' hero, I been hearin'. Fought agin the Frenchies at Waterloo an' come back sportin' all sorts o' medals." He gobbled another tart before he added grudgingly, "Sits his hoss good, anyways, an' 'pears to be a hand with critters, packin', an' sichlike."

That last remark recommended the Brit somewhat. When I said so, Black snorted and declared, "The snooty sumbitch treats his hosses better'n he does the rest of us! The way Bobby's tellin' it, Stewart's one o' them 'ere English aristercrats! Sez he's got hisse'f a castle an' sarvints an' ever'thin' what goes with it, over in Scotland!

I let Black cool off before I enquired further about the captain. "Who else is he bringin' along?"

"Reckon the prize hasta go to ol' Tippecanoe's drunken doctor boy, name o' Ben, same as his ol' man, but that's as fur as it goes fer bein' like his daddy. He's young, hardly even thutty yet, but a dedicated drammer, wuss'n me! 'Pears ol' Gin'ral Harrison figgers the mountains'll dry 'im out afore he drinks hisse'f to death." Black sniggered. "Reckon the gin'ral don't know nuthin' 'baout ronnyvoo. Young Doctor Ben'll likely drown hisse'f up thar—pervidin' he gits that fur!"

I was surprised. Drunk or not, any son of the Hero of 1812 was sure to be a celebrity amongst trappers old enough to remember much about the War of the British Return. I pursued my inquiry. "Who else?"

"Wal, thar's a Sain' Looie moneybags feller, name o' Ed Christy, lookin' to jump in on gittin' even richer offa beaver, from what I been hearin' 'im tellin' when I'm ridin nigh." He chuckled derisively. "Reckon he ain't never had no dealin's wi' the likes o' Fitz an' Bridger an' the rest. They'll skin 'im alive!" Harris reflected for a spell before he confessed, "Cain't tell ye nuthin' abaout t'other three young fellers, not even their names, 'ceptin' they 'pear to be well-heeled fer money an' still wet a'hind the ears." Somebody from amongst the hostlers called Black's name. He uttered a half-hearted curse, but he rose and went to see what required his attention.

While Harris was absent, Robert Campbell strolled by, bade us good evening, and extended a cordial welcome to his caravan. When he spied my several bulging packs of plunder and my numerous critters grazing nearby, he asked, only half-joking, "Ye planning on trading at rendezvous, are ye, Temple?"

"Ye know me better'n that, Bobby," I replied. "Trappin's good enough for me. No, what's in those packs'll be goin' to the fellers in my bunch, them an' their women an' kids, just for presents, nothin' else. It won't be costin' you a single plew. You an' Rocky Mountain Fur'll likely be gettin' all they've got."

Reassured, Campbell said, "There's not much for you to do 'til after Lexington, but after that I'll look for your help on night guard and hunting when we get to buffalo country."

I assured him that such was my understanding with Harris from the beginning. Then I said, "If it'll square better with your partner, Bill Sublette, I'll be happy to pay what ye ask in cash money, right now, for lettin' my pard an' me tag along with ye."

Campbell reddened and replied quickly, "No such a thing, Temple. You're always welcome with any outfit I'm running. I wouldn't think of it." He broke off, his attention captured by my sunburnt-black saddlehorse grazing nearby. He gazed long and longingly before he remarked, "That's a magnificent creature you've come by, Temple. Easily the finest of all the livestock here." I allowed that I thought so, too. A shout from Campbell's camp interrupted our palaver. He turned to respond, calling back, "I'll see you on the trail. We'll have more time then!" and hurried off.

Greedy though he always is for your vittles, Moses Harris rarely shows up empty-handed or without a comical yarn. When he returned, we passed around a quart of his good Kentucky whiskey whilst he entertained me with tall tales of mountain life and Saint Louis bordellos. What Zeetlah got out of it besides some hair o' the dog, I can't say, but then, I never can tell what's in his mind.

The next few days passed uneventfully, trudging westwards across Missouri towards Independence and Lexington, changing mounts frequently, training them to our custom, wrangling with our packmules until they accepted their servitude, and making night camp under mostly kindly skies. Zeetlah and I mostly hung back towards the tail of the caravan, keeping clear of the frequent fracases betwixt hostlers and obstreperous mules still unaccepting of their employment. Often we rode at the very tail-end, alongside Louie Vasquez, an old friend who was paying his way back to the mountains by chousing up laggards who strayed from the disorderly caterpillar inching across the prairie. Sometimes we were joined by François Lajeunesse, another longtime mountaineer, working as Campbell's clerk, leastaways until we arrived at rendezvous. I reckoned my presence at the head of the procession or at Campbell's gentlemen's mess wouldn't be welcome, so I refrained from making the acquaintance of Bobby's refined guests.

☙   ☙   ☙

More than halfway across Missouri, we camped one night in good weather beside a measly branch on a mostly treeless prairie. Zeetlah and I hustled through our chores, relieving our critters of saddles and packs, letting them roll and rubbing them dry, leading them to water, then hobbling and staking them out to graze, before we gathered enough dry sticks to build a fire to cook our meager supper. "Long time no buffler," Zeetlah said mournfully, a disgusted look on his face as he munched on sowbelly and spooned up a mouthful of boiled cornmeal.

"Yep, and it'll be a long spell yet before we get any decent meat. It's a long hike from here to the Platte. Buffalo don't come any closer to the settlements than that, nowadays."

Zeetlah grunted and looked sour, which wasn't much different from his usual expression. By time I returned from washing our cups and spoons in the crick, my companion was already rolled up in his sleeprobes. Night was falling, too dark to read, so I followed his example.

Images of loved ones flickered through my mind—my four-year-old daughter Iris, her long-dead mother Rainbow, most beloved of all, my father, and Ned Godey and his beautiful wife Cat, who were caring for Iris, and all the rowdy, rugged men who had become my brothers in the years that we had been together. If I dreamed that night, it was of them.

☙   ☙   ☙

Shouts and laughter and hostlers' grumpy curses, the neighing and braying of critters indignant at being recalled to servitude, jangling harness, and all the general clamor of a camp galvanizing into another day roused me from my slumber. When I returned from my morning chore, I expected to see Zeetlah tending our cookfire, but he was absent. I performed the job myself, striking sparks into tinder and blowing it into a tiny flame. Soon I had a tidy fire of driftwood sticks burning under the coffee kettle and last night's warmed-over vittles.

I had finished my breakfast, washed my utensils, and gone out amongst our critters to bring them in for water, saddling, and loading, when I realized that my Delaware friend was nowheres about. His saddle horse and one of the mules were absent. So were his saddle, rifle, and his sack of possibles.

I had long since given up trying to fathom the recesses of Zeetlah's capricious mind. He is a walking, seldom-talking conundrum. With a sigh and a muttered curse, I performed the loading chore by myself, but when it was finished, there was still no Zeetlah.

I waited, seated at my smoldering cookfire, smoking my pipe and sipping coffee, watching the caravan form and move out, until Black and Louie Vasquez rode up, questioning looks on their whiskery faces. "Whyn'tcha gittin' on the move, Temple?" Harris wanted to know. "Ever'body's nearly gone, as ye kin see." Vasquez also mumbled something along that line.

"Old Foot ain't here," I replied lamely. "Don't know where the hell he's got off to. His critters, too."

Black looked perplexed, but no more than I felt right then. "Wal, are ye comin' or ain'tcha? Time ye git a move on."

"Reckon I won't," I told him. "I'd best hang on here an' wait a spell. He'll likely come back from wherever in hell he's gone. Go on. We can catch up, slow-movin' as your menagerie is."

Vasquez harrumphed and Harris grunted. "Don't like it nohaow, leavin' ye back like this, all by your lonesome. 'Tain't right! Ye cain't never tell, out hyar."

At last they relented, wished me well, and loped off to join the unruly column, then disappear into its ranks. I watched the caravan out of sight, dwindling into the hazy blue horizon until it disappeared completely.

After an hour or so, I led the critters to a place nigh the crickbank that hadn't been occupied the night before, unloaded them, watered and staked them out on fresh graze, and set my camp in the midst of our packsaddles and plunder. I left my saddle on my black horse, howsomever, in case I might need him in a hurry. As Black said, ye can never tell.

The day dragged on. I strained my eyes in every direction, seeking a sign of my errant companion, but all I could see was the featureless plain dotted here and there with lonely, wind-twisted cottonwoods and a sparse fringe of willows along the crick. I tried to read, but my attention wandered. Bored, I dug out fishhooks and silk line, cut a willow pole, dug up some earthworms, and proceeded to reduce the catfish population in a deep hole in the crick, which somewhat relieved the tedium. Now and then I scanned the horizon whilst I fumbled for an answer to account for Zeetlah's desertion.

At length I concluded that he was likely calling on kin. Any number of Delaware and Shawnee villages are scattered over Western Missouri and it was not unreasonable to suppose that he was paying a visit to relatives he hadn't seen in more than a decade. Naturally he could have informed me of his intentions before he departed, but such polite behavior is alien to his character. Now I wondered if he would return to our overnight camp or if he would simply ride off in pursuit of the packtrain, assuming that I had gone along with it. It was a conundrum. I decided to stay put.

A dozen fat, foot-long catfish sizzling in sowbelly grease in a spider skillet are rather too much for one man to eat at a sitting, but I ate them all, anyways. After which I unsaddled my black and hobbled my picketed livestock as an extra precaution against ambitious Delawares or Shawnees, then retired to my robes at dusk for restless slumber disturbed by every cricket call and nightbird trill that might signal a horse thief.

Morning overcast soon burned off to reveal another sunny spring day, but still no sign of Zeetlah. Whilst my coffee kettle boiled, I watered the stock and moved them to fresh graze, the while searching the prairie for movement. There was none. After breaking my fast and cleaning up, I tried to read a novel entitled *Ivanhoe,* written by an English lord named Walter Scott, but my attention kept straying. I replaced the book in my saddlebag, loaded my new fowler with birdshot, and hiked off afoot in search of prairie grouse that might provide my dinner—never, howsomever, out of sight of my livestock and plunder. Ye never can tell.

The sun had reached its zenith when I returned to camp, three plump birds dangling from my belt. I dressed them and spitted all three on a steel ramrod over driftwood coals before I led the critters to water. By time I finished that chore, the air was redolent with the aroma of roasting grouse. My belly rumbled in anticipation of the feast that awaited me.

I should have thought of it earlier. The fragrance of roasting birds wafting over the plain proved to be the magic charm that had been lacking. I caught sight of movement at the prairie's edge, then the distant figures of two mounted men growing larger as they loped in my direction. A minute later I laid aside my rifle and greeted my truant partner and his unknown companion.

With scarcely a nod to me, Zeetlah swung down from his horse and made a beeline for the cookfire. His companion remained mounted on the mule, straddling Zeetlah's canvas possibles sack, which, I noticed, was empty now.

His canvas shirt and leggin's were in tatters. A shabby quiver of arrows and a short, yard-long bow were slung across his bony back.

"Hold on there!" I yelled. "Keep your damn hands off o' my dinner! Where in hell have ye been?"

Zeetlah skidded to a halt, looking surprised at my outburst. "Home," he replied simply, as if that were explanation enough. He turned once more to my roasting birds.

"No ye don't!" I yelled again. "You're goin' to tell me where ye been and why! I don't give a damn if ye starve to death! Ye ain't gettin' a goddamn bite less'n ye speak up!"

For the first time, he cracked a smile. "I go sister lodge. Not far. Brung present. Dey ver' pore. Nuthin' fer eat. No vittle. No blanket. No robe. Nuthin' much. I know you wait. Why mad?" The hand signs he made as he spoke conveyed much more meaning than his stingy English did.

I was still steaming, but I had to admit that in his place, I would have done much the same. I pointed to his companion, still slouched aboard the mule. "Who in hell is that? Why'd ye bring him along with ye?"

For the first time, Zeetlah appeared to take notice of the fellow aboard the mule. He signaled for him to join us. I saw that he was young, hardly more than a boy, tall and scrawny, ragged, half-starved, eyes downcast, a hang-dog look on what I could see of his face. He remained where he was. Zeetlah explained, signing as he spoke. "My sister boy. No life dere. No work, no vittle, no t'morra!" Perhaps for the first time in all the years that I had known our Delaware healer, I saw true emotion, compassion, in his normally stolid features, even a hint of a tear in his obsidian eyes. "I no let 'im die dere! Better I take boy to mountain. He Lenapee. He be man dere purty damn quick."

My anger fled. As my friend spoke, I recalled my own condition eleven years before—nineteen years old, broke and hungry, without a trade and with no prospects, when Lucette lent me a hand and let me make a whole new life for myself. In the mountains, a man learns to make up his mind in a hurry, lest he gets himself killed whilst he's doing it. "All right," I said, "but he's your boy and it's you who'll be lookin' after 'im. Don't look to me for any wet-nursin!" I glanced at the barely-smoldering cookfire. "G'wan! Tell 'im to get down and come eat, before dinner's ruint!"

Zeetlah rattled off a string of Delaware talk in a sharp voice. The boy stirred, then slowly untangled his tall frame, slid reluctantly off the mule, and shuffled to our side, staring at the ground the while, pausing only to tether the mule and Zeetlah's horse to a pack-rope. Which spoke well for his attention to critters.

I dug out a passel of hard biscuit and the three of us made short work of the birds. The lad sucked every last shred of meat off the bones and licked his fingers afterwards. The biscuit disappeared like magic. Whilst Zeetlah and I smoked a pipeful, I enquired after the young fellow's name. "Lenapee call 'im Tompsey-naha-aniungas, like 'Merican say, Half-hoss. He good wid critter. People not so much."

"Well, ye'd best tell 'im I'll be callin' 'im Half-horse in American from here on, so's he'll know it means him." Zeetlah barked out a few words in Delaware, including the name Half-horse. The boy nodded and almost smiled as he moved his lips, mouthing the unfamiliar syllables of his American name. Fact is, after that, sign-talk worked handily for him and me to communicate, once he got the hang of how Mountain Indians sign, which isn't a great deal different from the way Delawares do in Missouri.

The sun was still high in the sky and I was itching to catch up with Campbell's packtrain. We had already lost more than a day and a half. "Let's be packin' up an' gettin' after 'em," I announced. Zeetlah nodded as he rose and Half-horse surprised me by springing to his feet, acting like he understood what I said. I realized then that he had read my hand-signs, with which every mountaineer accompanies his spoken words, like Indians do, almost without being aware that we're doing it.

It required little time to saddle our critters, rearrange packs to free up a mule for Half-horse to ride, load the others, and to rig up a surcingle with rope stirrup-slings for the newcomer. A grown man riding bareback without stirrups will break a critter down in half a day. The bare-boned-skinny Delaware kid, tall as he was, weighed hardly more than a child, but I value my animals too much to take a chance.

I reckoned the three of us could travel considerably faster than Campbell's unruly column. Overtaking them shouldn't require more than a couple days. Which we did.

⁂   ⁂   ⁂

We caught up with the column a day's ride out of Independence without pressing our critters overmuch. The young Delaware lad owned a large share of credit for our rapid progress. He possessed an almost-magical way with animals, especially mules and our already-good-natured jackass, cooing into their long ears, stroking their cheeks, and blowing into their nostrils, gentling them, coaxing them to put aside their ill-tempered manners. They nuzzled into his armpit and brayed their disappointment whenever he deserted them to tend to other chores.

Black Harris greeted us warmly and said it made no nevermind when I told him that the young Delaware would be joining us for the rest of the journey. "Hell, I daon't give a good gawddamn who ye bring along. Bobby's ramroddin' the outfit this time an' he likely won't even notice, busy as he be with them 'ere dandies o' his'n." He spat disgustedly. "The most of 'em cain't hardly even saddle their own critters an' that 'ere mostly drunk Ben Harrison won't even try! He's got us totin' an' fetchin' fer 'im 'til I got no time fer hardly nuthin' else!" He heaved a sigh and added, "Onliest one amongst 'em wuth a damn be that 'ere Scotty sojer-boy Stewart. He's a proper hand, even if he does treat ye like dirt." Somebody called out from Campbell's camp. Black cursed and muttered, "See what I mean?" and hustled off.

Harris joined us for supper, still complaining about fops, but the whiskey he brought along made his jeremiads tolerable. Afterwards, smoking and passing the bottle amongst us, his mood brightened and he spoke cheerfully of the rendezvous that waited at the end of our journey. "It'll be good seein' the fellers agin an' 'speshly Injun wimmen up thar." He sighed. "It's gonna be a long dry spell afore we git thar, but I reckon we'll 'preciate 'em the more fer it."

When he offered the bottle to young Half-horse, sitting silent, intent upon every word we spoke, although he understood naught of it, Zeetlah held up his hand and growled, "No veeskey fer Half-hoss! He Lenapee boy! No want 'im crazy-drunk!"

Black backed off. "Reckon ye be right. Thar'll be time enough fer 'im larnin' bad habits, come ronnyvoo. Best we be keepin' 'im on the straight-an'-narrer whilst we kin."

꜇ ꜇ ꜇

Next day in Independence, whilst Campbell and Harris went off to buy a flock of sheep and several beeves, I left Zeetlah in camp with our critters and plunder and took Half-horse into town to outfit him for the trail. He hadn't appeared to mind riding bareback with his rope-sling stirrups, but I reckoned it was best to provide him with a Spaniard saddle, which would be useful in performing many of the chores we were sure to encounter ahead. I purchased a good used but serviceable saddle, bridle, bit, britching, and such from a saddler who offered to show me some horses he had for sale out back. They turned out to be much better stock than I expected. I acquired a decent bay and an even better sorrel at a price that would have made Charlie Bowden weep.

Half-horse had arrived in my camp with only the rags he stood up in, moccasins in tatters, his quiver and bow, and naught else. A brief visit to Aull's Mercantile clothed him head-to-foot in new moccasins, a couple hickory shirts, a wide belt for his skinny waist, and a couple pairs of long-legged britches—which he converted to leggin's immediately upon returning to camp. He regarded the broad-brimmed felt hat I offered with a dubious stare, but I convinced him with sign that he would be glad he had it, once we encountered rain and hail on the westward trail. *Capotes*, rain-shrouds, and blankets I already possessed aplenty in my packs. Buffalo sleeprobes would have to wait for rendezvous.

A few minutes in a bakeshop provided a sackful of still-smoking meat pies for our supper in camp, which produced the first and only hint of a smile on the young man's sullen phiz during the entire shopping expedition.

~o   ~o   ~o

The hike from Independence to Lexington, where Campbell picked up most of his trade plunder, crossing Muddy Crick, a couple more days to the spring-swollen Kaw River and ferrying across, until we arrived at the Kaw Indian Agency was a traveling nightmare. It was especially hard on Campbell's hostlers. They had already had their hands full with cantankerous pack animals. Now they also had to deal with a score of cattle, including a couple belligerent bulls, and a flock of woolies that brought to mind the difficulty of trying to hold a handful of quicksilver. They were forever running every whichaway, spooked by every unfamiliar sight or sound. Only when Bobby bought a billy-goat in the little French-Cree village on the Kaw did matters get somewhat better. From then on, the sheep mostly followed wherever he led.

When I commented on the cattle as a welcome addition to our diet, Harris cautioned, "Don'tcha be gittin' yer appertite too honed up. More'n half o' them 'ere cattle ain't fer eatin'. Them two bulls an' all o' the cows be fer breedin', once Billy Sublette gits his forts built. We're jist deliverin' the most of 'em. Bobby says jist the steers'll be fer eatin' on the way 'til we git to buffler." Campbell called a three-day halt at the Kaw Indian Agency—which was run by some shirttail kinsman of General Clark's—in order to rest and restore the critters on the good grass thereabouts.

It was a welcome respite, for it gave Zeetlah and me a chance to instill some practical smarts in Half-horse. His affinity for mules and horses was a valuable quality, but growing up fatherless in his impoverished Delaware village had failed to equip him with many of the skills he would need in the months and years ahead. For one thing, he had never fired a gun. He was handy with his short bow and stone-tipped arrows, but it is guns and knowing how to use them that allows a small party of strangers to survive against overwhelming numbers of hostiles eager for scalps and plunder.

First off, I presented Zeetlah with one of the brand-new Hawken rifles to replace his own long gun, which he had wisely converted from flintlock to percussion some years earlier. His old rifle, battered but serviceable, went to Half-horse, who proved to possess a keen eye and steady hands. The three of us burned up a passel of powder and lead, shooting at targets, until we were satisfied that the youngster could hit what he aimed at, then reload quickly and properly. There was something about the young fellow that convinced us that he would remain steady when the target offered to shoot back, but there's no explaining such a thing. You just know it, or think you do.

Naturally we equipped him with a tomahawk and a good English Sheffield butcher knife and Zeetlah undertook to tutor him in their use in close combat. I dug out a couple of the grass *reatas* I had received for boot from the old Spaniard saddler and showed Half-Horse how to coil the rope, build a loop, and throw it overhand to snare a horse or mule or whatever else he might wish to capture. Fortunately Campbell never caught us using his woolies for targets, which were somewhat the worse for wear after we got done with them.

Most other skills, such as assembling a pack and balancing it on a packsaddle, the various knots required, adjusting harness, and suchlike are best acquired by paying attention, trial-and-error, and practice. Half-horse exercised all three, with few errors after a couple tries. By time we resumed the march, the young Delaware was pretty much earning his keep.

-oOo-

CHAPTER II
TRAILING WEST

alf-horse's presence often relieved me of trailing pack animals, granting me freedom to ride where I chose in the column—admittedly showing off my Coffee horse—chatting with men I knew and getting acquainted with others. I avoided joining the cluster of gentlemen guests who usually rode in the van with Bobby Campbell, but I was able to observe them. In the saddle, most of them resembled so many sacks of potatoes, but I agreed with Harris that the British Captain Stewart's horsemanship was admirable. Mounted upon his flat English saddle, clad in smart britches and knee-high cavalry boots, he was straight-backed and square-shouldered, elbows snug to his ribs, flexible in response to his horse's every movement, heavy in the stirrups, gifted with what horsemen call Irish hands, sensitive to the animal's mood and intentions.

His treatment of men he considered his inferiors, which was nearly all of us, was something else.

My first encounter with Stewart occurred one late afternoon, soon after we departed Kaw Agency. When Campbell called a halt to the day's hike and after my chores were done, I propped against a tree nigh the crick and proceeded to catch up on my journal, the ledger on my lap and a volume of Mister Shakespeare's tragedies beside me. Intent upon my scribbling, I didn't notice his approach until a shadow fell across the page. Looking up, I beheld Captain William Drummond Stewart standing beside me, a thin smile on his lips but not in his eyes. "I believe that you are called Temple Buck," he said in a flat voice, neither friendly nor otherwise.

I allowed that I knew no other by that name. "I've to come to learn if you might be willing to sell your black horse," he said without further preamble. He rattled the pouch on his belt, announcing the presence of ready cash. I made no reply, rising instead to my feet to meet him on more equal terms. We were much the same height, an inch or so under six feet. He was what most folks would call handsome, clean-shaven, ruddy complexion, blue-eyed, a prominent Roman nose, dark brown hair tinged slightly with grey at the temples. I guessed his age at seven or eight years beyond my own thirty winters. He was somewhat more thickset than I, well set-up, muscular under his snug military-style tunic, ramrod straight, his manner imperious.

"Let's make short of it," I said. "I'll not be selling that horse under any circumstances. I have no need of cash money, either here or in the settlements. I already possess all I will ever need." For emphasis, I shifted my own money-poke, producing the dull clink of gold pieces. Which I immediately regretted. It was a childish rejoinder to his brash offer.

It was plain to see by his rising color that Captain Stewart was not accustomed to being denied, but he said merely, "Oh, very well," and half-turned to depart. Then, glancing down at my open journal and letting his gaze stray to the Shakespeare volume, he ventured, "I see that you are a man of parts, Mister Buck. Is that not uncommon in your profession?"

Bristling at his condescension, I replied as calmly as I was able, "Not so uncommon as ye might think, Cap'n. There are many men of superior intellect who have chosen the trapper's life. If ye make it all the way to rendezvous, you'll learn that any man who survives a couple winters in the mountains has all the smarts ye could wish for. Some are well-schooled. Most aren't, as ye say. But any man who rightfully calls himself a mountaineer is anybody's match for brains. Stupid men go under in a hurry."

Striving to appear unruffled, Stewart said vaguely, "That may be as may be, Mister Buck. I intend to see for myself."

As we spoke, I became aware that the Englishman was staring at my forehead, somewhere around my eyebrows, not once looking into my eyes. When I was sure of it, I couldn't refrain from saying, "It appears to me, Cap'n Stewart, that ye be more'n somewhat shy about lookin' a man in the eye, lest ye find that he's as much a man as you claim to be, maybe moreso." Stewart bridled, indignant at my impudence, but I went on. "That stick don't float in the mountains, Cap'n. P'raps such a trick works with your redcoat soldier-boys, but, hereabouts, mountaineers'll soon let ye know they reckon a man that can't look ye in the eye ain't much of a man an' he sure-as-hell can't be trusted."

Stewart made no reply. Redfaced, he merely harrumphed, turned on his booted heel, and marched stiff-backed to Campbell's tent. For a moment, I halfway regretted calling him out for using on me a well-practiced aristocratic trick intended to cow social inferiors, but then I shrugged and decided that he deserved what he got. That stick don't float in the mountains.

After supper, Harris, Zeetlah, Half-horse, and I were lazing about, smoking and palavering—leastaways, Harris and I were palavering—when Bobby Campbell came by and asked if he might have a word with me. I knew what was coming, but I reckoned it was best to get it over with. We walked off a few paces distant from our cookfire before Bobby demanded, "What in hell were ye thinkin', Temple, insulting our guest? Don't ye realize that man is a nobleman from one of the finest families in Scotland, a decorated British officer, and a hero of Waterloo, where Wellington defeated Napoleon and broke the back of the bloody French Army?" He paused, redfaced, breathless after his long question.

"Ye damn bet I do!" I replied, my temper rising to match his own. "And I ain't impressed one damn bit! He's here now, in America, where we don't give a good goddamn about noble titles an' such foolishness! Out here, as ye well know, Bobby, it's handsome is as handsome does an', hoss, what kin ye do! Nothin' else!"

"He has proved his mettle, Temple, and he has the medals to prove it! His courage in warfare is unquestioned. Stewart has been tried in battle and found worthy of the honors his country has bestowed on him!"

I mostly avoid strong arguments, but this time my dander was up. "That may be, Bobby," I responded hotly. "I don't take a mite away from his credit for whatever he did at Waterloo or anyplace else, but he's headed for the mountains now, where us hivernants don't get medals for fightin' Injuns and grizzly bears an' livin' through winters that freeze your arse solid and summers that boil your blood, starvin' an' thirstin', takin' our chances and askin' no man's help or leave, only the respect that one man owes another! Stewart didn't grant me that respect, Bobby, so I treated him likewise."

Campbell remained silent for a spell, but he wasn't mollified. "Just the same," he resumed, "brave men like Wellington and Captain Stewart deserve our gratitude for stopping Napoleon in his tracks and defeating the French, once and for all!"

I really didn't care much, one way or another, about Waterloo or anything that happens in Europe, but Bobby Campbell had put me in an arguefying mood. "Now that ye brought it up, Bobby, let me tell ye that I ain't so sure that Americans ought to be happy about how that war came out! What have the French ever done to hurt us? Hell, it was the French that saved George Washington's arse at Yorktown, where we won the war. Ye know that! Philadelphia, where you come from, would've been one big bonfire, if the Brits'd had their way. We fought two goddamn wars against the Brits tryin' to hold onto us Americans! Not one, that I ever heard of, against the French!"

"I know my history, the same as you do," Campbell responded lamely, "but England is still our Mother Country. We speak English here, not French."

I should have quit right there, but I didn't. "One more thing, Bobby Campbell, if it hadn't been for Napoleon sellin' all this land we're standin' on to Tom Jefferson for a song, we likely would've had to fight for it, but we didn't need to. So we can be thankin' ol' Nappy an' not some English king for our beautiful Shinin' Mountains."

Campbell made no immediate reply. He just glared at me before he cracked a smile and said, "You're a man of strong opinions, Temple Buck, but please favor me by not picking fights with our guest. He's really not such a bad sort, once ye get to know him."

I genuinely like and respect Robert Campbell. My ire evaporated. "Hell, Bobby," I assured him, "I bear no grudge against Cap'n Stewart. Just tell him to mind his manners with me and everybody else he comes across here in America. As ye know well, we don't take to highfalutin aristocrats treatin' us like less'n we are."

Bobby didn't reply directly. He just clapped me on the shoulder, wished me well, and mumbled something about how he hoped the matter was resolved.

He must have spoken with Stewart, howsomever, for the next time I met with the Hero of Waterloo, he fixed a steely gaze directly into my eyes and kept it there whilst we palavered about nothing much. I regretted my shouting match with Bobby Campbell, but perhaps the cause of it was for the best. I reckon Captain William Drummond Stewart learned an important lesson in mountain manners.

∾   ∾   ∾

The Hero of Waterloo continued to be a burr under just about everybody's saddle throughout the entire journey. "That 'ere gawddamn nosy Scotty sumbitch cain't never let well enough alone!" Harris exploded, after Stewart interfered with Black's disciplining of a hostler caught sleeping on his guard post, insisting that the man's punishment wasn't severe enough. The customary penalty for that offense, as well as for anyone who failed to keep his weapon clean and oiled, was a five-dollar fine deducted from his already meager wages and being required to march afoot for a full day, leading his animals, subject to the taunts and jeers of his fellows. Stewart recommended strongly that the punishment be tripled on both counts, which even Campbell thought was too severe.

Upon our departure from Kaw Agency, Bobby had imposed strict rules on the night guard. We were entering the sprawling domain of predatory Pani Indians, always on the lookout for critters, plunder, and scalps. He appointed Stewart, Harris, and me to be guard officers, which meant that, every third night, one of us was obliged to stay awake all night, patrolling the men assigned in pairs to guard positions for a two-hour stint. It was a difficult chore for dog-tired hostlers required to remain hunkered down in silence, unmoving, peering into the darkness, alert for any sound or movement that might betray a hostile incursion. Men frequently nodded off, especially at first, and it was our job to see that they didn't do so.

Black and I had performed that chore before. Usually a severe tongue-lashing and a warning sufficed to convince the usually-apologetic first-time miscreant to mend his ways, instead of levying punishment. Stewart harbored no such tender sympathies. He appeared to relish inflicting harsh penalties on our hard-working hostlers and even free trappers who were tagging along with the packtrain. Significantly, the gentry residing in Campbell's charmed circle were not required to stand guard duty. Stewart had volunteered his services.

Especially irritating was the Scotsman's practice of intruding on our authority on the nights when he was supposed to be off-duty. Time and again, I resisted an impulse to shoot him myself when I spied his erect figure tromping amongst the guard posts, standing straight up, making no attempt to conceal himself from a possible Pani marksman, single-mindedly intent upon catching a man who might be drowsing, as if it were some sort of military exercise.

At last, Harris and I confronted him. "These hyar men ain't yer gawddamn red-belly sojer-boys, Cap'n," Black told him, "an' this ain't no gawddamn game! Ye don't know nuthin' 'baout thi'shere country ner nuthin' abaout Injuns ner nuthin' else out thisaway! My men'll do the job jist fine, the way Buck an' me's got 'em doin' it. We been at it long afore naow an' we been keepin' the gawddamn Pawnee offa the critters an' our gawddamn ha'r! Ye be gawddamn lucky somebody ain't shot ye awready, the way ye been gallivantin' abaout in the dark, 'stid o' sneakin' 'round quiet-like, like y'oughta!"

It did no good. Captain Stewart remained impervious to experienced counsel. Apparently His Majesty's military officers always know best.

❧   ❧   ❧

Although Harris constantly complained about their wandering ways, Campbell's sheep provided better vittles than the sowbelly and boiled cornmeal that had been our constant fare before Lexington. Every evening, Zeetlah and Half-horse scoured the crickbanks and nearby prairie for roots and herbs to flavor and supplement the mutton stews on which we supped and then warmed over to break our fast. Naturally Black made sure that our mess received generous portions of the best cuts, since he was in charge of such matters.

Early on, our mess was enlarged to five with the addition of George Holmes, a handsome, gentle young man of good family from the East, who had signed on with Campbell in order to get a taste of adventure by traveling to the Rockies. "I reckon young George hyar'll be gittin' a bellyful of adventurin' afore we git to ronnyvoo," Black declared goodnaturedly when he introduced the young fellow to us. "'Sides his reg'lar chores, lookin' arter the cattle an' woolies," Harris explained, "Bobby put 'im to fetchin' an' totin' fer Cap'n Stewart, but natcherly nobody thought to feed 'im over thar 'mongst them 'ere nabobs an' he don't rightly fit in with most o' the hostlers an' drovers. They be allus funnin' 'im fer bein so good-lookin', callin' 'im Beauty an' sich. I reckoned he mought be welcome 'mongst y'all."

Which he was. George Holmes proved to be well-spoken and well-read, mannerly, a willing worker, quick to learn, and eager to please. He was delighted to discover the stock of books I carried with me and he returned in good condition each one that he borrowed. In turn, I enjoyed our bookish palaver, a commodity sorely lacking in my otherwise satisfactory traveling companions. He told me that he had no intention of remaining in the mountains. He wished to make this one trip to the Rockies only in order to broaden his education. When the weather was fair, nobody bothered with nighttime shelter, but when it rained, Holmes shared my skimpy canvas. Zeetlah and Half-horse bedded down in their own digs. Although Black joined us at mealtimes, he kept his sleeprobes amongst the hostlers and drovers.

❧   ❧   ❧

Whenever possible, overnight camps were set nigh watercourses, mainly in order to water the critters, but it also allowed Zeetlah, Half-horse, and me—and rarely anyone else—to indulge in our daily bathe—a custom, I might observe, that gives the lie to the common American expression *dirty Injun*. Indians of every tribe that I have known in my several years in the mountains and on the prairies bathe every day, if they can, which, as ye know, is regrettably not the habit of most Americans.

One early morning, as I trotted back to camp after my morning bathe, naked save for my dripping britchclout, I spied Captain Stewart seated on a rock by the crickside, his silver-ornamented toilet articles spread before him, squinting into a small, ornate hand-mirror as he scraped the last wisps of shaving soap from his cheeks. It was a customary sight. The Scotsman shaved his whiskers every morning, without fail. He was the only member of the company who did. Just about everybody else, except for Campbell and a few of his guests, pretty much gave up shaving and cutting their hair during the long, womanless journey from Saint Louis to the Rockies. Stewart had also arranged with a hostler who had put aside the barber's trade to try his luck in the mountains to keep his topknot more or less properly shorn.

The captain surprised me by beckoning me to join him. Without so much as a good morning, he enquired, "How is it, Mister Buck, that you and I are the only two men in this entire company who shave every day?"

To which I replied simply, "I don't," which wasn't altogether true, but it made a better response. I might have explained that I owe my mostly hairless features and body to the fact that I am the bastard son of Powatawa, a Shawnee Indian, formerly headman of his band, who awaited me now with my trapping bunch in the mountains, but I reckoned that my heritage was none of Stewart's business. My mother was a beautiful well-born lady of a respectable Virginia family who fell in love with a handsome, intelligent, young Shawnee warrior in the Ohio wilderness. I am proud to be heir to the blood those two bestowed on me and I strive to be worthy of them both.

I noticed that Stewart was running his gaze over the many scars that I have accumulated on my body over the years that I have been in the mountains, but he refrained from comment and I had no wish to discuss the circumstances of how I acquired them.

As I left the Scottish captain with a puzzled look on his smooth-shaven phiz, it occurred to me that I had never seen him bathe. It appears that he accounts his tonsorial attentions to be hygiene enough. I reckon Europeans are much the same as most Americans when it comes to laving their bodies.

≈   ≈   ≈

’D’ye git the feelin’ we been runnin’ ’twixt the raindrops, do ye?” Black Harris asked. “We been out more’n a for’night since Lexin’ton an’ we ain’t seed hide ner ha’r o’ Pawnees. ’Tain’t natcher’l!”

I agreed that it was indeed unusual that we had suffered no Pani raids on the packtrain, not even sneaky nighttime attempts by young bravos to make off with a critter or two from the herd. It was a happy situation, but queersome.

“I’m almost sorta wishin’ they’d make some kind o’ try,” Black mused aloud. “Nuthin’ much, mind ye. Jist enough to let us know whar they be. Some o’ the fellers’re gittin’ daownright slack on night guard, ’speshly them as ain’t never made thi’shere trip afore naow.” He spat and shook his head. “Course, I ain’t lookin’ fer no trouble, mind ye.”

It was true. It is difficult to maintain a high state of vigilance amongst inexperienced men, who tend to become complacent unless they are challenged. “Mebbe them Pawnee heared abaout that ’ere Scotty sojer-boy comin’ along this time an’ got skeered off,” Black offered with a grin. “Ye think?”

I laughed and allowed that it might be so, before I touched spur to Coffee’s flank and loped out ahead of the column to make a broad sweep of the country ahead, just in case Panis or some other band of hostiles might be lurking, all too willing to make Black’s humorous wish come true. I was grateful for the scouting chore. It gave me a chance to school my Coffee horse. He was responding nicely to his training, now that I had more time to provide it, thanks to the presence of Half-horse, who often relieved me of the tedium of looking after our pack animals in the column.

Hotblood though he was, Coffee possessed an agreeable disposition, a willing personality anxious to please. He learned quickly. Soon, a mere shift of my weight or a twitch of the rein told him my intention as if he could read my mind. Teaching him to swap leads occupied only a single morning—that is, schooling him to switch his leading foreleg in response to abrupt changes in direction at a lope or gallop, which is absolutely essential when running buffalo over uneven ground. A sharp turn on the wrong lead can cause a fatal spill of horse and rider amidst a stampeding herd.

Watching out for possible marauders was only a part of my scouting chores. Equally important was discovering buffalo, which unfortunately failed to appear by time we crossed the Big Blue. Our flock of sheep was dwindling fast. Boiled cornmeal and sowbelly once again became our dinnertime staple, with only skimpy portions of mutton for supper. The sheep were history by time we reached the Forks of the Platte, but still no buffalo.

Weather changed for the worse. Day and night, we were soaked with rain or pelted with hail the size of rifle balls. Cricks overflowed their banks and the prairie turned treacherous with bogs and quicksand as we plodded along the South Fork of the Platte until we found a fording place shallow enough to let us cross over to the North Fork.

My Coffee horse resumed his servitude, lugging a pack, like it or not. I rode my saddle mule each sopping-wet day, hunched over my saddle pommel, flinching beneath my rain-shroud against driving rain or pummeling hailstones, peering out from under the drooping broad brim of my hat, as Harris and I sought a passable trail for the packtrain to follow. I became increasingly pleased with my long-eared critter's easy-going gaits, judicious choosing of his footing, and agreeable personality. Until then, I hadn't bestowed a name on him. I had owned such a saddle mule before, actually one of his distant half-brothers, whom I called Sugarfoot because of those same qualities. Upon my departure from the mountains the previous fall, I had gifted that mule to my Flathead father-in-law, Iron Bow, who had long admired the critter. Now, stuck for a proper name, I decided that Iron Bow, who speaks no English, wouldn't likely be calling his critter Sugarfoot, so it was reasonable that my new saddle mule inherited that name.

Long days in the saddle as we forged westwards in the rain were bad enough, but nights were worse. Firewood was scarce along the crickbanks and what we could find was soaked. Cookfires sputtered and smoked, giving off barely enough heat to boil cornmeal and fry sowbelly. Campbell was stingy with his beef, trying to parcel it out until we ran into buffalo, which appeared to have forsaken that country. Trying to sleep was a miserable failure. We pooled our canvas, in order to have enough above us to keep off the rain and some on the ground to keep our sleeprobes from getting soaked, without much success. Nighttimes, the four of us, Zeetlah and Half-horse,

Holmes and I huddled together in our scant shelter for warmth, which situation wasn't improved when Black Harris burrowed in amongst us, claiming that his added presence did us a favor by adding his body heat. Nobody thanked him for that gift.

Once clothing and bedding got wet, there was no way to dry it. Constant rain and drizzle kept everything damp. Weapons rusted, no matter how much whale oil a man might use to wipe them down, and Captain Stewart was beside himself, levying fines and punishment which even Bobby Campbell countermanded.

Night guard was the worst. Hunkered down in the rain for a two-hour stint, shivering with cold and forbidden to move about or even stand erect, peering into darkness and straining their ears for a sight or sound that might signal a marauder was almost too much to bear for many of the men, especially those who were making the journey for the first time. There was much grumbling but, to their credit, no mutiny.

Even after a man stood his spell at guard duty, there was little chance to get warm, for always, no matter the weather, fires were forbidden after dark, lest their glow attract unwanted visitors and illuminate a target for them.

Fact is, there was little likelihood of a raid. Black summed it up. "Shee-it! Them 'ere Pawnee ain't likely to be gittin' out'n their lodges an' off'n their squars 'til the sun gits to shinin' agin! Wet bowstrings don't 'low makin' war Injun-style."

Grass was short and watery, which took its toll on the critters' good fettle. Their manure was loose, which made them weak. Ribs and hip bones commenced to show under shaggy hides. Constant wet softened hooves and thrush cropped up. The animals' crankiness was exceeded only by that of their hostlers, whose curses echoed from dawn to dusk and into darkness, until they fell into exhausted slumber.

Despite the weather, Robert Campbell doggedly pushed on, striving to put twenty to thirty miles behind us every day, ever mindful that he must reach the rendezvous before the competition gobbled up every precious beaver plew. Every morning, he urged Harris and me to find buffalo, which, try as we might, we were unable to do. Zeetlah suggested gloomily that maybe the Great Spirit had lifted them all into the heavens as punishment for whitemen's ways. As the days wore on, the beef cattle were consumed one by one, until only Sublette's breeding bulls and cows remained. Sowbelly and cornmeal became our sole sustenance. I wondered if the old scoundrel might be right.

Black and I, together with our Indians and the other free trappers, Vasquez and Lajeunesse, likely minded the weather less than most. Our years in the mountains equipped us with patience during present hardship and confidence that matters would get better.

The only cheerful face in the company belonged to Captain Stewart. He appeared to thrive on hardship and glory in privation. Always clean-shaven, he somehow maintained a reasonably dapper appearance. Peeking out from under the sagging, soggy brim of his once-jaunty palm-leaf hat, he constantly wore the tight-lipped, fixed half-smile of a man determined to meet every challenge with grace and bravado. No matter the boggy terrain, Stewart declined to ride a sure-footed mule, insisting that his blooded Kentucky steeds would do nicely. Black and I noticed with amusement, howsomever, that the captain took care to follow our hoof tracks with close attention, lest he flounder in quicksand.

Hugging the bank of the Platte's North Fork as best we could, we continued slogging westwards, passing Chimney Rock, its jutting stone needle barely visible in the driving rain, then Scott's Bluff, looking for all the world like some medieval castle with battlements and bastions, its watchtowers poking up here and there. "Reckon we awready come abaout five hunnerd mile from Independence by naow," Black opined. "But we still got a helluva lot o' miles to cover arter this, even afore we git to South Pass. An' gawd only knows haow fur it'll be to ronnyvoo arter that, wherever in hell they 'spect to have it thi'shere year," he concluded gloomily.

Soon after Scott's Bluff, the rain quit. Grass sprang up hock-high in golden sunshine. The treeless prairie blossomed with wildflowers, but still no buffalo. Alkali in some of the streams caused loose bowels in man and beast and did nothing to brighten the general mood of our travelers. Zeetlah saved us from the worst effects of the alkali water by mixing up an evil-tasting potion that relieved most of the symptoms. He was stingy with his nostrum, doling out doses only to those whom he considered worthy.

Campbell's retinue of settlement guests had become scruffy and sullen, except for Captain Stewart. He appeared to bloom in the good weather.

Uninvited, he took to riding out with me on my daily scouts. At first we spoke rarely, but after a couple days he peppered me with questions concerning the mountains and especially hunting the critters there, particularly buffalo and bears. One time, I dismounted and drew an outline of a buffalo on a bare patch of ground, then pointed out where to aim and where not to shoot. Stewart usually cultivated an air of snobbish disinterest, but on that occasion he appeared to be totally absorbed.

Riding side by side with him provided an opportunity for me to observe and admire his .70-caliber weapons, beautifully-crafted double-barreled percussion rifles. One was equipped with a smooth bore which could be used as a fowler. Both were adorned with intricate carving and silver and ivory inlays worthy of a skilled jeweler. Stewart abandoned his customary reserve. He couldn't keep from bragging. "Both of 'em the finest work of Joe Manton, Britain's finest gunsmith, which means, of course, the best of all Europe!" he crowed. "Forty guineas apiece I paid for 'em! And worth every farthing!" I recalled the thirty-eight dollars I had paid Jake Hawken for my own .54-caliber rifle, the best gun in his shop, and I calculated that Stewart had laid out at least five times that amount for each of his weapons. Aloud, I allowed that the captain's rifles were indeed admirable. Privately, I questioned the need for all that galena and gunpowder to charge those big bores and I reflected on the mountaineer's common maxim—handsome is as handsome does.

∾   ∾   ∾

Captain Stewart proved his marksmanship if not his judgment when we topped a gentle rise and spied a lone buffalo cow grazing nigh a huge jumble of boulders at the mouth of a ravine, her calf at her side. I saw by her shrunken hump and hollow flanks that she was still nursing her young one, but before I could speak, Stewart leapt from his saddle, knelt, took aim, and fired. His shot was true. The cow took hardly a step before she crumpled onto her forelegs, coughing out her life in a gush of blood. The calf caught a whiff of fresh blood and fled into the rockpile, impossible to follow.

Stewart was jubilant. "First blood!" he cried, his face alight with a victorious grin. I was less sanguine about his accomplishment.

"We'll see," I said, choking back a flood of words that sprang to mind. When I was reasonably composed, I added, "Too bad ye couldn't wait long enough so we could get 'em both. The calf looked pretty hefty."

Stewart, flushed with pride and pleasure, was unabashed. "I shot the big one, Mister Buck! Dropped her in her tracks! There'll be meat enough for all, this night!"

"Oh, more'n enough," I replied, choosing not to elaborate, letting him enjoy his triumph, while it lasted.

We had barely turned the cow onto her belly and commenced to split the hide down the backbone when the packtrain caught up with us. I turned the butchering chore over to a couple of drovers and joined Harris, who commented dryly, "She don't look like much. What d'ye think?"

"I think ye'd best be honin' yer choppers," I replied.

"Too bad we lost her young'un." I let it go at that. Black understood.

It was fairly late in the day and the Platte was nearby, so Campbell called a halt for the night. To do otherwise might have caused a mutiny amongst the hands, all of them eager for fresh meat.

As soon as the livestock was picketed, hobbled, and left to graze, the men scoured the prairie and crickbank for firewood and came up empty-handed. Nary a stick was found. The recent heavy rains had washed away every scrap of driftwood and, because buffalo had so far avoided that neighborhood, there were no dry buffalo chips for fires. All they found was dried-out sunflower stalks, which smoldered and sputtered and smoked and disappeared before they produced enough heat under the cookpots to boil the lean, stringy flesh of that nursing cow. We much prefer buffalo cows to young bulls, but later in the year, not in springtime, when nursing calves are draining off their mamas' strength and succulence.

When the men tried to eat whatever meat they managed to get halfway cooked, a general howl went up. They found that they could hardly cut it, let alone chew it. Black and I, the two Delawares, Louie Vasquez and Lajeunesse and a few other old hands didn't even try. We contented ourselves with sowbelly and let it go at that, assuring one another the while that better days were coming, but this wasn't one of them.

Better days took their good old time coming. Campbell's caravan grumbled its way west along the Platte, every eye straining in vain for a glimpse of buffalo, which helped to speed our progress. Every man was convinced that the farther we traveled, the better chance we had of finding fresh meat. Flat, featureless prairieland gave way to country broken by scattered low hills sprouting sparse greenery amongst rocky slopes and ravines.

Black and I spied the first pair of young bulls grazing near the riverbank, upwind of us, poor eyesight causing them to be unconcerned about the presence of two mounted men. Without a word, we quickly dismounted and, leading our horses, crawled within a hundred yards of them before we fired together, dropping one where he stood, the other no more than thirty yards distant before he stumbled and sprawled, stiff legs poking skyward. "We kin be thankin' Gawd ol' Fancy-pants Stewart warn't along t'day!" Harris growled as we swung onto our mounts. "He'd'a shore-as-hell figgered out somethin' to queer gittin' them two!" I made no comment, but I, too, was grateful that Stewart had chosen to spend the day with Campbell's group at the head of the packtrain. Good shot though he was, the Brit's know-it-all manner kept getting in the way of his learning from men he considered his inferiors. Which was all of us.

Black's mood brightened when we reined up beside the first bull. "Would'ja look at that'n, Temple!" he crowed. "Rollin' fat he be! I could eat that'n plumb raw, tender as he looks!" Fact is, we wasted no time in doing just that, rolling the young bull onto his belly, splitting and yanking the hide free, and diving inside, slicing off strips and gobbling smoking-hot liver, then went for the bladder and sprinkled gall on the liver for even better flavor. Looking across the critter, I burst out laughing at Harris's blood-besmeared phiz as he chomped happily on a chunk of liver.

"It's been entirely too long, Black, since I've tasted anything this good," I managed to say between mouthfuls. Then, "Ye'd best ride on back an' let 'em know what's for supper. I'll hang on here an' make sure we get to keep some good parts for our own mess."

Harris looked reluctant, but at length he nodded and allowed that it was best that he do so. He carved off another slice and, still chewing, mounted his horse and loped back to the column. I untied my rain-shroud from behind my saddle, took a moment to calm my Coffee horse, who was stamping and snorting nervously at the smell of blood, spread the rain-shroud on the ground, and proceeded to carve out generous portions of hump ribs and blackstrap, boudins plump with half-digested grass, marrow bone, and whatever else struck my fancy. The steaming heap of meat on my rain-shroud assured our mess a generous feast at suppertime and for next morning, as well. There was still plenty of good meat to go around and I felt no guilt in claiming the choicest parts. To the victor belongs the spoils.

By time the hands finished with the two carcasses, there was little left but bellow and squeal. Naturally we camped there that night. Bobby Campbell was as eager as the rest of us to indulge his appetite. There was deadfall aplenty on a nearby rocky hill and soon cookfires were blazing and the air was fragrant with the aroma of roasting meat. Good-natured cursing and snatches of song rang out through the camp. Weeks of pinched bellies and habitual complaining were forgotten by men stuffing themselves with nature's bounty, content to live for the moment, unconcerned about the morrow.

Wherever you find buffalo it is likely that Indians are not far off. The general jollity notwithstanding, a substantial night guard was posted and Captain Stewart volunteered to be its officer. The British gentleman neglected to congratulate Black and me on our good fortune, but that wasn't surprising. We reckoned he was miffed at the contrast betwixt his kill and our own. We shrugged and wished him *bon appétit*, wherever he was, and reached for another hump rib.

๑   ๑   ๑

Scattered bunches of kicked-out young bulls, in pairs and sometimes as many as half-a-dozen, which we shot from cover, kept us in meat and good spirits as we followed the North Platte to where the Laramie spills into it and the Black Hills lie off to the North. Harris couldn't refrain from grumbling about how Laramie Fork came by its name, just as he had done five years before, when I first came that way with him. "From what I hear," he groused, "ol' Joe Laramie warn't much a-tall afore he got hisse'f kilt by Injuns hyarabouts. Right off, folks got to callin' thi'shere river arter him. 'Pears to me, a feller oughta make some sort o' mark, 'stid o' jist gittin' kilt, afore he gits hisse'f remembered by gittin' a whole gawddamn river named arter him."

I realized that Black was plainly jealous of Joe Laramie's minor fame and I found it amusing. "Would ye like folks to be callin' some river or crick after you, Black?" I asked, trying to keep a straight face. "Or better, maybe some big ol' rock—like Chimney Rock, say, stickin' 'way up in the air—especially considerin' the reputation you've got amongst the Saint Louie whores?"

He shot me a hard look, but he replied somewhat seriously, "Wal, it'd be a helluva lot more fittin' than haow Joe Laramie went an' got hisse'f famous, 'speshly cornsid'rin haow, 'twarn't fer me, most trappers wouldn'a never found their way to the mountains. It war me, Black Harris, what showed 'em haow to git thar!"

"Tell ye what," I said, stifling my mirth, "when we get to rendezvous, I'll pass the word around amongst the fellers to keep a look-out for a crick or maybe a river that nobody has put a name to yet an' we'll call it Black's Fork. How would that suit ye?"

Harris colored visibly under his sun-weathered complexion before he replied, "Aw, ye be jist funnin', ain'tcha?" Then, more seriously, "Not that I don't desarve it!"

Just then, we topped a rise and beheld a sizeable valley below and three-score or more buffalo grazing in the middle of it. The same thought struck both of us. Without a word, we wheeled our mounts and loped back to the column, where we informed Robert Campbell of our discovery. "Thar's a passel o' buffler jist up ahaid," Harris told him, "an' we got a chance o' makin' a purty big killin', if we do 'er right an' run 'em, 'stid o' jist pickin' off a couple-three."

"There's hungry times ahead, Bobby," I chimed in. "This'll let us lay by a store o' jerked meat for when we're crossin' South Pass. There's no tellin' when we'll get another chance." Campbell hesitated not a jot. Although it was only mid-forenoon, he gave the order to halt for nooning and told us to get moving.

I rode back along the column in high spirits, thrilled at the prospect of running buffalo once again. I had been riding my buckskin gelding, whom I now called Davey, for lack of a better name, but now I could hardly wait to put my Coffee horse to the most trying test for a horse that the mountains offer. Whilst I switched saddles and readied my weapons, I told Zeetlah what we planned to do. As usual, he betrayed hardly any enthusiasm. Half-horse, howsomever, picked up on my sign-talk and commenced to chatter excitedly. It was clear that he wished to join me. Zeetlah's features retained their customary gravity, but his eyes sparkled. "Half-hoss, he wanna go 'long wid you. Whaddaye think?"

I hesitated whilst I summed up what I knew of the lanky young Delaware. He was certainly a good hand with horses and a competent rider and he had proved himself an able marksman shooting at stationary targets. Galloping in the midst of a stampeding buffalo herd over uneven ground and aiming at a small, specific spot on a huge, running, lurching target that might rip the guts out of your horse, or you, at any moment is something else again. Still, the only way to learn that particular skill is by doing it. I shrugged and nodded and signed that he could come along.

Zeetlah, usually short-spoken and impassive, erupted in a spate of Delaware lingo and a flurry of hand-talk, likely instructing his nephew in the do's and don'ts of running buffalo, whilst he scurried about gathering up the fixin's Half-horse would need for the hunt. The tall youngster looked grave, attentive, soaking up whatever his uncle was telling him, nodding and signing that he understood.

Riding back to the head of the packtrain, which had already commenced to scatter for an overnight stay, I did my unsuccessful best to curb my excitement, which naturally was infecting my high-strung horse. Weeks on the trail had schooled him well, but what lay just ahead would determine if he and I had become a team worthy of a dangerous game. Half-horse, trailing behind me, his rifle slung next to his ever-present quiver and bow, appeared calm, almost disinterested, although I daresay he wasn't.

Harris joined the hunters at the same time I did. "Thar ye be, Temple!" he called out. "Time we be gittin' on the move," he addressed to no one in particular, "afore them bufflers git to movin' on!" Louie Vasquez and François Lajeunesse were mounted and ready. Captain Stewart arrived aboard one of his tall, leggy Kentucky-bred saddlers, one of his handsome rifles slung, the other across his saddlebow, a look of almost boyish enthusiasm crowding out his customary dignified demeanor, in spite of his efforts to control it.

Campbell and his guests, together with a score of hostlers, had assembled to wish us well. Even frowzy Doctor Harrison, paunchy, unshaven, and blear-eyed, had managed to stagger along to see us off. Bobby called out that he would hold his hostlers back a half-hour or so before he sent them after us to help with the butchering.

"Let's be goin' naow!" Black yelled, touching spur to flank, and set off at an easy lope. "I see ye brung yer Half-hoss kid along," he said as we settled in side-by-side. "Ye figger to use 'im fer the butcherin'?"

"Nope," I replied. "He'll do what he can in the hunt. He's Delaware and he's gotta learn sometime."

Harris grunted, frowned, and said at last, "Reckon so. Jist hope he don't git hisse'f kilt out thar."

I dropped back to ride alongside Half-horse and proceeded to advise him to ride fairly close behind me when the chase began, watching what I did, before attempting to kill a buffalo on his own. He signed that he understood, but I had little confidence that he would do as he was told. Few youngsters ever do.

We slowed to a trot, then a walk, as we neared the crest of the hill. Black reined up, dismounted, and crept to the edge. He returned, grinning, and announced, "They be still right whar we left 'em. Ain't hardly moved on a-tall."

Fortunately the breeze was in our face. Whilst we inched cautiously down the hill we could see that the herd, composed mostly of young bulls, was grazing westwards, moving slowly away from us across the broad, grassy valley floor. One important advantage for the hunter is the buffalo's poor eyesight, which he mostly makes up for with a keen sense of smell, but being downwind as we were let us mosey within a couple hundred yards of the herd before an old bull threw up his head and squealed, which sent the whole bunch off in a shambling trot.

I glanced down to make sure that the pistols in my pommel holsters were capped and ready. When I looked up I spied Captain Stewart galloping out in pursuit of the herd, no doubt eager, once again, to claim "first blood." I barely tightened my leg on his side before Coffee bounded forward, eager to join the chase. Grass stood belly-high in the valley, making it impossible to see badger holes and such fatal traps. I could only hope that he would avoid them. Looking ahead as we closed the distance, I admired Stewart's easy grace in the saddle, his perfect control of his mount. I lost sight of him as we passed the laggards at the rear of the herd and surged forward into the main bunch, leaving the slowpokes for my comrades mounted on horses slower than my own.

Dodging amongst gangs of shaggy backs running together, I saw with satisfaction that this herd was composed mainly of young bulls, two- and three-year-olds driven out of the main herds by big seed bulls jealous of their harems. From what I could tell, they were healthy and rolling fat, thanks to abundant spring grass thereabouts.

As we closed on a husky young bull I had selected for my first kill, I glanced over my shoulder to see if Half-horse was following. He wasn't. I was not surprised.

I chose to take my first buffalo with a pistol, riding up on his near side, so that I could control the inexperienced Coffee with the rein as I reached out with the pistol in my right hand to make my shot. The herd was running flat out now, legs pumping furiously, massive heads swinging threatening horns, snorting snot and bleating and grunting as they sought to escape. We gained on our quarry, and I guided Coffee closer to his flank, then forward, striving to keep his head just behind the horns, but my over-eager horse surged ahead just enough to allow the bull to swing his head in a vicious swipe that almost put a full stop to Coffee's paragraph and likely my own. He must have seen or sensed it coming, for he suddenly shied half-a-rod outward in a single bound, never losing his galloping gait, howsomever, then plunged in pursuit of the bull. This time he was more cautious. He stayed where he belonged long enough for me to swing up my pistol, aim at the fatal spot behind and below the shoulder, and fire. The bull took no more than a stride or two before his forelegs crumpled and the bearded chin ploughed a furrow in the grass, blood gushing from his mouth and nostrils.

I patted Coffee's neck and shouted encouraging nonsense as we set off after another likely target. I holstered my empty pistol and yanked out the other one, choosing to shoot from the near side one more time in order to make sure that my too-willing novice had learned his lesson concerning buffalo horns. Apparently he had. This time he came up smoothly, then matched his speed to that of the bull, staying just out of reach of the huge swaying head and its deadly horns but close enough for me to make a clean shot. This time the bull threw up his great head, eyes wide and mouth agape. His hindquarters collapsed and he skidded nearly erect until he fell over and lay still, legs stiff as lodgepoles.

The valley was narrowing and we would soon lose the herd in a jumble of low hills. I unslung my rifle and went after our final kill, the while thrilling at the raw power that flowed from my magnificent horse into every fiber of my being. This time I rode up on the off side of a roly-poly youngster, risking that Coffee could apply what he had learned and allow me, without using the rein, to bring my rifle to my shoulder and make a clean shot across the saddle. Which he did. I am sure that the air in that vicinity turned rosy with my shouted compliments to my young horse and to Charlie Bowden for finding him for me. My new, previously-untried Coffee horse was a natural buffalo runner, worth, to me, tenfold the dollars I had paid for him.

Coffee was barely breathing hard whilst I rode off to one side of the dwindling herd to reload my weapons and to learn how my companions had fared. I was half-afraid to look for young Half-horse, but I needn't have worried. I spied him riding up to my last buffalo and loosing an arrow into the shaggy hide, doubtless obeying Zeetlah's instruction to claim our kills in that manner. Every Indian bowman's arrows bear his personal mark.

I hailed the young Delaware and he loped over to join me, his usually expressionless face split in a wide grin. Without my asking, he let me know by signs and a gibber of Delaware lingo that he had downed two young bulls, one with his rifle, the other with arrows. Then he told me that he had claimed all three of my kills. I marveled that this neophyte could have paid attention to what I was doing whilst he was running buffalo for the first time. But then, I reckon I will never fully understand how wild Indians do what they do. They likely get it in their blood.

An euphoric Captain Stewart joined us as we walked our horses back down the valley, his carefully-studied dignity put aside for the moment. "Capital sport, Mister Buck! Absolutely capital! Joe Manton would be proud of his guns today!" he crowed. "Nothing like it anywhere!" "If my friends in England ever chased a buffalo, I swear they would never again bother with foxes!" "Jolly sport!" and similar sentiments. I asked how many buffalo he had shot and he replied that he had killed two. I nodded in what I hoped was an approving manner and politely refrained from mentioning what Half-horse and I had done. Naturally he didn't enquire.

Harris, Vasquez, and Lajeunesse were already huddled around a carcass by time we rode up, their faces smeared with blood, happily munching still-smoking-hot raw liver. Half-horse and I lost no time in swinging down and joining them. Captain Stewart remained in his saddle. I paid him no further mind until Black called out, "C'mon, Cap'n! Gitcherse'f daown hyar an' jine us! Ye ain't never et nuthin' as good as this afore! Ye earned it! I seed ye git them two bufflers! C'mon naow!"

Reluctantly, Stewart stepped to the ground and approached, plainly hesitant to participate in what must have appeared to him to be some pagan ritual. I busied myself carving off thin strips of liver for Half-horse and myself until Harris shouldered past me and sliced out a sizeable chunk, then reached a bloody hand into the bladder and sprinkled it with gall. "Hyar ye be, Cap'n!" he cried, shoving the meat into Stewart's hand. "Buffler liver an' a pinch o' bile fer flav'rin'! Ain't nuthin' better! Try it!"

The noble Brit looked apprehensive, squeamish in fact, but he refused to be shamed by the likes of Black Harris and the rest of us. He took a tentative bite, then another, before he beamed and exclaimed, "I say! Jolly good, isn't it?" and proceeded to munch happily on our barbarian fare.

The spirit of goodfellowship was apparently sufficient for the Hero of Waterloo to reach into his shot pouch and bring forth a silver flask, which he passed amongst us after draining a healthy draught himself. When the flask came to me I noticed that it bore a coat-of-arms with the word *Provyd* inscribed upon it. "Whew!" Black exclaimed after his first swig. "That be some good likker!"

"Single malt whiskey from our own still at Murthly," Stewart explained. "We grow the barley ourselves. I prefer it above all others."

"Me, too!" Black rejoined and helped himself to another deep swallow. Privately I reflected that my friend Harris always prefers his most recent tipple to all others.

❧   ❧   ❧

Cookfires blazed and dripping fat sizzled on the coals under a dozen great gobbets of roasting meat in the camp that early evening. Copper kettles bubbling with boiling tongue, spider skillets heaped with tasty boudins, and even more boudins and marrow bones seething in the coals added more rich fragrance to the air that rang with loud talk and good-natured cursing and cheerful song amongst the drovers and hostlers.

Our mess was equally jolly. Zeetlah had seen to it that our camp acquired a plenitude of the choicest cuts from the five buffalo bulls that Half-horse and I had harvested. Harris had generously contributed all of his three kills to the common good of the hands. Fourteen fat bulls assured that there was more than enough to go around. Campbell declared an extra day's halt so that most of the meat could be made into jerky, to be used when buffalo were scarce. Already the camp was festooned with long, thin strips of flesh hung on ropes, drying in the crisp, dry prairie air.

When we had stuffed ourselves to surfeit, Harris passed around the last of his whiskey. I chose to keep my packsaddle kegs of spirits intact until rendezvous. Black's unquenchable thirst would have drained them by time we reached South Pass. Besides, we were already drunk on self-satisfaction with the day's accomplishments, full bellies, and goodfellowship.

Whilst we smoked our pipes and palavered, I couldn't help but notice the remarkable change in the starveling Delaware kid Half-horse since he joined us on the Missouri plain. Regular vittles, even cornmeal and sowbelly, had put meat and muscle on his bones. More important, the hangdog look he had worn in the beginning had gradually faded and nigh disappeared, especially after that day's buffalo running, where he had proved himself our equal. Now, seated beside Zeetlah, speaking softly in Lenapee, he wasn't afraid to smile and even to laugh out loud. What I could pick up from his hand-talk told me that he had developed a passel of pride in himself.

Black was feeling expansive, his good spirits warmed by satisfaction with the day's work, as well as the spirits he had consumed. He commenced a gentle teasing of Zeetlah about our healer's amorous conquests over the wintertime in Saint Louis. They are old friends who frequently indulge in harmless joshing of each other. Although he usually has little to say, Zeetlah can make himself perfectly clear whenever he has a mind to do so and precious little gets past him when Americans are talking.

"From what I been hearin'," Black was saying, "thar's a passel o' wimmenfolk back in Sain' Looie feelin' plumb put aout abaout yew leavin' 'em a'hind—an' they ain't even whores! Nope! Temple hyar's been tellin' they's all good an' proper wimmen what jist couldn't git enough o' what ye war sarvin' up to 'em, mornin', noon, an' night. What's yer secret, Foot? How do ye charm them 'ere wimmenfolk the way ye do?" He continued in that humorous vein for a spell.

Zeetlah declined to enlighten Harris on a topic that is dear to Black's lubricious heart. He merely smiled smugly, eyes twinkling, obviously enjoying what amounted to high praise from a man of Black Harris's reputation for lechery.

"I say, what a curious coincidence! Imagine! Finding, here in the wilderness, the precise counterpart of our own Jamie Anderson! Remarkable!" I was startled by Captain Stewart's unmistakable voice coming from just behind me. He stepped forward and it was plain to tell by his slurred speech that the captain had been imbibing freely of Murthly Castle's delicious barley broth. He squinted owlishly at Zeetlah, who returned his gaze with a calm, inquisitive look. "Oh, yes!" Stewart went on, "The very image! Another dwarf who exerts a fatal charm over women! Ye wouldn't expect it, would ye? We have just such a little man at Murthly, scarcely four feet tall, awkward and ugly as mortal sin, like this one, but a devil with the housemaids and all the servant gels! I daresay he's swived 'em all! And perhaps not only them!"

I sat open-mouthed at such a display of bad manners. Harris's grin was frozen on his face. Holmes was blushing, staring at the ground. Zeetlah's smile disappeared, replaced by a hard, quizzical look. Stewart was oblivious. "Ah yes. My father the baronet keeps little Jamie about as our fool—a jester, don't ye know—for his comical quips and impudent jests. He is also our gatekeeper, greeting our guests, and other little tasks." He trailed off and tipped up his flask, then, "I say. Does your little fellow tell comical tales for his keep?"

In order to keep the Hero of Waterloo from meeting an inglorious end at the all-too-capable hands of my friend Zeetlah, I sprang to my feet and suggested that our uninvited guest might wish to return to Robert Campbell's camp, inasmuch as we were preparing to assemble the night guard, or some such excuse. Stewart looked surprised and somewhat offended at my interrupting him, but he quickly regained his composure, stiffly bade us goodnight, and returned to his quarters.

Later, as I made my rounds from one guard post to another, I marveled at the Englishman's callous disregard for Zeetlah's pride. Does Stewart's lack of respect for men he regards as his inferiors, men whom he might need to send to their death, make him a good soldier? Or does being a military officer by birth and tradition deprive men such as Stewart of the common sympathy that is due every man? Are aristocrats born with the comfortable assurance of their natural superiority over others already installed in their blood or is it drummed into them by their fathers or fed into them with their mothers' milk? Which latter possibility isn't likely, considering that most of them are suckled by wet nurses. Like the chicken and the egg, it's a conundrum.

Next morning when I met him at the riverbank, he wished me a curt good morning and mentioned nary a word about the night before.

≈   ≈   ≈

When we resumed our march up the Laramie, the white canvas packs on the critters were candy-striped with strips of buffalo meat still drying. Springtime lavished a riot of color on the prairie. Wild flowers and blossoming currant bushes bestowed a rainbow of hues on hock-high grass, which kept scattered bunches of buffalo grazing within an easy ride out to harvest a couple-three for each night's supper. Night guard was more important than ever, for wherever you find buffalo, you can be sure that Indians are not far off, come to hunt meat but always eager to raid a packtrain for plunder and especially horses to enlarge their herds and raise their standing in the tribe.

From time to time, far off on the prairie, we caught glimpses of Indians running buffalo. "Too fur east'ards fer Crows," Harris opined. "Most likely Lahcotahs movin' daown thisaway from up Nawth, gittin' crowded out by whites. Reckon that's why we been runnin' 'twixt the raindrops so fur, not gittin' hit by Pawnees like we mostly do. Likely they been too busy fightin' off Lahcotahs grabbin' up their huntin' ground to be messin' with us, much as they'd like to."

After a few days of following the river, Campbell called a halt nigh a sizeable stand of willows and announced that we would cross the Laramie. The river was running calm but too deep for critters to swim across carrying their packs. Bullboats were needed to float our plunder across. That meant cutting willow saplings, fashioning them into a frame tied together with sinew and strips of buffalo hide, then lashing a green buffalo hide onto it to make a bowl-shaped vessel. We didn't need to be very careful about caulking leaks, for the bullboats were abandoned after the crossing, which went off with only the customary catastrophes.

We stuck with the Laramie for a couple days after that, until Bobby called another halt and set up a more or less permanent camp in a big meadow nigh a patch of woods. He regretted losing precious time getting to rendezvous before the competition did, but he had no idea where the rendezvous would be held. "Cain't be traipsin' from hell to breakfast trailin' all o' these hyar critters an' plunder an' men 'thout knowin' whar in hell we be headin' in the fust place!" was the way Black Harris put it.

Next day, Campbell sent Louis Vasquez and François Lajeunesse on ahead to learn the rendezvous location, then settled in to await their return. It is never a good idea to let men be idle, lest they get to hatching mischief, so Bobby put his hostlers and drovers to work throwing up a sort of breastworks of logs and dirt around the camp to defend against attack and protect the livestock at night. Naturally Captain Stewart assumed command of the construction, which happified Black and me, for it freed us to spend our days keeping the camp in meat.

The weather held fair, graze, firewood, and water were plentiful, and a steady trickle of buffalo drifted through the neighborhood. Divided amongst Zeetlah, Half-horse, Holmes, and me, camp chores were light, so I enjoyed plenty of leisure for reading, catching up on my journal, and trying to teach Half-horse to speak American. Not surprisingly, he already knew most of the cusswords. Placing them properly was a more difficult task, but the Delaware youngster proved to be bright and eager to learn. It was a pleasure to see the scarecrow kid developing into a strong young man and to help him grow in his skills and knowledge of my language. I reckon my schoolmarm mother would have smiled upon our efforts.

There was time, too, to get acquainted with some of the other men. In the absence of Lajeunesse, Campbell appointed one of his hostlers to the clerking duties, a young Frenchy named Charles Larpenteur. He was an odd duck amongst the rough crowd of trail hands, fresh-faced, polite, eager to please, hardworking, and studious, albeit a trifle fussy. He told me that Campbell had been reluctant to engage him, warning that the toil of the trail might be too much for the bookish young fellow. But he had pleaded so passionately with Bobby and Bill Sublette that they relented and hired him on. Larpenteur confessed that it had been his lifelong ambition to go to the Rocky Mountains and make his fortune there. I admired him for his pluck, but I entertained serious doubt that he had the grit for it, although I refrained from saying so.

I reckon it was only a matter of time until Captain Stewart got his wish. Naturally he never came right out and said so, but it was plain to see that the Brit was itching for a fight with Indians, a chance to test his mettle against the savage American aborigine. His constant concern with the night guard, his unflagging attempts to impose an iron discipline on free-spirited hostlers and drovers who had no wish to behave like soldiers bespoke his nostalgia for the Army and the good old days of Iberia and Waterloo. Stewart was a restless soul, never content unless he had an adversary or a hardship to overcome.

Campbell's holding the packtrain in one place for a long spell was an invitation that marauding Indians could not ignore. Black and I knew it and Bobby knew it, but he had no choice but to remain where we were until Vasquez and Lajeunesse returned with word of where the rendezvous would be held. So, like it or not, we continued to dangle a tantalizing prize of healthy American horses and mules and fabulous wealth in whiteman's plunder before the greedy eyes of nomadic prairie bandits. We were sitting ducks, a prey that no hungry hunter can refuse.

When we were on the move, changing location every night, it was much more difficult for Panis, Arikaras, or whatever hostile bunch to organize a raiding party of sufficient size to overcome us, before we moved on out of their neighborhood, but now there was time to spare for them to get together whatever strength they reckoned would get the job done. "An' all we kin do is sit on our arse an' wait hyar 'til they take a mind to jump us!" Black lamented. "They'll be comin' on, mark me, but ain't nobody kin know jist when!"

Harris and I became nearly as pernickety as Stewart about keeping the night guard awake and alert and seeing to it that every man's gun was clean and oiled, loaded and primed. We didn't enjoy it nearly as much as our resident British martinet did, but we were just as finical as he when it came to keeping our sentries on their toes. What pained us, howsomever, was when Stewart had the gall to compliment us on our improvement.

"Hell! I don't mind the fightin'!" Black complained. "Ye git used to sich doin's. It's the waitin' an' not knowin' when!"

❧   ❧   ❧

Early on, several of us had taken to keeping our best horses saddled, hobbled, and tethered near us at night. The rest of the stock grazed inside a flimsy fence during the dark hours and under guard on the prairie in daytime. Once he got his fence built, Campbell kept his trail hands busy fetching armloads of prairie hay for nighttime feed.

Like Harris, I almost yearned for a fight, just to get it over with. I was sleeping badly, waking at every unusual sound. Often, even when it was Black or Stewart in charge, I took to scuttling from one sentry post to the next, just making sure.

When it came, just before daybreak, I was returning to my robes after visiting with Black, keeping low, dodging this way and that in order to make a difficult target of myself in the dim light of a quarter-moon. A shot rang out, followed by an agonized yelp that came from no American throat. I stood and ran full tilt for our shelter, intending to get my Coffee horse, so that I might help to keep our critters from being run off in the confusion that was sure to come.

Shouts and gunshots filled the air. As I rounded a clump of willows, I saw him, on his knees, sawing at Coffee's hobbles, flinching when my horse reared, neighing loudly with displeasure, striking with his forefeet at the unfamiliar-smelling intruder. I was fully armed, my rifle slung, both pistols in my belt, but I dared not shoot, lest I injure my horse. I jerked my tomahawk from my belt and fairly flew over the remaining rod or two. He must have heard my moccasin scrape on the earth. He half-turned from his chore and tried to rise, but too late. I swung the tomahawk to where I reckoned his liver was and felt it sink halfway down the handle—a stifled shriek, brief scrabbling facedown in the dirt, and then no more.

I yanked my bloody tomahawk free and led my excited horse aside whilst Bobby Campbell and Captain Stewart burst out of their tent and rushed to their tethered horses. Stewart, clad in a white nightshirt and barelegged, his rifle slung, struggled to buckle his belt over his billowing nightclothes as he ran. I laughed aloud when I spied a long cavalry saber in its sheath dangling from the belt, together with his holstered pistol and gun-fixin's.

I didn't laugh for long. By time I swung aboard my horse and headed for the livestock pen, Stewart was already ahead of me, brandishing his saber above his head and calling out commands that nobody heard or heeded if they did. When he came to the fence, he never checked his mount. They lifted gracefully over the barrier and disappeared amongst the swirling mob of horseflesh.

I had never asked Coffee to do more than jump a downed tree trunk, but I was willing to wager he could equal Stewart's horse. And so he did, altering his stride a mite as we approached the fence, then surging up and over without any help from me.

Whoever fired that first shot spoiled a heap of scheming by the raiders. Although the enemy appeared to be everywhere, our gunfire cracked and boomed from every quarter. The air was alive with American shouts and Indian yells. Christian curses mingled with terrified neighing and braying. We plunged into a maelstrom of thoroughly-scared livestock giddy with fear and excitement.

Pale moonlight revealed a lanky, half-naked buck trying his best to haul my stubborn jackass towards the fence. My critter was having none of it. Long ears laid back, stiffened forelegs plowing, he skidded on his rump, refusing to budge. Once again, I couldn't shoot, for fear of killing my father-in-law's precious gift. We shouldered through the milling herd at a high lope and swerved to confront the miscreant. He saw us coming only at the last moment, too late. I swung my tomahawk at arm's length as we sped past, catching him just below the eyes.

Something plucked at my leather shirt. I felt a searing hot stab at my left shoulder just as I spied a bare-chested, long-haired Indian, greasy torso glistening in the half-light, musket still at his shoulder, standing beside the fence, where he had succeeded in removing the top rail. Horses milling all around still forbade using my pistol. He tried to grab his empty musket by the barrel to use it as a club, but we were upon him, Coffee's shoulder spinning him off-balance just as my tomahawk caught him full in the face. He fell away and we swung back to the critters, now running in a vast hairy circle, pretty much staying put. A few mounted drovers were by that time keeping them bunched up inside the pen. I reckoned I could be more useful elsewhere.

Blood was running down my arm and chest, but I felt no pain. That would come later. Grey dawnlight cast a silvery sheen on the prairie, revealing Captain Stewart, his saber held aloft, galloping in pursuit of two Indians running for their lives through the tall grass. I wheeled about and went for the low place in the fence. Coffee cleared it without losing stride. I shoved the tomahawk into my belt and drew a pistol from its holster. We caught up with Stewart just as the Indians—Teton Sioux, by the look of them—despaired of making it to safety and turned to fight. A brace of arrows flew past. The Captain, his face flushed and smiling, called out, "Jolly good sport, eh, Mister Buck?" There was no time to reply. We were upon them. I rode within a fathom of a tall young buck painted for war before I fired my pistol, striking him in the breast and flinging him backwards into the grass, still clutching an arrow nocked to the bowstring. From the tail of my eye I espied Stewart, long curved blade glinting in the first rays of sunshine, swinging his arm up and chopping downwards in one smooth motion, cleaving the skull nigh to the shoulder blades.

"Oh, I say, this *does* bring back old times!" Stewart crowed through his laughter as he wiped his dripping blade on the hem of his nightshirt. He was in his element, doubtless reliving past glory.

I swept my gaze over the prairie and saw no movement. "Time we get back where we can do some good!" I yelled, wheeling Coffee about and heading for camp, reloading my pistol as I went.

Stewart rode up beside me, still grinning, his naked blade swinging at arm's length. "I warrant we'll give the bloody beggars comeuppance this day!" he shouted, kicking his horse into a faster gallop and pointing the saber forwards, as if he were leading a charge.

"Take care ye don't go to choppin' our own men! Hear?" I yelled after him. I doubt he heard me or cared if he did.

We rode into camp at a full gallop, then reined in our mounts so abruptly that their tails swept the ground skidding to a halt, lest we trample our people. Fighting was hand-to-hand in dueling pairs and small bunches, whites mostly using empty rifles and muskets like clubs, the Sioux forced by close quarters to rely on knives and tomahawks instead of their bows.

Stewart let out a most ungentlemanly throaty war cry and plunged his horse into the midst of the fray, swinging his saber, thrusting and chopping, scattering whites and marauders alike as they dodged the glittering blade, not all of them successfully. I followed close behind, pistols cocked, seeking likely targets. I emptied them both, then unslung my rifle in time to fire at a fleeing invader. Abruptly the scene fell mostly silent. Only the groans of the wounded and scattered gunshots that testified to *coups de grace* bestowed here and there broke the quiet. Suddenly the camp erupted in a pandemonium of cheers and joyful cursing. Men clapped one another on the back and hugged. Even wounded men smiled if they could.

A gleeful Moses Harris showed up as I swung from the saddle. "Muh fellers done better'n I could'a hoped fer!" he crowed. "Stuck to their guns an' never quit! Kep' shootin' long as they could an' went after 'em with ever'thin' they had when they couldn't! Not a one tried to cut an' run!" Then, "Haow 'bout you. Ye git any of 'em?"

"A couple." There was no profit in describing that morning's work.

"I seed ye war ridin' 'longside o' Stewart when ye come up out'n the medder." He spat out his cud and stuffed in a fresh chaw. "Daon't care much a-tall fer that 'ere stuck-up sojer-boy, but he shore is plumb sumpin' wi' that 'ere hossback sword o' his'n! Ain't he, naow?"

I allowed that the captain was indeed handy with his saber. Harris was bleeding slightly from a gash on his temple. "What about you? How did ye get that?" I asked, pointing at his wound.

He swiped at the seeping blood and grinned. "Hell, t'ain't nuthin' much. The one that gave me that'n damn near got me proper, but he won't be thievin' no more hosses." He jerked his chin at my blood-crusted shoulder. "Speakin' o' sich, what abaout you? That bad?"

"Nope. Nearly missed me. Foot'll get us patched up." I realized then that I hadn't seen either Zeetlah or Half-horse. "Ye seen 'im lately?"

Harris laughed. "Yep. Jist whar ye mought expect 'em to be. Goin' after dead Injuns' duds an' sich. They shore-as-hell earnt anythin' they kin grab up. Fought like catamounts, the both of 'em!"

"Any of our own get killed?"

Black's mood sobered. "A couple, fur as I know. Mebbe more. I ain't had time to see to all of 'em yet." He mentioned the names, which were unfamiliar to me. He looked away and added in a dull voice, "Reckon ye gotta expec' losin' some in a fracas like this'n."

I hastened to change the subject. "How many of 'em do ye reckon they were?" For all I could tell, there might have been a hundred raiders.

"Daon't rightly know. Mebbe thutty-forty. A helluva lot, fer damn sure!" He shifted his cud and spat. "Reckon they be Tee-ton Sioux from over on the Muddy, judgin' by them 'ere twisty topknots on some of 'em. Ain't never seed ha'r put up like that on no other kind o' Injun, 'ceptin Sioux."

"They're a long way from home, if so."

"Yep, but we'll be seein' more of 'em, I'm thinkin'. Steamboats, 'stid o' keelboats, on the Missourah been puttin' a crimp in their piratin' an' tax-collectin', movin' upriver fast as they do, an' packin' cannons, fer boot."

Black looked reflective before he prophesied, "Reckon we kin expec' to see more an' more Lahcotahs ri'chere an' mebbe in the mountains, too. They're gittin' crowded out by whites up nawth an' headin' daown thisaway. They be a mean bunch. Mark me. Purty soon, you'll be seein' a passel of 'em headin' west, grabbin' up huntin' ground offa Injuns what are awready thar."

Licentious and rough-talking as he is, Moses Harris is a thoughtful and observant man. I nodded. He is most likely right.

Somebody called his name and he turned to go, promising to join us when he could. As I prepared to return to camp, Stewart and Bobby Campbell, still mounted, ambled by. "Jolly good show, would ye say, Mister Buck?" Stewart called out jovially, his smiling face still flushed with excitement. "Pity we didn't get 'em all. Some o' the rotters succeeded in running off!" He had sheathed his saber, but his white nightshirt was bloodsmeared where he had wiped it clean.

"Just as well," Campbell opined. "P'raps they'll pass the word that packtrains aren't such easy pickin's." Then, "Take care of that shoulder, Temple, and much thanks for your help today." He clucked to his horse and the two of them rode off to their tent. I had to smile at the comical figure that

Stewart cut, bare feet in the stirrups, clad only in his bloodstained nightshirt. Just the same, he proved his mettle that morning.

I tethered Coffee in camp, loosened the *cincha*, heaped up hay for him, and headed for the crick. My hands were itching, sticky with blood, an unpleasant reminder of that morning's chore. Kneeling in the shallows, I first scoured my gory tomahawk with handfuls of sand, removing every trace of its recent occupation. Getting unwelcome images out of my mind proved more difficult—fact is, impossible. Whilst I splashed cold water over my head and arms, I kept revisiting each of my victims, seeing each startled, terrified face and blood spurting at my fingertips. Memory swept me back to the Musselshell, so many years past, and the first time I killed a man, an Assiniboine horsethief who meant to kill me, and my friend Brass Turtle's sage counsel—"Don't ye be frettin', Temple. It war him or you an' he would'a bragged on it arterwards, if ye hadn'a got thar fust." Such practical advice helps, but only time allows those unhappy pictures to fade and they can never be completely erased.

∿ ∿ ∿

Zeetlah and Half-horse returned to camp just long enough to dump armloads of loot beside their bower and for the healer to clean my bullet-creased shoulder and slather it with soothing unguent, assuring me the while that the wound was "long vay from yer heart," his favorite witticism. Half-horse was already resplendent in scavenged Lahcotah clothing, quilled and beaded leggin's and moccasins and a fancy leather shirt that reached to his knees. He tossed his faded hickory garments to the rear of the bower with an air that proclaimed that he would never wear them again.

As soon as Zeetlah finished tending to me, he grabbed up his medicine sack and summoned Half-horse to accompany him, then set off to assist wounded men, of which there were many. He had company in the person of Doctor Harrison, who had apparently sobered up enough to remember his oath. I spied that gentleman hurrying about, satchel in hand, kneeling here and there to lend his medical skills to injured hostlers and drovers.

I busied myself with camp chores, building up the cookfire and setting the coffee kettle on to boil, replenishing hay for our tethered saddle horses, and helping a couple hostlers bury the naked corpse of the thief who had attempted to steal my Coffee horse. A drover passing by assured me that nary a single horse or mule had been lost to the raiders. When Harris and George

Holmes showed up, soon followed by Zeetlah and Half-horse, I relented in my resolve to conserve my ardent spirits until rendezvous. I tapped a kettleful of good whiskey from the keg and we all toasted and congratulated ourselves on surviving the raid.

"How many of our own killed?" I asked Black.

His face darkened. "Jist them two I tol' ye 'baout." Then, more brightly. "More'n a few more got bunged up purty good, but they likely ain't gonna die of it. S'prisin', ain't it? Cornsid'rin' all the fightin' thar war. An' it 'pears we'll be stuck here long enough fer 'em to mend afore we git to movin' agin."

Nobody had a mind to venture out onto the prairie to pick off buffalo, lest we encounter lingering Lahcotahs. We made do with yesterday's vittles, of which there was a plenitude, and passed the rest of the day eating and dramming and smoking and recounting the events of that early morning. There was no need to exaggerate our exploits. They had been exciting and gory enough without embroidering on them. Old habits die hard amongst mountaineers, howsomever, so we did it anyway.

Except for gathering deadfall and prairie hay and hauling water from the Laramie and standing guard, there was little to occupy the hands. When chores were done, most of them passed their idle time yarning and gambling at cards. There were fewer quarrels than formerly, possibly because resisting the Lahcotah marauders had drawn them together, but I can't say for sure.

Small bunches of buffalo continued to wander by, not far off on the prairie. Harris, Half-horse and I, often accompanied by Captain Stewart, were able, with little effort, to keep the camp supplied with meat. Butchering chores were mostly left to the hands after we claimed prime cuts for our own messes. There was plenty to go around, so nobody grumbled.

Stewart took particular delight in the killing. He was an excellent marksman, so we often let him pick off lone young bulls that had wandered from their bunch. Harvesting meat was a common thing for Black and me, but the novelty of killing the huge beasts appeared never to wear thin for the Scottish sportsman.

The monotony of camp was broken one forenoon by a musket shot from a nearby hillside, followed by a couple more. Instantly every man, fearing a return of Lahcotah warriors bent on revenge, grabbed up his weapon. One fear replaced another, howsomever, when we beheld a huge grizzly sow lumbering in pursuit of three men running for their lives. Her half-grown cub disappeared in the brush. She was the first grizzly we had seen on our journey. Captain Stewart, engaged just then at his morning toilet, let out a howl of pure delight, snatched one of his precious Manton rifles from its stand, and dashed through our camp, scattering our cookfire on his way, eager to deliver the killing shot. Zeetlah, Half-horse, and I followed at a slower pace, ready to help if required.

Unfortunately for him, accomplished veteran soldier that he is, Captain Stewart had neglected to keep his guns loaded. The hammer fell on the percussion cap with a harmless pop. Red-faced and cursing, the Hero of Waterloo hotfooted back to his tent to retrieve his powderhorn and gun-fixin's. Meanwhile the hostlers poured one volley after another at the advancing mother bear without inflicting any apparent harm, likely because most of our hostlers were equipped with small-caliber deer rifles and muskets common in the settlements. From time to time she rose up on her haunches, standing nigh seven feet tall, pawing and rending the air with horrendous roars and screeches, then dropped to all fours to continue her charge.

I tried to aim, but with so many men jostling my arms and gun-barrel, I gave it up and stood back, ready to shoot if need be. Howsomever, when Stewart returned, panting, grimly resolute, they parted, fell back, and allowed him through. By then, the slavering she-bear was no more than three rods distant. She halted, heaved herself onto her hocks, and let out an ear-splitting bellow, cavernous mouth agape, jagged teeth and claws threatening sudden death. Almost casually, Stewart swung up his rifle and, without appearing to draw a bead, squeezed off his shot at the towering grizzly. She screamed, jerked, her wide-open jaws suddenly drenched with blood, tottered, feebly batted air, then crumpled into a hairy heap and lay unmoving.

A triumphant shout went up from the men. Wisely, no one offered to approach the carcass. Stewart, a smug, confident smile wreathing his features, was surrounded by cheering men, none of whom, I noticed, dared to crowd close to him. Instead of the hugs and back-slapping you might expect, they contented themselves with shouting his praises from a respectful distance, which likely pleased the noble captain as appropriate deference to his exalted social station.

William Drummond Stewart is a first-rate marksman. When they butchered out the big sow, they discovered more than fifty rifle and musket balls in the carcass. Stewart fired only once. That was enough.

My impatience at being stuck on the Laramie, awaiting the return of Vasquez and Lajeunesse bearing word of the rendezvous site, was exceeded only by Bobby Campbell's. Normally easygoing and good-natured, he became short-tempered, strained, fearing that American Fur and half-a-dozen other traders would get there before him and scoop up the fur harvest. "I miss the old days, Temple," he lamented, "when Ashley or Bill Sublette called all the shots, when we were the ones who decided where to rendezvous and set prices, too. It's a different world now—dog-eat-dog and nobody in charge!"

I bit my tongue, forbearing to mention that competition meant that trappers would likely get more for their plews and pay less for the goods they need to continue trapping in the year ahead. Bobby is a righteous mountaineer, but he has always sided with the booshways and the suppliers. Now he and Bill Sublette were just one more trading outfit amongst several. I mumbled something about how it was indeed a shame, but I didn't mean a word of it.

Fact is, Campbell's packtrain of goods would be delivered to Rocky Mountain Fur, which would do the actual trading. Sublette and Campbell would make their profit from hauling goods to rendezvous and furs back to Saint Louis. Three years earlier, Sublette and his partners, Jed Smith and Davey Jackson, sold their company to five good friends of ours, Tom Fitzpatrick, Jim Bridger, Bill's younger brother Milton Sublette, Henry Fraeb, and Jean Gervais, all of them seasoned trappers but not a one of them possessed of Bill Sublette's flinty business smarts and rapacious hunger for profit. The new partnership, Rocky Mountain Fur, was born in serious debt to Bill and would likely remain so if the elder Sublette had aught to say about it. Which he usually saw to it that he did.

Campbell came bounding out of his tent, all smiles, when a sentry reported that white men were approaching the camp. His smile faded, howsomever, when he discovered that the newcomers weren't Vasquez and Lajeunesse, but

Henry Fraeb, mostly called Frapp, and a small party of trappers. Bobby's gloom increased when Frapp confessed that he wasn't sure where rendezvous would take place that year, that he had come to meet Campbell only to assure him that Rocky Mountain Fur would take possession of the goods when they were delivered to rendezvous, wherever that might be.

Whilst the two of them dickered and palavered, I contented myself with renewing acquaintance with Frapp's traveling companions, especially good-natured Grover Weed, commonly called Buzzard because of his omnivorous appetite, which has included everything from buffalo hump to lizards and ants, although he claims to prefer buffalo. I bombarded Grover with queries about the men in my trapping bunch, the women, the children, especially my daughter Iris, hardly giving him time to reply, so eager was I to gain knowledge of their well-being.

"Last I seed of 'em," Grover managed to say when I paused to take a breath, "they war all doin' purty good, fur as I could tell, 'ceptin', natcherly, fer Ned Godey, as ye mought be s'posin'."

An icy blade stabbed into my heart. "What d'ye mean, Buzzard? What about Godey? What's happened to 'im?"

"Thought ye knew," he responded at last. Grover isn't precisely slow, but living the often solitary life of a free trapper working mostly by his lonesome has damaged whatever slight communication skills he might have possessed to start with.

"What do ye mean? Knew what? I've been in Sain' Looie since last fall! What's happened to Godey?"

"Oh. I din't know. Come to thinkin' on it, howsomever, ye warn't with yer reg'lar bunch when I run inter 'em a couple months past, war ye?" He raised his hand to ward off my agitated queries. "Wal, best I be knowin', Ned got hisse'f kilt this early sprang when yer bunch run inter a passel o' Grovants. Had theirse'fs a helluva fight somewhars nigh the Big Horn, like they war tellin', an' Godey din't make it." He brightened. "He war the onliest one, howsomever. Rest of 'em come through it 'thout gittin' hurt much a-tall. Kilt a passel o' Big-bellies, too, whilst they war at it." He sighed. "Gonna miss ol' Ned, though. Allus liked 'im."

I was fairly jumping out of my skin. "What about his wife Cat? My little girl? Do ye know aught about them?"

"Don't rightly know, Temple. Din't hear nuthin' consarnin' losin' nobody else but Ned, so I reckon they be awright, fur as I be knowin'.

Further questioning produced nothing useful and Frapp was unable to contribute anything more than I had learned from Grover. "*Ja*," the doughty German told me sadly, "dey don't make 'em like Ned Godey purty much no more, I be t'inkin'. *Gottverdampt* Big-bellies alvays makin' troubles, killin' undt schtealin' undt makin' efrybuddy crazy mit dere *gottverdampt* schkelpin' undt such!"

I had to smile at Frapp's self-righteous indignation at Grovant scalping. His own leggin's were liberally decorated with Indian scalp hair.

I wandered back to my camp, numb, bewildered, trying to come to terms with the dismal fact of Ned Godey's death. Aside from my concern for my four-year-old daughter, it was impossible to imagine our trapping bunch deprived of Ned's quiet good humor, his sage counsel born of years of hard experience as a trader with Manuel Lisa in the upper Missouri wilderness long before any of the rest of us had set foot there, his steadfast loyalty, friendship, and tireless devotion to our bunch, and, for me, his unhesitating willingness to take my infant girl into his childless lodge, treating her as if she were his own child, when I was unable to care for her. My grief at Ned's death was mixed with fear for the well-being of his Flathead wife Kathleen—Cat, who had unselfishly mothered my daughter Iris since the death of my wife Rainbow two years before. A woman alone, no matter how well regarded by my fellows, would find herself in precarious circumstances.

Such dark thoughts haunted me until that night, when we made Frapp and Buzzard and the other men welcome at our cookfire. Apparently none of them measured up to the social requirements of the booshway's circle of gentlemen guests. After we stuffed ourselves on hump ribs, tongue, and boudins, I tapped one of my kegs of grain alcohol and everybody got gloriously drunk. Everybody but me. I got drunk enough, but *glorious* is not the word. *Sodden* is more like it. The more I drank, the worse I felt. Grief and gnawing fear for my loved ones overwhelmed me, until I crawled to my robes and fell into fitful slumber.

Next morning I awakened with a thousand imps pounding on my skull and a growing resolve to wait no longer for Vasquez to guide us to rendezvous. An icy bath in the river restored my well-being somewhat, but it altered not a whit my intention to go it alone from there on. I spoke of it to Zeetlah, who greeted my proposal with one of his rare smiles. "'Bout time," he said. "Too much hangin' one place. Goin' 'lone, mebbe gotta fight Injuns. Mebbe no. Hangin' here, Lahcotah comin' back, sure-as-hell!"

There was no need to consult Half-horse. Although the youngster had matured remarkably in the course of the journey, he jumped to do without question whatever his uncle told him to do. Besides, he was absent from camp that morning. Some hostlers had discovered bee trees in the neighborhood, testifying to the westward migration of honeybees from eastern settlements.

When Zeetlah explained to him what all the excitement was about, Half-horse grabbed up a couple of kettles and ran to join the men rushing out to harvest the sweet stuff.

Tom Fitzpatrick and some of his trapping brigade showed up that afternoon, only to disappoint Bobby Campbell once again. Fitz wasn't sure about the rendezvous site, either. He was confident, howsomever, that he would run into somebody who did know, amongst the trappers who would be streaming in from every quarter of the compass. Fitz had interrupted his spring harvest in order to meet with Campbell to finalize terms for the purchase of trade goods and to assure Bobby that Rocky Mountain Fur had already cached a plenitude of beaver plews to pay for them.

I was on pins and needles until I had a chance to quiz Fitzpatrick on what he knew of my trapping bunch. When he emerged from Campbell's tent, I pounced, but I learned hardly anything new. "'Tis a bloody shame concernin' Ned, sure'n it is, but they tell me he went down fightin' hard an' proud as any man iver did. 'Tis a fate, as ye well know, Temple darlin', that iv'ry man-jack of us is after flirtin' with iv'ry day of our lives. It comes wi' the terry-tory, as ye might be sayin'." The Irishman's long, lantern-jawed face clouded as he said it.

"Did ye see Ned's wife Kathleen and my little girl, Tom? Were they safe? Are they still with the bunch?"

"Indade I did, lad. And yes, they were. The woman was takin' it hard, as ye'd be expectin'—scratchin' her face an' cuttin' off her hair and all—but she's bearin' up an' lookin' after your darlin' colleen as if the child were her own."

There was little else that Fitz could tell me, other than assuring me that the rest of my comrades and, as far as he knew, their families, were pretty much as they were when I bade them farewell the previous fall. When I told him of my intention to go on alone, with only Zeetlah and Half-horse, to try to find the rendezvous on my own, Fitzpatrick frowned and shook his head before he said, "Sure'n 'tis a risk, as I'm sure ye know, trav'lin' on yer own hook, wi' so few o' ye and all o' yer stock an' plunder. We'll be leavin' first thing t'morra mornin'. You're welcome to come along with us 'til we turn off, this side o' the Pass, to finish up our spring trappin'."

That was welcome news indeed. Every mile that we traveled with a company of armed men provided greater assurance of arriving safely at our destination, wherever that might prove to be.

Fitz's intention to trap the eastern slope piqued my curiosity. "How come you're trappin' so far east, Tom? 'Pears to me, that's a long way this side o' your reg'lar stompin' ground."

Fitzpatrick scowled, spat, and cursed softly. "Indade it is, Temple, and we wouldn't be doin' it, save for all the bloody Johnny-come-lately competition overrunnin' iv'ry last one of our reg'lar high-country places, harvestin' iv'ry last hair an' leavin' naught fer seed! The blaggards're after creatin' a bloody beaver desert up there!"

That was cruel news, but not completely unexpected. Too many greedy companies and too many trappers would inevitably destroy the wild, free life we had supposed would go on forever. I merely nodded, unable to think of a reply. Fortunately somebody called for Tom's help and he hustled off to attend to whatever it was.

I hunted up Moses Harris and huddled with him, scratching out a rough map of the best passage through South Pass and on to the Big Sandy, then to the Seeds-kee-dee. I had made that same journey five years before, but only that single time. Black reminded me that much had changed. "Three year ago, when Billy brung all o' them 'ere big wagons to ronnyvoo, he like to worked me an' my fellers half to death. Built hisse'f whatcha mought be callin' a proper boolyvard across the Pass. T'ain't nuthin' like ye seed it last time. It's a helluva sight easier naowadays than it war." Considering that we wouldn't be encumbered with wagons, he went on to sketch in some shortcuts off Sublette's road. "They'll stretch ye some," he cautioned, "but they'll cut a couple-three days off'n yer trav'lin', mebbe more."

Fitzpatrick's hunters had brought in three packmules loaded with fresh buffalo meat and cookfires were blazing merrily when Half-horse returned toting two kettles brimming with honey. Trappers starved for the taste of sweetness slathered it onto hump ribs and slabs of smoking-hot backstrap, exulting in that rare delicacy. There was still a great deal of it left over, howsomever, so, lacking a suitable container to carry it with us, I poured the remainder into my partially-empty kegs of grain alcohol. By time we reached rendezvous, if we managed to get there, we would be able to celebrate with toasts of sweet metheglin.

æ   æ   æ

We gathered up our critters by moonlight and led them to water, then to camp to brush them down, saddle up, and load them with their considerable burdens. Naturally they were cranky at being recalled to service, but they had prospered, seal-fat now from good daytime graze and nightlong feeding on prairie hay during a near fortnight of working little, some not at all. They were in excellent fettle, well-fed and trail-toughened, much stronger than at the start of the journey.

The night before, I had informed Campbell of my decision to part from his packtrain, going on ahead on my own. He took it in good grace and wished us godspeed and good fortune. He understood my concern for my daughter. I expected no less of him. Bobby is a gentleman and a righteous mountaineer.

We broke our fast hastily on cold meat and coffee, lashed kettles and such atop one of the packs, and swung into the saddle, eager to quit the camp, Fitz and Frapp and their trappers to grab up a final few springtime plews, I to reunite with Iris and Ned's widow Cat, my father, and my longtime comrades.

At the last minute, I heard my name called and beheld an excited Charles Larpenteur running towards me, holding a book aloft. "Oh, M'sieu Bock, I regret!" he panted. "I did not know you would leave wiz ze *trappeurs*. 'ere is your book, your *Satyricon*."

"Have ye finished it?" I asked, impressed by his punctilious honesty.

"No, not yet, but I am grateful for your generous loan of it. I 'ave enjoyed it immensely, as far as I 'ave read it."

"Keep it then," I told him. "You can give it back at rendezvous." Just then, Tom Fitzpatrick called out, "Time, lads!" and swung his arm forwards as he touched spur lightly to his horse. Coffee needed no urging. Excited but controlled, he champed and stamped until I allowed him to join the file of trappers moving past the scattered tents and bowers of the hostlers. A final backward glance revealed Campbell, arm raised in a farewell salute, a solemn Captain Stewart at his side, and a rumpled Doctor Harrison grinning owlishly and waving languidly. As we passed almost out of earshot, Campbell's purebred seed bulls bellowed a final goodbye.

When the column pretty much sorted itself out, I rode forward to join Fitz at the head of it. "Come to show off your foine animal, have ye, Temple?" He ran his gaze admiringly over my horse, stem to stern, and added, "He's worth your boastin', surely, and ivr'y penny ye paid."

"No finer than your own, Tom," I replied modestly, if somewhat insincerely.

He allowed himself a satisfied grin. "Handsome is as handsome does. I've had Liffey here fer more'n a year now and I couldn't be askin' fer better! I've niver asked 'im fer aught that he didn't provide, and a passel more fer boot."

"It was your horse, Tom, that I had in mind when I told Charlie Bowden to find me the best. I'll never forget your pleasure the day ye got him back from the Grovants. I saw then that he was somethin' special."

"Charlie Bowden was it?" Fitz exclaimed with a laugh. "The runty little Sassenach horse-coper in Sain' Looie? He's the very bandit who found this'n fer me!"

"I wish I had known that," I told him. "It would've spared me a heap o' tellin' him what I had in mind."

We palavered a spell about Fitzpatrick's loss of his Liffey horse to Big-belly Atsina Indians the year before, touching only lightly on the terrible ordeal Tom suffered afterwards, and our winning battle with that same bunch of Grovants at the close of last year's rendezvous. The wound I received in that fracas took me to Saint Louis afterwards. Fitz recovered, too, but that experience aged him a great deal, turned his black hair mostly white, and etched indelible lines on his handsome Irish features. He was, howsomever, still the same tough, savvy Mick, the natural-born leader of men I first met in 'twenty-three, but, I daresay, much wiser now.

❦ ❦ ❦

The lightly-loaded trappers traveled much faster than the slow-moving packtrain. I had feared that my pack animals might slow Fitz's progress, but their good condition and fairly light loads—thanks to the extra mules I had purchased at the last minute in Saint Louis—let us keep up without undue exertion.

Flat prairieland gave way to broken country. Game grew scarce and we made do with jerkmeat until we reached the Sweetwater, so named, according to mountaineer lore, because of a mishap caused when a packmule loaded with a traveling party's entire stock of sugar fell into the river and spoiled all of it. We followed the Sweetwater upstream for another day and came in sight of a lone promontory that looks like a huge stone turtle stranded on the plain. Travelers to the mountains call it Independence Rock. Fitzpatrick called an overnight halt nearby, giving a few of us a chance to ride over to get a closer look at the names carved on its sides. Fitzpatrick's name was there and so were those of Bill Sublette, Robert Campbell, Nathaniel Wyeth, and that of Captain Benjamin Louis Eulalie de Bonneville, which likely required half-a-dozen hostlers to hack such a monstrous moniker into that rocky surface. Even James Bridger's handle is inscribed there, although somebody else must have done the job for him, for Jim Bridger, smart and knowledgeable though he is, can neither read nor write even as much as his own name.

There was still plenty of daylight remaining, so I borrowed a hammer and chisel from one of Frapp's trappers when he finished with it and etched the names of Zeetlah, Half-horse, and Temple Buck to show that we, too, had passed that spot. You can see them for yourself, next time you come by.

By time we got back to camp, fat meat from a fresh-killed buffalo was sputtering over the coals for a farewell feast. Next morning we parted, Fitz and his people headed off to rejoin their comrades trapping on the East Slope, we to continue on our own to South Pass.

ೞ   ೞ   ೞ

Five miles up the Sweetwater we came to Devil's Gate, where the river narrows into a tight notch hundreds of feet high filled with a torrent of wild white water forced high along its rocky sides, impossible to follow. A fairly well-worn trail led us around that obstacle, howsomever, and we rejoined the Sweetwater several miles upstream.

A day or so later we spied Cut Rock, far off, a huge triangle sliced into a mountain, assuring me that we hadn't strayed from the trail. Soon afterwards we got our first glimpse of the pine-girdled, snow-crested peaks of the Shining Mountains looming overhead in all their rugged majesty. Even

Zeetlah was open-mouthed at the sight and Half-horse looked almost stricken as he beheld mountains not even imagined on the Missouri flatlands.

Although it was June, nights of freezing cold seesawed with sweltering daytimes as we plodded first through the gently-sloping shoulders of South Pass, then weaved our way upwards, mostly sticking to Sublette's wagon road, sometimes scrambling through Harris's tortuous shortcuts to save time, until at last we reached the uppermost ridge of what Indians call the Backbone of the World, the Continental Divide, where cricks and streams and rivers split into some that flow into eastern oceans and others that feed the Western Sea.

By time we crossed the Big and Little Sandy Rivers, heading for the Seeds-kee-dee, our critters were considerably tuckered, and so were we. We had run between the raindrops. We hadn't encountered a single Indian hunting party on our journey through the Pass, let alone one looking to make war. Either one would have spelled trouble. The plunder and animals we possessed would have been too much for even friendly Indians to resist. It was time to celebrate and jerkmeat wouldn't do. We needed a buffalo.

After we made camp, Zeetlah offered to keep an eye on the plunder and critters while Half-horse and I went off to harvest supper. Which required hardly any time at all. We traveled not more than a mile before we came upon a small bunch of bulls grazing in a clearing. Half-horse dropped a fat young yearling with a single shot. Less than an hour later we rode into camp, the packmule tottering under more meat than we could possibly eat, our faces smeared with blood from gorging on the liver.

Zeetlah was nowheres to be seen. We heard not a peep from him. The packs were undisturbed and our critters were all there, cropping grass in the clearing. No answer greeted our calls for him, which scared us more than somewhat. Without a word, quick as scat, Half-horse and I dropped from our saddles and dived into the midst of the piled-up packs, lest we present easy targets for hidden hostiles. Nothing stirred.

Rifle ready, pistols loaded and primed, I swept my gaze throughout the glade, the crickbank, and the brushy edge of the clearing, seeking movement, alert for any unnatural sound. Still naught. At last, I reckoned it was best for us to start the fracas, if there was to be one, rather than provide that advantage to a foe. I cocked one barrel of my belly-gun and fired at a tree trunk.

"No shootin'! No shootin'!" The voice yelling in alarm was unmistakably Zeetlah's. A shallow blanket of dead aspen leaves at the edge of the clearing stirred, rustled, then exploded into the figure of the ageless Delaware, pistol in his sash, rifle in hand, my fowler slung over his shoulder, face split in a grin, advancing and calling out, "Purty good, huh? You lookin' right on me! You seen nuttin'!" He rattled off some Delaware talk to Half-horse, who hung his head sheepishly. In my own case, there was naught to do but laugh and feel relieved.

The aroma of roasting meat wafting from our cookfire proved to be a blessing. We were happily gorging on flavorful vittles of which we had been too long deprived, when a hoarse halloo came from the forest. We grabbed up our rifles, never distant from a mountaineer's hand, but we were reassured by somebody calling, "Thet yew, Temple Buck? Hell! I figgered yew fer a goner, arter las' year's ronnyvoo!"

A moment later, first one man, then a second, appeared at the forest's edge, leading their saddle horses and trailing half a dozen lightly-loaded pack animals. I recognized them as Gideon Moon and Willard Stringfellow, free trappers of long acquaintance, an ill-assorted pair in appearance, but fast friends, close as brothers. Stringfellow is a Kentuckian, short in stature, built like an oaken barrel and as sturdy, good-natured and loquacious, ever ready with a quip and a jest. Gideon hails from Tennessee, tall and buggy-whip lean, dour in manner, thoughtful, slow to judge but unshakeable in his opinions, once he decides.

"Put up your critters an' set yourself down to vittles," I called out in greeting. "We got plenty."

Which they wasted no time in doing. They stripped off saddles and packs, turned their hobbled critters out to graze with ours, and commenced carving generous slabs off the buffalo hump sizzling over the fire. At last Moon wiped his greasy chin with his buckskin sleeve and enquired, "Whar ye been, Buck? Hain't seen ye all year long. Not in winter camp ner nowhars."

I described as briefly as I could my whereabouts since the previous fall and why I had traveled to Saint Louis. Then I asked, "Would ye be knowin' where they'll be holdin' rendezvous this year? I need to be gettin' there in a hurry."

"Easiest thang in ther world!" Stringfellow said. "Me 'an Gid hyar, we be headin' thetaways ourownse'fs." He chewed off another mouthful before he added, "'Tain't fur from hyar, noways, jest mebbe a couple-three days er so, down on ther Siskerdee, nigh Hoss Crick. Reckon yew know whar it be—ol' Baldy Bonnyville's Fort Nonsense! Thet's whar! We be callin' it home, nowadays. We been trappin' fer Bonnyville ther past coupla seasons. We'll take ye thar 'thout no trouble a-tall."

"Yep!" Moon seconded. "That's whar we be goin', quick as we kin."

I was greatly relieved. My goal was not far off and five rifles traveling together amount to a considerable challenge to all but a large war party. My curiosity was piqued. "How come ye gave up trappin' free, Gid? Ol' hivernants like ye be."

Will was quick to reply in his stead. "'Cause ther money's gawddamn good, thet's how come! Ol' Cap'n Bonnyville, he don't know much a-tall, but he's payin' top dollar an' then some fer plews."

"'Sides," Moon cut in, "he's payin' extry on top o' that, jist fer stayin' on with his brigade—an' his *segundo*, Joe Walker, he's savvy enough fer the two of 'em! Joe be from Tinnessee, natcherly."

"Jist as well, too," Will sighed, "thet 'ere extry cash, I mean to say. Beaver's gittin' scarcer'n hell hyarabouts. We oughta be packin' twice as many plews as we got, fer all ther hard work we done this year."

Moon disagreed. "Fer one thang, 'tain't as bad as all that. 'Tain't the beaver runnin' out. Thar's jist too gawddamn many trappers! Ever' time ye turn about, thar's anuther new outfit comin' up thisaway, cashin' in on what we been larnin' fer ten year an' more!"

"Like Bonnyville, naow thet ye mention it," Will admitted, which saved me from making that same comment. Captain Bonneville had arrived in the mountains only a year before.

They lapsed into silence until Moon chuckled quietly and opined, "Hell, it'll git better. Allus does." Which is a sentiment that keeps mountaineers going, no matter the hardship or privation.

The sun had dipped below the tree tops, which prompted Stringfellow to suggest, "Best we be gittin' some shut-eye, 'count o' gittin' on ther way early t'morry. Ye reckon?" Nobody disagreed. We doused the fire and rolled out our sleeprobes, sorted out the order of our two-hour horse-guard stints, then scattered to our chosen hidey-holes amongst the surrounding thickets. A quarter-hour later I was dreaming of my daughter and reunion with my beloved bunch of ruffians.

-ooo-

1833 Rendezvous

It was by then the end of June. Warm sunshine spilled into the valley of the Seeds-kee-dee, shimmering on the water, bathing woodlands and meadows in a golden glow. Footing was firm and game was plentiful as we followed the river as close as the country permitted, nigh the riverbank when we could, other times trailing onto high bluffs overlooking the river, splashing through the numerous cricks, streams, and rivulets that feed the ever-broadening river. Will's confident prediction of a couple-three-day journey stretched into a week. Anxious to learn my daughter's circumstances, I chafed at what seemed to me to be our leisurely progress, but Moon and Stringfellow refused to be hurried past the twenty miles or so that we put behind us each day.

We dined well on fat wapiti and stray young buffalo bulls and occasionally plump grouse that fell to my new fowler. Whenever we camped nigh the river, Zeetlah and Half-horse supplemented our diet with firm-fleshed trout-fish.

Half-horse had prospered on our westward journey, gaining meat and muscle and a passel of new skills taught mostly by Zeetlah, sometimes by me. He had always been a gifted hand with horses and mules. Now he was eager to try his hand at any chore. The sullen look had gradually faded from his features as his self-confidence improved and his grasp of American palaver grew less shaky. Zeetlah's faith in his nephew was vindicated.

∾   ∾   ∾

We got our first glimpse of Bonneville's ramshackle fort as we scrambled up the bank of a puny crick that meanders to the Seeds-kee-dee. Crowds wandering amongst trappers' dirty white tents and brush bowers scattered around its walls, surrounded by scores of Shoshone lodges and horse herds in grassy meadows, proclaimed that this was indeed the place of rendezvous. Instead of racing down to the fort, all of us immediately dismounted and without a word spoken, commenced rummaging through our packs in search of our go-to-meetin' duds.

I hesitated in my choice of fancy leather shirts between one made for me by my late wife Rainbow, the other by Ned's wife Cat, as a parting gift to me when I left on my journey to Saint Louis the year before, both beautiful garments, lovingly embroidered with intricate quillwork and tiny beads. At last I chose the one made by Cat, as a gesture of gratitude to the woman who had unselfishly cared for my daughter as if my child were her own. Rainbow and Cat had been devoted friends from childhood, as close as sisters ever can be. Rainbow would understand and approve.

Whilst Zeetlah, Half-horse, and I splashed in the crick, Stringfellow and Moon cursed colorfully as they scraped away months of accumulated beard. Naturally they declined to join us in our bathe. White trappers who may be unfazed by grizzly bears possess a deep-seated fear of more water than they can drink. Shaving is equally onerous, but Indian women insist upon smooth-shaven chins on trappers seeking their favors. Dog-faces are not esteemed by the dusky maidens of our mountain land.

Getting rid of my own measly whiskers never takes long. After I dressed and attended to my hair, I busied myself currying and brushing my Coffee horse until his hide shone like polished jet. At last, attired in our most extravagant coxcombry, we mounted and proceeded down the slope at a brisk trot, breaking into a gallop as we approached the outer ring of Indian lodges, trailing our pack animals, firing rifles skyward and yelling our throats hoarse as we scattered kids and dogs and laughing women scurrying to protect their young'uns from our furious charge. There were only five of us, far from a whole brigade, but we did our noisy best to make a grand entry into rendezvous.

We slowed our gait to an amble as we neared the fort, where the crowd grew increasingly dense in the crooked lanes amongst trappers' shelters, giving us time to hail old comrades. Pleased though I was to be once again in the midst of the mountaineer fraternity, I was anxious to find my own trapping bunch. I looked in vain for them. At last I called out, "Anybody know where's Rocky Mountain Fur?"

Half a dozen men replied, pointing upstream. One man made his voice heard above the others. "Ye kin find 'em a fur piece up the Green, but they ain't tradin' yet!" That was the first time that I heard the Seeds-kee-dee called the Green by newcomers not content to let well enough alone.

Another trapper, glancing at my string of loaded pack animals, remarked, "That all ye brung fer 'em? 'Tain't much fer tradin' fer ronnyvoo!"

"Hell, no!" I shouted back quickly, lest they spread word that Rocky Mountain Fur would be short of trade goods this year. "This is all my own plunder I fetched up from Sain' Louie. Bobby Campbell's on the way, not far behind! Best ye hold onto your plews until he gets here!"

❧ ❧ ❧

My Delaware companions and I rode off amid cheers at the word that Campbell would soon be there, mixed, naturally, with grumbling at his tardiness. Stringfellow and Moon parted with us at the fort. On the way, along the riverbank, we passed clusters of trappers' digs and meadows where their critters grazed, interspersed with Indian villages, mostly Shoshone bands, and their sizeable horse herds. When Indians travel, they carry along everything they own. There is no safe place to leave anything behind.

I kept looking for Iron Bow's Flathead band, but in vain. Half-horse was fascinated not so much by the whitemen, but rather by the different Indian tribes there—Nez Percés, Crows, Kootenai, Pend d'Oreilles, Utes, several bands of Snakes—each garbed in their distinctive dress, hair arranged according to tribal custom. Zeetlah kept up a chatter in the Delaware tongue, likely expressing his opinion of each tribe's virtues and shortcomings.

As we passed by, Half-horse's Lahcotah clothing excited curiosity amongst the various Indian bands, especially the womenfolk, who are always attentive to new beadwork and quill patterns that might enhance their own art. The young fellow, conscious of the women's admiring stares, doubtless supposing they were meant for him, sat rather more erect in his saddle than is his custom.

At last I spied a familiar face, then another, two men who have been my closest friends in the years since I first left my birthplace in Whynot, Ohio, Tuttle Thompson and Micah Buck. I tossed the halter-shank of my packstring to Half-horse, touched spur to Coffee, and raced to greet them. Their look of surprise and pleasure when they saw who it was made my heart big.

"Thar ye be, begawd!" Tuttle strangled out between bursts of laughter. "I knowed nuthin' could put ye under! I been tellin' 'em all ye'd be comin' back fer thish'yar ronnyvoo an' hyar ye be!" He grabbed me about the waist and dragged me from the saddle, crushing me in a grizzly hug against his broad, slat-ribbed chest.

Micah said naught that I could hear, but the big grin on his handsome black face was warm greeting enough. Tuttle, meanwhile, was hauling me towards a big white tent, bellowing, "Buck's back an' lookin' fit as hell!" and a passel of similar nonsense. Soon we were surrounded by dear friends, men who had peopled my best dreams for nigh onto a year, calling out greetings and piling on questions that I had no time to answer. Painfully missing was Ned Godey.

The babble lessened and the crowd parted to allow my father through. Tall, slim, square-shouldered, ageless, immaculate in creamy Nez Percé leathers, a smile kindling his handsome features, Powatawa gripped my shoulders and gazed into my face, profound love flowing from his dark eyes. He said naught at first, then clasped me to his chest in a powerful embrace. I heard him murmur, "The Spirit has returned you to our fire, my son. Now I am whole."

There was no time to reply. Jim Bridger's big voice rose above the clamor, shouting, "'Pears thish'yar's a fust-rate occasion fer a swaller! We still got a dram or two left over! Whaddaye say, Temple?"

Amongst mountaineers, ceremony always loses out to free booze. Amid an assenting roar, Powatawa and I were hustled off to RMF's big trade tent, its trade tables set up but bare of merchandise. Whilst Bridger sloshed well-watered spirits into a thicket of outstretched cups, I saw that his face was strained and he moved about with difficulty, but the noisy crowd allowed me no time to enquire the cause. When he finished his chore, he enquired anxiously, "Ye come up with Bobby? When's he gittin' hyar?"

I told him of Campbell's reluctance to leave Laramie Fork until he was sure of where rendezvous would be held, that I had come ahead on my own hook, but I reckoned supplies wouldn't be long in showing up.

He looked somewhat relieved. "Yep. I heared Louie Vasquez an' LaJernesse run inter some trappers what tol' 'em whar we'd be an' they high-tailed it back to Bobby. That war a spell back, so they likely ain't fur ahind o' ye." Someone called his name just then, so my curiosity about his infirmity remained unsatisfied.

When the greeting and back-slapping lulled somewhat, I asked my father, "Iris? She all right?"

Powatawa's face brightened at thought of his granddaughter. "Your child is safe and happy. Godey's woman keeps her like her own child."

"Where are they? Here? In our camp?"

"No. Three days past, the band of Iron Bow arrived. She took our child to see her other grandfather," he said in the careful, precise English that my mother had taught him. "Now she has no man. She says she must return to her people."

A swarm of worrisome thoughts stung like hornets. Naturally Cat, widowed now, could not continue with our bunch without a man. Then what of Iris? Neither I nor Powatawa, nor the two of us together, living a trapper's life, could properly care for my four-year-old daughter. But even if Cat were willing to keep Iris with her amongst Iron Bow's Flathead band, who would look after them there? A woman with no man of her own fares poorly amongst Indians. It was a conundrum.

I bade a hasty goodbye to my fellows and asked my father to show me the way to Iron Bow's village. We stopped first with the crowd of Delawares and Iroquois clustered around Zeetlah and Half-horse. "Thar ye be, Temple Buck!" cried Brass Turtle, the unofficial leader of the Delawares and Iroquois in our bunch. Smiling, he hooked a thumb towards the youngster. "Ain't bad enough ye come back to pester us, but ye went an' fetched along thish'yar young'un fer us to be wet-nursin'!" Turtle's humor always has a sharp edge to it, so I paid no nevermind to his joshing.

"He's one o' your own, Turtle," I flung back. "You Delawares ain't gettin' any younger. I reckoned ye could use some new blood!"

He chuckled and replied. "Somebody been honin' yer tongue, down thar in Sain' Looie? Yer daddy thar'd best be teachin' ye yer manners agin'!" He winked and grinned at Powatawa, who smiled and nodded. Turtle grew serious. "Us Lenapees be much obliged, Temple, fer bringin' the young'un along with ye. Foot's been tellin' o' hard times fer the People down thar in Missourah."

"Don't ye worry none, Turtle, about wet-nursin' that lad," I told him. He'll learn fast. He's got a lot o' smarts already."

"Natcherly," he said with a smug grin. "He's Lenapee, ain't he?"

Zeetlah promised to look after my packstring and plunder when he got to camp. It occurred to me that I had best not show up in Iron Bow's village empty-handed. Besides, it was best to get the Jesus-burro stud off my hands before some enterprising Snake or Crow did it for me. A critter like that one was too much to resist, even considering the law of rendezvous which decrees that tribal rivalry and serious theft be put aside until trading is completed.

Half-horse helped me unload the jackass, curry and brush him, and distribute his burden amongst the other critters. When our Indians realized that the big fellow wasn't just a packmule, their hands flew to their mouths, lest their souls escape. He was truly a magnificent animal. They admired, too, the Jesus-cross on his back and withers, reminiscent of the four-directions design common in almost all Indian artwork.

Powatawa had already mounted. I swung up onto Coffee and we headed for the Flathead camp, my brain awhirl, feelings torn betwixt joy at seeing my daughter and Cat and uncertainty about what must be done to assure their well-being.

∾ ∾ ∾

On the way, Powatawa kept running an approving gaze over my new horse. "He is truly a fine animal," he said at last. "You learned your lessons well in our village in Ohio." I smiled, gratified at the compliment. He continued to appraise my well-bred Kentucky horse. "Yes," he declared, "even if the Great Spirit Himself gave me such power, I cannot think how to make a better animal." This time I blushed on behalf of my critter. Such fulsome praise is rarely expressed by my father.

Talking about horses let me avoid the topic uppermost in my mind—what to do about my daughter after rendezvous and in the years ahead. Powatawa's ingrained reluctance to meddle barred his offering advice and my own reticence kept me silent.

The Flathead encampment was not far distant. As we approached a bunch of young children playing on the riverbank, I heard a joyful shriek. Iris broke away from her companions and came running through the tall grass, screaming "Papa! Papa!" laughing and babbling a macaroni of English and Salish, joyful tears running down her chubby cheeks. I reached down and scooped her onto the saddlebow, my eyes blurring, laughing and nattering myownself, making no more sense than she was doing.

She continued to hang around my neck, kissing my cheeks and chattering Salish endearments, whilst I did much the same. The children had run on ahead, screaming news of our coming. It takes but an instant to alert an Indian village to anything unusual. In a blink the alleyways between the circles of lodges swarmed with women and children, young girls and boys and men, come to learn about this latest prodigy.

As we drew nigh the center ring of lodges, I spied Iron Bow and my brother-in-law Fast Horse standing with half a dozen other headmen, awaiting our approach. Although my departed wife no longer bound us together, they and I considered our tie unbroken. I stepped to the ground, Iris still clinging to my neck, and stood before Iron Bow. "I greet you, Father," I said in sign and Salish syllables. "I bring you a gift from whitemen's country." Just as I handed the halter-shank to Iron Bow, the big jackass let loose an ear-splitting hee-haw that nearly rocked the assembled Flatheads out of their moccasins, then provoked a huge burst of laughter amongst them.

The old gentleman's eyes fairly bugged. At first he strived to hang onto his dignity, then gave it up. A broad smile lit his face. "Now," I told him, "you can have all the fine mules that you desire. He is young and will father many children amongst your mares."

Iron Bow's dignity was in tatters for that day, anyway. He embraced me, right there in front of the whole village, signing that I was always welcome at his fire, bearing gifts or not. He was doubtless sincere in that sentiment, but his eyes kept straying to the handsome jackass whilst he spoke. My own eyes weren't idle, either. I was trying, without success, to find Cat amongst the crowd.

With difficulty I loosened Iris's fingers from my neck, set her upon the ground, and asked her to find Kathleen for me. Reluctantly, she nodded and ran off amongst the lodges. A few minutes later, Cat appeared at the edge of the throng. Fascinated as they were by the new critter with the mystical markings, it is likely neither Iron Bow nor Fast Horse noticed me sneaking off before they had a chance to invite me to their lodge for customary smoking and eating.

I caught up with Cat beyond the outer circle of lodges. She led the way to a grassy grove of aspens, where I loosed Iris's grip on my leg and sat down opposite her. Cat's features, thinner than I remembered, were calm, composed, betraying neither joy nor sorrow, her eyes bright and penetrating. Her once-waist-length hair was shorter now but not cropped off, and whatever scratches she might have inflicted on herself at the time of Ned's death had long since healed without leaving scars. She wore a loose, shapeless leather work dress that failed to conceal the lithe, supple form beneath. She smiled then, a dazzling flash of perfect white teeth in her dusky complexion, and greeted me in the Salish tongue, mouthing formal phrases as she signed a welcome in more friendly terms. I fumbled for a reply whilst I admired her loveliness. Ned had bestowed on her the name Kathleen, in memory of his departed mother, but we English-speakers soon commenced calling her Cat, prompted by her quiet independence, her fluid grace and strength and dark beauty, so like a sleek, healthy, powerful young catamount, pleasing to the eye but menacing if challenged.

Whilst we exchanged commonplaces about my return to the mountains and I expressed condolences on Godey's death and my gratitude for the care she had provided Iris in my absence—fact is, ever since the death of Rainbow two years before—my daughter grew fidgety. At last she jumped to her feet, pecked my cheek, and ran off to rejoin her playmates, vaguely promising to return soon.

Left alone together, our palaver dwindled. Cat offered no details about Ned's final hour and I was reluctant to open that wound. She had suffered enough. As we fumbled for safe conversation, I felt a certain electricity between us, much like the eerie tingling one feels immediately after a lightning bolt strikes nearby. Naturally we didn't speak of it, but I'm sure that she felt it, too. It made further talk difficult, uncomfortable.

During her four years with Ned and the rest of us, Cat had acquired a workable if ungrammatical grasp of American speech and I possessed a sufficiency of Salish words and phrases. Besides, we had sign-talk to fall back on, but now, both of us were tongue-tied. We two old friends had much to share, but neither could think of aught to say. We ended by simply staring at each other, until Cat, as embarrassed as I, rose to her feet in a smooth liquid motion and announced that chores awaited her. As she retreated, I called out that I would return next day with gifts. She paid me no nevermind, leaving me to stare after her, feasting my eyes on her swaying hips beneath her dress as she returned to her duties.

When Powatawa and I returned to camp, Micah and our Irish *medico* Finn McCool were just finishing erecting a spacious bower for me, nearby the riverbank, facing the Seeds-kee-dee for added privacy. I tethered Coffee to a nearby tree and we dragged my packs into the shelter before I rewarded their kindness with cups brimful of good Kentucky whiskey. Whilst we sipped, I put off Finn's queries about how I had survived my wound of the year before, insisting, instead, on learning the circumstances of Ned Godey's death, painful as I knew it would be to hear. At mention of Godey's name, McCool raised his cup and said in a low voice, "May the light of Heaven shine ferever on his grave." We clinked cups and drank in silence, until Finn added, "May darlin' Ned be rollin' in luxury in a bloody mansion in Heaven's best neighborhood. No man ever desarved such a reward more'n Ned Godey hisownself!" Which sentiment naturally demanded another deep draught and the refilling of our cups.

Micah saw my impatience and launched into what happened on Godey's final day. "There ain't that much to tell. Early last spring, nigh the Big Horn, not long after we split off from winter camp on the Salmon, our bunch was gathered together, gettin' ready to move on to fresh trappin', when a bunch o' Grovants hit our hosses, just at dawn, like they 'most always do. Pretty Hoss an' Little Mountain were on guard an' they commenced shootin' an' yellin'. Nat'rally, we chased after 'em, shootin' with ever'thin' we had, grabbin' up our critters an' pushin' 'em back to camp. Ye know how it goes." He took a deep breath before he proceeded quietly, his handsome dark features clouded, grim.

"One way or t'other, Ned got himself parted from the rest of us. He was afoot an' off by his lonesome when half-a-dozen Big-bellies jumped 'im. He must've put up one helluva fight. By time we heard the ruckus an' got there, three mostly-dead Grovants were layin' on the ground an' Ned was layin' on top of 'em, his rifle an' both pistols empty, his butcher knife still in his hand."

McCool could not restrain himself. "An' one o' the other t'ree o' thim red haythens was in the act o' scalpin' im!" Finn broke in. "Had his bloody fist in Godey's long hair, he did, yankin' up his head, gettin' ready to slice off his topknot, whin Cesár Pérez come runnin' up an' chopped the bloody beggar nigh half in two wi' that *machete* sword o' his! We kilt the ither two where they stood, but it was too late fer darlin' Ned."

"He was still breathin'," Micah resumed, "but his eyes were all glassy an' he couldn't talk, just looked at us an' tried to smile up at us. That hurt most of all."

"I did what I could," Finn said quietly, "but there was nothing useful to be done. T'ree arrows and a couple gunshots in the body was too much to survive."

"He lasted just long enough for Cat to get there," Micah said. "She must've felt somethin' in the air, 'cause she came runnin' up almost as soon as the rest of us got there, throwin' herself down beside 'im, huggin' 'im an' cryin' an' tellin' 'im things only the two o' them could understand an' Ned smilin' that quiet smile o' his until he couldn't smile anymore. His eyes closed an' he was gone."

"Kathleen showed herself to be the lady she is, then," Finn observed reflectively, "the loikes o' which ye wouldn't expect to be meetin' up with here in the wilderness. Oh, to be sure, she cut off much of her pretty hair, right on the spot, an' scratched up her face an' arms, loike her own people'd expect her to do, but she did her keenin' mostly to herownsel', not visitin' her sorrow on the rest of us. She kept her grief inwards, niver flauntin' it, loike, ye may be sure, most others would be after doin'."

They fell silent then and naturally I could add nothing to what had been said. We drank a few more quiet toasts, each of us wrapped in his own recollections of the man who had generously given us so much of himself, until the rattle of an iron spoon on a kettle and Yves Dureau yelling threats to throw the vittles to the prairie wolves if we didn't hurry up announced that the campkeepers had finished their supper chores, a summons never ignored amongst our forever-hungry bunch.

After supper, naught else would serve but that I dig out carrots of fresh tobacco and tap a keg of my grain alcohol, water it down to a drinkable state, and fill the cups of my thirsty comrades. Traders' packtrains had not yet arrived at rendezvous and Captain Bonneville's fort was bereft of spirits. Bridger's watery dram had merely whetted our appetite for strong drink and I had no wish to delay a celebration of my return to their midst. In no time at all every man in our bunch—and most of their Indian wives, as well—were happily drunk. Men deprived of ardent spirits for a year at a time possess little resistance to John Barleycorn. They were careful, howsomever, to restrain their merriment, lest too much noisy glee attract a mob of bone-dry trappers and drain our scanty resources. Anse Tolliver offered to unlimber his fiddle, but they quickly hushed him, cautioning against drawing unwonted attention to our camp.

Indian-like, nobody offered a toast to Ned Godey's memory, leastaways not out loud. I sipped and sent a silent salute his way, howsomever, and I daresay I was not alone in that respect.

A red-faced Finn McCool waved his arms for silence and offered a toast. "Temple, darlin'! 'Tis the Lord's own blessin' to be seein' ye back amongst us!" He raised his battered cup aloft and roared, "Let iv'ry man here drink to your coffin!" A storm of protest greeted that grisly sentiment—all but Paddy McBride, who likely knew what was coming—but Finn was undaunted. He shouted them down, stomping around the cookfire until they quieted, then declared, "An' may that coffin be built from the wood of a hunderd-year-old tree that I'll be after plantin' t'morra mornin'!"

A rendezvous that lacks stimulating popskull offers little invitation to wander. That, together with their unaccustomed drunkenness, sent my comrades to their robes at an early hour. I made sure that my Coffee horse, tethered beside my bower, had enough prairie hay to last the night, before I headed to my robes for a well-earned rest.

Which didn't come easily. I should have been pleased and contented to know that my daughter was safe, happy, and in good health and that I was at last reunited with my trapping bunch. Instead, I was beset with blurred yearnings and nagging doubt. Cat's beautiful face, closed, unreadable, floated in a troubling fog of conflicting loyalties, troublous feelings that hung just out of reach, a formidable riddle that held sleep at bay until the long day's exertions and excitement triumphed and I slipped into fitful slumber.

❧   ❧   ❧

Golden sunshine filtering into the bower, a breeze-borne tang of boiling coffee, and the myriad sounds of a wide-awake trappers' camp, brought me out of my robes with a bound. I stripped to my britchclout, raced to a nearby thicket for my morning chore, then ran to the river and plunged in amongst our Indians frolicking in the chill current. A huge hand appeared on my shoulder, then clamped my skull, shoved me under, and held me there. Choking, sputtering, cursing, I wriggled free and beheld our huge Delaware Little Mountain, his good-natured face split ear-to-ear in a grin. "Now ye got yer Jesus-bath, Tempo!" he shouted. "Now you go happy to Grey Land!" His features straightened in mock gravity before he added, "No too quick, mind ye!"

Gasping and laughing too hard to reply, I splashed water in his face, then extended the favor to the others ringed about me, my father, Zeetlah, and Brass Turtle amongst them. "Good havin' ye back, Temple!" Turtle called out. "Time ye be washin' Sain' Looie stink off'n yer hide!"

"That's a fact!" I rejoined, although, much as I enjoyed the company of my companions, not for an instant would I have traded away a single bubble of the perfumed lather I had enjoyed with Lucette in her copper bathtub. But naturally I would never mention such urban affectations to my fellow-trappers.

There was not a single whiteman amongst us early-morning bathers, except for myself, and I am only half-so. Quick and handy as righteous trappers are to learn the skills and customs of the wilderness, the universal Indian practice of daily bathing remains alien to my lily-hided brethren. They render lip-service to the axiom that cleanliness is next to godliness, but most of them prefer to keep both of those things at arm's length.

When we tired of sporting in the river and straggled to shore, wringing out sopping britchclouts, I spied Tuttle Thompson and Paddy McBride lounging on the riverbank. "I tol' ye an' I tol' ye, Temple," Tuttle yelled in a mock schoolmarmish voice, his Kentucky twang even more pronounced than usual, "I been tellin' ye an' tellin' ye, ef water'll rust ar'n, like ye sartinly know it'll do, jest think what it'll do to yer gawddamn hide!"

"Indade!" Paddy joined in. "If the Heavenly Father intended mankind to be after swimmin' loike a fish an' all o' thim other wahter craytchures, He'd'a pervided us wid fins an' gills an' one o' thim wavy tails fer boot, now wouldn't He now?"

I made no reply except to throw a handful of mud at them, which they dodged adroitly. Back in camp, most of the gang was gathered around the cookfire guzzling coffee that Zeetlah had thoughtfully provided from my stores before heading for his bathe. Their own supply of that luxury had long since been used up over the long winter months since last rendezvous. Steaming hot and black as a trader's soul and syrupy with sugar, the welcome draught washed away whatever cobwebs remained of last night's troubling thoughts. I broke my fast with crispy slivers of leftover hump meat, taking time to renew acquaintance with our French-Canuck campkeepers, Yves Dureau and Jean-Luc L'Archévêque. "*Bienvenue*, Temple," Jean-Luc greeted me. "*Ton siege parmi nous a été trop longtemps vide. Nous t'avons manqué beaucoup.*" Yves merely grinned a warm welcome. I assured them that I had missed them at least as much as they had me.

The feeling of goodfellowship could not be allowed to wither. There could be no better time for the gifting of plunder I had hauled up from Saint Louis. I summoned Zeetlah with a nod and the two of us plunged into my bower, ripping open my packs and grabbing up armloads of shirts for the men, bolts of woolens and calicos for the women, four- and six-point Witney blankets for everybody, English-made butcher knives, gunpowder and galena pigs, coffee beans, tea, sugar, and carrots of fresh tobacco, just for a start. The rest could be passed on later, according to what I knew of individual tastes and need.

We heaped most of the goods in piles, making no attempt to distribute it, letting each trapper and his woman, if he had one, sort through it and take what he required according to size, taste, and need. Our bunch had been together long enough to erase selfish greed that might have caused conflict amongst a different group. Zeetlah made sure that young Half-horse, shyly hanging back at the fringe of the excited crowd, got his fair share of the plunder.

"Hey, Temple!" Tuttle hollered out. "Ye got some o' thet'ere girly-smellin' soap ye brung up, las' time ye come from Sain' Looie? I be studyin' on doin' some serious courtin', soon's thi'shere ronnyvoo gits itse'f together!" I scurried back into the bower and grabbed up a poke of lilac shaving tablets and the case of fine English razors I had brought for my stiff-whiskered friend. His eyes popped when he opened the box. "Glory be! Ye din't fergit! I might'a knowed!" he crowed happily. "Thet'ere las' lot o' razors ye fetched up be purely wore down ter nubs by naow from honin' an' stroppin', 'twixt shavin' myownse'f and borryin' 'em out to all ther other fellers what's been usin' 'em!" His expression sobered, howsomever, when he added, "'Course, it don't matter how much shavin' ye do, less'n ye got trade plunder fer closin' the bargain wi' them'ere Injun gals."

Finn McCool was uncustomarily speechless when he opened the medical kit that Doctor Yuan had assembled at my request. Mouth agape at first, then lips pursed in concentration, he fingered carefully through its contents, marveling over the scalpels, forceps, pincers, and probes, a shiny medical saw, and I don't know what-all. At last he closed the wooden lid and, still too choked up to speak, he flashed me a smile as big and bright as summer sun.

When the last scrap of plunder had been whisked away, I tapped the alcohol keg once again to prolong the merriment and my own good feeling. In the midst of our celebration, two visitors ambled in a-horseback, Milton Sublette and his strikingly beautiful Shoshone wife he called Isabel. When Milton dismounted awkwardly and walked with considerable difficulty, I saw with regret that his leg hadn't healed completely from a serious knife wound he had received, nigh two years before, at winter camp on the Salmon, in a brawl with an ill-natured Iroquois free trapper, John Gray, employed by American Fur.

Milt was cheerful as ever, howsomever, especially when I filled his cup to brimming, and even more so when I ducked into my bower to retrieve a handsome Chinese silk shawl for his lady. "Ye be more'n gin'rous, Temple," he called over his shoulder as he shared his cup with his woman, who remained seated in her richly-caparisoned saddle. "I'll be gittin' even with ye, soon as Bobby shows up."

"No need, Milt," I replied. "You an' your pardners have always done right by me and all our bunch. A dram or two and a swatch o' foofurraw don't come close to makin' up for it."

We let it go at that, but small gestures of that sort strengthen the ties that bond righteous mountaineers together.

∾ ∾ ∾

When the copper kettle was at last drained of every drop, there was time to visit more or less quietly with a few of my comrades and catch up on the doin's that had occurred in my absence.

First off, Finn McCool, the closest thing we have had to a proper medico, thanks to his brief medical studies in Dublin, insisted upon learning the details of how I was cured of the gunshot wound that sent me to Saint Louis the year before. As briefly as I was able, I explained how a measly powder charge behind a pebble had propelled the lightweight little missile only far enough into my chest to hide it behind a rib, instead of busting my heart, as a proper galena pistol ball likely would have done. Finn and Zeetlah had worked manfully but unsuccessfully to dig it out, but they couldn't find it. "Och," the Irishman snorted, "we should ha' known 'twould be somethin' o' the sort!" He actually blushed. "But as ye know, I've niver claimed to be a surgeon, nor a proper physician, nayther, me schoolin' bein' interrupted loike it was."

"Don't ye fret, Finn," I assured him. "In the kingdom of the blind, the one-eyed man is king. There's many of us here today who wouldn't be, but for your care." A chorus of voices echoed that sentiment. "That's the long an' short of it," I declared, anxious to get off that particular topic. "I'm fit as ever I was. Tell me, now, what's been happenin' hereabouts?"

The grumbling response boded no good news. "Ther gawddamn trappin' trade's goin' ter hell like greeze through a gawddamn goose, thet's whut!" Tuttle growled.

"Puttin' it in jist one word, it's the compertishun!" Brass Turtle declared. "Too many newcomers climbin' on our backs an' peelin' off the profits!"

"'Speshly Amurrican Fur!" Anse Tolliver snarled. "They be the wust!"

I recalled that at the close of last year's rendezvous, Bridger, Fitz, and the other Rocky Mountain Fur partners, exasperated by American Fur dogging their footsteps and encroaching on their trapping grounds, offered to split the trapping territory with AMF, but Major Vanderburgh and Andy Drips spurned their offer with the arrogant response that they saw no profit in settling for half the country when they could have it all just by following the RMF brigades.

Brass Turtle volunteered to fill me in and the others let him do so—not, howsomever, without interruptions. "Wal, arter las' year's ronnyvoo, our bunch j'ined up with Gabe an' Fitz an' about threescore or so o' their trappers an' some other free men fer the fall hunt, headin' gen'rally fer the Missourah Forks."

"Then shore-as-hell," Anse broke in, "along come ol' Drips an' Vandyburg an' their sorry mob o' greenhorns snufflin' up our arse, grabbin' up our leavin's, crowdin' us sumthin' fierce."

Turtle shot him a hard glance and growled, "I'm tellin' it, Tolliver. Let it be." Some others hushed Anse and urged Turtle to continue. "Wal, Anse is right. That's abaout how it war. No matter whar we went ner how fast ner sneaky, thar they war—trailin' on our heels like a pack o' coondogs! 'Twarn't long afore Fitz an' Gabe reckoned the fall hunt war jist about ruint awready, so they hatched up a scheme fer givin' Amurrican Fur some proper comeuppance." He paused to fill and light his pipe before resuming his tale.

"We led 'em a merry chase, but they hung on like cockleburrs, 'spectin' us to show 'em prime doin's fer beaver. We jist abaout quit lookin' fer plews—stayin' clear o' good places, intendin' we'd teach 'em a lesson an' git 'em off our arse."

"We could'a had a better hunt, by gawd, ef Anse warn't allus preachin' 'gin killin' white-eyes!" Tuttle hollered out. "Don't matter who they be, most of 'em desarve no better!"

Turtle nodded tacit agreement and resumed. "We din't try hidin' our tracks no more. Naow we *meant* fer 'em to foller us an' they took the bait. We din't tarry 'round the Missourah Forks fer trappin' ner try steerin' clear o' Blackfoots. We headed over the Divide, straight inter Blackfoot country, up thar on the prairie, whar there ain't hardly no beaver nohaow. An' Amurrican Fur kep' on follerin' arter us, like Tuttle snarf'lin' up a purty gal's skirts." He flashed a grin in response to Tuttle's howl.

"It took a spell fer Drips an' sojer-boy Vanderburgh to catch on that naow they war somewhars in the middle o' the whole Blackfoot Nation, but even when they did, they reckoned they had traipsed all the way up thar arter beaver, so they bygawd meant git theirse'fs some plews. They split their brigade in two an' went to trappin', which, tharabaouts, warn't hardly wuth the trouble o' doin' it."

"Tell 'im haow it come out fer 'em, Turtle!" Anse called out.

"I war gittin' to that, natcherly," Turtle snapped. "Nobody in our bunch seen it ourownse'fs, but what we heard war, one o' Vanderburgh's scouts come upon some serious Injun sign an' he tol' the major abaout it, but 'stid o' makin' tracks out o' thar, that'ere sojer-boy—what never war up to Blackfoots ner much o' nothin' else he should'a knowed abaout—he takes a dozen men an' goes chasin' out to see fer hisownse'f. Which he sure-as-hell got his wish fer! Blackfoots cornered 'em in a narrer gully, kilt Vanderburgh an' a coupl'a others, an' chased the rest o' them'ere 'Murrican Fur greenhorns off to whar they holed up with a bunch o' frien'ly Pend d'Oreilles that war campin' not fur off.

"They say ol' Vanderburgh put up a helluva fight, but it din't do no good. Blackfoots kilt 'im an' chopped 'im up in pieces an' went to paradin' his parts around a-hossback. Same with t'other two."

My mind swung back to our early days on the Seeds-ke-dee and John Smiley, one of our original bunch, who had suffered a similar fate at the hands of Blackfoots.

Brass Turtle's brief telling summed up the sorry fate of American Fur's hapless field commander. Howsomever, I was still curious about Jim Bridger's ill-health. "Tell me," I asked Turtle. "Why is Gabe lookin' so peakèd."

"Paykèd, indade!" McCool commented sourly. "Seamus Bridger'll be blessed by the Good Lord Himsel' if he survives what he got last autumn."

"An' none of it would'a happened, 'ceptin' fer 'Murrican Fur meddlin' with us!" Anse insisted. "Cain't find their gawddamn arse with both hands, let alone no beaver, 'thout us p'intin' the way fer 'em! We wou'nt'a never been up thataway in the fust place, nohaow, if'n it warn't fer Jake Astor's igner'nt sumbitches!"

Turtle sighed. "Natcherly ye'd want to know haow that come abaout. It war sorta like what ol' Mister Shakespeare called a Comedy of Errors."

"Ye damn betcha!" Tuttle butted in. "'T'warn't nohaow comical, but thar war shore-as-hell a passel o' arrers flyin' abaout, 'fore it war over!"

Turtle ignored him. "What I mean to be tellin', Fitz an' Gabe an' all of us reckoned it war best we be leavin' Amurrican Fur up thar an' fer us to git daown to the Forks fer some proper trappin' 'fore the big snows come on. Which we did, trav'lin' fast an' careful-like, allus hungry, keepin' our critters nigh, lookin' 'hind ever' rock an' tree, an' sleepin' with one eye open, but we come through jist fine, 'thout losin' hide ner hair ner the few measly plews we scraped up when we warn't dodgin' Drips an' Vanderburgh."

"Tell 'im abaout Joe Meek's turkey-shoot," Tolliver sang out.

"Hell! 'Twar more like shootin' fish in a bar'l!" Tuttle corrected.

"I'm gittin' thar!" Turtle barked. "Wal, Joe Meek an' Doc Newell an' that'ere Irisher harpooner an' a coupl'a others war comin' back from runnin' their traps. They war 'longside a lake when they spy half a dozen Siksikas fishin' off the shore. An' when they saw them Blackfoots din't have no guns with 'em, Joe an' the others reckoned it'd be fust-rate fun to go shootin' at 'em, 'thout runnin' no risk to theirownse'fs. Which they did, havin' theirse'fs a merry ol' time, shootin' an' laughin' their arse off, 'speshly when them Siksikas jumped into the lake to save theirse'fs an' Joe's bunch kep' on shootin' at their heads, sorta like floatin' punkins.

"Problem war, all the ruction they war raisin' with their gawddamn shootin' caught the 'tention o' the main bunch o' Blackfoots what war campin' nigh the lake, more'n a couplescore of 'em, an' they come roarin' up a-hossback, lookin' to take some white-eyes ha'r!

"Seein' as haow the tables war all-of-a-sudden turned abaout, ol' Meek an' his Merry Andrews reckoned 'twar time to be high-tailin' it out o' thar. Which they did—a couplescore mad-as-hell Blackfoots close on their hocks.

"Course, when Joe an' his pals come bustin' into our camp o' fourscore fightin' men, them'ere Blackfoots did some serious recornsid'rin' abaout takin' on that many of us. They like the odds long on their own side.

"On t'other hand, their pride wouldn't let 'em jist quit an' go home, so one o' their chiefs, a big young feller, come ridin' out, aimin' to parley. He's carryin' a peace-pipe an' nothin' else ye could see, an' Jim Bridger rides out to meet 'im, takin' along his rifle an' that'ere young Spanyard Loretto's Blackfoot wife fer doin' the talkin' fer 'im.

"What happened arter that warn't precisely plain to see. The chief holds out his hand, like he means to be friendly, but jist then Gabe seen somethin' funny happ'nin' 'mongst some o' the other Blackfoot headmen standin' nigh, so he cocks his Hawken, which natcherly upsets the peacemakin' chief no little when he hears it. Quick as scat, he grabs a-holt o' Bridger's gun, which goes off into the ground, an' he yanks it out o' Gabe's hands, an' then he knocks ol' Bridger plumb off'n his hoss with his own gun!

"Right then, all hell busts loose! The Blackfoots commence yellin' an' whoopin' an' shootin' muskets an' fillin' the air full o' arrers 'til hell wou'n't have it! Jim gits hit in the back by two of 'em. An' natcherly we're shootin' back an' tryin' to git Bridger safe to our side o' the clearin'. Our li'l Blackfoot gal's hoss spooks an' r'ares an' throws her daown an' the Siksikas grab 'er up an' run 'er off to their side o' the medder, whilst the shootin' gits hotter'n hell on both sides an' keeps up the rest o' the day, ever'body crawlin' amongst rocks an' trees fer cover."

"'Twarn't as bad as it mought'a been," Tuttle declared. "'Spite of all thet shootin', we lost but three of our'n an' a couple-three more bunged up purty good. Them'ere gawddamn Siksikers carted off nine o' their own, close as we could count."

Brass Turtle nodded to McCool. "Mebbe you'd best tell it from hyar on, Finn, abaout Bridger's arrers an' all, seein' as haow that be your line o' work."

The tall Irishman swallowed hard and plunged into his part of the story. "I did all that my poor skills allowed," he said in a low voice. "Seamus was bleedin' bad—two arrows stickin' in his back, one o' thim deep in the muscle, the other not so serious, which I was able to cut out, stanchin' the blood wi' spiderweb from Little Mountain's stock o' medicinals. Try as I might, I've not been able to remove the other one. The iron point is lodged deep in the muscle. I fear attemptin' to dig it out'd be the death of 'im."

He frowned, his long Irish mug the very picture of gloom. "What I fear, as well, is the infection that's sure to result from that filthy haythen arrow point. That'll surely kill 'im." He looked thoughtful, glum, before he brightened somewhat and added, "But it's been more'n six months now and Seamus is still gettin' about. Cripplin' more'n somewhat, to be sure, but he hasn't died yet." He took a deep breath, shook his head, and said, wonder in his voice, "A most amazin' man, he is, Seamus Bridger."

Brass Turtle picked up the account, telling how the Siksikas refused to give up the young woman interpreter, claiming her for one of their own, even when young Loretto rode into their camp, carrying their infant child, and pleaded for her return. He told them how he had rescued her from the Crows, saved her from being tortured and killed. She added her pleas to his, but the chief insisted that she belonged to his tribe. Surprisingly, he allowed the brave young Spaniard to return to the trappers' lines, instead of killing him on the spot. Blackfoots admire courage, even in their enemies. Broken-hearted, young Loretto returned to his fellows, bereft of both his beloved wife and babe.

That accounting pretty much satisfied my curiosity, leastaways for the time being. In any case, the aroma of cooking vittles wafting on the summer air put an end to further confabulation, which rarely wins out against appetite.

∾   ∾   ∾

Scattered bunches of buffalo still grazed on the surrounding hills. Little Mountain, Acorn, and Pretty Horse had ridden out and harvested a fat young bull whilst the rest of us were palavering. By time we returned to the cookfire, boudins were sizzling on the coals, tongue bubbled in cookpots, and fresh raw liver was laid out on bark trenchers. Our French-Canuck campkeepers, resplendent now in new *tuques*, colorful shirts, and bright sashes and garters, greeted us with a flurry of cheerful *bienvenues, bon appetits*, and similar Frenchified pleasantries.

After Powatawa and I had eaten our fill, I invited him to accompany me on a gifting visit to Iron Bow's band, which he readily agreed to do. My father and the Séli chief had developed a strong friendship during the years since I took Rainbow to wife. They are natural leaders, strong, capable, thoughtful men, confident in themselves, respectful of the other's qualities.

I admit to a certain self-interest in doing my giveaways before the traders arrived, assuring that my truck would be appreciated and remembered, before the rendezvous became awash in trade goods. By time I finished assembling my heap of presents, my packmule fairly tottered under his load. Even so, it was but measly compensation for the generous treatment I had always enjoyed at the hands of Iron Bow and his son Fast Horse.

I chose to ride my Coffee horse on that pleasant mission, showing off my worldly worth Indian-style to my former in-laws. Hardly anything impresses

Indians more than a fine horse. The only thing that could have made it better would have been if I had stolen that magnificent critter from an enemy.

What warmed me most about the visit was the prospect of seeing Cat, although my feelings concerning the widow of my longtime friend were somewhat conflicted. My long-standing affection for her as a friend was complicated now by a hint of lust and tinged with a vague guilt over betraying the respect I owed Ned Godey's memory—and Rainbow, too. Still, I owed Cat a huge debt for her devoted care of my motherless child and I was genuinely concerned for her well-being as a woman alone now, deprived of her husband, an orphan who lacked even brothers to look after her. And always prominent in my mind was concern about how I, a rootless, wandering trapper, might provide for my four-year-old daughter.

I admitted to my father most of what tormented me, confessing that I was unable even to understand, let alone solve, that conundrum. Powatawa received my torrent of words with his customary calm. He said naught at first, appearing to be lost in his thoughts, but after a spell he smiled and replied. His words were carefully measured, thoughtfully chosen, delivered with gravity but warmed by affection. "Shawnees say that when two men choose to become brothers or when a man and a woman are meant for each other, we say they have walked together under the rainbow.

"You and Cataleen walked in the shadow of your Rainbow for many years. She loved you both. She will smile upon your union. Ned Godey will thank you for protecting the woman he loved, for he can no longer do so. Godey was a generous man. He would not begrudge the happiness you two can have together." He fell silent then. After a time he said with a gentle smile, "Perhaps they will comfort each other in the Grey Land. They could do worse."

I was comforted by his words, likely because they were what I wanted to hear. Then, doubt assailed me. "What if she won't have me? What then? She appeared cold when I saw her yesterday."

My father allowed himself a quiet chuckle. "There are some things men are not meant to understand. Woman is one of those things." He sighed, perhaps recalling his own youth. "Some things must be accepted without questions." He was quiet for a spell, then, "I believe in the sun, even when it is not shining. I believe in love between man and woman, even when I have no woman of my own. I believe in the Great Spirit, even when He is silent." Whilst I mulled over how I might apply his words to my own case, he finished with, "Not all things must be understood. Do what you can do, then listen to your heart."

We were by that time threading our way amongst the lodges of Iron Bow's village, which prevented further fathoming of my plight. I concluded that my father, wise as I know him to be, had only presented me with yet another conundrum.

Hardly anybody can approach an Indian village without giving plenty of warning, certainly not in the light of day. By time we arrived at the inner circle of lodges, Iron Bow, Fast Horse, and half-a-dozen other headmen had assembled there, together with a passel of men, women, and children crowding the alleyways between the lodges, curious, as always, to learn what errand had brought us there.

As soon as we dismounted, two boys took charge of our critters and I directed a couple more to tote the mule's heavy pack into Iron Bow's lodge. Then, after a brief welcoming speech from Iron Bow and a couple of the other headmen, Iron Bow led us all into his lodge, where we smoked and palavered mostly in sign until a couple-three women brought in bark platters of steaming buffalo meat, without which Indian hospitality would be remiss.

The palaver became livelier, comical, sometimes *risqué*, as we ate and licked our greasy fingers, until I reckoned it was time to commence the gifting. A fine Sheffield butcher knife, a pound of gunpowder and a galena pig, a hefty carrot of tobacco, a firesteel and English flint, and a fancy pipe-tomahawk went to each man present, but I let it go at that. It was best that Iron Bow be the one to distribute as he saw fit the rest of the plunder I had brought.

The other headmen soon drifted off, lugging their presents, grinning and mumbling and signing their thanks, leaving my father and me to continue our visit. Further palaver was forestalled by our hosts' sidelong glances at the bulging pack, even though etiquette forbade their asking to see what was in it.

I chose not to save the best for last. My first gift to Iron Bow, then another to Fast Horse, was a brand-new heavy-caliber Hawken percussion rifle, complete with bullet mold and gun-fixin's, as well as gunpowder, galena, and a sack of percussion caps. As I handed the weapon to Iron Bow, I explained in signs and syllables that it was only fitting that the man who had been first amongst his people to capture an enemy firearm should own the best gun available now. Even whitemen had none better. The carefully-studied dignity of the chief almost cracked, but not quite. His dark eyes were dancing, howsomever, as he studied every inch of the rifle, lips moving, running his fingers over the highly-polished stock and gleaming brass furniture.

The rest of my gifts—gunpowder and galena, tobacco, coffee, sugar, woolens and calico cloth, packets of vermilion, beads, thread, needles, shiny brass thimbles, knives and files and tomahawks, and a passel of other trade goods prized by Indians—were greeted with gratitude, but they paled to unimportance compared with the rifles, which never left the hands of either Iron Bow or his son, even when we smoked a final pipeful before I begged leave to depart in order to visit my daughter and the widow of my fallen comrade.

As I retrieved a last bulky parcel from my canvas pack, I thought that I detected a faint glimmer of amusement in the eyes of Iron Bow and Fast Horse, but good manners prevented them from expressing what was surely in their minds. My father discreetly chose to remain with his old friend.

When I emerged from the lodge, my daughter sped to my side, shrieking, "Papa! Papa!" and leapt into my arms, chattering a mile-a-minute, hugging my neck and kissing my face, happy tears flowing down her chubby cheeks, then grabbing my hand to drag me to the little lodge that she occupied with Cat, the same dwelling, I noticed, that Godey and Kathleen had used in their traveling, the lodge that Iris had called home for the past two years.

Cat met us at the doorway and invited me inside, her manner friendly enough but a mite too formal between old friends who had shared so much together. Her dark eyes were clouded, her smile reserved. I recalled my father's counsel that it is not given to understand the workings of a woman's mind, whilst I dragged my parcel past the low doorway.

Seated cross-legged on either side of the cold firepit, Cat and I laughed together at my daughter's joyous excitement as I presented her with a French doll and half a dozen brightly-painted toys from Europe, hung sparkling necklaces at her throat, draped her in woolens and calicos that would become new garments for her, and daubed her cheeks and forehead with vermilion. Iris was beside herself with glee, one moment admiring her new-found treasures, the next flinging herself around my neck, smothering me in wet, childish kisses, babbling her gratitude mostly in Salish with here and there an English or French word or phrase thrown in.

At last she could no longer contain her need to show off her new riches to her playmates. She planted a hasty kiss on my cheek, burbled a farewell thankee, and fled outdoors, her pretty French doll and a couple toys clutched to her bosom.

When our laughter subsided to chuckles, I commenced laying out my gifts for Cat. These produced an altogether different, unexpected response from my friend. She, who had always in times past expressed an almost childlike delight with settlement goods and foofurraw, now greeted my presents with a cool, detached air. She thanked me, but politely, without warmth.

I bit my tongue whilst I continued to heap woolens and cotton fabrics, Chinese silks, a nest of copper tin-lined kettles and a spider skillet, packets of vermilion and colored dyes for quills, beads, awls, needles, thread, thimbles, mirrors, metal tweezers, knives, firesteels and English flints, all manner of settlement plunder and foofurraw that is usually dear to the heart of an Indian woman.

At last I could restrain myself no longer. "What's wrong, Kathleen?" I demanded. "My presents don't please ye? They're the best Sain' Looie offers."

She sighed. This time her smile was sincere. "I be t'ankin' you, Tempo, fer zis good stuff, but I have no need. One winter pas', I be dancin' an' singin' fer havin' purty sings fer makin' my man who call me Cataleen proud when I walk wiz heem, fer makin' my hoss purty when I ride wiz heem. Now I no need purties fer makin' my man proud fer hees Cataleen. He no walk noplace no more. He no ride 'longside hees Cataleen no more. Never no more. Cataleen by lonesome now. No man by her. No need white-eyes foofurraw."

I quote Cat's words here pretty much as I heard her say them that day, but I won't offend her dignity further in the coming pages by rendering her speech verbatim. Fact is, she spoke her English remarkably well at that time, considering that she had picked it up by ear mostly from the ill-spoken hillbillies that make up our trapping bunch, myself included. Her spoken Salish is impeccable. You might have noted in her words quoted above that, observing Indian custom, Cat declined to speak Ned Godey's name, out of respect for her dead husband, using, instead, roundabout expressions to identify him.

Further talk stalled. Somehow, at first, I couldn't bring myself simply to tell her that I wanted her for my woman. Problem was, although I love language and glib as I can sometimes be in other circumstances, I am not blessed with the silken tongue and silver syllables that many of my comrades possess, a gift which enables them to charm Indian maids into their robes apparently at will. From what I've seen, they go merrily about gathering up bouquets of willing prairie flowers, then, when ardor cools, bidding those damsels farewell with no regrets. Even craggy, crabby, unwashed Anse Toliver rarely lacks a woman for his temporary use when he wants one.

I am not onesuch, nor wish to be. Although I had been no stranger to feminine companionship in the years before Rainbow, invitations to intimate relations were extended by the women, not by me. I was receiving no such signal from Cat. She was, apparently, not interested. At last, when I blurted out my intentions, silence greeted my overture. Nary a flicker of interest was visible on her comely features.

After an eternity or two, she replied in words and signs. No, she said quietly. I will not be your woman. I need no charity. You worry for Irish, for me, with no man in my lodge to hunt and fight for us. Be not worried. We go with Iron Bow. He will protect us. We will eat when he eats. He will keep us safe.   She knew that I could not look after Iris unless I had a woman of my own, but she refused to become my wife either for pity I might feel for her or for purely practical reasons. I found myself tongue-tied. I wanted to tell her that Iris was only a part of it, that I wanted her for herself, that I had long admired and loved everything about her. I wanted to add all the fine sentiments that a lover heaps upon his beloved. I could say none of it. Instead, I blushed and stammered and mumbled regrets before I retreated into silence.

Apparently it was too late for me to come a-courting with a flute and a blanket outside her lodge. Or too early. The spectres of Rainbow and Ned stood between us. Maybe it was too soon after Ned's death. Perhaps she and I knew each other too well. Maybe we had shared as friends, with other mates, too many perils and hardships, good times and lean, to put all of our history aside now and assume different roles.

Her eyes had softened somewhat by time I bade farewell. I promised to return soon to visit my daughter. She said nothing more about my awkward proposal and neither did I.

I collected my father from Iron Bow's lodge and we rode back to our camp in silence, until Powatawa said, pretty much repeating his earlier counsel, "It is not given for a man to know what a woman thinks." I merely grunted and retreated further into my gloom. We continued on our way without another word spoken.

~o   ~o   ~o

The mood amongst our bunch was not much more cheerful than my own. Traders still had not arrived. Trappers were restless. The married men were tormented by constant nagging by their spouses, whose unhappiness could be cured only by white-eyes plunder. Single men grumbled that it was fruitless to go a-courting Indian women without the beads, baubles, and gimcrackery that made their rough charms acceptable to intended lights-o'-love.

Although I might have relieved their discontent by distributing the remainder of my Saint Louis plunder, I reckoned there would likely come a time when we would need that trade goods to buy our way out of difficulty.

Tuttle Thompson was loudest in complaining about his enforced abstinence, until I privately slipped a string of sky-blue beads into his hand. Micah and Tuttle had been my earliest friends in my Rocky Mountain odyssey. I could not, in good conscience, fail to aid Tuttle in his amorous endeavors. Half-an-hour later, freshly-shaved and beaming, togged out in a new calico shirt and his Sunday-best buckskins, Tuttle set out for the Pend d'Oreille village, confident that his fistful of blue beads would guarantee a night of lubricious delight.

Micah has no need of material bribes. His handsome ebony features, athletic physique, and deceptively gentle demeanor suffice to mystify and attract a sufficiency of pretty Indian women, maidens and matrons alike, curious to see for themselves if his color will rub off.

Disappointment settled upon my spirit like a sodden cloak thrown over my shoulders, smothering the joy I should have felt at being reunited with my daughter and my comrades. I sneaked off to my bower, lest I be forced to feign good humor that I could not feel.

Cat's rejection of my proposal—of myself, as I saw it then—was not precisely a new experience for me, but it rankled just the same, made me doubt my own worth.

Six years before, on the eve of our wedding, my childhood sweetheart in Ohio, Sarah Rutledge, recoiled from me in horror when she learned that my true father was the admirable Shawnee chief Powatawa, not the lying, lecherous, murderous, whiskey-soaked hypocrite who went to hell believing that he had sired me. Sarah was willing to overlook Pap's evil reputation. He was, after all, a whiteman, but she could not stomach marrying the love of her life whose blood, as she saw it now, was tainted.

Fact is, Sarah did me a favor. For her sake, I had been willing to give up the bold, free life of the mountains and settle down to a dull, monotonous existence as an Ohio dirt farmer. Her disgust and disdain of my Indian ancestry released me from a bondage that would have shriveled my soul.

Seeking solace or oblivion or both, I filled my cup with fine French brandy, a noble cognac, liquid sunshine that had always thrilled and warmed my soul. But instead of boosting my spirit and driving off the imps of self-doubt, the alcohol merely deepened my dejection, dragging me farther into depression. A second cup made it only worse.

I crawled to my robes and drifted into troubled sleep, seeking unsuccessfully to blur Cat's lovely face and form. With a single word, a simple *no*, she had set me adrift on a sea of self-doubt and indecision. My pride was injured. I was uncertain of what I must do to ensure the well-being of my daughter. I am not sure which troubled me most.

-oOo-

A single delighted whoop from somewheres downriver, in the direction of Bonneville's fort, announced that a trader's packtrain had arrived. No other event could convey such enthusiasm in a single vocal note, announcing relief and reward for a couple hundred trappers yearning for tobacco, booze, and traders' goods—common stuff in the settlements, but, in the mountains, plunder more precious than rubies. Most highly prized was booze, the fuel and lifeblood of rendezvous!

There was a mad scramble to snatch up our saddle mounts and ride to greet the caravan. Within minutes most of our bunch was galloping furiously alongside the river, laughing our heads off, mingling with a horde of trappers and Indians eager to be foremost in welcoming the long-overdue travelers. We had no idea which trading outfit it might be, but that made little difference. Now there would be booze and foofurraw aplenty, whoever brought it.

Even so, it was with pleasure that we spied Bobby Campbell leading the packtrain splashing across Horse Crick. He was flanked by a grinning Black Harris and Captain Stewart, whose stiff, dignified expression crumbled into smiling excitement as he got caught up in the spirit of the noisy, colorful savages, red and white, come out to greet the packtrain.

With an ear-splitting roar and a welcoming fusillade of musketry fired into the air, our thirsty company charged into the ranks of newcomers, startling the greenhorn hostlers as much as their critters. Most of Bobby's men were strangers to the exuberance of rendezvous. My Coffee horse and I were swept up in a torrent of horseflesh and carried past the leaders, into a mob of terrified packmules intent upon bucking off their loads and cursing hostlers struggling to keep them from doing so. It appeared the mules were winning.

By time I was able to work my way back to the head of the column, we were nearing Bonneville's rude little fort. I heard Harris holler, "Whar's

Rocky Mountain Fur?" A dozen voices told him to move upstream. Which he did.

On the way, the young Frenchy Larpenteur caught sight of me and called out, "I 'ave your book still, M'sieu Bock, *le Satyricon*! Many sanks for ze use of eet." Sure that a reply would be lost in the hubbub, I merely waved acknowledgement and crowded Coffee close to Harris, who stood in his stirrups, leaned out, and wrapped me in a bear hug.

"Damn ef'n it ain't good to see ye, Temple," he muttered in my ear. "We war more'n a mite consarned fer ye, comin' up hyar on yer own hook like ye done."

I assured him that we had traveled without mishap and that the concern was mutual, that we had feared for the well-being of Campbell's caravan. "Aw, hell!" he replied with a chuckle. "'Twarn't us y'all war worried fer! It war the likker an' foofurraw we be fetchin'! Cain't be havin' no ronnyvoo 'thout 'em!" Falling into his jovial mood, I allowed that it was likely so.

∾   ∾   ∾

The arrival of Campbell's packtrain struck a spark that created light and mirth, merriment and good feeling. Only a few hours earlier, men had been grouchy, sullen, touchy, given to brawling at the slightest fancied slight. Now cookfires blazed and the air was redolent of roasting meat and filled with laughter and fiddle music from scores of roistering trappers along the riverbank

Times had changed. In the early years, there had always been just one trader at rendezvous. First, it was William Ashley, then later, Bill Sublette and his two partners. Back then, the trader needed to be in no hurry to spread out his merchandise. He could take his own sweet time to serve up tobacco and booze. But those days were gone. This year Campbell and Rocky Mountain Fur made haste to heap their trade tables with goods and to water down their kegs of pure grain alcohol for the horde of thirsty trappers and Indians who flocked to their trade tents toting plews and demanding strong drink and plunder, even before the traders had finished putting up their canvas.

Rocky Mountain Fur was happy to oblige. They needed to grab up every beaver plew possible while they enjoyed a brief monopoly, before the supply caravans of Captain Bonneville, American Fur, and god-only-knew-how-many other traders arrived.

As soon as the pack-animals had been stripped of their loads and turned out to graze, along with Sublette's seed bulls and milch cows, Campbell's hostlers were fetching up trade goods and ladling out watered-down booze at five dollars the pint. The trapping brigades of Tom Fitzpatrick and Henry Fraeb arrived later that day. Several of their men who possessed a keen eye for the quality of beaver fur were pressed into service, grading pelts and calling out the value of each plew to a clerk who scribbled the amount under the trapper's name in the Company's big ledger book.

"Hyar's wishin' 'em well!" Brass Turtle said, raising his cup in a toast as he and I watched from a distance. He and I had no need to join the rowdy throng clamoring for service. Our own cups contained good Kentucky sippin' whiskey. "Ol' Billy Sublette's holdin' enough paper on RMF to choke 'em. They'd best git 'im paid off whilst thar's still enough beaver left to git it done. A few more years like this'n an' thar won't be naught but empty traps!"

I refused to share the gloomy view of my Delaware friend. Even considering the increasing number of new trappers coming to the mountains each year, as well as all the Indians who were realizing that beaver plews could be converted into muskets and powder, copper kettles and blankets, foofurraw, and popskull booze, I still could not believe that we could ever use up all the beaver in the Rocky Mountains.

❧   ❧   ❧

Amid the circle of Rocky Mountain Fur's trade tents and tables were the modest, weather-stained traveling lodges of the partners and the rather more elaborate canvas dwellings of Robert Campbell and his guests. Conspicuous amongst the latter was a bright red canvas marquee owned by Captain William Drummond Stewart, which he had refrained from erecting during the journey from Saint Louis.

Even more startling was the spectacle of the gentleman himself that first evening, when he emerged from his scarlet digs, just before supper, clad in the most outlandish get-up ever seen or imagined amongst our unwashed multitude. The Scottish dandy was attired in a form-fitting white leather jacket equipped with more pockets than you might suppose a tailor could find room for, a ruffled white shirt, lacy stock flowing at his throat, snug-leggèd woolen trousers made of the Stewart family tartan plaid, a hint of white stocking showing between his trouser bottoms and shiny black slippers, the entire confection surmounted by his soft, wide-brimmed palm-leaf hat, which looked surprisingly none the worse for wear after its arduous journey from the settlements.

The expression on Stewart's phiz, the confident jut of his well-barbered chin, and the glint in his cold blue eyes dared any man to make fun of his garb. Not many did and those few kept their distance. Campbell's hostlers had, early on, spread word of the Scotsman's courage and his prowess with firearms and cold steel.

~ ~ ~

Rocky Mountain Fur's monopoly lasted only three days. Lucien Fontenelle and Andy Drips arrived with supplies for their American Fur Company brigades and a plenitude of trade goods for free trappers and Indian customers. They were soon followed by Captain Bonneville returning from the settlements with a fresh stock of plunder to outfit his people and to trade with whoever had plews. Even the crabby New England Yankee trader Nat Wyeth showed up, fresh from wintering on the shore of the Western Sea, where he likely had been consorting with the Hudson's Bay Company, although nobody knew for sure.

Bobby Campbell, with a few RMF men, set off for Pierre's Hole to raise a cache of beaver plews from the previous fall hunt. Tom Fitzpatrick took charge of business in camp, relying heavily on the teetotaling clerk Charles Larpenteur, the only sober man in camp, white or red. The creaking and groaning of RMF's hide press baling cured green beaver pelts into solid bundles must have been music to the partners' ears. Fitz and the other partners went about smiling as their stock of plews grew ever larger. Each hundred-pound pack represented a step towards freedom from the mounting interest on the substantial debt they still owed to Bill Sublette.

~ ~ ~

An exotic character such as William Drummond Stewart was certain to attract a bevy of hangers-on amongst our rude company, some who thought they saw an opportunity for gain, but most out of simple curiosity. Joe Meek, a big, handsome, blackheaded, boisterous, carefree young Virginian who had taken to mountain life like a duck to water in the four years that he had been plying our trade, was of the latter sort. Joe asked naught of any man, except friendship and respect and a swig or two from his kettle. He was fiercely loyal to Milton Sublette, but Joe was drawn as if by a lodestone to the colorful

Scotsman, whose military reputation was quickly bruited about the camp. Bumptious Joe Meek lost no time in scraping acquaintance with the Hero of Waterloo.

The interest was mutual. Stewart could not fail to be intrigued by young Joe's innocent swaggering, his harmless braggadocio founded in genuine madcap courage, and the outrageous coxcombry with which he bedecks himself, his favorite horse, and whichever Indian maiden who captures his fancy at rendezvous. By the end of every rendezvous, howsomever, his frippery is gone, along with his light-o'-love, sacrificed to buy ardent spirits for himself and his friends.

Another who was drawn to Stewart's coterie was Antoine Clement, a handsome French-Cree trapper who, although still in his mid-twenties, enjoyed a substantial reputation as a trapper, hunter, and Indian-fighter. Antoine's English is good and his French is better, beside his grasp of half-a-dozen Indian tongues. Most people, deceived by his fair complexion, red hair, and hazel eyes, take Antoine for a whiteman, which he encourages. Even so, he retains strong ties with his mother's Cree Nation up north, on the fringe of Grandfather's Land. The Scottish nobleman could not help but take notice of Antoine, whose customary colorful duds and gleaming weapons outshine Joe Meek's temporary finery. The two of them struck up an instant friendship which lasted as long as Stewart remained in the mountains.

Good-natured George Holmes continued his service with the captain, performing minor chores and sleeping in the crimson marquee on nights when Stewart chose not to entertain a dusky paramour or two from one or another of the surrounding Indian camps.

❧   ❧   ❧

I filled most days with hunting jaunts with Brass Turtle and the other Delawares and Iroquois in our bunch, harvesting young bulls for our cookfire, shopping at traders' tents, where my gold and silver coin was welcome, even if I had no plews to trade, and frequent visits to Iron Bow's band to play with my daughter Iris and to tiptoe around what had become a prickly relationship with Cat. Her distant manner towards me bruised my feelings, but there was naught I knew to do to change her manner towards me, so I made the best of it.

Daytimes were pleasant enough, for there is always plenty of amusement at rendezvous, all manner of physical contests—footraces, horse races, shooting at a mark, chucking knives and tomahawks at targets, rough-and-tumble wrestling matches, and other manly competitions—gambling at cards and the Indian game of Hand, yarning and elaborate story-telling at which Black Harris excels, and always music, wild dancing, and drunken singing. Whenever a fiddle or two might strike up a tune, they were soon accompanied by Indian flutes, hand drums, and sometimes a tinwhistle or a battered brass horn.

Naturally the most popular recreation for lusty young trappers is provided by young and not so young Indian maids and matrons who, for a handful of shiny glass beads, a swatch of woolen trade cloth, or a copper kettle, willingly accompanies her temporary swain to his bower or a convenient clump of bushes to satisfy her uxorial obligation.

Tempting as such casual dalliances might be for a healthy young man, I have been ever mindful of Ned Godey's counsel when I was still a callow youth ascending the Missouri River. Ned warned me then of the danger of contracting clap or the pox and he provided me with a useful test to avoid those maladies, which are commonly spread by whitemen. He advised me that if an Indian woman were ignorant of the custom of kissing, it was likely that she had never had intimate commerce with a whiteman and was likely free of disease. That useful rule had preserved my health for a decade, leastaways in that regard.

During daylight hours we wandered up and down the Seeds-kee-dee, visiting one camp and another, inspecting trade goods and haggling over prices at American Fur, Bonneville's rude fort, Wyeth's, or some of the little shirttail trading outfits trying to whittle a modest profit off the rendezvous. Our roaming was mostly done a-horseback, for the rendezvous stretched some ten miles along the river. Camps were constantly changing location, especially the Indian villages, as grazing for their large pony herds got used up and the middens became unbearably noisome in the summer heat.

Brass Turtle is a full-blood Delaware, but at rendezvous he mostly hangs with the white-eyes in our bunch. I use the term *white-eyes* loosely, for it includes Powatawa and me, Micah, who is black as ebony, and our dark-skinned Spaniard Cesár Pérez, as well as lily-white Tuttle Thompson, Anse Tolliver, and our two Irishmen, Finnæus McCool and redheaded Paddy McBride. At rendezvous Turtle prefers our company to that of most of our Lenapees and Iroquois, who, if they drink at all, display a single-minded dedication to getting blind drunk as rapidly as possible and passing out.

Turtle is too fun-loving for that, so he spends most of his time with us. Anse Tolliver's company is rarely available at rendezvous, for he is much in demand for his fiddling talent, and Tuttle Thompson is also often occupied otherwise, baffling his opponents in the Indian hand game or working profitable magic with his greasy deck of cards, dealing Old Sledge and bilking unwary hostlers and newly-recruited Company trappers out of their wages. Veteran trappers steer clear of Tuttle's gaming. They know him too well.

Often we followed Tolliver out of camp, trailing behind until he hooked up with Cap'n Billy, a seafaring German fiddler, and Harpoon Harry Yeats, a young Irishman whose big baritone voice, musical skill on his travel-scarred cittern, and seemingly endless repertoire of racy ballads and sea chanteys endeared him to our rude assemblage. Our campkeeper Yves Dureau and his little Frenchy concertina squeezebox completed their quartet. Whenever they got together to make music, trappers streamed in from every direction, anxious to listen and raise their voices in song and kick up their heels in riotous dancing, all of them more than willing to keep our rustic troubadors well-lubricated with trader's booze.

Nighttimes were less pleasant for me. After supper, when dusk commenced to settle, most of my *compañeros* drifted off to one or another of the Indian camps along the river. Most of them—often even our married men, Turtle and Paddy—headed for the Snakes or the Kootenais, my father to the Nez Percés. They urged me to come along, but, tempted though I was, I declined, vaguely promising to join them next time. Even now I can't explain what made me hang back, denying myself a pleasure that I have always esteemed highly. I was alone and beholden to no one, free to do as I pleased, and yet, horny as I was after the many months since Saint Louis, the idea of riding off to an Indian camp and offering a copper kettle, a string of pretty glass beads, or a packet of vermilion in a businesslike exchange for the temporary use of some female stranger's warm, young body was something I wasn't ready for.

Most nights I retired shortly after nightfall, seeking in sleep solace from the nagging self-doubt that lurked never far off during my waking hours, try as I might to dispel it with physical activity, palaver, or a bonhomie that was all too often forced. A gill or so of ardent spirits as I went to my robes helped to conduct me into the arms of Morpheus and pleasant dreams or, just as welcome, none at all.

After a week's absence, Bobby Campbell and his crew, which included Micah and Cesár, returned unscathed from Pierre's Hole with ten packs of beaver that RMF had cached from the fall hunt. Nigh half a ton more of prime plews and no loss of life or limb gave RMF good reason for a celebration and the partners were not behindhand in declaring one. They sent Joe Meek to our camp with their invitation.

"Bobby an' Tom an' t'others sent me over to fetch y'all fer celebratin' raisin' ther cache an' gittin' back with all o' their ha'r."

Such a welcome summons did not need to be repeated. In no time at all we were mounted and thundering off to Rocky Mountain Fur. After warm greetings and our cups had been filled, serious business commenced, that of sorting through the newly-recovered plews and retrieving those bearing the marks of members of our bunch.

I had no part in that commerce, so I occupied my time palavering with Tom Fitzpatrick, who interrupted himself in the midst of a comical story he was telling when a thought came to him. "Ah, Temple," he said, "it struck me jist now that Godey's woman, who's been lookin' after your little colleen this long while, has a passel o' credit comin' fer all the plews that Ned left with us last fall. Be a good fella—would ye now, Temple darlin' ?—an' let 'er know she's welcome to come an' get her money's worth."

I was more than happy for an excuse to see Cat again. I wasted no time in complying with Tom's request. I drained my cup, trotted to the picket line, swung aboard my Coffee horse, and departed the RMF camp at a gallop.

My daughter spied me as soon as I entered the Séli camp and came running to greet me. I reached down and swung her onto the saddle bow whilst she hugged me and chattered excitedly in what sounded like a couple-three tongues, garbled even more by the peppermint stick I had brought for her. She paused in her welcoming babble only to direct me to the new location of Cat's lodge. Iron Bow's band had needed to move their horses across the river to fresh grazing since my last visit. When we arrived, Iris jumped down and darted into the lodge, announcing my presence in childish shrieks, whilst I tethered Coffee to a bush.

Cat looked puzzled, wary, when she stepped past the door-flap of her little traveling lodge. I hastened to put her at ease, blurting out news of the recovered cache and Fitzpatrick's assurance that Ned's earnings were now her own. "You're a woman of means now, Cat," I told her in an awkward attempt to sound jolly, "a wealthy widow who's a prime catch for an ambitious bachelor!" I swept off my broad-brimmed hat in a courtly bow for comical punctuation.

My clumsy humor fell flat as a flannel-cake. If she understood my feeble effort at wittiness, she gave no sign of it, striving instead to maintain a demeanor of polite but distant cordiality. My breath caught in my throat at the sheer natural beauty of this strong woman of the mountains and high prairie. I silently swore that I would overcome her refusals and that she would one day be mine, and I hers, as long as the two of us might live.

Our stiff, formal behavior brought to mind the precise patterns of the minuets and quadrilles I had observed at Lucette's, the gentlemen customers and Lucette's ladies decorously dancing a coquettish courtship that both knew would inevitably end in bed before the night was over. I had no such assurance, but, like they say, hope springs eternal.

Although Cat appeared pleased at the news of her windfall at Rocky Mountain Fur's trade tables, she gave no indication of when she might visit there. I took my leave with no more reason for hope than I had possessed when I arrived.

৵   ৵   ৵

The merriment in the RMF camp continued unabated. It had, in fact, increased considerably in my absence, thanks in large part to the fiddling of Anse Tolliver and Cap'n Billy, Harpoon Harry's big baritone voice and his cittern, and Yves Dureau happily squeezing his Frenchy concertina in drunken delight, besides any number of tipsy trappers joining in with any utensil that was even remotely musical, hand drums, Indian flutes, beating on copper kettles, and the like. Music warms a trapper's heart almost as much as trader's booze and draws him to its vicinity as surely as a moth to flame.

Paddy McBride lurched to my side as I tethered Coffee at the edge of camp. "Ah, Temple darlin', ye've returned to us," he slurred, "an' about time, too! Afore that bloody Sassenach soaks up all o' Fitz's booze!" He jerked his chin in the direction of Captain Stewart, who was holding court in the midst of his toadies and likely sipping his own fine Scotch whisky from his personal flask. "Come now," Paddy insisted, "we'll fill yer cup whilst there's still a dram or two remainin'." He led me to a trestle table where the teetotaling clerk Charles Larpenteur presided over a tub of watered-down grain spirits flavored with molasses, hot peppers, plug tobacco, and likely several other ingredients that best remain unidentified.

"Ah, M'sieu Bock," he called out as we approached. "'Ow good you 'ave arrive! Allow me to feel your cup." Whereupon he ladled my cup brimful of hooch and topped off Paddy's outstretched kettle for good measure. I thanked him and we retreated to hobnob with comrades and friends, many of whom I hadn't seen for a year and longer. When he spied me, Joe Meek detached himself from Stewart's circle of admirers and joined us.

"It's good to see ye amongst us agin, Temple. Ye had us purty worried thar, wond'rin' if ye war goin' to make it, arter las' year's woundin', don'tcha know?" I assured him that I was completely mended, as fit as ever, and naturally all three of us drank to our mutual continued good health.

Paddy insisted on making still another toast, which went something like this:

"I drink to meself an' one other!
An' may that one other be he
Who drinks to himself an' one other.
An' may that one other be me!"

I drifted amongst the crowd, chatting with trapper friends and admiring the splendiferous raiment of their Indian wives and the Indian girls and women who came with bachelor trappers. Especially striking was Milton Sublette's Shoshone wife, the beauteous Mountain Lamb, or so Joe Meek assured me she was named.

I noticed that Captain Stewart was not accompanied by a woman, which was noteworthy, for the gallant Scotsman had already acquired a considerable reputation as a ladies man. He had discarded his tight-fitting tartan trews and the white coat-of-many-pockets for an outfit of elaborately-quilled, butter-soft buckskins, which signaled his willingness to blend in with our mountain fraternity, albeit in colorful duds that most trappers could not afford.

Stewart's single condition was short-lived, howsomever, for soon Antoine Clement shouldered through the crowd, conducting a pair of young Shoshone beauties to the Captain's side. At first I thought that only one of the girls was meant for Stewart and the other for Antoine, for the Scotsman and the colorful French-Cree redhead had become close chums, but I quickly revised that thought. Antoine twirled first one, then the other, young woman in a graceful pirouette, displaying her charms to an appreciative Stewart, who smiled broadly, nodded his approval, gathered both girls under his outstretched arms, and led them off in the direction of his crimson marquee. Clement stared after them, shrugged, then headed for Larpenteur and his liquor tub.

"So naow he's got Antoine pimpin' fer 'im!" Tuttle exploded from behind me. "Allus thought thet'ere Frenchy had more style than lettin' hisse'f be doin' thet sort'a thang!"

"An' the pity of it is," Finn McCool chimed in, "young Antoine will niver be aught more than a servant to that Sassenach soldier-boy, niver a friend."

I allowed that it was likely so and the three of us clinked cups and drank in solemn sympathy for Antoine Clement's stumble from mountaineer respectability.

Dusk was gathering fast and I was beginning to feel somewhat befuddled by the liquid hospitality of Rocky Mountain Fur. I decided to retreat before it got any worse. I retrieved Coffee from the picket line, mounted, and picked my way through the crowd of trappers and Indians that had gathered to enjoy the music. My route took me past Stewart's marquee, where I spied George Holmes, the handsome young man who often served as the Scotsman's unpaid servant. Why Holmes performed menial chores for the high-handed Brit, I have never known—perhaps because Stewart allowed him to sleep in the marquee when he wasn't entertaining. At any rate, George was spreading out his bedroll under a tree when I ambled past.

I halted and we exchanged good-evenings, for we had become reasonably good friends on the journey from Saint Louis. "So you'll be sleeping under the stars tonight, George," I said by way of sociable conversation.

"Yes," he replied, smiling ruefully. "The Captain has guests tonight, so that's no place for me inside. I'll be fine if it doesn't rain."

I glanced upwards and saw a few twinkling stars in the gloom. "Yep, reckon ye will. No reason to worry. Pleasant dreams." I gathered my reins and continued on my way and Holmes returned to his chore.

≈   ≈   ≈

Although L'Archévêque had piled up a plenitude of prairie hay under the tree where I usually tethered a saddle horse overnight, I decided to indulge my Coffee horse by letting him stretch his legs by running free with our herd that night. I stripped off his saddle and pads, hung them from a low-hanging limb, rubbed his sweaty back dry with handfuls of hay, then scrambled onto his bare back and loped off to the pasture.

Little Mountain's huge bulk loomed out of the darkness as I dropped to the ground and slipped off the bridle. I slapped Coffee's rump and sent him off to join the herd before I called out, "It's all right, Mountain. Just me."

"I know you, Tempo, night an' day." Then, with just the slightest concern in his voice, he asked, "Eb'ryt'ing good?"

I assured him that everything was just fine and explained that I wished to give my favorite saddler a few extra hours of freedom overnight. The big Delaware was close enough now that I could see him nod. Then he surprised me by saying, "I t'ink bettah you go you robes now, Tempo."

For a brief moment I was stung, before I reminded myself that the Indians in our bunch, Delawares and Iroquois alike, don't trust the whites to stand horse guard at rendezvous. They reckon we are all drunks and unreliable at that important chore, so they split it up amongst themselves. After rendezvous, when booze is just a memory, we all take our turn.

Although I wasn't precisely drunk, I chose not to argue with Little Mountain just then. I bade him goodnight and trotted off to camp.

❧ ❧ ❧

Something made me slow my step and loosen the pistol in my sash as I rounded the corner of my bower. It was nothing I could identify, but years of living in the wilderness, where peril might lurk behind any bush or tree or bend in the trail, sharpens your senses and makes a man trust his hunches. I dropped to my knees and crept to the doorway, pistol cocked and ready in my hand, when a familiar voice giggled and called out softly, "I seenk you weel be sorry eef you shoot me."

I eased down the hammer of my pistol and laid it aside before I lunged forward and seized the intruder in a bear hug that caused her blanket to fall away, revealing her naked charms in the dim starlight. Fervent lips sought mine and her frantic hands tore at my clothing, darting beneath my britchclout and scrabbling at the knots and buckles of my various belts and sashes. I shrugged out of my clothing and we tumbled onto my robes, feverish lips glued fast, tongues darting and probing, eager hands caressing and exploring, her impassioned moans suddenly punctuated by her muffled shriek when we became a single natural animal, each striving to lose oneself in the other.

We achieved a writhing, gasping, groaning mutual climax and fell slightly apart, drained of strength, laced in close embrace, struggling for breath, still hugging tightly, as if we feared falling off the edge of the earth if we parted, breath rattling, at first unable to speak. When I tried to do so, she placed a finger firmly upon my lips and murmured, "No talk now. Better sings to do."

Indeed there were and we explored a passel of them in the next several hours, learning the personal arithmetic of an adventurous new lover's lovemaking, falling into exhausted slumber after an encounter, then slipping down the bank and into the chill waters of the Seeds-kee-dee to lave away sweat and amorous ichor, only to race back to our robes, shivering, and do it all over again in an effort to get warm—or so we facetiously assured each other was our intent.

All the while, Cat refused to explain her sudden change of heart. When I tried to question her, she grew solemn and withdrawn, saying only, "Is it not enough zat I am here now? We must live in today. Maybe tomorrow we are in ze Grey Land." I accepted her at her word.

During one lull in our lovemaking it came to me why Little Mountain had urged me to go to my robes. The sly Delaware had known that Cat was waiting there for me. She had left her horse with him for safekeeping and sworn him to silence if I happened by. No doubt he was chuckling now as he stood his lonely sentry watch, warmed against the chilly night air by his imagination.

Our lovemaking became more thoughtful, leisurely, inventive, our earlier frenzy mostly replaced now by a mutual wish to assure the other's pleasure. Even so, once, I thought I felt in Cat's embraces and stimulating caresses a mysterious urgency, as if she feared to fail in some purpose. Naturally I didn't put that notion into words, lest I offend her. I conveniently told myself that her concern might be for my pleasure and approval, even though such a sentiment ran counter to everything I knew about that independent-minded woman. The thought evaporated half a minute later when she drew me into herself and we commenced still another journey to mutual ecstasy.

We never got there. The stillness of the sleeping camp was shattered by hoarse yelling with a scared edge to it, pounding hoofbeats and moccasined feet running past my bower, an incoherent babble of frightened voices, then a chilling realization of what all the excitement was about, as the uproar jelled into meaningful sense. Fragments of terrified shouting came to us—"Mad wolf!" *"Prenez garde! Il y a un loup enragé!"* "Hyderphoby critter runnin' loose!" *"¡Lobo rabioso!"* "Don't try shootin'! You'll git somebody kilt, sure as hell!" And the like.

My ardor wilted but I clasped Cat even closer, impulsively seeking to shield her from harm. I felt her arms tighten around me, doubtless impelled by a similar impulse. That protective tightening of her arms did more to convince me that Cat loved me than a passel whispered endearments and feverish coupling.

I made sure that my guns were loaded and primed and ready to hand, against the unlikely event that the rabid wolf might invade my bower. Our location, perched only a few feet away from the swift-running river, made it extremely unlikely that any hydrophobic creature would come near. As is so often the case, fear, excitement, and especially the imminent possibility of death are powerful aphrodisiacs. And so it was with Cat and me. Without our realizing it, we were soon engaged in furious lovemaking, as if, somehow, we might assure immortality through procreation. Which is a ridiculous notion, but it appeared to be a good idea at the time.

≈ ≈ ≈

Rosy dawn was fingering into the eastern sky when Cat departed my bower. She slipped down the bank and followed the riverbed downstream to the meadow where our horse herd grazed, taking that route beside the water as much to avoid the gossip of my companions as to assure her safety from the rabid wolf. Just the same, I insisted that she take my pistol with her, in case the hydrophobic critter happened to ignore the common symptoms of his malady.

My daughter's safety was assured by Iron Bow's fortunate move across the river in search of fresh graze for his horses. It was unlikely that there was more than one rabid wolf thereabouts and even if so, that he would be on the other side of the Seeds-kee-dee.

I had enjoyed but little sleep the night before, but a brief swim in the chilly river, combined with the exhilaration produced by Cat's visit and the excitement engendered by the rabid wolf restored me as much as a proper night's rest might have done.

The crowd around our cookfire was abuzz with palaver concerning the wolf, all of it hearsay, for none of our bunch had actually seen him. I grabbed a few mouthfuls of buffalo hump and gulped a cup of strong coffee, then snatched up my bridle and hotfooted to the meadow to recover my Coffee horse. Little Mountain was just coming off his stint of nighttime horse guard duty, but he turned back to help me retrieve my saddler from our herd. While we rode back to camp together, he pulled my pistol from his sash, handed it to me, and said, "Cataleen she say she no need your gun nomore. She say she be crossin' river. No loco lobo over dere."

Back at camp, I saddled Coffee and trotted off to Rocky Mountain Fur to learn what I could of the wolf's depredations. As I drew nigh, William Drummond Stewart was just emerging from his scarlet marquee, clad in his nightshirt, yawning and stretching, when he spied Joe Meek sprawled nearby, sound asleep and snoring, evidently still lying where he had fallen the night before, gloriously drunk and indifferent to the peril posed by the rabid wolf. Stewart prodded Meek with his slippered toe and, when Joe sleepily acknowledged his presence, the Scotsman shouted, "Joe! Joe Meek! Don't ye realize that terrible animal might have bitten ye and killed ye and given ye a horrible death in the bargain!"

Joe grinned sheepishly, sat up, and replied, "Aw, hell, Cap'n! I went an' got m'se'f sech a skinful o' hooch las' night thet ef he'd'a bit me, it shorely would'a kilt 'im, fer damn sure, ef it din't cure 'im outright!"

Stewart laughed in spite of himself, and turned away, his attention suddenly captured by something considerably more serious. A short distance away, under the tree where I had talked with him the night before, sitting amid his sleeprobes, nursing his bloody ear and torn cheek, was George Holmes, a woebegone look on his handsome face, testifying to the source of his wound and his awareness of its fatal consequences. I rode to his side, dismounted, and mumbled an offer to assist him, although I had no idea what I, or anyone, could possibly do to help. The captain joined me, an anguished look creeping onto his face, as he admitted to himself that Holmes had suffered the wolf's attack because he had been obliged to sleep out-of-doors because of Stewart's amorous entertaining.

In the Scotsman's defense, howsomever, it should be mentioned that the balmy summer weather—as well as overindulgence, as in Meek's case— prompted many men to sleep under the stars at that rendezvous.

When I spied Finn McCool and Zeetlah making their morning medical rounds, I hailed them and waved them to our side. No explanation was necessary. Holmes's condition and its cause were obvious. Finn cleansed the young man's tattered ear and cheek with grain alcohol, which must have stung terribly, but George showed little reaction. While Zeetlah treated the lacerations with a soothing balm, McCool said quietly, "Ach, the pity of it is that naught we know to do will be of the slightest help to the lad. He's doomed and his dyin' will be most cruel." Zeetlah said nothing, but the expression on the old Delaware's features was grim.

We offered to help further, but Stewart and Holmes insisted that we had done enough. They gathered up George's belongings and retreated to the red marquee. Finn acquainted me with what he knew of the damage suffered the night before. "Siftin' out the gossip an' tittle-tattle that'd have ye believin' half the camp was bitten, it appears that only two men were harmed—this young fellow the lads've been after callin' Beauty and a Delaware trapper workin' for American Fur. Jist those two and one o' Bobby Campbell's prize bulls out in the meadow. An' not a single solitary thing that eyether Foot or I—or Doctor Harrison, drunk or sober—can do to help any one of 'em!"

∾   ∾   ∾

The incident of the mad wolf sent a chill through the rendezvous, nothing you could put your finger on, but the wild, drunken sprees tapered off and trappers attended to refurnishing their outfits for the coming season, replacing traps and replenishing supplies of powder and galena, flints and percussion caps, knives, tobacco, blankets, bright-colored woolen shirts, and, for experienced trappers, a stock of useful goods and trinkets for trading with Indians.

As you might suppose, that neighborhood became exceedingly unhealthy for the lupine breed, both wolves and coyotes. At least a hundred men claimed to have killed the rabid predator. Perhaps one of them actually succeeded, but none of them was inclined to investigate closely the critter's state of health.

Whenever I visited my daughter in Iron Bow's camp in the following days, Cat managed to be discreetly occupied elsewhere, so I was unable to learn if I would be gifted with any more nocturnal visits.

As always, Rocky Mountain Fur was gasping for breath under Bill Sublette's stranglehold. And much as I like Bobby Campbell, he can be nearly as hard-fisted as Sublette in business matters. Compared with the other outfits, this had been a good year for RMF, with sixty-two 100-pound packs of beaver ready to transport to Saint Louis. American Fur got 51 packs and Sublette & Campbell's Saint Louis Fur accumulated another 30 packs. Problem was, in the old days, RMF would have got it all. Now, even though they got more plews than any of the others, it wasn't enough to pay off Sublette and Campbell and interest on what they still owed continued to pile up.

I almost felt sorry for Captain Bonneville, who, in spite of his large cash outlay and feverish efforts to succeed, ended the year with not quite 23 packs that Mike Cerré would be taking to Saint Louis. Bonneville could be seen every day, visiting trapper camps, trying to recruit seasoned trappers, offering them as much as $1,000 to work for him, but most free men were leery of Bonneville's ability to meet such a high-dollar payroll.

I obtained most of my information from the young Frenchy Charlie Larpenteur, who was highly-prized as a clerk by both Robert Campbell and Tom Fitzpatrick for his literacy, honesty, and trustworthiness, but mostly because he was the only white teetotaler in the entire rendezvous. He and I had early on formed a friendship based on our mutual love of books. I allowed him free access to my stock of books and he never failed to return them promptly after reading them.

It was Larpenteur who told me that Mister Edmund Christy, who had accompanied Campbell's party on the journey from Saint Louis, had completed arrangements to buy a partnership in Rocky Mountain Fur. Fastidious fussbudget that he is, Charlie even provided the exact amount, $6,607.82&1/2¢, that Christy invested with the always-cash-strapped RMF partners—which figure I dutifully entered into my journal, mostly as a matter of curiosity.

Christy intended to be a working partner. Soon he was canvassing the free trapper camps, attempting to enlist men to trap the Snake River country. When he approached our bunch he met with a cold reception. None of our people was willing to work under the command of any man, much less that of a rank greenhorn fresh from the settlements.

The end of July was fast approaching. The rendezvous was commencing to splinter apart and our bunch still hadn't decided where we would trap in the fall. Brass Turtle, usually the most clear-thinking, decisive member of our bunch, now that Ned Godey was gone, was of little help this time. Turtle was thoroughly disgusted with the influx of new trading outfits and the horde of greenhorn trappers overrunning the mountains. He wasn't alone in his gloom. Last season's nightmare experience of American Fur dogging their tracks had soured every man in the bunch. Still, time was running out. We needed to decide.

As it turned out, Anse Tolliver, our crabby, selfish, opinionated fiddler, solved the conundrum. After still another day-long debate that came nowhere close to resolving the issue, Anse leapt to his feet, scarecrow arms waving excitedly, roaring, "Y'aint never gonna be satisfied with no place hyar in the mountains! Slim pickin's las' year an' Amurrican Fur ruint it fer all of us! I say we oughta look fer new stompin' grounds! Someplace we ain't never been afore naow an' whar Amurrican Fur ner Yankee Doodle Wyeth ner nobody else'll be follerin' us!"

"An' whar'd thet be, Tolliver?" Tuttle challenged. "Any place we go, thar's nothin' keepin' 'em from taggin' arter us—'thout we shoot 'em, an' yew won't never tolerate us doin' thet!"

A triumphant grin spread over Tolliver's craggy features. "Californy!" he crowed. "Thar's a galore o' beaver thar fer the takin' an 'tain't likely we'd be suff'rin' compertishun thar from nobody!"

As soon as Anse uttered the word Californy, every one of us guessed what our Tennessee hillbilly had in mind. For the past week or more, Captain Joseph Walker, Bonneville's second-in-command, had been recruiting trappers for an expedition bound for the Spaniard colonies on the western shore. Walker originally comes from Tennessee and Tolliver claimed some shirttail kinship with the captain, whom Anse greatly admired. Which was a prodigy in itself, for our fiddler is infamously peevish, bilious, acidulous in his opinions, and notoriously harsh in his judgments, usually according respect to no one.

"We be lookin' plumb through ye, Tolliver!" Brass Turtle exploded. "Ye'd be havin' us chasin' off to Californy, crossin' that'ere sorry-arse desert, thirstin' an' starvin' all the way, jist so's we kin be helpin' Cap'n Joe Walker spy on them'ere Spaniards fer Bonnyville an' the 'Murrican gov'mint, jist like Diah Smith war allus up to, usin' up good men like wipin' rags, 'til them'ere Comanches put 'im under!"

Tolliver bristled at the comparison. "Joe Walker's a sight diff'ernt from Jed Smith, Turtle, an' yew know it! He looks arter his men an' they respect 'im fer it. Jist ask any of 'em over thar in Bonnyville's camp. They'll tell ye!"

Tuttle Thompson stood and waved his arms for quiet. "P'raps ye'd both best settle daown an' let some others talk some." He turned to Toliver. "Anse. How come ye be so all-fired hot to foller Joe Walker to Californy? Jist 'cause yer mama's a Rutherford and so's his'n?" Anse nodded without thinking, then shook his head, before he spat angrily and stuck out his tongue at Thompson. "Thought so!" Tuttle said with a grin. "Naow, I'll 'low thet blood be thicker'n water, but I shore-as-hell prefer to keep my own blood whar it be, inside o' muh carcass 'stid o' spillin' it all over Californy, if we even git thet far." Tuttle paused a spell, looking thoughtful. "Jest the same, what ye say mought be wuth cornsid'rin'. Allus wanted to see ther Westren Sea . . . ." His voice trailed off and he sat down.

Nobody offered to lead the debate. Instead the bunch broke into a gabble of palaver, everybody voicing half-baked notions and making enquiries of their neighbors, who possessed no more knowledge of California than they themselves did. I kept my own counsel, but the more I mulled over Anse's proposal, the better it appeared to me. I had been restless, drifting, lacking direction and purpose, especially since Cat had spurned me. A brand-new adventure might fill the empty place in my spirit.

An hour later I had come to no decision and apparently neither had anyone else. Brass Turtle stood up and declared, "Best we sleep on it. It's mebbe a harebrained notion an' then, mebbe it ain't, but we'd best hold off afore we decide on it. What'say?" An assenting mumble greeted that sensible suggestion and the assemblage broke up.

As I rose to depart, Little Mountain clapped me on the shoulder and said in a jovial tone, "Ye comin' 'long, Tempo? Plenty beaver, plenty wimmen, plenty summertime. No snowtime whar Big Water be, I'm thinkin'."

It was plain that the big Delaware had already made up his mind to make the journey. "It's too soon to say, Mountain," I replied, "but it's worth thinkin' about. Maybe so." I let it go at that and we parted.

On the way to my bower I ran into Black Harris. He was uncharacteristically sober but in remarkably high spirits just the same. "Thar ye be, Temple," he called out from a distance. "I been lookin' fer ye to let ye know it's been decided. Next year's ronnyvoo's gonna be on Hoss Crick, jist nawth o' what from naow on an' ferever arter'll be knowed as Black's Fork!" He saw the pleased look on my face at the news that a landmark had at last been named for him. "Yep! Arter nigh a dozen years o' me guidin' greenhorns up thisaway, they fine'ly put muh name on sum'pin! 'Tain't as big as Henry's Fork ner the Seeds-kee-dee, mind ye, but it's a purty li'l crick, jist the same!"

Naturally such an event demanded a toast and I was not slow to offer one. We repaired to my bower, where I soon remedied Harris's uncommon sobriety with a plenitude of good Kentucky whiskey.

Which naturally loosened his tongue. He commenced with what most of us already knew, that Bobby Campbell and Tom Fitzpatrick were preparing to head for the mouth of the Bighorn, where it spills into the Yellowstone. There Campbell intended to build enough bullboats to float his plews and those of Rocky Mountain Fur down to the Missouri, where they expected to meet up with Bill Sublette.

"An' then, once Bobby gits on his way, Fitz's brigade an' that'ere English sojer-boy mean to keep on headin' east inter Absorkee country, trappin' beaver an' likely exterminatin' all the game-critters tharabaouts, if His Lordship gits his way. Thar won't be a buffler ner a grizzle-b'ar left standin', time he gits done!"

Not much gets past Moses Harris, drunk or sober. He proved it then. "Milt Sublette's goin' downriver with Campbell, 'long with that'ere Yankee trader Wyeth. Them two 'pear to be hatchin' up some kind o' scheme fer outfoxin' Billy Sublette, come next year's ronnyvoo. Fitz an' Bridger an' the others are in on it, too. Don't know jist what they got in mind, but it better be purty shrewd if they mean to git ahead o' Billy."

"Ye goin' to tell Sublette what ye know?" I asked.

"Hell no!" he replied hotly. "Sublette don't pay me to be his spy an' I wou'nt do it if he did! I'll guide his packtrains to hell an' back, but I won't never do no goddamn snoopin' fer 'im!"

Further palaver was cut short by the welcome clamor of Jean-Luc beating a big iron spoon on a kettle, announcing suppertime. Black and I repaired to the cookfire, where great slabs of fresh buffalo hump, ribs, and backstrap smoked and hissed and crackled over the coals, crowding out all other considerations until a score of healthy appetites were satisfied. Only when we had stuffed ourselves to a standstill did anyone allow himself to indulge in what folks back in the settlements might call table talk. Once begun, howsomever, the sole topic was California and the pluses and minuses concerned with getting there. As the lively debate progressed, I noted with amusement Harris's anguish and disappointment at not being able to make that journey, because of his promise to Campbell and Sublette. Trappers are a nosey bunch, always eager to see what's on the other side of the mountain, and Moses Harris possesses the itchiest foot of any mountaineer I have ever known.

It had been three days since I had seen Cat, which was not surprising, considering the attack of the rabid wolf was the only time she came to me. Cat has always been a rock of reliability and she became even more so when she took on the responsibility of mothering Iris. Cat possesses as much courage as anyone I have known, but her devotion to my child made her cautious.

What I couldn't comprehend was her recent behavior. I was unable to grasp why she had come to my sleeprobes after spurning my offer to make her my woman. It was a riddle worthy of the Sphinx.

It was still daylight when I decided to call it a day and retreated to my robes. I lay in restless discontent, staring at a patch of darkening sky, mulling over thoughts about a journey to California, others of Cat and Iris, then memories of Rainbow and that happy time of my life when I just did the next thing, hardly ever needing to make hard decisions. Leastaways that is how I remembered those times. At last it all blurred into fitful slumber and I knew no more, until I felt a gentle touch on my cheek and a finger firmly on my lips, commanding silence.

I obeyed, contenting myself with gazing upon her fine features limned in the cool light of a waxing moon. At last she spoke, her voice husky with serious intent. I will not try to reproduce here the exact words that Cat spoke to me that night, lest I trivialize her intent. She leaned back to free her hands to supplement her speech with signs. "You wonder, Temple," she said in a low voice, "why I come to you now, in dark time, alone in your lodge, yet I do not offer to share your robes."

Naturally I felt a pang of disappointment at hearing this. Her cool manner hadn't encouraged much hope for a night of love-making, but that remark totally poured cold water on it.

She continued. "I must tell you. I am an honest woman and you are a good man, a very good man, and you have made me happy in your robes. Very happy."

Hope kindled anew. I opened my mouth to speak, but once again she placed her fingers upon my lips to silence me. "No," she insisted, "I must say it all before you talk." I nodded my assent and slumped against the roll of blankets and clothing that served as my pillow. A brief smile flitted across her features. She resumed her speech. "You wonder, too, why I refuse to be your woman. There are many reasons. One is that it is too soon after the death of him who called me Cataleen. Only five moons have passed. I still mourn for him." Even in the dim moonlight filtering into my bower I could see grief clouding her lovely face. I recalled how deeply I had suffered at Rainbow's death and how long that wound had taken to heal. I gained a new understanding of Cat's reluctance to accept my offer.

She spoke rapidly now, lest I try to interrupt. "Also, if you take me for your woman, it must be only for me, not for your girl-child Irish or because you wish to protect us—only because you feel for me what you felt for her who was my friend and what he who called me Cataleen felt for me. Irish and I will go with Iron Bow. Next summer, we can decide if you and I will walk together always. Not now."

Once again her finger touched my lips when I tried to speak. "Many of your friends wish to see the Great Water where Father Sun sleeps. I think you also wish this thing." I did not reply but I silently cursed Little Mountain for being a tattletale. Cat continued. "If you wish to go with them, do not worry for Irish. Iron Bow will care for us. We will eat in his lodge. He will keep us from harm."

I don't recollect that I spoke any words in reply. If there was a suitable response to what she had told me, I couldn't think of it. I merely nodded, although my brain was buzzing with questions, especially one that kept asking why she had lain with me the night of the rabid lobo and then never again. As she rose to leave, Cat, ever practical, bestowed a generous parting gift. "Temple," she said, "you are a man. A man needs woman. I can wait. You must not." Then she was gone into the night.

Breaking our fast around the cookfire next morning was even noisier than usual and the noise had a hard edge to it. In all the years since our original bunch had come up the Missouri in 1822, we had stuck together in a kind of loose brotherhood, looking out for one another's welfare and sharing good times and bad. Not everyone wanted to go to California and even if they did, Captain Walker's westward expedition would be composed only of single men. No women or children allowed. Now the prospect of splitting up, even if just for a year, was causing a passel of bruised feelings.

As it turned out, the married men—Paddy McBride, our two Iroquois, Stone Bird and Acorn, our most recent benedict, who had taken a Shoshone wife only a couple weeks previous, and the Delaware Pretty Horse—would remain in the Rockies, trapping with Jim Bridger's brigade, along with our French-Cree campkeepers Yves Dureau and Jean-Luc L'Archévêque.

The sole exception was Brass Turtle, whose good-natured wife Tallymesko—which means "I'll go with you" in the Delaware tongue—had consented to remain with her Shoshone family during the coming winter. "She's with child agin," Turtle explained, "an' consid'rin' how bad she had it birthin' the girl-child, Tally reckons havin' her own womenfolk nigh'll be a sight better'n some cold beaver camp this comin' winter." Which might have been so, but it was hard to imagine that our resident daredevil Brass Turtle would willingly miss out on a grand adventure such as the one we contemplated.

Once that matter was settled, eleven of us saddled up and rode downriver to Captain Bonneville's rickety fort to enlist in Joe Walker's expedition. As we rode along at an easy gait, not one of us betrayed any doubt that we would be accepted—nay, welcomed!—into Walker's company. And so it turned out, almost.

Apparently Anse Tolliver had extolled our virtues to his shirttail cousin some time before most of us decided to make what was certain to be a long and arduous journey across a barren desert, unlike anything we had ever experienced. Captain Walker greeted us warmly when we rode into the well-ordered camp he had set up next to Bonneville's establishment. He invited us to step down and waved towards a couple-three big kettles steaming over the cookfire, offering morning coffee. I had seen Joseph Walker at a distance during the rendezvous. He was hard to miss. He stood well over six feet tall and packed a couple hundredweight on his well-muscled frame. Now, observing him close up, while he moved from one newcomer to another, introducing himself and making small talk, I saw that he was likely a good-looking fellow under his substantial dark-brown beard, about 40 years of age, neat and clean and modest in his dress, alert, strong, and athletic.

Anse Tolliver surprised us all when he called out, "Whatever ye mought be wantin' to know about our bunch, Cap'n, I reckon Brass Turtle hyar'll be able to tell ye." He clapped Turtle on the shoulder, then stepped quickly away when the Delaware swung to face him, a quizzical look on his face.

Micah, who was standing beside me, leaned close and said in a low voice, "I reckon Tolliver elected Turtle to do the talkin' so he himself won't have to say anything nice about us."

Turtle shrugged and said in a clear level voice, "Most of us kin speak for ourownse'fs. Fer them as can't or won't, I'm hyar to help."

While I waited for Walker to make his way to me, I recognized several trappers whom I knew well, among them Gideon Moon and Willard Stringfellow, the beanpole and the barrel, who had guided us to rendezvous. Another was a well-set-up young fellow who hovered close behind the captain as he made his way amongst us. He was Zenas Leonard, the young Pennsylvanian we had pretty much outfitted the year before when he showed up at rendezvous broke and ragged after Gantt & Blackwell went bust and abandoned their greenhorn trapping crew. His fortunes had obviously improved since that time. He conducted himself now in a manner that bespoke confidence in himself. I was pleased to see that his star had risen, for he had earned my admiration by the courage he had shown during our bloody battle against the Big-bellies the previous year. Leonard's close attendance upon Walker indicated that young Zenas had been engaged as clerk of the expedition, which made him second-in-command or *segundo*, as trappers had lately come to call that job.

Walker spent little time with Tuttle, Powatawa, and me, likely because Anse had already assured him that we were experienced and reliable. He shook hands with us and welcomed us warmly before moving on to the others. He appeared to be particularly keen on McCool when he learned that we regarded Finn as our resident medico, although the Irishman confessed that he hadn't completed his medical education in Dublin.

Brass Turtle and Little Mountain were immediately regarded as valuable recruits. Experienced Delawares are highly-prized in the fur trade. And dark-skinned Cesár Pérez, who would likely have been the subject of the Tennesseean's prejudice in different circumstances, was now considered an asset because of his ability to speak the Spaniard lingo. The same applied to Micah, who had become proficient in the Spanish tongue, thanks to his close friendship with Cesár.

It was only when he came to Old Foot and his young nephew Half-horse that Walker balked. He peered into the old healer's wrinkled face and announced, "I cain't be carryin' along an old-timer like this'n on the journey we've got in mind. A man his age wouldn't last the half of it and he surely couldn't pull his weight on the trail!"

Brass Turtle had been lagging a step or two behind Walker and Leonard. Now he stepped forward, dark eyes snapping, and addressed the captain. "I'm hopin' ye got better judgment than what I jist heard ye say, Cap'n. Thi'shere old man'll walk ye into the ground an' wear out a herd o' hosses afore he quits. He's Lenni Lenapee, Delaware, an' I daresay ye know what that means. He's tougher'n old saddles! Hell! He war older'n sin when we fust come up the Missourah ten year back an' he ain't a day older naow than he war then! Not only that, he's our healer! Zeetlah hyar knows more abaout physic than a wagonload o' Boston *medicos* an' he'll be keepin' your people spry an' full o' pluck when they'd be dyin' without 'im!"

Walker looked puzzled, uncertain. Then he grinned at Turtle and said, "All right, I'll take your word for it, but you'll be the one that'll be buryin' 'im if he goes under afore we get thar." Old Foot hadn't uttered a word throughout the entire exchange. He had stood ramrod straight, arms folded across his chest, staring into Walker's eyes, his expression impassive, unreadable, a tiny hint of a smile lurking at the corner of his lips, until he heard the expedition leader's words granting approval, at which he grunted and spat and stalked off to join my father in the shade of a tree.

Walker stared after him, shook his head, and chuckled before he turned and appraised young Half-horse before he declared, "And this'n? He's purty young for the chore we got in mind. Thar'll be no time fer wet-nursin' a young'un on this trip." His choice of words made it clear that he meant to pique Brass Turtle. Walker obviously enjoyed their bickering, which spoke well for the leader's sense of humor. Turtle rose to the bait.

"That'n'll be needin' no wet-nursin', Cap'n! He's Delaware tough an' he's the same stock as Ol' Foot thar, who's his uncle! We call 'im Half-hoss, 'cause that's what he is—half hoss. Young as he be, he savvies critters better'n any growed-up man I know. We wou'nt'a brung 'im if we hadn'a knowed fer sure he war wuth takin' along. Ye won't be sorry if ye do!"

Walker laughed and shook his head. "All right, he can come along, too, Turtle. Ye surely missed yer callin'! Ye should'a been a hoss-trader or a parson! Mebbe a lawyer! Ye be plumb wasted out thisaway, trappin' beaver!"

Half-horse had picked up enough American lingo to understand that he had passed muster. A shy grin crept onto his normally solemn features and he raced to join his uncle under the shade tree.

Walker turned then to address all of us, sweeping his arms inward to gather us together. "Welcome to the expedition! Fust off, meet Zenas Leonard hyar! He's clark o' thi'shere oufit an' you know what that means. He'll he'p ye when he kin an' when he passes along an order, it's the same as me givin' it. 'Nuff said.

"I don't need to tell ye thar's a tough trip ahead afore we get to Californy—crossin' deserts, climbin' mountains, in heat and cold, likely sometimes thirsty an' hungry, amongst kinds of Injuns mebbe no whiteman ever saw. It ain't goin' to be easy, which is why I'm pickin' the best men I can find hyarabouts.

"Some o' ye might know that I already tried gettin' to Californy, some years back, but I didn't make it. That hurt more'n somewhat, but I learnt a passel o' things I should'a knowed afore I tried it the fust time. This time's diff'rent! I'm takin' only the best men an' I'll be outfittin' ye with ever'thin' you'll be needin' fer a long, hard hike!

"Every man will be issued four good hosses in time to get to know 'em afore we set out an' we'll be supplyin' good English Witney blankets an' buffler robes fer sleepin' warm, powder an' flints, galena an' caps, traps if ye need 'em, a passel o' groceries an' tools, cookin' pots an' such, proper hoss-clothin' an' packsaddles and ever'thin' else ye mought need fer an expedition o' thi'shere kind. We'll be lookin' at yer shootin' irons, makin' sure ye'll be ready fer a fight if need be." He paused for breath before he added, "If ye got any questions, see me or Zenas arterward."

Only Anse Tolliver had a question. As Walker turned to depart, our fiddler called out, "Four good hosses, ye say, Cap'n? What about mules? Ye got mules?"

Walker turned back with a laugh on his lips. "Natcherly we got mules, Anse! Good'uns, too. Go choose yer pick!" He walked off to Bonneville's fort, still chuckling.

We took Joe Walker at his word and rode off to the meadow where a sizable herd of horses and mules grazed. Zenas Leonard rode along with us. "How many men are ye plannin' to recruit for your expedition, Zenas?" I asked.

"Captain Walker says he'd like about sixty for the trip," he replied, "but it looks like we'll be fallin' short o' that number. He was really pleased when you'uns showed up this mornin'."

"Yep, that's eleven more he doesn't have to worry about. How many ye got so far?"

He took a moment to tot up the figure. "Thirty-four, thirty-five now." His expression sobered somewhat. "Some real hardcases amongst 'em, though.

Mountaineers are generally a hard-bitten lot, tough enough to deal with the hardships and perils that are part and parcel of our trade, so I was surprised to hear Leonard describe some of the recruits in that manner. "Like who?" I asked.

Zenas reddened, obviously regretting his remark, but he replied, "Well, old Bill Williams, for one, and some of the gang he brought up with him from Taos—that redheaded bully Levin Mitchell an' Crazy Bill Craig, for a couple more."

I didn't know the other two, but Bill Williams was an old acquaintance of mine. When I was still fairly new to the mountains, he and I spent a couple days and nights together in the hills above Sweet Lake, dodging a bunch of murderous Blackfoots, until Williams showed me how efficiently bloodthirsty he can be, wiping out the lot of them almost single-handed. I owe my life to him, so I can't fault him overmuch for his savagery. I didn't mention that experience to Zenas.

We arrived at the meadow about that time, so further palaver was cut short. The next hour or so, I was occupied with selecting and cutting out two suitable horses, a five-year-old bay gelding and a six-year-old gray mare, and a pair of sturdy jack mules. I didn't need any more livestock, but no sensible mountaineer passes up free horses, especially critters as good as Walker offered.

Half-horse again proved his worth that day. After acquiring a first-rate foursome for himself, he lent the rest of us a hand by pointing out the most desirable critters in the herd. Even Tuttle Thompson, who prides himself on his knowledge of equines, was impressed by the young Delaware's uncanny skill in detecting physical flaws that likely would have gone unnoticed by the rest of us. Especially valuable is his talent for divining the animal's character and temperament, able to judge on the spot if a horse or mule will be willing and useful.

∾ ∾ ∾

After we drove our new livestock to our own meadow and turned them in with our regular herd, we rode back to camp in time for a hearty dinner of fresh-killed buffalo. Pretty Horse, Paddy, and Acorn had ridden out early that day in search of meat, which was becoming scarce in that neighborhood as the rendezvous dragged on and trappers commenced to stock up on dried meat in anticipation of their winter needs. Every camp was surrounded with a cobweb of ropes festooned with jerkmeat, looking like so much red laundry drying in the crisp mountain air.

Now it was time for a difficult chore, sorting out my plunder and winnowing it down to the few essentials that I would need on the westward journey to California. My task was much greater than that of my comrades, for I was burdened with the plenitude of gifts and trade goods that I had transported from Saint Louis. First off, I put aside what I would be carrying for my own needs, keeping in mind what Walker would be providing all of his recruits, as well as some easily portable trade goods, groceries, and gifts for my fellow-travelers and for those who would be staying behind.

Paddy McBride has become an avid reader in the years since I first taught him and Tuttle to read during a long-ago winter camp. Now I entrusted to his safekeeping the stock of books I had carried from the settlements. Paddy whistled with pleasure when he beheld my collection of romances by Sir Walter Scott, a Scottish novelist whose colorful tales of medieval derring-do are favorites amongst the trapping fraternity. Most trappers can't read, but they will tease, coax, and bribe their literate brethren into reading aloud from whatever text is at hand, be it the works of William Shakespeare, the Holy Bible, or more contemporary works of fiction. The little Irishman's eyes fairly glowed as he mouthed the titles of the books before him—*Quentin Durward, Rob Roy, Waverley, The Talisman, A Legend of Montrose, Old Mortality, The Heart of Midlothian.* "Och, Temple!" he exclaimed, "I'll be the bloody hero Cuchulain meownsel' this winter camp, possessin' these foine books an' the wunnerful tales they contain! Sure'n I'll pertect 'em wi' me very loife an' return 'em safe an' sound when ye come back."

I saved out two volumes, *Ivanhoe and Kenilworth,* for my own amusement and to entertain my companions on the trail. The rest of my modest library I carefully wrapped in oilskin and turned over to Paddy.

After I heaped up as much plunder as I thought Cat could possibly carry with her, there remained several times that amount of valuable goods.

Nothing goes to waste in the mountains, so I sought the assistance of my companions to help me cache that merchandise and some of their own plunder until our return to the Rockies, when we would need it.

We set out that day to a spot that Tuttle assured us would be perfect. And it was, a wooded area atop a bluff overlooking a fast-running crick, which was handy for dumping the soil excavated from the cache, high enough to escape springtime flooding, and screened from prying eyes by a surrounding grove of willows and aspens while we worked. Many hands make light work, as the saying goes. The cache was sealed, the earth tamped down, and the sod carefully replaced before the sun dipped below the western ridge.

Naturally we didn't cache all of our ardent spirits. I kept out one of the curved metal kegs that contained grain alcohol well-imbued with wild honey that Half-horse had gathered on the journey from Saint Louis. Diluted with water from the clear-running crick below, it made a heavenly potation equal to metheglin. So delightful was it, in fact, that not one of us was capable of riding back to camp that night. We slept where we fell.

Next morning, back at camp, I hastened to complete my preparations, which required painful decisions concerning the livestock that I would take on my westward journey. Much as I hated to do it, I decided to leave my Coffee horse with Cat until my return, together with the pack animals she would need to carry the extra plunder that I would deliver to her that day. I reckoned Iron Bow would consent to include my other critters with his own large herd until I reclaimed them.

Besides the two saddle horses and two pack mules provided by Captain Walker, I intended to take only the lineback dun gelding I called Davey and my easy-going saddle mule Sugarfoot. They were both well-trained and rawhide-tough and, much as I would have regretted losing either one of them, it was better than risking my Kentucky-bred darling to the rigors and unknown perils of the western deserts and mountains.

My father rode with me to the Séli camp and remained to visit with Iron Bow after I turned my extra livestock in with his herd, then proceeded on to Cat's lodge with the loaded packmules and Davey. Naturally I rode Coffee that day, savoring every minute of pleasure he provided. I told myself the while that my decision to leave him with Cat was best but I didn't believe a word of it.

Cat's composure nearly crumbled when she beheld the heap of plunder that I unloaded from the packmules, but I assured her that it contained not much foofurraw, that most of it was useful goods that she could swap with her neighbors for whatever help she might need for Iris and herself.

She looked astonished when I stripped off the saddle and bridle from Coffee and tethered him beside her piebald mare at her doorway. I explained my reasons for leaving him behind, telling her to treat him as her own, and asked only that she do what she could to prevent my former brother-in-law Fast Horse from racing him.

Parting from my daughter was the most difficult chore of all. Looking back at what I have just written about parting with my favorite saddle horse, I realize how inadequate my scribbling is when it comes to expressing my feelings for my little girl. Indian-like, neither of us cried tears, but my eyes were smarting as I hugged her and my voice caught in my throat as I promised to return to her. She was unbelievably stoical for a four-year-old, but her deep-blue, almost purple eyes, so like my mother's, betrayed her, welling up until she buried her face in my neck and made me promise that I would come back to her and Kathleen.

Spoken farewells between Cat and me were brief, noncommittal, but her eyes revealed more feeling than she let herself to speak. I recalled her words from the final night we were together and tried to believe that she would be waiting when I returned.

~ ~ ~

Joe Walker kept his word regarding the outfit he supplied to every man he recruited. Some of the horses and mules he provided were better than others, as you might expect, but they were all sound and serviceable. Tools and equipment, gunpowder and galena, flints and percussion caps, and a modest amount of trade goods provided to each man were all of first-rate quality, most of it from England or France. Groceries such as coffee, tea, sugar, molasses, and suchlike were issued in generous amounts. Brand-new *capotes* and pairs of thick woolen four-point Witney blankets were luxurious. Buffalo sleeprobes were fresh and clean, tanned butter-soft. The Rocky Mountain fur trade has never seen, before or since, such a well-equipped brigade.

Much of the equipment Walker had accumulated was not intended to be distributed amongst his recruits. His compound contained a considerable store of tools—axes, picks, crosscut saws, spades and shovels, and what looked like half a mile of stout rope. He had already failed once in his intention to complete that difficult journey. This time, he would be properly-equipped. It was reassuring to know that our leader wouldn't be going off half-cocked.

⁕   ⁕   ⁕

"Whar d'ye reckon that'ere sojerboy Bonnyville got enough cash together to pay fer all o' thi'shere plunder," Brass Turtle asked of nobody in particular during our final supper at rendezvous. Nobody spoke up. "I'm thinkin' that'ere road, all the way to Californy, better be paved with beaver plews if he's expectin' to show a profit."

"Thet be his concern an' none o' mine," Tuttle observed. "But, like ye say, thar likely ain't enough beaver in all o' Californy to let 'im break even."

"Cain't speak fer Bonnyville, natcherly," Anse Tolliver put in, "but Joe Walker ain't short o' brains, nohaow. I reckon he knows what he's abaout."

"I reckon the both of 'em do," Turtle responded. "An' jist so ye know what ye signed up fer, I'm wagerin' the 'Murrican guv'mint paid fer ever' last stick an' crumb they'r givin' us an' we're settin' off t'morry mornin' on a sure'nough military expedition to see how hard it'll be takin' Californy away from them'ere Spaniards!"

A rumble of mild protest mixed with laughter greeted Turtle's pronouncement. Most of our number allowed that even if it were so, it made little difference to them, but Finn McCool got no argument when he said, "Even if you're right, Turtle darlin', I'm thinkin' 'tis better that Americans claim that territory, rather than lettin' the bloody Brits come down from Hudson's Bay an' make it their own!" Which is what one might expect to hear from an Irish revolutionary. Finn drained the final drops of metheglin from his cup and declared, "No matter, 'tis a grand adventure we're embarkin' on in the mornin', gentlemen. Let's be makin' the most of it!"

-oOo-

CHAPTER V
SLIM PICKIN'S

Every mile we put behind us lifted a little more of the burden that had weighed down my spirit throughout the Fort Nonsense rendezvous, even though most trappers judged it to be one of the best. Gloom commenced to wrap itself around me even before I got there, when I first learned of Ned Godey's death. Then, Cat's puzzling behavior, first rejecting my proposal, then sneaking into my sleeprobes, telling me no, then a possible maybe, left me confused, whipsawed, and feeling guilty about leaving my daughter with her, although there was no way to do otherwise.

Now the die was cast. There was no going back on my decision, or hers. Late-July sunshine warmed my soul and baked out the last lingering doubts that I had chosen the wisest course in joining Walker's cavalcade to the mostly unknown Pacific shore. The prospect of adventure unlike any I had known thrilled me to the marrow, honing my appetite for all the sights and sounds, the smells and sensations that lay ahead, as well as the camaraderie of like-minded men whose dedication to mountain life was as absolute as my own.

Captain Joe Walker's column had departed the rendezvous that morning within an hour of when he said it would, testimony to his efficiency and notice to us all that the tall Tennesseean meant what he said. Walker and Leonard had failed to recruit their intended sixty-man company. Only forty men had volunteered to make the journey, but the leaders reckoned they could pick up the rest of his intended complement along the way. With that in mind, they brought with them a sizeable herd of horses and mules, as well as enough plunder to outfit a score of additional recruits.

Naturally, that first morning, there was a passel of stragglers, many of whom didn't catch up until the midday dinner halt. Most of those Johnny-come-latelies looked the worse for wear, especially Anse Tolliver and Tuttle Thompson, who had apparently tried to soak up enough traders' popskull on their final night at rendezvous to last them all the way to California.

Our immediate destination was the mouth of Bear River, where it spills into the Great Salt Lake, a four-day hike from rendezvous. Walker intended to halt there long enough to lay in a supply of buffalo jerk-meat, at least 60 pounds for each man, because, word was, that neighborhood would be the last place we would see buffalo until we returned to the Rockies the following year.

Most men scoffed at that notion. They refused to believe that any place west of Missouri would lack plenty of buffalo. Most of the old-timers griped, too, about tarrying long enough to lay in a supply of dried meat. Indian-like, the custom is to gorge when meat is plentiful and to starve when it ain't.

∾ ∾ ∾

Walker and Leonard were pleased to discover a sizeable community of free trappers camped nigh the mouth of the Bear. It was still too early to commence trapping, but most of them had quit the rendezvous broke and crapulous, most of them too impoverished to replenish the supplies they would need for another trapping season. Their prospects were grim, which made those prodigals fertile ground for Walker's recruiting efforts.

Among the most destitute was our young friend Joe Meek. He was ragged and dirty, unshaven, obviously suffering the effects of extended hobnobbing with John Barleycorn. His faithful companions, Doc Newell and the seagoing Irish harpooner Harry Yeats, were hardly better off. Except for their rifles and powderhorns and the Irishman's musical instrument, they were bereft of nearly every item of property they had been able to sell or swap for a final dram of trader's booze.

In Joe's case, it was neither Walker nor Zenas Leonard who convinced the young Virginian to join up. It was his older brother, Stephen Hall Meek, who had come north from Santa Fe with Bill Williams and his rowdy crew. When Joe beheld his brother, he rubbed his eyes and shook his head and wailed, "Oh, Gawd save me! I still ain't sobered up! I be seein' thangs!"

Stephen Meek stepped down from his horse, closed the distance between Joe and himself in a single stride, and playfully cuffed his younger brother on the side of his head, which nevertheless sent Joe sprawling in the dust. "What in hell are ye doin' out hyar, Joe?" he demanded. "I thought ye war still back on ther farm in Virginny."

Joe sat up, rubbing his ear, and replied, "Hell, Stephen, I been four year hyar in ther mountains an' ye hadn't oughta be doin' me like thet! I been a free trapper fer nigh two of 'em an' 'tain't proper fer ye to be treatin' me like a kid no more!"

The elder Meek stared long and hard at his kid-brother before he declared, "Proper! I'll tell ye what ain't proper! What ain't proper is makin' a gawddamn rum puncheon o' yerse'f, a gawddamn whiskey-soak hawg sleepin' in ther gutter!" His lip curled in contempt. "Us Meeks're better'n thet, Joseph, an' I ain't abaout to let ye shame ther fambly like ye been doin'!"

Joe was obviously deeply affected by his big brother's scolding. He reddened and hung his head, searching without success for words to frame a response. Apparently even Doc Newell and the Irishman felt chastened by Stephen's censuring Joe. They, too, stared at the ground and offered no excuses for their protracted drunken spree, tacitly granting Stephen Meek authority he hadn't claimed.

Addressing his remarks directly to Joe, Stephen spoke in a commanding tone. "I'll tell ye what you're goin' to do, Joseph! You're goin' to shag yer arse down to thet'ere crick an' wash ther whiskey stink offen yer hide an' then you're goin' to shave off them'ere gawddamn whiskers afore ye go tell Cap'n Walker thet ye be ready an' willin' to jine up with his Californy expedition! Ef he takes ye on, he'll set ye up with an outfit an' hosses, too!" Joe opened his mouth to speak, but Stephen shushed him with an imperious glare. "Ye say ye be a free trapper naow, do ye? Wal, thet oughta he'p recommend ye to ther cap'n. Naow git a move on!" He spun on his heel, returned to his horse, stepped into the saddle with one smooth motion, and loped off to join his Santa Fe companions.

Big, bluff, tough Joe Meek said not a word before he trotted off to the riverbank and dived into the fast-running stream, fully-clothed. Not long after, he was joined by Newell and Yeats. Soon the three of them were laughing and splashing and indulging in carefree horseplay, a decided improvement over their previous near-paralysis from their extended revels.

Tuttle Thompson and I witnessed the Meek family drama with considerable amusement and a certain smug self-satisfaction, although neither he nor I was a stranger to alcoholic excess. The three sots are our friends, so when they emerged from the river, Tuttle offered to lend them his razors and even some of his precious lilac shaving soap. I dug out clean calico shirts so they might present a halfway decent appearance when we introduced them to Captain Walker and recommended that he include them in his caravan.

Once Joe was decently scrubbed and shaved and mostly sobered up, he opined, "Ye know, ther more I think on it, ther better ther whole idee 'pears to be. Reckon makin' a jaunt like that'n'll put a feather in a feller's cap, wou'n't ye say?

∽   ∽   ∽

An additional score of such feathers was made available by Captain Walker in the next few days, which brought his complement up to the originally-desired sixty-man company. As each new recruit was accepted and outfitted, he was ordered to join up with others to hunt buffalo and to dry at least sixty pounds of jerkmeat for his own use, against a time when game would be scarce.

When our bunch headed out to run a small herd of buffalo cows that Little Mountain had discovered early one morning, Brass Turtle advised, "Git yer enjoys whilst you kin today, fellers. From what they're tellin', this'll be the last buffler we'll be seein' 'til we git back hyar to the Rockies next year."

An unbelieving howl greeted his remark. "Whatcher sayin', Turtle?" Tuttle demanded. "No buffler? What'll we eat? Cain't live 'thout no buffler!"

"Don't rightly know, Tuttle," Brass Turtle replied, "but I listened in on ol' Black, the onliest one what come back from Californy with Diah Smith, back in 'twenny-nine, an' he war tellin' haow thar ain't no buffler west o' the Big Salt Lake, ner in Californy neither. Fact is, he said thar ain't much of anythin' wuth eatin' 'twixt hyar an' Californy, so ye'd best git yer fill afore ye start."

Turtle possesses a wry sense of humor and he dearly loves a prank, but something in his tone and his expression told us that what he was saying now was gospel, leastaways according to what he honestly believed. We took him at his word in all respects, running fat buffalo cows that day with wild abandon and harvesting a plenitude of prime meat that had our pack critters tottering by time we returned to camp.

I sorely missed the pleasure of running those cows on my Coffee horse, but my lineback dun Davey, on whom I had chased buffalo only once before, proved to be a natural buffalo runner. He never flinched and he dodged and forged and matched the buffalo's pace like a veteran. It was a happy discovery and a further regret that this would be the last time he would be able to prove his buffalo-running ability until the following year.

Cookfires blazed night after night during the week we stayed there. The air was perfumed with roasting meat and filled with loud palaver and goodnatured shouts and curses and hoarse singing whenever Tolliver unlimbered his fiddle and Irish Harry joined in with his cittern and his big baritone voice. Men gorged on as much as ten pounds of meat at a sitting, only to return to the cookfire an hour or two later to eat that much again.

The camp was a sober one after the first few days, for, although Walker did not forbid drinking ardent spirits, neither did he provide any.

Daytime was occupied with drying meat and tanning buffalo hides for making a supply of moccasins. Keeping in mind what Brass Turtle had said about the scarcity of game critters in the country that lay ahead, we put extra effort into drying buffalo meat. Every man in our bunch had brought a couple extra critters of his own, favorite horses or mules, besides the livestock Walker provided, so each of us was able to carry along at least a hundredweight of jerkmeat for the journey.

҂   ҂   ҂

By mid-August we were skirting the northern shore of the Great Salt Lake. Although we forded any number of small watercourses feeding that inland ocean, we failed to discover the famous Buenaventura River that was supposed to flow westward from somewhere in that neighborhood. So, early on, Captain Walker achieved his first success. He proved, once and for all, that the Rio Buenaventura was a myth and should be removed from the maps of that region.

Soon after we put the Salt Lake behind us, we met up with a band of ragged-arse Bannock Indians hiking eastwards on their once-a-year buffalo hunt. That particular band had been driven out by other tribes to live in desert country where not enough grass grows to let them keep horses, so, once a year, they set out walking in an easterly direction until they meet up with buffalo. Then they kill and dry as much buffalo meat as their women can lug home on their backs.

Naturally our bunch bristled at the sight of Bannocks, recalling the fight we had with a band of those treacherous prairie pirates, just two years earlier, that resulted in the death of my wife Rainbow. We were not alone in our hostility towards them. Every experienced mountaineer regards Bannocks, whether afoot or horseback, as murderous, thieving bandits, never to be trusted. So it was with considerable consternation that we were obliged to bite our tongue when Joe Walker called on us to camp overnight beside them and gifted them with beads and trinkets while he pumped them for information about our westward trail.

Bannocks are shirttail kin to Snakes and the lingo they speak is close enough to proper Shoshone talk to let us understand them, especially with their hand-signs, which weren't much different from what we were used to. Apparently Walker got what he wanted from them, for next morning he struck out directly west through a salt desert. It was thirsty going, with sparse forage for our livestock and no game critters to supplement our diet. Days were scorching hot and the nights chilly enough to make us appreciate our buffalo robes and thick-pile Witney blankets.

After a week we met up with another band of Indians heading east to hunt buffalo. This bunch was also afoot, but they were much cleaner and looked to be somewhat more prosperous and rather more civilized than the ragged, dirty Bannocks we had first encountered. After Walker explained by signs where we intended to go, the chief and his headmen advised us to stick to the well-worn paths that run from one waterhole to the next in a southwesterly direction, until we came to a certain high mountain, its top covered with snow all year 'round, then to follow the river that flows westward from that mountain. They explained that the river forms a chain of lakes, until at last it sinks into the earth and disappears. Some distance after that, they said, there is another high mountain. They warned that between those mountains there is no game, only very poor Indians who are likely not friendly.

Walker followed the Indians' advice and continued on a mostly westerly course, keeping to the chain of waterholes, which also provided meager forage for our critters. After the first three days we commenced to see what you might call human life, but only in a manner of speaking—totally naked Indians, skinny and stunted and sunburnt nearly black, leathery bodies daubed with mud, their hair filthy and wildly disheveled. They offered us lumps of salt in trade for whatever we might be willing to part with. When we camped that night, we noticed our horses and mules busying themselves licking the rocks scattered around the spring, which turned out to be lumps of nearly pure salt.

A few more days brought us to the snow-topped mountain we had been told about. It stood alone in the midst of a barren desert, jutting into a cloudless sky, its craggy shoulders bereft of trees or any vegetation that we could see. We camped that night at the foot of the mountain, taking advantage of a spring of icy-cold pure water gushing from between massive boulders and the skimpy grass that it sustained.

Zenas Leonard often joined us at our scanty cookfire, which was comprised mostly of dry reeds that burned quickly without providing much heat. After a hasty supper of stew made from boiled jerky and dried corn, Zenas told us that we weren't the first whitemen to visit that spot. He said Bonneville had provided Joe Walker with a copy of Jedediah Smith's journal of his journey to California in 1826, which prompted Brass Turtle to observe, "I reckon Cap'n Bonnyville din't have a whole heap o' trouble gittin' that'ere journal from the Army, whar Diah war sendin' ever'thin' he l'arnt abaout the Spaniards an' all abaout gittin' thar, jist like we'll be doin' thi'shere time out!"

Zenas was fiercely loyal to Joseph Walker and to their mission. He flushed beet-red and sputtered, "Ye hadn't oughta be talkin' like that, Turtle! This is a worthy undertaking and Captain Walker is an honest and honorable man!"

Turtle stood his ground. "Nobody's sayin' he ain't. I b'lieve he's both o' them things an' I reckon Bonnyville gave him a chance to try gittin' to Californy agin an' Walker took it. Cain't fault him fer that."

Anse Tolliver, always ready to defend his kinsman, chimed in. "An' so fur, ever'thin' the cap'n's done has turned out right, jist like he war sayin' it would."

Tuttle Thompson was already wrapped in his sleeprobes. He yawned and stretched and declared, "Yep an' ther last thang I heard 'im say war thet we'll be on ther trail bright an' early t'morra mawnin'! What'say we git some shut-eye whilst we kin?"

Nobody had a better idea, so we did.

~ ~ ~

Next day, just in time for our dinner halt, we arrived at a sizeable stream that Leonard called the Barren River in his journal. He told me that Jed Smith referred to it by a couple different names in his journal, the Mary's and also the Ogden River, but I reckon Zenas was closer to the truth than the other two. A more desolate and uninviting watercourse is hard to imagine, muddy and turgid, its banks almost completely devoid of vegetation, save for reeds growing in the shallows. Even so, it was wet and it afforded easy traveling for our critters along its banks. We saw beaver sign aplenty, broken dams and deserted lodges, but no beaver, likely because the Indians thereabouts hunt them for food. Our line of march and everywhere else that we could see lacked firewood of any kind, unless we happened upon a stick or two of driftwood here and there along the riverbed. After several nights without a cookfire, we learned to grab up firewood wherever we found it and carry it along with us.

The original light-hearted mood of the company gradually sobered as we realized Walker's California expedition was serious business and that we were committed to a long and arduous journey before we might be able to enjoy any reward for our efforts.

After a few days travel we commenced meeting up with what you might call human beings, if you are inclined to be generous in your opinions. We finally made out from their gabble that they call themselves Paiutes, distant kin of the Shoshones. A more pathetic excuse for humanity is hard to imagine. Men and women alike go about unshod and naked except for a skimpy shield of plaited grass worn around their loins. They are all filthy dirty, their hair a mucky, tangled mess. Most of them are small and weak and some are exceedingly hairy. Even Tuttle Thompson showed no disposition to dally with the females we encountered amongst the Paiutes. When I facetiously enquired regarding the cause of his unaccustomed celibacy, he shuddered dramatically and chucked a handful of mud at me.

Apparently the Paiutes have no memory of whitemen traveling through their country and they know naught of civilized merchandise or its worth. The captain bargained for a large robe of beaver skins with an old man who appeared to exert some authority over his neighbors. The robe was easily worth forty or fifty dollars. Walker obtained it in exchange for two awls and one fish-hook.

As we traveled downstream, mostly sticking close to the river, we were able to observe the manner in which these unbelievably primitive people live. They subsist on grass-seed, insects, frogs, lizards, snakes, and, when fortune smiles, an occasional fish, which they usually spear. They obtain much of their food by poking sharp sticks into burrows along the crick banks and prying out whatever critters are secreted there, which provoked some of our people to call them Diggers.

When we arrived at the first lake formed by the Barren River, we learned how the Paiutes cultivate their major winter food source. The water in that lake is stagnant, totally disagreeable, its surface covered with green scum, similar to a frog pond. In warm weather there is a fly—about the same size and color of a grain of wheat—that breeds on this lake in great numbers. When the wind rolls the waters onto shore, vast quantities of these flies are left on the beach. The female Paiutes carefully gather these flies into baskets and expose them to the sun until they are dry, when they are laid away for winter provender. These flies, together with grass seed and a few rabbits, make up most of their food supply during the winter season.

I was at first amused when I observed some of our trappers trading for some of that fly-food from the Indians, but then, considering my dwindling supply of jerk meat, I bought some, too, just in case.

"'Ceptin' fer fire, these hyar Pye-ute critters ain't hardly a-tall diff'ernt from a bunch o' badgers in ther way they live," Tuttle opined, referring to the common habitation of the native population. He was pretty nearly right. What serves as their housing is a round hole dug into the ground, in the shape of a potato hole, over which they place sticks covered with reeds and grass and earth to form a roof of sorts, with a doorway at one end and a shallow fire-pit at the other.

They do their cooking in a pot made of stiff mud or clay, which they lay upon the fire and burn until it hardens. After using it a few times for cooking, the pot falls to pieces and they make a new one.

~ ~ ~

As we proceeded downriver we passed a chain of small lakes connected by the river. Some of our people commenced trapping a few beaver, which, in the absence of trees, have adapted to living on reeds growing in the river. The principal result of our trapping prompted Finn McCool to observe in mock admiration, "Och, at last I've discovered the single cultural accomplishment of these benighted Paiute craytchures! They have refined thievery to a bloody art form!" It was true. If a trapper set out a beaver trap overnight, however carefully concealed, there was a better than even chance that the trap would be stolen before daylight.

Naturally such thievery fomented resentment amongst our people. One early morning, I happened to be nigh when Joe Meek shot a Paiute who was loitering near one of Joe's traps. Zenas Leonard heard the shot and came running to enquire its cause. Joe explained simply, "Wal, it 'peared to me thet'ere Digger war thinkin' on stealin' muh trap."

"But he hadn't done it yet," Zenas objected.

"Thet be so," Joe replied, "but he war hangin' 'round too close to thet'ere trap fer muh comfort an' if he gone ahead an' stole it, it'd be too late an' whar d'ye reckon I kin git anuther'n out thisaway?"

Joe got away unpunished for his rash deed because it was the first time, but his action elicited a rapid response from our leader. When he learned of the incident, Walker immediately called the entire company together and warned against provoking hostility amongst the natives. He issued a stern order forbidding any repetition of Meek's action, promising swift punishment of any transgressors.

As you might suppose, howsomever, the wisdom of Walker's warning fell upon many deaf ears, especially the unruly Santa Fe bunch. Paiutes continued stealing traps and anything else they could lay hands on. Resentment amongst the trappers finally boiled over. One day, Old Bill Williams, a madcap young scoundrel named Bill Craig, the redheaded bully Levin Mitchell, and a man called Frazier were out hunting at a considerable distance from the main column, when, just for the fun of it, they shot and killed three Paiutes. Naturally, they couldn't refrain from bragging about it that night in camp, although they tried to keep Walker from learning of their deadly prank. Next day, they repeated their murderous behavior, but this time the captain heard about it.

Punishment was swift and harsh. Without hesitation, normally easy-going Joseph Walker established his authority and his leadership, once and for all. He ordered the four miscreants to march afoot for three days, leading their critters, deprived of their firearms, which obliged them to keep up with the mounted column, lest they fall prey to vengeful natives hovering never far off from our line of march. In pronouncing that severe sentence, Walker repeated his earlier warning about stirring up hostility amongst the natives. This time, most of the party accepted his authority.

Whether or not the Santa Fe rowdies learned their lesson was unimportant. The damage was already done. A week after Joe Walker pronounced judgment on the rascally quartet, we arrived at what he described as a *sink*, a place of marshes and small lakes, where the river flows into low land that provides no outlet and simply sinks into the earth and disappears. We rejoiced at the prospect of restoring our livestock on the abundance of fine grass that the swampy land afforded, but our satisfaction was short-lived. Whilst he was surveying the nearby country through his spyglass, the captain saw smoke rising from the surrounding marshland, then discovered hordes of Paiute Indians hiding in the tall grass around our position, doubtless eager for revenge and especially anxious to claim whatever booty they might plunder from our corpses.

There was no timber thereabouts in which to establish a defensive position, so Walker ordered a retreat to the edge of the lake, where we built a breastwork of saddles, baggage, and whatever else might deflect an arrow, then picketed our livestock inside. While we were thus engaged, six or seven hundred Paiute men emerged from the tall brush and reeds and advanced.

They halted some 150 yards from our makeshift fort and five of their headmen came forward to make medicine, swinging smoking clay pots, waving feather fans, and chanting, before they signed their demand that they and their people be allowed to enter our compound and smoke with us. Joe Walker, standing tall and imposing, signed his refusal, but he offered to meet them halfway betwixt the two lines to parley. The chiefs retreated somewhat and put their heads together for a spell before they returned to announce that they would enter our compound anyway.

Every man amongst us stood ready with his guns loaded and primed, awaiting the captain's commands. Walker ordered a dozen of us to mount the breastwork, rifles ready, before he signed to the elders that they and their people would be killed if they came any closer.

His message was greeted at first with a ripple of laughter that grew to a general roar as word spread amongst them of Walker's threat. The chiefs and several of their people signed the same question: How could we possibly hurt them at such a great distance?

We realized then that the Paiutes had no knowledge of guns. Rather than demonstrating their lethal power with human bloodshed, howsomever, Walker ordered a few of us to pick off some ducks that were swimming out on the lake. When a volley of half-a-dozen rifles fired at once blasted into the still air, most of the Paiutes fell flat upon the earth, terrified at the sound. I doubt that many of them even noticed the dead ducks floating on the water.

When they had somewhat recovered their shabby dignity, the chiefs ordered some of their people to pin a beaver hide to a tree, then asked us to shoot at it. Which we did, enough to educate them, we hoped, regarding the killing power of our firearms.

When we quit shooting, most of them appeared to lose interest and drifted into the brush. Several approached the riddled beaver hide and fingered the bullet holes, grinning and chattering and shaking their heads in wonderment, before they wandered off. Naturally nobody could be sure that they were gone for good. Walker posted a heavy guard that night. I daresay no one slept soundly, but the Paiutes did not return.

We saddled our mounts and loaded our pack animals in the dark and took to the trail as the first streaks of dawn light fingered into the eastern sky. As soon as there was enough daylight to see, we became aware that Indians were converging on us from all directions, growing bolder as their numbers increased. A few large groups commenced cutting in front of our leaders, seeking to delay our advance until the entire Paiute fighting force could assemble and surround us completely.

Walker halted the column and rode forward to sign a warning to their headmen, telling them that if they did not disperse, there would be terrible consequences. They greeted his peacemaking effort with raucous laughter and insulting gestures. Then a bunch of nigh a hundred bowmen, saucier and bolder than their fellows, trotted forward and challenged us with belligerent shouts and obscene hand-talk.

Joe Walker, usually cool and in control of his temper, flushed beet-red and called out, "Awright, that rips it! Thar's nothin' equal to a good start in a case like this'n!" He swung about and pointed out about thirty men, our bunch amongst the lot, and ordered, "'Pears they be lookin' fer some eddication! You men kin larn 'em! Git onto yer best hosses, loaded an' primed, an' go teach them sons-o'-bitches some gawddamn manners!"

Those were welcome words to the ears of mountaineers whose pride had been rubbed raw by weeks of putting up with the Paiutes' persistent thieving and growing insolence prompted by Walker's reluctance to punish their forays, which they apparently attributed to cowardice. I was mounted on my Sugarfoot mule in anticipation of traveling that day through boggy country bordering the sink. Now I leapt to the ground and quickly swapped saddles with Davey, my lineback dun, who had proved himself steady and fearless in running buffalo. This chore promised to require much the same qualities.

Whilst I busied myself snugging my saddle *cincha*, making sure my rifle and pistols were loaded and capped, and tethering my idle critters, I stole glances at the men in my bunch who were similarly occupied. Brass Turtle and Little Mountain were gleeful, anticipating a fight that had been too long delayed. Old Foot's countenance was as inscrutable as ever, but his nephew, young Half-horse, striving mightily to appear grave and matter-of-fact, looked like he might burst with excitement. The others betrayed no emotion that I could see, exchanging small talk and jests as they awaited Walker's order to attack, except for Cesár Pérez, whose grin threatened to swallow his ears, so eager was he to enter the fray.

Preparations took less than five minutes. Zenas Leonard rode amongst us, making sure all was in order and briefly describing the plan of attack, before he signaled our readiness to Joe Walker, who roared out, "Go git 'em, boys! Give 'em hell!"

The sight of thirty horsemen, brandishing weapons and shouting bloodthirsty war cries, bursting into the clearing and bearing down on them at an all-out gallop so nearly petrified the hundred-or-so Paiute warriors gathered there that most of them could hardly lift their bows or nock arrows to their bowstrings, let alone aim them, in defense against our onslaught. Following the plan, as we neared the throng clustered in the field, we split our charge into a flanking attack and rapidly surrounded them, trampling several who attempted to flee and herding the rest into a screaming, terrified mob fighting one another as they sought to escape. A couple ragged volleys sufficed to kill or seriously wound about forty of them. The rest, dismayed at the ferocity of our attack, ran howling into the swamp reeds and underbrush. Within minutes, not a single Paiute remained in that neighborhood.

Captain Walker immediately rode out to inspect the carnage and to thank those of us who had taken part in the attack. Although his words expressed approval of what we had done, the look on his face testified to deep regret that such an action had been necessary. Mindful that gunpowder and galena must not be wasted, he ordered us to take up the Paiute bows and dispatch those Indians who were still alive but fatally wounded. Our Delawares and Cesár saved the rest of us that grisly chore, swiftly delivering the *coup de grâce* with tomahawks and Cesár's machete.

Walker wasted no time in resuming our westward journey. All of us were anxious to quit that neighborhood, although we saw neither hide nor hair of any Paiutes as we made our way back to the Barren River. There was little rejoicing amongst those of us who had taken part in punishing those primitive Indians, but neither did we suffer guilt for teaching them a hard lesson in order to preserve our own lives. We were threescore men traveling in the midst of thousands of hostile natives who would happily kill us without a flicker of conscience in order to rob us of our livestock and plunder. If they had succeeded in overrunning us, we had no hope or expectation of aid or succor to deliver us from a merciless enemy. The sacrifice of a few of their number served to instruct the vast population of Paiutes that it is unwise—and likely fatal—to victimize outlanders traveling through their domain.

We made camp when we reached the bank of the Barren River and immediately set to work gathering large quantities of reeds and rushes and lashing them together to make rafts on which to ferry our plunder to the far side. Many hands make light work. That chore and swimming our horses and mules across was completed the following day.

❧   ❧   ❧

Next morning we commenced what turned out to be six weeks of journeying across a dull, drab landscape that might have been the moon, lacking as it does significant landmarks or memorable geographical features, offering only an endless vista of deadly monotony, a mind-numbing sameness that robs the traveler of interest and enthusiasm, curiosity, wit, and humor. Day after day, we squinted into an unchanging dry, dreary ocean of dingy grey shale and pale red rocks that stretched forever westward under a cloudless iron canopy until it blurred into a hazy horizon fading into blood-red sundowns at day's end.

Every day, hunters fanned out in advance of the column, but except for a few stringy jackrabbits our efforts proved fruitless. The hunters' other mission was to seek out waterholes and patches of greenery that might provide graze for our critters, whose increasingly visible ribs and sunken flanks attested to hard work and scant rations.

That selfish, barren country denies sustenance to every sort of animal, yet we rarely passed a day when we did not see Indians or fresh signs of them, and some days, hundreds of them, at a distance. Word of our violent confrontation with their eastern kin had evidently spread amongst Diggers everywhere, for they immediately took to their heels and hid themselves when our caravan approached.

We gained some knowledge of the Paiute diet when a couple of our hunters surprised a Digger family, who fled in panic. The hunters ransacked their meager belongings and discovered a couple of rabbitskin sacks which contained what the hunters supposed was dried fish. Naturally they brought their ill-gotten booty back to camp and added it to the stew that was being prepared for their mess that night. Finnæus McCool happened by their camp during their suppertime and, curious chap that he always is, inspected the contents of the rabbitskin sacks. The foragers and the other members of that mess lost their supper when Finn informed them that the mystery ingredient was not dried fish, but insect larvae, commonly called grubs.

🛶 🛶 🛶

September was drawing to a close by time we came to another large, shallow lake that lacked an outlet and sank into the earth, then a fresh-water lake and a fast-running river of considerable size flowing east, but still no game, save a few jackrabbits. There we had our first sight of the forbidding wall of high, jagged, snow-capped mountains that stretched darkly to the north and south as far as the eye could see, blocking further westward progress. They made my heart small. I recalled the first time I saw the Rocky Mountains, a decade past, and how that sight had happified me and my companions, how those sun-lit pine-clad heights and snowy pinnacles had welcomed us, promising adventure and a better life than we had known. This was different. These mountains chilled my spirit. Their bleak, rocky slopes and towering crags beetling over the barren plain on which we stood brought to mind a great iron door forever shut and barred against intruders.

Then I reminded myself that getting to these mountains was what we had been striving so hard to achieve, why we had struggled through the drab desolation of the sterile desert, often thirsty and always ill-fed, sleeping poorly with one eye open lest Paiutes return to avenge their fallen fellows, and being constantly concerned for the well-being of our animals and our comrades. Those lofty heights presented a final challenge before we could claim victory in our effort to reach California and the Western Sea. Nobody had said or believed that it would be easy.

Brass Turtle thoughtfully appraised the forbidding eminence, his gaze ranging across the rocky mountainside, before he declared, "Wal, we been callin' ourse'fs mountaineers an' thi'shere is sure-as-hell one helluva mountain. One way or t'other, we'll git acrost it."

Tuttle seconded Turtle's opinion with enthusiasm. "Yew kin wager all ye got on it. We'll git 'er done! Hell! I kin awready smell them purty *señoritas* Caesar's been tellin' abaout!"

Turtle was quick to respond. "I don't know about that, but I reckon they kin smell you, not jist in Californy, but all the way to China!"

Spirits perked up amongst the whole party at the idea that only one more obstacle separated us from our goal, even when the search parties that Walker sent out to find a pass through the mountain failed to discover one.

The one chance we had of obtaining guides to show us a trail through the mountain ended in disaster. Walker and Leonard set out to scout a trail and came across a couple of Indians, who bolted at the sight of the whitemen and fled down our leaders' backtrail. Walker and Leonard pursued them, hoping to allay their fear and convince them to guide us. Unfortunately, George Nidever, the best rifle shot in our entire company, was out hunting in that neighborhood, following that same path. When he saw the Indians dashing pell-mell towards him, running one behind the other, he whipped up his rifle and fired. The ball passed through the first Indian's chest and mortally wounded his companion, as well. Any hope of finding a guide through the mountains died with them.

We tarried there for half a week, seeking to restore our critters on the scanty forage that we found thereabouts. Winter was coming and food was running short. Our dried meat, corn, and such were nearly gone and getting across the mountain would likely take a month. We couldn't stay where we were. On the first day of October 1833, sixty-two men and some three hundred horses and mules set out on a skimpy game trail that wound up the mountain, with no idea of where it might lead us.

The following month was a frigid, hungry hell, a grim comedy of false starts and disorderly retreats from blind trails blocked by slides of huge boulders or snow-choked gullies. The threat of rock slides and avalanches was a constant worry. Although we style ourselves mountaineers, most of us were not accustomed to the kind of mountain-climbing we encountered, but we learned in a hurry how to tread slippery paths.

Know-it-all old-timers who had disdained to stock up sufficiently were the first to run out of dried meat. We cursed them but we shared our meager store with them. Firewood was always scarce and often there was none at all. We often slept without a fire, shivering in wet buckskins, huddled in our *capotes*, blankets, and buffalo robes, bellies threatening to gnaw through our backbone. When trappers ran out of dried meat, many were reduced to eating juniper berries—we called them gin berries—and, for those who had had the foresight to buy any, Paiute fly-food.

I shared some of my fly-food with Joe Meek, who, improvident as always, had been among the first to run out of jerked meat. He was starving but too proud to admit it. Nevertheless, he gobbled up every crumb I provided and licked his fingers afterwards, commenting as he did so, "Never thought I'd go to eatin' bugs—an' likin' it, too. Got any more?"

After the first week in the mountains, the horses ganted up badly. They became stiff and stupid from cold, exhaustion, and starvation. Mules handled privation rather better, but they, too, suffered severely from lack of forage. We served in shifts breaking trail through the snow so that the critters could pass. When a horse or mule floundered and fell, we stripped off his pack, wrestled him onto his feet, restored his load, and returned him to the packstring. Naturally nobody rode the critters in their weakened condition.

My grey mare had become devoted to my lineback dun gelding Davey and my bay gelding was devoted to her. And my three jack mules, for some reason known only to mules, would unquestioningly follow any grey mare to hell and back. So all I needed to do in order to keep track of my critters was to hang on to Davey or at least to know where he was.

Naturally that much hardship caused a passel of grumbling amongst a certain kind of men, whose discontent finally boiled over into open rebellion against Captain Walker's authority. I was not surprised to see Bill Williams at the core of it, along with Levin Mitchell and crazy Bill Craig. The rest were mostly malcontents amongst the Santa Fe crowd. After a fortnight of failing to find a trail through the mountains, about a dozen trappers balked, declared that we were lost, and demanded that Walker lead them back to buffalo country. Joe Walker is a patient man. First off, he refused to turn back. Then he explained that attempting to retrace the trail on their own would be foolhardy—suicidal, in fact—that they lacked food and strength enough even to reach the plains, let alone get back to the Rockies.

The rebels were adamant. They insisted on turning back. At last, Walker appeared to give in. "All right, if that's what ye wish, I won't keep ye from it. Ye kin go—with my blessin' an' my prayers. But that's all ye git! The hosses b'long to me an' I ain't about to let ye take a one of 'em. An' as fer gunpowder an' galena, whatever ye got in yer horn an' yer pouch is all you're gonna git. If that suits ye, good enough. I wish ye godspeed an' the best o' luck. You'll be needin' it."

The mutineers stared in stunned silence, shocked that easy-going Joseph Walker had turned into a stone wall. They stood open-mouthed, obviously weighing their chances of surviving a retreat to the valley floor, providing they could find their way, and then confronting the impossibility of making it back to the Salt Lake afoot, lacking horses, food, and ammunition, past hundreds, maybe thousands, of riled-up Indians. Their resistance collapsed. Even Bill Williams, often called Old Solitaire, who prides himself on his self-reliance, didn't fancy hiking back to the mountains alone, afoot, and without supplies.

Walker didn't strut about overcoming that challenge to his authority, nor did he inflict punishment on the insurgents. Perhaps he reckoned that the shame of being forced to back down in front of the rest of us was punishment enough. He acted as if the incident hadn't happened. Then he ordered the slaughter of two horses that were at death's door anyway and saw to it that the flesh was distributed equally amongst the various messes, which raised our spirits more than somewhat. That horse meat was black and stringy, lean and tough, but we feasted on it as if it had been the choicest buffalo hump. It was the first fresh meat that we had tasted since we departed Bear River nearly three months before and every man ate his fill that night. We broke our fast with horse meat next morning. What little remained was shared out to each man equally. Not a mouthful was wasted.

Full bellies spawned a festive air that night. Anse Tolliver unlimbered his fiddle and Harry Yeats unpacked his cittern for the first time since we commenced our ascent of that rugged mountain. The young Irisher's big voice attracted a score of others. Ere long sentimental ballads and saucy sea chanteys were ringing off the rocky hillsides. Although it was difficult to be sure in the flickering firelight, I could have sworn that I saw a smile crack Bill Williams' craggy features.

Ω Ω Ω

We continued to wander across the mountain top in a snowy, rocky nightmare, seeking in vain a pass or passable trail that might lead us downwards. Walker sent out several search parties every day, but nobody discovered a descending route that might free us from our mountain prison. From time to time we came upon small mountain lakes fed by melting snows—McCool called them *tarns*—which sustained along their shores patches of indifferent grass, which our livestock eagerly cropped to the roots. Naturally there were no fish in those high mountain ponds, nor did we discover a single game critter in those lofty regions.

What timber that neighborhood afforded was mostly scrubby pine, cedar, juniper, and a tough red-barked wood that burns ideally hot for cookfires. From time to time Captain Walker ordered the killing of horses that had become utterly worthless because of hard work and little grass. That meat is all that kept body and soul barely together for us human critters. Most of the horses and mules were unable to assist our traveling. Rather, they had become a burden. We had to help many of them along, as we might have done for a feeble old man. Most of us shouldered that chore without question or complaint. Many times, over the years, our critters had done the same for us.

Now I was doubly glad that I had left my Coffee horse with Cat. It was bad enough that Davey, Sugarfoot, and the others had become tottering skeletons, barely able to put one foot in front of another.

One day we came upon a precipice that overlooked a beautiful broad wooded valley that contained wide streams sparkling in sunlight and lush meadows flanked by dense timberland, a veritable Eden, but it was a mile below the crag on which we stood.

Several men tried to find a way down the cliff, only to admit defeat and climb back up. Even if a very agile man could have scaled that rock face, it would not have been possible to transport our animals and our baggage down that sheer mountainside.

As much as the broken terrain permitted, we traveled in a westerly direction, which led us along a rocky spine between two chasms, working our way around rock slides and snow banks, making no more than two or three miles a day. Walker continued to send out several search parties every day, exploring every slope that might permit us to descend from the ridge. Near the end of a chill late-October day, Brass Turtle and Half-horse were among the last searchers to return from an unsuccessful scout along the mountainside. They had discovered neither game nor a likely downward trail. "Ye seen Li'l Mountain, have ye?" Turtle enquired when he emerged from the thick underbrush that grew along the canyon rim.

"Nope," Anse replied. "He war s'posed to be with yew two."

"I know that," Turtle responded testily, "but he ain't! Fer a big man, he surely kin make hisse'f scarce when he takes a mind to!"

"Ye mean to say ye went an' lost Li'l Mountain, big as he be?" Tolliver persisted, plainly enjoying Brass Turtle's discomfort. "'Pears to me, one o' yew two Delawares could'a kep' track of 'im. He's kinda hard to overlook, wou'n't ye say?"

Turtle bristled but he clamped his mouth shut, declining to provide Anse with further amusement at his expense. He was clearly anxious about his friend's absence and so were the rest of us. Clambering about those steep, slippery hillsides was dangerous business. Any one of us, any day, when we were scouting those icy slopes, might make a false step and plunge to our death. Captain Walker joined us in our concern. So far, our leader had achieved a kind of minor miracle. In spite of all the hardships we had endured, as well as threats from hostile natives, we had not lost a single man, nor had any of our company suffered serious injury. Even our livestock had survived remarkably well. Most of the horses that died had been slaughtered on purpose to provide food for the men.

Tuttle summed it up best. "Measurin' Joe Walker agin Diah Smith fer ramroddin' an outfit like this'n, thar ain't no doubtin' which one gits ther prize. Joe wins somethin' like thutty-to-nuthin'!" Tuttle was referring to Jedediah's second and final California expedition. Only two of Smith's men survived.

Walker's perfect score remained intact. About sundown Little Mountain's smiling countenance poked into view above the scrubby brush that framed the canyon rim. We greeted the big man with joyful whoops and heartfelt curses expressing relief. "Ye big dumb sumbitch!" Brass Turtle exploded. "Ye skeered the hell out of us! Whar ye been?"

Little Mountain brushed it all aside with a grin. He is forever cheerful, no matter the circumstance or what he might be doing, whether it is running buffalo, wooing a shy maiden at rendezvous, killing and scalping an enemy, patching up a wounded comrade, or gentling a fractious green horse. Little Mountain greets each new chore with great good humor and boyish enthusiasm. When he stepped onto flat ground, we saw that he was toting a large basket filled with what appeared to be reddish-brown pebbles. "Whatcher got thar, Mountain?" Anse wanted to know.

"Acorns," the big Delaware replied. "Big'uns, too. Biggest I ever seed." Joe Walker thrust himself into our midst, dropped to his knees, and shoved his fist into the basket, bringing out a handful of the largest acorns any of us had ever seen, all of them a couple-three inches long and of comparable girth.

"Whar'd'ja git these?" Walker demanded, sifting acorns from one hand to the other, a warm grin meanwhile seeping onto his features as he realized the import of that basket of acorns.

"Got 'em off an Injun down below. He run off an' dropped 'em when he spied me. I chased 'im but he got away. Them acorns be good. Best I ever et."

Walker ignored Mountain's gastronomic evaluation of the acorns. "Which way war he headin'? Could ye tell?"

"Yep. I seed 'im a spell afore he spied me. He war headin' thisaway, comin' over thi'shere mountain, best I could tell."

This was apparently the answer that Walker had hoped for. A broad smile spread over all of his face not covered by his bushy brown beard. He looked up and addressed us. "I reckon ye know what this signifies. That'ere Injun come up some kind o' trail an' he war headin' thisaway, so it means thar's gotta be a trail somewhars nigh that kin take us down to the flatland."

This was the best news we had heard since we first set foot on the California Mountain, as we had come to call it. Now that we could be sure that there was, in fact, a trail somewhere on that mountainside, it would be only a matter of time until one of us discovered it.

Little Mountain hadn't lied about the acorns, either. Roasted in the ashes of the cookfire, they were tastier than the best chestnuts I've ever eaten, although, as Zenas Leonard wryly observed, the culinary judgment of people who have been living on stringy old horse meat can hardly be trusted.

∾ ∾ ∾

Next day, nigh half the company swarmed over the mountainside seeking the trail of the Indian that Little Mountain had startled and routed. At first it appeared that descending that sheer precipice would be impossible. From where we stood to the valley floor appeared to be a distance of about three miles, almost all of it pretty much straight down. But now that we knew that Little Mountain's runaway Indian had somehow traveled it, hope and confidence surged in our collective breast. Every man was certain that we could find a navigable passage to salvation.

Little Mountain led the way to the place where he discovered the Indian the previous day. After that, we all spread out in search of a path that we could travel to the plain below. After a few hours of fruitless exploration on my part, I spied Micah and Cesár scrambling up the face of the rocky hillside, a gleeful look on their faces. "We found it! Or, rather, Cesár did!" Micah crowed, when he was able to catch his breath. "It ain't much. It's a measly path, but it'll take us off this mountain!" Cesár kept nodding and grinning fit to swallow his ears. Micah gulped a lungful of air and added, "We're on our way up to tell Cap'n Walker the good news. Ye might as well come along."

Now that my companions had succeeded in our quest, I could see no good reason to cling to my precarious perch on a rock face. I followed them to the top.

❧   ❧   ❧

Micah and Cesár also reported that they had also seen tracks and droppings of deer and bear nigh the Indian trail, which happified our leaders and whoever was within earshot almost as much their discovery of the path. Early next morning, Cesár and Micah led us a mile or so along the canyon rim before they slipped over the edge and called back for us to follow them down the path. It was not an easy trail to travel, but because it was our only means of escape from the cold and starvation of the mountain top, we valued it as if it were a highway. The slope was steep and difficult. Our only way to descend with any speed was to traverse the nearly-vertical cliff face in a zig-zag manner, first traveling in one direction, those in the lead spading out footholds, then those who followed widening the narrow downward path as we went, then reversing direction and repeating the process, gaining a couple yards downwards with each reversal. More picks and spades came into play as relays of shovelers followed the leaders, smoothing and widening the path enough to allow our critters to be led along behind.

All went well until our descent encountered a rocky ledge over a steep drop-off that completely stalled our progress. Walker sent men out in either direction to find a way past the obstruction. One by one, they returned to report failure to find a safe passage around the rocks. George Nidever also failed in that quest, but he brightened our spirits considerably when he showed up carrying a small deer on his back.

The little critter was skinned, dressed out, cooked, and eaten in less time than a hungry wolf would have taken to devour a lamb. Except for tough, dry, stringy horsemeat, that was the first fresh meat larger than a rabbit that any of us had tasted since we killed the last buffalo near the Great Salt Lake. Moreover, it had been a fortnight since we ate the last of our jerkmeat and had depended since on stale, unsavory horse flesh to keep from starving altogether.

Those few morsels of fresh meat allotted to each man did wonders to raise our spirits. There I gained additional respect for Joseph Walker's foresight. The many fathoms of stout rope that we had hauled from the Rockies proved its worth at last. Some men found a place that was fairly smooth and gradual enough in descent to let us sling our critters on ropes and let them down, one at a time, to a safe landing past the rocky barrier. Our poor animals had lost so much flesh during their lean times in the desert and the starving time atop the mountain that slinging them in a canvas sheet and supporting their weight was hardly a strain for three or four men engaged in the chore. Hunger had made them so spiritless that they offered no resistance when we swung them off the ledge and carefully let them down to safe footing on the trail.

Once over the rocky rampart, we exerted every effort to get as far down the mountainside as possible before darkness stalled our progress, widening and smoothing the original path, which was growing plainer and well-traveled as we proceeded downwards. Meanwhile, several hunters set out in search of more substantial game than our earlier meager snack had provided. We worked on the trail until it grew too dark to see, by which time we had arrived at a fairly level place where green oak bushes grew. We encamped there, hobbled the critters to keep them from straying into trouble, and awaited the return of the hunters.

They arrived not long after dark, well-rewarded for their efforts. They brought in two big, rolling-fat blacktail deer and a black bear that had fattened well in anticipation of his winter slumbers. The meat was dressed in short order and was soon sizzling over a dozen cookfires. Every man ate his fill and, for most of us, soon afterwards did likewise again. Full bellies foster jollity and it wasn't long until somebody broke into song and Tolliver commenced sawing out lively Tennessee tunes on his fiddle, which naturally prompted our Irish harpooner to join in with his cittern. I have no idea how long the gaiety lasted for I dropped off to sleep almost as soon as I crawled into my robes and rested my head on my saddle.

From that place downwards, we encountered little snow and a greater amount of greenery. Grass grew more abundantly and improved in quality as we neared the valley floor. Naturally the critters grazed greedily at every opportunity. Their ribs commenced to disappear and their sunken flanks began to fill out. Although they were still weak as kittens, I hadn't lost a single one of my critters, nor had anyone in our bunch. Most of us made a point of letting Half-horse know that we valued his judgment in selecting sound animals from Walker's herd and for his care of them during the starving time.

Captain Walker still maintained his perfect record in regard to the well-being of the men in his company and he had lost only 24 horses from the herd of more than 300 head. Seventeen of those horses had been used for food. If it hadn't been for that horse flesh, it is likely that some men would have died.

As we proceeded down the mountain, timber grew much larger. Some of the red-wood species are incredibly immense, measuring as much as 16 to 18 fathoms around the trunk. The farther down the mountain we traveled, the more plentiful game became, mostly wapiti, blacktail deer, and black bears, all of them rolling fat from lush graze and large acorns that littered the earth beneath the oak trees that grew in abundance on the gentle slopes. On the 30th day of October 1833 we reached level ground. It had taken us nearly a month to cross over the mountain.

-ooo-

CHAPTER VI
GOLDEN DAYS

That was a glorious time for those of us who enjoyed hunting. Every day we harvested a plenitude of game critters and feasted to surfeit every night. Our starveling horses were still too stove up to ride, but we didn't need to hike very far afoot in order to shoot elk, blacktail deer, and bears that were unused to hunters equipped with firearms. If we chanced to startle them, they would run off a short distance, just beyond bowshot, then halt to look back at us, offering an easy target.

As you might expect, some men are never satisfied, no matter how much fortune might smile on them. One night at supper, after we had stuffed ourselves to bursting, Tuttle Thompson wiped his greasy chin whiskers and grumbled, "Thi'shere bear meat's awright, I reckon, but I shore do miss buffler hump ribs an' boudins! Cain't b'lieve thar ain't no buffler hereabouts. 'Tain't Christian, gawddammit!"

Brass Turtle was quick to respond. "Thar ye go agin, Tuttle! Bellyachin' when y'oughter be thankin' the Sperrit fer yer full belly! Ain't but a week since ye war chawin' on yer gawddamn mockersins an' glad ye had 'em fer eatin'!"

"I'm thinkin' you'll be goin' without your bison ribs until we return to the Rockies, Tuttle darlin'," Finn McCool added. "I recall readin' somewhere that those craytchures have never succeeded in crossin' the coastal mountains."

"And now that we've gone an' done it ourselves, it's easy to understand why," Micah put in. "Why would a buffler, dumb as they be, leave all that good Rocky Mountain grass behind an' hike across that bare-arse desert, just so he could starve to death tryin' to get over that godforsaken mountain?"

Tuttle wasn't the only mountaineer who yearned for buffalo. We all did. Many men refused to be convinced and continued to keep a lookout for their favorite foodstuff until Joe Walker led them back to the Rockies.

అ అ అ

We continued traveling afoot, but our horses and mules had improved enough by that time to let them carry most of the baggage as we followed a mighty river downstream across a grassy level plain. Its powerful current slices a deep channel across the prairie, the banks often more than a hundred feet high, racing with great speed and turbulence, only to broaden out here and there in beautiful serene bays, until it narrows again and goes mad in a series of violent rapids.

The plain through which the river runs is watered by several feeder streams and the soil is rich, producing large quantities of wild pumpkins, as well as a rich variety of wild oats, which our livestock gobbled enthusiastically as they traveled through it.

When we encamped one night beside the river, Captain Walker announced that it was time that we commence trapping, in order to earn some profit for the expedition, which so far had been a dead loss, except for the benefits in natural curiosities we had seen.

Our progress downriver slowed considerably as we searched the tributary streams for beaver sign, which also provided more time to recruit our critters. Their condition was still much impaired from their starvation on the mountaintop, as well as from strains incurred in descending rocky precipices.

When we weren't running traplines or dressing plews and such, we busied ourselves laying in a large supply of elk, deer, and bear meat of the best kind. Graze for critters was abundant and the large acorns I described earlier thrive in that country. Bears likely ate naught else than those acorns and all of the game critters thereabouts were full-fleshed and fat. I had brought along several fathoms of English silk fishing line and fishhooks, which let us vary our diet with large trout taken from the chill waters of the rushing river. No man could reasonably ask for better surroundings.

It was hard to believe that it was November. Weather continued sunny and warm under clear skies and the prairies swarmed with wild horses of every color, piebald, sorrel, jet black, bay, dapple, and mouse grey that Cesár called *grullas*. They were in excellent fettle and surprisingly tame, but we made no attempt to capture them.

❧   ❧   ❧

Although we had seen smoke and moccasin tracks and had come upon the ashes of cookfires, we had not laid eyes on a single Indian since we got off the mountain. Now, as we moved downriver, trapping the feeder streams as we went, moving camp every other day or so, Indian sign became more common, until at last we spied a cluster of five huts, housing about a score of natives, who fled at our approach. We tried to coax them back with peaceful signs, offering to smoke with them, and inviting them to share the fresh meat that we commenced to prepare on their cookfire. The aroma of roasting meat and our offer of tobacco caused a few of the men to put aside their fear. Soon the rest of them crept back into their village.

Looking around at the men in our company, it was no wonder that we presented a frightening spectacle for those Indians. Hardly any of the whites had bothered to shave since we left Bear River more than three months earlier, which lent them a wild look that must have terrified the smooth-faced natives. Besides, most of our people stood half again as tall and were much sturdier than those short, fragile-looking, mostly-naked, dark-skinned natives. Moreover, our firearms, knives, tomahawks, and warlike hardware with which every man was girded must have struck terror into any people not similarly equipped.

Whatever spoken language they possessed seemed to consist only of hog-like grunts and their hand-signs bore little resemblance to the universal sign-talk of the Rockies and northern plains. Our attempts to obtain information regarding the Big Water, white people, beaver, or whatever met with no success. Walker decided to camp there overnight, howsomever, perhaps in the hope that some happy accident of communication might occur.

Staying overnight gave me an opportunity to observe our hosts. They are a small people, not very muscular, and much darker in complexion than Indians of the Rocky Mountain prairies. A gentle climate allows most of them to run about entirely naked, except for a few older individuals who wear a skimpy shield of animal skin about their loins. Shelters consist of walls made of poles set upon end and roofed over with thatch. Bedding is merely a pile of dried grass. They live pretty much on horse meat and acorn mush and not much else, which might account for their delicate physiques and general weakness, which in turn may be the reason for their almost total lack of industry.

Whilst we were settling in for the night, Stephen Meek and another Santa Fe trapper, Powell Weaver, were passing through the Indian camp when they espied a couple blankets and a steel-bladed knife, sure signs that the natives had some commerce with whitemen. Walker resumed his enquiries, holding up the blankets and signing repeatedly his questions regarding their origin.

At last, amidst their garble of grunts and whistles, we distinctly made out the word *español*, accompanied by the Indians' enthusiastic pointing towards the west, which we took to mean that a Spaniard settlement was not far distant.

Next morning, the Indians brought several horses into camp and offered them in trade. All of them bore an elaborate Spaniard brand, further proof that there was a whitemen's establishment in that neighborhood. Once again, Joe Walker proved himself to be a shrewd trader. He chose five of their best horses and got them all in exchange for a yard of scarlet trade wool and two butcher knives. Brass Turtle awarded the palm to the Indians, howsomever, opining, "I reckon they figger they put one over on Joe, cornsid'rin' they likely be fust-rate hossthieves an' the hosses cost 'em nothin' to start with."

☙   ☙   ☙

We continued down the big river, moving camp every other day and trapping the feeder streams without much success or observing anything of particular note, until the night of November 13th, 1833. We encamped beside the river and treated ourselves to a hearty supper. Beaver were scarce in that neighborhood, but game critters abounded. Full bellies make for early nights, so most of us headed for our robes when dusk gathered in the last rays of sunshine.

My head had hardly touched the saddle seat when a horrendous explosion ripped through the darkness and catapulted me to my feet. The heavens yawned wide, spilling out streams of multi-colored meteors falling to earth, some exploding in air, others appearing to smash into the ground at a distance. The entire sky was lit with an eerie brilliance. The din from bursting meteors was deafening. Men who could calmly face the charge of an enraged grizzly bear or an attack by a horde of Blackfoots went white-faced with terror. The shouts and curses of the men were barely audible above the frantic neighing and braying of our critters, hauling back on their tethers and falling down in fright, yanking picket pins loose in a frenzied attempt to flee. Many of us rushed to restrain our own horses and mules and calm them by our presence. A few men dropped to their knees, clasped their hands, and prayed for forgiveness.

I didn't know what to make of it all, but I didn't take it personally. If the Great Spirit ever has a mind to punish me for my misdeeds, I daresay He won't employ such spectacular means to do so.

Captain Walker bustled from one group of men to another, calming them as best he could, assuring them that the meteor shower offered no harm to them or their property, providing they kept their critters from injuring themselves. Most men took him at his word. The panic subsided abruptly, testimony that Walker had earned our trust and respect by his quiet strength and natural authority. When the camp settled down to something like normal, Tuttle summed up the extravagant display. "I'm callin' thet'n ther damnedest shootin' match thet ever war seen!" Nobody disagreed.

∾ ∾ ∾

That was a season of prodigies for us Rocky Mountain mountaineers. We continued to follow the big river downstream, plying the trappers' trade with indifferent success and literally living off the fat of the land. The valley got much wider and black bears gave up their place to their huge grizzly cousins, which are mostly a golden color, but which share the ferocious character of their silver-tipped kin of the Rockies in all other respects. Grizzlies and wild horse herds grew more numerous as we traveled westward. We came across a fair amount of Indian sign, but no natives or their dwelling-places. Here and there, tree stumps that had been chopped with an axe told us that whitemen frequented that neighborhood.

The valley floor was generally level thereabouts, so the river flowed with a gentle current, running clear and clean, and broadened to two or three hundred yards. A few days after the meteor shower, we encamped in a beautiful spot beside the river. We had traveled a considerable distance that day, so most of us went to our robes when it got dark. Not long afterward, when the camp grew quiet, we felt a trembling of the earth beneath us, accompanied by the rumble of distant thunder, constant and unceasing. Somebody hollered that it was an earthquake, which prompted several men to yell out that we were sure to be swallowed into the bowels of the earth. Others thought the noise came from a cataract upstream and we were doomed to be drowned in a giant wave of water. It made no difference to our panicky companions that we had never seen a waterfall during our long hike down the river valley.

Once again Joe Walker allayed the fears of his company. He supposed that the tremors we felt and the distant noise we heard were caused by waves of the nearby ocean dashing upon the rocky shore. That explanation was willingly accepted by one and all. It meant that we were getting close to the Western Sea, the lodestone that had drawn many of us to make that long and difficult journey in the first place. Our fatigue magically disappeared. Most of

us passed the night in lively talk about reaching, at last, the westernmost end
of the continent.

❧   ❧   ❧

We quit trapping and traveled rapidly for the next day and a half beside the
river, which became brackish, confirming that the thundering noise and
tremors had been caused by ocean waves striking the shore. We continued
down the river until it mingled with briny ocean water in a large bay. There
we discovered a great many Indians engaged in fishing. Unlike their inland
brethren, howsomever, these Indians appeared indifferent to our presence,
which suggested that they were no strangers to whitemen.

The Indian fishermen's distant manner, although not hostile, made most
of the company uncomfortable, so the captain determined to quit that place
and set off immediately for the main coast. Which we did.

Another day and a half of brisk southward travel gave us our first glimpse
of the broad Pacific Ocean bursting into view, its endless dark blue waters
laced with curling whitecaps stretching forever westward. The months of
toilsome travel, privation, hardship, and danger were compensated in that
first instant of filling our vision with that magnificent panorama.

We camped that first night not far from the beach in a grassy hollow
watered by a fresh-flowing spring, our animals munching contentedly in
belly-high graze, cookfires burning driftwood dancing with multi-colored
sparks. In the morning I wandered along the beach, picking up seashells and
sea-polished bits of rainbow-colored shells Finn called abalone as presents
for my little girl, when I espied Powatawa seated alone on the sand, staring
out at the breaking waves.

I had not heard my father speak a single word since we arrived at the
shore. He appeared transfixed, gazing out to sea. As I sat on the sand beside
him, he turned to me and said in a faraway voice, "I have seen such a great
water before—sweet water it was that time, we drank it, too far to see across—
when I was young, younger than you are now, when I journeyed to
Grandfather's Land to fight beside Tecumseh." He fell silent and returned his
gaze to the ocean for a spell, before he said, "Now I have walked the entire
circle. I can begin again." He didn't elaborate what he meant by that and I
respected his privacy too much to press him about it.

We fell silent, comfortable in each other's company, each absorbed in his
thoughts, enthralled by the mystery and power of the restless sea before us. A

cloud drifted across the sun, blotting its golden brilliance, darkening the far-stretching waters, recalling Homer's epithet concerning the wine-dark sea, then by a freak of glinting sunshine glancing off the wave-tops, momentarily turning the vast ocean the deep violet color of my mother's eyes, a hue that I had seen in only one other place, the eyes of my daughter Iris.

Even as I yelped in delighted surprise, I felt Powatawa stiffen and heave himself to a sitting position beside me, grunting in pleasure, a broad smile lighting his features. Then it was gone.

The sun shrugged off the clinging rags of cloud and returned the sea to its former radiance. The brief moment had passed but my father had also seen that matchless color dancing on the waves. He bared his strong white teeth in a grin. "I think your mother welcomes us to this new land, Sauwaseekau. It is a good sign."

I had to agree.

❧ ❧ ❧

Next morning Walker called a meeting of all the men who weren't wandering along the water's edge, marveling at the vast blue expanse and trading trinkets with Indian fisherman for fish and clams and the corn and melons they grow in little garden plots. What Walker said went something like this: "I reckon you noticed by now how cheeky the Injuns hereabouts are actin'. I cain't say why, but I don't much care fer it. I been thinkin' the Spaniards have got these Injuns under their thumb—lock, stock, an' bar'l—an' mebbe they could turn 'em loose on us if they take a mind to. So I'm thinkin' it's best we git a move on an' go find the Spaniards an' let 'em know that we mean 'em no harm by comin' into their country."

Walker sent out a few parties of men to see if they might discover signs of a Spaniard settlement. When they returned, the men who had gone north had failed to discover any trace of whitemen. The scouts who went in a southerly direction reported signs of what they supposed were white settlements, but they had been unable to come up with any actual people. Next morning, we headed south along the ocean, traveling well away from the water, for a strong wind had come up overnight and huge waves were crashing against the rocky shore.

Late in the forenoon, we came upon the carcass of a whale thrown upon the beach, a huge critter some ninety feet long. Harry Yeats, our Irish harpooner, assured us that it was a sperm whale, the species most highly prized by whalers because of the large quantities of valuable whale oil that can be obtained from each one of them.

About noon of the third day, we spied what appeared to be a ship far out to sea. Naturally none of us knew from whence it came nor to whom it belonged, but it was the closest link to civilization that we had seen in months. Accordingly, we fastened brightly-colored blankets to long poles and commenced waving them in a manner to attract the attention of the ship. Our efforts succeeded and the ship veered shoreward, much to lour satisfaction. Our pleasure increased considerably when the ship approached closely enough for us to behold the broad stripes and bright stars of the American flag fluttering proudly from the mainmast.

The ship anchored at a safe distance from shore and boats were put out to discover who we were. The manner of the Yankee seamen warmed up greatly when they learned that we, too, were Americans. They sent a signal to the ship informing the captain of that fact, which prompted him to fire several cannon salutes in recognition of our meeting on that foreign shore. Then he had himself rowed to the beach in order to greet us in person.

He introduced himself to Captain Walker as John Bradshaw, master of the *Lagoda*, a trading ship out of Boston. He was an affable chap, as were his officers and men. They shook hands all around and Bradshaw described his mission to the California coast before respectfully enquiring about our reason for being in a place so distant from our customary stomping grounds.

Bradshaw won the unqualified approval of every man in our company when he invited us to come aboard the *Lagoda*, absolutely assuring our acceptance when he announced, "I've got a few casks of untapped cognac aboard that I'd be proud to share with my newfound countrymen. All o' ye be welcome aboard my ship." We had gone without ardent spirits since Bear River or shortly thereafter, so the Yankee captain gained instant popularity with us.

"Ol' Hick'ry kin jist be steppin' aside," Tuttle declared. "Fur as I be consarned, it's Cap'n Bradshaw fer prezzydent!"

"Indade!" Finn McCool agreed enthusiastically. "For my part, he can bloody well be the king hisownself if he so desires!"

Fifteen men remained on shore to tend our animals and guard our plunder. The rest of us were rowed out to the ship to enjoy the hospitality of Captain Bradshaw and his crew. The guests of Lucullus were never treated more handsomely than we were at the *Lagoda's* festive board. The Yankee mariners were unbelievably lavish with their groceries, setting out heaps of delicious cured meats, a variety of cheeses, butter, fresh-baked bread, and sweet pastries, luxuries that most of our company hadn't tasted for years, as well as copious draughts of brandy, beer, and wine. No cup was allowed to remain empty for more than a blink of an eye.

The *Lagoda's* crew were a hardy lot, strong, agile men, most of them bearded and sporting tarred pigtails, clad in loose duck trousers that reached barely past the knee, checkered hickory shirts, and tarpaulin hats, mostly barefoot, all of them deeply tanned and leathery from constant exposure to wind and salt spray and tropic sunshine.

One of the crewmen brought out his fiddle and naturally Anse Tolliver joined him, along with Irish Harry Yeats and his cittern. Our transplanted harpooner astonished our hosts with his vast repertory of lively sea chanteys delivered in a booming baritone, until somebody informed them of Harry's earlier seagoing career. The captain thereupon showed a keen interest in our Irisher, engaging him in conversation during a pause in the music-making. Seeking to repay, in part, Bradshaw's generous entertainment of our company, Harry told him about the sperm whale we had discovered on the beach and urged him to take advantage of it. "I promise ye, Cap'n," he assured him, "there be enough spermaceti oil in the critter's head alone to make a handsome profit fer yer ship. It'd be a cryin' bloody shame to pass it by." Bradshaw thanked him and assured him that he would certainly attend to the matter before weighing anchor, then insisted that Harry accept, as a reward, a brimming beaker of the *Lagoda's* finest cognac, which our mannerly Irisher courteously consumed to the very last drop and licked his lips in gratitude.

Intrigued by the young Irishman's knowledge of whales and such, Bradshaw asked him why he had seen fit to quit the sea and take up the trapper's trade. The ordinarily self-assured Harry stammered and blushed and finally admitted that although he had excelled in throwing the harpoon truly to its mark and was competent in all other seafaring duties and skills, he had been unable to overcome a fatal flaw in a man who means to be a sailor. Harry Yeats, a very able seaman and harpooner extraordinary, gets seasick whenever the ocean becomes stormy.

The ship's crew and our buckskinned brethren continued to trade toasts to each other's health until we became aware that a brisk breeze had sprung up and the deck beneath our feet had commenced to pitch and roll. Several men amongst our landlubberly company commenced to turn green and head for the ship's rail, where they proceeded to make generous donations to the sea critters. Zenas Leonard was amongst the stricken and so was our big Delaware Little Mountain, who lamented, "Damn shame, Tempo, losin' all that good grub!" Harry Yeats resisted the urge to retch as long as he could, but at last he surrendered to the frailty that had cut short his seagoing career.

Captain Bradshaw took pity on the suffering mountaineers and ordered a longboat to take them to shore. The rest of us remained aboard and continued our celebration until dawn, at which time the sailors rowed us to the beach, where we continued the festivities by offering them a mountain-style breakfast. Naturally we couldn't match the exotic foodstuffs with which they had regaled us, but fresh meat was a commodity they hadn't tasted since they departed Boston's rocky shores. The Yankee seamen assured us that it was a more than fair exchange and we made sure to supply them with generous slabs of elk, deer, and bear meat when they returned to the *Lagoda*.

Later that morning we showed Captain Bradshaw the beached whale, whereupon he ordered his crewmen to return to the ship to obtain several empty hogsheads, axes, siphons, and other tools, so that he might salvage the precious spermaceti oil sealed in the monster's huge head.

Harry Yeats had recovered from his seasickness as soon as he set foot on solid ground the night before. Now he volunteered his knowledge of the whaling trade to assist the merchantmen in recovering as much as possible of the valuable whale oil, baleen, and other useful materials from which they might turn a profit. He expressed regret that they lacked try-pots and other tools of the whaling trade that might have allowed them to render out large quantities of oil from the blubber and thereby greatly increase their gains, but Captain Bradford assured him that he was quite satisfied to settle for the easily-accessible spermaceti.

Bradford had thoughtfully ordered his men to bring back from the ship a number of empty bottles, which they filled with whale oil and presented to us as a gift of gratitude. It was a welcome present, for the damp sea air along the coast caused our rifles and other tools and weapons to rust much more rapidly than is the case in the dry Rocky Mountain air.

As we moved off from the giant carcass, I noticed Harry Yeats casting longing glances at the remains of the enormous critter thrown upon the beach, then gazing wistfully out to sea. It was plain to see that, in his heart, the young Irish harpooner had never abandoned his first love, a seafaring life on the oceans of the world, even though he literally lacked the stomach for it. Harry had adapted admirably to our mountain life, but anybody who saw him at that moment could tell that he still pined to return to a whaler's life.

As the *Lagoda* prepared to set sail and continue its trading activities along the California coastline, Captain Bradford advised Joe Walker to make haste to present himself to the Mexican Governor Figueroa at a town called Monterey, some 70 miles south of where we were. He promised to meet us there and to introduce our leader to the governor, as well as to interpret the Spaniard tongue for him if necessary.

Bradford assured Walker that he would be well-received by the governor. The Mexican government in California was weak and it feared encroachment by British and Russian forces coming down from the north. The Russians had already established a colony on the coast. Walker and his men might be welcomed by Figueroa as a possible deterrent against future incursions. Our captain assured Bradshaw that we would get to Monterey as rapidly as our still-recovering livestock would allow.

The *Lagoda* sailed next day on the morning tide and we set off southward as soon as its sails disappeared in the mist. At first we hiked through marshy meadows along the shoreline, where late on the first day we discovered another huge fish thrown up on the beach by the angry sea. This one measured 47 feet long and possessed a 12-inch horn or spear projecting from its nose. Harry informed us that it was not a whale and, because it had likely been there for a spell, its meat was probably unfit to eat.

Traveling through the marshlands nigh the ocean was hard on man and beast, so we turned inland and struck out across a level plain, which provided better walking and an opportunity to trade for pumpkins, beans, and corn with Indians we encountered there. The soil is rich and well-watered, which lets the natives grow melons of enormous size, as well as a galore of other garden truck, without demanding much effort on their part.

Leonard was particularly scornful of the Indians we encountered in that neighborhood, forever calling them "ignorant, dirty, stupid, shiftless" and similar unflattering terms. I am fond of Zenas, but at last I called him on it. "C'mon, Zenas," I challenged, "how can you justify callin' these Indians *dirty,* when you and most of the white-eyes amongst us hardly ever bathe? The Injuns hereabouts are frolicking in the water morning, noon, and night!"

Before Zenas could stutter out a reply, Brass Turtle chimed in. "An' whilst you're at it, why are ye allus callin' 'em *igner'nt* an' *stupid*? 'Pears to me, they know 'bout as much as they need to. What they grow in their gardens an' the fish they catch gives 'em all the vittles they need. Warm as it be hyarabouts, they don't need clothes, an' they be smart enough to stay put an' not be allus traipsin' off somewhars, lookin' fer someplace better'n what they awready got ri'chere!"

"Speakin' o' which," Finn McCool put in, "if ye wish to be usin' yer bloody adjectives, I suggest ye be after applyin' 'em instead to those Paiutes on t'other side o' the mountain we jist crossed." He drew a deep breath and launched into a heartfelt rant. "Dirty, lazy, ignorant, stupid? Those'll do fer a start, but be sure ye add cowardly, thievin', an' murderous, whilst you're at it! If those benighted Paiutes possessed an ounce of enterprise at all, do ye s'pose they'd be starvin' an' shiv'rin' an' scratchin' out a mis'rable existence in that misbegotten purgatory. No, they'd be stirrin' their naked arses an' marchin' out o' that hell-hole an' climbin' the mountain like we did an' findin' a daycent place to be livin'!"

Zenas stared open-mouthed at the three of us, astonished at our defense of California Indians, before he clamped his jaw tight, heaved himself to his feet, and stalked off with nary a word of reply.

"Think we changed his mind?" I asked innocently, convinced that we hadn't.

"Not a chance in the bloody world," McCool averred.

"He dassn't ever admit he's wrong," Brass Turtle declared. "If he ever does, his whole world'll come tumblin' 'round his gawddamn ears. Hell! I reckon he has trouble enough puttin' up with us Injuns an' Irishers, as it is!"

In the last week of November, whilst we were still traveling to see the governor at Monterey, the captain called a halt in the midst of an area of rough hills, near a fresh-flowing crick, surrounded by tall stands of timber, abundant graze for our animals, and plenty of game critters of every kind, except, naturally, buffalo. Our traveling afoot for lack of horses to ride had completely worn out everybody's moccasins. The entire company was nearly barefoot. Winter was coming on and nobody knew how the Spaniards might greet us when we came up with them at last. Joe Walker reckoned that where we were was a good place to halt and get ourselves reshod. Accordingly, early next morning he sent out half the company to get hides to make moccasins. We were more successful than Walker dared hope. We returned to camp at dusk with the tongues and some of the hides of 93 deer and elk, as well as those of several wild cattle, with which that neighborhood abounds.

Although the wild cattle can be ferocious when cornered or wounded, they are exceedingly shy, hiding out in the daytime and feeding mainly at night. Compared with those cattle, the deer and elk thereabouts are relatively tame. We butchered some of the cattle on the spot and carried the choice parts back to camp, where the beef, which was quite fat, was pronounced edible but naturally much inferior to Rocky Mountain buffalo. If the Greek gods of Mount Olympus had feasted our company with their private stock of ambrosia, I am sure that our people would have requested buffalo hump instead.

We spent the next few days curing and tanning hides, making moccasins, and feasting on the enormous amount of fresh meat that we harvested. It was a pleasant respite from our constant traveling and we made the most of it with story-telling, music and song, and reading aloud from the works of the Scottish poet and novelist Sir Walter Scott, the Holy Bible, and Mister William Shakespeare. Our company of rough and ready, hard-bitten trappers, strong men unfazed by peril or hardship, gathered like schoolboys, hushing the rowdies amongst them, to listen enraptured to romantic tales of princes and rebels and heroes and villains in faraway lands and days of old.

After a pleasant few days in that hilly region, we resumed our southward hike, well-rested and stoutly-shod, still leading our critters, which were regaining strength enough to carry an increasing amount of our plunder, although not yet ourselves. Zeetlah and Half-horse had long since gained the respect and gratitude of Joe Walker by the care they bestowed on our animals and as many others as they had time for, including those of Walker and Leonard. Since we arrived in California, Zeetlah had been forever poking about in the brush, seeking herbs and roots and suchlike natural truck, brewing it into medicines, and dosing the critters with it. Our livestock had commenced to bloom under his care and we reckoned it wouldn't be long until we would be traveling astride instead of on shank's mare.

Wild cattle scattered at our approach, but we gained an occasional glimpse of them as they fled. They are very tall, rangy, and their horns are enormous, especially the cows. As we departed the hill country, we found one of those horns which measured three-and-a-half feet long and a foot around at the base, far bigger than any of us had ever seen at home.

Leaving the hills behind, we continued across a level plain and by day's end arrived on the bank of a measly crick, where we encamped. The smoke of our cookfires attracted the attention of a party of eight Spaniards—fine, affable, well-dressed, well-mounted, portly-looking men—who rode into camp and made themselves pretty much at home, joining us at supper and spreading their bedrolls alongside our own. Neither Walker nor Leonard knew a word of the Spaniard tongue and, not surprisingly, our Santa Fe trappers' knowledge of Spanish proved to be limited to the few words and phrases they had needed to get drunk and laid in Santa Fe and Taos. Cesár Pérez and Micah Buck rose to previously unattained heights in Joe Walker's esteem.

Our visitors explained that they were on their way to the town of Monterey and volunteered to guide us there on the morrow, which offer was gratefully accepted by our leader. From their clothing and easy-going manners it was apparent that these were well-to-do gentlemen, although Zenas unaccountably insisted that they were outcasts like ourselves. I was fascinated by their garb, tall-crowned, broad-brimmed *sombreros*, enormous six-inch jingling spurs, a colorful small blanket called a serape flung over one shoulder. Each of them wore a short, waist-length, richly-embroidered *charro* jacket and bell-bottomed *pantalones* with triangles of red satin inserted in the seams at the cuff, leather *chaparreras* worn over their *pantalones* when they were on horseback, and a colorful sash around their middle, in which a flintlock *pistola* and a long-bladed dagger were half-concealed. Naturally I learned the Spanish words I just used rather later in our California journey.

~o ~o ~o

Next morning we resumed our journey, accompanied by our Spaniard guides, who showed us the way to the home of Mister John Gilroy, a native of Scotland who had been living in California for nigh twenty years, after being left there to die of the scurvy by his British ship's captain. He had employed that time well, converting to the Roman Catholic religion, which California's

Mexican government requires of all its citizens, acquiring a Spanish bride and a sizeable estate as her dowry, and developing his acres into a productive farm. Once Mister Gilroy got over the shock caused by the barbarous appearance of our people—dirty, unshaven, and bristling with weaponry—he appeared delighted to receive us in his home. At first we experienced considerable difficulty in understanding his welcoming words. He explained that he rarely had an opportunity to speak his native tongue, that he had ceased even to dream in English. Zenas kept calling him an old man, but the gentleman was scarcely forty years old, which testifies more to Leonard's youth and *naiveté* than to any debility on the part of our host, who appeared to be in the prime of his life.

Mister Gilroy explained that we were only 35 miles distant from Monterey and that we would pass by the Mission of San Juan on our way. Then he threw open the doors of his larder and his cellar and entertained our company with the best of his produce. Naturally we reciprocated by contributing a plenitude of wild game to the feasting, which went on until late in the evening. Our host and his shy Spanish lady particularly enjoyed the music of Anse and Harry and the spirited singing that rocked the rafters of their whitewashed country home.

₧   ₧   ₧

Shortly after we bade farewell to Mister Gilroy and headed in the direction of Monterey, Captain Walker called a halt on the bank of a crick and announced that it was time that we all made ourselves presentable. What he said was, "I di'nt reelize jist haow hard-lookin' all of us've been gittin', cornsid'rin' that we di'nt git this ugly all of a sudden. We been addin' jist a mite o' dirt an' ugly ever' day, until we be lookin' naow like Satan's Legion come' straight out o' hell!

"When I saw the look on that'ere Scotty feller's face when he fust laid eyes on us, it come to me that that'ere Spaniard guv'nor ain't abaout to roll aout no welcome mat fer a pack o' hairy ragamuffins lookin' like we do! Naow I don't 'spec ye kin quit lookin' ugly—that's likely yer nature an' yer pa's fault—but ye kin all git yorese'fs a whole lot cleaner than ye be right naow an' ye kin scrub the dirt off'n yer clothes. Those o' ye what shave fer goin' to ronnyvoo had oughter do it naow an' them what wears a beard all the time, like me, had oughter trim it down to lookin' halfway decent. If ye don't have scissors, ye kin borry mine.

"We'll be comin' on to one o' them Spaniard missions purty quick an' I don't want the word gittin' aout that Satan's imps are on the prod! So git to it!"

The foregoing pretty well captures the spirit and flavor of Joseph Walker's style of command. He usually laced his orders with enough humor and commonsense to make even unwelcome requirements acceptable to men who are normally hostile to any authority.

Naturally Tuttle Thompson groaned the loudest amongst our bunch at the prospect of bathing, but he brightened somewhat when Brass Turtle reminded him that we would likely be encountering women at the mission. "Ye cain't be keepin' downwind of 'em all o' the time, Tuttle," he advised, "so ye'd best be scrapin' off some o' that'ere muck an' ha'r afore we git thar."

"S'pose you're right," Tuttle admitted ruefully, "but what ef thar ain't no wimmenfolk thar at ther mission? All o' thi'shere bathin' an' shavin'll be purely wasted!"

"Then there's sure to be some women elsewhere, Tuttle lad," Finn advised, "an' you'll be ready fer 'em whin ye find 'em."

The Delawares, Micah, my father, and I had already bathed in the crick that flowed behind Gilroy's farmhouse, as we do each morning whenever we can, but now I took that opportunity to shave off the scant amount of whiskers I had accumulated during the several months since we departed Bear River. I don't possess much hair on my body or whiskers, either, but it felt good to run my hand over smooth cheeks and chin once again.

As you might expect, once they got to it, there was much horseplay amongst the trappers frolicking in the crick, ducking one another and splashing like schoolboys, but gradually, as a ton or two of desert sand and soil and untold gallons of ancient sweat washed away downstream and razors, scissors, combs, and hairbrushes came into play, our hirsute brigade commenced to resemble actual human beings instead of a battalion of grizzly bears. By day's end, most of the men were clean-shaven, possibly because somebody, likely Tuttle, had circulated a rumor that the mission was staffed exclusively by women.

❧   ❧   ❧

Which wasn't altogether true, but there were plenty of Indian women at the Mission San Juan Bautista, where we arrived at dusk the following day after a brisk march over rutted roads across a broad prairie. There was also a great number of Indian men there, about six or seven hundred in all, counting both sexes, all of them being Christianized by a score of Franciscan friars and being taught civilized skills by another score of lay teachers.

Naturally the Indians we saw at the mission were fully clothed, as you might expect in a place run by priests, but the sly looks many of the women directed at our men indicated that getting them naked under the right circumstances would not be a difficult chore.

Immediately upon our arrival, Captain Walker summoned Cesár and Micah and went directly to the monastery to present himself to the abbot, explaining who we were and why we were in that country, assuring the reverend gentleman that we meant no harm, and requesting permission to remain in that neighborhood for a spell, which was granted.

The abbot assigned one of his friars to guide us to a desirable location well-furnished with grass, plentiful timber and firewood, and a sizeable fresh-running crick, where we pitched our camp. Next day, we commenced building a breastwork to fend off a possible attack and to discourage thieving Indians from pilfering our plunder. Building the breastwork turned out to be a mostly gratuitous effort, for in no time at all, every night, there were nearly as many Indians of the female persuasion inside our bulwark as there were trappers.

The behavior of the mission Indians toward us was rather different from what we had experienced with the coastal fishermen farther north. Although these people were apparently of the same racial stock, they were of a sturdier build, likely because they were better fed, and much more direct in their manner with us, especially the womenfolk.

Considering what we had experienced in previous months, our situation at the mission was idyllic. That country abounded with beaver and game critters and the friars were happy to trade their garden truck in exchange for deer, elk, and bear meat, which we harvested from the countryside without much effort. The captain's early concern about a possible attack by Spaniards or Indians appeared to be groundless and he determined that the company would be well-advised to remain where we were and not proceed farther into the country, where graze and game might be scarce and where the arrival of sixty well-armed men might arouse fear and hostility amongst the Spaniards.

On the first day of December 1833, Captain Walker obtained what is called a *visa*, a local passport, from the abbot, who is also the *alcalde*, like a mayor, of that district, so that he might travel unimpeded to visit the governor of California in Monterey. He left Zenas Leonard in charge of the camp with Cesár Pérez to interpret for him if need be, then summoned Micah and me to accompany him to Monterey.

The town of Monterey is only 20 miles distant from the Mission of San Juan Bautista, but Captain Walker thought it best that we ride horseback into the capital city of California, so we saddled the three best horses he had obtained from the Indians on our way to the coast and used the other two to carry our sleeprobes and other belongings. We covered the distance in half a day, then sought out Captain Bradshaw at the harbor, so that he might introduce our leader to the governor, as he had offered to do.

Riding through Monterey, I was struck by how small the capital of Upper California is. By my reckoning, it contains hardly more than four hundred people, who occupy fewer than fifty houses, one Catholic church, a courthouse, and a military fort overlooking the bay, which boasts several pieces of ancient artillery. The place looked prosperous enough, howsomever, and the few Spaniards we saw strolling about appeared to be well-to-do.

When we arrived at the residence of Governor Figueroa, whom Captain Bradshaw referred to as *el Gobernador*, we were shown into a beautifully-appointed drawing room which apparently functioned as that gentleman's office. I was immediately struck by the almost comical contrast between the three buckskin-clad ragamuffins who had come a-calling and the dignified patrician who welcomed us into his quarters. *El Gobernador* was clad in what Captain Bradshaw told us later is the Castilian Spanish style, white silk stockings, black velvet knee breeches, shiny leather slippers fastened with jewel-encrusted buckles, a fine Toledo sword on his belt, a scarlet silk sash around his ample middle, from which gleamed the well-polished stock of a flintlock *pistola* and the ornate haft of a sheathed dagger. Even indoors, he wore a tall-crowned, broad-brimmed *sombrero* gleaming with gold thread. His short, waist-length, braided, velvet *charro*-style jacket was trimmed with intricate gold embroidery and it shone with massive gold buttons. Whilst Micah was interpreting Walker's introductory remarks, Captain Bradford whispered that *el Gobernador* Figueroa was one of the genuine *sangre azul*, aristocratic bluebloods. He certainly dressed the part. The gentleman was past middle age, but his leathery face was handsome, and his calloused hands were those of a man who was no stranger to outdoor work.

Captain Walker presented his Mexican passport that Captain Bonneville had obtained from the Mexican consul in New York a year or more before, which authorized Walker and his company of men to enter the province. Figueroa barely glanced at it, scribbled a brief endorsement, and returned it to our leader, saying that Captain Bradford's confidence in us was good enough for him. Then he told Walker what we had hoped to hear. He said that we were free to hunt and trap as much as we wished, but not on Indian lands, and that we were free to trade with Spaniards, but not with Indians. He said, too, that our people must refrain from brawling or molesting either Spaniards or Indians. All of which conditions Captain Walker readily agreed to abide by.

Captain Bradford returned to his ship, after informing us that he would return to Monterey at Christmastime and inviting all of us to celebrate the holiday with him and his crew.

In spite of the innkeeper's protestations, a single glance at the flea-bitten accommodations offered at the only *posada* in town convinced us that we would be wise to roll out our sleeprobes in the woods somewhere out of town. Which we did.

❧ ❧ ❧

Now that he had secured the governor's approval and protection, Walker encouraged the men to make our quarters more comfortable at our San Juan encampment. We continued to occupy bowers covered with animal skins and scraps of ship's canvas, however, much as we do in the Rockies. We received daily visits by Indian men and some of the Spaniards who worked at the mission, all of them curious to see how we lived, which, except for our shelters, wasn't much different from their own way of life. And the giggles and moans of female voices after dark attested to an equal curiosity on the part of the native women concerning the amorous nature of the big, leather-clad men from beyond the eastern mountains.

Game critters and beaver continued to be plentiful thereabouts, although we needed to range farther afield as time went on, for sixty men require a plenitude of meat, besides the amount we traded for garden truck with the friars. Grapes from the mission's vineyards provided a supply of strong wine and a fiery raw brandy called *aguardiente*, which were intended solely for the friars and their Spaniard employees, but the Indians were adept at spiriting off ardent spirits from the mission cellars. A thriving bootleg traffic in potent alcohol traded for beads and trinkets and suchlike soon developed between the Indian dormitories and our sylvan encampment.

The friars mostly occupy themselves with civilizing their Indian charges by instructing the men in religious matters for several hours each day, after which the lay teachers devote the rest of the day to teaching them the arts of farming food crops and animal husbandry, as well as methods of simple construction and irrigation. Indian women are trained in cooking, sewing, child care, and other skills of civilized housewifery.

The church buildings at San Juan are admirably built of sun-dried clay bricks called *adobes*, with remarkably thick walls, a belfry, and roofs covered in red tiles. Zenas continually flattered himself and his kind by harping on the superiority of the whiteman over the Indian by comparing San Juan's sturdy religious buildings with the simple pole-and-thatch shelters which house the mission's native residents, until, once again, Turtle, Finn, and I got fed up and took him to task by pointing out that the durable buildings required in cold European and eastern American winters are not necessary in the mild California climate, so naturally the natives never learned to build them until the *padres* enslaved them to do so. Again, Zenas stalked off in a huff. Significantly, only San Juan's friars and the European laity occupy the *adobe* structures. Pole-and-thatch is apparently adequate for Indians.

The mission's Indian cowherds, called *vaqueros*, excel in both horsemanship and courage. Soon after our arrival there, they showed us how they capture wild cattle, which abound in that neighborhood. They work in pairs, each man mounted on his fastest, most manageable horse, each equipped with a braided rawhide rope equipped with a noose, called a *reata*. Our bunch were no strangers to that very useful tool, for Cesár Pérez had taught us how to use it seven years before when he first joined us, but, amongst us, only Cesár possessed the skill of those Indian *vaqueros*. All of us soon traded for new, well-oiled *reatas* to replace our worn old lassos.

When a wild bull or cow is first started out of the brush, both *vaqueros* give chase. The rider who first catches up throws his loop around the head or horns, yanks the noose tight, wraps the rope several times around the pommel post of his saddle, then brings his mount to an abrupt halt, which ideally throws the animal to the ground without breaking its neck. If the cow-critter escapes serious injury, the second *vaquero* rides forward with his noose and snares one hind leg, which lets them control the stoutest, most ferocious bull by pulling in opposite directions until the animal is exhausted. If the critter stalls and refuses to advance, the man in the rear whips him and the leader teases the brute until he charges, in which event that *vaquero* takes off at a gallop, dragging the bull behind him, the second man urging him on with a horsewhip called a *cuarta*. They may run as far as two or three miles in this fashion until they bring the exhausted animal into camp, where they stretch him and throw him once again and one man dismounts and cuts his throat with a large knife. It is an occupation reserved for excellent horsemen on well-trained courageous horses, an activity that is not for the faint of heart.

Vaqueros, both Spaniards and Indians, prefer to perform all of their chores a-horseback, if at all possible. If they need firewood, they ride into the forest, find a suitable log, throw their loop around it, and drag it home. They are all expert horsemen, constantly in the saddle, either at work or training their horses to ever higher degrees of perfection.

∽ ∽ ∽

About a week before Christmas 1833, Captain Walker proposed to make a tramp through the countryside to observe California life and manners and he invited Zenas, Micah, and me to accompany him. He left Cesár behind in case some matter came up that required better communication than sign language or shouting louder and louder, which is the customary American method of communicating with non-English-speakers.

Our horses had by that time recovered from their earlier privation and were once again able to carry us and the modest amount of plunder we took with us. Each of us brought only two animals. I mostly rode Davey and my favorite mule Sugarfoot was usually loaded with my sleeprobes and other gear. It was a pleasure to have my own fine animals, lately grown seal-fat and frisky, once again under saddle.

When we departed our San Juan camp we headed southeast, intending to return by way of Monterey. The well-forested country through which we passed possessed rich, well-watered soil that appeared to offer rich farming opportunities, but it was sparsely-populated with few Indians and even fewer Spaniards, whose principal interest and enjoyment, and, in the case of wealthy Spaniards, their sole occupation, appeared to be the chase. It was hard to fault them, for the country abounded with elk and deer and wild cattle lurked in every copse and gully.

After a time, Micah and I took to riding some distance in advance of our two companions, for Zenas Leonard's sour observations concerning the ignorance and indolence and lack of ingenuity of the local populace commenced to chafe on Micah's usually easy-going personality and on my own. Zenas had somehow managed to transport his hidebound provincial values and attitudes intact from his little backwater Pennsylvania village all the way to the Rocky Mountains, then on to California. Nothing suited him or gained his approval, whether it be the dark complexion and puny physiques of the Indians or their rude habitations, their clothing or lack of it, and especially their indifference to productive work. Well-to-do Spaniards fared little better in his severe judgments. They universally failed to measure up to Pennsylvania standards of housekeeping, cuisine, building standards, cultural achievement, ambition, industry, agriculture, or animal husbandry.

From what we could tell, Joseph Walker paid no nevermind to Leonard's constant carping about the shortcomings of California's native residents. Apparently he cultivated a deaf ear when Zenas voiced his harsh opinions, a talent that Micah and I envied but never succeeded in acquiring.

Indian dwellings consist of a single room composed of *adobe* brick walls with a pole-and-thatch roof and well-beetled dirt floors pounded perfectly level and nearly waterproof, with a small fireplace at one corner. Beds consist of blankets spread on a large hide, which are rolled up in daytime and used for seating. They eat well enough, mostly wild game and soup made of beef and beans, together with a small amount of unleavened bread.

Wealthier Spaniards occupy much more elaborate houses that boast *adobe* walls a yard thick, tiled roofs, and windows covered with oiled parchment. Although their floors may be covered with costly imported furniture and oriental rugs, those floors are always earthen.

The Catholic missions supply most of the Indian labor that supports the very productive agriculture that makes possible the easy life and leisure of the Spaniard ruling class—all, naturally, in the name of Christianizing the benighted natives, called *neófitos—neophytes*—by the *padres*. Their principal crops are wheat, corn, and beans and they also cultivate many vineyards, which produce a large quantity of wine, their principal drink, as well as a powerful native brandy called *aguardiente*.

Micah, as you might expect, took a less than sympathetic view of the forced servitude of the mission Indians, especially the harsh discipline and severe punishments inflicted by the *padres* on unruly Indians who try to resist their bondage, including the branding of repeat offenders. He held his tongue, howsomever, around Walker and Leonard, for his opinions were not likely to fall on a sympathetic ear with either of them.

The large unpaid work force of mission Indian *neófitos*, together with the rich, mellow soil and mild climate, allow the friars to reap large harvests of wheat, corn, beans, and wine grapes, in spite of primitive farming methods and tools. Plows are made from a forked branch from the forest hauled by a yoke or two of oxen. Harrows consist simply of a big bush weighted down with heavy rocks and dragged over the ground. Only in California's rich and tender soil could such methods succeed.

In all our travels we never saw a barn or stable. Livestock roams free, except for a few favorite horses or prize cattle confined in open-air paddocks called *corrals*. Even cultivated cropland isn't fenced, although it may be invaded by herds of horses, mules, or horned cattle, protected only by young Indian boys charged with driving them off. On the rare occasion when a *vaquero* might wish to milk a cow, he mounts his horse, runs her down, ropes her head and throws her, ties her feet, and milks her, whilst his well-trained horse pulls back on the rope to keep her in place.

Horseback skills are essential tools in every mountaineer's kit for survival and success in the trapping trade, so we naturally admired the Spaniards for their magnificent horsemanship, their ability to train and control their horses to hold steady and obey in situations that normally would cause a horse to rear over backwards in an effort to escape. What we couldn't understand or stomach, howsomever, is their casual cruelty to those admirable creatures. The same romantic fellow who weeps over a sentimental ballad and courts his intended *señorita* in a most gentle manner treats his horses in the most barbarous way imaginable with nary a blush or twinge of conscience.

Needle-sharp six-inch rowels on the common Spaniard spur often rip a fatal gash in a horse's belly and the cruel Spanish spade bit can, in reckless hands, sever the critter's tongue at the root. Time and again, we've seen young *vaqueros* ride in with a gaping hole in their horse's belly caused by vicious spurring, half a yard of gut trailing from the wound. Instead of sewing up the gash, they merely strip off the saddle, rope another mount from their numerous *remuda*, and ride back to their chore, leaving the unfortunate creature to die from gangrene or, more likely, as coyote bait.

"They keep sayin' it don't matter 'cause they got so many hosses runnin' free all over Californy," Tuttle fumed in disgust, "but it ain't right to be treatin' no critter like thet—not ef ye got jest one hoss or ten thousand of 'em!"

Tuttle's revulsion was mild compared with that of young Half-horse, who on several occasions had to be restrained by his uncle or Little Mountain from attacking Spaniards who treated their animals in the manner described above.

Spaniard cruelty isn't confined only to horses. A popular sport amongst those people is the *carrera del gallo*, or rooster-pull, which involves burying well-greased chickens neck-deep in the ground, then riding past at a full gallop and leaning down to snatch off the head.

Their most common method of gentling young wild horses is brief and not at all gentle. The critter is roped and thrown to the ground, haltered, blindfolded, and saddled before an adventurous and extremely athletic *vaquero* slides into the saddle and urges him to rise. If the horse proves to be unmanageable—and almost every wild critter is bound to object to an unfamiliar presence on his back—the rider spurs and whips him unmercifully with a stout leather *cuarta* and gallops him out onto the prairie, urging him onward until he can no longer stand and sinks to the ground, totally exhausted and cowed. After such an experience, a horse is usually reasonably docile and ready for training.

California offers only two seasons in the year, one wet, roughly October through January, the other mostly dry, which is the rest of the year. During the driest months, some *Californios* gather large droves of mules and drive them some 1400 miles through the southern deserts to market in Santa Fe, where they find a ready market amongst Missouri traders who buy them for a price of from $6 to $10 each in gold and silver hard money, as well as bartering for silks, jewelry, and groceries.

When we learned of that practice, Micah and I turned to each other and, with almost a single voice, wondered aloud why Joe Walker chose to climb that godawful mountain to get into and out of California. We reckoned that, after all, one desert is bound to be much the same as another. We had come to rely on Walker's otherwise good judgment, howsomever, so we refrained from mentioning the matter to him.

On Christmas day we arrived at the Catholic mission of San José, about ten miles north of Monterey, which is much like the San Juan mission, except that it boasts a much larger and better-appointed church. We remained there for two days, giving our mounts time to restore themselves in the mission stables. A hasty glance at *el Gobernador's* endorsement on Walker's passport was all it took for the abbot to welcome us to the best that the mission could offer, which at Christmastime proved to be especially lavish.

Half a day's journey from the Mission San José brought us to Monterey, where we tarried with Captain Bradshaw, who had returned there with the *Lagoda* from trading northwards along the coast as far as the Russian colony. We were awaiting the arrival of some of our trappers, who were expected to bring some of the peltries that we had collected in California.

Our people arrived on the 29th, bringing with them enough beaver plews to trade with Captain Bradford for a stock of gunpowder, galena, and percussion caps, as well as a supply of trade goods and groceries required for the return trip to the Rockies.

Although we had been absent from our San Juan camp less than a fortnight, it was good to see men from our own bunch—Brass Turtle and Little Mountain, Cesár, Tuttle, and Anse Tolliver—as well as Joe Meek, Doc Newell, and Harry Yeats, amongst others. Besides a substantial load of beaver plews, our men brought with them a supply of Mission wine and *aguardiente*, as well as a plenitude of elk, deer, and bear meat and choice cuts of wild cow beef they had harvested along the trail to Monterey. Captain Walker invited Captain Bradshaw and his crew to spend the last day of 1833 ashore with us, celebrating our successful journey to California, which the master of the good ship *Lagoda* accepted with the *proviso* that all of us would observe New Year's Day aboard his vessel. Which, naturally, we did.

Thus followed two days of riotous feasting, drinking, fiddle and cittern music, singing, and swapping outrageous yarns of impossible deeds of derring-do at sea and in the Rocky Mountains, first on shore, next day aboard the *Lagoda*. Although our trappers did their manful best to out-fib the mariners, Bradshaw's tars easily took the palm for their mendacious skill. Joe Meek lied most colorfully, employing great feats of imagination and invention, but he was no match for our salty friends. "Them'ere sailor-boys're jist damn lucky Black Harris ain't along with us," Brass Turtle observed with a grin. "He'd'a had 'em tongue-tied fer sure with his tall tales. Thar ain't a better liar on land ner sea!"

Fortunately the bay at Monterey remained calm throughout the celebration, so Zenas, Little Mountain, Harry, and others who are prone to seasickness were able to enjoy the festivities as much as those of us who are blessed with sturdier stomachs.

Naturally we mountaineers itched to get even after our ignominious defeat at tall-tale-telling, so when we returned to shore on New Year's day, we staged a shooting-match with the sailors, which convinced them that although they could best us in telling "long yarns," we were, by far, their superiors with the long rifle.

Next morning, the 2nd of January 1834, Captain Bradshaw insisted that we return to his ship to "take a glass" with Governor Figueroa to celebrate the new year, which naturally we did, happily. When we returned to shore, the governor was apparently in an ebullient mood. He called to Cesár and Micah to come to his side to interpret for him. Then he offered Captain Walker a tract of prime agricultural land seven miles square if he would bring to California fifty families of American settlers skilled in various mechanical arts. Joe Walker actually blushed and stammered, which is something nobody ever saw our normally decisive and resolute leader do before. At length, he declined Figueroa's princely offer, choosing his words with extreme care, in order to avoid offending our benefactor. Micah and Cesár, neither of whom is skilled in polite diplomatic parlance, took turns trying to phrase Joe's refusal in words that wouldn't upset the governor. At last Figueroa took pity on all three of them and assured them that he understood our leader's reluctance to renounce his citizenship and declared that he admired Walker's patriotic loyalty to his homeland.

We departed Monterey soon thereafter, likely sooner than we might have done otherwise, bidding the *Gobernador* a courteous farewell and expressing our gratitude for his protection.

On the ride back to San Juan Bautista, Joe Walker confessed to mixed feelings concerning his refusal to accept Figueroa's offer. "I war hard put fer a spell thar to turn 'im down. A feller could git rich as hell in jist a couple-three years hyarabouts, but I jist couldn't bring m'se'f to turn muh back on ever'thin' I hold wuthwhile about Amurrica. Nope. Couldn't do it."

                                                                        ર   ર   ર

Everything was in order in our camp at the mission, except for Levi Phillips, who had had a serious run-in with a sow grizzly and her cubs early that day. He had been out hunting and killed a fat deer, which he gutted, then hung the carcass from a tree limb before heading back to camp afoot to get a horse to bring in his kill. About a mile along the trail, he topped a low rise and came face-to-face with an old grizzly sow trailing a pair of cubs. She naturally r'ared up on her hocks and roared her displeasure at Levi's intrusion, batting air with her paws and threatening to send him off to the Happy Hunting Ground. Levi was in a quandary. He was too close to the bear to run, yet he feared that if he took a shot and only wounded her, she would make mincemeat of him. He ran. She caught up within a stride or two and proceeded to rip him to shreds. Levi did the only sensible thing he could do. He covered his head with his hands and played dead. Still snorting and growling, she quit her attack and shambled off, leaving our trapper shocked, dazed, and bleeding so badly that several hours passed before he was able to rise and stagger back to camp, where he arrived shortly before our party returned from Monterey.

Zeetlah and Finn McCool were attending to Phillips when we rode up. So intent were they on treating his wounds, laving dirt from the horribly-mangled flesh, applying spider webs to stanch the bleeding, and splinting his broken arm that they scarcely acknowledged our presence. Zeetlah stepped away from the wounded man and rummaged in his saddle bags, bringing out an assortment of horns, hollow bones, and little glass bottles, then stirring a mixture of their contents into half a cup of water. Joe Walker squatted nearby, closely observing the old Delaware's every move. Zeetlah looked up at me and winked. "Remembah sleep-vittle, Tempo?" he asked me. "Gonna quit hurtin' purty damn quick." Then he propped Levi against his chest and forced the contents of the cup into his mouth. The wounded trapper gagged, coughed, quit groaning, and commenced snoring, which allowed our two makeshift *medicos* to proceed unhindered with their life-saving ministrations.

I remembered Zeetlah's "sleep-vittle" very well. The vile-tasting concoction had twice left me with a couple blank places in my memory instead of what would have been unpleasant recollections of two very painful surgeries the year before. Levi Phillips was indeed fortunate that Zeetlah happened to be nigh.

Zenas was visibly upset by Phillips's misfortune, but, it turned out, mainly because Levi's serious injuries and near-death marred the perfect record that the expedition had maintained up to that point. At first I thought Zenas was showing off some wry comical antic, but I soon realized that he was deadly serious. In the months since we had departed Bear River,

Leonard's loyalty and admiration of Joseph Walker had grown into something like a literal worship of his hero. He bragged excessively on Walker's success in losing only 24 horses on our torturous passage of the mountains and he implied that the number would have been fewer if we hadn't eaten 17 of them. Now his manner suggested that Levi's life-threatening mishap was somehow an affront to our leader.

"'Pears to me," Tuttle observed dryly, "Zenas be takin' thet'ere job o' bein' seegundo fer Joe Walker a mite too serious. Ain't nobody keepin' no scores fer thi'shere expeedishun."

"That's about so," Brass Turtle agreed. "A year arter we git back, ain't nobody goin' to remember we ever made this hike 'ceptin' them few as done it."

"An' besides, Joe don't need no defendin', nohaow," put in Anse Tolliver, ever mindful of his kinship with Walker. "He be runnin' thi'shere brigade jist fine!" Which was so. By and large, the men were content with our situation and satisfied with Walker's firm but easy-going style of leadership.

Now that our horses were restored to good health and strength, groups of our people took to visiting Spaniard communities in the neighborhood of the Mission San Juan Bautista. Mindful of Captain Walker's repeated warnings concerning the need to pay proper respect to the Spaniards and their womenfolk, lest we all suffer reprisals, they mostly conducted themselves with restraint and reasonably decent manners. If a trapper got too liquored up and attempted to visit his amorous intentions on a married lady, his companions were usually quick to discourage such behavior. Most of our trappers agreed with Tuttle when he observed, "Hell! Thar ain't no p'int in killin' ther gawddamn goose what's layin' ther golden aigs hyarabouts, jest fer gittin' a-holt o' one partic'lar woman, when thar's a plenitude o' willin' fillies jest waitin' ter git asked."

Even Bill Williams and his wild Santa Fe cronies appeared to be content to enjoy themselves within the bounds of reasonably decent behavior that Joe Walker required of his brigade. *Californios* are sufficiently given to indulging in the customary vices concerning gambling, indulgence in ardent spirits, and the pleasures of bed that the rowdies amongst us had no need to demand more than what was freely given.

The Spaniards were as curious about us as we were about them. They were generous with their hospitality, their brandy and wine, and their invitations to join them in the hunt, their *fandangos*, and other recreations. Both men and women are devoted to the use of tobacco, which most of them smoke in the form of *cigarillos*, the tobacco shredded and rolled in a twist of corn husk. It is a pleasant form of smoking, depending, naturally, upon the availability of corn husks.

One particular entertainment may be unique to California, for it requires the occupation of two critters with which that country abounds, grizzly bears and wild cattle, as well as expert horsemen adept in the use of the rawhide *reata*. A number of well-mounted gentlemen, called *caballeros*, ride out onto the prairie seeking a herd of wild cattle. When they find one that suits their purpose, they make wagers on who shall be first to snare a large bull with his loop. At a signal, they all ride off in pursuit of the likely bull. Usually it is the man who owns the fastest horse who wins, for all of them are expert with the *reata*.

When he successfully ropes the critter's horns or head, he secures his rope with a few wraps around the pommel post and turns the bull in a wide arc while his companions assist in roping the hind legs and throwing the bull to the ground, which ends the contest for the time being. The bull is then led off, in the manner I described earlier, to a strong pen, or *corral*, for safekeeping, and bets are paid off. But that is only part of the game.

Next they set off in pursuit of the largest grizzly bear they can find. This is the most dangerous part of the sport, because of the grizzly's tremendous strength and ferocious nature. When they come upon one of the great golden grizzly bears of California which is of suitable size, one man first drops a loop over the bear's head, draws it tight around his neck, and snugs the rope on the pommel post, backing his horse meanwhile to take up slack in the rope, which causes the bear to quit running and prepare for war, at which time a second man sneaks his horse up behind the animal and snares a hind foot. Then the sport really begins, with almost unbelievable feats of dexterity and horsemanship and incredible courage and agility on the part of the well-trained horses.

Naturally the bear is furious and bats at the restraining ropes, seeking to rush at his captors, only to be restrained by one or the other horseman checking his charge. After a time, the bear grows sullen and throws himself down, refusing to move, letting his leg be stretched until the pain becomes too severe, at which he draws up his leg almost effortlessly and pulls his tormentor towards him, horse and all, and the rider is forced to pay out more rope in order to stay clear of the grizzly's teeth and deadly claws.

Now, still another rider snares one of the bear's forelegs or his neck and commences yanking, which infuriates the animal. He beats the ground with his feet and jumps up to do battle, which allows the men to get him moving, dragging, whipping, and coaxing him along to the *corral* where the bull is penned.

After the grizzly is confined in a separate pen, bets are settled and refreshments are consumed. Then the Spaniard gentlemen commence their favorite part of the entertainment. They begin by enraging the bull by pricking him with a sharp nail fixed to a stick, until his anger rises to a warlike pitch, at which time the grizzly bear, which usually needs no goading, is let into the pen with the bull. If, howsomever, the animals refuse to fight, they are tormented by sharp sticks until one or the other delivers a thrust or blow. Then the battle is on without let-up, sometimes lasting as long as half an hour, goring and raking and biting, roaring and bellowing fit to split your ears, hot blood spurting from a hundred wounds, until one of them crumples in defeat. The grizzly is stronger but the cramped quarters of the pen won't let him escape the bull's sharp horns. Usually the bull, battered and bleeding, emerges victorious.

Mountaineers are no strangers to bloodshed and making split-second choices that cause an adversary's death, but pitting animals in bloody contests for pure amusement rubbed most of us the wrong way. "I got no love fer grizzle b'ars," Joe Meek declared after the huge golden bear tottered and fell for the last time, blood gushing from a gaping horn wound ripped in his belly, "but it flat turns muh stomach, makin' 'em suffer an' killin' 'em like thet, jest fer the fun of it!" That remark was especially significant coming from Joe, who had by then already acquired a considerable reputation in the mountains for killing grizzlies for food and in self-defense.

Bets are settled once again and if it is the bear that is defeated, new wagers are made on a different game, which requires a man to enter the pen with the enraged bull, slap his palm upon a specified place on the critter, and escape untouched. When all the bets are made, the daredevil waits at the *corral* gate, his *serape* in hand, while his fellows prick and prod the bull to a fever pitch. Then the hero—or idiot, according to how you view it—steps into the pen, dodges the bull's furious charge, blinds him by throwing the *serape* over the animal's eyes, slaps the designated spot, snatches the *serape* off the bull's head, and dances to safety. If he succeeds in this folly, he wins for all those who bet on him and he receives a substantial percentage of their winnings. If he fails, howsomever, he is treated with contempt and indifference, even by the men who have profited from his failure.

Such was the fate of an old, time-worn Spaniard who volunteered to enter the *corral* and touch the bull, one day when our bunch watched the spectacle. All went well for him until he tried to retrieve his *serape*. The bull gored him in the thigh, throwing him to the ground. The only assistance he received was the other Spaniards plaguing the bull to distract him, while the old fellow crawled unassisted from the *corral*.

Both Tuttle and Joe Meek had been fidgeting throughout the early parts of the old Spaniard's performance, anxious to try their hand at this dangerous sport, until they actually saw the huge bull's massive horn shoved clear through the *vaquero*'s upper leg, great gouts of blood gushing from the wound, and the ashen-faced man scrambling frantically for his life. Our daredevils hastily reconsidered and chose to postpone that particular exploit until another day.

Gambling is a major pastime of *Californios*, men and women alike. Cash money, livestock, merchandise, and personal possessions are freely exchanged as wagers are paid off at horse races, bull-and-bear-fights, card games, and every sort of athletic competition. This custom suited Tuttle Thompson admirably and he may be remembered amongst *Californios* as the man who introduced Old Sledge to their sunny shores, as well as a new card game called Bragg, which Captain Stewart had brought from England and taught to an eager circle of mountaineers, of which, naturally, Tuttle was one.

We stayed on at our encampment nigh the Mission of San Juan Bautista, for we enjoyed excellent relations with the *padres*, the Spaniard teachers, and especially their female Indian charges, until one night when six of Joe Walker's best horses were stolen. Naturally we assumed that Indians had done the thieving. Next morning, Captain Walker sent out scouting parties in several directions to track down our missing livestock. Only one horse was retrieved, that one not from an Indian village but from a Spaniard settlement, which was a great disappointment to us. We had assumed that our hosts would treat us fairly and honorably, but that was not the case.

Walker hustled off to complain to the abbot, who was also the *alcalde* or mayor of that district, enquiring how we might regain our property or how we might be repaid for its loss. Our leader was shocked to learn from the *padre* that custom thereabouts dictates that if a Spaniard is traveling through the country mounted on a poor horse or one that goes lame, he is legally at liberty to help himself to a good horse, either wild or tame, if he can find one, no matter who might own it, and continue his journey. This quaint custom helps to explain why a Spaniard is never seen away from home without his trusty *reata* and is never afoot.

Horse-thieving is the most common kind of theft in California, but it is not considered to be a crime, likely because of the great number of horses thereabouts and how cheap they are. Unbroke colts and fillies can be had for a dollar and well-trained saddle horses rarely cost more than ten dollars.

Walker thought it best that we pack up and move out of that neighborhood before any of our people came in conflict with Spaniards helping themselves to our livestock. Most mountaineers tend to be fond of their horses and mules. We don't take kindly to horse-thieving, local custom or not.

Within a day Walker supplied our company with flour, corn, beans, and whatever other provisions he deemed necessary. And recalling our famine times in the desert and crossing the mountains, many of us stocked up on our own provender, just to be on the safe side.

We set out on a generally eastward course on a sunny mid-January morning, most of us happy to be exploring new country and moving on to untrapped beaver streams. Two days of leisurely travel brought us to the bank of a handsome river, clear-running and sizeable, shaded by tall oaks and elm trees, and bordered by a broad plain of wild oats that stretched to the horizon, providing excellent graze for our horses and mules, as well as affording lush cover for a plenitude of rolling fat elk, deer, and bear. It was unlikely that we could improve on that situation, so Walker decided to establish a permanent camp there until spring, when he planned to cross the coastal mountains and return to the Rockies.

The surrounding hills were laced with beaver-rich streams that fed the large river. After a couple weeks of hunting on the broad prairie and trapping the nearby streams, our bunch grew restless and we left the main camp, telling Captain Walker only that we wished to trap farther afield. The truth was, howsomever, that we had commenced to chafe under the discipline that is necessary to maintain order and good behavior amongst five dozen strong-minded free-trappers. Joe Walker governed his expedition with a light hand, albeit a firm one when required, but our bunch had been successfully leaderless for nearly a dozen years. We regard all authority as bothersome and well-nigh intolerable. Moreover, an abrasive rivalry had sprung up betwixt Rocky Mountain trappers and the Santa Fe crowd led by Bill Williams and his fellow bullies Levin Mitchell and Bill Craig. Trapping the surrounding country on our own hook provided an excuse to escape from both for a spell.

Now that we were no longer competing with other Americans, our daily harvests of plews increased remarkably. The mostly untrapped California streams teemed with beaver and even though their fur was not as thick and luxuriant as it would have been in the much colder Rocky Mountain winter, their greatly increased numbers in our traps more than made up for the lesser quality. We grew ever more greedy in our search for plews, extending our trapping territory eastwards and southwards, probing into the foothills and higher mountain streams, congratulating ourselves the while on having discovered a mountaineer's idea of heaven. "An' best of all," Tuttle observed, "ye don't hafta be wond'rin' ever' gawddamn minute ef some Blackfoot ain't drawin' a bead on yer back whilst ye be payin' mind to yer trappin' chores."

"That's a fact," Brass Turtle agreed. "We'll hafta be eddicatin' ourse'fs all over agin, once we git back to the Rockies, lest we go to actin' like greenhorns fresh out o' the settlements."

"Speakin' o' the Rockies," Finn McCool remarked, "whin d'ye s'pose Cap'n Walker'll be after pullin' up stakes an' headin' east?"

"Not yet, I reckon," Tolliver declared emphatically. "Joe war sayin' we'd best wait 'til spring afore we tried gittin' over that'ere mountain agin an' it ain't springtime yet, even if the weather hyarabaouts allus feels like it."

Nobody wished to quit trapping or, for that matter, to give up our respite from authority, so we assured ourselves that we still had plenty of time before we had to return to the main body of Joe Walker's expedition. We continued trapping and hunting, amassing a wealth of beaver plews that soon had our pack animals tottering under their loads. We lived richly off an abundance of fat game animals, swapping extra meat and trinkets with Indian villagers for corn, beans, acorn meal, and whatever else we desired, often including feminine favors from all-too-willing native women eager to scrape casual acquaintance with the big leather-clad men from another world.

❦   ❦   ❦

We were camped beside a sizeable stream on the open prairie, taking a day off from trapping, occupied in dressing plews, repairing gear, and performing other necessary chores—time, too, for Micah and me to catch up on our journals—when we were visited by a score of well-mounted Spaniard gentlemen who informed us that they were on their way to capture wild horses. Our hunters had been even more successful than usual that morning and we had a plenitude of fresh meat on hand, as well as a goodly supply of other comestibles, so we invited them to join us for supper and to stay with us overnight. Tuttle was feeling especially hospitable, for he had spied one of our visitors swigging from a wineskin, which he was sure contained the fiery brandy Spaniards call *aguardiente*. "I kin smell thet'ere argywenty half a mile off," he confided to me. "Injuns don't make it, nohaow, so we'd best be makin' these hyar Spanyards welcome."

Our guests were not stingy with their wine and brandy. Full bellies and ardent spirits inspired the general good feeling that prevailed that evening, especially when Anse brought out his fiddle and regaled us all with sprightly tunes from his native Tennessee, as well as a few new ones in the Spaniard style he had picked up at *fandangos* we had attended in California.

Cesár and Micah were kept busy explaining to the Spaniards who and what we were, where we had come from, and what we were doing in California. Our visitors were especially intrigued by our trapping of beavers, an occupation not much practiced thereabouts. Although they likely supposed that all of us beaver-hunters were somewhat addled, they were apparently willing to overlook our peculiar lunacy. They invited us to accompany them to a neighborhood where wild horses roamed in abundance, promising to reward us with some of the captured critters in exchange for our help in capturing them.

Our own pack animals had become seriously overloaded with the windfall of plews we had acquired, so the Spaniard gentlemen's offer was welcome. Besides, an opportunity to witness their manner of taking wild horses was an experience none of us was willing to forego. We promised our guests that we would join them. Most enthusiastic of all was young Half-horse, once Zeetlah explained to him what we expected to do on the morrow.

❦   ❦   ❦

Half a day's brisk trot brought us to our destination, a large, strongly-built pen, called a *corral*, enclosing about three-quarters of an acre. Two long wings extend out in the shape of a V from a wide gate at the front of the *corral*, reaching out on the left and right to a distance of about a mile and a half and roughly a quarter-mile wide at the mouth. These wings are made of posts set in the ground joined by poles tied to them by elk- or horsehide thongs, about four feet high. The *corral* at the juncture of the V is built much higher and stronger than the wings and appears to have been in use for many years.

All of us were occupied the remainder of the day in repairing weakened places in the *corral* and the wings, until our hosts were satisfied that the structures were strong enough to contain our intended quarry. We made do that night with cold meat from the night before and I daresay none of us slept soundly, eager as we were for the next day's adventure.

At the first glimmer of light in the eastern sky, we mounted our swiftest horses—in my case, Davey, my dun horse buffalo-runner—separated into several parties of half a dozen each, and rode out in search of bands of wild horses. When we encountered a large bunch, we fanned out around them, turned them, and, whooping and hollering and waving blankets and serapes, drove them into the wide mouth of the giant V, where they were joined by other bunches driven by other bands of horsemen. We followed them into the wings, driving them towards the *corral*, until at last a couple hundred snorting, neighing wild horses thundered into the *corral* and commenced milling about, eyes rolling in fear and excitement, while two men slid strong poles across the entrance to prevent the captured critters from breaking out.

Now we all dismounted and passed close to the outside of the *corral* fence, letting the wild horses get used to the smell of humans and the sound of our voices as we spoke to them in a calm, reassuring manner. When the critters appeared to settle down somewhat, half a dozen men entered the *corral* with their *reatas* and proceeded to rope and tether all the young horses, three years old or less, about a hundred in all. Animals older than that are considered too difficult to tame and were turned loose, once the desirable youngsters were securely tethered to the fence.

Each of the captured horses was fitted with a blindfold, then turned loose inside the *corral* with our saddle horses and mules, where they soon settled down and abandoned much of their scared, distrustful behavior. When he wasn't gathering prairie hay, young Half-horse spent most of his waking hours inside the big *corral*, cooing and chatting with the youngsters, gaining their trust, caressing them, blowing into their nostrils, letting them nuzzle his armpits. By the second day, they hardly shivered when he ran his hands over them.

After two days, the Spaniards announced their intention to return to their homes. They selected twenty-two of the captured horses and presented them to us, two critters for each man in our bunch, even taking care to include the two largest animals for Little Mountain, in the event that he might wish to train them as saddlers. Then they gathered the rest and drove them off, still blindfolded, in the direction of the seacoast, the young captives snuggling close to the men's tame horses for reassurance. As the Spaniards rode out of sight, their laughter and easy banter fading in the distance, Tuttle shook his head and declared solemnly, "Never thought I'd be sayin' this, but them'ere Spanyard fellas'll sartinly do fer knowin' what's what fer gentlin' hosses. It's been a lesson to me!"

"If them young hosses knew what kind o' hurtin's waitin' fer 'em, they'd bust loose an' go runnin' fer their life!" Little Mountain observed sourly.

"Ye'd best be savin' some o' your admiration fer our own Delaware lad, Tuttle," McCool suggested. "He's after teachin' those wild craytchures loike a bloody schoolmarm! An' they 'pear to be lovin' it!"

∾ ∾ ∾

And so it appeared. Now that Half-horse's charges had been reduced to only two-and-twenty, he was able to devote much more time to each of them, getting them halter-broke, accustomed to being led around by a halter-shank, and, most difficult of all, accepting a weight on their back. Even though he is remarkably handy with critters, our young Delaware suffered a passel of scrapes and bruises as he hurried to ready our new animals for our return to Walker's brigade.

Micah, Cesár, Powatawa, and I helped out whenever Half-horse asked us to do so, leading blindfolded horses around the *corral*, slipping a rope halter over their sensitive ears, crooning to them in a soft, reassuring voice, and avoiding vicious cow-kicks whenever we snugged up the cincha on a packsaddle. Meanwhile, the rest of our people were busy building packsaddles and fashioning other horse gear needed to equip our new livestock for their packing chore.

At the end of the second day Zeetlah announced with a sly smirk that Half-horse reckoned his green-broke horses were ready for the trail. The smirk was not lost on the rest of us, who were accustomed to the old man's wry humor, but, next morning, Half-horse gave his uncle the lie. Our new livestock proved to be surprisingly docile, accepting their unfamiliar burdens with hardly any more objection than experienced pack animals offer after a long layoff, say, at winter camp. They were still blindfolded, howsomever, and Half-horse advised us to secure the halter of each new horse close to the neck of a steady experienced pack animal, at least for the first day or two.

The first day's route led over a broad, level prairie which offered no obstacles or difficulties for our blindfolded animals. Once they fell into the rhythm of overland travel and came to rely on the comforting presence of their seasoned equine companion, most of them plodded along like veterans. The few who didn't were soon educated by nips and kicks from their yoke-mates. At day's end, we hobbled the new critters no differently from our other livestock, removed their blindfolds, and turned all of them out to graze overnight.

❧ ❧ ❧

A few days steady travel returned us, on the second day of March 1834, to Walker's campground, which, to our dismay, was mostly empty, except for the bowers and grazing critters of half a dozen trappers. Their surprise appeared to equal our own, for it was plain to see, even at a distance, that the expedition had given up on ever seeing us again. George Nidever was first to hail our arrival and came riding out to greet us. "Howdy!" he called out. "Whar the hell ye been? We plumb gave up on ye!"

Anse Tolliver spurred his mule to the front of our bunch. "Whar's Joe? Cap'n Walker? Ever'body else?" he yelled at Nidever, who shrugged off our fiddler's excited queries.

"They be gone, that's what," he replied calmly. "Gone more'n a for'night past, headin' fer the Rockies—lock, stock, an' bar'l—'ceptin' fer we'uns what chose to stay behind—an' yerownse'fs, natcherly."

"But he warn't s'posed to be leavin' 'til spring!" Tuttle exploded. "Thet's what he tol' us, gawddamnit!" He swung about in his saddle to face me and demanded, "How long be it 'til spring gits hyar, Temple?"

I realized the futility of raging against the simple fact of Walker's departure, but I replied dutifully, "Nigh three more weeks, Tuttle." I might have added some mollifying remark to ease the strain on Nidever, who was bearing the brunt of our disappointment, but Brass Turtle broke in just then.

"Whar'd they go, George? Which way war they headin'?"

Nidever was obviously pleased to be asked a purely practical question. "Nawth'ards. Purty much the same way we took gittin' hyar, Turtle, 'cept they'll likely be lookin fer Injuns to p'int out a better trail fer gittin' through the mountains than the one we took gittin' hyar." He paused, spat a stream of tobacco juice and added, "Like I said, they been gone more'n a for'night. If ye be thinkin' o' catchin' up, ye got some hard ridin' ahead."

Turtle's face lit up with a broad grin. "No sich a thang, George!" He wheeled his horse to face the rest of us and declared, "I don't know 'bout the rest o' ye, but fer me, I'm damn glad I won't hafta be climbin' them'ere gawddamn snowy mountains agin, tryin' to git my arse out o' Californy. Word is, thar's better ways o' gittin' back to the Rockies. I reckon we kin find a good 'un!"

Turtle's words were sunbeams bursting through storm clouds. Instead of worrisome disappointment at being left behind by Walker's expedition, we realized in a flash that we had been blessed. Thanks to Joe Walker's capricious change of mind, we were released from our pledge to him, free to take our chances and make our own luck, as we had done since we had first joined together on the Missouri in 'twenty-two.

As we made our way across the meadow towards the nearly-empty camp, Finn McCool asked Nidever how it came about that he and his five companions had remained behind when the expedition departed. "How is it, Jarge, that you're after stayin' on here amongst the Spaniards, 'stid o' returnin' to Santa Fe an' trappin' thereabouts, like always?"

Nidever looked thoughtful. He drew a deep breath, putting his thoughts in order before he replied. "Well, now," he said at last, "it warn't an easy choice, I tell ye. I love the trapper life, but I'm pilin' on some age an' winters are gittin' colder, I'm thinkin'. Beaver are gittin' scarce an' I'm tired o' gittin' cozened out o' most o' my proper earnin's by sharp-dealin' traders. My brother got hisse'f kilt by 'Rapahoes whilst he war trappin' 'long the Purgatory an' I'd as lief not be goin' under like he did. Then, natcherly, thar's all o' them purty *señoritas* hereabouts an' thar comes a time to be settlin' down an' sirin' some kids I kin call my own." He winked at McCool and me and added, "That enough reasons fer ye? I got more if ye need 'em, like these hyar Spanyards surely make good drinkin' likker an' they sell it cheap."

"But how will ye make yer livin' here, Jarge?" McCool wanted to know.

"That's the easy part," Nidever responded with a smile. "Early on, as a lad, my step-dad apprenticed me to a turner, makin' furniture an' cabinets an' such. It's a trade I know well an' one that's sorely needed hereabouts. Have ye noticed the sorry work these Spanyards turn out, have ye? I'll have no trouble makin' a handsome livin' here in Californy, startin' with the *padres* at San Juan."

"And the others?" Finn persisted.

"Much the same as me," Nidever replied. "All of us own a trade. Milligan's a hatter an' Schmidt was a bootmaker in Germany, afore he come west. Jones is a smith an' Yount an' Higbee are both carpenters fer buildin' houses."

Finn nodded solemnly and clamped his jaw, a sign that he was seriously mulling over what Nidever had imparted. We had by that time arrived in the camp, which forestalled further palaver.

While we were putting our critters out to graze and setting up our shelters, the men who had elected to remain in California informed us that we had caught them just in time. They planned to pull up stakes next day and travel to the seashore. They meant to meet up with trading ships and exchange beaver plews for the tools and supplies they needed to establish themselves in their respective trades. None of them doubted that they would be successful in their intended endeavors.

"An' what about religion?" I asked. "I daresay ye know the Spaniards'll demand that ye accept the Roman Catholic religion if ye wish to remain here as citizens." My question elicited a general laugh.

"We know it," Nidever replied. "T'was the fust thing Joe Walker warned us about, but it makes no nevermind. Milligan an' Schmidt are awready Catholics an' the rest of us reckon one church'll do as good as another. Ain't none of us been doin' much in the way o' churchin', anyways, since we been plyin' the trappin' trade."

"Or afore that, neither!" Jones called out, which provoked another spate of laughter and settled the matter once for all.

⁎ ⁎ ⁎

We watched them out of sight next morning, until the hardy half-dozen and their critters faded into the horizon and disappeared. "Ye reckon they be makin' a mistake, j'inin' up with Spanyards like they mean to do?" Tuttle wondered aloud.

"Not if the Spanyards let 'em do it," Brass Turtle averred. "They all got a trade they kin make a good livin' off of, like Nidiver was sayin', makin' stuff an' buildin' things folks hereabouts'll pay money fer."

"Which is more than the rest of us possess, I'm thinkin'," Finn McCool commented sourly. "If it weren't for the lowly buck-toothed beaver, the lot of us'd be starvin' in the streets!"

"C'mon, Finn, the beaver's not so lowly!" Micah rejoined. "Those furry critters have given every man amongst us the best life any man could wish for! I warrant free trappers are the only free men who ever lived on this earth, in all of history and even before!" he declared vehemently. "We're governed by no man's laws. Nobody tells a free trapper what to do or how or when to do it! As long as we're willin' to take our chances, puttin' up with hostile Injuns, hurtful critters, bad weather, an' starvin' times, a mountaineer calls no man boss!" He ignored a ripple of surprised but approving murmurs and plunged ahead. "An' who can we thank for makin' us the only truly free men there ever was an' likely ever will be, here on God's green footstool? I'll tell ye who! It's the beaver! God bless 'im!"

Micah sat down then and refused to say another word. I am not sure if Micah meant everything he said that morning or if he was just pulling our leg with a mock-serious rant. But there is a lot of truth, just the same, in what he had to say about mountaineers being the only free men there ever was and likely ever will be, which is why I included it here.

McCool tried to pick up the thread of his original remark, mumbling a denial that he valued the beaver less than the rest of us do, explaining that he meant to say that none of us would fare well in the settlements, lacking, as most of us do, any useful skills with which to earn a living amongst civilized folks.

Brass Turtle's satisfaction at being free of Walker's authority was contagious. Nobody regretted being left behind. Now we looked forward to making our own way home to the Rockies, confident that we were equal to any challenge or hardship that circumstance might throw our way.

Only Anse Tolliver clung to his resentment at being abandoned by the man he claimed as blood kin, but Tuttle soon jollied him out of his injured feelings. "Hell, Anse," he chided our sour-minded fiddler, "it ain't like Joe Walker reckoned ye cain't take care o' yerownse'f amongst these hyar

Spanyards, ner ther rest of us, neither. He knows ye fer a feller what lands standin' straight up in his mockersins, like a gawddamn catamount, no matter what, else he wou'n't'a gone off an' left ye. I'd be takin' it fer a compliment, ef'n I war yew."

∾   ∾   ∾

Once again we made our way southwards, retracing our route, passing up rivers and streams we had already trapped, seeking an ever-greater harvest of plews. We were not disappointed. The streams teemed with colonies of castors. California Indians and their Spaniard overlords apparently lacked either the skill to trap beaver or any interest in learning how, which accounts for the wealth of fur that we garnered without difficulty. We found this puzzling, for we recalled that Captain Bradshaw had been eager to accept Joe Walker's beaver pelts in exchange for generous quantities of gunpowder, galena, and groceries. Other coastal trading ships must also value beaver fur as a commercial commodity as much as the master of the *Lagoda* had done.

My best reckoning tells me that the reason might lie in the fact that Indians never needed furs to keep warm in California's gentle climate and Spaniards descended from the soldier class who first conquered that territory have never recognized any good reason to learn the hard-working useful trades practiced in every civilized place. Indian labor costs them naught and the fertile land provides a generous bounty of everything the ruling Spaniards require for their sustenance, as well as plenty extra for trading to acquire whatever foreign comforts and luxuries they might desire. So why bother to engage in arduous trades and to acquire laborious skills when Providence has blessed them with endless leisure and opportunity for enjoyment?

-oOo-

CHAPTER VII
RANCHEROS DE LOS PUEBLOS

Traveling in a southeastern direction, we encountered more Spaniard settlements, mostly Franciscan missions and large private holdings devoted to raising sheep and cattle. Sheep are closely herded in meadows by Indian boys, but the rangy, slat-sided, long-horned cattle are allowed to roam freely in the thick brush that covers the gullies and mountainsides. Once the proprietors were satisfied that our band of heavily-armed ruffians meant them no harm and that we were merely passing through their neighborhood in pursuit of beaver, most of them were generous with their hospitality, usually inviting us to camp nigh their houses and treating us to delicious suppers.

Our packhorses and mules were by that time once again struggling under their burden of plews, so we quit trapping and traveled in a leisurely fashion, enjoying the countryside, often visiting with friendly Spaniard stock growers called *rancheros*. We enjoyed the hospitality of *caballeros* by name of Sanchez, Carrillo, and de la Guerra, amongst others. Sometimes we tarried a couple-three days to help our hosts gather cattle or sheep that had strayed into the wilderness. Wolves and catamounts are a constant threat to their livestock, especially sheep. We further ingratiated ourselves and gained the *rancheros'* respect for our accurate marksmanship in killing predators. They marveled at our percussion rifles and several wealthy ranchers offered princely sums to buy our guns from us, but naturally none of us was willing to part with his weapon.

Sometimes the landowner would host a *fandango*, which brought *paisanos* from every corner of a vast neighborhood, members of the *ranchero's* large family, his *vaqueros* and their wives and children, as well as Indian servants and their families, all of them eager to dance to lively Spaniard tunes played on homemade fiddles and *guittaras* and sometimes a battered brass cornet or two.

These were occasions for elaborate feasting. We learned to respect the local cuisine that, delicious as it was, was almost always seasoned with blistering hot *chiles* that, at first, had most of us gulping great draughts of water, wine, or the rich black beer they call *cerveza* and chomping *tortilla* bread to quench the fire on our palates as tears ran down our cheeks. Cesár Pérez was unaffected. He continued to munch away at fiery red and green *chiles* as if they were plums, commenting happily in his broken English that this was indeed the food of the angels—*la comida de los angeles.*

"The food of the devil's own imps!" Micah snapped through his tears. His diligent study of the Spanish tongue had done nothing to prepare his palate for those scorching Hispanic comestibles.

Once the music commenced, Anse could never resist joining in with his fiddle, which helped greatly to warm the Spaniards towards us outlanders. Heaps of delicious food and free-flowing wine and *aguardiente* didn't hurt, either, to soften our ingrained suspicion of people who spoke a tongue other than our own. Before long, our men were amusing the *campesinos* and their unmarried sisters and daughters with clumsy attempts to speak the Spanish tongue. After that, it took hardly any time at all before trappers were drifting off into the shadows with hot-blooded *señoritas* leading the way.

At last old Zeetlah gave up trying to shield his young nephew from the wiles of young Indian girls who were fascinated not only by his youthful good looks, but also by the showy Lahcotah warrior finery he always donned for such occasions. "It's about time the old man quits tryin' to pertec' young Half-hoss, anyway," Brass Turtle snorted. "That'ere kid's been gittin' laid more'n anybody since we fust set foot in Californy!"

Little Mountain nodded and grinned. "It's mighty hard sayin' no when ye feel a hand inside o' yer britchclout an' it ain't yer own. That's a pow'ful argyment."

Tuttle seconded his sentiment. "Yup! It's allus hard!" he declared with an evil chuckle.

Our intended trail led southeastwards through the Spaniard settlements, most of which hugged the seashore, to the desert country, then directly east to the southern Rockies, before turning north to return to the Seeds-kee-dee and the summertime rendezvous on Horse Crick. So far, our presence in California hadn't been challenged by anyone in authority, which was just as well, for we lacked papers of any kind which might have authorized our being there.

Our route brought us to a chain of low mountains that gently shunted us towards the seacoast and the most beautiful country we had seen since we first entered California. Rich belly-high grass sprang from fertile black soil in every quarter that wasn't thickly grown with a dense forest of oaks and pines and a curious, low-growing, red-skinned hardwood called *manzanita* or a larger variety they call *madrone*, which burned long and hot in our cookfires. Game was plentiful and traveling was easy along a fairly well-worn trail that ran more or less beside the seashore. Springtime air was soft and sunny and flavored with a whiff of salt from the nearby ocean.

One morning, lingering over coffee, none of us in a particular hurry to take to the trail, palaver ran to admiring the natural beauties that surrounded us, then to discussing taking up life in California. "Mebbe ol' Nidiver warn't so wrong, arter all, stayin' on hyarabaouts fer good," Tuttle ventured.

"Don't be fergittin'," Brass Turtle reminded him, "Nidiver an' t'other fellers what chose to stay on hyar all l'arnt a proper trade they be good at afore they come out to the Rockies. We awready talked about that, Tuttle, an' not one of us, 'ceptin' mebbe McCool hyar, ever l'arn't nothin' much 'cept' huntin' an' trappin' beaver."

"'Ceptin' me!" Anse Tolliver chimed in. "I war he'pin' muh pap b'ilin' corn mash fer whiskey afore I war old enough to walk, I reckon. I had me a trade makin' some o' the best squeezin's aroun' afore I lit out o' Tinnissee in twenny-one! I reckon I could do 'er agin!"

It was plain to see by the look on their faces that some others were wishing they had mastered a useful trade that might let them earn a living in California. Such palaver halted abruptly when a horseman appeared around a bend in the trail.

"*¡Buenos días!*" he called out in a cheery voice when he spied us.

A macaronic chorus of "g'mornin's" and uncertain "*buenos diáses*" responded to his greeting. Our friendly waves beckoning him to approach evidently assured him of our good intentions, for he rode closer before he checked his mount, a magnificent sturdy, cream-colored stallion, and looked down at us.

He was a handsome, well-built, sandy-haired, blue-eyed, rosy-cheeked young fellow, attired in the clothing of a well-to-do Spaniard *ranchero*. He wore a huge brown felt *sombrero*, stylish waist-length, embroidered *charro* jacket, and fancy tight trousers adorned with red satin insets from knee to cuff, protected by brush-scarred leather *chaperreras*. A well-used rawhide *reata* hung from the pommel of his high-backed saddle. Except for his fair complexion, our visitor looked to be a typical California *ranchero*.

Micah made haste to invite him, in the Spaniard tongue, to step down and join us for coffee and Tuttle and Finn did likewise in American—or leastaways Tuttle did. McCool always sounds rather English. When the horseman heard the English words, he beamed and exclaimed, "Ah, you are the *Americanos* they speak of in Santa Barbara!" Although the gentleman's use of English was impeccable, it was strongly flavored with the Spaniard tongue.

He swung down from his saddle, led his horse to a nearby tree and tethered him there, then returned to us, saying, "I will be most grateful for coffee, if you have no tea." Something about the way he said tea, even through the Spaniard accent, pronouncing it *tay*, caught Finn McCool's ear.

He stepped up to our guest and enquired, "Is there a chance that you've somethin' Irish in your background, sir?"

The gentleman colored and replied in his Spaniard-flavored English, "I certainly do. I am Nicholas Den, born and bred in Waterford, County Kilkenny. And you?"

"Finnæus McCool, at your sarvice. Killimor in County Galway, born in the shade o' Henry Castle!"

The two shook hands warmly and Finn resisted an urge to engage his countryman in reminiscence about the Auld Sod long enough to introduce all of us to our guest. Fact is, Den's easy manner amongst us, which bespoke a quiet authority, made us guess that it was we who were his guests.

Although I enjoy attempting to render the speech of my comrades and others in my writing, I confess that I have failed completely in trying to do so with the accent of Nicholas Den. His Spaniard-flavored Irish-tinged English utterly evades my clumsy attempts to capture it on paper. My readers—if any exist—must content themselves with imagining what that well-spoken gentleman of two different cultures sounded like as he recounted his adventures.

He joined us at the cookfire, sipping strong coffee and peppering us with friendly questions about where we had come from and what we were doing in California. We told him that we had traveled from the American Rocky Mountains with a much larger expedition and had been left behind through a misunderstanding and that now we were making our way back to the Rockies.

Den showed particular interest in our trapping, especially when he learned that we considered beaver plews to be valuable enough for us to carry them all the way back to the Rockies for ultimate sale in the States. Brass Turtle showed him a cured beaver hide and explained that the soft woolly underhair is more valuable than gold—by weight, for it is very light in weight—to people in the hatter's trade. "That'ere purty hat you're wearin' is made o' beaver felt an' I daresay ye paid a purty penny fer it, too, big as it is." A thought struck Turtle and he asked, "They make them'ere big hats hyar in Californy?"

"Oh, no," Den assured him. "*Sombreros* and almost everything manufactured comes either from *Mejico—Ciudad Mejico*, the capital—or from *España*, Spain, or elsewhere in Europe or America, where the best merchandise comes from. There is little industry here in California. We produce mostly cowhides and tallow, wool, and little else for trading with the ships that call at our ports."

During a lull in the palaver, Finn asked his fellow countryman, "What brought ye here to Californy? 'Tis a long way from Waterford."

Den sighed and smiled before he replied. "'Tis indeed. Truth to tell, I came here from Dublin by way of Newfoundland, Nova Scotia, Boston, and bloody cold Cape Horn before I set foot on this darlin' place." Sensing a good tale in the offing, our people leaned a little closer to the gentleman. He cleared his throat and paused, evidently putting his thoughts in order before he plunged into his history. "I was in the final year of my medical studies at Trinity College in Dublin—a mere half-year from hanging out my shingle, as they say—when word came from my father that he had suffered severe financial reverses, to the point of bankruptcy, and could no longer afford to keep me in school. 'Twas a terrible blow, to be sure, but soon after, along came a letter from a cousin of ours in Saint Johns, Newfoundland, offerin' me a position in his mercantile. I had no other prospects, mind ye, so I jumped at it. Within a week I was aboard a ship sailin' across the Atlantic."

"Studyin' medicine at Trinity, ye say!" Finn erupted at Den's first pause. "Me, too! Ye must've been close behind me, then!"

Before Nicholas Den could reply, we hushed McCool and begged the other Irishman to proceed with his tale. Den winked at Finn, promising to catch up on their school days at Trinity at a later time. "When I arrived in Saint Johns," he continued, "I learned to my sorrow that losin' my schoolin' was only the first of my disappointments. Instead of offerin' me a clark's position in his grand mercantile, Cousin Felix made me a slavey in his household, puttin' me to common chores and payin' me a pittance for my hard work, practically nothin' at all!" Den's ice-blue eyes snapped at the recollection, but he swallowed hard and continued his account.

"I was miserable, but I had no place to turn. Then one cold morning, Cousin Felix hands me a muddy pair o' boots an' orders me to clean and black them before I broke my fast. It was too much. I saw red. 'Black your boots?' I yelled at him. 'I'll bloody well see you in hell first!' Before I knew it, I swung that pair o' boots at his head, fetchin' him a mighty clout on his noble Irish nose, and knocked 'im to his knees.

"His nose was streamin' blood, but Cousin Felix got to his feet, cursin' me back to the day o' me birth, and came at me with both fists cocked for battle. This time I stepped back and took his measure before I walloped him proper across the temple and Cousin Felix hit the floor like a pole-axed ox!" Den grinned, recollecting his youthful triumph.

"There was no time for celebratin'. Felix Fitzpatrick is a citizen of great influence in Saint Johns. I could expect to be spendin' a year in gaol at hard labor for hittin' him. I ran.

"There was no time even for grabbin' up my hat and coat. I ran to the docks and galloped up the gangplank of the first ship I saw, a packet castin' off its lines, bound for Nova Scotia. I gave the captain a false name and signed on as a green hand.

"As soon as we docked in Nova Scotia, some of the hands told me the ship in the next berth was about to sail for Boston in America, so I hopped aboard her, changed my name again, and signed on."

Hearing the tale of his youthful trials, which were not much different from what most of us had suffered growing up, made us regard this richly-dressed *ranchero* in a new, more sympathetic light. We urged him to go on.

"I didn't much like Boston. The weather's harsh and so are the Yankees. Tight-fisted they are, with no love for anybody Irish. I worked when I could, tryin' to put together a nest-egg, but with little success. Waterfront pubs were my favorite haunts, hobnobbin' with sailors fresh returned from tradin' in California, list'nin' to their tales o' pretty girls and sunny weather and the easy life o' the Spanish dons an' gettin' rich with little effort. Most of it was blarney, but it fired my ambition to come here to see for myself. At last I could wait no longer. I shipped out, once again, as a common hand on the

Yankee windjammer *Kent*, this time under my own name, bound for California.

"My fortunes soon improved. I spent only a short time in the fo'c'sle before Captain Hickney discovered that I possessed a college education. He made me his supercargo, tradin' my marlinspike and holystone for an inkhorn and a quill, lookin' after the ship's bookkeeping. 'Twas a great improvement, to be sure.

"Five months later, after roundin' bloody Cape Horn and beatin' our way past South America, we docked at Monterey in Alta California, where the authorities inspected our cargo and collected duties. 'Twas there that I met Mister Thomas Larkin, the American consul. I told him that I wished to leave the ship and stay in Monterey, but he advised me to stay aboard until we reached Santa Barbara, which he assured me was, by far, the best place he had ever seen this side of the Sandwich Islands."

I noticed that the longer Den spoke to us, the more his Spaniard accent faded from his speech, not completely but considerably. When I mentioned this to him later, he explained that he rarely has occasion or opportunity to speak English. Most foreigners who reside there speak *español* exclusively, even amongst themselves, at times when they might revert to their native tongue if they wished to do so.

Several times he attempted to cut short his history of how he came to reside in California, pleading embarrassment at monopolizing the palaver, but we urged him to continue. Den possessed that inborn Irish ability to create vivid pictures and human feelings with his colorful speech, even in a language that had grown rusty with disuse. He resumed his tale.

"I took Mister Larkin at his word and stayed aboard the *Kent*. It was December and the Pacific was stormy and rough until we tacked into the lee of Point Concepción. As soon as we entered Santa Barbara Channel, the sea smoothed as if by a miracle, thanks to the sheltering chain of islands on our starboard. When I beheld the shore, I was overcome by its beauty. All I could think of was pictures my father had of the French Riviera. Mister Larkin had advised me well.

"The *Kent* had come to trade for cowhides, *arrobas* of tallow, and wool. The beach was crowded with ox-carts loaded with all of those items. Stacks of cowhides stiff as boards, bullhide sacks of tallow, and bales of Merino sheep's wool littered the sand. Handsomely-dressed *rancheros* came down to the shore to greet us when at last our boat made its way through the surf. They called us "Bostons" and I learned to call them *Barbareños*." Den paused and glanced skyward, as if he were revisiting his first glimpse of that place. "'Twas a colorful scene," he said at last, "and I swore right then that I would become a part of it."

We had by that time moved into the shade of a nearby grove of pines. Zeetlah, Half-horse, and Cesár, their attention wandering from Den's discourse, busied themselves at the cookfire, spitting a brace of elk haunches on a slender green *manzanita* sapling and suspending them over the coals. The sun had climbed to its zenith, time to offer dinner to our guest, lest he plead hunger and depart, depriving us of our entertainment. While the meat hissed and crackled and smoked, dripping rich fat onto the coals and wafting an appetizing aroma over the glade, Den continued his story.

"'Twas there on the beach at Santa Barbara that day that I met Daniel Hill, who became the author of all my good fortune in the New World. He is now my father-in-law and I bless the day that I met that excellent Yankee gentleman. After the day's commerce was completed, he invited me to supper at his *casa*, his home, where I met his wife, Doña Rafaela, and his young daughter, Rosa Antonia, who is now my wife and will soon be the mother of our child.

"After a delicious dinner and over brandy and cigars afterward, he and I traded our histories. He told me that he had arrived here several years before as a mate aboard a Yankee trading ship and had fallen in love with Doña Rafaela as soon as he saw her. He immediately quit the sea, converted to the Catholic faith, and settled here as a loyal and proper citizen of *Mejico*.

"I told him that I, too, wished to remain in California and in the course of our conversation he learned that I had studied medicine in Ireland. Hill seized on that and insisted that I establish a medical practice in Santa Barbara, which hadn't a single *medico* in the entire town.

"I resisted his arguments, insisting that I hadn't completed my studies and that I possessed no license to practice medicine. He waved away my objections, declaring that in the kingdom of the blind, the one-eyed man is king. Then I confessed to him what I had never revealed to anyone, that I had never really wished to become a physician, that I had merely acceded to my father's wishes, and that my true ambition was to become a farmer, a cattle grower, *un ranchero, en español.* I went on to say that I had been told that it was possible to obtain land just for the asking. The man who would one day be my father-in-law slapped his knee and exclaimed, 'True! True! Ye can get as much as 48,000 acres here just by askin' the Governor for it! But first ye must become a citizen of *Mejico!'* I assured him that I had no qualms about doing that and that I was already a Catholic. We shook hands, then, on my decision to remain in California. Daniel Hill invited me to accompany him, next day, to look at the land I occupy now, my *Rancho los Dos Pueblos*, to the *casa* of which I invite all of you to accompany me as soon as we finish the delicious dinner you have so generously offered me."

෨   ෨   ෨

As we ambled along beside the ocean on the rutted, dusty trace that Den said was called *el Camino Real*, the Royal Road, our host described how he learned the skills to become a proper *ranchero*.

"Next morning, Captain Hickney released me from my duties aboard the *Kent*. I was free to pursue my ambition. I immediately joined Daniel Hill and we rode out along the seashore west of Santa Barbara to the land that makes up *Rancho los Dos Pueblos*, some fifteen thousand acres that lie between the ocean and north to the foothills. It's a small parcel, as land grants go in California, but every inch of it is divine! It's as green as Ireland, as ye can see!" Den's eyes sparkled when he uttered those words. It was plain to see that he loved his land and the life he had chosen. "Decide for yourself," he said. "You've been on our land since we met this morning."

Nobody was surprised. Most of us had guessed it soon after he commenced relating his California history. He was right, too, about how green his land was. Elsewhere, fields were turning coppery, scorching in springtime heat. Here, all was lush grazing land under spreading oaks and woods watered by running cricks and streams that were spaced like mileposts along the rutted road we traveled.

"This parcel of land owned me, body and soul, long before I was able to lay claim to it!" Den declared. "I had much to learn before I could even apply for a land grant from the Mexican Government. Two things I needed to do were, first, learn to speak the Spanish language fluently, and second, learn the cattle business. Fortunately, languages have always come easily to me. I studied Latin and Greek at school and French has been a private family tongue amongst the Dens since we first came over with William the Conqueror." He added this last with a noticeable trace of pride.

"Regarding the cattle business, Daniel Hill came to my aid once again. That very day, we left the *Dos Pueblos* parcel and rode directly to Hill's father-in-law's *rancho* in Refugio Canyon, where he offered my unpaid services to Don Jose Vicente Ortega for what turned out to be nearly two years of the hardest labor, by far, I had ever performed. They were also my happiest years—up to that time, at any rate.

"I learned the trade of *vaquero*, a *bucaro*, how to use a *reata*, taming wild horses and dealing with wild cattle that roam the hills and valleys and forests of *Rancho Nuestra Señora del Refugio*. After a time, I also supervised the *rancho*'s vineyards. For that, Don Jose paid me in barrels of wine and *aguardiente*, which I bartered for what I needed to establish myself as a squatter on the *Dos Pueblos* property. As I'm sure you've noticed, hardly any cash money is used here.

"In all that time I hardly ever spoke a word of English, except now and then with Daniel Hill. And once I became fairly fluent *en español*, neither he nor I used our native tongue."

Just then our procession rounded a bend. A house and outbuildings appeared at the far end of a tree-lined meadow. Our host hastened to conclude his history. "After nearly two years of working for Don Jose Ortega and practicing medicine whenever I was in Santa Barbara, I was still as far as ever from being able to establish myself as a proper *ranchero* on *Dos Pueblos*. Then an American offered me five hundred head of neat cattle at a very attractive price, in cash. Unfortunately, I had nothing like the amount he asked, either in cash or in kind. Time was running out on his offer. I despaired. Then, on the final day, Padre Durán of the Franciscan Mission came to my door and presented me with a basket of silver coins in the exact amount I needed to purchase the cattle. When I asked him why he was being so generous, he replied only that it had been noticed that I always attended mass whenever I visited Santa Barbara. Owning those cattle qualified me as a proper *ranchero*. From that time on, people began to call me Don Nicolás, a title that makes me exceedingly proud.

"When I applied for Mexican citizenship, it was granted without difficulty. Soon after that, I obtained ownership of *el Rancho de Los Dos Pueblos,* to which I welcome you now. *Mi casa es su casa.* My house is yours."

We had by then arrived at a large *adobe* dwelling, some of it still under construction. An Indian servant ran up to take Don Nicolás's horse as he dismounted. When his foot hit the ground a silvery jingle caught my ear and I saw that his spurs were equipped not with the customary huge needle-sharp rowels but rather with smooth Mexican silver pesos. I had already noticed that his bridle bit was an ordinary curb, not the cruel spade bit that is commonly used by California *caballeros*. When I commented on this later, Den told me that all of his *vaqueros* were required to blunt their spurs and none of them was allowed to use a spade bit on his horses.

Several servants appeared and Don Nicolás fired off a rapid string of Spanish. They bustled off in several directions and our host turned to us, an apologetic expression on his features. "I regret that I cannot offer you quarters in the *casa*," he explained, "but, as you see, we haven't finished building it. I have arranged for you to set your camp in that glade." He indicated a grassy, shaded grove nearby, watered by a small stream. "I trust you will be comfortable there."

"Hell, Don," Tuttle assured him, "we wou'n't be able to draw breath inside o' thet'ere *casa* o' your'n, nohaow. Ain't none of us slept inside o' nothin' bigger'n an Injun lodge since we come to ther Rockies, anyways. Thet'ere purty patch o' ground over thar'll do us jest fine!" He spoke for all of us and our assenting rumble of voices assured Den that Tuttle spoke for all of us.

ℛ ℛ ℛ

By time we hobbled our critters and turned them out to graze in the meadow and pitched our shelters, Den's servants had set up several trestle tables in the tree-shaded courtyard alongside the big house. Tantalizing aromas from a kitchen inside the dwelling were already drifting across gardens planted with vegetables, a riot of flowers, and flowering cactus plants. Indian servants commenced lugging loads of firewood to our camp from the nearby woods and others placed earthen jugs of water beside each of our bowers.

Don Nicolás soon emerged from the house and called to us to join him. He was accompanied by another man, well-dressed in the Spaniard fashion, somewhat older and stouter, who added his big, booming American voice to Den's invitation. When most of our bunch had straggled onto what Den called the *patio*, he introduced his companion. "I wish to present Don Daniél Hill, my father-in-law and my dearest friend. Without his efforts on my behalf, we would not be standing here this day."

Hill shrugged off his son-in-law's kind words and strode forward, grinning broadly, both of his big, work-hardened hands extended in greeting. "Welcome to California, me buckos," he barked in an unmistakable Yankee accent diluted with a strong Spanish flavor and seasoned with a generous sprinkle of salt from his seafaring career. "'Tis always good to see Americans here. Have ye come to stay?"

Brass Turtle was first to speak up. "No longer'n it takes to make our way back to the Rocky Mountains," he declared emphatically.

"Not that we haven't enjoyed our visitin' here," Finn put in hastily, lest our host take offense at Turtle's abrupt response. "'Tis a darlin' place, to be sure, California, but so is the Rocky Mountain country and we make our livin' there."

Anxious to relieve an awkward moment, Don Nicolás called out, "'Tis dry work, visitin' and meetin' people. Come, gentlemen, and relieve your thirst." He waved towards a table laden with bottles and carafes, a scatter of earthen cups, and a trio of wineskins hanging from a trellis beside it. Mountaineers are never behindhand in accepting strong drink. Fortunately our hosts were not injured in the ensuing stampede.

Servants flitted in and out of the *casa*, bringing a seemingly endless variety of delicious dishes, from zesty tidbits rolled in flaps of flat bread called *tortillas* to substantial portions of chicken, pork, and beef, much of it spiced with garlic and fiery red and green *chiles* that could sear the palate of an unwary mountaineer accustomed to a diet of little else but fresh meat with no seasoning of any kind. We had learned to approach Spaniard cuisine with respect, howsomever, at the *fiestas* and *fandangos* we had attended elsewhere in California. Now we were careful to keep a *tortilla* in hand before we bit into an unfamiliar delicacy.

Both Don Nicolás and his father-in-law appeared to be fascinated with my father, who evidently impressed them with his quiet good manners. They drew him aside and plied him with questions concerning the fur trade and how it was that some American whitemen and Indians worked and lived together as equals.

I had sidled nigh at the start of their palaver, so I heard most of it.

"That was never so in New England afore I came here," Daniel Hill asserted. "We kept apart, unless we were takin' more land away from the red men. And it's the same story here in California. First the Spaniards, then the Mexicans, claimed all the land an' drove the natives off to parts that no white man wants."

"The lucky ones were driven off," Den commented dryly. "Those that stayed soon died—or bloody well wished they had."

This was a tender subject for Powatawa, but he kept his good manners and replied in a level tone. "It is no different in America. Indians are drowning in a white sea. A few of us swam to the mountains. We are valued there for what we do, not for color or tongue. Perhaps that will last until we die of too many winters. Perhaps not for long. Already there is talk of settlers coming."

The two Yankee Dons nodded gravely and glanced at each other, as if considering if they would continue the palaver. Powatawa spied me then and beckoned me to join them. Den made haste to introduce me to his father-in-law. I was impressed that he remembered my name. Powatawa mentioned that I am his son, which caused a faint ripple of surprise in the two men. My father doesn't look old enough to have a thirty-year-old son.

I had by then picked up enough Spaniard lingo to be curious about how the *rancho* had got its name, *Dos Pueblos*, which, I was told, means Two Towns or Villages. Don Nicolás and his father-in-law explained how that came about and then launched into the history of that particular chunk of land. I was almost sorry that I had asked. But not quite. It was a bloody story, but fascinating.

Don Nicolás took the lead. "As you already know," he said, "El *Rancho de Los Dos Pueblos* means the *rancho* of the two villages, named after the two Chumash Indian villages that used to be located on either side of the creek that flows through the beach and into the bay at the southern boundary of this property. Chumash Indians lived in those two villages forever, since long before Juan Cabrillo ever spied this darlin' land—and that was three hundred years ago!"

"Those two big *rancherias*, Mikiw and Kuyamu, were still there in my time." Daniel Hill interjected. "There were still some old Chumash Injuns goin' out in their *tomolo* boats an' fishin' ev'ry day, livin' off the land and the sea like they always did. But most of 'em had already been carted off to the Mission in Santa Barbara. The Franciscan *padres* called 'em *neófitos*— neophytes in English—claimed to be teachin' 'em Christian ways and the True Faith. They worked 'em nigh to death all day, workin' on Mission farms or buildin' the Mission bigger, then tearin' it down an' buildin' it even bigger, feedin' 'em scraps or hardly nothin' at all, then locked 'em in behind the Mission gates come nighttime, boxin' 'em up worse'n cattle in stinkin' little *'dobe* huts, 'thout a breath o' fresh air!"

"The *padres* justified that cruel treatment by insisting the *canaliños*, the Chumash Indians who lived along the Channel, were pagans doomed to hellfire unless they converted to the True Faith," Don Nicolás put in. "I am a lifelong Catholic and I will remain so, but I cannot approve of using human beings in that manner."

"I doubt those particular *padres* thought of *canaliños* as humans, anyway," Hill said, his tone growing more heated, "workin' 'em so fearful hard as they did, treatin' 'em like property, and sellin' 'em off for cash money to *rancheros* to labor for no pay and little food until they dropped dead in their tracks! Starvation, overwork, rotten lungs, an' the pox were killin' 'em off like flies—and all the while the Grey Robes kept on preachin' salvation to 'em and sayin' prayers over their graves! If hadn't kicked Spain out in 'twenty-two and grabbed back Alta California from the missions, there wouldn't be an Injun left alive in California today!"

"As you can see," Don Nicolás said in a milder tone, "my father-in-law feels very strongly about the ill-treatment that the Chumash suffered here. There aren't many of them left, but word has gone out that they are welcome to come back here to *Dos Pueblos* to live and work. Don Daniél does the same on his *Rancho Arroyo Tajiguas*. Some have come trickling back and we do what we can to make amends for those awful years. It'll never be enough, but we do what we can."

"We've got a better class o' *padre* nowadays," Hill assured us, "but, just the same, we're still keepin' 'em away from our Injuns."

Festivities had pretty much petered out by that time. Most of our people had departed, alone or in company with an Indian servant woman. If Don Nicolás noticed, he didn't let on. The few trappers who remained, slumped against the *casa* wall, were snoring peacefully, sleeping off too much *aguardiente*. We reckoned it was best to leave them there. Powatawa and I thanked the Yankee Dons for their hospitality and for relating the unhappy history of the Chumash Indians and took our leave.

Walking back to camp in the gathering dusk, I asked my father, "What d'ye think o' what those two were tellin'?"

Powatawa took his time putting together his reply. "I believe," he said at last, "they were asking two Indians for forgiveness for crimes they did not commit." He fell silent for a moment before he added, "They are good men, but it is not for you or me to forgive. Their holy men must answer for it."

∾ ∾ ∾

Several of our people were nursing severe headaches next morning. "Thet'ere argywenty ol' Nicholas sarves up shore is tasty," Tuttle lamented, "but it's got a kick like a loco Blackfoot mule."

"Nat'rally drinkin' it like it was crick water had nothin' to do with it," I chided, but Tuttle looked so distressful in the aftermath of his over-indulgence that I couldn't bear to add more scolding to his suffering. Instead, I reminded him that he had best get a move on, breaking camp and saddling up, if we intended to travel any considerable distance that day, which comment was equally unwelcome. He groaned and prepared to rise, when Don Nicolás rode up on a handsome bay stallion, dressed in well-worn work clothes, a quizzical expression settling on his features when he saw that several of us had already packed our plunder and saddled our critters, ready to depart.

"*¡Buenos días!*" he called out in greeting. "Are you leaving so soon? We hoped to have the pleasure of your company for more than one night. You are welcome to stay much longer.

"Besides," he added with a mysterious smile, "we have arranged an entertainment for you, a *rodeo* in preparation for the *matanza*. I believe you will find it a pleasant diversion."

"What's a ro-dayo?" Tuttle asked, eager to delay any effort to pack up and depart. Anse and Finn had roused by that time and they added their voices to Tuttle's, doubtless for much the same reason.

"'Tis a gatherin' of our cattle from the brush and the forest," Den replied. "We'll be bringin' 'em together and drivin' 'em to *Bahía Refugio*, up the coast a ways, where *las matanzas* take place before the trading ships arrive."

"Tradin' ships?" Brass Turtle sounded interested. "What're they tradin'? What kind o' stuff?"

"'Most anything ye like. We depend on 'em for everything from the States and Europe. As I told ye, California manufactures hardly anything. We sell what we grow, little else."

Turtle addressed the rest of us. "I reckon ye noticed we're runnin' short o' gunpowder an' galena an' thar's no tellin' whar, or even if, we kin git any more afore we git to ronnyvoo. Tobacco's runnin' out, too. If it don't take too long, mebbe we oughta be swappin' some plews fer plunder we need afore we git goin' agin. What'say?"

A rumble of assenting voices granted Don Nicolás his wish. He had successfully recruited almost a dozen unpaid novice *vaqueros*.

"What is a *matanza*?" Finn enquired politely. "You mentioned that word, Don Nicolás."

"It means the killing of the cattle," Den replied. "We drive the animals to where the ships come near to shore and kill them there. We take the hides, scrape them clean and dry them, retrieve the tallow and pack it into bullhide sacks of about one *arroba* each. You will not be expected to perform such labor. The *obreros* do all of that. Once the animals reach *la matanza*, your work will be finished. You have only to trade with the Bostons and enjoy the many *fiestas* that take place there.

"I warrant you'll not regret staying for *la matanza*. From the moment *los rancheros visitadores* arrive here with their herds, it will be one long string of *fiestas*, each night at a different *rancho* on our road, until we arrive at *Bahía Refugio* on the *rancho* of my wife's grandfather, where the Ortegas are renowned for their hospitality. Our *criados*, our servants, look forward with great anticipation to *las matanzas*. It is their favorite holiday!

"Come then! It is time that we break our fast. *El desayuno* is ready and waiting for us!"

So it was that our bunch agreed to perform some of the hardest labor any of us had done in years and had the most fun doing it. Don Nicolás hadn't lied. The *matanza* and all that led up to it turned out to be one big *fiesta*.

⁞⁞⁞⁞⁞⁞⁞⁞⁞

After we broke our fast at the food-laden tables on the *patio* beside the *casa*, Don Nicolás led the way to a large *corral* that contained nigh a hundred horses. "These will be your mounts, gentlemen, for the work that lies ahead. I don't expect you to use your own horses for this difficult, sometimes dangerous work, unless, naturally, you wish to do so. I suggest that each of you choose half a dozen *caballos* for your own *remudas*. A *vaquero* who is familiar with our *rancho* will work with each of you and he will show you what is required to capture, brand, and collect the cattle that we will drive to the *matanza*. None of our *vaqueros* speak English, but, no *importa*, no matter, this is a task that is best learned by seeing and doing."

As I neared the *corral*, expecting to pick out some likely horses for the chore ahead, a swarthy, smiling young fellow appeared at my side. He was nearly a head shorter than I but sturdily-built, booted and spurred, shabbily-dressed in a patched but clean hickory shirt and *pantalones*. Brush-scarred leather *chaparreras* covered his legs. A mop of straight black hair straggled from under his ragged straw *sombrero*. Most notable were his broad smile and sparkling black eyes. He carried a bundle of halters and shanks and hobbles over one arm and his rawhide *reata* in his other hand.

All I could make out from the torrent of Spanish lingo he sputtered at me were the words *vaquero*, *caballo*, and Paco, the last of which was evidently his name, for he kept punching his thumb at his chest and repeating the word Paco. I nodded, poked my thumb at my chest, and told him that my name was Temple, which he pronounced "Tempo," which is about as close as most people come to it.

Paco handed the halters and such to me before he darted into the *corral*, dragging the open loop of his *reata* behind him. He appeared to be looking anywhere but at the deep-chested bay horse he suddenly snared with a single snake-like fling of the loop that settled deftly over the critter's head and was instantly snugged around his neck. The bay made as if to run, but as soon as he felt the rope tighten, he settled down and allowed Paco to lead him quietly to the *corral* gate. Seeing that response, I immediately felt better about the horses that Don Nicolás was providing for our chore.

I haltered the bay and tethered him to the fence while Paco strolled nonchalantly amongst the milling horses, dragging his *reata*, his gaze studiously avoiding his target, until his arm shot out like a striking rattler and the loop settled on the animal of his choice. There were, by now, other *vaqueros* in the *corral*, securing mounts for my companions. Paco continued his single-minded search for certain animals he apparently had chosen beforehand. One by one, he smilingly turned them over to me and returned to his quest, until half a dozen excellent horses stamped and snorted at the *corral* fence. Paco loosed another flood of Spaniard talk at me, likely letting me know that these horses would be my personal *remuda* until we returned from *la matanza*. Then we led them back to our meadow, hobbled them, and turned them out to graze with my own critters.

On the way I noticed that Anse Tolliver's preference for mules had been accommodated. He and the *vaquero* assigned to him were leading six fine-looking saddle mules to the pasture where our critters were grazing.

～ ～ ～

Day after day, for a week, from early morning to nearly dusk, Den's *vaqueros*, paired up with our bunch, combed the hills and gullies, crick bottoms, and woods of *Rancho Dos Pueblos*, seeking the Yankee Don's rangy, slat-sided longhorn cattle. They skittered like startled quail at our approach, charging through the underbrush and seeking refuge in gulches and woodlands and on the tree-shaded slopes of the low mountains that loomed above the *rancho*. Each of us, *vaqueros* and trappers alike, wore out five or six horses every day.

Paco showed me how not to flail my *reata* before launching the loop, but to open it with a single flick of the wrist before sending it truly to snare the huge horns of my prey, then to jerk it snug, take a turn or two around the pommel post, and haul the struggling *vaca* behind my horse so that Paco could rope a hind leg to hold him in check, before we dragged and goaded the critter to a holding *corral*, where a branding crew waited to burn the NAD *marca a fuego* of Nicolás Antonio Den into the animal's skinny flank before shunting him into a holding *corral* to await the drive to *Bahía Refugio* and the *matanzas*.

We gained tremendous respect for the *vaqueros* and it turned out that our differing languages didn't pose much of a problem. Our years in the mountains provided us with sign-talk that we use constantly, unconsciously, even when we're talking amongst ourselves. And even though *Californios* don't know our Indian sign-talk, Mexicans talk with their hands so much that it works out pretty much the same.

The work was never easy, but the *vaqueros* saved us much hard work and wear and tear on the horses and our own hides by employing a stratagem invented, they said, by Don Jose Ortega to lessen the labor required to round up wild cattle. The *vaqueros* killed a bull and skinned him, then draped the bloody hide over a tree stump. When the range bulls picked up the scent of the gory hide, they drifted to that spot and commenced bawling and pawing the ground in a most pitiful manner. Their laments could be heard for miles and it brought bulls and cows trailing their calves hurrying out of canyons and down from the mesas to the site of their slain *compañero*, which spared us much of the chore of chousing wild cattle, one by one, out of thorny thickets and treacherous crick bottoms.

Even so, it was hard, gritty, sweaty, exhausting work, but it was also exhilarating—not as thrilling as running buffalo, but fun just the same. Our bunch, along with our assigned *vaqueros*, vied amongst ourselves to capture the greatest number of *vacas* each day, most of us refusing to quit until darkness made further effort impossible. Don Nicolás never shirked. We often caught a glimpse of him and his heeler plunging through the *chapparal* in pursuit of a cantankerous longhorn, hallooing much like an English fop in pursuit of a fox.

Don Nicolás did his best to keep us happy and he succeeded admirably, especially with the heavy drinkers in our bunch. When at last, each day, we rode into the yard surrounding the *casa*, Indian servants scurried to help us dismount and lead our horses off to be fed and watered and otherwise cared for. Every night, a lavish variety of delicious foods, some smoking hot simmering on braziers, others *picante* hot, covered plank tables set out on the broad *patio*, under hanging wineskins bulging with *vino* and *aguardiente*, the produce of the *Dos Pueblos* vineyards.

Sometimes Doña Rosa, the beautiful young wife of Don Nicolás, would join us for a brief spell in the evening. She was with child, her first, and it was plain to see that she was more than somewhat uncertain about the loud, sweaty, whiskery, hard-drinking, leather-clad crew of outlanders that her husband had recruited to help him prepare for the *matanzas*. She spoke no English and as far as we could tell, she never spoke a word of Spanish, either, leastaways to us. She smiled prettily, howsomever, and that was good enough for us.

Doña Rosa's father, Daniel Hill was often present, although he never joined us to chase wild cattle. His chore was of a different nature. His work crew was installing a wooden floor in the *casa*, which would make the house of his daughter and Don Nicolás only the second dwelling in Alta California to be so provided. "There ain't hardly an *hombre* in all o' California who can saw a timber or dress a block o' stone besides meself!" he told us proudly. "My *casa* is the only *'dobe* in California that has a wooden floor in it, by God! Now there'll be two. Some o' these Mexican Dons are stinkin' rich, but they put their Chinee rugs on a rammed-earth floor, damned if it ain't the gospel truth!"

At last the rodeo was complete. More than twelve hundred wild *vacas* milled and complained loudly in Den's pasture, awaiting the day when we would herd them onto *el Camino Real* and drive them along the coast to their fate at the *matanza*. Our most difficult chore had been accomplished. Now all that remained was to await the arrival of *los rancheros visitadores*, the visiting *rancheros* who would come from the south driving their own herds to *Bahía Refugio* and the Boston trading ships. Those Mexican dons would be expecting a *gran fiesta* at *Dos Pueblos* and the Dens did not intend to disappoint them. Servants bustled about their chores from dawn to dusk, fetching foodstuffs and drink from the butchery, smokehouses, vegetable gardens, and the winery to the kitchen inside the *casa*. Delicious fragrances of cooking foods enveloped the *casa* and the scatteration of outbuildings that surrounded it.

There was no work for our bunch to do until the northward cattle drive. Tuttle and Anse, and sometimes Little Mountain, occupied much of their time sampling the products of Den's winery and distillery. Cesár told me he had learned that Doña Rosa was fond of wildfowl, so I often took my fowler to the field early in the morning and brought back a brace of plump partridges or sometimes wild ducks for her table. Micah engaged Den's servants in palaver whenever he could steal them away from their chores, constantly seeking to enlarge his vocabulary *en español*. My father read the Walter Scott novels I had brought with me. Cesár and Half-horse kept themselves busy seducing scullery maids, when they weren't putting a handle on the horses we had captured on the prairie up north. Sometimes a few of us amused ourselves by riding out to the hills to shoot wolves that were a constant menace to the *Dos Pueblos* sheep flocks or to harvest a couple-three wild hogs lurking in the oak groves. Mostly I used my leisure to catch up on my journal and Finn McCool and Zeetlah were often closeted with Don Nicolás.

Finn had been eager to reminisce with Den over the days they had spent at medical school at Trinity, but once they exhausted their stock of recollections of classmates and professors, favorite Dublin taverns, and memorable schoolboy pranks, their palaver naturally ran to their mutual interest, medicine, and—because they had studied to be physicians, not surgeons—from there to pharmacopœia. Which naturally brought our old Delaware healer Zeetlah into the picture.

While Zeetlah was with me in Saint Louis, he and the Chinese physician-surgeon who healed me became well-nigh inseparable, the two of them roaming fields and forests in search of all manner of herbs and useful weeds, testing them, and cataloguing them. Finn has tremendous respect for Zeetlah's knowledge and skill. He recommended our cranky old Delaware most warmly to Don Nicolás, who, although he much prefers his life as a *ranchero*, is still the only *medico* in Santa Barbara town. Whenever Den was not taken up with the business of running the *rancho* or overseeing preparations for his expected visitors, the three of them had their heads together, exploring the meadows and woods and along the seashore of *Rancho Dos Pueblos*, collecting specimens and testing their usefulness.

Whenever time permitted, since we first set foot in California, Finnæus McCool and Zeetlah had been assembling a collection of medicinal recipes of California Indians and adding them to knowledge they already possessed of their own various nostrums. Here follows a passel of herbal cures that Finn scribbled into my journal for safekeeping, until he was able to record them elsewhere. I include them here in the hope that they might prove useful to someone.

Bitterroot and sage for digestive ailments. Fennel for colic. Desert tea for rheumatism. Rosemary for disinfecting. Watercress for liver ailments. Willow bark for throat gargles. Garlic and *calabaza* seeds to expel worms. Foxglove (digitalis) for heart tonic. Flaxseed for poultices. Cascara sagrada for cathartics. Pennyroyal for kidney disorders. Elderberry blossoms for reducing fever.

The three *medicos* all profited in new knowledge by their association, each one learning from the others, even Zeetlah, who drew me aside to boast that he had eliminated the vile taste from his "sleep-vittle" by substituting a newly-discovered herb that grew near the seashore on the *Dos Pueblos rancho*. When I asked him how he could be sure that it was just as effective as his original formula, the old scoundrel sniggered and winked and confessed that he had laced the drinks of Tuttle, Brass Turtle, and Little Mountain with his new concoction. "All t'ree go sleep-time purty much all day. Dey remember nuttin' when dey wake up. Dis'n bettah sleep-vittle, betcher arse!"

McCool and Zeetlah earned their keep and Nicolás Den's gratitude when word came from Santa Barbara that a foreign ship had arrived in port with a crewman suffering from smallpox. Den, accompanied by Finn and Zeetlah, immediately galloped to town, where the Irish doctor treated the sick sailor, but too late. The patient died, but Den was able to obtain from the dead man a quantity of serum. Den, McCool, and our Delaware put their heads together and concocted a smallpox vaccine, which they administered to the ship's crew and several of the Santa Barbara townsfolk. When they returned to the *rancho*, they treated Den's *vaqueros* and Chumash *criados* in like manner, as well as our bunch. Most of us had witnessed the ravages of that dread disease, so there was not much resistance to rolling up our sleeves and letting Finn scratch our hide.

∝ ∝ ∝

The lazy pleasure of a drowsy early-April afternoon was shattered when a *vaquero* galloped into the *patio* shouting the welcome news that *los rancheros visitadores* had been sighted no more than a *legua* distant from *Dos Pueblos*, a distance of maybe three miles. Instantly the entire *rancho* was galvanized into feverish activity. Don Nicolás, roused from his siesta, tousled and frowsy from his nap, appeared in the doorway of the *casa*, bellowing orders to a platoon of servants, who passed them on to a small army of *criados* and *vaqueros* who scampered and galloped hither and thither to carry them out, laughing all the way, for the arrival of *los rancheros visitadores* is regarded as a great holiday thereabouts. The honor of *el Rancho de Los Dos Pueblos* was at stake and every man, woman, and *muchacho* was determined to make it shine.

When at last the procession rounded a bend on *el Camino Real* and came fully into view, it provided a colorful spectacle. Don Nicolás, wearing his Sunday best and mounted on his cream-colored stud, rode out to greet the leader of the first party, a handsomely-dressed Mexican Don astride a spirited, richly-caparisoned stallion, surrounded by his retinue of *caballeros*, family members and gentleman friends. They rode in the forefront of a herd of upwards of a thousand bawling longhorn bulls and cows, flanked by smiling, shouting *vaqueros* cracking long whips and crowding the cattle together, keeping them on the road until the *Dos Pueblos vaqueros* directed them into a pasture reserved for that particular herd. Each herd was trailed by a string of creaking ox- and mule-drawn wooden-wheeled carts piled high with bags of wool, kegs and barrels of wine and *aguardiente*, smoked meats, and garden truck intended for trade with the Bostons. Bringing up the rear of each procession were the *remudas* of the *vaqueros* and the extra horses of the mounted gentlemen who accompanied each herd.

The caravan appeared to be endless, stretching around the bend in *el Camino Real* as one herd after another came into view, each one composed of a thousand or more cattle, each led by an elegant *Don* and his entourage of *caballeros*, each herd trailed by a score or more heavily-loaded wagons screeching and groaning along the deeply-rutted road.

At last the noisy parade came to an end with six companies filing into *Dos Pueblos* pastures and the colorful tents and pavilions of the *Dons* and their retinues sprouting in a vast circle bordering the *casa*. The riders were helped from their saddles by *criados* who led their mounts off to stables and *corrals*, whilst others conducted the guests to the *patio*, where Don Nicolás waited to greet his guests and offer refreshment. A few of the *caballeros* had brought along their wives and daughters and these ladies were welcomed into the *casa* by a smiling Doña Rosa.

My trapper companions had risen to the occasion as soon as they spied the cavalcade. The whites retreated to the nearby woods to scrub off a fortnight's accumulation of sweat and grime in the crick that flowed there and emerged freshly-shaved and clad in their cleanest buckskins, most of them sporting bright-colored calico shirts. Our Indians likewise got themselves gussied up in their best bib and tucker, which in their case meant elaborately quilled and beaded war shirts, leggin's, and moccasins—myself included. Half-horse strutted in his captured Lahcotah finery, grinning in anticipation of new conquests of toothsome young *criadas* arriving with the caravan.

Tuttle Thompson was fragrant with the bouquet of lilac shaving soap and his cheeks almost shone through a faint blue stubble that no razor could remove completely. His bright red calico shirt was wrinkled but clean. When I complimented him on his appearance and aroma, he snorted and replied, "Shee-it, Temple! Cain't be shamin' Don Nicholas in front o' his comp'ny! Not arter the gen'rous way he's been treatin' us since we got hyar." As an afterthought he added, "'Sides, thar's bound to be a purty li'l Spanyard filly er two, come 'long with thi'shere new bunch, what might cotton to ol' Tuttle ef'n he don't smell too bad."

By unspoken common consent, none of us ventured near the *patio*, where Den's guests crowded around the richly-laden tables of food and drink, until Don Nicolás came hurrying over to our camp, a concerned look on his face. "Where have ye been? What are ye waiting for?" he called out as he approached. "I've been boasting about ye to our guests and they wish to meet you. Please come over." Then he noticed the unaccustomed neat appearance of our usually grubby bunch. He blushed and stammered, "Oh, please forgive me! You've been waiting to be invited! I never thought . . . ." His voice trailed off uncertainly. Then he recovered and declared, "By all means, gentlemen, you are as welcome and as honored as any guest who has ever graced this *rancho* with his presence! Please join our *fiesta!*"

That's all it took. Fortunately Don Nicolás wasn't trampled in the stampede as our thirsty bunch rushed to the wineskins and *aguardiente* kegs. Zeetlah, my father, and I followed with Don Nicolás at a more leisurely pace.

When we joined the others on the *patio*, our host introduced each of us to the assembled Dons, an impressive gathering of splendidly-dressed, deeply-tanned, vigorous gentlemen, who displayed great interest in us. I noticed with satisfaction that although Den naturally spoke the Spanish language in addressing his *ranchero* guests, he distinctly pronounced the proper name of each of us when he introduced us to them. The names of Tuttle Thompson, Anse Tolliver, Zeetlah, and even Half-horse stood out in the spate of *español* that he rattled off, describing each man's distinctive traits and skills and accomplishments that he had observed, as Micah told me later.

I paid particular attention when he came to Micah and Cesár Pérez, but Don Nicolás accorded both of them the same praise and respect in describing their merits as he did for the rest of us. Micah confirmed it afterward when he described the event. Den was so generous with his compliments that both black Micah and swarthy Cesár would have blushed if their complexions had allowed it.

Two richly-fatted young beeves, the carcasses of a pair of wild hogs, and a large sheep turned on spits suspended over pits filled with glowing *manzanita* embers, buttery fat hissing and crackling as it dripped onto the coals, wafting a mouth-watering fragrance over the *patio* and surrounding meadows, promising feasting not only for the aristocrats gathered on the *patio*, but full bellies for the army of *vaqueros*, *criados*, drovers, wagoners, ox-tenders, and muleteers scattered throughout the pastures of *Rancho Dos Pueblos*. Nobody went hungry that night.

As long as they remained out of doors, none of the *caballeros* removed their huge felt *sombreros*, most of which were heavily embroidered with gold and silver thread. Almost all of them were mustachioed but otherwise clean-shaven. The few who wore beards kept them closely-trimmed. Lacy shirts and colorful cravats peeked out from waist-length velvet and corduroy jackets bedizened with gold and silver buttons and elaborate embroidery. The gleaming stock of a flintlock *pistola* and the jeweled hilt of a dagger jutted from a richly-hued satin or silken sash around every aristocratic middle. A long Toledo blade with an ornate basket hilt of gleaming silverwork swung at the side of every *caballero*. Leather *chaperreras* protected *pantalones* decorated with bright red triangles inserted from knee to ankle, covering high-heeled riding boots equipped with jingling silver spurs. Lest my description of their colorful garb suggest that those men were ineffectual dandies, grasping their work-hardened palms in a handshake quickly dispelled such notions.

Besides Don Nicolás, there were a couple other English-speaking Yankee Dons amongst Den's guests. Most memorable was Abel Sterns, a wealthy merchant from the City of Our Lady of the Angels, a hundred miles or so to the south of where we were. When he spoke of his town, Sterns shortened the complicated Spanish name simply to *Los Angeles*. His outfit was much the same as the other *Dons*, but Stern's ruddy complexion and the nasal Yankee twang that flavored his fluent *español* gave him away as our fellow countryman. Sterns showed a lively interest in our beaver-trapping, asking a host of questions concerning where beaver might be found in California and under what conditions, traps and necessary tools, trapping and preparation methods, market value of plews, and I don't know what-all. He put all of his questions to us in such a friendly, genuinely-interested, easy-going manner, howsomever, that we didn't resent what we might have regarded as an insistent grilling by a different man. He finished by extending a warm invitation to our bunch to stop by his emporium in Los Angeles on our return to the Rockies, offering to provide us with reliable maps showing the best route to Santa Fe.

Den's father-in-law, Daniel Hill, was not present. He and his crew had completed building the wooden floor in the *casa* a few days earlier, after which Don Daniél had hastened home to his *Rancho Arroyo Tajiguas* to oversee final preparations for his own *fiesta* for *los rancheros visitadores* when we would arrive there the following night.

There was a plenitude of wine, both red and white, and a bottomless keg of *aguardiente*, but there was no drunkenness amongst the *caballeros*. I can't say the same for some of my companions, who are dedicated to draining every bottle, jug, and barrel of ardent spirits they come across. Fortunately, trappers are forced to stay cold-sober from one summer rendezvous to the next, simply for lack of opportunity, otherwise many of our number would become hopeless sots.

Doña Rosa and the ladies joined us briefly on the *patio*, but they retreated indoors when supper was announced. The *caballeros* flocked to benches at the plank tables, but all of us trappers squatted or sprawled on the floor tiles after filling our plates, which doubtless amused the Mexican guests. There are no chairs in the mountains and, except for perching on a convenient log, now and then, mountaineers soon abandon the use of chairs and benches, even when they are available.

Musicos had commenced playing lively Mexican tunes on *guitarras* and fiddles and a couple of cornets when supper was announced. As soon as he emptied his plate, Anse Tolliver hotfooted back to camp and reappeared shortly with his fiddle case in hand. The Mexican musicians welcomed him, especially when it became clear that Anse's presence amongst them assured them all of staying well-lubricated throughout the evening.

Most of the lavish spread of cured and roasted meats, beans, corn, rice, *chiles*, and other dishes remained after the gentlefolk's supper, but naught went to waste. Everything was whisked away to feed the *Dos Pueblos* workers and the mob of newcomers, who likely made short work of it.

The gentlemen guests soon drifted off to their tents and marquees, anticipating rising early to resume the cattle drive. Most of our bunch had already departed, likely headed for the cattle camps, where their romantic aspirations might be gratified. My father and I and a somewhat tipsy Zeetlah bade Don Nicolás goodnight and started for our camp. When we moved out of the light of the flickering candle lamps on the *patio*, a titter of feminine laughter came from the darkness. Without a word of farewell, Zeetlah left us and disappeared into the gloom. A moment later we heard his throaty chuckle mingled with girlish giggles. Powatawa's quiet laughter matched my own as we paid tribute to the old Delaware's remarkable stamina.

Next morning, by time I emerged dripping from my swim in the crick, Paco had already rounded up my *remuda* of *Dos Pueblos* horses and saddled a tall, deep-chested grey for me, ready to join the cattle drive. Don Nicolás rode up and assured our bunch that, in our absence, his people would look after our livestock and extra plunder and keep our packs of beaver plews safe. We bolted a hasty breakfast with the *rancheros* and the other *caballeros* on the *patio*, then hurried off to join the *Dos Pueblos vaqueros*, who were already gathering Den's herd of longhorns in the big *corral*, preparing to turn them loose onto *el Camino Real* at the tail-end of the other six herds and their accompanying carts and wagons.

Paco and the other *Dos Pueblos vaqueros* had tied long cattle whips called *azotes* to each of our saddle pommels, alongside our rawhide *reatas*. The *azote* proved to be a most valuable tool to keep our unruly bovine charges on the trail and moving in the proper direction. The short time they had spent crowded together in the *corral* had given the cattle a mite of herd sense, but they were still crazy-wild critters used to being strictly on their own in the woods. "Look at 'em," Brass Turtle observed sourly, peering over the *corral* fence, "if them sumbitches had claws, they'd be climbin' trees!"

"Don't be too damn sure they cain't, anyways!" Tuttle cautioned.

At last came the order to slide back the long poles that served as the gate of the big *corral*. A horde of long-horned, slat-sided, orey-eyed bulls and cows spilled out, grunting and bawling, crowding and threatening to trample the half-grown calves amongst them, all of them desperate to regain their freedom, only to be met by the crew of whip-cracking *vaqueros*, whose long *azotes* snaked out and popped like pistol shots over their backs, at first painfully flicking off tufts of hair, soon making them flinch just at the sound and retreat amongst their fellows, thus compacting the disorderly mob into a manageable herd that could be collected and controlled and pushed along the road in a single moving mass.

Our trapper bunch hung back for a spell, watching and learning from Den's *vaqueros*, getting the feel of aiming and cracking the long cattle whips. Trappers lead a mostly physical life and clumsy, dim-witted newcomers to the mountains rarely survive their first winter there. It didn't take long for us to acquire the knack of persuading Den's wild-eyed critters to join up and follow the leader. Don Nicolás and a venerable grey-haired *vaquero* led our noisy procession. Doña Rosa's *enceinte* condition prevented her from accompanying her husband that year, although she had done so the year before. Unlike many of the older, long-established *rancheros*, Den had not yet acquired a retinue of gentlemen hangers-on, nor had he any grown sons to bring along. At first our two leaders were frantically busy keeping excited wild cattle from surging past them, but soon the critters sorted themselves out and settled in behind a few natural leaders, content to plod forward more or less in place.

Even so, a herd of more than twelve hundred mostly-wild animals is bound to harbor some single-minded bunch-quitters within its ranks. Almost anything—a chittering squirrel, a covey of quail flushing, a screeching crow— could startle them and set them off at a breakneck run, which required a rider to gallop in pursuit, head them off, turn them, and bully them back into the herd before their defection became general. Which used up our horses in a hurry, especially at the start of our journey. Every hour or so, it was necessary for each of us, *vaquero* and trapper alike, to ride our sweaty, lathered critters to the tail end of the column, where our *remudas* of extra horses followed along, and change mounts.

Riding past Den's caravan of ox-drawn carts and wooden-wheeled drays hauled by mule-teams, I marveled at the industry that Don Nicolás had inspired on his *rancho* in the few years since he obtained title to that land. Den had truly found his proper vocation as a farmer. The wooden axles groaned and screeched under kegs and hogsheads of wine and *aguardiente* from his vineyards, casks of olive oil, cured hams, flitches of bacon, and ropes of sausages from his smokehouses, bales of raw wool from his flocks, sacks of wheat and dried corn, strings of garlic and *chiles*, and bulging bags of lemons, oranges, and dried vegetables piled high on the creaking wagons. His servants, the good-natured, smiling *criados*, men and women alike, who were driving the mules and oxen and looking after the precious produce, attested to kind and generous treatment they received at the hand of the Irish lord of *el Rancho de Los Dos Pueblos*.

❧ ❧ ❧

Don Daniél trotting towards us along *el Camino Real* on his tall saddle mule signaled the completion of a long, taxing journey, leastaways for that day. When Hill came up with Don Nicolás, the two men leaned out of their saddles and embraced. The older man pounded his son-in-law on the back, apparently congratulating him on a successful cattle drive.

It was appropriate praise. We hadn't lost a single *vaca* along the way, although there were several longhorn bulls and cows that were somewhat the worse for wear, as well as a passel of *vaqueros* and trappers and their hardworking horses who could use a good night's rest. Running runaway cattle ragged made no nevermind, for the critters were valuable only for their hides and whatever tallow that could be salvaged from their skinny frames. Most, if not all, of the meat would be left for the buzzards, crows, and coyotes.

The *ranchos* of Daniel Hill and Nicholas Den were popular with *vaqueros*, for they both fenced their pastures, unlike most California *rancheros*, who might, at most, build a pole *corral* for a couple-three favorite horses or a small pen for a beef steer being fattened for slaughter. Once a trail-weary herd was turned out in a fenced pasture on the *rancho* of either one of the Yankee Dons, after a hungry, fast-moving day on the trail, the cattle were content to stay inside the fence and graze. Fences made it possible for as few as one or two *vaqueros* to look after a large herd at night.

I rode to the rear of the wagon train to retrieve the horses of my *remuda* and to see that they were properly fed and secured for the night. A couple of them also needed attention to some deep scrapes they had received from vicious swipes aimed at man and mount by the long-horned cattle. "'Tis surely loike herdin' a troop o' bloody enemy hussars, it is," McCool complained, "iv'ry one o' the bloody divils armed with a brace o' sabers, 'stid o' just the one!"

Zeetlah, Half-horse, and Little Mountain were already moving amongst our extra horses, treating minor cuts and rips with healing salve and sewing up a few deeper wounds in shoulders, flanks, and thighs. All of our people had become fond of the horses which Don Nicolás had provided for us for gathering and driving his wild cattle. Every one of them was sound and well-trained, possessed of intelligence and that indefinable quality horsemen call heart. Already Anse Tolliver was scheming how he might buy or otherwise gain possession of his borrowed mules.

I obtained some of Zeetlah's salve and smeared it on the shallow wounds that my animals had sustained. The old healer inspected my handiwork and nodded approvingly. "Iss long vay from heart," he pronounced. "Dey be all good purty qvick."

"How 'bout me?" Little Mountain wanted to know, smiling and jerking a thumb at a long rip in his blood-soaked leggin'.

Zeetlah rattled off a spate of Delaware lingo, which provoked a guffaw from his huge apprentice. Zeetlah turned to me and said, "I tell 'im he be too beeg for hees head be tellin' hees arse be movin' qvick!"

Little Mountain roared again at the English translation, then dropped to the ground and let Zeetlah tend to the gash in his thigh, which turned out to be not as deep as it first appeared to be.

Assured that Little Mountain's wound wasn't serious, I wished them well, swung into the saddle, gathered my *remuda*, and drove them off to the pasture that Don Daniél had reserved for Den's *vaqueros* and our bunch. It had been a long, hard, sweaty day and the swift-running crick that ran through the pasture beckoned invitingly.

❦   ❦   ❦

Don Daniél and his beautiful wife, Doña Rafaela, were experienced hands at entertaining the visiting *rancheros*. They provided a lavish spread of food and drink for their guests, made all the more delicious by the warmth and sincerity of their hospitality. The rafters of the *casa* rang with Don Daniél's hearty pledge, "*¡Mi casa es su casa!*"—My house is your house!—delivered over and over again in Hill's booming bass voice. The mistress of *el Rancho Arroyo Tajiguas* made a sincere effort to make us foreigners feel at ease. Although she, like her daughter Rosa, Den's wife, spoke no *Inglés*, her beaming smile and sunny tone of voice, even in a tongue foreign to our ears, conveyed genuine welcome.

This was the last overnight stop before we reached our final destination, the deep-water moorage for trading ships on the seacoast at the edge of the hacienda of Doña Rafaela's father, the renowned Spaniard grandee Don José Vicente Ortega. Don Daniél and his lady were determined to make this visit memorable for *los rancheros visitadores*. The tiled *patio* blazed with dozens of colorful glass candle lamps and a troupe of gaily-dressed *musicos* filled the air with lively Mexican melodies, their spirited tunes competing in the atmosphere with mouth-watering aromas from half-a-dozen glowing firepits, where two plump young beeves, a couple wild hogs, and a brace of stout muttons were turning on spits, dripping savory fat onto hissing coals, creating an intoxicating fragrance that had my belly rumbling in anticipation of the forthcoming feast.

Anse had anticipated the presence of the *musicos*. He arrived at the *fiesta* surprisingly neat and clean and even freshly-shaved, fiddle case in hand, and, most remarkably, with a smile on his customarily crabby phiz. Doña Rafaela was enchanted by Tolliver's joining in with her entertainers. She clapped her hands with pleasure at the sight and sound of Anse sawing away for the pleasure of her guests and fired off a string of commands to her servers, who saw it to it that our cranky comrade stayed well-oiled throughout the evening.

The rest of our bunch were respectably turned out in our best rendezvous duds, which also pleased our hostess, for she had never seen American Indians from the Rockies and the plains. The colorful quillwork and bead-encrusted foofurraw we sported on our leather shirts, leggin's, and go-to-meetin' moccasins are unknown arts amongst the *Indios* of California.

Even more prized by my fellows than Doña Rafaela's approval, howsomever, were the shy glances and furtive smiles of her pretty *mestiza* serving girls, who discreetly let it be known that our attentions might not be unwelcome, once their chores were completed. Which was, naturally, the main reason that most of our bunch got all gussied up in the first place.

❧   ❧   ❧

Even before we glimpsed the ocean, the joyful sound of lively Mexican music penetrated the bawling and squealing of our long-horned cattle, announcing the end of our journey and the start of the bloody *matanza*. As my horse topped the low rise that brought us in view of the sea, I spied a dozen colorfully-dressed *musicos*, their polished *guittaras*, fiddles, brass cornets, and one giant viol gleaming in the sunshine, standing on a low hill that overlooked a broad stretch of beach. They formed a half-circle behind a splendidly-attired, grey-haired *caballero* mounted on a tall black stallion that stamped and curvetted in place, champing and rattling its ornate silver bit. The proud animal's caparison, its rich trappings and harness, rivaled the magnificence of its rider.

As I drew nigh the knoll, Paco rode by, smiled broadly, jerked his chin in the direction of the colorful horseman, and called out, "Don José Ortega! *el jefe grandioso!*" before riding on. I shouted a *gracias* over the din of the cattle, but Paco's identifying the gentleman wasn't needed. The patriarch of *el Rancho Nuestra Señora del Refugio* was one of a kind, unmistakably "the boss," as Paco had called him. It wasn't only his distinctive clothing that set him apart, but mostly his manner, his hawk-like features and imperious glance, his natural assumption of authority and the universal respect that was his due.

Don Nicolás rode to the foot of the knoll and bowed from horseback, sweeping off his big *sombrero* in a respectful greeting to his grandfather-in-law, who acknowledged the younger man with a brief smile, a nod, and a friendly wave of his hand. Den wheeled his horse, regained his position at the front of the herd, and led us to a designated stretch of the beach in front of a shallow canyon at the foot of a high bluff, where our carts and drays were already filing into a formation that formed a kind of *corral* to confine the cattle.

As soon as the herd was secured, Den's *vaqueros* sorted themselves into two-man teams consisting of a roper and a lancer. Each mounted pair commenced to drive individual animals out of the herd and onto the beach, where the roper secured the horns with his *reata* and dragged the critter, while the lancer swiftly overtook him and slashed the *vaca*'s hamstrings with his razor-sharp spear, causing the hindquarters to collapse. The *vaqueros* immediately abandoned the fallen animal and headed back to the herd to obtain another *vaca*, while a trio of *criados* , both men and women, rushed to the frantically thrashing critter, one expertly cutting its throat, then two more skinning off the hide and scraping it clean, taking care to preserve the fat and suet clinging to the hide and the carcass. The fat was thrown into huge iron cauldrons suspended over driftwood fires to be boiled into tallow for sale to the Bostons.

If an animal was sufficiently fat, which was rarely the case, choice cuts of flesh meat, usually only the backstrap, were put aside. Otherwise, the carcass was left for catamounts, wild hogs, wolves, and coyotes that haunted the killing-ground after dark. Insolent buzzards, ravens, and crows perched and pecked unafraid during daylight hours.

Hides were stretched and pegged out to dry and tallow was molded into cakes and stuffed into raw leather bags stripped from the legs of the slaughtered cattle, amounting to about twenty-five pounds each, a weight called an *arroba* in the Spaniard tongue. We learned that one-third of the value of the tallow would be divided amongst the *vaqueros* and the other workers at the *matanza* as a special reward for their labor there. Shipmasters paid two dollars apiece for hides and tallow sold for four cents a pound, so an *arroba* of tallow was worth a dollar.

Don Nicolás kept his word. He rode up whilst we were watching the bloody business on the beach and called out, "Come, gentlemen! Your work is done! You have my deepest thanks for all your efforts. Now all you need to do is enjoy yourselves at the many *fiestas* here, until the ships arrive and trading begins." He wheeled his horse and signaled for us to follow him. "Come! Let's pay our respects to Don José Vicente Ortega, the lord of this magnificent manor!" We fell into a file behind him whilst he led the way inland, through Refugio Canyon, to the *hacienda* of his wife's grandfather, which lay about a mile and a half uphill from the beach.

I, for one, was happy to get away from the monotonous carnage of the *matanza*. Mountaineers are certainly not put off by the sight of blood. We are used to killing, skinning, and butchering critters for meat and hides or for their valuable fur, but standing by and witnessing the gory spectacle of more than a thousand cattle being reduced to a pile of hides and a heap of tallow bags commenced to get my gorge rising.

We passed by lush, unfenced pastures where young boys tended flocks of grazing sheep, through dense forests of oak and pine, past well-tended vineyards, olive groves, and orchards of orange, lemon, apple, and fig trees, with here and there a scatteration of low *adobe* dwellings and outbuildings, called *jacals*, that housed the *rancho's* married *vaqueros* and their families.

When at last we came in sight of the palatial main house, the *casa grande*, Brass Turtle snorted and exclaimed, "Hell! It ain't much, but it's home!" Which provoked general laughter, including Den's.

"Impressive as it is now," he said, "I'm told that it used to be even more so, before my time here, twenty years ago, before a pirate raid destroyed much of what was here then. Even so, this *rancho* is still one of the grandest in all of California!"

That was easy to believe as we gained a better view of the whitewashed *adobe* mansion that sprawled over the crown of a high, tree-shaded knoll, surrounded on its lower slopes by a village of *adobe* walls—a harness shop, a saddlery, a cooperage for making barrels and kegs, horse barns, a couple smithies, and dozens of shacks and huts that housed the *mayordomo* and his Indian and Mexican *vaqueros* and a small army of artisans who plied the many trades that supported the splendor of the Ortega barony—wool combers and hide tanners, carpenters and stonemasons, weavers and winemakers, seamstresses and laundresses, as well as a platoon of page boys who carried the *mayordomo's* commands to a regiment of farmers who worked the corn and grain fields, vegetable gardens, orchards, and vineyards scattered over Ortega's far-flung domain. The huge main house itself employed scores of butlers, housekeepers, cooks, and scullery maids to keep the vast establishment running smoothly.

When we approached the large tiled *patio*, stablehands came running to take our horses and help us dismount, which naturally wasn't required. They looked surprised and uncertain when they caught sight of our shabby, trail-worn buckskins, so different from the elegant attire of the *ranchero dons* assembled on the *patio*. A few words from Don Nicolás reassured them, howsomever, and they went smilingly about their chore, leading our horses off to a nearby picket line.

A chorus of *¡holas!* and *¡bienvenidos!* greeted us as we entered the *patio*. We had become friendly with several of the Mexican dons during the previous couple of nighttime *fiestas* and they had apparently spread the word amongst their *amigos* that we weren't quite as uncivilized as our appearance might suggest. Even so, we were a curiosity in that place, outlanders from the distant eastern mountains, which, for most of them, was as faraway as the moon. Several of the gentlemen made sure that our cups were filled before they led us off to the presence of the ruler of that rich kingdom, but the task of introducing us fell to Don Nicolás, our protector thereabouts and the exalted gentleman's grandson-in-law.

Fancy feathers are commonplace amongst the aristocrats of California, but not since we enjoyed the company of *el Gobernador* Figueroa in the capital at Monterey had we been treated to such a picture of sartorial splendor as Don José Vicente Ortega presented. He was standing and chatting amid a group of attentive *caballeros* when we arrived, but he waved them to silence when he spied us. He had changed his outfit since we first saw him on horseback earlier that day.

As Figueroa had been in Monterey, Don José was dressed now in antique Castilian Spanish fashion. His *pantalones* were deep-green velvet knee-breeches, with white knee-length silk stockings and jeweled buckles on soft leather slippers. His dark-brown steeple-crowned *sombrero* was richly embroidered with gold thread, adorned with tiny ball tassels around its broad brim, which danced whenever the handsome old gentleman gestured, which was constantly. His wine-colored waist-length *charro* jacket, tailored from the richest velvet, gleaming with gold embroidery, adorned with massive gold buttons buffed to a mellow brilliance, framed his ruffled white shirt and flowing cravat. A folded multi-colored striped serape was flung carelessly over one shoulder and his substantial middle was snugged by a vivid scarlet sash that partially concealed the polished brass-and-rosewood grip of a flintlock *pistola* and the bone haft of a dagger. Most notable was the fine Toledo sword at his side. Late-afternoon sunbeams bounced off its glimmering silver hilt as he advanced with widespread arms to greet Don Nicolás, a broad smile lighting his leathery face. As he neared, I saw that his eyes were blue, in startling contrast with his swarthy features, but undeniable testimony to his claim to be one of the *sangre azul*, the blue bloods of Spanish nobility.

The two men hugged in the customary *abrazo* before Den launched into a spate of *español*, explaining our presence there, then introduced us to the venerable gentleman, naming each of us in turn, as Don José moved from one of us to the next, clasping our hands in his work-hardened palms and muttering what we took to be welcoming words, out of which I was able to extract only "*Mi casa es su casa*," which was, naturally, music to our ears.

The next several days are a pleasant blur in my recollection and, I daresay, in the memory of my comrades, an endless round of *fiestas* and goodfellowship, of rich food and too much wine and *aguardiente*, of dark eyes and firm bosoms and straining thighs and murmured endearments in a foreign tongue that were nonetheless tender and sincere, leastaways at the time.

We divided our time between the festivities at Don José's *casa grande* and the nighttime *fiestas* at each of the workers' camps on the beach, after darkness halted the slaughter of cattle and the preparation of hides and tallow. Then the hardworking *vaqueros*, *criados* and their dark-eyed women put aside their tools, laved away the sweat and gore, and donned their simple holiday finery, all of them eager to enjoy the *matanza*, which, for them, was one of the most joyous festivals of the year. Every camp offered a plenitude of wine and *aguardiente* and the air was redolent with the fragrance of meat roasting on a dozen cookfires crackling and sparkling with the rainbow flames of blazing driftwood from the seashore. *Guitarras* and fiddles, their lively rhythms pierced here and there by the brassy bray of a cornet, filled the darkened beach with a festive spirit that often translated to amorous attachments that thrived in moonlight but withered in the rising sun.

At last the *matanza* came to an end. Mountains of stinking green hides and heaps of tallow-stuffed bullhide arrobas littered the beach. Three tall-masted trading ships, their sails furled, rode at anchor offshore in the deepwater harbor. Now began the serious business that had summoned *rancheros* from their various domains along the coast and their inland empires.

Ox-carts and drays hauled by mule teams trundled onto the beach, bringing for trade the produce of each *ranchero*'s flocks, vineyards, distilleries, smokehouses, fields, gardens, orchards, and groves. Even so, cattle hides—the two-dollar bills of the California trade—and tallow were the principal items of interest for the sea captains and their attendant supercargos, the ship's officers who oversaw the actual exchange of commodities. Barter is the method of trade in California. By day's end thousands of dollars worth of the ships' merchandise had been delivered to the *Californios*—hardware, arms, building supplies, drygoods, furniture, foodstuffs, Oriental carpets, liquor and fine European wines, and assorted luxuries—without a single copper cent changing hands. Cash money—except for actual gold, silver, or gems—is mostly unused in California.

Don Nicolás made sure that we were able to offer our beaver plews to the captains and supercargos of all three ships before we swapped our furs with the highest bidder. We were pleasantly surprised at the high price that our plews earned from the Yankee traders and regretted that we hadn't brought more of them with us.

Brass Turtle did most of the trading for our bunch, driving hard bargains that would have been miracles at a Rocky Mountain rendezvous but which likely left those sea-going hucksters laughing up their sleeves. We acquired large amounts of galena, English gunpowder, and, best of all, a passel of percussion caps, for which, the seamen told us, there is virtually no market in California. Besides groceries for our trip back to the mountains, we also bought new shirts and colorful woolen ponchos for all of us and, recalling the searing daytime heat of the desert on our journey to California, a handsome straw *sombrero* for each man. It seemed odd to be buying these typical *Californio* items from Yankee traders, but that's the way it was. Not much is manufactured there.

Don Nicolás was particularly elated at acquiring a large quantity of wooden shingles from one of the ships' captains. "Now," he crowed, "I'll not only possess one of the two wooden floors in California, but *mi casa* will also have the only shingled roof!"

About that time the festive air of the trading holiday was suddenly chilled by the arrival of a troop of mounted soldiers, lancers clad in bulky leather armor, the first we had seen during our time in California. They were about a score in number, attending a plump, gaudily-dressed officer astride the tallest horse in the troop. He wore a ridiculous high-crowned shako surmounted by a tall crimson plume. Even at a distance it was possible to develop an instant antipathy for him. His arrogant manner, the imperious eye, the curling lip under a wispy moustache and the militant jut of his soft double chin, recklessly curvetting his horse, spurring him through a crowd of workers, who scattered like chickens at his approach, instantly earned my dislike.

Daniel Hill had been standing with us. He and Den exchanged a look of disgust before he announced to us, "It's that bloody scoundrel Narcisso Batista and his bully-boys, up from *Mejico* an' claimin' rights an' authority the most o' which he likely invented on the way up here!" His face clouded with anger.

Don Nicolás, too, had sobered at the sight of the chubby, overdressed officer, but he held his temper in check long enough to explain to us who the newcomer was and why his presence so infuriated Don Daniél. "He calls himself *Coronel* Narcisso Batista. He arrived in Santa Barbara several weeks ago with his troop of *lanceros* and a handful of written orders he claims appoint him to the post of *alcalde*, not only of Santa Barbara, but of the entire *condado*." I didn't understand precisely what Den meant by all that and neither did my comrades, but we didn't interrupt him. "Since he and his men arrived here, they've been acting in a bloody high-handed manner, confiscating property, demanding taxes from merchants with trumped-up laws that no one ever heard of, and allowing his drunken bullies to abuse citizens in the streets, with no possibility of redress!"

Den's anger increased as he catalogued the tyrant's sins, the color mounting in his normally placid features. "Naturally we complained to *el Gobernador* Figueroa about Batista's disgusting behavior and he has sent an enquiry to *la Ciudad Mejico* questioning Batista's authority, but it'll take months to receive a reply. Until then, we suffer his outrages!"

While Don Nicolás was speaking, Batista had ridden up to the station of the trader with whom Brass Turtle was still dickering over a purchase. The Mexican halted his horse with a savage jerk of the reins on the cruel spade bit that set the poor critter back on his hocks, eyes rolling, grunting in pain. Immediately one of the lancers leapt from his saddle, caught the reins of his superior's mount to hold him fast, then dropped to one knee, offering his thigh so that the officer could step on it to dismount. Tuttle snorted in disgust. "Didja see thet, Temple?" he demanded loudly. "Ain't no kind o' proper man'd do thet fer nobody, boss er no! Any feller what'll do a thang like thet shore-as-hell has to squat to piss!"

When the colonel stepped onto the soldier's thigh, then onto the ground, I saw that he was of considerably less than average height. He swaggered to make to make up for it, but it didn't work. Limping slightly, he headed straight for the haggling pair and barged into Brass Turtle, evidently expecting our Delaware friend to retreat. Turtle didn't budge and the little popinjay bounced backwards and nearly lost his balance. Without turning around, Turtle growled, "Ye'd best wait yer turn, sonny. We be busy hyar."

Although he likely didn't understand Turtle's words, the little Mexican flushed with anger and his hand darted to the saber at his side. He thought better of it, howsomever, and let the blade slide back into its scabbard. Which was just as well, for my tomahawk was already in my hand and so were those of Tuttle, Anse, Little Mountain, and Finn.

Red-faced and fuming, Batista stomped back to his horse, stepped from his slavey's leg to the stirrup and into the saddle, then sat glaring first at Brass Turtle and the Yankee trader, then directed his attention to the beaver plews heaped on the ground beside them. His stony gaze swept over the rest of our bunch gathered around the two Yankee dons, evidently noting that we were foreigners. When he caught us staring back at him, he jerked his horse's head about, gouged him savagely with his saucer-sized spurs, and thundered off to a different trader's station, his lancers trailing obediently in his dust.

"That'n'll do to be keepin' a close eye on," Finn McCool opined. "Did ye see how his mouth was fairly waterin' when he was lookin' at our furs there next to Turtle? He wasn't seein' plews. What he could see was money. That'n'll be hatchin' up mischief, ere long. Mark me."

🍠 🍠 🍠

Then it was over for another season. Trading came to an end and the tall-masted ships weighed anchor and disappeared in the misty distance. Mountains of green hides and acres of tallow had been stowed in the ships' holds, along with countless bags of wool, casks of wine and brandy, and tons of dried farm produce destined for American and European dinner tables after it completed the perilous voyage through the stormy seas around Cape Horn.

It was time, too, for sentimental farewells and emotional *abrazos* at the Ortega *hacienda* as dear friends embraced and bade one another a heartfelt *adios* or *vaya con dios* before mounting their horses and returning home to resume their pastoral occupations. Parting from the *casa* of Don José was difficult for our hosts, especially Doña Rafaela, who shed copious tears when she hugged her father for a final time before stepping onto her saddle mule, but she soon regained her customary cheerful spirits, once the *casa grande* disappeared behind a bend in the trail. Spaniards are an emotional folk, but much of it is a matter of custom.

Now that we were no longer encumbered by a herd of rebellious cattle, we made good time, arriving at Hill's *Rancho Tajiguas* in half a day, then *Rancho de Los Dos Pueblos* by late afternoon. The ox-carts and drays had departed the *matanza* as soon as they were loaded with trade plunder. We had sent our *remudas* of extra horses back to Den's *rancho* with the *vaqueros*, keeping with us only one saddler and another to pack our sleep robes and such.

As we rode along *el Camino Real* with Don Nicolás, he, too, got to feeling more than a mite sentimental. We had told him that now that the gathering and herding chore was done, we meant to make tracks for the Rockies. When we reached a shady spot under a spreading oak tree, he reined up his big cream-colored stud horse he called a *palomilla* and waved for us to gather around him. "Gentlemen, *amigos*," he said, "I don't know enough words in any language to tell you how grateful I am to all of you, not only for your hard work in gathering and driving our cattle to the *matanza*, but especially for your friendship during these past weeks. As you know, we don't deal much in cash money here, but I have seen and admired how well you have treated the horses—and the mules, Anse," he interjected with a wink at Tolliver—"that you have been using in your *remudas*. I know how fond a man can become of a good horse, especially when you've shared much hard work with him. So I would like to gift you with the horses in your *remudas*. They'll be waiting for you in your pasture when we get back to *Dos Pueblos*. May they serve you well on your journey to your beloved Rocky Mountains!"

Naturally there was a plenitude of thankees flying about right then. What had been a pleasant afternoon ride turned into a downright merry one. I had been reluctant to let myself get too fond of the excellent horses in the *remuda* that Nicholas Den had placed at my disposal, lest parting with them be too painful when we moved on. Now that they were truly my own, I considered myself rich in a way that money can never achieve. I daresay that my comrades felt much the same way, especially Anse Tolliver, who could quit conniving, now, how to rustle the saddle mules in his *remuda*.

∾ ∾ ∾

The cheerful mood of our company was dampened and chilled by the eerie quiet that greeted our arrival at the *Rancho Dos Pueblos*. Instead of smiling servants running up to welcome their *patrón*, a sullen silence enveloped the *patio* and the surrounding buildings. The few servants we could see hung back, as if waiting for something to happen.

Almost without thinking, I unslung my rifle and loosened the pistols in my pommel holsters. My comrades did likewise. With a muttered oath, Don Nicolás spurred his mount towards the front door of the *casa*, but as he neared, the door swung open, revealing, first, a white-faced Doña Rosa, and behind her, the portly figure of Colonel Narcisso Batista, an evil grin pasted across his swarthy jowls. Two of his soldiers, muskets in hand, flanked the pair. Den skidded his horse to a halt, flung himself from the saddle, and ran to her. The soldiers brought up their muskets to cover him, but Batista waved them back, allowing Den to embrace his wife.

As soon as Batista and his captive showed themselves in the doorway, a score of mounted lancers appeared between the buildings that surrounded the *patio*, gigging their horses into a ragged line facing us. Some of them carried their lances more or less erect, seated in stirrup-cups. About half their number pointed muskets in our direction. I'm not sure if those Mexican soldiers were ready for a fight, but we were. Problem was, they had us stalled. And they knew it. We didn't dare start a ruction, lest Den and his wife come to harm at the hands of the fat little colonel and his bullies.

About that time, Batista commenced waving his pudgy arms and yelling a passel of Spaniard talk at us, like he expected us to understand what he was hollering about. When he finally shut up, red-faced and out of breath, Micah told us what he had been ranting about.

"He says he came to get the furs that we stole from the people of California an' the Mexican Government, which he represents, an' just 'cause he couldn't find them yet doesn't mean he's about to quit lookin'. He says, too, that we better not be thinkin' about fightin' his men, 'cause Don Nicolás and his lady are bound to get killed if we do. He says we hafta give up our guns an' such, right now, an' surrender, an' if we don't, Don Nicolás and Doña Rosa'll be payin' for it."

Bedlam sings soothing lullabyes compared with the uproar that ensued amongst our bunch when we heard Batista's challenge. Everybody had an opinion but nobody could come up with a way out of the trap that the wily little poseur had set for us, using our friends and benefactors as bait. Much as we hated giving up without a fight, none of us was willing to sacrifice Den, his pretty little wife, and their unborn child. Brass Turtle summed it up. "I'd ruther slide daown a razor than be givin' in to thi'shere measly li'l dandy 'thout even a fight, but he's got us caught in a crack an' thar ain't no way out, 'ceptin' lettin' 'im win this'n. We been in tough spots afore. We'll git out o' this'n, too."

Scowling and cursing, one by one, we stepped down from our horses and laid our rifles, pistols, and other hardware on the ground. As we were doing so, several lancers rode forward, dismounted, gathered up our weapons, and stowed them aboard a rickety wagon that Batista had brought with him, likely intending to haul our plews back to Santa Barbara in it. Then they commenced searching us for weapons we might have concealed on our persons, which is how they found my hideout belly gun and the poniard strapped to my leg. Close up, Batista's *soldados* were even more unsavory than they appeared at a distance. They were dirty, smelly, unshaven, and, besides their battered blue shakos, they were clad in patched and ragged bits and pieces of faded blue army uniforms, supplemented by whatever other clothing they had managed to scrape up. Evidently the pompous little peacock's sartorial pride did not extend to his subordinates.

Whilst we were giving up our weaponry, Don Nicolás called out, "Be of good heart! We will come to your aid! Your property is safe!" before one of his guards jabbed him savagely in the back with his musket and sent him reeling. Although we had no idea who might come to save us from that military despot and little faith that anyone would or could, Den's assurance that leastaways our plews were safe was some small consolation.

We were told then to mount our horses and the soldiers closed in and surrounded us, lances tilted menacingly over our heads. The leader's big charger was led up then and Batista bowed elaborately to the Dens, waved away the two guards, and limped across the *patio*, where a soldier sank to one knee and helped his under-sized boss clamber aboard his over-sized horse.

Except for their fright and the unfulfilled threat of violence, Don Nicolás and Doña Rosa and their child were unharmed and their people and possessions remained intact. We had, leastaways, bought them that much by losing our freedom.

The chubby colonel called out a command and the company lurched onto the *Camino Real*, headed toward Santa Barbara, Batista leading the van, his preposterous lofty red plume bobbing comically amid the *soldados* clustered around him. Unaccountably, Batista had neglected to commandeer the pack animals we had brought back from the *matanza*. As we reached a bend in the road, I glanced back and spied several of Den's *criados* whisking them off to safety.

Even amid our sorry circumstance, Tuttle couldn't resist gibing Tolliver. "Hey, Anse!" he called out. "Still thinkin' on mebbe settlin' daown amongst these'shere Spanyards an' startin' up yer still fer makin' yer corn-squeezin's?" Tolliver said not a word in reply. Sticking out his tongue sufficed.

-ooo-

Much of what I will tell about in this chapter will be what Micah related to us about what occurred during the next day and a half, for Narcisso Batista chose him to be his interpreter—and, whilst he was at it, his personal manservant—likely because the evil little conniver reckoned that a negro would possess only limited intelligence and likely could be persuaded to divulge the hiding place of our furs. Fortunately for us, he couldn't have made a worse choice to achieve his larcenous aims.

Within an hour after we arrived in town, Micah was conducted to the *alcalde's* residence, which Batista had appropriated for his own use when he arrived in Santa Barbara from Mexico, waving papers that—according to Daniel Hill —nobody ever got to read and claiming absolute military and civil authority granted, he said, by *el presidente* of that nation. The rest of us languished in a thick-walled *adobe calabozo* nearby, guarded by lancers, who devoted little effort to attending to our needs.

Our prison was a single large, dirt-floored dungeon room lighted only by narrow slits sliced into yard-thick walls. We possessed only the clothes on our back. Our sleep robes and *capotes* were still on our packsaddles at the *rancho* of Don Nicolás, so we passed the night shivering in the chill sea breeze that swept off the nearby bay. Food consisted of thin, cold soup poured into a big earthen pot called an *olla* and flaps of moldy flat bread called *tortillas* and not much of either one. Conditions were as harsh and filthy as you might imagine with a dozen men crowded into a gloomy, stinking, dank, rat-infested hole.

I daresay our Indians experienced even greater hardship during that dreadful time than those of us whose early lives had been spent in houses and cabins. Men who had never known solid walls and roofs but only flimsy, portable shelters against the elements must have experienced a constant nightmare at being deprived of fresh air and sunshine. My father was onesuch, but he remained resolute. He betrayed no ill-effects from our incarceration. Instead, he devoted much of his attention to counseling young Half-horse, assuring him that we would survive the ordeal.

None of us believed that Batista would set us free if he gained possession of our beaver plews. Refusing to reveal their hiding place was the only bargaining chip that we possessed. And that secret was absolutely safe, because not one of us had any idea where Don Nicolás had hidden our furs. Two other prisoners shared our filthy dungeon, Mexican army deserters who told Cesár Pérez that they would likely be hanged soon. They appeared to be resigned to that dismal prospect, accepting death as preferable to serving under the brutal conditions they had known in the Mexican military. Both of them had been California *vaqueros* before they were conscripted and both had made the journey to Santa Fe a couple times. Our ears pricked up when we learned that, for not a man amongst us doubted that we would somehow regain our freedom. We told Cesár to encourage them to be of good heart, that we would take them along when we escaped. They appeared to be unimpressed by our promise, which, considering our situation, was not surprising.

With Micah gone, Cesár was our main source of information. He kept an attentive ear to the rusty iron grating that separated us from the guard station, where he learned that the *lanceros* were somewhat less than enchanted with their selfish commander. They resented the *coronel* indulging in luxury while they enjoyed little of what had been confiscated from the Barbareño populace. At the time of our arrest, they expected that our horses, saddles, guns, and other weapons would be shared amongst the troopers. Instead, Batista had ordered everything locked up and even forbade them to use our horses, which they suspected he planned to sell and pocket the profit.

A notable exception amongst the grumbling *lanceros* was their skinny sergeant, Emilio Gomez. His men called him *Flaco* behind his back. He was almost fanatical in his devotion to Narcisso Batista. Evidently the *sargento's* loyalty hadn't been purchased with material rewards, for his uniform was as shabby as those of his men, his only marks of authority the faded chevrons on his sleeve and a jangling bunch of keys on his belt. Despite his unimposing scrawny appearance, Flaco was a petty tyrant. He carried out Batista's commands with fervent zeal and imposed severe punishments on his men for the slightest infractions. He spent most of his time with Batista, but whenever he visited the guardhouse, a collective shudder ran amongst the *soldados* on duty.

Which was often. Gomez came to the *calabozo* twice a day or more, standing outside the iron grating and shouting demands that we surrender our peltries, sometimes threatening us with a forced march afoot to Mexico City, which would amount to a death sentence, if we refused to comply. At other times he employed a conciliatory tone, offering to set us free if we gave up our furs.

∾ ∾ ∾

When *Sargento* Gomez first plucked Micah from our midst and conducted him to the *alcalde's* residence, our comrade was greeted by the comical spectacle of the pompous little *coronel* stripped to his underdrawers, reclining in a padded chair, one leg propped on a footstool, the foot swathed in bandages. His arrogant sneer had flown, replaced by a mask of agony on his flabby features. Micah's early years as a slave, serving masters who held life-and-death power over him, stood him in good stead now. He neither laughed nor gloated.

The invalid merely glared at his bond servant before turning away with a whimpering groan. Gomez immediately put Micah to work tidying the officer's quarters, washing dishes, scouring cooking utensils, and stowing away a clutter of boots and clothing. Micah kept his eyes peeled for a weapon—a pistol, a saber, a dagger—but the wily Gomez had made sure that no such opportunity was available to the prisoner. The only visible weapon in the house was the *pistola de chispa* tucked securely in the *sargento's* belt.

Whilst he went about his chores, Micah kept his ear cocked to pick up whatever might prove useful, especially the nature of the Mexican officer's disability. His curiosity was piqued, as well, by the unusually close relationship between the colonel and his sergeant. Although they had chosen Micah to be their slavey mainly because he could follow orders given in their tongue, they kept forgetting that he could understand everything they said to each other. When he heard the words *la gota*, Micah understood that Batista was suffering from gout. He was sure of it when a waiter arrived from a nearby eating-house with their supper and Gomez unlocked a cabinet and brought out two bottles of sweet Madeira wine. When the sergeant whisked away the napery from the serving dishes, Micah saw that they contained steaming heaps of lobster and crab swimming in butter.

Gomez moved a low table beside the colonel's chair and the two soldiers pitched into the rich vittles, clinking their wineglasses in toasts of Madeira, punctuated by Batista's frequent yelps of pain from his gouty toe, and chatting in low tones, which were not always low enough to muffle the occasional use of the words *querido, enamorado, caro*, and *cariño* in a most unsoldierly manner. Micah grinned behind his hand, but he was neither surprised nor judgmental. Such relationships between tough trappers are not unknown in the mountains.

While he washed dishes and tidied up, Micah was allowed to make his supper from the scraps, which was better fare than what was offered to the two *soldados* stationed outside the *coronel's* door, which was nothing at all. When Micah's finished his chores, Gomez locked him inside a narrow cupboard, where he passed the night huddled on the bare earth, now and then drifting off to sleep, only to be jolted awake by Batista's agonized shrieks whenever he chanced to jar his gouty foot.

Next morning, when Gomez released him from the cupboard, Micah beheld a greatly-altered Narcisso Batista. The much-weakened officer was sweaty, pasty-faced with prolonged suffering, writhing in his padded chair and squealing in distress whenever a twinge from his gouty foot sent him into yet another paroxysm of misery.

Between catnaps during the night, Micah had devised the bare bones of a scheme that he hoped might lead to our liberation. What he saw now in the colonel's condition encouraged him to put his plan into action.

After he brewed morning coffee and served it to his captors, Micah spoke up. Risking their ridicule and certain punishment by Gomez if he failed to convince them, Micah adopted a simple-minded, childlike manner and professed sympathy for the torment that the *coronel* must be suffering. Then he informed the pair that gout is a common ailment in the mountains, caused by the large amount of buffalo meat that the Indians and trappers consume, which, he assured them, has resulted in many medicinal cures for that malady being discovered by Indian medicine men, *curanderos indios*. The sergeant's interest perked up and Batista demanded that he tell them more.

Now that he had their attention, Micah revealed that fortunately they had in their power, in every sense of that word, the means to relieve the agony of their esteemed *jefe*. He told them there was at that moment, in their own *calabozo*, a genuine Indian healer, an *indio médico brujo* who would almost certainly be able to relieve the *coronel* of his distress, providing that el *sargento* allowed the Indian healer access to the herbs and other medicines in his saddlebags.

So it came about that Zeetlah was liberated from the *calabozo* and was escorted to the *alcalde's* residence. *Sargento* Gomez accompanied the old man to the storeroom where our saddles, bridles, and all of our weapons were kept under lock and key. Zeetlah pointed out his saddle and its bulging *alforjas* and Flaco himself hefted the bulky saddlebags onto his shoulder and lugged them back to the colonel's quarters, so eager was he to commence the healing of his beloved commander.

Zeetlah immediately set to work concocting a substantial dose of whatever it was that he put together for the temporary relief of Narcisso Batista's pain. After Micah assured him that the Mexicans couldn't understand their American palaver, Zeetlah explained that the first dose or two would kill the colonel's pain but only for a spell, giving them time and opportunity to execute a scheme that would get our whole bunch out of the pickle we were in.

When our Delaware healer finished preparing the initial dose of painkiller and offered it to the stricken colonel, the always-suspicious Gomez called a halt and insisted that Zeetlah and Micah first taste some of it. The old man shrugged and took a healthy sip of the bitter-tasting concoction, grimacing whilst he assured Micah that no harm would come from ingesting the vile brew, explaining that he had expected such distrust, so no harm done.

Confident now that the prisoners did not intend to poison his *jefe*, Gomez allowed Zeetlah to administer the medicine to the tormented man, who was by that time fairly writhing in anticipation of relief from his suffering. Which occurred soon after he choked down a substantial dose of Zeetlah's nostrum. Within minutes he was snoring peacefully under the approving eye of the greatly-relieved skinny sergeant. Zeetlah returned to fussing with his herbs and seeds and whatnot, while Micah explained to Gomez that a complete cure would require several treatments.

Micah experienced a numbing sensation in his feet after imbibing Zeetlah's medicine, a not unpleasant feeling that passed after a few hours.

Batista awakened after a time and he and his sergeant broke their fast with vittles delivered from the eating-house. Not surprisingly, they offered naught to their prisoners, who nevertheless sustained themselves well enough on what was left over.

In time, the painful twinges returned to the colonel's gouty toes and once again the Delaware healer was called upon to relieve his pain. For a second time the untrusting Gomez demanded that Zeetlah and Micah sample the dosage, which they did without protest. Batista was pretty much exhausted from his sleepless night, so he soon dropped off after swallowing a second copious draught of our old wizard's brew. Shortly thereafter, a knock at the door informed the sergeant of some duty that required his presence. When he departed to attend to it, he ordered the guards at the door to come inside in order to protect their sleeping commander and to keep an eye on the prisoners.

Zeetlah busied himself now in preparing a sizeable batch of what he told Micah was his new recipe for his sleep-vittle, which lacked the foul taste of his earlier elixir and the effects of which lasted much longer, thanks to certain California herbs he had discovered in his ramblings with Don Nicolás and McCool. Whilst he puttered and powdered and sliced up his makin's, he instructed Micah in how best to administer the sleep-vittle.

When Zeetlah at last fell silent, concentrating on his preparations, Micah played the simpleton with the two *soldados*, chatting them up with mindless nonsense, seeking to convince them that he was harmless and well-intentioned and that Zeetlah was too old and weak to be a threat, hoping to gain their trust if not their friendship.

Upon his return, Sergeant Gomez sent the two guards back to their post, threw an irritated glance at Zeetlah but didn't offer to interrupt him, and put Micah to work cleaning Batista's scuffed and muddy riding boots, which had been a frequent chore for Micah during his years of servitude. He took particular care now to remove every speck of dirt and grime before carefully waxing and polishing the leather to a brilliant high gloss, which earned him the closest approximation of an approving nod and smile of which Gomez's vinegary features were capable. More important than Flaco's approval, howsomever, was the hour or more that the task had occupied, which brought the time close to the suppertime hour that Micah had fixed in his mind from the day before.

Batista roused from a fitful slumber and crankily demanded another dose of Zeetlah's nostrum, lest the pain return to plague him, which the old Delaware obligingly provided. This time Gomez neglected to require that the prisoners first taste the concoction, a sign that they had acquired some degree of trust with the sergeant. Relieved of his pain, leastaways for a spell, the invalid's testy nature reasserted itself. Scowling at the foul taste of Zeetlah's potion, the crabby little colonel ordered Gomez to fetch a bottle of Madeira to rinse away the unpleasant flavor. Flaco hastened to comply. He unlocked the wine cabinet and removed two bottles in anticipation of their supper. He pulled the corks of both bottles, set one aside to breathe, and rushed to fill Batista's goblet, then his own. The peevish little officer slurped down half a glassful in a single greedy gulp.

Zeetlah's obsidian eyes fairly glittered at the sight of the unprotected bottle of wine. He nodded at Micah, who caught his meaning and walked to the far side of the room, where he clumsily tripped over a chair and went sprawling, bawling in pain, then struggling to his feet uttering elaborate apologies in Spanish and English and French to the colonel and his sergeant, who stared at him in disgust, while our venerable Delaware healer deftly slipped a liberal dose of his soporific elixir into the Madeira and retreated to his work table undetected.

The sweet wine and relief from his suffering greatly improved Batista's humor. Soon he and his sergeant were clinking wineglasses and chuckling over some shared experience. The jollity increased when supper arrived from the eating-house, especially when the colonel saw that the serving dishes contained his favorite seafoods, which Gomez had ordered especially to celebrate his *jefe*'s recovery.

Both Micah and Zeetlah held their breath when Flaco emptied the last remaining drops from the wine bottle, cast it aside, and rose to retrieve its mate. He brought it to the low table beside Batista's chair, filled both their goblets brimful, and raised his glass in a heroic toast, bragging on their courage and prowess in capturing the despised *yanquis* without a shot fired and anticipating a rich reward from the furs they would certainly obtain from their prisoners, by torture if necessary. They were both by that time somewhat tipsy, so even if some alien flavor from Zeetlah's elixir failed to be disguised by the sugary sweet Madeira, neither man was likely to notice.

Batista's slurred reply to the sergeant's braggadocio was cut off in mid-sentence. His eyes rolled back and his mouth fell open. He slumped sidewise in his padded chair and lay unmoving, his breath rasping in his throat. Alarmed, Gomez lurched forward to assist his chief, only to stiffen and halt midway, clutching at air, staring, his bony cheeks frozen in rictus, hands scrabbling feebly at the *pistola* in his belt, before he crumpled in a pathetic heap at his commander's one healthy foot.

Micah stepped forward and yanked the flintlock from the sergeant's belt, then relieved him of his keys, a dagger, his shot pouch, and gunpowder flask, lest the wiry *soldado* manage to revive and put up a fight. Zeetlah merely grinned and shook his head, confident that neither man would regain consciousness. Then he drew his finger across his throat, suggesting a sure way to guarantee that their jailers would cause no trouble. Micah has no qualms about killing in a fair fight, but he has no stomach for cold-blooded murder. Instead, he found some stout cord in a cupboard and trussed the pair like geese going to market.

Then he unlocked the wine cabinet and commenced hauling out bottles and pulling corks, so that Zeetlah could lace each one with a substantial dose of his sleep-vittle. Then they gathered a dozen bottles into a straw hamper which Micah carried to the outside door, calling out to the guards as he cracked it open and shoved the hamper onto the sill, announcing in a loud voice that *el jefe coronel* was observing the *fiesta* of his patron saint and he wished all of his *soldados* to join him in the celebration. He claimed to be passing on an order that they keep a bottle for themselves and carry the rest to the barracks and the guardroom, with the colonel's compliments and those of *Sargento* Gomez, as well. He kept his fingers crossed that the guards wouldn't smell a rat at their commander's uncharacteristic and no doubt unprecedented generosity and raise an alarum, but apparently so great was their joy at getting their hands on some of Batista's private stock of Portuguese Madeira that they neglected to question the source of their extraordinary windfall.

Fact is, Micah crossed his fingers only briefly. After he pushed the hamper onto the threshold, his hands were filled with a *pistola* in one and Flaco's dagger in the other, in case he needed to dispatch the guards to prevent their spreading an alarum. He was saved that bloody chore when he peeked out and saw only one guard guzzling wine. The other guard was absent, doubtless delivering Zeetlah's slumber swill. Micah hoped only that he might complete his errand before losing consciousness.

He waited by the door for a few more minutes before he risked another look-see outside. He was rewarded with the sight and sound of the snoring sentry slumped against the doorpost. Micah made haste to drag him indoors and tie him up before one of his comrades spied him in that condition.

After an agonizing quarter-hour, Zeetlah showed Micah the way to the storeroom where the *soldados* had locked up our weapons and other plunder.

Whilst Micah was fumbling one key after another into the rusty padlock, Zeetlah suddenly flung his arm around Micah's belly and snatched Flaco's *pistola* from his sash. By time Micah could spin about, Zeetlah fired and a *lancero* was tottering, crumpling, pitching onto his face in the dirt, his musket clattering to the ground. Zeetlah handed the pistol back to Micah, saying only, "Bettah load now," before he trotted off to retrieve the fallen soldier's musket.

Once inside the storeroom, they each slung a couple-three rifles on their shoulder and raced to the *calabozo*, which was in an uproar. All of us inside clamored at the iron grating, trying in vain to get our hands on the unconscious guards sprawled just out of our reach in the guardroom. After an eternity or two, Micah got the padlocks open and handed out his extra guns as we poured out of that pigsty into the alleyway that led to the storeroom that held our weapons and other belongings.

The two *soldados* who rounded a corner and confronted our mob likely still wore that same look of surprise when they saluted San Pedro in the Happy Hunting Ground half a minute later. "Hell," Micah said with a laugh, "some days ye can't win fer losin'! Poor souls didn't even get a taste o' Zeetlah's wine!"

❧ ❧ ❧

Within minutes we retrieved our guns and plunder, found our horses and saddled up, and were racing out of Santa Barbara town, along *el Camino Real* to the *Rancho de los Dos Pueblos*. Happiest of all at regaining his property was Anse Tolliver, when he pried open his fiddle case and discovered the precious instrument was undamaged. The two Mexican Army deserters were with us, well-mounted now on the personal horses of *Coronel* Batista and *Sargento* Gomez and sitting astride their fancy saddles besides.

A smiling, laughing Don Nicolás ran onto the *patio* when we thundered into the yard and reined our horses to a rearing halt. His people came running from every direction, from fields and workrooms and corrals, cheering and laughing, delighted to see us free and apparently unharmed. They surrounded Cesár and Micah, besieging them with questions. Don Nicolás was equally curious, but he deferred his queries long enough to issue a string of commands in which the welcome words *comida, carne,* and *vino* caught my ear. Smiling young boys caught hold of our bridle reins and led our horses off to water and hay, whilst our host beckoned us onto the *patio*, where *criados* were already hanging up wineskins and lugging a keg of *aguardiente* to a table. Others were bringing trays of foodstuffs from inside the *casa*.

After we slaked our thirst with wine or brandy—for most of us, both—we exchanged *abrazos* with a jubilant Don Nicolás, who was barely able to contain his eagerness to show us how he had outsmarted Batista's greedy attempt to steal our property. "Everything of yours is absolutely safe," he assured us. "I'll show you how we foiled that bloody cockalorum and his thieving toughs." He summoned a couple of *criados*, who trotted off and soon returned carrying spades. "Now, come. Follow me." We trailed after him to the rear of the *casa*, to a dense grove of willow saplings. He plunged in amongst them, shouldering through the slender stalks until he reached the foundation of his house, where he rattled off a command to his workmen, who nodded and grinned, for they were obviously in on Den's surprise. They proceeded to dig away a wall of dirt that formed the foundation until they unearthed a stout wooden door, which, when it was freed from the surrounding soil, swung wide to reveal our bales of plews and all of our plunder, snug and dry, wrapped in sailcloth, safely preserved under Don Daniél Hill's sturdy wooden floor, a luxury unknown in California, whose existence Batista, Gomez, and their men had never suspected.

Den instructed his people to carry our property to our camp in the meadow and then led us back to the *patio*, from which, he assured us, we would not leave hungry. On the way, we told him how we had regained our freedom and explained that we durst not tarry long with him, lest we expose him and his lady to Batista's revenge. We had come only to retrieve our plunder, our peltries, and our critters and the sooner we made tracks and put Santa Barbara town behind us, the better it would be for all of us.

Don Nicolás expressed regret that we could not remain longer, but he agreed that it would be unwise for an individual *ranchero* to stand up to Batista and his troop of lancers. We assured him, howsomever, that it was unlikely that the military could mount a pursuit sooner than the morrow, so there was time for refreshments, a bathe, and a change of clothing.

While we stuffed ourselves with delicious vittles from Doña Rosa's kitchen, our host confided that the most personally rewarding aspect of the entire recent adventure, even better than the satisfaction of deceiving Batista, was knowing that not one of his people had betrayed the cache beneath the wooden floor of the *casa*, even though Batista, Gomez, and several *lanceros* alternately threatened them and offered bribes.

I reckon Don Nicolás Den can congratulate himself, as well, for earning the loyalty of his *criados* and *vaqueros* through the fair and humane treatment he has accorded them since he became a *ranchero*. Loyalty is a trail that runs both ways.

Our route to the Rockies lay south and eastwards, but Den advised against our passing through Santa Barbara, lest we encounter members of Batista's command who might have escaped Zeetlah's revenge. He proposed that we follow a trail through the hills north of the town and offered to send along a couple *vaqueros* to show us the way.

After we said goodnight to Don Nicolás and his shy young wife, our entire bunch headed for the crick in the meadow and laved away the filth and stench of the *calabozo*. "Never thought I'd be gittin muh en-joys like thi'shere sittin' in ther crick," Tuttle crowed, splashing and ducking his head under water, "but gittin' rid o' ther stink o' thet'ere gawddamn calaboose makes bathin' halfway tol'able!"

His unlikely companion in the water, Anse Tolliver, growled, "Jist be handin' over some o that'ere girly soap ye got thar, Tuttle. Cain't let ye be smellin' sweeter'n me, if some o' them'ere Messican gals come a-callin'!"

The two young Mexican Army deserters, who had been imprisoned much longer than we had, couldn't get their fill of the cool, clean crick water. They frolicked like otters, swimming back and forth, scrubbing themselves with sand, ducking each other, and laughing like zanies. When at last they crawled out of the crick, we burned their filthy uniforms and clothed them in extra shirts, britchclouts, leggin's, and moccasins that we dug out of our possibles.

A long journey lay ahead and our Mexican guides required a proper *remuda* of saddle horses, so each of us donated a horse from our own plentiful *caballadas*, which provided each of them with half-a-dozen critters, counting the two they had commandeered from their intended executioners. Stingy Anse Tolliver was allowed to keep all of his mules. When Micah and Cesár explained our gift to them, they were open-mouthed with disbelief and with gratitude. Both men had armed themselves with the muskets and fixin's we took from Batista's fallen *lanceros*, so we didn't need to share our weapons.

It felt good to help those men, but Brass Turtle saw it in practical terms. "We got a long trail ahead an' thar's no tellin' what we'll be meetin' up with. A couple extry guns'll likely be comin' in handy."

❧   ❧   ❧

We bade farewell to Don Nicolás and a tearful Doña Rosa by candlelight in the early morning, on the *patio*, where we had broken our fast with delicious comestibles that must have kept the *casa*'s cooks in the kitchen all night long. Our critters, already saddled and loaded with our plunder, snorted and stamped impatiently in the yard. Thanks to Den's generous gift after the *matanza*, each of us now owned a wealth of horseflesh. A final present from Don Nicolás was a score of packsaddles, which let us lighten each animal's load. Lighter loads would let us travel faster and longer each day.

At last it was time to go. A few coppery rays glimmered through purple clouds on the eastern horizon. Paco, the young *vaquero* who had squired me through the cattle gather and was now one of our guides, called out, "*¡Andale!*" which means something like 'Let's go!' Which we did.

We crossed the *Camino Real* and followed a narrow game trail northwards into the hills that beetle over the *Rancho Dos Pueblos* and the seacoast beyond, strung out in single-file, our pack-animals tied nose-to-tail, the newer ones interspersed with our original critters to get them used to one another, so that later on, when we let them run free, they would more likely stay together.

Riding alone, separated on the skimpy trail by our packstrings, I had plenty of time for reflection. Parting with California was, as Mister Shakespeare says, a matter of sweet sorrow. Saying goodbye forever to the Dens and their generous kinfolk was painful, but our final experience there with Batista's troops provoked not a shred of regret at leaving those sunny shores and returning to our own kind in our belovèd Rocky Mountains. My thoughts strayed to my daughter Iris, who would be a year older and smarter and more beautiful by time we arrived at rendezvous. I reminded myself, howsomever, that a year is a very long time in the life of a five-year-old child. Would she still love me or even wish to know me?

Naturally, thinking of Iris put me in mind of Cat, conjuring up a passel of painful and confusing recollections of Ned Godey's beautiful widow, whom I reckon I had loved, in one way or another, ever since Rainbow first introduced her as her lifelong best friend. Her rejection of my proposal to make her my woman still rankled, even though the reasons she offered were sound. My pride had been injured, especially when, after we shared my robes one sleepless night, she still said no. I had done my best to lose myself in all that was strange and new in California, but even in the most intimate moments, Cat's image intruded, and the remembered feel and fragrance of her stole away much of the present pleasure.

We passed high above sleepy Santa Barbara town, catching glimpses of its red-tiled roofs and whitewashed *adobe* houses through a screen of trees on the heavily-forested slopes that shielded us from view. Few people stirred in its narrow lanes, which we took to be a good sign. We reckoned that if Batista and his *soldados* had recovered from Zeetlah's toxic cocktail, the scene below would have been a sight more lively.

We continued on the high trail until it sloped downwards and joined the *Camino Real*, well past Santa Barbara town. Paco and Den's other *vaquero* bade us farewell there and returned to *Dos Pueblos*. Threading our way along steep deer trails had been slow-going travel, so it was dinner time when we reached the main road. We halted in a deep gully a discreet distance from the road, safe from the eyes and ears of passers-by, before we attacked the hampers of delicious foodstuffs that Doña Rosa had insisted that we take with us.

Our two Army deserters—whose names, we had learned, were Pablo Torres and Diego Valenzuela—became extremely excited when they saw where the mountain trail had brought us. They took barely time enough to chew their food, so eager were they to impart some secret information to Cesár Pérez, whose smile grew broader every second, until he waved Tuttle and Little Mountain to his side and whispered in their ear. They, too, commenced to grin like cats in a creamery.

One by one, without a word of explanation, they retreated to their saddle horses. Soon we heard a clatter of hoofs on the hard-packed trail. Nobody thought to challenge them. That is the way our leaderless bunch prefers it. "Now, what d'ye s'pose them damn fools are up to, slippin' off like that," Brass Turtle asked nobody in particular.

"Ye can wager it'll have a healthy slice of revenge in it, however it turns out," McCool assured him. "Those soldier lads suffered too much to let Batista off with naught besides a long night's sleep."

"An' whilst you're wagerin', ye kin wager, too, thar'll be a profit in it, any time Tuttle Thompson stirs hisse'f," Anse observed sourly.

"Cain't see nothin' wrong with that, nohaow," Turtle rejoined, "pervidin' it don't take too long an' they ain't kickin' over a hornets' nest fer us."

We felt them and heard them before we saw them. The ground shook beneath our hams, then the pounding of hundreds of hooves filled our ears, before a cream-colored avalanche exploded out of the woods onto the *Camino Real*, more than a hundred beautiful horses, young mares and stallions of the golden color Spaniards call *palomilla*, wild-eyed, long manes flying, crowding onto the road, running free, then milling into an equine maelstrom when Pablo and Diego turned back the leaders. Tuttle and Little Mountain riding the flanks, laughing and whooping like banshees, swung stout leather *cuertas*, crowding them together. Grinning Cesár, riding drag, crisscrossed the tail of the herd to prevent them from turning back.

When the dust settled somewhat and the snorting, neighing horses calmed down, we learned that our comrades had raided Narcisso Batista's personal herd of stolen horses. "Hell!" Tuttle fumed, "Tain't like they war his'n in ther fust place. Diego hyar's been tellin' haow Batista an' thet'ere Sahjint Gomez feller been grabbin' up hosses an' cows an' whatnot fer theirse'fs from folks hyarabaouts, claimin' people got to pay taxes to 'em. It's dreadful hard sayin' no when you're starin' down thutty musket bar'ls in ther hands o' Batista's sojer-boys!"

"Now that ye got 'em," Brass Turtle wanted to know, "what do ye figger on doin' with 'em?"

"Why, takin' 'em home to the mountains an' sellin' 'em, that's what!" Little Mountain chimed in. "Jes' look at 'em, Turtle! Purtiest hosses I ever did see! Not a one of 'em cut! All mares an' studs!"

"They'll bring a pretty penny, to be sure." McCool agreed. "If we can get 'em there."

"We kin do it," Tuttle insisted. "They'll drive easy enough. They be herd-broke gentle. Din'tcha see haow easy we brung 'em daown hyar, fust time we tried?"

"Howd'ja git these critters loose, Tuttle?" Brass Turtle wanted to know. "I reckon ol' Batista had somebody lookin' arter 'em, din't he?"

Tuttle chuckled. "Wal, I reckon he did, but not fer long. One sojer-boy got uppity, p'intin' his musket at us, but arter he fell off o' his hoss, t'other two turned tail an' headed fer ther hills. Thet's ther last we seen of 'em!"

"Fell off his hoss, ye say!" Turtle queried. Before Tuttle could reply, Cesár drew his finger across his throat and grinned, which was explanation enough. The gesture produced short barks of laughter from Torres and Valenzuela, who likely had settled a score with Batista's horse herders.

Zeetlah, Powatawa, and Half-horse had been engaged in private palaver of their own. Now my father spoke up. "We own these fine horses now, no matter how we came by them," he said. "It will do no good to return 'em to thieves who stole 'em. We say," he waved towards Half-horse and Zeetlah, "We say these horses belong to us. If the fat little soldier can take 'em, he can have 'em. If no, we keep 'em."

Nobody had a better idea. We retrieved our packstrings from the gully and returned to the trail at a brisk trot, some of us looking after the pack animals, others herding our spoils of war. Tuttle hadn't lied. The new horses were completely herd-broke, staying together as long as they kept moving, which suited our situation perfectly. We were eager to put as much distance as possible between us and Santa Barbara.

℞   ℞   ℞

The morning of our third day on the eastward trail dawned with a feeble springtime sun trying to burn its way through low-hanging clouds. We had camped the night before in a broad valley ringed by low hills, amid lush pasture that kept our critters nigh, with no need to wander in order to get a bellyful of tender green grass.

Now we ascended a grade leading to a notch in the hills, on the far side of which, Diego assured us, was the *pueblo* of Los Angeles, where we hoped to see the merchant Abel Sterns and obtain maps to guide us through the eastern deserts. Although we now had the benefit of Torres and Valenzuela in our party, both of whom claimed to have traveled that route to Santa Fe, it would do no harm, as Finn said, to furnish ourselves with braces and a belt, so we wouldn't be caught with our britches down.

The mindless monotony of keeping pack animals, extra saddlers running free and unburdened, mingling now with our captured horses, all crowded together and moving forward on the narrow road was disturbed by Half-horse galloping past, an urgent look on his face, heading for the head of the column. The gait quickened to a fast trot, then an easy lope, which rapidly brought the tail end of our cavalcade through a narrow notch and over the crest. Below on the far side, critters were milling. Our leaders beckoned us forward for what appeared to be urgent palaver.

There wasn't much doubt in anybody's mind what caused the excitement. A hasty glance at our backtrail when Half-horse first rode past confirmed what we had been expecting. Batista's *lanceros* were in hot pursuit, fast closing the distance betwixt them and us. Stealing his horses had erased any uncertainty Batista might have had about which direction we were traveling. We had humiliated and beggared the greedy little popinjay and his ruthless sergeant. They were sure to be thirsty for our blood.

Dividing our force took no time at all. We had decided the night before who would stand and fight and who would retreat with our livestock and plunder. Four men took charge of the critters and got them moving at a rapid gait into a broad valley. In the distance, the whitewashed *adobe*s of a sizeable *pueblo* surrounded by groves of green trees were visible.

There was little that needed to be said as we prepared for battle, but Brass Turtle said it anyway. "Fust off, we don't want to be fightin' a-hossback agin them'ere long-handled frogstickers. Them'ere Messican sojer-boys make their livin' with them lances. We kin pick 'em off better an' safer from a'hind these big rocks, whar they cain't hardly get at us. It's best we git our hosses someplace safe, like up that'ere li'l draw thar." He jerked his thumb at a narrow break in the canyon wall. All but two of us stepped down. Little Mountain and Pablo Torres trotted off, leading our saddlers by their bridle reins. "The rest o' ye split up two-by-two. Make sure ye don't both shoot at the same time, else they'll catch ye with empty guns an' split yer gullet, sure as hell!" He turned to Cesár Pérez. "Tell them two Messican sojers what I been sayin', Caesar. It'll mebbe save their arse." What he said was likely useful only to Torres and Valenzuela. The rest of us had learned, years before, never to get caught with empty guns.

Powatawa and I paired off together and found a defensible nest amongst a clutter of big boulders that commanded a broad swatch of the road that the invaders would be forced to take in coming at us. The others scattered to similar positions, all of us facing the notch in the hilltop that would frame the horsemen when they reached the crest.

It was still early forenoon. The sun at our back cast long shadows in front of us, which would be an advantage for us if the enemy attacked before the sun rose high in the sky. A faint smile played around my father's lips and his dark eyes crinkled with pleasure, as if he were listening to a favorite jest, instead of bracing for a battle that might cost his life. I had observed that behavior in him before, a lust for worthy warfare that belied his otherwise calm and thoughtful nature.

At last we heard a thud of hoofbeats and the rattle of bit-chains and sabers and spied colorful pennons fluttering from a pair of lances as two mounted *lanceros* rose into view in the narrow notch at the crest of the hill, then two more, and two more after that. But they didn't advance. Instead, they peeled back on either side of the notch, in plain view but just beyond convenient rifle range. Besides the lance that each of them had in hand and the saber on their hip, they all carried a musket slung across their back. Outnumbered as we were, we held our fire, letting them advance to a range that assured a possible kill with every shot.

When half-a-dozen *lanceros* were positioned along either side of the narrow gap in the hillside, we caught sight of His Flabbiness, *Coronel* Narcisso Batista himself, flanked by his skinny sergeant Emilio Gomez, coming through the gap. The two of them commenced waving their arms in apparent displeasure with their *soldados*, who showed no disposition to charge our rocky stronghold. Instead, a dozen *lanceros* let their lances fall to the ground and swiftly unslung their muskets, took careful aim at their officers, and in one deadly volley, swept them out of their saddles, flinging their lifeless bodies to the ground like a pair of rag dolls, the portly colonel's tall shako rolling in the dust, its ridiculous red plume limp and broken like its owner.

At once a cheer went up from the *soldados* assembled at the gap. They commenced waving at us in a friendly fashion, while more and more *lanceros* surged through the narrow opening, some of them firing in the air to show peaceful intent, others discharging their muskets into the riddled corpses in the road. Some others replaced the bright-colored pennons on their lances with makeshift white flags of surrender.

"Reckon we jist seed a mutiny, fellers!" Brass Turtle called out gleefully. "Jist the same, keep yer guns ready, 'til we kin be sure," he cautioned as an immediate afterthought, which proved to be unnecessary. Two of the *soldados* rode towards us, hands held aloft, gigging their horses forward with oversized spurs, toothy smiles stretching their swarthy cheeks. They halted within speaking distance and one of them stood halfway up in his stirrups and commenced gushing a flood of *español* that ran on for a minute or two, whilst his companion contented himself with nodding and smiling to demonstrate good intentions.

While the soldier was talking, a couple of his comrades were going through the pockets of their fallen commander and his faithful sergeant.

Micah and Cesár put their heads together, jabbering for a spell before they sifted out what was worth repeating in what the talkative soldier had to say. Micah stood up and announced, "As ye likely guessed, it's good news for us. Turns out, these fellers didn't much care for ol' Batista, any more'n we did—an' ol' Flaco Gomez even less—an' they ain't even reg'lar Mexican Army, anyway. They're just Batista's private troop. Comin' after us this time was what tore it for them. Most of 'em were purty used up on soldierin', anyway, always suckin' hind tit while Batista an' Flaco were livin' high on the hog.

"After we kilt a couple-three o' their people, gettin' ourselves loose back in Santa Barbara, when we didn't even have our own guns, they reckoned it warn't worth any more of 'em gettin' kilt for Batista's sake.

"This whole bunch is up from *Mejico* an' they're lookin' to settle down somewheres in California, so, this feller says, if it's all the same with us, how about we call it square an' no harm done?"

That was music to our ears. Even so, fearing mischief, Brass Turtle called out to Micah and Cesár and the rest of us with a cautious response. Sounds good, but jist the same, tell 'im we're sittin' tight fer naow. We ain't showin' ourse'fs 'til they go back down that'ere trail, out o' rifle range, headin' out o' these parts, so we kin be sure they ain't got some trick in mind. What'say, fellers?

Some men are natural leaders and Brass Turtle is onesuch. Even our leaderless bunch values how Turtle is always thinking half a step ahead of here and now.

Assenting shouts echoed throughout our rocky fortress. Micah relayed Turtle's message to the emissaries of the mutineers. They heard him out, shrugged, threw us a half-hearted salute, wheeled their horses, and loped back to their comrades waiting at the gap. A few minutes later, they filed through the notch. A few of them waved farewell as they disappeared down the trail. All that remained of Batista's private army was a clutter of discarded lances, a few faded blue shakos, and the riddled bodies of *Sargento* Flaco Gomez and *Coronel* Narcisso Batista himself.

~δ~ ~δ~ ~δ~

We caught up with the herd in a broad meadow close by the *pueblo* of Los Angeles. Zeetlah, Finn, and the others had already pitched camp for the night, mainly because Anse had shot a fat elk there as they were passing through. The free-roaming *palomillas* were sticking close to their new domesticated friends and naturally the young *palomilla* stallions were especially attentive to our saddle mares.

Half-horse was turning a big wapiti backstrap and a couple fat haunches skewered on steel ramrods over glowing coals of hot-burning pin-oak wood. Its mouth-watering fragrance floating on soft springtime air would have drawn us to the spot, even if we hadn't spied it from afar. "Thar's a passel o' thangs in Californy I'll be missin'," Tuttle said wistfully. "One of 'em's hardwoods, which ye cain't hardly never find in ther mountains. Ain't found no hick'ry yet, hyarabaouts, but thi'shere oak an' them'ere redskin madrono an' manzerneeter woods'll sartinly do fer makin' hot cookin' fa'rs."

"I'd'a thought ye'd be missin' that'ere Spanyard argywenty drinkin' likker an' all o' them purty *señoritas*, Tuttle, 'stid o' some ol' measly fa'rwood," Anse chided. "Ye gittin' old?"

"An' yew mought miss it, too, ef ye ever turned a hand to he'p out with ther cookin' chores, Tolliver!" Tuttle flared. "'Stid o' allus makin' yerse'f scarce when thar's camp work to be done!"

"Camp work!" Anse exploded. "That'ere elk meat you're chawin' on is some o' my camp work, Thompson! An' if ye don't like it, jist quit stuffin' yer greedy craw with my camp work, begawd!"

Tuttle ignored Tolliver's outburst and sliced another slab off a haunch. "Naow thet ye mention it," he said thoughtfully, "p'raps I'd best be gittin' inter thet'ere town over thar an' git m'se'f some o' thet'ere argywenty afore we head out t'morry. Ain't likely we'll be findin' ary drinkin' likker in thet'ere dry country we be headin' fer."

Tuttle wasn't the only one of our bunch who thought to stock up on ardent spirits before we set out on our return to the mountains. As far as we knew, except for a few scattered *ranchos*, there would be no settlements between Los Angeles and Santa Fe. Half a dozen of us rode into the *pueblo* of Los Angeles and enquired as to the whereabouts of Don Abel Sterns' mercantile. It wasn't difficult to find in the dusty little village.

Diego and Pablo stayed with the livestock. They reckoned it was best not to risk running into authorities who might apprehend them as deserters from the Mexican Army. We agreed. We had just avoided one battle. There was no profit in risking another on their behalf, for we wouldn't have given them up without a fight.

When his clerk informed him that a band of wild Indians had invaded his emporium and asked for him by name, Sterns emerged from a back room and greeted us with a broad smile. "Welcome, gentlemen, to *el Pueblo de Nuestra Señora la Reina de los Angeles de Porciuncula*! But you can call it Los Angeles, as the rest of us do! As you see, the proper title of our little *pueblo* is rather larger than the town itself, but we are growing! One day we will be a proper *ciudad*." He caught himself up and flushed. "But enough of my enthusiasm for my adopted land! It's good to see you here, all safe and sound!" A shadow passed over his features and he added, concern in his voice, "I hope that is so. We heard that you had run afoul of that rascally impostor and his brigands from Mexico City. Is that true?"

We assured him that all of us had emerged unscathed from our scrape with Narcisso Batista. Then, as briefly as we could, we described our recent experience with the scoundrelly colonel and assured him that neither Santa Barbara nor Los Angeles need ever concern themselves with that particular gang of rogues. He appeared to enjoy especially learning the circumstances of Batista's demise and that Don Nicolás and his wife were unharmed. In celebration of which he called for his clerks to bring out a keg of his best brandy. We celebrated the favorable outcomes of many recent events with fervent toasts that left us stumbling back to our horses when we finally bade him goodnight.

Before we got ourselves completely pickled, we gifted Sterns with a couple beaver traps and a wooden flask of castoreum, so that he might furnish his future trappers with the right kind of equipment to get started, and we traded half-a-dozen beaver plews for merchandise and groceries we needed for our journey across the desert. In turn, the Yankee don kept his promise to furnish us with maps to guide us across the mostly waterless desert waste that lies between Alta California and Santa Fe. The maps had been compiled over a number of years by Franciscan monks conducting their annual drive of California mules to Santa Fe. The most valuable feature of the maps was the location of waterholes in arid stretches of country where a traveler ignorant of their presence would likely lose his livestock and his life.

When Don Abel offered to provide us with a compass, Anse and Tuttle declined, bragging that we didn't require such a contraption, that they relied on the sun and stars for directions. Sterns overrode their objections. He pointed out that in late springtime the deserts commence to heat up and thick, low-hanging clouds drawn from the cold ocean often obscure both the sun and the nighttime sky for several days at a time, leaving desert travelers wandering aimlessly until the sun reappears or they die of thirst, whichever comes first. The rest of us thanked Don Abel for his guidance, even if our two know-it-alls didn't. McCool pocketed the compass.

-ooo-

etting across *el Desierto Mojave* on our eastern journey to the Rockies proved to be a trial for both man and beast. By time we got our first glimpse of the southern Rocky Mountains looming on the horizon our horses and mules were seriously ganted up after our long, often waterless, retreat across the southern deserts. We had pressed them hard every day, begrudging every mile we were unable to leave behind, striving to make California a distant memory, in every sense.

Fact is, howsomever, except for our unpleasant run-in with Batista and Gomez, our California adventure had been a pleasant experience, and profitable besides. Although the beaver we harvested in that gentle climate lacked the deep, rich quality of prime Rocky Mountain winter fur, the large number of plews we took helped to make up a substantial difference. At least as valuable were the *palomilla* horses we had acquired from Batista. We didn't reckon that we stole them. As Brass Turtle piously pronounced, "Ye dassn't call it stealin' when ye take critters off'n a hoss-thief. It's jist doin' the right an' proper thing—squarin' accounts, as ye might say."

Right or wrong as the taking might have been, the well-bred golden horses were sure to command a hefty price at rendezvous, especially from Indians who wished to strut on those handsome critters—which includes every Indian man I have ever known—and most trappers, too—as well as improving the Indians' breeding stock. All of the *palomilla* mares were in foal by then, and all of our other mares, as well. They had all come in season during the month and more it had taken for us to cross the desert country and the healthy young stallions had not neglected a single one of them.

We counted ourselves lucky to have brought our critters across that barren waste without losing any of them. Diego and Pablo were knowledgeable guides and whenever their memory faltered, Don Abel's maps had charted the way to cricks and waterholes, a couple sizeable streams, and one really big river that kept us, man and beast, from perishing of thirst. We saw no fresh horse or mule tracks at the waterholes, so it was likely we were that year's first California party to pass that way, heading towards Santa Fe. Grass was sparse, but there had been just enough to let our animals continue traveling.

We were mostly always hungry after we used up the groceries we had purchased at Abel Stern's mercantile and there are few game critters in the desert. Now and again, howsomever, a curious runty deer would stand just outside of bowshot range and stare at us passing by, which allowed a careful rifle shot to collect it for the cookpot. Desert deer aren't very big or fat and the meat tastes strongly of sage, but it kept us going.

It was too much to hope that we could complete that long journey unchallenged by hostile Indians. As we were leaving behind the easternmost Mexican *haciendas* and entering a dry wasteland, Pablo and Diego warned us to be on the lookout for desert-dwelling Mojave Indians, who consider it their right to exact a toll on the *padres'* caravans of mules traveling through their domain on the trail to Santa Fe. The desert doesn't support enough year-round forage to let the *Mojaves* keep critters for riding. They eat the mules they extort as blackmail from the friars passing over land they claim as their own. It was a safe bet that they would see our young, well-fed horses as a toothsome target.

Memories of Joe Walker's experience with the Paiutes a year before were still fresh. This was a different desert, howsomever, and these were different Indians, so we called a council of war.

"I don't give a good gawddamn what y'all decide," Anse Tolliver declared. "I ain't partin' with a single one o' muh mules, nohaow!"

"Aw, hush up, Tolliver!" Tuttle growled. "Ain't nobody had a chance to say nawthin' abaout what we're gonna do!"

"'Pears to me," Brass Turtle started off, "from what our Messican sojer-boys hyar be tellin' us, we be runnin' into what amounts to another Paiute sitchy-ayshun hyar."

"Diego's been sayin' if we give 'em what they ask for," Micah put in, "the Injuns hereabouts'll surely take it as a sign o' weakness an' we'll never get rid of 'em."

"Which isn't any different from any other bully-boys ye'll be meetin' up with anywhere, red or white," Finn observed. "The more we give 'em, the more they'll be after demandin'!"

"I'm sayin' we oughter stand pat an' give 'em nawthin' 'ceptin' a dose o' galena pills when they come a-callin'!" Tuttle declared. "I ain't abaout to give up a one o' these'hyar purty hosses fer pervidin' some gawddamn Mo-havvy's supper, nohaow!"

"Like Turtle war sayin'," Little Mountain announced, "thi'shere ain't no differ'nt'n what we had wi' them 'ere Py-yoots. We're gonna be fightin' 'em sooner or later. Mought as well make it sooner, when we kin see 'em comin', an' git it over with!" He bent down and cupped his ear to listen to something our old healer was telling him, then stood up and added, "An' Zeetlah says that goes fer him an' Half-hoss, too!"

Cesár nodded and grinned in agreement with Little Mountain's declaration of war, so I saw no profit in adding my own ha'p'ny's worth. My companions were likely correct in assuming that the *Mojaves* wouldn't be satisfied with a horse or two and we would have to fight them sooner or later. Besides, I suspect we were still itching for the battle that never happened with Batista's *lanceros*.

໕ ໕ ໕

When it arrived in the forenoon of the next day, the showdown was over almost as soon as it commenced. Suddenly a double score of mostly naked Indians armed with half-drawn bows, arrows nocked and ready, appeared as if by magic on the sandy landscape, blocking the trail and cutting off retreat in all directions. Three of them stood in our line of progress and commenced making menacing signs, one of them yelling in a tongue unknown to us.

"Don't be wastin' no time on 'em, fellers!" Turtle called out. "Them arrers mebbe got rattler pizen on 'em! Don't let 'em git no closer!" He whipped his rifle to his shoulder and fired, dropping the foremost member of the trio that stood in our way. The other two leaders and half a dozen others wilted in the volley that erupted from the rifles of the rest of us. Fast as we reloaded, nobody was able to get a second shot. For a moment the *Mojaves* stood frozen, transfixed, likely astonished by the thunder of our weapons. When the rest saw so many of their comrades flung to earth, they took to their heels, many of them dropping their bows in their haste to depart.

"Time we be gittin' out o' hyar!" Tuttle shouted. "Let's git these'hyar hosses movin' afore them Injuns git to thinkin' 'baout comin' back agin!"

Which we did. At a gallop.

໕ ໕ ໕

As fast as we traveled, almost always at a brisk trot or an easy-going lope, word of our deadly encounter with the *Mojaves* traveled even faster across the desert wasteland. Whenever we drew nigh a waterhole or river crossing, Indians scurried to depart, snatching up their belongings and hotfooting into the *chapparal* as soon as they spied us approaching. Even so, we never relaxed our vigilance, especially at night. Half our number stood guard while the others slept.

❧   ❧   ❧

Tuttle and I were riding scout one early forenoon, seeking a safe trail, when we first caught sight of the mountains, a purple-grey blur on the eastern horizon looming off the sandy plain. Tuttle reined his horse to a fidgeting halt and sat staring, open-mouthed, straining to make out familiar features. As we rode closer, he said, wonder in his voice, "Reckon ol' Daddy Mose an' his band o' Hebrews warn't no happier to see thet ol' Promise Land than we be right naow, lookin' out thar at ther Rocky Mountains an' knowin' we be purty soon comin' home."

His voice trailed off, then erupted in a yelp. "Lookee thar! Buffler, begawd!" I followed his gaze and his finger pointing eastward, where purple foothills fringed with greenery thrust up from the sunny plain. Sure enough, a cluster of perhaps a double score of shaggy brown bodies peacefully grazed their way across the prairie, blissfully unaware of our presence. It was all I could do to keep myself from rushing into their midst. Tuttle was fighting the same impulse, but we both realized that the ever-present western breeze at our back would carry our scent far in advance of our galloping horses, alerting the herd and scattering them into the foothills long before we could get close enough to shoot.

Without a word spoken, we wheeled our mounts and sped back to the column, where Tuttle roared out, "Buffler! Thar's buffler up ahead 'til hell won't have it, begawd! We gonna be chawin' on hump ribs afore thi'shere day's done!"

Whilst I switched my saddle to my Davey horse, my best buffalo runner, and Tuttle did likewise, we described to the others where the herd was grazing and how we might best flank them, staying downwind and at sufficient distance to prevent their catching sight of us. Fortunately for hunters, buffalo possess poor eyesight, but even so, they can spot movement from a long way off and their keen sense of smell makes up for their weak vision.

Six of us rode out from our column—Tuttle and me, naturally, because we had discovered the herd, Brass Turtle and Little Mountain, Micah, and young Half-horse, whom the Delawares considered to be most in need of experience running buffalo. Everybody was in high good spirits when we started out, but our mood sobered as we neared our prey. This was serious business. We had been too long without buffalo meat or a square meal of any sort. Every man's mouth watered at the prospect of fresh hump ribs, boudins, and raw liver.

The critters had remained pretty much where we had first espied them, moving on only gradually as they cropped the lush prairie grass. While the herd was still nigh half a mile distant, we cut sharply right until we discovered a shallow ravine that ran behind a gentle rise south of our quarry, which let us get to the leeward side of the herd without being detected. We filed through the gulch at a walk, nose to tail, hardly daring to breathe, for fear of betraying our presence. I made sure, once again, that my weapons were loaded and primed, pistols snug in their pommel holsters, rifle slung across my back.

When at last we reached the end of the narrow defile, we halted while Brass Turtle dismounted and crawled to the top of the ridge. He was grinning broadly when he clambered down and swung into his saddle. No words were needed. We had successfully flanked the herd.

My excitement flowed through my legs into my Davey horse as we emerged from our hidey-hole. His ears perked up and he tucked his chin against his chest, arching his powerful neck, forging against the curb, his choppy, mincing gait threatening to explode into a gallop, but he held himself in check, awaiting my signal. When it came with a slight forward shift in my weight, loosening the rein, and tightening my leg ever-so-lightly on his barrel, the spur barely grazing his hide, he threw himself into a headlong rush towards the buffalo grazing on the prairie, for the moment still unaware of our presence.

As we drew nigh, I saw that they were mostly two- and three-year-old bulls with a few old-timers amongst them. One of those veterans caught sight of us at last, threw up his great shaggy head, and bawled a terrified alarm to his fellows, which set them into a stampede, lumbering at first but rapidly gaining speed as they raced to get away, skinny tufted tails stiffly aloft, sturdy legs churning, huge bearded heads armed with deadly-sharp horns swinging wildly, snot and saliva streaming, gulping air to fuel their retreat.

Fast as they ran, we soon overtook them, scattering ourselves amongst the herd to harvest our prey. I spied a likely young bull and set off in pursuit. A twitch of the rein and a touch of my near-side spur brought us close alongside the furiously-pumping buffalo, Davey careful to stay clear of the huge swinging head and threatening horns, matching the critter's pace exactly, keeping me in place on the near side long enough to let me swing up my pistol at arm's-length, aim, and fire a ball cleanly behind the shoulder, shattering the lungs and likely busting the heart. The bull shuddered and broke stride, stumbled, and collapsed onto his knees, blood gushing from the mouth, bearded chin plowing a furrow in the sod. I shoved the empty pistol into its holster, patted Davey on the neck with a muttered endearment, yanked out my other pistol, and sped off to harvest a second bull.

The herd was running full-tilt now. Davey was taxed to close the distance on our quarry, but he called on some reserve of strength, flattening into an all-out gallop that had my moccasins combing the prairie grass, when suddenly I heard a loud, sickening, popping sound and Davey's agonized scream as he came to an abrupt halt, as if he had run into an invisible wall. He collapsed and spilled to his knees, hindquarters rising up and catapulting me out of the saddle and over his head, pitching me a rod or so out in front, my chin digging a furrow as I hit the ground—much like the young buffalo, I thought antically, until the rifle slung across my back caught up with my head and sent me off into blessèd darkness.

ॐ   ॐ   ॐ

The strained, anxious faces of Zeetlah and Finn McCool hovering over me swam out of a swirling red haze that faded into golden sunshine and a cloudless blue sky. I lay on my back, head propped on my saddle, a pounding headache throbbing in my temples, the acrid taste of prairie soil in my mouth, acutely aware of aches and pains throughout my entire body when I struggled to sit up. Which action was greeted with smiles on the faces of McCool and Zeetlah and a rumble of approving voices, in the midst of which I recognized Tuttle Thompson's Kentucky whine—"Gawddammit, Temple, ye gotta quit gittin' yerse'f bunged up like ye been doin'! Ye ain't much, mind ye, but I don't cotton to breakin' in anuther pardner!" He broke into a raucous horselaugh without waiting for the others to join him in appreciating his witticism.

McCool shoved his arm under my shoulders and helped me sit up, then tilted a flask to my lips. Fiery *aguardiente* flowed down my throat, welcome as much for washing away the taste of dirt in my mouth as for its restorative properties. Now I could see my father and Micah, the two of them grinning and nodding, now that it appeared that I wasn't knocking on death's door. Brass Turtle and Little Mountain sat with them and Turtle called out, "Best ye gitcherse'f together purty quick, Buck. Buffler hump's 'bout ready fer comin' off the fire. Ye cain't never tell if Mountain hyar'll fress up the whole shebang!"

I became aware of the tang of a cookfire of dried buffalo chips and the aroma of roasting meat suspended over the blaze on steel wiping rods, liver bubbling in copper kettles, and boudins sizzling in a couple spider skillets. Half-horse and our *Californio vaqueros* squatted around the fire, tending to cooking chores. Everybody's lips and cheeks bore traces of dried blood from indulging in fresh-killed liver. I felt a twinge of jealousy that I missed joining in that delicious ritual, before I reminded myself that I was lucky to be alive.

Tuttle hung back and waited for my father and Micah to visit with me, assuring themselves that I suffered no serious injury. When they departed, Tuttle told me what he had seen and done. "Fust thang I seed war yew and yer Davey hoss streakin' past, goin' like a bat out o' hell arter anuther buffler, when all of a sudden ever'thin' quits an' ol' Davey's screamin' somethin' pitiful and turnin' what 'peared like a whoppin' big cartwheel an' you're flyin' out in ther air like some kind o' big ol' bird an' fetchin' up on yer face, plowin' up ther prairie, an' out cold as Chris'mas!

"Wal, I ride up an' make sure ye ain't daid, afore I run back to yer Davey hoss an' see thar ain't nothin' I kin do fer ther pore sumbitch. He went an' stuck his nigh foreleg inter a badger hole! Goin' lickety-split like ye war doin', it broke off clean! He war suff'rin' somethin' awful, squirmin' an' screamin' an' thrashin. I done ther same as yew would'a, Temple. I put 'im out o' his mis'ry, quick as I could. 'T'warn't nuthin' else to do."

I nodded and thanked my friend for doing what must have been a painful task. Tears stood in his eyes by time he finished describing his chore. Privately I marveled at the compassion that Tuttle had felt for my injured horse, this man who had, time and again, killed, and usually scalped, enemies who had threatened our lives, without an apparent flicker of conscience, almost always exhibiting high good humor afterwards.

Tuttle astonished me then. He dug at tear-filled eyes with a grimy fist and said seriously, "I reckon I know what you be thinkin', Temple. You be wond'rin' haow come ol' Tuttle 'pears to be cryin' over a hoss, jes' naow, arter you seen me doin' a heap o' killin' durin' ther years you an' me been together. Wal, them 'ere Injuns I kilt war meanin' to be takin' our hair an' yer pore li'l innercent Davey hoss war jest doin' ther best he knowed haow to please ye. He din't desarve to be hurtin' like he war!"

He swallowed hard and spat. Then he fixed a hard look on me and added, "An' don't ye never dare be tellin' nobody thet ye saw Tuttle Thompson cryin', neither! I jest got somethin' in muh eye. Thet's what it war!"

I assured him that I had observed nothing unmanly in his behavior and would have said nothing if I had. Friends don't tattle on friends. Just then, Micah called out that we had best get a move on, else Little Mountain would eat it all. Tuttle helped me to my feet and half-dragged me to the cookfire, where the hump ribs were as tender and delicious as any I had ever tasted.

As for Davey, I saved my grieving for a private time.

⁎ ⁎ ⁎

I had more time than I would have wished to heal up from my bumps and bruises. Although we had arrived at the southern end of the Rockies, we were stalled. None of us knew a reliable trail northwards through the mountains. Diego and Pablo had been dependable guides up to then, but their knowledge was confined to the eastward trail to Santa Fe, and Cesár Pérez, years before, had come to the Rockies by way of Saint Louis. Normally we wouldn't have hesitated to strike out in a northerly direction and trust to luck that we would find our way through the mountains. This time, howsomever, we were encumbered by our wealth of livestock, especially the *palomillas*. They were by then pretty much herd-broke and mostly inclined to run with our saddle stock, but they were still half-wild, and unpredictable, especially the studs. They were too valuable to risk seeing them stampede off a mountain trail and into a deep canyon, likely taking our saddlers, pack animals, and all our plews and plunder along with them.

Meanwhile we tarried in a pleasant little valley, restoring the critters on rich forage, keeping ourselves well-fed on gangs of young buffalo bulls that wandered through, and jerking the extra meat against possible lean times when at last we would be able to commence our journey through the mountains. Each day, we sent out a couple pairs of scouts to discover a northward trail, but without success.

"Never thought I'd be wishin' to see aught o' them'ere gawddamn Santy Fee trappers ever agin," Tuttle lamented, "but I wou'n't mind a-tall ef jest one of 'em showed up along abaout naow to p'int aout ther way thet'ere bunch taken last year, gittin' to ronnyvoo on ther Siskerdee."

࿔ ࿔ ࿔

Tuttle got his wish sooner than he could have expected, although the Santa Fe trapper wasn't one of the rowdy bunch with whom we had parted company in California. Most of us were gathered at the cookfire later that day when Half-horse loped in from tending the herd and announced, "Li'l white-eyes comin' plenty quick!" He held up one finger to indicate a single rider and pointed east.

We hadn't long to wait. A couple minutes later, the rider, long hair flying and hallooing at the top of his voice, galloped straight up to our cookfire, skidded his horse to a halt, and flung himself from the saddle, laughing and yelling out, "Who'd'a thought it'd be you boys I come high-tailin' over hyar to warn! Anyhow, ye best be gittin' yer arse out o' hyar, quick as ye kin! Thar's a passel o' 'Rapahoes nigh what's likely seen yer purty yeller hosses an' got eyes fer 'em!"

As ye might suppose, the pleasure of meeting up with our old friend Kit Carson was somewhat tempered by the disagreeable news included in his greeting. Even so, we crowded around him, slapping him on the back, everybody talking at once, nobody hearing what was said, stooping to exchange *abrazos* with the sturdy little trapper, who stands not much more than five feet tall.

Once the hubbub subsided, Carson repeated his warning about an impending Indian raid on our horse herd. That wasn't surprising. We had tarried too long, every day increasing the chance that some sharp-eyed hunter would espy our animals and alert his band to easy pickin's.

We retired to the cookfire and Kit helped himself to hump ribs sizzling over the coals. "Do ye know a good way out o' these parts, Christopher, a daycent trail through the mountains we might be takin' to get this menagerie safely to the Seeds-kee-dee?" McCool asked our visitor, waving vaguely in the direction of our sizeable herd.

"'Deed I do," Kit responded. "Reason I come thisaway is 'cause I be headin' nawth, myownse'f, headin' fer ronnyvoo up thataway. Gawddamn Messican gobernador in Santa Fe's gittin' too gawddamn grabby lately, conferscatin' plews off us 'Merican trappers in the name o' the law an' then sellin' 'em on his own hook! I ain't abaout to let ol' Greedy Guts Alvarez stuff his gawddamn poke off my hard-workin' arse!" He quit talking, carved off another meaty rib, and attacked it with ferocity likely meant for the governor, after which he wiped his greasy chin on his leather sleeve and announced, "I left muh critters in a draw not far off. I'll go git 'em naow. Meantime, ye'd best gather yer hosses and git ready to pull stakes. The sooner we make tracks out o' hyar, the better off we'll be."

Gathering the herd and loading our plunder was quickly accomplished. By time Kit returned with his string of pack-animals, we were ready to fall in behind him and head into the mountains looming overhead. They seemed to stretch forever northwards, purple peaks poking into the clouds, a rugged stairway returning me to the only life I ever wish to lead.

~ ~ ~

The following days and weeks took us through high mountain passes where snow never melts in shady corners, into sheltered valleys lush with belly-high grass, home to a plenitude of wapiti, deer, and, now and then, stray bands of buffalo, across icy cold streams teeming with fat trout, following narrow trails threading amongst towering peaks, snaking high above blue valley floors, where critters wandering far below appeared no bigger than bugs.

We wasted no time trapping on our journey through the southern mountains, although we saw beaver sign aplenty. It was too late in the season for prime plews and every man in our party was itching to get to rendezvous. Tobacco was running short and whatever *aguardiente* we had carried along with us had long since disappeared.

It had been five years since Kit had traveled through that country, but he never faltered. Carson possesses an unerring sense of direction and an unfailing memory of landmarks and natural features of which few men, even amongst our mountaineer fraternity, can boast. From what I have seen, Kit is equaled in that regard only by Moses Harris and Jim Bridger. And of that distinguished trio, Black Harris is the only literate member. Neither Gabe nor Kit can read or write, which detracts not a whit from their smarts or sound judgment. Whatever it is that keeps those two very capable men from fathoming the mysteries of the printed page is more than balanced out by other qualities that guarantee their place amongst our natural leaders and most gifted wilderness guides.

Kit was fascinated by our descriptions of the California country we had visited and the people we had known there. Day and night, during long hours in the saddle and around the cookfire when we camped, he pumped us for our recollections of our experience there. Even Diego and Pablo were not immune from his interrogations. Kit's long residence in Santa Fe and Taos has equipped him with fluency in the Spaniard tongue and his friendly, easy-going manner immediately gained their trust and respect.

"Yep," he said dreamily one evening after supper. "Shore do wish I'd'a been up thar to ronnyvoo las' year when ol' Walker war hirin' on fer Californy. I'd'a gone along with y'all in a minute! Jes' settin' foot in that'ere country agin an' seein' an' doin' what y'all done whilst ye whar thar'd shore put a feather in a feller's cap!"

That remark brought Joe Meek to mind. They are much alike, despite Joe's great muscular bulk and Kit's wiry but diminutive build.

"I been thar oncet, early on, trappin' fer Ewin' Young when I war jist a kid, but we war sneakin' abaout, keepin' clear o' the Spanyard guv'mint, so we never got close to folks thar an' we pulled out fer Taos agin afore I had a chance fer gittin' to know hardly any of 'em or doin' any o' them'ere thangs ye been tellin' of."

∾   ∾   ∾

If horse-thieving Arapahoes were indeed on our trail, as Kit had warned us when he joined us at the foot of the southern Rockies, they never did catch up. The threat of a raid, howsomever, made us cautious during the daytime drive and especially at night, when we posted double the usual number of sentries on the herd. We lost not a single critter and Carson's trail through mountain valleys lush with plentiful springtime graze left our animals fat and sassy and full of vinegar, although we crowded every possible mile into every day.

Long hours in the saddle were rewarded by the pleasure of watching the well-bred young *palomillas* loping easily together along the trail, powerful muscles rippling in fluid grace under sleek creamy hides in the soft springtime sunshine for some reason called to mind the velvet melodies of Lucette's Negro musicians plying their fiddles and viols, creating tender music that nevertheless possessed a sturdy core of purpose and inspiration. Naturally I never expressed those notions aloud, but such thoughts helped to make the hours fly. Also, for a pastime, I amused myself by closely observing every possible detail of conformation and manner of going of each of our more than a hundred *palomillas*, so that when it came time to choose the individual horses that I would claim for my share, I knew which particular critters I wanted.

When we caught our first longed-for glimpse of the Seeds-kee-dee, Tuttle hollered out, "Thar she be! Ther Siskerdee! Ain't fur to Hoss Crick an' ronnyvoo naow! An' soon's we git thar, we're all gonna git rich! Once them Injuns an' some o' them'ere trappers git an eyeful o' these hyar purty yeller hosses thar won't be a beaver plew left in camp fer ther traders, 'ceptin' from us! We'll git 'em all, begawd!"

That night we drew straws to divide up the *palomilla* horses, allotting an equal share to Carson and the two *Californios*. At first, Kit modestly declined to accept his portion, saying that he had been heading thataway, anyhow, and he was grateful for the company, but we insisted that we would likely have lost most, if not all of the critters in the mountains without his guidance. As for the Mexican Army deserters, trading off their share of the *palomillas* would provide the two young Spaniards with the wherewithal to equip themselves with a proper outfit to join a trapping brigade after rendezvous.

Both Diego and Pablo were picking up American lingo at a rapid rate, starting, like most men do, with the cusswords. Neither Spaniard was literate in his native language, which usually indicates a limited vocabulary, so acquiring the couple hundred or so useful words in the new tongue was no great chore for either of them and the universal application of the present tense satisfied their simple needs without cluttering their minds with the complexities of English grammar.

The educated man is saddled with a much more difficult task in acquiring a foreign tongue, for he will inevitably insist on making fine distinctions in time, degree, and precise description in the new language, which demands a vocabulary several times greater and infinitely more precise than the meager lexicon required by his illiterate brother. The scholarly newcomer will likely also feel himself compelled, largely involuntarily, to master the unfamiliar orthography, mentally spelling out each new spoken word and phrase instead of merely mimicking the alien noise, and he will tax himself to fathom the origins of idioms he encounters in the foreign tongue, bothersome concerns of which his unschooled counterpart is blissfully unaware.

ॐ   ॐ   ॐ

We were tardy breaking camp the last morning before we arrived at rendezvous. The whites were shaving off at least a month's growth of whiskers and digging clean shirts out of their plunder and our Indians were bathing in the crick and primping like belles headed for a dance, donning their finest apparel and daubing colorful designs on their favorite saddlers. I was no different. Rummaging through my plunder after my bathe, I came upon the fancy quilled-and-beaded shirt that Kathleen had gifted me with, nearly two years before, when nobody had been sure if I would return alive from Saint Louis. As I slipped the butter-soft leather over my head and shrugged into that beautiful garment, I confess that I was hoping that Cat would recognize her handiwork and take it kindly that I was wearing it on this festive occasion.

At last my companions completed their fussing and preening and we were ready to gather our numerous herd of horses and mules and set out for the rendezvous, more than two hundred critters, of which more than half were the creamy *palomillas* which we had lifted from Narcisso Battista. Abundant graze and fresh water and easy traveling unburdened by riders or packsaddles had restored their original excellent fettle after the rigors of crossing the southern deserts. Warm, early-summer weather had let them shed the last of winter hair. Now they were fat and sleek and running free amongst our pack animals and spare saddlers.

"Would ye look at them'ere purty Messican hosses, would ye, naow?" Anse Tolliver crowed joyfully. "Jist one o' them'ere critters'll buy me booze enough to git me drunk an' keep me thataway fer the whole damn ronnyvoo!"

"An' a passel o' foofurraw, fer boot, enough to git a feller laid day an' night, long as we be hyarabaouts!" Tuttle chimed in. "Damn if them critters ain't easy on ther eyes! Ever' one of 'em'll bring a purty penny from whites an' Injuns alike!"

Anse and Tuttle, my father, and I were riding drag behind the herd, chousing up strays and laggards, the four of us feasting our eyes on the fat rumps of the *palomillas*, their snowy manes and tails flowing on the soft morning breeze as our charges loped easily towards Horse Creek on the last leg of our long journey, first crossing Black's Fork, a pretty, clear-running stream, where we paused to let the herd slake their thirst. Brass Turtle was riding point, choosing our route, and the rest of our people were scattered out on the wings and flanks, keeping the herd moving together in a more or less compact mass. The animals had been running together for a couple months, so even the unbroken *palomillas* showed little disposition to stray.

Now that we had divided up the *palomillas*, I was able to amuse myself as we loped along by observing the seven horses that I could now safely call my own. I had already chosen the one tall stallion that I intended to keep for myself, as well as two pretty mares that would be presents for Iris and Cat. A breeding pair, stallion and mare, would go as gifts to Iron Bow and his son Fast Horse. Which still left two *palomillas* for which I had no plans. I doubted that I would sell them. I didn't need the extra money they might bring and, even without counting those two, I already had more critters than I needed, several of which I intended to trade off at rendezvous. It was a happy concern, howsomever, and not worth troubling about.

The closer we got to Horse Creek, the more eager I became to be reunited with my daughter and, in spite of past disappointments, to renew my suit for Kathleen. I had tried, with indifferent success, to avoid thinking overmuch about Cat during my California wandering, choosing to lose myself in the here and now, declining to fret about matters I couldn't influence, let alone control. Cat's refusal to become my woman no longer rankled as much as it had a year before, but my determination to make her my own was stronger than ever. I reckoned that living with her would be a challenge, but I had always known that she was strong-minded. I found that somehow attractive. If she and I would make our life together, it must be as equal partners.

I had long admired Kathleen when I knew her as Rainbow's lifelong friend and Ned Godey's beloved wife—and then, after Rainbow's death, Iris's adoptive mother and a devoted friend to me. Only a friend, mind. Thinking of her otherwise would have been disloyal to Ned and unworthy of the friendship the three of us shared. Although I confess that hadn't always been easy.

Naturally my thoughts strayed to the possibility that she might have taken up with one of Iron Bow's warriors during the year we had been apart, but I quickly dismissed that idea as absurd. Strong-willed and determined as I knew her to be, no Indian man that I ever knew would be willing to put up with her independent nature. One or both of them would not have survived the honeymoon.

Now, after a year, my resentment at being denied had pretty much faded away. I was ready to enter the lists again, even if it meant risking rejection still another time. And truth be told, I was privately grateful to Cat for turning down my initial proposal. If she had accepted my offer the year before, I would never have experienced the wonders and pleasures of the California adventure.

And it was best that another year had passed since Ned's death, another year to heal and to accept the reality of life in the mountains, where sudden death might lurk beyond the next bend in the trail, from our fellow man, critters, or the vagaries of nature and circumstance. I recalled how very long it had taken for me to accept Rainbow's death. Now I chided myself for my impatience with Cat for declining my offer after only a few months since she had lost Ned.

Which naturally brought to mind that single memorable night of frantic lovemaking the summer before, when I discovered a naked Kathleen in my robes, eager for my caresses and insatiable in her demands for yet another coupling, then, next day, once again cool, distant, indifferent to my attentions. I had often revisited that frenzied scene in my imagination, trying in vain to fathom her intention, always forced to dismiss it as mere feminine caprice.

I expected to find Iris and Cat amongst Iron Bow's Séli band, likely already encamped at rendezvous. Passing the winter with the numerous, well-armed Flatheads was much safer for the two of them than if, under ordinary circumstances, they had come along with our trapping bunch. It has usually been our custom to shun the large company brigades during the fall and spring hunts, avoiding competition with company men and, trapping on our own hook, reaping a greater harvest of plews. Naturally such policy risks inviting hostile Indian attacks on our small bunch, which never numbered even a full score of men, but greed is a powerful influence on men's judgment. That behavior had become ingrained during our bachelor days and such habits are difficult to alter.

My heart was in my mouth when we splashed across Horse Creek and the tall lodges of Iron Bow's Flathead band came into view as we scrambled up the far bank. I strained to catch sight of a familiar face amongst the few people I espied walking amongst the lodges, but without success. My comrades commenced yipping and hoorawing as soon as we entered the outskirts of the trapper camp. Our critters, responding to our excitement, commenced whinnying and neighing and breaking into a faster gait. I was borne along on a torrent of free-running horseflesh. Renewing tender ties would need to wait until later.

-ooo-

1834 Rendezvous

We created more than our customary stir when we galloped into rendezvous with more than two hundred horses and mules. More than half were the golden *palomilla* horses of California. Trappers tumbled out of their bowers and tents and Indians raced from their villages to gaze in wonder upon the unusual blond horses thundering along beside the riverbank, long flaxen manes and tails streaming as they swept past the trappers' camps, their golden coats shimmering in mid-morning summer sunshine. Naturally we made the most of all the attention, yipping and hallooing and calling out to old trapper friends we spied in the crowd, glorying in the sheer delight of being amongst our own kind once again.

Anse Tolliver kept standing in his stirrups, craning his bony neck, hard blue eyes darting up and down the lanes between shelters, searching for trade tents amongst the cluster of trappers' lodges, tents, and bowers. "Any traders hyar yit?" he called out from time to time. The response was universally negative, always accompanied by a flurry of cusswords from trappers suffering from unsatisfied thirst.

"'Tis a blessin' fer us the traders be slow gettin' here this toime," Finn McCool observed, riding close beside me. "The free-trappin' lads'll still be full up wi' their stock o' plews an' likely willin' to part with a passel of 'em fer the sake o' flauntin' theirsel's on a handsome horse."

Tuttle overheard Finn's remark. Never one to neglect an opportunity for profit, he commenced yelling to the staring trappers, "Ye like the look o' these hyar purty hosses, do ye? Ef'n ye do, come on to our camp an' we'll dicker. They be fer sale, ever' one of 'em! Fetch yer plews along an' we kin git to dealin'!"

Brass Turtle was attempting to lead us away from the crowd, heading out of the trappers' camp in search of open ground where we might pitch our camp and pasture our livestock, when we spied Paddy McBride and Pretty Horse struggling through the sea of horses and mules, the chunky little redhead grinning and waving his arms, pointing upstream, his yelling drowned in the equine bedlam. At last they managed to force their mounts through the press of crowding horseflesh and get close enough to Turtle for Paddy to shout directions. Turtle nodded and gestured for us to fall in behind him, heading out of the encampment and into open country.

Some three miles farther upstream, on the tree-shaded banks of Horse Creek, we spied the lodges, bowers, and cookfires of the stay-behind remnants of our bunch, the married men and their wives and children, and our French-Canuck campkeepers, Yves Dureau and Jean-Luc L'Archéveque, who were first to come running out to greet us and were nearly trampled by the mob of excited horses and mules.

"Look out thar, ye damn idjits," Tolliver roared, "afore ye gitcherse'f trompled to a gawddamn jelly! Most o' these hyar critters ain't broke, nohaow!"

The two Frenchies paid him no nevermind. They were too busy pouring out a welter of *bienvenues* and *bon accueils, bras ouverts*, and the like, their whiskery faces wreathed in smiles, welcoming us prodigals back to the closest thing to home that any of us had known for a dozen years.

Red-faced Paddy McBride rode from one of us to another, leaning out of his saddle to wrap us in a welcoming hug, his bright blue eyes misty with sentiment. "Och, Temple darlin'," he yelled into my ear, "'Tis a blessin' to see the lot o' yez, it is, surely! A sight fer sore eyes, it is! And all o' yez, too! Not a one o' ye gone under, thank the good Lord!"

Naturally the Iroquois Acorn and Stone Bird and the Delaware Pretty Horse were more reserved in their greeting than their Gallic and Gaelic comrades, but their quiet smiles conveyed an equally warm welcome. The two Iroquois had caught up their saddlers before coming out to meet us. Now they helped drive our herd to the meadow where their own animals were pastured.

By time we returned to camp to unload our pack animals and set up our bowers, the campkeepers had built up their cookfires. Great gobbets of buffalo meat crackled and hissed on steel ramrods suspended over the fire, dripping flavorsome fat onto the coals, misting the camp in a mouthwatering brume of delicious fragrance. Boudins sizzled in a brace of spider skillets nestled in the coals and thick slices of fresh tongue bobbed and boiled in tin-lined copper kettles slung over the flames. Especially appetizing were stews of meat and wild onions and all manner of prairie roots and tubers gathered by Paddy's wife Molly and the other Indian wives.

"Och, 'twas truly a sign from heaven, it was, surely," Paddy was saying. "Our Eerie-quah hunters come along this foine mornin', one after t'other, each of 'em bringin' in all the best parts o' two differ'nt bufflers. T'was far too much fer our little camp as it was, mind ye, but jist enough fer feastin' the lot of us now!"

"While you're after lookin' fer heavenly signs, Paddy," McCool suggested with a chuckle, "be a good lad an' see if ye can 'spy a sign that shows us where to lay hands on a jug or two o' poteen fer wettin' our whistle. The lads downriver were sayin' there's not a drop to be had in all o' the rendezvous."

"Ah, would that I could, Finnæus darlin'!" Paddy replied. "Your thirst can be no greater than me own an' those lads are after tellin' no lies. Not a solitary trader has shown his face so far!"

It was not surprising that no traders had yet managed to put in an appearance. Pack trains rarely departed Saint Louis before the last days of April, lest they bog down in the muddy prairies east of South Pass. Scarcely ten days of June had passed so far, which meant that we would likely need to wait as much as a fortnight more to slake our thirst. I shuddered at the prospect of listening to my comrades' grumbling for that long.

"I be as dry as anybody hyar," Brass Turtle advised, "but bitchin' about it ain't goin to hurry 'em up any. We might as well make the most o' the time we got fer tradin' off our Californy hosses. The longer them'ere free trappers hafta wait fer traders to show up, the more their plews'll be burnin' holes in their packsaddles, an' the better our purty Californy critters'll be lookin' to 'em. Same fer Injuns. If we play it right, thar won't hardly be a beaver plew left in the whole damn ronnyvoo, 'ceptin' with us!"

It was the best advice available. There was naught else to do right then. At that precise moment, howsomever, our ideal course of action was doing our best to founder ourselves on the heaps of tender buffalo meat that our cooks were serving up. Which we nearly did.

After supper, Tuttle, Brass Turtle, my father, and I gathered the others who had made the California trip in council to discuss a delicate matter, upon which the future harmony of our trapping bunch might have depended. As it turned out, howsomever, we could have saved our worry. Almost as soon as we brought up the matter, every man amongst us, including Kit and the two

Mexicans, voted to donate one of his *palomillo* horses to the four married men who had stayed behind, which amounted to fourteen critters, a convenient number which let us gift each married trapper with three *palomillo*s, with one pretty critter left over for each of our faithful campkeepers.

~ ~ ~

Next morning Half-horse lent me a welcome hand halter-breaking the *palomilla* stud and mare that I meant to present to Iron Bow and his son Fast Horse. Once again I marveled at the young fellow's natural gift in gaining the critters' confidence, convincing them to accept without resistance the unfamiliar rope halter around their sensitive ears, then to follow the lead of the haltershank, all while he cooed and murmured endearments, running his hands gently over their bodies, letting them nuzzle his armpits, and blowing his breath into their nostrils. Within two hours' time, the stallion and mare were ready to be led off to their new owners.

The night before, it had been all I could manage to stay put with the bunch and not go running off to the Séli camp to see my daughter and Cat, but custom dictated that I not show up empty-handed. Now my arrival at Iron Bow's lodge trailing these two handsome horses, the like of which had almost certainly never been seen in the mountains, assured me of a warm welcome by my former father- and brother-in-law. Less predictable was the kind of greeting I might expect from Kathleen. Just the same, I was nigh giddy at the prospect of renewing my suit for her affections.

I chided myself for devoting so much attention to thoughts of Cat, rather than to my daughter, but, ever practical, I told myself that if Iris remembered me at all, after a year's absence, she would love me, but I could have no reasonable expectation of encountering such a sentiment on Cat's part.

I was saddling my mouse-grey gelding—called a *grulla* in Spanish for its similarity in color to the long-legged marsh bird called a crane—when my father volunteered to accompany me to the Séli village. I welcomed his offer. His presence would make it easier for me to excuse myself from Iron Bow's company when I wished to go a-calling. The two older gentlemen had always enjoyed each other's company.

They recognized in each other many of the leaderlike qualities which they value in themselves, even though Powatawa no longer aspires to lead anyone. He had willingly abdicated his chieftainship amongst the Shawnee when he chose to accompany me to the mountains six years before. My half-brother Chiksika had leapt at the chance to succeed him and Powatawa greeted his younger son's ambition with a feeling of relief. My father had been a changed man, lighthearted and free of care, since the day he had put aside his headman duties and we had set out to begin his new life. Even so, some men always carry the air of easy authority of the natural leader, whether they mean to do so or no, and my father is onesuch.

ॐ   ॐ   ॐ

My sharp-eyed daughter espied us even before we reached the outer ring of Flathead lodges. She came running through the tall grass, joyful tears streaming down her chubby cheeks, screaming "Papa! Papa!" swallowed up in a string of Salish syllables, then more shrieks of "Bon papa!" when she saw that my companion was her grandfather. I leaned down and swept her onto the saddle bow, hugging her close and bathing her cheeks in kisses. Suddenly I choked up when I let myself admit how much I love my dark-eyed girl-child.

Powatawa and I handed her back and forth, from one saddle bow to the other, hugging her and talking nonsense, as we threaded a passage amongst the rings of lodges to the center of the Séli village where Iron Bow and his son would likely be waiting. On the way, I dug into my belt-pouch and brought out a handful of colorful seashells that I had gathered on the shore of the Western Sea. They produced appreciative squeals from my little girl, especially when I described the vast ocean that produced them.

Iron Bow's people crowded into the alleys between the lodges, eager to get a close look at the cream-colored horses with the beautiful flowing flaxen manes and tails and enormous kind brown eyes. Of all the tribes I have known in the Rockies, I believe the Flatheads possess the greatest love for and understanding of their horses, but if that is so, every other tribe in that horse-crazy culture runs them a close second.

Iris's childish prattle cut short when we caught sight of Iron Bow and Fast Horse standing with half a dozen other headmen outside Iron Bow's big lodge. She fell silent out of respect for her grandfather and the other leaders, hastily pecked my cheek, slipped to the ground, and scooted off, looking back over her shoulder and flashing a shy smile, gesturing that I should follow when I was able to do so.

The venerable chieftain was barely able to tear his eyes away from the two *palomillas* long enough to welcome Powatawa and me to the village. Fast

Horse never did. The stallion and mare were much more than a pair of pretty hides. They both possessed excellent conformation and every good physical quality that a discerning breeder might possibly wish for, coupled with a willing disposition bred into their bloodline centuries before in their native Spain, while retaining the proud, fiery spirit demanded by every serious horseman. These two were no more than five years old, so if Fast Horse were able to keep the Crows and Snakes from stealing them, they would provide excellent breeding stock for Iron Bow's band for many years to come.

Truth be told, the only reason that I could bear to part with this stud and the mare was because the stallion and two mares that I had chosen to keep for my own were even better. Naturally I saw no good reason to mention that to Iron Bow and Fast Horse.

I have never mastered the flowery, formal, ceremonial speech so beloved by Indians, but, somehow or other, by signs and my limping Salish syllables, I stumbled through the presentation in sufficient style to satisfy the requirements of custom. I doubt that any of my auditors were paying much attention to what I was saying, anyway. They were much too occupied with examining the *palomillas* from every angle, running their hands over their sleek quarters, and chattering about their qualities in a most admiring fashion.

At last Iron Bow had his fill of admiring the *palomillas*, leastaways for the moment, and remembered his manners sufficiently to invite Powatawa and me into his lodge, along with the other headmen, to smoke and palaver and, naturally, to eat. While the pipe traveled around the circle, Iron Bow, Fast Horse, and the other elders belabored my father and me with surprisingly astute questions about our travels in the western regions, especially concerning the great Western Sea, the Indian people we met, the whites who live thereabouts, the weather, the critters we discovered there, and especially the food people eat in those parts. They were shocked and unbelieving when we told them there are no buffalo west of the Great Salt Lake. One of the headmen was sufficiently astonished by that revelation that he so forgot his manners that he suggested that perhaps we had simply failed to see them, his manner implying that he wondered if we might be lying, which elicited a sharp clearing of the throat by Iron Bow and a hasty, mumbled apology on the part of the offending elder, who doubtless remained unconvinced of our veracity.

Which was not surprising, considering that most of our mountaineers had also refused to believe that there are no buffalo in California and kept looking for the great shaggy beasts for as long as we remained there.

After an hour and more of feasting and passing the pipe, when the palaver commenced to run somewhat shallow, I reckoned it might be acceptable to our hosts for me to make my exit. I was unprepared, howsomever, for the genial manner in which Iron Bow greeted my request and somewhat mystified by the fleeting, faintly amused, almost conspiratorial look he exchanged with Fast Horse when I did so. But anxious as I was to be on my way, I shrugged off my puzzlement, told Powatawa I would join him later, and retreated from their company.

I hadn't traveled five paces, squinting in the bright summer sunshine, unsure where to find Cat and Iris, before my little girl popped out from behind a lodge, grabbed my hand in hers, and commenced pulling me along to the lodge she shared with Kathleen, never ceasing her excited chatter, except, now and then, to giggle and shriek in childish delight. Glancing back, I chuckled when I spied Iron Bow and his guests come spilling out of the lodge, anxious to feast their eyes once more upon their pretty new horses. My little girl and I quickly acquired an entourage of noisy children trooping along with us. My presence there was apparently not unexpected. Women smiled at us and men nodded gravely but in a friendly manner as we trotted through the alleyways between the lodges.

My Coffee horse standing hock-deep in prairie hay, tethered at the doorway identified Cat's lodge as plainly as if he were a painted sign. His eager nickering was more than likely directed towards Iris, but right then I preferred to think that he recognized me after my year-long absence. Iris dropped my hand and streaked to the lodge, ducking past the low doorflap, squealing news of my arrival. Uncertain of the reception I might encounter, I hesitated in the alleyway for a spell before closing the distance to my Coffee horse and reaching up to scratch his ears. This time there was no doubting that he remembered me. He nuzzled my armpit, snuffling and blowing delightedly, his velvety muzzle caressing my cheek, vigorously butting his brow against my belly in affectionate recognition, nearly knocking me off my feet.

When I regained my balance I found myself staring into Kathleen's smiling eyes. I could not have wished for a more desirable sight right then. My concern about how she might greet me instantly washed away. I feasted my eyes upon her lovely features, unable to think of aught to say, deciding that what I was thinking right then would likely be inappropriate to mention anyway, content merely to bask in the presence of that beautiful woman. Cat appeared more lovely just then than I had ever known her to be. She glowed with a rosy inner warmth, an easy grace, so different now from the way she had been the year before, when she had appeared to attack life rather than merely meeting and dealing with it.

Her body, under her soft doeskin dress, looked softer, slightly fuller, her bosom somewhat rounder than I remembered it. Which resulted in what might have proved my downfall. She caught me staring, dropped her eyes, and blushed, her deeply tanned cheeks coloring deep rose, which, fortunately for me, resulted in a girlish giggle instead of a scowl.

At last she spoke, her strong, slender fingers complementing and enriching with graceful sign-talk the meaning of her words. "Your place at our fire has been too long empty, Tompo. You are welcome here."

I managed to strangle out a suitable reply, which led to her enquiring about the well-being of my companions on the journey to California. Since everyone had survived without mishap, that smoothed the way to further pleasant palaver, carefully avoiding anything personal or intimate between the two of us. After a time, howsomever, we ran out of talk while we were still standing beside my Coffee horse outside her lodge. Our encounter was becoming awkward. By that time, custom required that she invite me inside for coffee or tea.

Iris, bored with our grown-up palaver and likely feeling the tension, commenced to fidget. Soon she scampered off to show her pretty seashells to her playmates. Cat first looked relieved, then anxious. Now she could no longer put off whatever was causing her discomfort. She kept glancing towards her lodge.

Without another word, she caught hold of my hand and half-dragged me to the modest traveling lodge she shared with my daughter and pulled me inside. When I stood erect, my eyes slowly adjusting to the dim interior after the bright sunshine outdoors, I made out what I recognized as a colorful quilled cradleboard hanging from one of the lodgepoles. Cat reached up and pulled loose the slipknot that held it up, caught it in the crook of her arm, then thrust it into my arms, taking care not to turn it completely loose, for, surprised as I was at her next words, I likely would have dropped it.

"Here, Tompo," she said with a throaty chuckle, obviously relieved now that she had traded anxious hesitation for decisive action, "it is time you meet your man-child."

I surely would have lost hold of the cradleboard and its precious cargo if she hadn't kept a firm grip on it. While the full meaning of her words seeped into my mind, I went weak in the knees, striving to wrap my mind around this startling news, memory racing back to our single night of passionate coupling a year before, brain awhirl with a thousand thoughts, weighing the odds against Cat conceiving a child in just that single encounter, while at the same time exulting over fathering a son, hope surging that now Cat couldn't refuse to be my woman, then—as nearly every man except possibly Adam has likely questioned at such a moment—wondering if the child were truly mine.

Although I hadn't uttered a single word, Cat divined that fleeting doubt. "So, Tompo, you are thinkin' maybe he is not your boy?" She ignored my sputtered protests and took the cradleboard from me. Then, clutching it to her bosom, she bent down and ducked through the doorway, calling back over her shoulder, "Come. I will show you."

I followed her outside, still insisting that I never doubted her, but she merely giggled and paid me no nevermind. All the jostling roused the infant. He came awake with a lusty bellow worthy of a young buffalo bull. Cat calmed him by giving him her breast. When he had drunk his fill and settled into a fitful doze, I was able to see what a handsome young fellow he was, even if his eyes were squinched tight shut against the bright sunshine. "Come," Cat ordered, and carried the infant to the shady side of the lodge, where she commenced to jiggle the cradleboard ever so gently and croon into his ear until he opened his eyes and dispelled for all time any doubt that I or anyone else might have regarding his paternity.

He was mine and no one else's, for in all the vast Rocky Mountain wilderness only his sister Iris also possessed the deep violet eyes of my mother.

Now I understood Iron Bow's sniggering exchange with Fast Horse when I excused myself to go to visit Cat. They had known about the baby since his birth and long before then and that I was ignorant of his existence. I reckoned, too, that Powatawa had learned that he had a grandson before I did.

"How will you call him?" Cat asked, rousing me abruptly from my thoughts.

"Ben," I replied without thinking. "We'll call him Ben."

"Ben," she repeated and said it a time or two more, as if testing its weight upon her tongue. "Yes, it is a good name—to begin with."

I didn't mention that it is not a white-eyes custom to keep changing our name throughout our lives. I was aware, howsomever, that young Ben would collect a passel of Séli names in the course of his growing-up, according to his character, exploits, and accomplishments and very likely from what he might see at the time of his vision quest.

Ben—the name had rolled off my tongue without my thinking about it, as if I had carried it in a secret chamber of my heart, waiting for the day that I might bestow it upon my son in the hope that he might carry on the sturdy character and honest virtues of my Uncle Benjamin Buck, who taught me to ride and shoot, to hunt and trap and survive in the Ohio wilderness. But most important, it was he who first showed me how to be a man.

Cat made as if to re-enter her lodge, but I caught her sleeve and tugged, inviting her to sit beside me in the shade. The child was sleeping peacefully on his cradleboard and Iris had run off with her playmates.

She sank down beside me and propped the cradleboard against the lodge. Ben blew a milk bubble or two before he settled into slumber. I was uncertain where and how to commence this long-overdue conversation, but I was equally sure that I would not, could not tolerate even one more day of uncertainty concerning my future with this woman, if, indeed, I was destined ever to have onesuch. Whilst I was trying to gather my thoughts, I glanced down at her smooth brow, dusky cheek, and soft lips curved in a gentle smile. I felt my resolve melting, lest I speak clumsily and offend her and lose her forever.

Before I could get a word out, she swung about and stared me full in the face, the smile gone now, before she demanded, "You still want me for your woman?" Without waiting for my reply, she declared, "I told you no, before. I was not ready. It was too soon. I needed no pity. I needed time to grieve alone. My heart was small, dry. I could not be a proper woman for a man."

I opened my mouth to respond, but she reached up and placed a finger gently on my lips. Her words came now in a rush, her fingers flying in rapid sign-talk. "You were already in my heart, Tompo, but I could not give you half a woman. It was better that I lose you than cheat you. Then you spoke of your long journey with the others. Maybe you would return. Maybe not. If not, I wanted a child with you, my child and yours, so I came to your robes on a night I was sure I would get with child. The Spirit smiled. I have Ben."

I need to explain that Kathleen didn't precisely use that exact language. This was the general sense I derived from her torrent of excited words and sign-talk. I love and respect her too much to render her quaint English here. It sounds much better than it reads.

Actually, when we speak to each other we use a macaronic sort of speech made up of English and Salish mixed with some Shoshone and a smattering of Nez Percé. I had picked up a workable knowledge of Salish during my years with Rainbow almost without realizing that I was doing so, much the same as I had done with the Shoshone and Crow tongues. A couple-three hundred words, or even fewer, is all that one needs to get most useful things said. Almost all of our speech is accompanied by hand-signs. Misunderstanding rarely occurs.

I once asked Cat if she minded being deprived of her Salish name, Sin-gel-eh Sim, Coyote Woman. She told me she prefers her American name Kathleen, which she pronounces Cataleen, or Cat. The name Coyote Woman was apparently bestowed on her not as a compliment but a reproach for her nimble mind, independent nature, and effective arguefying, qualities not considered appropriate in a woman.

I never did reply to her first question—if I still wanted her to be my woman—leastaways not right then. Instead I took her in my arms and pressed my lips hard against hers. She responded with an eager ferocity that brought to mind her American nickname, Cat—more like a catamount in the wild, howsomever, than a house pet.

It soon became apparent to us both that mere kissing would not be enough. She rose, hauled me to my feet, picked up the cradleboard, and led me around the lodge to the doorflap, pushed me inside, and, as she retreated after me, set a pair of crossed sticks in front of the doorway as a sign that neighbors should not come a-calling.

Whilst she was hanging the cradleboard from a lodgepole, I spoke the single word "Iris," to which Cat replied that a neighbor woman had offered to look after our little girl overnight. I greeted this announcement with a snort and a chuckle. She had planned this outcome from the start. Any lingering doubts I might have had about her feelings and intentions instantly whisked away. In a flash of understanding it became clear to me what had driven Cat the year before, how she had risked her security and future happiness rather than deprive our union of a full measure of undistracted love and total commitment that she meant to devote to it.

I dropped down upon her sleeprobes, already spread out invitingly, and caught her hand in mine, pulling her down beside me. As she sank to her knees, she twisted out of her soft leather dress and tossed it aside, revealing completely the breathtaking coppery beauty that had filled my dreams for a year and more. Her eager lips found mine in a long, lingering kiss, whilst her busy hands fumbled at my britchclout until she succeeded in her search for the magical wand that granted our wish, again and again, until we fell into exhausted slumber.

Dawnlight peeking through the smokehole of the lodge roused us, calling us to our chores, chief of which that day would be returning my woman and children to their rightful place amongst my bunch. Now that Cat and I had at last pledged our love, neither she nor I saw any reason to part even for a single night.

❧　❧　❧

Packing up and moving never takes much time for Indians or trappers. Everything we own is readily portable. Even the lodgepoles of our dwellings serve as travois drags when we are on the move. After a hasty breakfast, Cat and I packed up her camp before we rode out to the pasture of Iron Bow's band to round up the horses she and Ned had owned and those that I had left in her keeping the year before. Early that morning, Iris had retrieved my *grulla* saddler from her grandfather and brought him to Cat's lodge, where I had the pleasure of stripping off my saddle and putting it on my Coffee horse.

The *grulla* was a first-rate animal, but, compared with my Kentucky-bred Coffee, he seemed almost like a different breed of critter. The moment I swung into the saddle it felt as if a lightning bolt coursed through my thighs, into the core of my being, Coffee's strength blending with my own, our spirits fusing into a single soul.

By time Cat and I finished gathering our animals, it was plain that we owned far too many horses. We couldn't take all of them with us, once trapping season commenced, especially counting more than a dozen critters of my own still in the trappers' camp. Cat assured me there was no need to worry. Before we departed the Séli camp that morning, custom required that we pay our respects to Iron Bow. Cat intended to gift him and Fast Horse with half a dozen horses in gratitude for the hospitality and protection they had provided during the previous year. Horseflesh on the hoof is the coin of the high prairies and no Indian warrior ever thinks he owns too many critters.

As we approached Iron Bow's lodge, I spied my father, already mounted, loping out to meet us, eager to see his grandson. Young Ben, swinging in his cradleboard from Cat's saddlebow, didn't disappoint his grandfather. He was wide-awake and bellowing like a bull-calf. Powatawa's grin grew even broader when he caught sight of the infant's eyes. He and Cat exchanged warm greetings, for they were long-time friends, drawn even closer now by kinship ties, before he dropped back amongst the loose horses to embrace little Iris, who had insisted on assuming the duties of horse-wrangler and was doing a good job of it. He leaned far out of his saddle to hug her and whispered something in her ear that made her laugh before he settled in beside her to help keep our critters gathered until we reached the chief's lodge in the center of the village.

Herd boys came running and took charge of our animals. We dismounted, greeted our host, and entered Iron Bow's lodge, where he strained tribal tradition by including Cat and Iris amongst his guests for the midday repast, otherwise an exclusively male affair, which he justified by using that occasion to adopt Kathleen officially as his daughter. It was a gesture long overdue. Cat had been mother to his granddaughter ever since Rainbow's death three years before. Iris had no memory of any other mother.

Cat gifted her new parent with six good horses as a mark of filial piety and respect. The custom fitted nicely into our own needs at that time, but it also prompted Iron Bow to declare that I was welcome to join his band and the Séli nation. He further promised that if I did so, the horses would be returned to us, together with the progeny of the mares.

℞   ℞   ℞

Our trapper camp was buzzing with commerce when our little party arrived. Powatawa and I lingered to observe the fun while Cat and Iris rode on into camp to erect our lodge. Tuttle was haranguing a cluster of trappers and half a dozen Indian men about the superior merits of a handsome *palomilla* stallion that Little Mountain was parading about, extolling the animal's superior qualities in physique and character, even insisting that it was an advantage that the horse was completely untrained.

"Thisaway, ye won't hafta be puttin' up with some other feller's bad habits when ye go to startin' off thi'shere beeyootiful critter what's got a couple hunnert years o' fust-rate breedin' in ther ol' country behind 'im, jest fer startin' off. I'd be keepin' ever' las' one o' these hyar hosses fer myownse'f, if'n I could, but natcherly I cain't be doin' no sech a thang, so yew git ther chance of a lifetime to own sech a magnifercent ee-quine fer yerownse'f to go paradin' in front o' all o' them purty Injun gals. An' thar ain't no gal that'll be tellin' ye no, once they git an eyeful o' yew up thar astride o' thi'shere fancy hoss!"

Most, if not all, of Tuttle's prattle was lost on the Indians in the crowd, but it was plain to see they were already sold on the *palomillas*, impressed by the young animals' obvious admirable breeding and sound condition, gentle disposition, and especially on their exotic blond good looks. Most white trappers waste little sentiment on their horses and mules. They value their animals purely for their usefulness. Indians, too, demand a great deal from their workaday critters, but Indians, men and women alike, regard their favorite saddle horses differently from whites. They treat them almost as a part of their own persons, adorning their hides with painted symbols and patterns, braiding ribbons and trinkets into their manes and tails, and lavishing much of their wealth on elaborate saddles, ornate quilled and beaded apishamores, elegant bridles, breast-collars, and other equestrian frippery. Tuttle might have saved his breath. The pretty *palomillas* needed no fast-talking huckster. They would sell themselves, leastaways to Indians.

As Powatawa and I rode off to join Cat and Iris in camp, I glanced back in time to see the young *palomilla* stud horse being led off by a Shoshone buck and Tuttle and Little Mountain hauling away a sizeable heap of plews and buffalo robes they had received in payment. My father chuckled and commented, "Tuttle talks purty pictures, but Injuns don't ride pictures. When they see our milky horses up close in their village, it will eat on them. Many more will come to buy."

And so it turned out. For the next week, every day saw more and more Indians riding into our camp, eager to swap their beaver plews and other fine furs and soft-tanned buffalo robes for a cream-colored California horse or mare. Often a couple-three Indian men pooled their furs and robes together to meet the steadily-increasing price as the craze to own a *palomilla* gained momentum, sweeping at last like a prairie fire through the entire rendezvous. The traders making their leisurely way from Saint Louis were contributing handsomely to the wealth of my companions by their continued absence. White trappers and Indians alike were bored, forced to stay sober, with little besides gambling to distract them, so they readily fell victim to the current craze to own a *palomilla*. It was merely a passing fancy, but it worked to the advantage of our bunch while it lasted.

By the time Bill Sublette's pack train showed up on Horse Creek on the nineteenth of June and moved in beside Rocky Mountain Fur, most of the *palomilla*s were gone from our pasture, scattered now throughout the rendezvous, mostly in Indian camps. A rivalry had sprung up amongst the various tribes to see who might claim to own the most pretty blond horses. Only the Nez Percés, smugly convinced of the superiority of their own spotted paloosie horses, remained aloof from such foolishness.

My comrades were giddy with glee as they gloated over the growing heaps of beaver plews and buffalo robes they were accumulating. Cookfire palaver in our camp concerned little else than calculating the probable worth of their growing stores of robes, beaver, and other fine furs. So great was the greed that had taken hold of them, some of them sold off all of their *palomilla*s, holding onto not even a single one of those excellent critters for their own use.

Except for the married men, who each kept at least one of the pretty blond horses for his wife to ride. As you might suppose, their restraint had little to do with their strength of character. A trapper would have known no peace and little marital comfort if he had dared to deprive his woman of the opportunity to parade on a stylish *palomilla*.

Listening to the chatter about how much booze and foofurraw they could afford now, it came to me how little cash-money wealth a proper mountaineer can use or appreciate. Once he renews his outfit and purchases supplies for the coming trapping season and buys enough trade plunder and gewgaws to guarantee his getting laid every night of rendezvous, besides affording a daily skinful of trader's booze for himself and his good friends, a trapper has little use for money. Unless he intends to return to the settlements. Which hardly any healthy mountaineer in his right mind is willing to do.

Even though Sublette's arrival at rendezvous meant booze was available at Rocky Mountain Fur and Nat Wyeth's showing up the next day signaled even more, our bunch showed remarkable restraint, trading only enough plews to guarantee a drunken spree and enough hair-o'-the-dog to cure the next-morning effects thereof. Brass Turtle advised, "It won't do fer us to be tradin' ever'thin' we got right off, afore all o' the traders git hyar. Thar's still Amurrican Fur an' Mike Cerré fer Cap'n Bonnyville what ain't got hyar yet. Once they show up, that's when the compertishun'll set in proper. Then beaver an' everthin' else we been pilin' up'll git a damnsight more dear."

Naturally our people weren't the least bit tardy about getting drunk, along with all the other trappers and Indians, as soon as Sublette first knocked the bungs out of his kegs. Rendezvous exploded into riotous action. The sullen pall that had hung over the camps scattered along the banks of Horse Creek whilst trappers awaited the arrival of the traders evaporated like morning dew in sunshine. Fiddle music, Indian drums, drunken laughter and raucous song, the cheers of spectators watching horse races and foot races, and gunfire from shooting matches filled the air around the traders' camps from early morning until far into the night.

Nathaniel Wyeth, the skinflint Yankee trader, arrived a day after Bill Sublette and, unaccountably, almost immediately commenced selling his booze cheaper than the equally tight-fisted Sublette had been doing. Naturally the rendezvous became even rowdier and some of us wondered what could have inspired such unprecedented generosity and good-fellowship on the part of the customarily rapacious New Englander.

Once again, Brass Turtle cautioned our fellows to exercise restraint in parting with their plews. American Fur and Bonneville's packtrain from Saint Louis had not yet arrived.

⇢ ⇢ ⇢

As soon as Nathaniel Wyeth's packtrain arrived on Horse Creek, rumors commenced flying about bad blood betwixt the Yankee trader and Tom Fitzpatrick, who was keeping close company with Bill Sublette. I recollected what Black Harris had told me the year before about a scheme that the Yankee was hatching up with Rocky Mountain Fur. As soon as Black was free from the chores he owed Bill Sublette, I latched onto him, a tried-and-true fount of mostly-reliable gossip, and led him off to a shady grove. On the way, I asked, "Whatever became o' young George Holmes, Black, that polite, helpful kid the hostlers were callin' Beauty on the way up thisaway last year?" I feared that I already knew.

Black's mood turned glum. "I know who ye mean," he replied sourly, "the young feller what got bit by that'ere hydrophoby wolf last year, sleepin' outside o' Stewart's tent. Wal, ye saw the fust part of it, when it looked like mebbe he war goin' to git away with jist a bunch o' bad scratches, but arter we got on the trail, headin' east, he got real quiet, quit talkin' to ever'body, an' then, arter a coupl'a days, comin' onto a crick, he hung back, refusin' to cross over, gittin' real wild-eyed, an' commenced ravin' somethin' awful, gnashin' his teeth an' foamin' at the mouth, afore he jumped off his hoss an' run off inter the brush screamin' an' never come back. We hung around a spell, but not fer long, 'cause it war plain he war sure to die—an' the sooner the better to put 'im out o' his mis'ry."

I handed him my booze kettle, always an effective tool to prime Harris's pump, and demanded, "What's happenin', Black? Word is, ol' Wyeth's mad as hell at Rocky Mountain Fur an' he's takin' the most of it out on Tom Fitzpatrick. Ye told me they had some kind o' deal."

Harris took a healthy swig before he replied, "Oh, whar to commence? Sounds like ye don't know nothin' 'bout what's been happenin' this past year, since I seen ye last." I assured him that it was so.

"Wal, naow, backin' up some'at, as I reckon ye do know, Billy Sublette an' Bobby Campbell been busy as hell fer more'n a year buildin' a string 'o tradin' forts 'long the Missourah an' some ways up the Yellerstone, lookin' like they war aimin' to crowd out ol' King McKenzie an' Amurrican Fur thar on the Yellerstone. Course, thar war fat chance o' their doin' that, but jist the same, they put the fear o' God inter McKenzie an' commenced a helluva compertishun fer beaver, which got Amurrican Fur to payin' up to twelve dollars the pound fer prime plews. Natcherly Billy couldn't come close to matchin' that kind o' cash, though McKenzie din't know that fer sure.

"What the two of 'em done then war, Bobby stayed up on the Missourah, runnin' the bizness an' seein' if he could make some kind o' deal with McKenzie, whilst Billy went on down to Sain' Louie with what furs they had, then on to New York fer talkin' bizness with the big bosses at Amurrican Fur. Turns out, he couldn'a got thar at a better time. 'Pears ol' Jake Astor's gittin' out o' the fur trade an' the other bosses are plumb skeered o' losin' his money an' spesh'ly all o' his pers'nal clout wi' the guv'mint in Washin'ton.

"'Sides, ol' Gin'ral Ashley's a Missourah senator naow an' he's been sidin' Rocky Mountain Fur with his friends in the Congress. Then, on top o' that, when Nat Wyeth stayed over a spell at Fort Union las' year, he tangled arseholes wi' ol' King McKenzie, which, as ye know, ain't a-tall hard to do fer either one of 'em, so, when Wyeth got down to Sain' Louie, he tattled to the guv'mint folks about the whiskey still McKenzie war runnin' thar at Fort Union an' tradin' booze wi' the Injuns. Which caused all kinds o' hell fer Amurrican Fur wi' the guv'mint in Washin'ton.

"As ye know, Billy Sublette ain't one to be overlookin' a weak spot in the oppersishun. I ain't sure perzackly how he done it, but Billy went fer the throat an' come out o' New York smellin' like a posy. He ended up sellin' Amurrican Fur all o' the tradin forts an ever'thin' else him an' Bobby had on the Missourah fer a helluva profit an' he even got 'em to promise to stay plumb out o' the mountains all o' nex' year, which, if ye ain't been keepin' track'll be eighteen-an'- thutty-five."

He grinned and added, "Course, a big part o' chalkin' up sich a big score in them'ere talks war 'cause Billy warn't dealin' direc'ly with ol' Jake Astor, neither. That'ere would'a been a dog-fight wuth payin' money to see."

Black leaned back against the tree trunk and reached for the kettle. "This be a thirsty chore ye got me doin', Temple," he said with a chuckle, lifting the kettle to his lips and gurgling down several mouthfuls.

What he had related whetted my appetite for more. "Thanks for all o' that, Black," I told him, "but what's got Nat Wyeth on the prod for Fitz? From what they're sayin', he's blamin' Tom for bankruptin' him."

"Wal, he mought be pert'near right. Last year, Wyeth made a deal with Fitz an' Milton an' the others to supply 'em at this year's ronnyvoo, 'stid o' Billy an' Bobby, fer a helluva lot less'n Sublette's been chargin' 'em." He paused and took another long swig. "But 'fore I git into that'ere part of it, I gotta back up an' tell ye 'baout Fitz an' that'ere English nabob Stewart gittin' robbed pert'near blind last year by a bunch o' Absorkee bucks.

"Fitz, an' thutty men an' Stewart, 'long with Antoine Clement, parted with Bobby an' me over on the Yellerstone, whar we war buildin' bullboats, an' went trappin' east o' thar in Absorkee country. That's whar they run into that'ere bunch o' sassy young Crows what got the drop on Stewart an' stripped 'em all damn near nekkid. Damn near lost their arse, they did—guns an' nigh all o' their plunder—even got Stewart's watch—nigh ever'thin' they owned, includin' all o' the plews they'd trapped up to then, which ended up with Amurrican Fur down on the Missourah. Fitz did some sweet-talkin' with the Crow chief an' got his guns an' hosses an' some o' their plunder back from the Crows, but ol' McKenzie jist laughed at 'im an' offered to sell the plews back to 'im fer fair market price.

"Fitz an' 'speshly Cap'n Stewart put most o' the blame on Jim Beckwith, what useta run with yer bunch, fer rilin' up them young Absorkee bucks an' gittin' 'em to steal their plunder. Ol' Jim claims to be some kind o' Crow war chief naowadays. He's married to a coupl'a Crow wimmen an', word is, he's on McKenzie's payroll daown at Fort Union.

"Natcherly that got Fitzpatrick madder'n he usually is at Amurrican Fur fer stealin' his plews an' he's also got some questions in mind abaout the deal they're hatchin' up with Wyeth. So he writes a couple letters, one to Senator Ashley, tellin' him abaout McKenzie stealin' his furs an' askin' him to put some more guv'mint pressure on Amurrican Fur in Washin'ton, an' t'other'n to Milton Sublette consarnin' the deal whar they're plannin' to bust loose from Brother Billy an' Campbell. Then, 'stid o' handin' them'ere letters to me, Fitz gives 'em to that'ere arse-kissin' tosspot Ben Harrison to carry down to Sain' Louie.

"Tom might'a figgered I war too close to Bill Sublette to be trusted with them'ere letters, but he couldn'a never made no bigger mistake than what he done. That sneaky drunken medico couldn't hardly wait to steam them letters open an' when he sees what's in 'em, soon as we git to Sain' Louie, quick as scat, he shows 'em to Billy afore he passes 'em on to Milton!

"An' natcherly, once Bill Sublette catches on to what Rocky Mountain Fur's schemin' on with ol' Yankee Nat, he ain't abaout to be lettin' his li'l birds be flyin' the coop, gittin' out from under his thumb, an' queerin' his deal with Amurrican Fur in the bargain!

"Ye see, Sublette's deal in New York mostly depended on guaranteein' that Rocky Mountain Fur war ready to fold, leavin' him the only big he-dog hyarabaouts, which is why they agreed to stay out of the mountains nex' year. But if Nat Wyeth got his trade goods to ronnyvoo afore Sublette did an' Rocky Mountain Fur war able to pay off what they owed 'im, Bill Sublette war bound to lose his edge an' a whole lot o' money!

"An' I reckon it stung Bill even more that his own li'l brother war a big part o' the problem. Fust off, he tried argyfyin' with Milton abaout how they war blood-kin, brothers an' all, an' then, when that got 'im nowheres, he threatened Milt with callin' in some drafts Milton owed him an' Bobby Campbell, but then, Wyeth lent Milton the money he owed Bill, so that din't work, neither. It war gittin' fearful plain to see that Billy had best be gittin' his packtrain to ronnyvoo afore Yankee Nat got thar or Sublette's whole house o' cards war gonna come tumblin' daown on 'im!

"Spite o' Wyeth gittin' a whole week's head start on us, we caught up with 'em arter jist a week on the trail—passed 'em in the dark, one night, we done. Grass war good this year an' our critters stayed strong. We would'a got hyar to ronnyvoo a whole lot sooner'n we done, 'cept fer holdin' up at Laramie Crick an' leavin' Bill Patton an' a dozen men a'hind thar fer buildin' a tradin' fort they'll be callin' Fort Willum arter Billy Sublette.

"Course, we know the trail a heap better'n ol' Nat does an' we war trav'lin' cornsidible lighter'n he war, too, startin' off with jist thutty-seven men an' ninety-five hosses an' mules an' even less'n that arter Laramie. Wyeth war packin' more'n twice that much. 'Twixt him an' Milt, they had two hunnert an' fifty critters an' more'n eighty men, with half a dozen greenhorns amongst 'em. 'Sides, Milton war hurtin' mortal bad from that'ere bum laig o' his'n, right from the git-go. Even wuss fer ol' Yankee Nat makin' anythin' close to decent time on the trail war his own herd o' beef cattle that he brung along fer rations 'til they come up on buffler, 'sides a couple-three milch cows b'longin' to a couple o' missionaries he 'lowed to jine up with 'im. He war countin' on his stock o' fust-rate horses an' mules fer makin' good time, but he couldn't move no faster'n them'ere milch cows'd let im.

"Milt's laig got to painin' 'im so fierce arter jist a week on the trail that he had to turn back an' that likely slowed 'em up more'n some'at, too." Black fell silent, staring into the distance, likely seeing naught, evidently recalling—as I, too, was doing right then—the brave, handsome, humorous, daring, always generous, madcap Milton Sublette we had known and loved from the first giddyap in our Rocky Mountain adventure and how he had suffered the stab wound that had crippled him, defending men who looked to him as their leader. Addressing no one in particular, Black said quietly, "If I ever run acrost that'ere Eerie-quah sumbitch John Grey, what cut Milton's laig fer no good reason, I'll be makin' damn sure he eats that gawddamn dirty blade o' his'n."

Knowing Harris as I do, I had no good reason to disbelieve him.

Returning to the here and now, Black said, "I don't reckon we'll be seein' Milton up thisaway agin. If that'ere laig don't kill 'im, it'll sure-as-hell keep 'im in Sain' Louie."

I saw that my kettle was nearly empty by that time, so I hastened to ask the question that had prompted Harris's whole discourse. "So what did Bill Sublette tell Fitz that made him crawfish out o' the deal that he an' the others cooked up with Nat Wyeth last year? That must've been one helluva powerful argument, Black, to make Tom Fitzpatrick go back on his word like that!"

Harris shook his head and looked almost sorrowful. "I cain't tell ye that, Temple, 'cause, try as I might to pry it loose, I cain't git neither one of 'em to tell. But, like ye say, it must've been one pow'ful argymint, er likely somethin' more, like a threat. Fitz has allus prided hisse'f on livin' up to his word, as ye know."

Then, in a loyal attempt to preserve at least a shred of Fitzpatrick's reputation, Harris added, "Wal, leastaways Fitz din't zackly cheat Wyeth out o' no cash money on the deal. He paid 'im back the five hunnert dollars Nat lent Milton fer payin' off Billy in Sain' Louie an' anuther five hunnert forfeit fer Rocky Mountain Fur backin' out o' what they promised last year. 'T'warn't near enough to cover his losses, but it war somethin'."

Harris tipped up the kettle and drained it before he said, "I 'spec' Bill Sublette called in all o' the markers he's been holdin' on Rocky Mountain Fur—an' Fitz, even smart an' tough as he be, had to knuckle under. Naow that Milton ain't hyar, Fitz an' Frapp are the onliest ones o' the bunch that kin read—not countin' Christy, but I reckon he don't 'mount to much wi' t'other'ns, anyways."

We stood up, preparing to return to camp when Harris said, "Aw, hell, I near fergot to tell ye—naow that Jake Astor's gittin' out o' the pitcher with Amurrican Fur, he went an' sold all his west'ren holdin's to Pratte an' Chouteau in Sain' Louie. 'Pears yer ol' companyero Pierre Chouteau'll be callin' all the shots fer Amurrican Fur hyarabaouts from naow on!"

Strolling back to camp, I chewed over Black's last bit of news regarding Pratte and le Cadet assuming ownership of American Fur in the Rockies and decided that who owned American Fur likely wouldn't make much difference in our lives. Chouteau had always been Astor's big he-dog in Saint Louis, anyway. Much more important to us, leastaways right at that time, was what Harris had said about Tom Fitzpatrick reneging on his contract with Nathaniel Wyeth, leaving the Yankee high and dry in the Rockies with a passel of unsold trade goods. That was sure to be welcome news to my comrades.

୭ ୭ ୭

As soon as I announced what Harris had told me, our bunch made a beeline to Nat Wyeth's trade tents with some of the plews and buffalo robes they had swapped for horses, as well as beaver and fine furs we ourselves had trapped during the previous year. After word went abroad that Rocky Mountain Fur had been dissolved, we took pleasure in making trade with Bill Sublette's competition. Crabby Nat Wyeth smiled with sour satisfaction from underselling his nemesis Bill Sublette. The Yankee charged only five hundred percent over Saint Louis prices for his merchandise, instead of the customary thousand percent and more that traders generally charge in the mountains.

We swapped plews and robes with Wyeth for much of the plunder we needed to outfit ourselves for the coming year—gunpowder, galena, tobacco, clothing, blankets, trade goods, and such, taking advantage of the lower prices he offered to spite Sublette, but we held back most of our plews against the arrival of American Fur.

Brass Turtle assumed the rôle of financial advisor to the bunch. Finn McCool and I did what we could to help him restrain our impetuous comrades from parting with their windfall of furs and robes before all of the traders arrived. "Jist sell off enough o' yer booty to that'ere Yankee trader fer makin' sure ye got ever'thin' ye'll be needin' fer trappin' this fall an' winter an' then sit tight," he counseled. "Oncet ever'body gits hyar, the traders'll be fightin' each other fer plews somethin' fierce. That's when the price o' fur'll go up. Robes, too."

Turtle, normally tough and leaderlike, was going about with a perpetual smile on his face—and with good reason. His woman, the always good-natured Tallymesko, had arrived at rendezvous at last with her Shoshone band and presented him with a strong, healthy son. She had survived the birthing in good health and was happy to be reunited with her man, eager to resume the life of a trapper's woman.

Turtle's good humor was exceeded, howsomever, by my own. I was able to glory once again in the joy of fatherhood with my new son and especially with that fascinating person who never fails to astonish me with her lively mind and ever-ready wit, my incomparable daughter Iris.

And every day and especially every night provided new pleasures that flowed from the inexhaustible cornucopia that was and is my union with Kathleen, who never fails to excite and comfort me—a passionate lover and a wise, trusted friend and counselor, protective and nurturing. She provides a bond that is hot as hellfire and strong, solid, and enduring as the Rocky Mountains. Two other qualities that keep my love for Cat burning bright are her insatiable curiosity and her unfailing sense of humor, neither of which are much prized in an Indian village, but which keep me forever fascinated. She constantly reminds me of Mister Shakespeare's description of Cleopatra, whom "age cannot wither . . . nor custom stale her infinite variety."

Waiting for the other traders to arrive, I spent much of my time in the pasture with Half-horse, working with the three *palomillas* I wished to keep for myself, Cat, and Iris, a tall sturdy stallion and two well-built mares. Breaking them to saddle and putting a proper handle on them turned out to be a much easier chore than I had expected. Their excellent breeding, coupled with the several months they had spent traveling with our well-trained saddle stock, made them surprisingly amenable to accepting their new responsibilities.

I still owned an extra *palomilla* stud horse, besides a dozen other mares and geldings that I wouldn't need when trapping commenced after rendezvous. I had already gifted Pablo and Diego each with a couple geldings to help them get established in the trapping trade, but the horses I had accumulated first from Joe Walker and then, later, those from Don Nicolás, added to Cat's personal *remuda* and the several excellent animals I had brought up from Saint Louis the year before amounted to a troublesome embarrassment of equine riches.

I considered selling off my extra animals, but I was reluctant to part with them. They were all good critters, well worth keeping, and I might need some or all of them in future. And I certainly didn't need the money I might have realized from selling them off. The capital I had invested with Pierre Chouteau in Saint Louis always accumulated much faster than I could spend it.

I parted with two more of my saddle horses as gifts to Paddy McBride, one, a gentle little mare, for his son Sean, a precocious little redhead for whom it was apparent Iris had developed a special fondness. He was a year younger than my daughter, but lively as he was, it was time that he possessed his own critter.

During my visits to Iron Bow's lodge I became aware of a certain coolness on the part of my brother-in-law Fast Horse—nothing I could put my finger on, but nevertheless disturbing, for he and I had always enjoyed a cordial friendship. When I mentioned it to Cat, she opined that Fast Horse was likely still miffed by my refusal to let him race my Coffee horse during my absence in California. One time, when he tried to do so, insisting that I would never be the wiser, she had forbidden him to lay a hand on my favorite saddler. She reckoned he was still sulking about it.

Which was likely. Indian men are powerfully prideful. They don't take kindly to being thwarted in their intentions, especially by a woman, even one whom they hold in high regard.

ﾌ　　ﾌ　　ﾌ

Confronting the matter head-on was the only sensible solution I could conjure up to melt Fast Horse's grudge and, at the same time, solve the dilemma of my overpopulated *remuda*. Which was how it came about that Half-horse and I herded ten of my extra horses, together with one handsome, freshly-groomed, but still unbroken *palomilla* stallion, across Horse Creek and through the Flathead camp, to Fast Horse's lodge, where Half-horse held them whilst my brother-in-law and I palavered and reconciled our differences.

His bruised pride healed instantly, you might say miraculously, when I gifted him with the *palomilla* stud as his personal property, separate from his father. He promised to look after my critters as if they were his own and assured me that he would return them to me whenever I wished. He told me that in passable English, which he said he had learned from Kathleen during the previous winter.

Riding back to camp, I mused on how easy it had been to resolve what had appeared to be a knotty problem, while making our friendship even stronger in the bargain. Would that all such problems could be settled so handily.

On the way, Half-horse and I fell in with three old friends who were just now getting back from California, Joe Meek and his constant companions Doc Newell and the Irish harpooner Harry Yeats. After calling out greetings and leaning out of our saddles to exchange *abrazos*, I asked them, "How come you're gettin' back so late? We left California a sight later'n you did an' we've been here more'n a week already. And where's Walker and the others? They comin' up behind ye?"

All three merely rolled their eyes in silent response. Joe Meek undertook to provide a reply. "Don't rightly know jest whar Cap'n Walker an' ther main bunch mought be, Temple. We parted with 'em comin' out o' Californy an' went 'long with muh brother Stephen an' ther rest o' ther Santy Fee bunch, which warn't ther smartest thang we ever done!" Joe's distressed expression and assenting groans from Doc and Harry punctuated his last remark.

"How come?" I asked.

Harry Yeats cut in with an attempt to explain. "Well, as ye well know, Cap'n Walker runs what ye might be after callin' a taut ship and after all the months in Californy jumpin' at his orders, such servitude was growin' more'n some'at tiresome, so whin Bill Williams and Levin Mitchell an' the others from Santa Fe proposed to be strikin' off on their own hook, it appeared to be a good idea to be jinin' 'em."

"Which it shore-as-hell warn't!" Doc interjected.

"Nope! It warn't!" Joe asserted. "'Ceptin' fer Brother Stephen an' thet'ere Dellerware Injun Mark Head, what both kep' actin' sensible, ther rest o' ther whole gawddamn Santy Fee crowd went plumb crazy, once Cap'n Walker warn't around, holdin' 'em daown. Got crazier'n a passel o' one-arm wooden clocks, sure as hell!"

"Tell 'im what they done to them'ere pore goddamn Moqui Injuns, Joe!" Doc urged.

"Yeah," Joe agreed. "Thet'll show ye haow they war behavin'. Wal, them'ere Moquis be a half-civilized nation o' hard-workin' farmer Injuns what raises melons an' beans an' *chilis* an' sech an' all kinds o' fruits in their orchards an' war willin' to swap their garden truck fer pratic'ly nuthin', when Ol' Bill an' Levin an' Crazy Bill Craig an' t'others run inter their gardens an' commenced stealin' all their stuff an' grabbin' up critters an' messin' with their wimmenfolk an' when them Injuns told 'em to quit what they war doin', they all went plumb loco an' commenced shootin' them innercent Injuns fer no good reason a-tall! Gunned daown nigh o' score of 'em, they done! Wimmen an' kids amongst 'em! Laughin' an' jestin' whilst they done it, too!" Joe was red-faced and trembling with indignation by time he paused for breath.

"We had no part o' sech doin's," Joe hastened to add. "Doc an' Harry an' me, we din't b'long to thet'ere crowd. We jest sat on' ther fence an' saw it, though. It war a shameful thang!"

"We parted company with those bloody blaggards soon after, we did," Harry offered, "as soon as we had a halfway sure idea of which way to travel, gettin' up thisaway to rendezvous."

"Which warn't very sure, at all," Doc commented wryly. "We follered jist about every wrong trail thar war, 'twixt thar an' hyar."

"Wal, but we got hyar, anyways," Joe said. "An' thet's all thet counts." Then, to me, "What's been happenin', Temple?"

I commenced describing events I knew about, describing what I knew about the current circumstances of the now-defunct Rocky Mountain Fur Company, since all of us were close friends with the RMF partners. Early on, telling about Bill Sublette's race with Nat Wyeth, I mentioned that Milton Sublette's injured leg had forced him to turn back on the trail and return to Saint Louis and that Black Harris, who had seen Milt at the time, reckoned that we had seen the last of Milton in the mountains.

Joe's interest peaked when he heard that. He kept pumping me for more details about Milt, although I told him I knew no more than what Harris had told me. I repeated all I could recollect of what Black had told me about Milton's condition, declaring at the end that it sounded to me like we would not be seeing Milton Sublette in the mountains that year or likely any other.

Joe's features took on a sober, thoughtful expression, which was understandable, for he and Milton had been close friends ever since Joe first came to the mountains six years before. What surprised me, howsomever, was when Joe suddenly pulled up and tossed the lead-ropes of all but one of his packhorses to Newell. "Take muh critters inter camp fer me, will ye, Doc?" he said. "I'll jine ye thar." Without another word, he reined his horse about and loped down his backtrail, the lightly-loaded packhorse traveling easily at his heels.

Harry and I stared after him, dumbfounded, but Newell burst out laughing. "What's that all about, Doc?" I demanded. "Where's he goin'?"

When Newell recovered from his fit of mirth, he choked out, "Cain't be sartin sure, but I'm wagerin' ol' Joe Meek's on his way to gittin' hisse'f a bride! He's gonna git married, by gawd!" He burst out laughing once again.

"Married?" I heard myself repeating. "What makes ye say that?"

"What ye jist tol' us about Milton prob'ly never comin' back up hyar thisaway no more, that's what. Ol' Joe's been plumb sweet on Milt's Snake woman Isabel ever since them two fust seen her in ol' Bad Gotcha's lodge, when she he'ped the two of 'em git loose from her ol' man an' his bunch o' red devils. Joe's been moonin' over that plumb purty gal ever since he fust laid eyes on her—calls her the Mountain Lamb—but Milt got 'er fust an' natcherly Joe wou'n't mess aroun' Milton's woman. They're friends. But now ye war tellin' how Milton ain't never comin' back no more. That makes a pow'ful heap o' diff'ernce. 'Tain't likely Joe's gonna be lettin' that'ere bee-yoo-tiful woman go to waste 'mongst the Snakes. 'Specially not a good-looker like that'n what's awready broke to runnin' in double harness with a white-eyes! Nosirree! Ye kin wager yer arse Joe Meek's gone a-courtin'!"

I recalled Milton Sublette's incredibly beautiful Shoshone woman from last year's rendezvous, Milt's obvious devotion to her, and her evident affection for him. I recollected, too, that Joe Meek had spent a lot of time hanging around their lodge, which, at the time, I attributed to his long-time friendship with Milton.

Now I recalled the story of how the two friends had first encountered the Shoshone beauty, how they had stumbled into the village of the treacherous Snake war chief Mauvais Gauche—so called because of his withered left hand—how his daughter had helped them escape a painful death at the hands of his warriors and how Milton had returned for her and made her his wife. It was a charming romantic tale and might even be partly true, but there could be no doubt that, right then, Joe Meek was adding another chapter to the story.

∾ ∾ ∾

Naturally I invited the two remaining wayfarers to our cookfire for supper and a place to sleep and safely stow their plews and plunder until Joe Meek returned and the trio could decide on which trapping brigade to join for the fall hunt. They were not our only guests. Henry Fraeb, whom everybody calls Frapp, and Jean Gervais, two RMF partners recently set at liberty, were also enjoying our hospitality. Actually, it was rather more of a case that we were enjoying theirs, for when Fitz and Bill Sublette bought out their former partners, they paid in livestock and merchandise, not cash, so, amongst a passel of other plunder, our guests brought with them a pair of curved horseback kegs of undiluted grain alcohol. A wild party was just getting into full swing by time we arrived and we joined it eagerly, a fitting culmination of a successful day.

A well-oiled Anse Tolliver was delighted to see Harry Yeats joining the festivities. "Hey, thar, Irisher!" he yelled in greeting from his perch on a fallen tree, resting his fiddle on his knee. "Time ye showed up! Didja brang that'ere cittern o' your'n 'long wi' ye? We been needin' ye hyarabaouts, lad! Music's been a mite thin without ye!" Likely because of their music-making together, crabby Anse had admitted Harry to a very select circle of people whom he mostly spared from the unwelcome attentions of his acidulous tongue.

"Better'n that! I've somethin' even better now!" the smiling young Irishman rejoined. "I'll show ye!" He busied himself loosing the cords that held a large leather case onto one of his packsaddles. When he lifted the lid, he revealed a shiny Mexican *guitarra*, its polished wood surface gleaming in the late afternoon sunshine.

"It's a purty 'un," Anse called out, "but have ye larnt haow to play it yet?"

"You decide," Harry replied with a grin and proceeded to twist the knobs and twang the strings as he tuned his new instrument. A few minutes later, he proved that he had indeed mastered the mysteries of the Mexican *guitarra*, its full-throated timbre booming Irish reels and sea chanteys beside Horse Creek in a manner never heard in Barcelona or Yerba Buena.

Yves Dureau sneaked off from his cooking chores and joined the musicians with his little squeezebox concertina and several of our Delawares, including Brass Turtle, commenced tootling on flutes. Cesár joined them with his little earthen yam, which prompted Frapp to dig into his possibles and emerge with an outlandish contraption composed of an Indian hand drum, a wood block, and a cowbell fixed on five feet of slender lodgepole topped with a pair of brass cymbals that he played with a single drumstick and an unbelievable amount of enthusiasm, red-faced and grinning and cavorting around the fire in high good humor, revealing no trace of regret or resentment at being euchred out of his share of Rocky Mountain Fur. Frapp claims his musical monstrosity is common in his native Germany, where he says they call it a *teufelgeigenspieler*, which means the devil's plaything.

Even ordinarily shy Kit Carson joined the fun, pulling his large silver spurs off his moccasins and chiming them together in time with the music, contributing a pleasing bell-like tone to the general din.

Jean-Luc was busy concocting a more potent mixture of Frapp's grain alcohol, molasses, fiery chili peppers, crickwater, and I'm not sure that I wish to know what else than the much tamer libation served up by profit-minded traders. It appeared to take no more than a dram or two of L'Archévêque's devil's brew to get Paddy McBride onto his feet and whirling like an inspired dervish in a wild frolic around the fire, laughing like a good-natured banshee, kicking high above his head, and performing intricate Irish jigs in response to Harry's musical urging. The years and the various wounds he has accumulated had apparently taken naught away from his native sprightliness, inspired as he was by the music, goodfellowship, and Jean-Luc's evil elixir. He was soon joined in the firelight by his Séli wife Molly, plumper now than when they first met in a scalp dance half a decade before in Iron Bow's camp, but proving that years of hard work and bearing three kids had not impaired her nimble footwork or her fun-loving nature. They were joined in their frolic by trappers drawn to the bonfire and the music, many of them toting their own kettles of booze, which they freely passed around.

The music swelled into pleasant pandemonium when Anse and Harry were joined by Cap'n Billy and another fiddler, which inspired their tuneful hangers-on to even great efforts. I was considering if it were possible for me to rise and make it back to Kathleen waiting at our lodge, after I had, say, just one more drink, when someone grasped my hands and hauled me to my feet.

It was Cat, her dark eyes flashing in the firelight, white teeth sparkling in a broad smile, pulling me into the midst of the dancers. "Come, Tempo," she urged, "come dance wiz me. We 'ave never done!" Which was true. And if it were left to me, we never would have done. I am an observer, not a performer, but I could not refuse her.

I stumbled after her into the revolving circle of dancers pounding their moccasined feet on the prairie, keeping time with the musical beat, laughing and hooting in high good humor, bumping shoulders and hips and bottoms as we gyrated past smiling onlookers. Cat's strong fingers locked firmly onto mine, drawing me towards the center of the spinning mass of damp wool and sweaty buckskin. Suddenly she broke into an intricate pattern of dainty dance steps, twirling energetically about, scattering the surrounding dancers, dodging under my outstretched arm, never turning me loose, now kicking high in the air, now rocking back on her heels in a low curtseying bow, her loving gaze urging me to join her, until at last the riotous pounding of the music, the heat and press of the crowding dancers, and certainly Jean-Luc's evil elixir blending with a powerful surge of desire for this remarkable woman all conspired to dissolve my customary reluctance to call undue attention to myself. I commenced moving my feet in time with the music, slowly at first, then faster, more deliberately, emphatically, intricately, pounding the earth for all that I was worth, thrilling to the sound and the wild rhythm and the freedom of losing myself in the dance.

As soon as the music ended, howsomever, Cat quickly led me away from the crowd, dragging me back towards our lodge. "Was my dancing really that bad?" I asked, halfway convinced that I done rather well by the end of the tune.

"Oh, it was ver' good, Tempo! Ver' good for you! But now is time for your reward!" With such a promise in store, much as I had begun to enjoy it, only a fool would have preferred to continue dancing.

❧   ❧   ❧

Henry Fraeb and I are old friends. Next morning, whilst he and I lolled in the shade of cottonwoods on the riverbank, recovering from the excesses of the previous night, Frapp showed me the agreements that severed him and Jean Gervais from Rocky Mountain Fur. I had my journal with me and Frapp let me scribble down the terms. Frapp had settled for forty horses, forty traps, eight guns, and a thousand dollars worth of merchandise. Gervais, who had invested less, received twenty horses, 30 beaver plews, and five hundred dollars worth of goods. In either case, pretty stingy wages for four years of hard, dangerous work.

Frapp was surprisingly good-natured about his recent ouster from Rocky Mountain Fur. "Oh, vell," he explained, "I vas neffer t'inkin' I vas gonna be gettin' rich trappin' bibers. Me, I still got dese bee-yootiful mountains undt all o' my frien's. All Veely Sublette's got is Sain' Louie undt his money!" After he said that, his laughter sounded like he meant it.

I asked Henry about the guns he had received in the payout. "Vell, dey aindt der best, mebbe not so goot like ye could be gettin' from Jake Hawken in Sain' Louie," he replied honestly, "but dey be purty goot rifle guns, all of 'em made fer usin' caps, an' dey be shootin' purty plumb."

I had been thinking about Iron Bow's return journey to Flathead country, and especially their annual buffalo hunt on the eastern prairie, both of which travels are always threatened by Pikunis, who resent any other tribes trespassing on what they consider their private hunting grounds. On an impulse, I offered to buy Frapp's extra rifles from him. At first he demurred, but the prospect of a substantial amount of cash deposited with interest with Pierre Chouteau in Saint Louis melted his resistance. I was able to buy five of his rifles and sizeable quantities of gunpowder, galena, and percussion caps— which relieved him of transporting those items when he returned to trapping after rendezvous. `

Whilst we were haggling over price, neither of us noticed the approach of two men until they were nearly upon us. When Frapp spied them at last and recognized them as members of Wyeth's party, likely missionary pilgrims, he blanched and scrambled to his feet, stuffing my payment order into his poke.

Gotta go, Temple!" he strangled out. "You, too, if ye be schmardt! Dem'ere be dose *gottverdammt predigers*, preachers, I be t'inkin', py *gott*! Allus preachin' *gottverdammt* hellfire undt *Schwefel* undt tellin' how all of us be goin' to *Hölle* if ve don't do chust like dey say!" He retreated at a shambling trot, not waiting for me to catch up.

By time I gathered up my belongings it was too late to flee. The newcomers had already arrived. "Good morning, sir!" one of the men called out in a cheerful tone. "Please do not disturb yourself on our account. We are just passing by." I looked up to behold a tall, middle-aged man of pleasant mien and sturdy build, equipped with a staff and a large canvas bag slung over one shoulder. His companion was somewhat younger and equally genial in appearance. I mumbled a greeting which my visitors evidently took to be an invitation to tarry a spell. "Allow me to introduce myself," the older man said. "I am Thomas Nuttall and my friend here is Kirk Townsend. We have accompanied Captain Wyeth's party from Saint Louis to your rendezvous."

"Ye came to preach to the Injuns, did ye?" The words were out of my mouth before I realized that I was uttering them. Both men looked shocked at my remark.

"Oh, good heavens, no!" Nuttall exclaimed. "We'll happily leave that chore to Reverend Lee and his people!"

"By all means!" Townsend rejoined emphatically. "They require no help from us, nor, I daresay, do they wish for any."

Their swift denial that they were missionaries and especially the fervent tone they used in doing so instantly warmed me towards them.

"No, sir," Nuttall hastened to explain. "Townsend here and I are scientists, naturalists, come here to study and attempt to catalogue the flora and fauna of this magnificent country—the plants and animals, that is to say, that are native to these parts."

"It is a task that will occupy considerably more time and effort than we will be able to devote to it on a single visit," the younger man explained. "Therefore, the souls of the aborigines, however precious or in jeopardy, must remain the concern of others, those who are best trained and equipped to guide our redskinned brethren to celestial bliss. Neither my colleague nor I is qualified to function in that regard." His bantering tone as he delivered those sentiments further assured me of the purely secular interests of those scholarly gentlemen.

I had meanwhile taken note of the large canvas bag each of them carried, likely to collect speciments, together with much the same sort of sketching pad that I had seen the artist George Catlin using at Fort Union the year before. After a brief but pleasant chat concerning the birds and furry critters that I knew about in that neighborhood, they bade me adieu and hiked off across our horse pasture, heading for the woods that bordered it, blithely ignoring my warning words concerning the possibility of encountering a grizzly bear in those parts.

❧   ❧   ❧

Jim Bridger led his brigade into camp on June 25, greeted with the bad news about the dissolution of Rocky Mountain Fur from an apologetic Tom Fitzpatrick, who explained that Bill Sublette and Bobby Campbell had called in the notes they held on RMF and there was no way their hard-pressed outfit could have survived. Black Harris told us that Jim was "natcherly madder'n hell" and sneered at Fitz's mention of forming a new outfit called Fitzpatrick, Sublette, & Bridger Company. Harris related that Bridger growled something like, "How the hell do ye reckon we're gonna put anuther comp'ny together when Billy ain't leavin' us a gawddamn bone to chaw on an' Milt ain't even hyar ner ever comin' back?" Black said Fitz got all red-faced and backed off.

Losing Rocky Mountain Fur to Bill Sublette's greed wasn't Bridger's only misery. According to Harris, "That'ere Blackfoot arrer war still in Jim's back, painin' 'im wuss'n ever, which ain't calca'lated to be makin' Gabe any more sweet-tempered'n a grizzle b'ar with a sore paw!"

❧   ❧   ❧

There was still plenty of game in the neighborhood—a plenitude of buffalo, wapiti, deer, prairie goats, and an occasional bear, both grizzlies and black bears—in spite of the increasing size of the gathering, at least six hundred trappers and several times that many Snake, Eutaws, Nez Percé, Séli, Kootenay, Pend d'Oreille, and Kalispell Indians, as well as a ragtag band of rowdy Bannocks, their crude brush shelters clustered on the southern fringe of the rendezvous. Indian villages and trapper camps were scattered along the banks of Horse Creek and Black's Fork, all the way to the Seeds-kee-dee, moving from time to time when nearby firewood got used up or the large Indian horse herds exhausted the graze in a particular spot.

Weather stayed mild through the month of June. Making meat was not a demanding chore. There were plenty of men in our camp to harvest all that we needed, both for the present and to jerk for future need, so we had much free time for visiting and indulging in the pleasures of the rendezvous. Tuttle occupied himself profitably at Old Sledge and the new English card game Bragg, shearing unwary sheep newly arrived from the settlements with the traders' packtrains, when he wasn't consoling comely widows in the surrounding Indian camps, an obligation which he piously described as his "bounden Christian duty." My old friend apparently possessed an unerring eye for identifying both incompetent gamblers who harbored an exaggerated opinion of their skill and desirable women who would prove susceptible to his good-natured advances backed up by foofurraw with which he supplemented his dubious charms.

The other bachelors in our bunch lack Tuttle's repute for amorous prowess, but they rarely spend a night alone at rendezvous if they don't choose to do so. The lure of white-eyes foofurraw and trade goods is a powerful persuader for fun-loving young and not-so-young Indian females unaware of the preachifying of doomsaying parsons. Although the women of some tribes are purely virtuous, there is a passel of playful womenfolk thereabouts who value chastity less than the material reward they receive in return for a brief and pleasurable dalliance with an amorous trapper.

I bade farewell to a bachelor's dubious freedom and the hasty couplings of rendezvous with nary a pang of regret. Union with Kathleen provides whatever I might desire—elaborate, leisurely robe games infinitely more enjoyable than the hurried pairings of brute appetites satisfied in haste in some darkened glade. I value, too, the practical comforts of domestic life, warm food and a fire waiting in a clean, well-ordered lodge when a trapper returns soaked and shivering from his wintry chores, clean clothes and dry moccasins, and, if you earned it, a smile and a warm embrace before you slip into exhausted slumber.

But that hardly describes Kathleen's virtues. Aside from her lean feline beauty that straightway brings the nickname Cat to mind, I feel in her the sinewy strength of a catamount in her graceful movements and perceive a smoldering intensity driving her to excel in whatever she undertakes, be it friendship, motherhood, pride in her own person and those whom she calls her own, unwavering loyalty to clan, tribe, and her chosen love, unflinching courage, keen intelligence, thoughtful judgment, and boundless curiosity.

Our union is built upon a more solid foundation than that of most couples, who know little about the other when they commit to spending their lives together. Cat and I were friends long before we were lovers. I had long admired Kathleen when I knew her as the faithful wife of Ned Godey, one of my dearest and most respected friends, and the lifelong friend of my beloved Rainbow woman. Childless herself, Cat unhesitatingly accepted the burden of mothering my infant daughter after Rainbow's violent death at the hands of renegade Bannocks. It is unlikely that Iris, young as she was then, remembers any other mother. Even when Cat and I were free to commit to each other, we were slow to act, but I have already described the rocky road that Kathleen and I traveled before she admitted that we belong together.

Although I am usually reluctant to call attention to myself, I am glad to show off this remarkable woman, especially at rendezvous, to join her as she struts as the wife of a free trapper, when we parade through the trapper camps and friendly Indian villages. I am especially proud to see her astride the prettiest horse I can provide, her Mexican saddle, crupper, breast collar, apishamore, *alforjas, cinchas*, and stirrups all bedizened with silver coins, glass beads, porcupine quills, and hawk bells, her fanciest tomahawk slung from one side of the pommel and our best tobacco pipe in an elegant otterskin bag on the other, her bridle jingling with silver dollars, she herself dressed in the most luxurious finery the traders offer, her skirt of fine broadcloth, the bodice of rich silks and velvets, her thick braids wrapped in red wool and dangling silver gauds, all covered with a bright blue silk kerchief, scarlet leggin's sporting shiny silver *conchas* I carried back from California, and colorful quill-encrusted moccasins that reach to her knees.

At Horse Creek in thirty-four, Half-horse and I hurried to gentle my remaining two palomilla mares, so that Kathleen and Iris might be suitably mounted when we toured the camps and Indian villages scattered along Horse Creek and Black's long-wished-for namesake crick. The mares were impeccably groomed, their coats smooth and gleaming like gold bullion, soft creamy manes flowing in the breeze, when Half-horse led them into camp to be saddled and otherwise caparisoned.

Cat's hand flew to her mouth in pleased surprise when she first caught sight of her tall, deep-chested mare and Iris shrieked with delight when she beheld her new mount. They hauled out their showiest horse clothing whilst Half-horse and I stood beaming with satisfaction that our gift met with such approval. As soon as they finished saddling, they tethered their animals and disappeared inside the lodge. They remained there what seemed like forever, whilst I paced impatiently outside. At last they scuttled past the door flap, dressed to the nines in their most colorful duds, Kathleen toting little Ben in his quilled and beaded cradleboard.

When I asked why so gaudy, Cat explained that receiving such beautiful new horses demanded a showoff visit to Iron Bow's village and she and Iris needed to show respect to the venerable chief by dressing appropriately. What she didn't say was that she really needed to let the women of Iron Bow's band know that she was restored to her former glory as a free trapper's woman. Although Cat had never told me so, I reckoned some of her spiteful childhood friends had gloated over her come-down in the world after Ned's death and her return to spend an impoverished winter back in Iron Bow's village, forced to trade off her possessions in order to survive. Widows do not fare well in Indian society, especially strong-minded females like Cat. Now that good fortune smiled once again on her and Iris, she deemed it only fair that they flaunt their finery now in retaliation for past injustice.

Kathleen led the way out of camp, her *palomilla* mare daintily picking her way through the sagebrush, Ben swinging gently from the pommel in his cradleboard, my five-year-old daughter chirping and giggling happily behind her, enchanted with her mare's splendid appearance, her smooth gaits, and her impeccable manners. Half-horse had devoted particular effort to gentling my little girl's new mount. He had excellent material to work with. The *palomillas* are the product of centuries of careful breeding in Spain and these had obviously experienced much gentle manhandling by their original owner before Batista and his bandits stole them.

I followed on my Coffee horse, my chest swelling in conscious pride as I beheld my two beautiful ladies glorying in the approving gazes and admiring comments of trappers and their Indian women as we paraded through the camps scattered along the riverbank. Ours was a leisurely progress. Kathleen s chose the long way around to reach Iron Bow's village, meandering through nearly every encampment along the way. I couldn't fault her for showing off her handsome new, well-mannered mare, as well as indulging in a mite of bragging on her recovered status as a free trapper's wife, which I took to be a compliment to myownself.

We tarried a spell on the way at Nat Wyeth's trade tents, where we purchased tobacco, gunpowder, caps, and galena pigs, presents for Iron Bow and Fast Horse, as well as cloth and foofurraw for their women. The Yankee trader was doing a brisk business amongst free trappers taking advantage of his lower prices. That should have softened his resentment against Tom

Fitzpatrick, but, considering Wyeth's tetchy nature, likely did no such thing. Even in the best of circumstances, Yankee Nat rarely has a good word to say about anybody or anything.

Our horseback stroll through Iron Bow's village must have warmed Kathleen's heart, although it was difficult to tell from the cool, distant expression on her features as we made our way through the alleyways amongst the circles of lodges to the center of the encampment. Iris, on the other hand, was all smiles and friendliness, waving and calling out to her former playmates when she spied them. They created a stir all along our route, men and women alike tumbling out of their lodges to gaze upon the handsome blond horses and their extravagant trappings, then to exclaim over the sumptuous costumes of their riders. Cat is an excellent rider, a pleasure to behold. With the slightest twitch of her fingers on the reins, she cued her tall mare into a high-stepping slow singlefoot, then an elegant gentle prancing and curvetting gait that elicited approving murmurs from the spectators—rare tribute from Indians whose entire life, from cradleboard to grave, is bound up with horses.

Cat didn't let on that she noticed. Her expression remained remote, tranquil, self-possessed, her posture ramrod straight but supple, shoulders squared, hands resting lightly on the pommel, staring straight ahead, as if she were hardly aware of the people on the ground, until we rode past the last circle of dwellings, into the broad open space where the council fire is built and headmen erect their lodges. Cat's haughty look evaporated instantly when she espied Iron Bow and Fast Horse standing amid several other elders. She gigged her mare into a jogtrot until she neared the group, then stepped to the ground in a single fluid motion and knelt before the chief, bowing her head and pressing his outstretched hand to her brow.

I halted some distance away and heard him use the word 'daughter' when he greeted her. The significance of that word was not lost on people who witnessed our progress through the village. Cat's triumph was complete.

Kathleen resumed her imperious expression and manner when we emerged from Iron Bow's lodge and maintained it until we passed the outer fringes of the Flathead village, whereupon she broke into a broad smile and exclaimed, "I sink now zey know zat I an' Irish are worse somesing more zen zey sought las' winter when we were zere wiz zem!" Kathleen, who still calls herself

Cataleen, was still having trouble pronouncing her tee-aitches in our tongue, a difficulty she shared with most people who have not been raised in our language. Although she has since mastered that thorny aspect of English, she never has quit calling my daughter Irish and I have never corrected her, reckoning that it pays homage to my mother's side of her heritage.

Iris never experienced difficulty with pronouncing her tee-aitches, growing up as she did around so many Delawares and my Shawnee father. Both of those tongues possess an abundance of thorny sounds.

The visit to the Flathead village was a success on several counts. Not only did it restore Cat's dignity and social standing amongst the womenfolk of her band, but it also strengthened our ties of affection and respect with the chief and especially with his son Fast Horse. Iron Bow insisted on showing me the newborn progeny of the tall jackass with which I had gifted him the year before, which he bred to some of his best mares. Young as they still were, they showed promise of soon becoming tall, sturdy, clean-limbed mules. Their sire's so-called Jesus-cross was beginning to show on the backs of some of them. When we were returning from Iron Bow's pasture, Fast Horse rode up on the *palomilla* stud that I had given him, showing off the young horse's gaits and good manners and bragging on the critter's speed and endurance, qualities that Fast Horse, who loves racing, holds in the highest esteem.

Back in the chief's lodge, I told them of my wish to train five of their young warriors in marksmanship with rifles I would provide and asked that they select young men best qualified to profit from such instruction. They were delighted with my proposal and assured me that they would choose the very best youths in the band.

Instead of returning directly to our camp, we rode by way of Sublette's trading outfit, which he shared with Tom Fitzpatrick, a couple miles above the mouth of Horse Creek, where they had moved in search of better pasture. As we approached the trade tents we spied a crowd of trappers clustered around a couple riders and their heavily-loaded pack animals. When we drew near I recognized Joe Meek. His companion was the Shoshone woman I had seen with Milton Sublette the year before, the woman Milt called Isabel. Even trail-stained and obviously fatigued, she was strikingly beautiful. She cradled an infant on her thighs, behind the pommel of her richly-adorned Mexican saddle. Her face instantly lit up in a broad smile when Cat called out and rode in close beside her, chattering in fragments of the Snake tongue supplemented with fluttering finger-talk. I recalled then that Ned and Milton had long been friends and that he and Cat had often visited Milt and his new wife at rendezvous.

The two women prattled on for a few minutes before Cat swung about and told me in sign-talk that Meek and his woman would be setting up in our camp. Whilst I was being apprised of that decision, Joe was learning about it also. For a moment he appeared inclined to object, or at least to comment, but at last he simply shrugged and grinned before he touched spur to his horse and joined me in the shade of a tree where I was waiting for the women to finish their confabulation.

"Hell, mought as well jine y'all t'night as go lookin' fer muh pals, wore out as we be," he allowed. "Spread out from hell ter breakfus like thi'shere ronnyvoo 'pears to be, I'd likely be at it 'til mawnin'. Thankee fer ther invite, Temple."

I refrained from mentioning that it was Cat who deserved his thanks. Instead I told him that Doc and Harry had settled in with our bunch during his absence in Snake country, so he wouldn't need to go searching for them. "Howsomever," I added, "I reckon ye never need to go lookin' far for Harry. Makin' music like he does gen'rally lands 'im plumb in the middle o' whatever's happenin', leastaways at rendezvous. Ye can hear 'im a mile off."

"Thet's a damn fact," Joe said with a grin. Then, "When ye war tellin' about Godey gittin' kilt ye din't mention nothin' about yew an' his woman jinin' up, Temple," he said, resting an appreciative gaze upon Cat. "How come?"

Whilst I was sorting out possible replies, he answered himself. "Ain't surprisin', though. Cain't be 'lettin' a purty woman like thet'n go to waste. Sides, she allus done a good job o' lookin' arter yew an' yer li'l gal, arter yer Rainbow woman went under."

It surprised me that rip-roaring, fun-loving, hard-drinking Joe Meek had bothered to notice what was happening in my life, Godey's, or anyone's besides his own. It revealed a tender, human side to Joe that he mostly worked hard to conceal. "Yep," I replied at last, "we teamed up about a month ago. She turned me down last year. It was too soon after Ned's goin' under, but we're together now. That's what counts."

Joe chuckled slyly when he commented, "Thet so? An' thet'ere chile swingin' off yer woman's saddle post? Thet'n be you'rn?"

"Damn right!" I responded testily. "Just look at his eyes, when ye get a chance! Same as my daughter's! Same as my ma's! Like nobody else's!"

Meek looked sincerely regretful for his quip. He hastened to apologize. "Hell, Temple! Din't mean no offense. Same color eyes, ye say, like yer li'l gal's? Hell! Ain't anuther'n like her in all ther Rockies. Then he's got to be your'n!" Once again I was astounded, this time that rollicking Joe Meek had ever noticed and remembered Iris's eye-color.

"Speakin' o' which," I said, eager to change the subject, "that child on your woman's lap, is it yours?"

Joe looked shocked. "Why, hell no, Temple! Thet'ere's Milton's li'l gal, but she'll be my own chile from here on. I wou'n't never be thinkin' o' courtin' Umentucken nohaow, even naow, 'thout ye tol' me Milt warn't never comin' back hyar to the mountains. Oncet I heared thet, haowsomever, thar warn't no way in hell I war goin' to leave her thar with ol' Bad Gotcha an' ther rest o' his gawddamn rennygade Snakes!"

Just then, Kathleen signaled that they were ready to go, so I lent Joe a hand bunching up his pack animals. The two women took the lead, Iris riding behind them, Joe and me bringing up the rear with their packstring.

Our camp was a few miles distant from Rocky Mountain Fur, so Joe and I had time to palaver. "Ye were sayin'," I said, picking up where we had left off, "that ye got your woman out o' the same camp o' bloodthirsty Snakes where you an' Milt almost got yourselves killed the first time ye met her?"

Joe puffed up a mite with obvious pride and declared, "Yep, thet's jest what I done. Warn't no other way to let 'er know what's been happ'nin' to Milt ner what I war thinkin' on, neither. So I jest waited 'til early mawnin' daylight, when ever'body war still sleepin', afore I rode in, fast as I could, an' jumped off muh hoss an' run straight inter ol' Bad Gotcha's lodge, whar ther ol' sumbitch war still sleepin', dropped muh rifle gun an' muh pistol on ther ground out o' reach, an' set m'se'f daown nex' to his sleeprobes!

"Wal, ther ol' bastard war fit to be tied! He r'ared up an' fust thang he says to me in sign-talk war somethin' like 'Yew agin!' Then, afore he kin do nuthin' else, Umentucken comes runnin' from her sleeprobes spoutin' a passel o' Snake-talk too quick fer me to unnerstan' much of it, but it 'peared to settle ther ol' man daown—enough, anyways, fer him to call off half a dozen o' his young bucks come bustin' inter the lodge chasin' arter me.

"Outside ther lodge, I heared a helluva racket, anuther bunch o' his bucks raisin' hell, tellin' 'im to turn me loose so they kin git at me. He looks at me hard, then he sorta growls at 'em like an ol' grizzle boar, tellin' 'em to back off, an' I hear 'em goin' off, mad as hell he won't give me up, leastaways not yet.

"Then he gives me a hard look an' tells me to sit tight 'til he gits back and goes out o' the lodge, likely fer doin' his mawnin' bizness. Which gives me an' Umentucken time to talk. Quick as scat, I tell 'er ever'thin' I know about Milton never comin' back no more, 'count o' his bad laig an' all, an' then I tell 'er I'd be proud as kin be ef she'd be willin' to jine up an' be my woman.

"Wal, she din't say no-thankee right off, so I had a mite o' hope thet mebbe I had some kind o' chance. About then, ol' Gotcha comes back an' says we best be eatin' a bait o' grub afore decidin' what ought'a be done about me. Which war a good sign, but it still din't mean I war off ther hook fer sure. Then Isabel goes out an' Gotcha's ol' woman comes in with soup an' buffler meat an' I don't know what-all an' the ol' man signs me to sit an' eat with 'im, which I war mighty glad to do, even skeered as I should'a been, fer gittin' thar war purty skinny trav'lin', 'count o' gittin' thar in a hurry.

"Whilst we're eatin', ol' Gotcha don't say nothin' a-tall, jest keeps lookin' at me hard-like, like he's tryin' to see what's goin' on inside muh head. Arterwards, when Umentucken comes back, they get to palaverin' so fast I cain't keep up, but when they git done, the ol' chief shakes his haid like he cain't b'lieve what he's been hearin'. Then he turns 'round to me an' says— mostly in sign but along with some real slow Snake-talk—he reckons I gotta be plumb crazy, bustin' inter his camp ag'in an thinkin' he won't kill me, which is why mebbe he won't, 'cause he reckons the Great Sperrit has tetched me an' it ain't proper to kill no lunatic. An' then he makes a real sour face an' goes on an' says like it must be ketchin', 'cause his daughter says she wants to go off with me!

"Natcherly I light up like a gawddamn Chinee lantern, soon as I heared thet, which is the fust I l'arn thet Isabel ain't meanin' to turn me down, an' thet's what all their palaverin' war about. Arter thet, it took hardly no time a-tall afore all o' Gotcha's womenfolk come along leadin' all o' these hyar packhosses an' mules, awready loaded up with all o' Umentucken's plunder thet she brung along home last year when Milton went back east. An' right arter thet, Isabel comes ridin' up with the little gal in her lap an' tells me I'd best git a move on an' git on muh hoss, 'cause her ol' man is plumb changeable in his mind an' ye cain't never tell what he's liable to do next. By then, a coupl'a sour-face young'uns come up with muh hosses an' I git aboard quick as scat an' we git ther hell out o' thar.

"Injun-style, as ye know, means thar warn't no good-byein' ner farewellin', jest a passel o' hard looks comin' my way, an' we war a couple-three mile along ther trail afore I quit feelin' thet'ere itchy feelin' in my back whar an arrer might'a showed up an' got me. Arter thet, wal, all I reckon I ought'a say about thet is, the trip comin' back thisaway war a whole lot nicer'n it war gittin' thar."

I nodded my thanks for Joe's witty story and we rode in silence for a few minutes before I asked, "How come ye mostly call her Umentucken, Joe, 'stead of Isabel, like Milt always did?"

Rough, tough Joe Meek actually blushed and faltered before he stammered out a reply. "Wal, truth to tell—an' dontcha be spreadin' around thet I ever said nuthin' like thi'shere—I been a heap more'n sorta sweet on Isabel ever since I fust laid eyes on 'er back in ol' Bad Gotcha's lodge ther fust time, but Milton got 'er an' I din't an' I allus respected thet. But when she tol' me what her proper Shoshone handle war, I commenced usin' it, 'stead o' Isabel, 'cause it 'peared to me it war more private-like an' pers'nal fer her than a white-eyes handle war."

Once again I was confounded by rowdy, unrefined Joe Meek's depth of feeling and considerate understanding. I commenced to get an inkling of why Isabel so readily accepted his proposal. "What does her name mean in the Shoshone tongue, Joe?" I asked.

"Wal, Umentucken be jest a li'l part of it. Ther whole thang be a proper mouthful. It's *Umentucken tukutsey undenwatsey* an' it means *young daughter o' ther mountain bighorn he-sheep*—what ye mought be callin' *Mountain Lamb* in Amurrican. Purty, ain't it? Hard to b'lieve ol' Bad Gotcha'd come up with a handle like thet'n, but he prob'ly din't hisownse'f, seein' she war jest a girl-chile."

I agreed that it was a pretty name and I thanked him for explaining it to me. Joe's tale had been a pleasant way of passing time on our way back to camp, which had just come into view.

Cookfires were already blazing. We could smell the aroma of roasting meat as we drew closer to the cluster of travel lodges and trappers' tents and bowers. When they spied the packtrain that we were bringing along with us, several men from our bunch came out to lend a hand. And naturally, when they recognized Joe Meek and Milton Sublette's erstwhile mate, an enthusiastic hurrah erupted from their midst, the loudest from a smiling Doc Newell, who rushed to bestow a welcoming *abrazo* on his oldest friend and partner in the mountains. Several kettles of booze were thrust at Joe, still mounted but not at all behindhand in accepting their hospitality, taking a swig from every one of them—"jest fer bein' perlite, don'tcha know," as Joe described it.

As soon as our womenfolk caught sight of Isabel and her young child, they surrounded her horse, helped her down, and conducted her to Molly's lodge, where they fussed over the newcomer and coddled her young one, before helping unload her packstring. Pitching in together, they quickly erected her lodge and stowed her belongings inside. Joe, assisted by Doc and Harpoon Harry Yeats, dragged up his plunder from their bowers. He and his new family were established in camp, leastaways for almost as long as rendezvous lasted.

The extra labor whetted already healthy appetites and the fragrance of roasting meat on a couple cookfires, together with stews and suchlike steaming from several kettles contributed by various wives, drew the entire bunch and a few passers-by to the center of camp where Dureau and L'Archévêque held forth, summoning laggards by drumming on copper kettles with iron spoons.

One of the first in line, busily carving off slabs of hump meat and scooping up stew from a kettle was Moses Harris, a frequent visitor to camp, especially at suppertime. Nobody objects to satisfying Black's substantial appetite, howsomever, for he never fails to sing for his supper, as the saying goes. He is always ready with yet another of his outrageous tall tales sprouting from his fertile brain, spiced with a hearty sense of humor. Behind him in line was another old friend from my earliest days in the mountains, a Missouri-born Frenchman, Etienne LeBref, who shares my love of reading and with whom I've been swapping books since I first met him. When he spied me in the crowd behind him, Etienne called out a greeting, quickly seconded by Harris, and bade me join them as soon as I filled my bowl. Black called out, "Don'tcha be fillin' yer cup, Temple! I brung along somethin' special!"

Which naturally hurried my efforts at the cookfire. It had been a long thirsty day in the saddle, visiting in the teetotaling Flathead camp, and confabulating with Joe Meek. Whilst I was folding my legs into a comfortable squat and propping my shoulders against a tree, Harris grabbed my cup and plunged it into his kettle, filling it brimful with delicious metheglin, a trapper's most esteemed libation, composed of fermented honey, malt, yeast, and hardly any water, which might displace too much of the raw spirits with which it is generously diluted. It's a rare treat, reserved mostly for rendezvous and even then not often served up.

"I reckoned y'all desarve some proper recompensin' in return fer all o' the vittles I been surroundin' hyar in yer camp thi'shere ronnyvoo," he said with a chuckle. "Drink up! Thar's more whar thet'n come from."

Naturally I didn't wish to hurt Black's feelings, so I happily obliged. Palaver was suspended for a spell, whilst we wolfed down the tasty comestibles provided by our Métis cooks and the Indian wives in camp, whose differing tribal backgrounds offer an appetizing variety in the foods they prepare when they can get hold of the makin's. The relative leisure our women enjoy at rendezvous allows them time to indulge their inventive fancies in gathering foodstuffs from woodland and prairie and preparing appetizing dishes for our grateful palates. Bachelors benefit equally with us married men from their efforts. The Plains Indian way of life dictates an annual cycle of feast or famine, so when food is plentiful, only too much is enough, and nobody goes hungry. Belly-shrinking skinny times lie always ahead.

When we had supped to surfeit, we put aside our bowls and lit our pipes. It was time for catching up on what was happening throughout the rendezvous and Black Harris was our herald.

"Have ye heard anything about American Fur gettin' here," I asked. The men in our bunch were getting restive about hanging onto the heaps of plews and robes they had traded their *palomillas* for and Brass Turtle was having difficulty holding them back.

"Nope," Harris replied, "ner Mike Cerré bringin' up Bonnyville's goods, neither. Lucien Fontenelle must have a doxy or two in Sain' Looie he jest cain't bear sayin' g'bye to, 'cause ever' year he gits hyar later'n we do, lettin' Billy git the jump on Amurrican Fur fer the early tradin'."

"Anything new in camp?" I asked.

"Nuthin' much that ain't what ye mought be expectin' amongst the trappers, but thar's a bunch of Injuns, from what I been hearin', what are more'n a mite upset abaout that'ere missionary name o' Jason Lee, what come up along with Nat Wyeth, 'speshly the Napercy bunch."

"How come?" I pursued. Anything that had to do with the Nez Percés interested me, for my father always spent most of his time in their village at rendezvous. I suspected that he had a lady friend there, but since he chose not to discuss the nature of his business there, I respected his privacy, as a dutiful son should do.

"Wal, 'pears that soon's the Napercy elders got wind o' thar bein' a Christian parson hyar at ronnyvoo, a bunch o' their headmen showed up in Wyeth's camp an' commenced beggin' 'im to come on home with them an' start teachin' 'em the Word o' Gawd, so's they kin git smart an' rich an' strong like the white-eyes!"

"So what happened?"

"What ye mought expect. Ol' Preacher Lee gave 'em the cold shoulder. Prob'ly din't care fer haow they smell or somethin' like that. From what I hear, same thing happened with some Snakes an' a passel o' Pend d'Oreilles what come lookin' to git theirse'fs saved!" Black snorted in disgust.

I wasn't surprised, but I held my tongue. "Anything else?"

"Wal, let's see," he drawled. "Oh, yeah, yer ol' friend Cap'n Stewart an' his pretty-boy Cree Antoine Clement dropped in jest yestiddy, the two of 'em keepin' purty close-mouthed abaout whar they passed the winter."

Brass Turtle had joined us whilst Black was enjoying himself drawing out the news about the Scottish hero of Waterloo suddenly surfacing in our midst after nearly a year-long absence. Harris removed Turtle's cup from his outstretched hand, filled it with metheglin, and returned it to its thirsty owner.

"What are they sayin', Black, about where they were and what they were doin' all that time away?" I demanded.

"Not much," he replied, "jest some kind o' trash abaout visitin' with Antoine's kinfolk up nawth somewhars."

"Ye b'lieve it?" I asked.

"Not fer a gawddamn minute."

"Only if Antoine's kin to ol' Doc McLoughlin up at the Aitch-bee-cee," Turtle sneered, referring to the Hudson's Bay Company's chief factor in Western Canada, headquartered at Vancouver on the Columbia River not far from the ocean. Doctor John McLoughlin, originally trained as a medico, has spent most of his lifetime as a fur trader, first as a Nor'wester, then rising rapidly in the HBC. Word was, he was an impressive man, standing six-and-a-half feet tall, with a mane of long white hair that earned him the name of White Eagle amongst the Indians, some who respect him, and others who, with good reason, fear him. "Din't take the cap'n long to hightail it up thar to git back with the rest o' the Brits, did it?" Turtle added.

"Cain't hardly blame 'im, though," Harris said with mock sympathy, "arter what he went through las' year with Tom Fitzpatrick, losin' nigh all o' his plunder to them'ere Absóraqa bucks, includin' that'ere fancy sojer-sword o' his'n. An' then, what shorely had to hurt their feelin's, arter Fitz talked the ol' Crow chief inter givin' some of it back, along with most o' their hosses, them young Crow scamps trailed 'em agin an' stole all o' their best critters, includin' Tom's purty black an' Stewart's high-blood English hosses."

That was the first I heard that Fitzpatrick had lost his prized Kentucky horse again. My heart went out to him. I myself had grown deeply fond of my own Coffee horse, an almost identical counterpart of Fitz's sunburnt black gelding.

"Reckon he went up to the Aitch-bee-cee lookin' to git hisse'f a new outfit?" Turtle observed dryly.

"Ye could be right," Harris rejoined. "Stewart don't look like he's missin' much a-tall anymore. Even got hisse'f anuther one o' them purty swords. Neither is Clement an' they both got theirse'fs some good-lookin' hosses."

"Mebbe so," Turtle replied, skepticism in his voice, "but I reckon he war likely reportin' in to the Brits, gittin' his orders an' tattlin' 'bout all he's learnt since he's been hangin' with Bobby an' Billy an' what he picked up at last year's ronnyvoo."

Brass Turtle is naturally suspicious of anyone who is even remotely connected with any government, but I wouldn't be surprised if he were right about Captain William Drummond Stewart in this case. At any rate, nobody ever did find out where the Scotsman and Antoine spent the winter and spring of 1833-1834 or what they might have been doing during that time.

"'Course, new duds an' guns an' hosses ain't all o' what Cap'n Stewart's brung to thi'shere ronnyvoo," Black said with a sly chuckle. "Somewhar's along the way—er mebbe it war hyar at ronnyvoo—Stewart went an' got hisse'f saddled with a ragged-arse Englishman name o' Ashworth, what claims to be some kind o' British lord. Showed up afoot, purt'near nekkid, an' starvin', so ever'body natcherly turned 'im over to Stewart, seein's how they both be English royalty er somethin' o' the sort. Nobody knows whar he come from ner how he got up hyar, but the cap'n gave 'im a hoss an' a gun an' a good Witney blanket or two an' naow it 'pears he cain't shake the sumbitch loose."

"I've seen 'im around Sublette's camp," Etienne put in, "always puttin' on airs an' tryin' to cheat at cards, but he's not very good at it. Everybody quit playin' cards with him, 'ceptin' for Tuttle, who cleaned 'im out an' told 'im to mind his manners before somebody teaches 'im a proper lesson he won't soon forget."

I marveled that Stewart would allow himself to be taken in by an obvious fraud, but perhaps their mutual Englishness was a tie that he couldn't ignore.

⨎   ⨎   ⨎

American Fur, ramrodded by Lucien Fontenelle and Etienne Provôt the *segundo*, arrived at the end of June, followed a day or two later by Bonneville's majordomo, Mike Cerré, leading his own packtrain. Captain Bonneville was otherwise occupied on some business of his own down on Bear River and never did show up at rendezvous that year. Now all the major traders were in place. Brass Turtle declared that it was time for our bunch to part with our own considerable stock of furs and the stacks of plews and buffalo robes acquired in trade for the California horses, selling to the highest bidder amongst the trading outfits. He offered to make the early arrangements and naturally everybody agreed that our tough, shrewd, fast-talking Delaware was just the man for that chore.

Preparing for his mission, Turtle asked me to accompany him to American Fur. "Ye got the Frenchy lingo down pat," he explained, "better'n the rest of us, 'ceptin' mebbe Micah, an' ye awready know Provôt an' Micah likely don't, so it won't hurt none to have ye along." He winked. "Jist so's thar won't be no cornvenient misunderstandin's, don'tcha know," he added slyly. I was curious to see how Turtle would conduct his commerce with Pierre Chouteau's sharp-witted traders, so I readily agreed to accompany him.

Turtle's first target was the trading camp Bill Sublette shared with Tom Fitzpatrick. They had moved a couple miles upstream from their earlier location near the mouth of Horse Creek to a meadow not far from our own diggin's. It was close by, so I went along to Turtle's meeting with Bill. Fitz took no part in the bargaining betwixt Brass Turtle and Bill, although he was a keen observer of everything they said. Later, Turtle noted, "Ol' Fitz 'pears to be suckin' hind tit in Sublette's camp. Wonder what's keepin' 'im hangin' 'round thar."

Bill Sublette's eyes grew bigger and I'm sure his mouth was watering when Turtle showed his samples and described in detail the huge haul of beaver, fine fur, and castoreum our bunch had amassed from trapping and trading, besides heaps of fine-tanned buffalo robes they had acquired mainly from selling off their *palomillas* to Indians at the rendezvous. He made it plain that he intended to offer that valuable plunder to other traders, so customary bullying tactics would be a waste of time. He was looking for the best deal for his people, take it or leave it.

I caught sight of the despairing look on Tom Fitzpatrick's face as Turtle reeled off the large quantities of beaver plews and numbers of tanned robes, as well as the fine furs and castoreum we possessed. I could almost read his mind as he calculated their value against RMF's indebtedness to Sublette and Campbell. It was, howsomever, too late. The door had closed on the once-bright ambitions of the RMF partners, even before rendezvous. Hard-fisted Bill Sublette was in charge now.

As Turtle haggled price with Billy, he scribbled, now and then, with a pencil stub on a scrap of foolscap he had got from me, recording Sublette's final offer for each of the various kinds of plunder we had for trade. When the bargaining at last arrived at its ultimate quibble, Turtle made a final notation, folded the foolscap and shoved it into the possibles pouch on his belt, and posed a final question to Bill Sublette. "As ye kin plainly see," he said levelly, fixing his regard squarely on Bill's hard blue eyes , "thar'll be a heap too much plunder comin' to us trappers fer us to be cartin' it off an' cachein' it—if, fer a fact, ye've even got enough trade goods on hand to pay fer ever'thin' I been tellin' ye 'bout. Nope. What we'll be needin' is a safe-an'-sure cache fer the extry money what's owin' to each of us, down in Sain' Looie."

Sublette grinned broadly and replied, "Don't ye be frettin' about that for a minute, Turtle. As ye likely know, Bobby and I have extensive holdings all over Saint Louis. Your money will be absolutely safe with us."

Brass Turtle returned his gaze straight to Sublette's eyes, his own as black and hard as lava glass arrow points as he asked, "An' how much inter'st de ye expec' to be payin' us fer the use of our cash money whilst ye be usin' it in yer bizness?"

Sublette was surprised and visibly shaken by Turtle's demand. "Interest?" he croaked. "Who said anythin' about interest? We'll be guaranteein' safe-keeping for your money, that's enough."

"Nope, 't won't do," the Delaware replied evenly. "I reckon ye know all about inter'st, Bill, seein' as how that's what squeezed Fitz hyar an' the rest o' the Rocky Mountain Fur fellas out o' bizness arter all o' their hard work all o' these years. How much ye payin' us fer usin' our money?"

Sublette remained silent for a spell, his eyes straying from time to time to our packmule loaded with samples of our horde of fur and robes. He swallowed hard and rasped, "Well, I reckon we can work somethin' out."

For reply, Turtle withdrew the foolscap from his possibles and fished out his pencil stub. I could see another long spell of dickering coming up, so I retreated to the shade of a big cottonwood on the river's edge. Fitzpatrick tagged along with me. Whilst we sat and smoked and watched the two antagonists yammering at each other, Fitz observed with a tinge of bitterness, "P'raps we should've asked your darlin' Brass Turtle along whin we were after drawin' up the bloody agreements that Billy's been shovin' down our throats this long while an' chokin' us to death in the end."

I merely grunted and held my peace. At last Turtle scribbled something on his foolscap and shoved it into his belt bag, which I took to mean that negotiations were at an end. I stood and trotted to where our critters were grazing, picked up their reins and the mule's halter-shank and returned to the trade tent.

The two antagonists were civil but not very friendly, which was not unexpected after the hard-nosed negotiations that had taken up most of the afternoon. Sublette was red-faced, drawn, and curt in his manner. Even Turtle showed signs of what had been a difficult chore. Bill extended a tepid invitation that we stay for a drink, but Turtle declined for the both of us, glancing skywards at the sun and declaring that we needed to return to camp.

Once out of earshot, he commented sourly, "Hell! I'm spittin' cotton, but I'll be damned if I'll be wettin' my whistle 'longside o' the likes o' that'ere cutthroat jackanapes what trompled his own gawddamn brother 'thout battin' an eye whilst he war chasin' arter one more dollar!"

After a moment of silence, he turned to me, smiling now, and announced, "Jist the same, I got what I been arter, rock-solid bids on all the plews an' sich from ol' Bill. Now ye kin wager Fitz'll be hot-footin' it over to Amurrican Fur, fust chance he gits, tellin' 'em all about it, chapter an' verse!"

Surprised by his mention of Fitzpatrick in that connection, I swung about in the saddle and demanded, "What d'ye mean? What's Fitzpatrick got to do with American Fur?"

Turtle barked out a short laugh that had no good humor in it. "Hell, Temple, ol' Tom's been hangin' out in their camp ever' chance he gits, ever since they got hyar, suckin' up to Fontenelle like a gawddamn orphan calf!

Tryin' to put together some kind o' deal fer hisse'f an' mebbe Bridger, too, whilst he still kin, I'm wagerin'!"

I was dumbstruck by Turtle's remark. Everything I had regarded as fixed and certain in my Rocky Mountain world was suddenly turning topsy-turvy. All the old allegiances and loyalties were becoming meaningless, adrift in a flood of unwelcome change over which I had no control, swept along by forces from far beyond our mountain wilderness.

At first I was stung by what felt like Fitzpatrick's betrayal of us who had believed in and supported our trapper friends in Rocky Mountain Fur, until I had to admit that he had little choice. His company was gone, fed into the greedy maw of Bill Sublette's voracious ambition.

Every mountaineer worthy of that title prides himself on his ability to survive, no matter what might come along. Tom Fitzpatrick was merely doing what has always served us well.

Whilst I struggled to come to terms with what I should have seen was coming all along, I sought to change the subject. "When d'ye reckon ye'll be talkin' with all the others?" I asked.

"Don't plan to," Turtle replied, "never did, 'ceptin' only fer Amurrican Fur, t'morra. Ol' Yankee Nat won't be comin' back arter this year, arter the hanselin' his pardners treated 'im to this time. He'll be lucky to git out o' the mountains with but half his hide, if'n he don't go pluperfec'ly broke. An' Cap'n Bonnyville ain't likely to be comin' back no more, neither. S'prisin' he ain't gone belly-up awready. Would'a, too, I reckon, if'n the guvmint warn't feedin' 'im money enough to keep 'im goin'. Anyways, that'ere Californy hike we took likely told 'im ever'thin' they sent 'im out thisaway to find out.

"'Sides, neither one o' them'ere outfits owns enough trade goods or cash money to buy all of our plunder an' neither one of 'em has roots in Sain' Looie, whar our extry money oughta be workin' fer us, fer when we're gonna be needin' it."

I didn't reply, mainly because I was utterly speechless, marveling at the depth and complexity of Brass Turtle's crafty reasoning, his knowledge and organization of the various factors that he must have ferreted out and considered as he wove them into his scheme, as well as his surprising ability to compete in trade with a seasoned hand like Billy Sublette, at the end, playing him like a tired fish until he gave up.

Who would have guessed that this untutored redskin was the conniving equal of a Machiavelli or Richelieu in achieving his ends? Not I, certainly, but I was mightily pleased to be so surprised.

At last I managed to say, "I reckon ye could be callin' this a pretty good day's work then, wouldn't ye say?"

Turtle favored me with a broad grin and replied, "Reckon we could at that. Cain't hardly wait 'til t'morra. You?"

After what I had witnessed that day, I was anxious to see our wily Delaware pitted against Fontenelle and Provôt, who, except for Pierre Chouteau himself, ranked amongst the best *marchandeurs* that shrewd old Saint Louis Money could put into the lists. My wager was still on Brass Turtle.

‽   ‽   ‽

Next morning, riding alongside Turtle to American Fur's trading tents, located where Ham's and Black's Fork meet, the packmule bearing our samples in tow, I mentioned what Black Harris had told me about Chouteau's eastern colleagues agreeing that American Fur would stay out of the mountains the following year, giving Sublette and Campbell an unencumbered field, free of major competition.

"Yep, Black tol' me that, too, but don't ye be countin' on it! The Rockies be a fur piece from New York an' ol' Cahday'll be figgerin' that what they don't know back thar ain't gonna hurt 'em." He fell into what appeared to be deep thought for a spell, then emerged with a bright smile. "On t'other hand, not knowin' fer sure exackly what's goin' on back east jist might make ol' Fontenelle a mite more anxious to beat Billy Sublette out of our plews an' sich, makin' 'im some'at more gen'rous with what he's willin' to pay fer 'em."

I was saved the need to frame a reply by our arrival at the sprawling collection of American Fur Company trade tents. The AMF counter-jumpers were doing a brisk business with their own company men that Andy Drips and the other brigade captains were daily bringing in from the field, a scatteration of free trappers I recognized, men who normally traded their plews with Rocky Mountain Fur but who likely resented Bill Sublette's brutal takeover of RMF from the partners, whom most of us regarded less as traders than working trappers like ourselves, and a mob of Indian men of various tribes seeking powder, lead, and booze and their chattering women whose eyes were big as they thirsted after gobs of colorful foofurraw prominently displayed on the shelves behind the long trestle-tables.

"'Pears they're doin' pretty good without us," I commented to Turtle as we tethered our horses. "Ye reckon that'll make 'em stingy about what they're willin' to pay?"

"Nope," he replied with a confident grin. "That might'a been so a couple years back, but beaver's thinnin' out somethin' fierce. Ever'body says so. They all been bitchin' about it since we got to ronnyvoo. Traders'll be lucky if they take back half as many packs this year as they did a couple-three years ago. Count on it, they all be hungry fer plews!"

Still impressed with Turtle's performance the day before, I held my tongue, content to be a silent witness to the hard dealing that was sure to come.

I waited with the packmule whilst Turtle went in search of Lucien Fontenelle, observing the while the buzz of activity in and around the trade tents—sharp-eyed clerks grading heaps of beaver plews for size and condition and recording the value of each on a ledger page assigned to each trapper. Other clerks piled up stacks of essential merchandise and trade goods and scribbling the cost on the opposite page of the ledger, instantly reducing the momentary wealth of the trapper to mere wages. What he doesn't spend on necessities such as gunpowder, galena, caps, traps, and suchlike and enough foofurraw to guarantee a brief interlude of romantic comfort usually goes for a kettle or two of watered-down trader's booze. When he and his pards drink that up, going into debt with the Company is a likely option.

In spite of what Turtle had said about that year's scarcity of beaver, I saw crews working two big fur presses in the open space behind the trade tents, weighing and squeezing stacks of bone-dry cured beaver pelts into compact bundles of ninety pounds each, about sixty plews to the pack. Two packs slung onto either side of a packsaddle make a substantial burden for a packhorse or mule.

Brass Turtle stepped out of a big marquee and gestured for me to join him, which I did, leading the mule past curious onlookers who doubtless wondered why I was taking a packmule to the *bourgeois*'s party. When I got to the doorway, a camp servant emerged and offered to hold the critter whilst I went inside.

As soon as I entered into the cool darkness of the marquee, Lucien Fontenelle strode forward and clasped my hands in his, exclaiming the while,

"Bienvenue, mon cher Monsieur Bock! *C'est un grand plaisir de vous voir ici, dans notre tente!"* Then, collecting himself and glancing at Brass Turtle, he switched to English. "M'sieu Chouteau sends 'is regards. Eet is good to see you again, especially een the 'appy *circonstance* zat your *compagnon* M'sieu Turtle 'as been tellin' of. But firs', let us enjoy *un* rare *plaisir* 'ere in ze *montagnes.* Our *chef de cuisine* 'as *prepare un riz au lait pour notre délectation!"*

Fontenelle's effusive vocabulary lost Turtle for a moment. He was used to the common patois of our Métis camp servants, not the polished Gallic accents of our host and soon-to-be adversary. "What's he sayin'?" he muttered in my ear.

"He's just invitin' us to have some rice puddin' with him an' Provôt before the hardarse hoss-tradin' commences."

"That's right neighborly of 'im," Turtle conceded. "Ask if he's got some o' that'ere Frenchy brandy to go along with it, whilst he's at it."

Fortunately I didn't need to do so. Etienne Provôt was already sloshing generous amounts of French cognac into tin cups and passing them around. Rice pudding was indeed a rare treat in the mountains and we appreciated the excellent cognac even more, as ye might suppose. Once, when Fontenelle and Provôt were conferring between themselves, Turtle leaned near and murmured, "Ye kin be sure ol' Fitzpatrick's awready been here an' told 'em 'bout ever' rag we got fer trade. An' they cain't wait to git their hands on all of it. These two ain't about to be sarvin' rice puddin' an' brandy to jist anybody that comes by."

Which was likely so.

❧   ❧   ❧

Riding back to camp that late afternoon was even more pleasant than yesterday's return had been. Brass Turtle had got everything from Fontenelle that he had bargained for. If my friend had any regrets about the transaction with American Fur it was that he wondered if he had triumphed too easily, if perhaps he could have got more out of them than he had demanded.

I disagreed. Although Turtle had done all of the talking on our side, I witnessed it all and it was plain to see that Tom Fitzpatrick had thoroughly informed the two Frenchmen before we ever entered their precincts. They knew just how much Turtle had been able to wring out of Bill Sublette for each kind and quality of fur or robe we had accumulated, which prepared them to outbid Sublette, but not by a great deal more than Turtle might be willing to settle for.

They wanted the entire lot, howsomever, which played into Turtle's hand, for he offered more than once to peddle portions of our stores piecemeal to other traders, who might be willing to pay him top dollar for certain items, even if they couldn't afford to purchase the entire amount. It was an effective argument, apparently, for at last Lucien Fontenelle shrugged his well-tailored shoulders, struck his fist into his palm, and cried out with a laugh, "*D'accord!* M'sieu Tortue, you shall have what you demand!"

Fontenelle's sudden capitulation caught Brass Turtle offguard. For a moment he was almost speechless, but he quickly regained his composure and covered whatever confusion remained by bending down to scribble the final figures of the transaction onto a fresh scrap of foolscap.

When Turtle opened his mouth to speak, Fontenelle once again interrupted our clever Delaware. "I believe I know your nex' *demande*, M'sieu, *la matière* of *l'intérêt* for *l'argent, la monnaie* which will remain wiz us in Saint Louis, in our keeping for *vos compagnons*. We weel pay you one pour cent more zen M'sieu Sublette 'as promised! *D'accord?*"

The cat was out of the bag. Fact is, it had been frolicking about the tent throughout most of the entire haggling. Fontenelle had known all along what Bill Sublette had agreed to. If he hadn't been willing to pay more than that amount, he never would have met with us.

Brass Turtle responded with a good-natured, although somewhat rueful, grin and replied, "Agreed. I gotta admit, ye got me fair an' square." Nevertheless, he scribbled the interest figure on his paper before folding it and stowing it in his belt poke.

Etienne Provôt was already filling tin cups with cognac to celebrate the successful conclusion of negotiations. Fontenelle waved us to seats on the wooden benches that flanked the long deal table on which were heaped our samples of plews, fine furs, and robes. "Come," he exclaimed heartily, "let us drink to zis, zat weel be only ze firs' of many profitable *affaires* between us!" There was a polite murmur of agreement and we all raised our cups in a toast to that sentiment. I thought that Lucien was surprisingly cheerful for a man who had just paid an extravagant price for our peltries. I glanced at Brass Turtle to see if he thought so, too, but the Delaware's face was, as usual, unreadable. He was responding just then to a question Fontenelle asked concerning our California journey, which gave me a few moments to study our hosts.

Fontenelle had risen to great heights in the world of fur trade commerce. Now, instead of the greasy buckskins of a working brigade leader in the field, as I remembered him from past years, his raiment now was downright elegant, still buckskins, but butter-soft and elaborately quilled and fringed, perfectly tailored to his tall, lean frame, his shoulder-length hair well-barbered and his short beard trimmed to perfection, altogether a portrait of a handsome, successful Saint Louis merchant sojourning in the mountains.

Etienne, on the other hand, hadn't changed much over the years, except to show the effects of an overfondness for the pleasures of the grape and whatever other inebriants that might come to hand, especially around his eyes and broken veins that marred his cheeks above his bristling grey-streaked black beard. Always rotund and seal-fat like a healthy horse, though muscular and powerful, now he bulged inside his stained deerhide shirt and his step had lost much of the spring that I recalled from earlier days.

Taking our leave from the *bourgeois* of American Fur, it was agreed that we would return the following day with our peltries and buffalo robes, so that grading and counting could commence and a final accounting be concluded, crediting each trapper in our bunch with the agreed-upon value of his merchandise in the Company's ledgers, the unused balance of which to be held in interest-bearing accounts for them at Pratte, Chouteau & Company in Saint Louis. Fontenelle promised to prepare the appropriate documents overnight, so that the business could be finalized when the transfer of merchandise occurred.

As I followed Fontenelle and Turtle out of the marquee, Provôt plucked my sleeve to detain me inside. "You yourself will be returning with the peltries tomorrow, is it not so?" he asked me in French. I assured him that I would certainly be in attendance, which apparently pleased him. "Good," he replied. "We will talk then." I was puzzled by this odd exchange, but I shrugged and attributed it to the celebratory libations we had just enjoyed.

Brass Turtle was jubilant over the outcome of his efforts on behalf of our comrades, flavored with sour satisfaction at depriving Bill Sublette of the coveted prize. Bill's shabby treatment of the RMF partners rankled all of us, but Turtle appeared to resent it even more deeply than the rest of us did, which likely had driven him to sharper dealing than he might otherwise have done.

That thought was in my mind when Turtle surprised me with his next comment. "Reckon we oughta be sorta grateful to ol' Bill, arter all." I gave him a sharp look which he greeted with a laugh. "Sure enough. If t'warn't fer Sublette, our dealin' with Fontenelle wou'dn'a been near so easy as it war. I reckon that'ere Frenchy could feel ol' Bill breathin' on his neck ever' minute we war thar!"

Which was likely so.

‽ ‽ ‽

Happily, next day, we actually lacked enough packhorses and mules to lug all of our plews and buffalo robes to American Fur's trade tents in a single trip. It was necessary to send several critters back to be loaded a second time in order to transport all of our wealth to Fontenelle's grading tables.

The route from our camp to American Fur led past Sublette's trade tents, where a crowd of his hands turned out to watch our cavalcade of heavily-laden pack animals passing by on their way to their competition, high-piled bales of precious plews and buffalo robes swaying precariously as they made their way across the uneven prairie. It was a festive procession. Our trappers had decked themselves out in colorful new calico shirts, sashes, and garters at Nat Wyeth's cut-price trade tables and our womenfolk were even more richly arrayed in their Sunday-best duds, anxious to splurge their new-found wealth and to flaunt their status as trappers' wives over their stay-at-home sisters, most of them mounted on their still-fractious, half-trained *palomilla* mares, curvetting and prancing and forging at the bit, but firmly under control of their practically born-in-the-saddle riders.

Joe Meek's Isabel, mounted on a handsome dapple-grey gelding, rode in the midst of Cat, Iris, Paddy's Molly, and Turtle's ever-loving Tallymesko, all of them riding their prized new *palomilla*s, the well-groomed hides gleaming like burnished brass in summer sunshine, creamy manes and tails flowing in the fresh morning breeze. Joe, Doc, and Harry trailed behind them, leading packmules loaded with their own plews taken during their California journey, evidently disdaining to trade with Sublette out of loyalty to their bankrupted RMF friends.

Glancing towards Sublette's establishment, I espied Bill standing amongst his people, bending a frosty glare on our light-hearted parade. When he caught me returning his gaze, he set that long blue-shadowed jaw of his in a sneer, spun on his heel, and darted into his tent. I could almost hear his disgusted harrumph from where I sat.

❧   ❧   ❧

Micah was our chief factor at the weighing and grading of pelts and buffalo robes, assisted by sharp-eyed Zeetlah and Little Mountain. Micah's several years in Chouteau's Saint Louis establishment, first as a slave, then as a valued free man, doing precisely that kind of work, earned him respect amongst Fontenelle's people and eliminated much of the quibbling over quality that might have occurred if any other man had been assigned that function. Finn McCool and I, together with a pair of American Fur clerks, presided over the bulky ledgers that recorded the value of our merchandise. He and I carefully credited each of our people with ownership of each pelt or robe that bore his branded mark, along with its assigned value.

As the long day wore on, heaps of hides cluttered the open space behind the trade tents and the crew of men operating the big log hide-presses sweated to keep up with a steady stream of beaver plews, buffalo robes, and fine furs—mink, otter, marten, fisher, white winter weasel, muskrat, fox of both red and white winter fur, skunk, nearly all in prime winter condition— flowing from the grading tables.

Our California beaver plews were not as prime as Rocky Mountain springtime pelts, but the large quantity of beaver that our bunch had amassed during our stay in that region assured us all of many more dollars in credit on Chouteau's books than any of us had ever dared dream of for a single year's trapping. Added to that, every man who made that trip, except myself, realized a tremendous windfall in plews, buffalo robes, and fine furs gained in trading off their extra *palomilla* horses, mostly to Indians, at rendezvous. Tolliver accumulated more than anyone else in that regard. Anse has always been exclusively partial to mules, but stingy as he is, he was not about to part with a single one of his California horses except for a handsome profit.

Anse's sudden prosperity provided Tuttle with an opportunity to claim the last word, leastaways for a spell, in their never-ending verbal feud. "Naow, Tolliver, ain'tcha kinda sorry 'baout all ther bitchin' ye done 'baout herdin' them'ere purty hosses all ther way from Californy? Them critters've gone an' made ye rich!" Anse merely glared at Tuttle, clamped his lean jaw tight shut, and replied not a single word.

Kit Carson was open-mouthed with wonder when McCool and I told him how much his own furs had brought, besides the tremendous profit he had gained from trading the horses he had reluctantly accepted from us. When Kit expressed doubt about keeping his money with Chouteau & Pratte in Saint Louis, for he intended someday to return to Santa Fe, we explained that Pierre Chouteau had many interests in that Mexican province. Fontenelle's signature on the document we gave him guaranteed payment in either town, likely in silver coin in Santa Fe, instead of trade goods. Kit can neither read nor write, but he took us at our word without question.

Although they possessed no plews of their own to trade, our *Californio* recruits, Diego Valenzuela and Pablo Torres, suddenly found themselves substantially well-to-do in credit on American Fur's books from the returns in beaver, fine fur, and buffalo robes realized from trading off their share of the *palomilla* horses to Indians and trappers, much thanks to Cesár Pérez and Micah for advising and guiding them in their new world of rendezvous commerce.

Several of us already had an account with Chouteau's establishment— Tuttle, Micah, Finn, Paddy, Turtle, Powatawa, and I, as well as Ned Godey, which was now assigned to Kathleen—but it was short work for Finn and me to prepare documents with Fontenelle's endorsement for the others. We encased the precious papers in oilskin packets and carefully explained their value to each of our illiterate comrades.

At last the enormous chore was accomplished. The scales and grading tables were finally bare, the ledger entries complete, and our people were free to celebrate their triumph. Which they were not slow to do. Every man promptly purchased a brand-new copper kettle and had it filled with trader's booze. Any envy or ill-will amongst other trappers that might have been prompted by our sudden good fortune was speedily dispelled by a fountain of liquid generosity on the part of our bunch, sharing their booze with all comers and sending them back to the trade tables, again and again, to refill their kettles.

As I prepared to depart the grading area and seek out Cat and Iris in the noisy throng of women besieging the tents that overflowed with AFC's treasure trove of splendid silks, satins, velvets, broadcloths, woolens, and all manner of gorgeous foofurraw intended to excite the material lust of Indian women, Etienne Provôt caught my sleeve and invited me into the *bourgeois*'s marquee. Once inside, he handed me a cup of cognac and said in his heavily-accented English, "Zis 'as been a mos' successfool day, n'est-ce pas? We 'ope zat it weel be only ze firs' of many such occasions! Let us dreenk to zat, *hein*?" We clinked cups and drained them, which action amounted to at least a venial sin, considering the excellent quality of that cognac, which deserves to be sipped slowly and thoughtfully. Then he produced a bulky wax-sealed packet of fine linen paper and handed it to me. Glancing at the seal, I recognized the ornate signet of Pierre Chouteau embedded in the red wax. I had often admired its design on that gentleman's large gold finger ring.

"Pair'aps eet would be bes', Temple, eef you would read zat in secret, when you 'ave time enough. Eet could be *très importante, hein*?"

I agreed. Any communication directly from le Cadet was not to be taken lightly. I slipped the packet into my belt-poke, thanked Provôt for delivering the letter and for the cognac, and took my leave.

Riding back to camp, the letter still unopened, I wondered how it was that both Provôt and Fontenelle were lately both so affable and polite with me, a common trapper in the Rocky Mountains. A personal letter from their powerful patron helped to explain why.

∾   ∾   ∾

Whilst Cat and Iris were preparing supper, I slipped down to the riverbank to read Chouteau's letter. The long summer day provided enough daylight to read le Cadet's tiny, crabbed handwriting that I recalled from previous years, especially on the contracts that he had personally prepared a dozen years earlier to be signed by Mike Fink and his henchmen Talbot and Carpenter—contracts, as it turned out, to which I owe the foundation of my own financial security.

When I broke the seal I saw that the letter was written in Chouteau's distinctive style of Creole French, which I won't reproduce here. I will instead render its meaning and intent in the most faithful English translation of which I am capable.

The letter was evidently written shortly before Lucien Fontenelle and Etienne Provôt departed Saint Louis with their packtrain destined for the Horse Creek rendezvous.

26 April 1834
My dear friend Temple Buck:

As you know well, I have for many years repeatedly invited you to join our establishment in pursuing your chosen métier in the fur trade in the Rocky Mountains, an invitation that you have always politely but steadfastly declined, preferring instead the unrestricted life of an independent trapper in the company of your several loyal and devoted friends, with most of whom you have been associated since your earliest experience in our trade with Major Henry in 1822. I admire your spirit of independence and self-reliance. In many ways, I envy the nearly absolute freedom afforded by the way of life you have chosen in the mountains.

Unfortunately the profession that you and your companions have practiced with admirable skill, courage, and dedication during these past dozen years is now in severe jeopardy. For several reasons that I am reluctant to disclose in this letter, I sincerely advise you to consider seriously the proposal that I shall make herein. I will say only that commercial forces beyond the control of any individual or entity may very well sweep away institutions that we have long considered permanent.

If you are reading these words, you are aware that William Sublette has foreclosed on the Rocky Mountain Fur Company and that he and Robert Campbell control all of its assets. The previous partners, Messrs. Fitzpatrick, Milton Sublette, Bridger, Fraeb, and Gervais have been discharged. By time you receive this letter, Thomas Fitzpatrick will form a new company with Lucien Fontenelle under the title Fontenelle, Fitzpatrick & Cie. It is expected that Mister Fitzpatrick's former partners and many of the trappers previously engaged by the now-defunct firm will join him in his new enterprise.

Regrettably, representatives of our firm residing in New York City, none of whom have ever visited the Rocky Mountains and who possess little if any knowledge of the practical workings of the fur trade, in a recent agreement concluded with Mister William Sublette, have unwisely committed the American Fur Company to refraining from all trade in the Rocky Mountains during the coming year 1835.

Naturally negotiations are underway to remedy that unfortunate situation, but at the time of this writing, no progress has been realized. Inasmuch as it is apparent that the new firm of Fontenelle, Fitzpatrick & Cie. will need to receive its supplies from the American Fur Company, which would violate the terms of the ill-advised agreement made with Sublette in New York, I propose that you and your immediate comrades enter the service of Chouteau, Pratte & Cie. of Saint Louis directly and that you enlist as many of your fellow independent trappers as possible, as well as willing Indian bands and tribes, to join you in selling their furs to that entity.

Arrangements will be made to conduct business and to provide adequate supplies in the coming year for you and your comrades and to all individuals whom you recruit to our service. In return for your effort, Chouteau, Pratte & Cie. pledges to reward you and your immediate comrades with a premium of fifty percent over mountain price for your peltries and a premium of twenty-five percent awarded to each of those trappers whom you recruit to our service.

The alternative to accepting this offer will be subjecting yourselves to the unrestrained avarice of William Sublette, who, relieved of all significant competition in the coming year, will certainly seek maximum profit at the expense and impoverishment of all who are forced to deal solely with him.

I have on good authority information that the year 1835 will be Sublette's final year in the mountain trade and that he and Mister Robert Campbell will, after that, concentrate their wealth and energies in mercantile and real estate activity in Saint Louis and elsewhere in Missouri. Their reputation in the mountains will be of small concern to them after next summer.

As a guarantee of the sincerity of this proposal I believe that I need offer only the history of our dealings since we first met on the eve of your great adventure in 1822. I have always conducted our commerce together honestly and honorably in every respect. You may expect no less in this and all future endeavors between us.

I remain Your Most Humble & Obedient Servant,

Pierre Chouteau, Cadet

I sat stunned and almost unbelieving the words that I had read, poring over the paragraphs to be sure that I understood what Chouteau had offered and why he had done so. He had shown himself to be almost clairvoyant in predicting the outcome of Bill Sublette's machinations. Everything that Cadet had predicted when he wrote that letter in April had come to pass, which lent credence to his veiled forebodings about what might lie ahead for our trade and our way of life. A dozen years of acquaintance, even at a distance, with the western master of American Fur had instilled in me a tremendous respect for his acumen and judgment, his uncanny ability to anticipate change or a rival's next move and turn it to advantage. I marveled, too, that Pierre Chouteau trusted me enough to confide in me a stratagem to outmaneuver Sublette and Campbell in the coming year, a scheme that could prove most embarrassing if it were exposed.

It was flattering that Chouteau had enough confidence in my judgment and discretion to entrust me with such potentially explosive and damaging information, but it was Cadet's apprehension concerning the future of all of us that convinced me that the matter warranted an early council with my comrades.

Further deliberation on the riverbank was forestalled by my daughter calling me to supper.

৯   ৯   ৯

I slept badly that night, my mind a jumble of unanswerable questions and serious doubts about the wisdom of our bunch committing ourselves to any authority beyond our own counsel. I awakened earlier than usual, my eyes burning, my mind whirling with conflicting ideas and emotions, and still no closer to a decision on what to say to the others in the bunch about what I thought of Chouteau's proposal.

Cat, always sensitive to my moods, had little to say past what suffices for a good-morning in Salish, busied herself with the little cookfire in the lodge and getting a kettle boiling for morning coffee. I grunted something unintelligible and ducked out the doorway, heading for the men's swimming-hole on the crick, where I dropped my britchclout on the bank and dived headfirst into the chilly depths. My dive took me all the way to the bottom, where I rootled in the rocky crick bed as long as I was able, seeking to clear my head in the cold water, until at last I rose sputtering to the surface, my long braids wrapped around my throat, and laughing in spite of myself at my plight.

I saw that I was not alone in the water. Several of our Indians were frolicking at the far end of the pool, Micah in their midst. It struck me then that I needed to consult first with him before I broached Cadet's proposition to the others. His French was much better than my own and he had known Pierre Chouteau as long as I had, with much more frequent association, and in more telling circumstances. Besides, I thoroughly trust Micah's level-headed judgment. I swam to his side and, after the customary greetings and small-talk which humorously touched upon his overnight escapade, I invited him to break his fast with us, which, like most bachelors would, he enthusiastically agreed to do.

৯   ৯   ৯

Micah is always a welcome guest in our lodge. Kathleen plied him with vittles and kept his cup filled with rich sugary black coffee, whilst Iris coaxed him to sing just one more song, of which he seems to possess an inexhaustible store of Negro religious hymns and humorous ditties. Afterwards, he and I retired to the shade of cottonwoods on the riverbank with our pipes.

I wasted no time in handing over Chouteau's long letter, which Micah read slowly and carefully, returning, now and again, to a previous portion and reading it a second and third time, assuring me that he was wringing every morsel of meaning and intent from his former employer's epistle.

At last he handed the letter back to me and emitted a low whistle, shaking his head in silent admiration, before he said, "Ol' Cadet surely ain't lost track of his trusty ol' crystal ball, nohow! How do ye suppose he figgers out what's goin' to happen months before it does?"

Naturally I had no reply then, nor since. Then Micah and I went over the letter together, word-by-word and line-by-line, making sure that we both understood the same things from its content. What you have read in the text I included above is the result of our collaborative translation.

We experienced no great sense of triumph as a result of our effort. Instead we were overwhelmed by a feeling of gloom inspired by the ominous implications of Chouteau's dimly-suggested but not specifically described prediction of impending disaster.

We both fell silent, chewing over what we had distilled from Cadet's sentiments expressed in his lengthy letter, what he actually said and what could only be surmised. After finishing a pipeful, Micah tapped out the dottle and broke the silence. "Takin' it all togethah, I'm inclined to go along with what the ol' gentleman recommends we do. It's plain to see, ever'thin's changin' hereabouts. Fitz an' Fontenelle are courtin' each othah, just like Chouteau said they'd be doin'. Sublette's grabbin' up ev'ry copper he can lay hands on an' not givin' a damn what us trappers might think about it. An' as far as what he's promisin' us for bringin' in free trappers an' Injuns an' payin' us an' them a galore of extra money for the plews we bring in to Chouteau's people, well, mebbe so. We can't be sure, natcherly, but in all the time I worked for ol' Cadet, bond an' free, and evah'thin' I evah heard about 'im, even from them as don't like 'im, nobody evah said he evah went back on his word."

I had to agree. Tough and exacting as Pierre Chouteau, Cadet could be in his business dealings, his honesty was never in question. As far as his scheme to get around the ridiculous agreement to keep American Fur out of the mountains all of the next year was concerned, it hadn't been Chouteau who consented to such a deal.

It was decided between us, then, that the two of us would convey Cadet's proposal to the bunch, starting with a few but leaving the final decision to a majority vote amongst our entire number, as we had always done. For the initial group we chose Brass Turtle, Finn McCool, Tuttle, Powatawa, Zeetlah, and Little Mountain, reckoning that they would be most likely to hold the plan in confidence until Sublette and Nat Wyeth departed the rendezvous.

Keeping Anse Tolliver in the dark made sense because, spiteful and contrary as Anse is wont to be, especially when he's in his cups, he might spill the beans simply as a mischievous prank. Regretting it afterward wouldn't repair the damage. Paddy McBride, loyal and lovable as he is, runs off at the mouth when he drinks. Rendezvous is no place to count on Paddy keeping a secret.

∾   ∾   ∾

We gathered that same afternoon in a secluded grove on the riverbank. Micah read the letter aloud, translating as he did so. When he finished reading it through, he went back and read each sentence separately to the group. The two of us took turns responding to questions as best we could, both Micah and I taking care not to advocate a decision either way on Chouteau's proposal.

Only McCool asked to read the letter himself, but he quickly gave up his attempt to fathom the murky meanings of Chouteau's colloquial Creole French. "Och!" he cried, shoving the letter back to me. "'Tis an abomination, surely, on the darlin' French language—what a hundred years or so in America have done to corrupt it!"

Surprisingly little debate ensued before the select group meeting that day decided to approve Chouteau's offer. Although our bunch would be acting as Cadet's cat's-paw, pulling his chestnuts out of the fire, so to speak, we would be well-paid for our efforts and, after next summer, not be further obliged either to Pierre Chouteau himself, Chouteau, Pratte, & Cie., or American Fur.

"Hell!" Tuttle crowed, "I'd a'most be willin' to do 'er fer nuthin', jest to be doin' Bill Sublette in ther eye, arter what he done to Fitz an' t'others!" He paused and grinned roguishly before he added, "Natcherly thet be jest a manner o' speakin'—doin' it fer nuthin, thet is to say."

Brass Turtle looked up from where he had been carefully explaining to Zeetlah and Little Mountain what Micah had been reading aloud, making sure they understood what was being proposed. "If it war anybody else'n ol'

Chouteau hissownse'f, I'd be more'n a mite leery, but cornsid'rin' he put his name to it, I'd call it solid!"

Everybody present nodded his assent and although the rest of our bunch hadn't voted, it was reasonable to assume that they would go along with our decision. Because Cadet's letter had been addressed to me, I was assigned the chore of replying to him when Lucien Fontenelle departed for Saint Louis.

❧　❧　❧

On most days I devoted a couple hours each morning to schooling Iris in reading, composition, ciphering, and practicing her penmanship. Kathleen usually attended those classes, as she had done in previous years, during Ned's lifetime, after Rainbow's death. I had always encouraged Cat's attendance at those sessions. Thirsty for knowledge as she was herself, I could count on Cat keeping Iris intent on her studies.

As the mysteries of the "talking leaves" resolved into a solid ability to read, both Iris and Cat became devoted to books, hungry for the stories they contained. Often I would overhear one or the other reading aloud from my personal stock of books, with the listener occasionally correcting the reader's pronunciation or interrupting to enquire the meaning of a word or phrase. They soon included Powatawa in their sessions, begging him to relate traditional Shawnee winter tales to supplement their store of white-eyes legends, which inspired Kathleen to introduce time-honored Séli stories into the mix, telling them in her accented English, which greatly increased their charm. Tuttle was often an attentive guest. He is able to read, but he much prefers to listen.

Although neither one of them appeared to tire of stories they had heard or read themselves many times, they constantly nagged me to acquire more books, which is not an easy thing to do in the fur trade, even at rendezvous, where few trappers can read or write. I enlisted Micah, Finn McCool, and Paddy McBride, along with my long-time bookish friend Etienne LeBref, to assist me in scouring trade tents and trapper camps in search of so-far-unread tomes to satisfy the literary appetite of my womenfolk.

Naturally, all that did not occur immediately at that one Horse Creek rendezvous, but gradually over succeeding years, as both Iris and Cat acquired increasing skill and knowledge and a growing demand for ever more grist for the literary mill.

❧　❧　❧

A day after Fast Horse rode into our camp and announced that he had selected five likely young men to be trained as riflemen, Micah and I loaded up a packmule with Frapp's percussion rifles and their fixin's, a plenitude of galena, caps, and gunpowder, and a score of beaver traps and headed for the Flathead village. Fast Horse had chosen well. All five were fresh-faced, sturdy youngsters, eager to learn, and proud of being singled out from the rest of their fellows.

Fast Horse asked if he might receive the training, as well, which we welcomed, not only for his willingness to interpret for us, but also the authority he exercised as a headman's son and likely future leader of the band.

First off, we taught them how to run a stock of rifle balls, melting the lead and keeping it clean and carefully pouring it into the bullet mold that would produce rifle balls to fit their particular rifle and possibly no other. Most of our pupils were familiar with smoothbore flintlock trade muskets that are much more forgiving about the precise size of bullets than the rifles we gave them. Often, in a pinch, a smooth pebble or a few nails or screws serves in place of a galena ball to secure the musket owner's dinner if distance and accuracy aren't critical factors. Rifles require precision ammunition.

We were aided in convincing our neophytes of the important advantages of rifles over muskets by Fast Horse, who had been using his Hawken percussion rifle with good effect since I gifted him with it a year before. Although the rifles I had obtained from Frapp were not as good as Jake Hawken's fine weapons, they were far and away superior to the poorly-made trade guns that traders usually swap for Indians' precious beaver plews.

Fast Horse also helped to overcome their skepticism about percussion caps over flintlocks. He admitted that originally he had shared those same doubts, but experience had erased them. Our novices were no different in that respect from most white trappers, who argued at first that they would be weaponless if they ran out of caps, until they were forced to admit that neither galena nor gunpowder grows on trees in the mountains. Nothing is perfect, but hangfires, flashes in the pan, and soggy priming in rainy weather are greatly reduced by using percussion caps.

Because our main intention was to prepare Iron Bow's Séli band to resist attack by Síksika Blackfoot raiders on the wide-open eastern plains during their annual buffalo hunt, Micah and I worked hardest to train our novices in long-distance shooting. Living as they mostly do on the prairies, Síksikas hunt mostly buffalo and they mostly do it a-horseback, which means that most of their shooting is done at a distance of only a few feet with their flintlock trade guns.

Flathead country is mostly in or near the mountains, where their usual game is wapiti, deer, and mountain sheep and goats, all of which require better marksmanship at greater distances than galloping alongside a running buffalo and delivering a fatal gunshot. If our training proved successful, our five riflemen could pick off Síksika hostiles at a comfortable distance before the raiders would be able to return effective gunfire. Losing half a dozen family, friends, and neighbors usually discourages even the most bloodthirsty Blackfoot.

Our keen-eyed youngsters proved to be apt pupils, handily increasing the distance of their targets to nearly two hundred paces. Micah began rewarding exceptional performance with a large-headed brass tack, which inevitably appeared next day decorating the stock of the shooter's rifle, which encouraged a lively competition amongst the group for those shiny trophies.

When we reckoned that their shooting at stationary targets couldn't be much improved, we took our tyros out to hunt real game critters. They rapidly graduated from wapiti and deer to the elusive, fast-running prairie goats some folks call antelopes, which convinced Micah and me that our chore was mostly finished.

Our efforts didn't always meet with success, howsomever. We tried to give our young men an edge over their enemies by training them to plan their attacks and to fight together as a single force under the command of a leader. No luck. The Indian war chief merely leads by example. Nobody follows orders. The warrior tradition of individual skill, personal courage, and achievement in battle is deeply ingrained, likely imbibed with their mother's milk. "I give up," Micah complained. "There ain't a coward in the lot, but gettin' 'em to take orders in a gunfight is worse'n herdin' turkeys. They ain't about to do it! Injuns be pluperfect democrats! Evah'body's got a vote and evah' one of 'em can't hardly wait to use it! Best we can do is just teach 'em how to shoot plumb an' try to get 'em to keep their guns clean."

I had to agree.

Our final gift to the young sharpshooters was a set of four beaver traps for each of them, so that they might earn the wherewithal to keep themselves supplied with gunpowder, galena, and percussion caps.

"Sorta wish I were goin' buffler huntin' with 'em this year," Micah observed wistfully, "just to see the look on those Blackfoot's faces when they run into these kids, 'stead of the easy pickin's they'll be countin' on."

ȣ   ȣ   ȣ

Kathleen's milk dried up a fortnight or so after my arrival at rendezvous, which fortunately offered no serious problem for young Ben. He was remarkably active, growing like a weed, and had already abandoned his cradleboard. Iris delighted in playing with him on the floor of our lodge, sometimes carrying him out-of-doors to show him off to her playmates. Weaning him to pap and soon after to more solid vittles proved to be an easy chore. I jested at the time that Ben's appetite threatened to interfere with my trapping in the fall, for I might be obliged to go hunting when I should be looking after my traps.

Like many fathers, my interest in him grew apace with my son's increasing size and activity. He became less a cherished object in my eyes and much more a valued person in his own right with each faltering attempt to take his place in the world of people. I caught myself daydreaming of when I would first put him on a horse and take him with me into the woods to learn the wonders of trees and greenery and the ways of wild critters. I had done these things with Iris, too, but now I felt somehow guilty about my eagerness to pass on my knowledge to my newborn son and to instill in him what it takes to become a proper man.

At last I realized that my impatience to see Ben grow to young manhood had its roots in my own early childhood, when the man I thought was my father ignored me when he wasn't using me as his slavey. I was twelve before his brother, Uncle Ben, who had no children of his own, insisted on taking me away from a steady diet of farm chores and teaching me woodcraft, hunting, and trapping in the Ohio wilderness. Ben showed me, too, that grown men could be decent and honorable. It wasn't until I turned sixteen that I came to know Powatawa, my real father, who saved my life and welcomed me into his Shawnee family, where I learned the masculine values and principles that have guided me ever since.

Powatawa, usually reserved in his behavior and measured in his expressions of emotion, puts aside his dignity whenever he comes nigh his grandson, cooing Shawnee baby-talk, cradling the little fellow in his arms, and bouncing him on his knees, all in a decidedly un-chieftainlike manner.

Often, when he and I are alone together, he speaks of the future day when he will teach Ben to ride and use a bow, reading a track, tying knots, and all the things my son will need to take his place in a grown-up world. I never interfere with those daydreams, nor will I do so when that time comes. I am thankful that Ben is blessed with such love.

⤜   ⤜   ⤜

Tuttle came by one morning whilst I was sitting outside our lodge, catching up on my journal, and, now and again, keeping an eye on Iris trying unsuccessfully to teach her little brother to walk, until the little fellow tired of being dragged on the tips of his toes and commenced to howl in protest, which prompted her to gather him into her arms to soothe his injured feelings. Tuttle stepped down from his horse, dropped the reins to the ground, and commented with wry grin, "'Pears ye be tryin' to git your boy ready fer he'pin' ye with your trappin', come fall, Temple. Don't ye s'pose ye mought be rushin' matters a mite?"

Playing along with his conceit, I replied, "Can't never be startin' too early, Tuttle. He's got to earn his keep."

My old friend burst into a horselaugh, which set Ben off into another fit of earsplitting bawling. Iris, exasperated, retreated, carrying the youngster into the lodge.

Tuttle watched her go, still chuckling, before he recommended, "Wal, ef he don't work out fer trappin', ol' Iron Bow kin train 'im up fer bein' his camp crier, don'tcha reckon?" Then he looked halfway serious when he said, "C'mon, Temple, why'n'tcha put thet'ere book aside an' come along to ol' Yankee Nat's with me? Hear tell he's pullin' stakes t'morry. Fellers say he's sellin' plunder purty cheap so's he won't hafta be packin' so much of it along." He glanced in the direction of our lodge and added, "Hell, mebbe ye kin find some foofurraw your woman ain't awready bought over t'Amurrican Fur."

I had been feeling sort of restless, anyway, that morning, after sticking close to camp for the past few days, so his invitation was welcome. It was the work of only a few minutes to saddle Coffee and tie on half a dozen plews behind, in case I found some exotic treasure that might please Kathleen. Although I had already traded off most of my peltry to American Fur, plews are the universal coinage of trappers at rendezvous and elsewhere.

We headed upriver for Wyeth's trading camp at a leisurely gait, mostly at a walk, chatting and enjoying the early July sunshine. The Yankee trader had moved some ten miles higher on Horse Creek from his earlier location in search of better grass for his critters and perhaps to put as much as distance as possible between his old partners and himself.

Coming around a bend in the trail alongside the crick, we encountered half-a-dozen well-dressed horsemen, amongst whom I spied my father, who was handsomely togged out in the Nez Percé style, as were most of the other riders. None of them looked happy.

Naturally we stopped to chat. Powatawa informed his companions, all of whom he described as Nez Percé headmen, that I was his son and Tuttle a member of our trapping bunch, using mostly sign-talk and a few words in their tongue. When that formality was completed, reckoning that none of the Nez Percés understood English, I asked my father why they all looked so upset.

Powatawa took a long moment before he replied, evidently boiling down a passel of information into a statement that wouldn't require half a day to relate, as well as striving to control his own strong feelings on the matter. At last he told us, "The Shahaptín are a godly people, more than most. When they learned that a Christian missionary has come to the mountains, they asked that I come with them, to speak for them in his tongue, to ask him to come home with them and put them on the Jesus Road. They think if they take the whitemen's god for their own they will receive all things whitemen have—guns and cloth and metal things. They say the medicine of the whiteman's god, who gives whitemen such things, must be stronger than their own gods. I have told them it is not so, but they will not believe what I say.

"I have told them of the Moravians back home, Indians who learned to walk the Jesus Road and forgot how to fight, until most of them were killed by other whitemen who wanted their land. My words fell on ears of stone.

"Today I went to speak for them with that Man of God in Wyeth's camp. He is a very proud man, this Jason Lee. He has no time for Indians or their needs. He said no, he will not come to the Napercys, as he calls my Shahaptín friends, that he has more important business in Oregon. Perhaps, he says, another missionary will attend to them.

"So now you know why the hearts of my friends are small today. We are not happy, although perhaps I should be so, for I was not surprised by the answer we received. Jason Lee proved me right, but that is cold comfort."

I looked over the assembled Indians and recognized two of the elders from Iron Bow's Flathead band. "So it's not only the Nez Percé who go seeking a white missionary," I said.

"No," he replied gloomily. "The Séli are just as eager as the Shahaptín to learn the whiteman religion."

"What about Iron Bow? Where does he stand?"

"He thinks like me. His people have many enemies. He fears that turning their cheek will cost them their scalps now and, later, their land. He tells them to stay with their own gods and sell beaver and buffalo robes for white-eyes plunder. Many close their ears to his words."

I had many more questions for my father, such as where and how and from whom he acquired his handsome new duds and when would we be meeting her, but his disappointed companions were obviously impatient to return to the Nez Percé camp, so we bade them farewell and continued on our way.

If moving upriver to avoid rubbing shoulders with his former partners had been Nat Wyeth's intention, he was sure to be disappointed. As we came in sight of Wyeth's white canvas trade tents, we ran into two other horsemen, Tom Fitzpatrick and Jim Bridger, whose destination was the same as our own. Fitz hailed us and Jim raised a hand in greeting, so we fell in with them for what remained of the distance.

"Heard ye made a killin' over at Amurrican Fur," Bridger said by way of opening conversation.

"Ye mought be sayin' thet," Tuttle allowed. Then, "Hell! We warn't abaout to be feedin' ol' Billy's kitty arter haow he's been swivin' yew boys!" he declared warmly. "'Sides, he had his chance. Ol' Turtle an' Temple hyar even let 'im bid fust!"

Fitzpatrick smiled thinly at that last remark, but he held his peace. Jim barked out a short, dry laugh. "Sorta got the range thataway, didja?" he asked, looking at me with a sly smile.

"Sorta," I replied, figuring it was all water under the bridge by then, anyway.

Tuttle, seeking to assure our companions of our friendship and loyalty, said, "It's past time Billy got some gawddamn comeuppance. He drives a bargain harder'n flint!"

Fitz grunted a wry assent and replied, "Given half a chance, Bill Sublette'd be after stealin' the Good Lord's last supper, he would, an' lettin' the 'postles go hungry in the bargain."

We rode in silence until we reached a stand of willows, where we dismounted and tethered our horses. Jim heaved a deep sigh as he swung to the ground. I fell into step beside him as we walked towards the crowded trade tents. "How's your back?" I asked, not sure if I should mention it. "Any better?"

"Nope," he replied curtly. "Ain't likely it'll be gittin' any better, neither." Then, apparently recollecting that he and I had been friends for a dozen years, since our earliest days coming up the Missouri, he added in a friendlier tone, "But thanks fer askin'."

Wyeth's trade tables were still heaped with plunder of all sorts. His hands were conducting a brisk commerce, howsomever, at the table where tubs of booze were besieged by a horde of thirsty trappers. Tuttle took my cup and joined them, whilst I continued to inspect the merchandise, which didn't appear to be any cheaper than I recalled from the last time I was there. He soon returned with brimming cupfuls of spirits much superior to most of the watered-down alcoholic concoctions purveyed by rendezvous traders. "Ahhh," Tuttle exclaimed, smacking his lips appreciatively, "thet'ere be some proper rotgut!" He took another swig, just to make sure. "Wonder why ol' Nat's suddenly gittin' so gawddamn gin'rous with haow he's makin' his redeye, 'speshly seein' as haow he's pullin' out t'morry."

"Likely because he reckons if he gets ye drunk enough, ye won't notice his high prices or ye won't mind 'em if ye do," I replied. Just the same, I parted with two good plews in exchange for a shimmering scarlet Chinese silk scarf for Kathleen and another plew for a brightly-painted wooden box for Iris to keep her precious girlhood treasures in.

A growing murmur amongst the crowd of trappers drew my attention to the open space in front of the large *bourgeois*'s marquee occupied by Nat Wyeth. Fitz and Jim Bridger were approaching the entrance when the Yankee trader stepped out, the look on his craggy features anything but friendly. "Uh-oh," a trapper standing behind me muttered, "'pears the booshway's fixin' to go to war!" I was reassured only by observing that Wyeth did not appear to be carrying a weapon.

The New Englander is notoriously cantankerous and quarrelsome under the best of circumstances. Now, in light of the very real injury that these uninvited guests had inflicted upon his enterprise, no matter their reasons, it was reasonable to suppose that he might be spoiling for a fight.

Bridger and Fitz, noting Wyeth's flinty glare, halted in their tracks half a dozen paces distant from their unwelcoming host. Fitzgerald raised his hand, palm outward, in a half-hearted salute. Jim attempted a greeting. "How d'ye do, Nat," he began.

"Not very well," Wyeth barked, "as I believe ye know! If my health is ever restored, it will be with no thankees to the two of you, nor to Milton, whom I trusted as a friend!"

Bridger looked stricken, but he made no reply. Fitz merely set his jaw and returned the Yankee's hostile stare. At last, they shrugged and turned to depart, but Wyeth's wrath was boiling over. "Ye may choose to call what you have done to me merely business, but ye know in your heart that it was betrayal of the foulest kind! Hear me now! Listen well and take my words to your Master William when ye return to his den! I will roll a stone into your garden which you will never be able to get out!" With that, red-faced and fuming, he spun on his heel and stomped into his marquee.

"What d'ye reckon he meant by thet?" Tuttle enquired. "Abaout thet'ere stone an' ther garden, I mean."

"Hard to say," I replied honestly. "Reckon we'll just have to wait an' see what he does next. Whatever he means to do, howsomever, likely won't be friendly."

Tom and Jim returned to their horses, heads held high, backs ramrod straight, with a firm stride, looking neither right nor left. Tuttle and I tarried, reckoning that our friends didn't require our company just then. Whilst Tuttle went to fill our cups, I struck up an acquaintance with one of Wyeth's clerks, a sensible, well-spoken young man, a newcomer to the mountains, who introduced himself as Osborne Russell, a native of Maine. He told me that they intended to depart the rendezvous on the morrow, their destination the Snake River and, after that, the Columbia and the Pacific Ocean, where his employer expected to meet a ship that he had chartered before returning west.

Whilst we spoke, I spied a gentleman whose unusual garb captured my attention, not the customary leather shirt, clout, and leggin's, but a reasonably fashionable frock, breeches, and riding boots, well-worn but respectable. "Who's that?" I asked.

Russell turned to see whom I meant, then replied, "Oh, that's Mister Ermatinger, a friend of Mister Wyeth's. He arrived here just yesterday. He's with the Hudson's Bay Company. He'll be coming along with us tomorrow, together with his friend Captain Stewart."

Riding back to camp, I didn't mention Mister Ermatinger to Tuttle and I still didn't know what kind of rock Nathaniel Wyeth meant to roll into which garden, but I had a somewhat better idea of where it might be coming from.

Two days later, Cat and I came springing out of our robes at dawn, startled by a blast from the brass cannon in Sublette's camp, quickly followed by another, farther away, from the American Fur encampment at the mouth of Horse Creek. As my sleep-befuddled mind groped for an explanation, Tuttle Thompson rode through camp yelling, "Gitcher arse outen them robes, ye slugabeds! Let's be hearin' three big cheers fer ther good ol' Yew-nited States of Amurrica! It's Independence Day, begawd!" and a passel of other such patriotic nonsense. A chorus of hoarse cheers and a ragged volley of rifle and pistol fire followed, as our sleepy comrades crawled out of their lodges and bowers to salute America's birthday. Even the Indians and French-Canucks joined in, for the Fourth of July always provides an abundance of free booze.

I thought to reassure little Iris that no danger was at hand, but I saw that my five-year-old daughter was still sleeping peacefully, blissfully unaware of the growing hubbub out-of-doors, and Ben was just commencing to stir, more concerned with breaking his fast than fearing any peril.

Cat was no stranger to the annual white-eyes summertime lunacy usually celebrated at rendezvous. Once she recovered from the initial artillery salute, she set about preparing our morning meal, whilst I tapped my tin packhorse keg, mixing equal parts of pure grain alcohol and water and a generous helping of molasses for flavor in a large tin-lined kettle to provide a celebratory libation for the thirsty patriots who were sure to be visiting our lodge.

Ned had taught Kathleen how to make flapjacks, frying them in bear fat in a sheet-iron skillet. So whenever wheat flour could be had at rendezvous, that became our special treat, slathered with sweet molasses or honey if we were lucky enough to discover any in a hive or on some trader's table.

No hound that I have ever seen or heard of has a keener nose than Tuttle Thompson. The first flapjacks were hardly out of the skillet before my old friend came scratching at the door of our lodge. "Figgered ye'd likely be havin' them'ere flannel cakes yer woman makes so good, speshly on a day like this'n," he announced by way of greeting. "Sorta like Chris'mus, only better, ain't it?"

Naturally there was nothing else to be done besides inviting him to join us. Cat's regard for Tuttle swings betwixt friendly affection and mere toleration. Fortunately for him and his appetite, she felt kindly disposed towards him that morning. Whilst she and Iris busied themselves at our cookfire, I filled his cup with my makeshift metheglin and, just to be neighborly, I joined him with one of my own.

Between toasts to Long Live the Union, Death to All Tyrants, and Let Freedom Ring, Tuttle said, "Natcherly ye'll be goin' over to Amurrican Fur fer ther sellerbrayshun, ain'tcha?"

"Hadn't thought of it," I replied.

"Why, ye gotta go! It's fer sellybratin' Amurrica gittin' loose o' them'ere Brits, not jest ther once but twice! Thet's what! Ever'body's goin'! Injuns, too! All o' ther wimmenfolks're awready gittin' all gussied up, paintin' up their hosses an' theirownse'fs an' gittin out their purtiest duds fer showin' off! Natcherly ye gotta be goin'!"

I glanced at Cat, who hadn't missed a word. She was smiling in anticipation of another opportunity to prove to her Séli sisters that she had indeed come up in the world and reclaimed her proper place. I knew that I needn't even bother asking if she wished to go when she handed the first plate of flapjacks to Tuttle.

∾   ∾   ∾

By time I returned from my morning swim, Cat had groomed and saddled her *palomilla* mare, painted the critter's shoulders and flanks with artful designs, and plaited the flaxen mane and part of the tail with colorful red, green, and blue ribbons. Her Mexican saddle, burnished with bear grease, sparkled in the sunshine with a wealth of shiny hawk bells and polished silver dollars and Mexican *pesos* dangling from the saddle skirts and the fringes of her elaborately quilled and beaded apishamore. A tack-studded tomahawk and a beaded otterskin pipe case hung on either side of the pommel. A new scarlet Witney blanket, neatly folded and tied on behind the cantle, spilled over the mare's flanks on either side.

I was idly speculating how many beaver had sacrificed their plews in order to decorate that saddle when Cat returned from her own ablutions in the women's swimming hole, her long black hair still wet and sheening in the sunshine, flowing freely over her shoulders, her face rosy and glowing from the chilly creek water. She paused only long enough to flash a brilliant smile at me before she vanished into our lodge, reappearing only long enough to set my kettle outside, before pulling the door into place, signaling that I was not welcome inside right then.

I had no time to be lonely. My kettle of flavorful booze was a lodestone for my comrades, who clustered about with broad smiles and outstretched cups. After I joined them with a cupful or two of my own, I, too, became imbued with the appropriate patriotic spirit or what might pass for that sentiment. When at last Kathleen poked her head out the doorway and beckoned me to join her, I was astonished at the change she had wrought in her appearance. From the simple, natural, healthy young woman who had returned smiling from her bathe, her hair loose and glistening with moisture, she had transformed herself into a paragon of feminine splendor. Her long black braids, glossy with bear grease, were partially wrapped with red wool and mink fur and decorated with tiny bright trinkets. My recent gift, the scarlet Chinese silk shawl, formed a colorful turban, its fringed ends spilling over her shoulders.

Her dress was of almost-white mountain sheep leather, as light and soft as the finest English woolen fabric, tastefully decorated with elk ivories, rich multi-colored quillwork, and tiny glistening glass beads in intricate designs. Its irregular hem fell just past her knees, showing off snug-fitting bright blue woolen leggin's spangled with Mexican silver *pesos* and knee-high quilled and beaded moccasins.

Cat rarely paints, but today a firm line of vermilion defined her high cheekbones and a small scarlet circle adorned her smooth brow. Half a dozen necklaces of bright-colored beads, fragments of lustrous seashell, and shiny coins completed her striking ensemble.

If the choice had been mine, we never would have left the lodge for the rest of the day and night, but Kathleen refused to be deprived of her promenade. I had to be satisfied with a chaste peck on the lips and a promising grin from my savage beauty.

Apparently my lady was not content to be the only showhorse in our family on that festive day. When I finished inspecting her from top to toe and complimenting her on her art, she presented me with an outfit of new duds that she had been making for me whenever I was absent from the lodge—new leggin's made from butter-soft but tough prairie-goat hide, quilled and beaded and fringed to a fare-thee-well, a scarlet woolen britchclout, new summer moccasins, handsomely quilled and ankle-high in the Séli style, and a bright blue broadcloth shirt from the settlements that reached nearly to my knees.

When I enquired why Iris's mare hadn't been groomed and saddled, I learned that my daughter had chosen to remain in camp with Paddy's wife Molly, who also offered to look after Ben in our absence. Cat tittered mischievously when she suggested that Iris was in puppy love with Paddy's son Sean. He had inherited his father's red hair, earning him the Shoshone name Woodpecker amongst the other children in camp. He was a bright, handsome little fellow, so she could have chosen worse.

The sun was at its zenith by time the bunch assembled to ride en masse to the celebration. From what I could see, it wasn't only the womenfolk who had delayed us with their primping. My comrades were a gaggle of peacocks, togged out in traders' finery combined with new leggin's, beaded moccasins, and clouts from half-a-dozen different tribes, even Tuttle, sporting a bright red shirt and freshly-shaven cheeks. I looked for my father, whom I hadn't seen since our chance meeting on the way to Wyeth's, but he was nowhere to be seen.

Our womenfolk were even more resplendent. Evidently released from all restraint by our recent windfall at American Fur, some of them had apparently indulged their every whim and fancy at the trader's tables, then did their best to wear it all at once. They rode together in pairs at the head of our column, Cat and Joe Meek's Isabel in the lead, followed by Turtle's pretty Snake wife Tallymesko and the Iroquois Acorn's new wife Mary. The Shoshone Nettaqueathy and the Crow Sally, the wives of Pretty Horse and Stone Bird, brought up the rear.

Although our bunch was hardly welcome in Sublette's neighborhood anymore, our ladies, unwilling to forego an opportunity to show themselves off, led us through the center of Billy's camp, past his trade tents and tables, waving and calling out to old friends and anyone else who saluted them, impudent behavior that would have been unthinkable for Indian women before they became trappers' wives. We had no trouble making our way through the alleyways of the camp, for there was sparse attendance around most of the trade tents. If Bill was in camp, he made himself scarce until we passed through.

At last we arrived at American Fur at the mouth of Horse Creek, tethered our horses, and engaged a brace of Flathead lads to keep an eye on them. The women made a beeline for the trade tents and the rest of us sought to fill our cups in order to render an appropriate patriotic salute.

The place was swarming with free trappers, likely expressing by their presence in the precincts of American Fur their disapproval of Bill Sublette's high-handed treatment of the RMF partners. Naturally there was also a large number of AFC *engagés*, together with a healthy sprinkling of free men regularly employed by that company. Whilst I waited in a queue to fill my cup, Andy Drips, one of their long-time field captains, clapped me roughly on the shoulder in a friendly albeit well-oiled greeting. "Welcome, Buck! Glad to see ye got here in time! Ye won't be wantin' to miss what's comin' today!"

He spilled some of his liquor into my empty cup and winked conspiratorially when I asked, "What's that? What's comin'?"

"Dassn't say yet," he replied solemnly, "but it's worth waitin' for." He grinned owlishly. "Yep. Ye won't want to be missin' it." He clinked my cup with his and we raised them in a toast to I knew not what, although I had a pretty fair inkling of what he might have in mind.

We hadn't long to wait. Shortly after my meeting with Drips, several hands circulated amongst the crowd, encouraging us to go to the open area where stood the Company's two big fur presses, idle now in respect of the holiday. As we arrived, Lucien Fontenelle, grinning broadly, and a rather more serious-looking Tom Fitzpatrick were clambering onto one of them, intending to use it as a stage. Jim Bridger and a smiling Andy Drips stood beside the press, saying nothing. When the unruly throng, composed mostly of free trappers, had crowded into the open space, Fontenelle raised both arms for quiet and commenced to speak. Lucien's English is heavily-accented at best and today it was obvious that several celebratory toasts had preceded his calling the assembly.

"As mos' of you know, many 'ard sings 'ave been 'appening at zis rendezvous an' zere 'ave been many deesappointments for our frien's een Rocky Mountain Fur, wheech ees no more. But now zere weel be bettair days au futur for all of us! We 'ave formèd a new *compagnie qui s'appelle* Fontenelle et Feetzpatrick! Wheech weel be even more successfool zan evair before! Alzough only two names are mention, our new *compagnie* ees composèd of men you know and 'ave workèd togezzer weeth—also Jeem Breedger an' Andrew Dreeps an' Meelton Sublette when he weel be able to return to ze *Montagnes!*"

He went on for a spell longer, but that is the gist of what I took away from it, which caused hardly a ripple of surprise amongst the assembled trappers who were sober enough to comprehend what he was saying. It had been common knowledge that Fitz had been cooking up something important with Fontenelle and it was not surprising that Drips and Bridger, both excellent field captains, had been included in the new company. Naming Milton Sublette was likely a mere courtesy or it represented some financial consideration, or possibly both.

Fitz added a few remarks of his own, mostly to rally support amongst the trappers who remained loyal to the RMF partners and who would be essential to the success of the new outfit. Tom's most welcome and significant announcement was an invitation to everyone present to drinks on the house, which provoked an immediate exodus back to the booze tubs.

I didn't join the stampede. Instead I set off to retrieve Kathleen from the Halls of Mammon and try to convince her to return to camp with me. Which she was surprisingly willing to do. I settled her account and the clerks bundled her purchases into a large canvas poke, which I slung onto my shoulder and headed for the alleyway. There I encountered Jim Bridger and a pretty Eutaw woman I assumed was his wife or, judging from the way she clung to his side, leastaways a close friend. I uttered some congratulatory nonsense about his new job, which elicited an unenthusiastic response from my old messmate. He shrugged and replied, "Hell, Temple, if ye cain't beat 'em, sooner or later ye gotta jine 'em."

I wasn't altogether sure if Bridger wasn't giving me advice about my own future conduct, but he didn't elaborate and I didn't enquire further. Cat and I continued on our way.

The weather had grown exceedingly warm, prompting us to return to camp at a jog-trot, foregoing unnecessary detours to strut and flaunt milady's finery. Evidently Kathleen had satisfied that desire during the earlier triumphal parade to American Fur and during her shopping spree, leastaways for that day. When we came in sight of our camp, howsomever, Cat, without a word, reined her mare sharply left and guided her down into the crick bottom, traveling at a brisk trot alongside the stream until we were well past the lodges and bowers of our bunch, then regained higher ground. I was somewhat mystified by her action, but I made no objection, content to follow behind, enjoying the sight of her bottom as she flexed to accommodate the mare's choppy trot.

As soon as smoother terrain allowed, she let the mare out into an easy lope for another quarter-mile or so, the red blanket streaming behind, when she abruptly turned back towards the crick and dodged under the low-hanging branches of cottonwoods that lined the riverbed. By time I caught up, she had dismounted and was spreading the blanket on the grassy bank. Her mare was grazing contentedly at a distance and Coffee was all too pleased to join her.

The glade was cool and shaded, screened by willows and cottonwoods from the prairie, an ideal setting for the thought that was forming in my mind. Evidently I was not alone in that intention. Cat was already kicking off her moccasins and removing her necklaces. "It is so hot today," she said with a sly smile, "it would be good for us to swim, no?"

That in itself was a surprise and a giant step forward in our relationship. For one thing ,Séli women, like most Indians I have known, almost never swim with men, no matter their intimacy otherwise, although Rainbow and I had flouted that prohibition, excusing our transgression on the grounds that our first meeting occurred, by happy chance, when we were swimming. Even more surprising was Cat's willingness to share with me an activity that had been exclusively Rainbow's, she who would not even utter the name of her departed friend. I agreed that, yes, it would be good for us to swim.

Fortunately, false modesty with a loving mate is not a trait in Kathleen's character. She was already wriggling out of her leggin's, then slipped her dress over her head, revealing all of her tawny, lean, muscular body that nonetheless possesses every desirable feminine attribute, flaring hips, a generous bosom, smooth, flat belly, and long tapering legs. It was hard to believe that she had given birth to our son only a few months earlier.

I threw myself down beside her and took her in my arms, my lips seeking hers, which she readily granted in a long, passionate kiss, but when I sought to go further, she demurred, holding me at arm's length and laughingly informing me that "Firs' we mus' swim. Zen zere will be time enough for ev'rysing."

Reluctantly I fell back and shucked my moccasins. She helped me pull off my new shirt and strip off my leggin's before she sprang to her feet and raced to the riverbank and dived smoothly into the deep pool, while I sat transfixed, staring at the miracle of womanly beauty with which I had been gifted. Then I wasted no time before I joined in our watery tryst.

The chill water flowing clean and fresh from the snowy heights of the mountains looming above struck me like a fist as I plunged to the bottom, eyes open, seeking in vain to catch a glimpse of her, then rising to the surface, breaking into warm air, gasping for breath and laughing aloud, glorying in the pure joy of being alive and healthy and in love with the beautiful woman who floated just a few feet away, tantalizing, just beyond reach, taunting me to catch her if I could, before she doubled over and disappeared into the depths, treating me to a fleeting glimpse of her delicious bottom before she vanished.

This time I waited until at last she broke the surface. Then, before she caught sight of me, I ducked below and swam under water until I spied her long shapely legs scissoring invitingly as she floated above, doubtless waiting for me to appear so that she might resume the merry chase. I gave a mighty surge and came up between her legs, raising her on my shoulders, clear out of the water, eliciting a startled shriek, followed by peals of mutual laughter quenched into gurgles as we fell back into the depths, only to rise embracing and sharing watery kisses.

Cat was first to clamber up the grassy bank. She was already seated on the blanket by time I struggled out of the chilly water. When I gained my footing on the slippery grass and stood erect, Cat exploded into merriment, pointing and giggling and bursting into still another torrent of laughter. My pride and joy had shrunk disgracefully in the frigid mountain stream.

I sprinted to her side, threw myself down on the blanket, and with mock-serious gravity declared it was all her fault. Now it was up to her to repair the damage. She, responding in kind to my humorous conceit, promised to do so. Which she did. And very efficiently and enthusiastically, too.

Afterwards, lying naked together in the late afternoon sunshine, my head resting on her velvety taut belly, admiring the vibrant rosy hue that underlies her tawny skin, on a whim I twisted about and took her nipple between my lips, nibbling and nuzzling, thoroughly enjoying myself.

I heard her throaty chuckle and felt a tremor of suppressed laughter before she gently lifted my head with both hands and brought my lips to hers. After a long, satisfying kiss, she pulled back, giggled, and said, "Zat is why Injun women like white-eyes men in zeir robes."

"Huh?" I responded, confused.

"All o' you white-eyes like kissin' our teaties. It is good feelin'. Injun men never do, mebbe almos' never."

I mumbled something like, "What makes ye think so?"

"I sink mebbe white-eyes women don't have no teaties or mebbe zey allatime keep zem all cover up, like zis." She put both hands around her throat, high under her chin. "Mebbe white-eyes men never see no teaties 'til zey come here." She pulled my head back onto her bosom and added, "Mebbe Injun men allatime see Injun woman teaties, so zey don't care. Zey more interes' in uzzer place, I sink so."

I did my best then to prove her point. Naturally, one thing led to another, until we lay gasping, laced in a loving embrace, reluctant to turn each other loose, until the sun slipped below the western mountains, causing shivers of a different, unwelcome sort.

A final cleansing dip in the chilly crick sent us racing to don our clothing. We gathered up my weapons and Cat's purchases and retrieved our horses, which had wandered off in their never-ending search of even better graze. As Cat led the way out of our tiny slice of Eden, I cast a grateful glance at the grassy bank and wished that our moment there might never end.

~ ~ ~

Bill Sublette left camp to return to Saint Louis on the tenth day of July with forty packs of beaver and a fistful of promissory notes from the RMF partners and Edmund Christy. He was accompanied by Captain Bonneville's packtrain boss Mike Cerré, returning to the settlements with this year's pitiful returns and to obtain next year's supplies. Mister Christy was giving up the mountains as a bad job at best.

American Fur stayed on for another month, picking up whatever plews that remained amongst the Indians and the few free trappers who hadn't already guzzled themselves into debt with the Company. Fitz and Fontenelle were close-mouthed about their business dealings, but gossip said they were working out details with other members of the new company, particularly Bridger, Fraeb, and Gervais, without whom the new outfit would collapse. Andy Drips, a longtime American Fur employee, would likely agree to almost anything that promised him even a modest slice of ownership in the new company.

Now that Bill Sublette had departed, our bunch commenced to enlist trappers and friendly Indians in Pierre Chouteau's scheme to get around the deal that his New York partners had concluded with Sublette. The twenty-five percent premium over mountain prices for plews was a powerful incentive for all concerned. Helping the RMF partners get even with Bill was a further strong inducement for many trappers.

Naturally my first recruits were Iron Bow's Flathead band. I encouraged Fast Horse to rally his young riflemen as the core of the trapping effort and to encourage them to persuade other young men to exert themselves in pursuit of beaver plews. Being able to purchase a new rifle and fixin's of his own, instead of depending on an old hand-me-down musket, would likely be a young man's strongest incentive.

Brass Turtle and Acorn did much the same thing with the Shoshone bands of their wives, Tallymesko and the pretty young woman we called Mary. Most Snakes are already kindly-disposed towards white-eyes, but extra plunder for each plew strengthened the ties of our comrades with their in-laws' bands.

Crows are always on the lookout for extra profit. Pretty Horse and Stone Bird reported that at least the two Absóraqa bands of their Crow wives would trade with Chouteau's clandestine supplier next year, whoever that might be and however he might be able to circumvent that unwise agreement in faraway New York.

Word gets around, so these early bands might prove to be seed for several more Absóraqa and Shoshone bands joining up.

Powatawa undertook to enlist his Shahaptín friends in our scheme, hoping not only to enrich the Nez Percé band with whom he spent much of his time at rendezvous, but also to convince them that the way to acquire whitemen's plunder was to employ the same methods that whitemen do. He argued valiantly but mostly in vain that the Jesus Road would lead only to their destruction, as it had for the Moravians, those unfortunate Christian Indian converts slaughtered by avaricious whites for their Pennsylvania land, the crime that had orphaned our own Brass Turtle as an infant.

Naturally such activity could not go unnoticed. I was not surprised when Tom Fitzpatrick came by to enquire the cause. "Ye fixin' to get into tradin' on your own hook?" he demanded suspiciously.

"Not on your life, Tom!" I replied, laughing. "We'll leave it to the likes of you and Fontenelle to lose your arse at that game! Nope, trappin's good enough for us." I realized, howsomever, that Fitz would not remain long in the dark about what we were doing and why and that Lucien Fontenelle likely already had a pretty good idea of what Chouteau had in mind. I decided to come clean. "Fact is," I told him, "I'm surprised ye don't already know why we're doin' what we're doin'. If ye can't trade in the mountains next year, you'll be out o' business before ye start."

I told him to wait whilst I went into our lodge to retrieve Chouteau's letter. Fitz read it carefully, whistling under his breath and shaking his head as he digested its contents, now and again asking my help with translating a Creole expression. When he handed back the letter, I said, "If this scheme is goin' to work, Tom, it 'pears to me that you an' Lucien an' some others'll have to be in on it, one way or t'other. Who else'd be bringin' up trade goods to pay for plews?"

I posed several other questions that Fitzpatrick couldn't answer, mainly how we expected to transact next year's business without Sublette tumbling to what we were doing. Fitz thanked me for my candor and turned to leave. I couldn't resist adding, "When ye come back up from Sain' Louie next year, Tom, ye'd best be bringin' an extra passel o' trade plunder, so's ye can pay top dollar an' then some for our plews, like Chouteau says ye'll do."

He made no reply. He merely looked glum. Still shaking his head, he mounted his horse and rode out of camp.

∾   ∾   ∾

Weather in the mountains remained much too warm to resume trapping. The rendezvous continued through July and into August, which gave us plenty of time to lay in a supply of dried meat against lean times in winter. Running buffalo a-horseback thereabouts was discouraged amongst trappers and Indians alike, which kept the herds nearby, and a plenitude of deer, wapiti, and bear, mostly grizzlies, still roamed that neighborhood. Pole racks in every camp groaned under the weight of drying meat strung like so much red laundry in the crisp mountain air. Camp dogs grew fat from gobbling scraps and what they could steal from unwary campkeepers.

Whenever Cat was able to put aside for a spell the many chores required for daily life or getting ready for winter, she attended Iris's schooling sessions, often combining the two, stitching clothing or moccasins whilst improving her reading and ciphering skills. Anxious though she was to improve her knowledge, she refused to allow me to assist in performing tasks that Indians consider women's work, which includes nearly everything except hunting and fighting, lest I be ridiculed as being unmanly and she be scorned as the lazy wife of an unworthy person. For some reason known only to the Indian mind, the bachelor members of our bunch, who must shift for themselves, as I had done for the several years before I married, are not subject to such demeaning judgment. I suspect that those rules and customs were established by Indian men, not the women who are obliged to do the work.

When I wasn't out hunting, sharpening knives and tools, or refurbishing weapons and horse clothing, I passed many pleasant hours in the horse pasture with Half-horse, training my tall *palomilla* stud horse. He was a handsome critter, only four years old, deep-chested and lean-limbed, with a kind eye and an easy disposition, always willing, a pleasure to train, a credit to his breeding. Yet he put me into a quandary, for I was unwilling to suffer the displeasure of my comrades by including a stallion in my *remuda* when it came time to go trapping. He was sure to cause havoc amongst the other horses, especially the mares, simply by following his natural instincts. On the other hand, I was equally reluctant to geld him, as several of my companions had already done with their *palomilla* studs. I already owned more than enough geldings. I didn't need another.

I would need to ask another favor of Fast Horse, but for the time being I indulged my pride by alternately riding either Coffee or my handsome Sunshine, as Iris had named him, garnering compliments on either one whenever I visited other camps. I was itching to try him at running buffalo, but the sensible ban on that particular sport prevented my doing so.

A summertime diversion that never failed to please were the afternoons when Cat and I were able to steal away to our secluded little glade on Horse Creek, where, oblivious of all else in the world outside, we bonded our bodies and souls in a marriage ceremony unrivaled by any ever solemnized in humble meetinghouse or towering cathedral. We pledged our vows in loving laughter and pleasurable groans, confident that a wise Great Spirit surely approved.

Rendezvous continued with all the customary recreations, foot races and horse racing, shooting matches, chucking butcher knives and tomahawks for sport, wrestling contests, and naturally plenty of fistfights amongst men who had imbibed too freely, as well as a passel of fiddling and singing and dancing and spinning outrageous yarns meant to mystify greenhorns and challenge seasoned trappers to contribute even greater flights of their own fancy.

As summer wore on, howsomever, even those rowdy manly amusements commenced to pall. American Fur's booze became increasingly diluted although the price remained firm. Tuttle had impoverished all the greenhorns unwise enough to try to best him at Old Sledge and the new game Bragg, in which, generous soul that he is, he was willing to instruct them. Experienced mountaineers gave Tuttle wide berth when they espied his greasy pack of cards. Even bibulous Anse Tolliver grew weary of cadging free drinks from drunks urging him to fiddle just one more tune.

It was time to pack up and go trapping. Problem was, we couldn't come to a decision on where, which wasn't unusual amongst our very democratic numbers.

Lucien Fontenelle's drinking had increased alarmingly after Sublette's departure, which likely prompted Fitzpatrick's decision to accompany the packtrain carrying that year's huge haul of peltries and robes back to the settlements. That left the new company's trapping brigades under the direction of Jim Bridger and Andy Drips, assisted by Henry Fraeb and Jean Gervais, all of them seasoned hands. They had no trouble attracting free trappers to join their brigades. Amongst the first to pledge his services was Joe Meek, whose longtime loyalty to Milton and Jim Bridger was unwavering. Naturally his devoted companions, Doc Newell and the Irish harpooner Harry Yeats, went with him.

Captain Bonneville's absence from the rendezvous relieved the new partners from competing with his extravagant promises of impossibly high wages to trappers willing to sign up with his trapping brigades. He attracted few veterans. "He'll be payin' ye with hot air an' little more!" was the universal verdict amongst experienced mountaineers.

Naturally Cat was distressed by Isabel's departure from our camp when Joe moved out to join Bridger's growing encampment, but there was plenty of work to take her mind off the loss of her good friend's company. She and the other women, along with Yves and Jean Luc, often worked until darkness scraping buffalo hides and drying meat, pounding some of it fine into the makin's of pemmican, mixing it with rich buffalo fat and adding dried plums and chokecherries for extra flavor and nourishment.

Nearly as unhappy as Cat at Meek's leaving camp was Tolliver, who lamented losing Harry Yeats and his Spanish *guitarra* from our circle. Most days, Anse mounted his favorite mule and rode to American Fur to join his fellow *musicos*. Our fiddler had become exceedingly fond of the young harpooner's seemingly inexhaustible repertory of sea chanteys and Irish folk tunes.

Meanwhile the debate continued amongst our bunch concerning where we would do our trapping, come fall. Several men, Anse amongst them, argued that we ought to tag along with one of the new brigades, but they were loudly opposed by last year's stay-at-homes, Paddy McBride the loudest in dissent. "That's what we done the year past!" he fumed. "The few of us remainin' had little choice, a pitiful handful left behind, lackin' the rest o' ye gone traipsin' off to Californy! So we jined up wi' Seamus Bridger an' he mostly left us suckin' hind tit, givin' all the prime waters to his own, natcherly lookin' out fer his own purse, but it did oursel's not a scrap o' good! Sich traitment surely don't shine wi' the loikes o' meownsel'! I say we need no bloody booshway tellin' where an' whin fer us to be after doin' our trappin'! I'm fer goin' off on our own hook, just ourownsel's, like we allus done! Jist be askin' the others," he cried heatedly, waving at Pretty Horse, Acorn, and Stone Bird, "they'll surely be tellin' ye!" Those worthies were pouring their gripes into the ears of Brass Turtle. It was obvious they agreed with Paddy's tirade.

Tolliver, not surprisingly, sang his old familiar tune of safety in numbers, but Tuttle, forever rejecting any man's say-so over him, heaved himself to his feet to challenge him. "I reckon I kin see whar ye be headin', Anse," he sneered. "Ye cain't feature gittin' along 'thout thet'ere Irisher lad an' his git-fiddle! Wal, I git muh en-joys hearin' 'im, too, but, gawddammit! we be talkin' trappin' hyar! Jest be leavin' yer moosic fer ronnyvoo an' winter camp an' pay some mind ter what's good fer the whole bunch!"

Tolliver sputtered and fumed, but angry as he was, he was unable to get out a coherent response.

Naturally every man who wished to do so had his say, either in person or, in the case of most of our Delawares and all of the Iroquois, mainly through the voice of Brass Turtle, who did his best to keep their opinions separate from his own. Three of the men who held their peace throughout the haranguing were Kit Carson and the two *Californio* former soldiers, who still hadn't attached themselves to a trapping brigade, nor had they shown any disposition to do so. They stuck like burrs to Cesár, Micah, and Kit and listened intently to every word spoken, now and again leaning close to one of them to enquire the meaning of what had just been said.

When everybody had pretty much used up his argufying urges, the bunch voted, which was overwhelmingly in favor of going it alone, which wasn't surprising, considering how close-knit and clannish our bunch has always been. Problem was, we still didn't know where.

Before we broke up, Micah got to his feet and signed that he wished to speak, Cesár standing at his side. Everybody got quiet, for Micah rarely voices his views and Cesár almost never.

"As ye know well," Micah began, "I be one o' the Johnny-come- latelies to this heah bunch, along with Powatawa an' Finn, an' afore that, Cesár heah and his old pardner Jim Beckwith jined up with ye a middlin' spell after the most o' ye first got together. Now I'm standin' up an' talkin' for takin' in two more good men most o' ye already know, Pablo an' Diego heah."

An immediate murmur rippled through the bunch, most of it coming from the Indians clustered around Brass Turtle, who repeated what he said in both Lenni Lenapee and one or another of the Iroquois tongues. I daresay our Indians understood what was said as well as I did, after a dozen years in the bunch, but it was an old habit and it insulated them somewhat.

Aside from being surprised to hear Micah taking a stand in any likely controversy, I was struck by how handily he altered his usually respectable diction to common palaver.

When the crowd quieted, Micah resumed his argument. "We just voted to go trappin' this time on our own hook, 'spite o' what Anse has to say about safety in numbers. Well, Anse is plumb right about that an' a couple more plumb-shootin' guns'll surely be welcome when Blackfoots come a-callin'. Those o' ye who've known these two from the git-go in Californy know they won't cut an' run in a fight. From what we've been hearin' lately, there's a passel more Blackfoots on the prod down thisaway, more'n ever.

"Cesár an' me, we've been teachin' 'em ever'thin' we know about rifle- guns an' how to use 'em —'stead o' muskets, which is about all they've got in Californy—an' they've learnt it all. I reckon they'll be proud to show ye how good they kin shoot. They're tough an' honest an' better'n most with critters. As for trappin', I reckon they kin learn that quick enough. 'Nuff said!"

He turned to resume his seat, then swung back to add, "I reckon all o' ye know ye kin be thankin' these two *Californios* for all those purty yeller hosses that've been makin' ye so well-off lately. That be all I got to say. It's up to y'all."

Micah and Cesár had barely folded into a sitting position before Tuttle and Brass Turtle jumped to their feet to loudly endorse Micah's proposal and Zeetlah and Little Mountain commenced jabbering at the Indians clustered around them, whose smiles signaled a favorable response. Finn McCool stood, arms raised, and called for an immediate vote, which resulted in unanimous acceptance of the *Californios*. They were orphans no more. Even Tolliver voted to accept them. But as Tuttle observed later, "Thet war purty 'cute o' Micah, don'tcha think, butterin' up cranky ol' Anse thetaway, usin' his own argufyin' 'baout safety in numbers to git 'im to come along."

❧   ❧   ❧

A few more days went by and our bunch still couldn't agree on where we meant to do our trapping that fall. The new company had pretty much sorted out its people into brigades and the leaders were waiting only for the departure of the fur caravan for the settlements before heading out. Drips intended to go west with Gervais as his *segundo* and Bridger was preparing to return to his favorite haunts in the north, in spite of Blackfoots they were sure to stir up once they got anywhere close to that country. Frapp was Jim's *segundo* and Joe Meek, Doc, and Harry Yeats had agreed to go along as free men, along with a passel of Flathead and Nez Percé trappers.

Joe has always turned down positions of authority. He prefers instead to command top dollar from his employers for his trapping skill, his courage and reliability in a gunfight and hard times, and his unflinching loyalty to a leader who earns his respect, which up to that time had always been the Rocky Mountain Fur partners. Few mountaineers would decline following Joe through the gates of hell, if he asked them to do so, but his rollicking good nature and his partiality for pranks and just one more drunken binge outweigh any ambition for leadership that might lurk in his generous nature.

At last Kit took pity on our seemingly endless indecision. One night, after supper, we had lit our pipes and had fallen into little groups palavering about nothing important, when Carson spoke up. "I been thinkin' on goin' along with Bridger fer trappin' thi'shere fall," he began, "but I reckon I owe you boys more'n some'at fer what ye done fer me at thish'yere ronnyvoo, fillin' up muh poke like ye done with what I got fer tradin' off them yeller hosses ye gave me. Ye din't hafta, an' I tol' ye so, but ye done it, anyway.

"Thar's some country I know abaout, south an' more'n some'at east o' hyar, whar, fur as I kin tell, ain't hardly nobody's ever been trappin' an' whar thar's a galore o' beaver sign. Thar's likely buffler aplenty the year 'round, fer makin' winter camp, 'cause, fur off as it be, we'd likely be stayin' thar'abaouts, waitin' out the cold time fer prime trappin' come spring. It's a fur piece from hyar, but if ye cain't make up yer mind whar else ye wish to go, I'd be proud to pilot ye thar an' trap along with ye 'til nex' year's ronnyvoo."

Kit's offer came at the right time. All previous suggestions had been debated and rejected and the prospect of trapping in new country appealed to everybody. Carson's quiet manner, together with his knowledge of our trade and the country where he proposed to lead us convinced us that Kit would be a proper pilot. His offer was accepted with a notable absence of squabbling.

I had held off parting with my Sunshine stud horse until the last minute, but when the women of Iron Bow's band commenced stripping their meat racks bare of jerk meat, I knew that I could delay no longer. I saddled the handsome *palomilla*, slipped a halter on my *grulla* gelding, and, with a heavy heart, set out for the Flathead camp.

Fast Horse's woman was already gathering their plunder into neat bundles and stowing loose items in *parfleche* boxes for the journey north to Séli country. She directed me to Iron Bow's horse pasture, where I found my former brother-in-law gathering his considerable herd, which included several of my own critters that I had entrusted to his care. His eyes widened with pleasure when I explained my mission, then, reluctantly but sincerely, without my asking, he assured me that he wouldn't race my stud horse unless I granted permission for him to do so. Which I refrained from doing, telling him instead that any foals sired by my stallion on his mares in the coming year would naturally belong to him. Which pleased him almost as much.

Riding the *grulla* back to camp, I reflected on the happy events that had befallen me since the day when I first splashed across Horse Creek a couple of months before, but also how much that I had considered solid and forever in the fur trade had become uncertain now, thanks to faraway forces and events beyond my knowledge or control. Lest I trouble my spirit needlessly, howsomever, I reminded myself that life in the mountains is a constant challenge and hardly anything remains the same for very long. A proper mountaineer deals as best he can with each new trial as it occurs. Borrowing trouble makes no meat.

-ooo-

CHAPTER XI
NEW COUNTRY

___

The heavily-loaded packtrain of American Fur, under the direction of Fontenelle and Fitzpatrick, departed the rendezvous on August 7, after more than a month of profitable trading, a substantial portion of which our bunch had contributed. The Company faced a happy dilemma which no trader would ever complain about. Their hefty haul of robes and peltries required considerably more pack animals than they had brought up from the settlements, which further enriched some of our people who found themselves burdened with more horses and mules acquired in California than they would need or be willing to look after when we set out for fall trapping. One last shopping spree at the Company's much-depleted trade tables provided all hands with a plenitude of additional ammunition, tobacco, groceries, and trade goods, as well as a final drunken binge fueled by the well-watered spirits remaining in the Company's booze tubs.

"Cain't tell, nohaow, what we mought be runnin' into," Tuttle observed, "headin' inter thet'ere country Kit's leadin' us to, so ther more powder an' galena we're packin' the better. T'other plunder, 'speshly vittles, won't hurt none, neither. It'll be lettin' us down easy from whar we been livin' high on ther hog hyar at ronnyvoo, gittin' use't'agin fer goin' hongry once'ta while." He sounded almost wistful for the lean times that every trapping season brings.

"I reckon we'll be seein' more'n enough skinny spells before it's over," I reminded him. "So ye needn't fret about gettin' soft. Enjoy it whilst ye can."

"Reckon so," he replied. Then, more brightly, "An' we never even had to raise thet'ere cache o' extry plunder we put aside las' year. I'm wagerin' it'll still be thar, safe an' sound, not fur off o' Hoss Crick, when we git back fur nex' year's ronnyvoo."

"Well, you picked the spot, so you oughta know if it's a good one. But it looked safe enough. Like ye say, we'd best let it be. It'll keep."

∾   ∾   ∾

"I'd say 'tis past toime we'd best be saddlin' up an' gettin' on our way," McCool observed sourly as he and I rode through mostly deserted campsites which only a few days before hosted crowds of roistering trappers and noisy Indian villages with their yammering kids and barking dogs. "'Tis niver a good idea to be tarryin' too long at the fair. 'tis too depressin' whin it's over."

I allowed that it was so.

"An' nigh all o' the charmin' little prairie flowers've gone, 'til next year," he lamented, revealing that what he likely missed most was the bevy of willing young Indian women who thronged the camps and traders' alleyways eager to swap their favors for foofurraw and a modest amount of trade goods.

"There's always winter camp," I suggested by way of consoling him. "There's no tellin' what that might bring."

"Och, from what Kit's been sayin' about where we're headin' to, it'll be a barren winter fer bachelors. There'll be no Snakes or Crows in that far country. An' no Flatheads or Napercys, as well."

I held my peace. There was no profit in reminding him that I anticipated no privation of feminine warmth for myself in the cold months.

Most of the trapping brigades had already pulled out and Iron Bow's band had departed Indian-style, without notice, a day before in the early dawn hour, without the tearful farewelling that clutters white-eyes partings. They left behind only blanched lodge rings on the grass and castaway rubbish that soon disappears into the prairie.

Our own camp was much reduced from its earlier population. Frapp and Gervais, as well as Joe Meek's trio, had joined the American Fur brigades, along with the occasional hangers-on who had been drawn by Anse's fiddle and Harry's *guitarra* and stayed for breakfast—and in many cases, dinner and supper, as well. Most regretted by our women, especially Kathleen, was Isabel, Joe's beloved Umentucken, to whom Cat paid a farewell visit before Bridger led his brigade northward, a most unusual gesture amongst prairie Indians, who rarely bid goodbye and almost never look back when taking their leave.

The drying racks had been stripped clean of jerk meat and their sturdier lodgepoles had been fashioned into travois drags for transporting bulky plunder and kids too young to ride horseback and too big to be carried all day on their mother's lap. Our lodge was a mare's nest of hide-wrapped bundles and painted *parfleche* chests, even though Cat had used some of her time at rendezvous to enlarge the traveling lodge she and Ned had shared in order to accommodate our larger family. Custom decrees that the lodge is the woman's property and hardly any Indian woman would sacrifice a useful dwelling merely for the sake of sentiment.

Kathleen had Iris scurrying hither and thither, performing myriad chores in preparation for our departure. My daughter, in turn, had dragooned Paddy's redheaded young son into helping her. Molly, his Flathead mother, would never think of demanding such demeaning labor from a male child, but my enterprising daughter, trading on his devotion to her, was apparently untroubled by such taboos.

When at last it came time to quit camp, confusion disappeared. Order prevailed. In the blink of an eye, our lodge was struck, folded, and expertly bundled onto a travois, the extra lodgepoles immediately lashed onto packsaddles and rawhide slings suspended between the drags were heaped with bulky items securely bound in place. Bulging canvas panniers slung on either side of packsaddles on a brace of packmules contained the rest of our plunder. Three more packhorses were burdened with a plenitude of dried meat and pemmican and most of our free-running extra saddle stock carried empty packsaddles acquired on our California trip, in case it became necessary to abandon the travois drags because of difficult terrain or a need for greater speed to avoid pursuit by hostiles.

We were a colorful caravan when we set out at dawn on August tenth, leastaways our women were. They were loath to miss a final opportunity to flaunt their finery before trappers' wives still in camp and the few remaining Indian villages. And noisy, too, with squalling youngsters competing for a better seat on a travois, braying mules and whinnying packhorses complaining about their unaccustomed burdens after the long summer layoff, and barking camp dogs yapping us on our way out of camp. Our women gabbled amongst themselves, calling out to one another, scolding squabbling children riding on travois, and hailing friends they spied in the remaining camps in an altogether white-eyes fashion. Naturally my trapper companions and I indulged in our share of shouted farewelling to old friends, wishing them good hunting and a safe return to next year's rendezvous, taking care, the while, not to mention where we were headed when asked.

Fact is, we really didn't know, but we wouldn't have revealed our intended trapping grounds if we had. No sensible trapper ever would.

Iris was old enough to ride her own horse, but Ben was still too young to be entrusted to a travois, so Cat was obliged to carry him astride behind the pommel of her Mexican saddle or in a sling resting on her breast when he dozed. I marveled at Cat's strength and fortitude and that of Turtle's wife Tallymesko, whose son was the same age as Ben. They didn't appear to mind the discomfort, but I admired them nonetheless.

Once out of camp our little cavalcade settled into a serious vein, everyone aware that our meager numbers, together with our evident wealth in critters and their loads, would be an inviting target for enterprising raiders. With Kit, we now numbered twenty men, counting our two French-Canuck campkeepers, whose courage in a gunfight is uncertain, at times remarkably plucky, at others, totally craven. They are creatures of whim and passion. There is no telling which disposition might prevail in a crisis. Just the same, they rode with muskets slung across their back, like the rest of us, and one could only hope for the best.

Of the six women in our party, as far as I knew, only Kathleen was proficient in the use of arms. Years earlier, Ned Godey and I had instructed Cat and my late wife Rainbow in loading and shooting our rifles, pistols, and fowlers loaded with slugs, a deadly weapon at close range. Rainbow had preserved her life and that of our daughter from a marauding Blackfoot with my flintlock fowler when Iris was an infant. Recalling that fearsome event planted a seed in my mind that ultimately bore useful fruit.

Iris, mounted on her dainty *palomilla* mare, was determined to be helpful. She attached herself to the young Delaware Half-horse, the principal herder of our loose-running *remuda* of spare saddlers and pack animals. Naturally the redheaded Woodpecker, scion of the House of McBride, tagged after her on his roan gelding, his tiny bow and quiver bobbing on his back, which prompted Paddy and me to fall behind and lend a hand to Half-horse, keeping the livestock bunched and maintaining a watchful eye on our impulsive offspring.

Early-morning summertime sun was still burning mist off the Seeds-kee-dee when we arrived at the ford and commenced pushing our critters across, Tuttle and Kit leading the way, choosing the shallowest passage to avoid soaking the plunder transported on the several travois. Mothers scooped children onto their laps for the crossing and their fathers reluctantly assisted if there was more than one child who needed a lift. Indian men of whatever stripe and occupation loathe performing any chore they consider women's work.

Once across, we followed the river upstream for a distance, taking advantage of the bordering treeline when we could, in order to escape the prying eyes of a possible enemy. Such precautions are second nature for mountaineers and Indians alike in that country, practiced almost without a conscious decision by people schooled in self-preservation.

We proceeded without incident across open, rolling country in a general southeastern direction until the nooning halt for dinner and turning the critters out to graze. Before pitching in to perform the cooking chores, the women gathered together, raised blankets in a circle to screen one another, and quickly changed from their colorful rendezvous attire into common workaday buckskin dresses, leggin's, and moccasins, carefully stowing the precious holiday garments until the next opportunity to parade their wealth and status.

After a quick bait of vittles left from the night before, carried from camp in copper kettles, there was time to laze about and smoke a pipeful before attending to packing chores, balancing loads, snugging *cinchas* and harness, and suchlike, whilst our stock grazed their fill of crisp buffalo grass. Golden sunshine beamed from a cloudless sky, turning the prairie into a shimmering El Dorado.

"Shore do wish thar war time enough fer takin' a snooze," Tuttle said plaintively. "Thet'ere sunshine's purely puttin' me to sleep." He was stretched at full length, head propped on his saddle, bloodshot eyes under his raggedy hat brim attesting to a final drunken revel the night before. "Sunshine an' all o' thet'ere popskull I drunk las' night, but it war wuth it, ever' dram."

"Just so ye had a good time doin' it," I said.

"Li'l woman I woke up with this mawnin' said I did, anyways!" he replied and broke into a horselaugh as he struggled to sit up. "Hell! I'll git over it! Allus do!" He heaved himself upright and strolled off to his ground-tied horse, toting his saddle in one hand, stirrups dragging.

I had ridden Coffee out of camp that morning, but the trail had been gentle and undemanding. He had barely broken a sweat, so I decided to stay with him for the rest of the day. He enjoyed the work and I derived immense pleasure from riding him.

My little girl's early-morning enthusiasm for herding chores was mostly used up by mid-afternoon. She abandoned Half-horse and fell into line behind the mounted women, drooping in the saddle, likely dozing from time to time, but maintaining her seat and balance in the stirrups, belying her tender age and limited experience. Watching from a distance, I swelled with pride at the sight of her.

Her carrot-headed little swain was forbidden by custom to join his intended light-o'-love in the women's group, but he positioned himself as close as he dared to my daughter's creamy little mare, gigging his gentle blue roan energetically by drumming his moccasined heels on the critter's shoulders, which was as far as his chubby legs were able to reach.

Paddy and I took turns keeping a watchful eye on our young'uns, trading the herding chore and maintaining vigilance on the surrounding prairie, constantly swinging our gaze forward and twisting about to the rear, alert to picking up suspicious movement in the tail of the eye. Frequently looking backward is particularly important when you are traveling a new trail, for what you see when looking ahead looks entirely different when you view it from the opposite direction. If you wish to be able to return the way you came, you'd best keep looking over your shoulder. Keeping your head on a swivel will likely let you keep your hair, as well, for trouble usually comes from behind.

By late afternoon, the trail took us into a range of low forested hills and grassy valleys where small bands of buffalo grazed. Kit called a halt at the edge of an aspen grove, nigh a clear-running crick flowing into a broad meadow, where we hobbled our critters after we arranged their loads into a makeshift barricade around our intended campground.

Whilst the women set about spreading out sleeprobes and unpacking utensils, our campkeepers and children big enough to help gathered deadfall from beneath the aspens for the cookfires, the preferred firewood for travelers anxious to avoid detection. Aspen burns with much less dark smoke than resinous pine and fir produces. Cat, scanning the cloudless sky, suggested that we forego erecting our lodge that night and I happily agreed. The long ride that day had felt delightfully liberating after our overlong residence at rendezvous. Sleeping in the open air on a warm summer night promised to extend that feeling of freedom.

Micah and I joined Brass Turtle and Little Mountain to harvest our supper from a band of buffalo grazing at the far end of the valley, a couple dozen young bulls so far undisturbed by our presence at the treeline. Coffee had worked hard enough for one day, so I saddled the *grulla* gelding I had begun to call Crane, for lack of a better name. He was strong and willing, good-natured, with a kind and knowing eye, and I had grown fond of him, especially since the death of my Davey horse. Then I slipped the hobbles off my Sugarfoot mule, who had enjoyed a holiday during our journey from Horse Creek, running free with the *remuda*, burdened only with an empty packsaddle, which I replaced now, along with canvas panniers to carry the meat we meant to acquire.

My companions apparently shared my feeling of liberation at being once more on our own in the wilderness, after nearly two months of living cheek by jowl with a couple thousand other people. When I expressed that thought as we rode out to the herd, Little Mountain surprised me with his response. "Yeh, we be allatime wishin' fer ronnyvoo an' what we be gittin' thar— wimmin an' drinkin' an' foofurraw an' some more wimmin—an' them ain't bad things—but it ain't good fer allatime. Out hyar's what's good fer inside me most o' the time."

"That's a fact," Turtle chimed in. "If I wanted all the plunder ye kin get at ronnyvoo all the time an' rubbin' elbows with a gang o' folks ever' day, I could'a stayed in the settlements. Ridin' out today with fellers I kin trust, jist our own bunch, takin' our chances, no matter what comes up, war sort'a like gittin' out of a trap."

Micah grinned at what he was hearing. "An' all the time I've been thinkin' it was just me feelin' thataway," he said. "Not that I don't get my en-joys from doin' a mite o' drinkin' an' not sleepin' alone, but educatin' white-eyes greenhorns thinkin' they got some kind o' right to be pickin' on me gets old after a spell."

"Not to mention gittin' your knuckles all skun up," Turtle said with a laugh. "We seen ye doin' it, more'n once."

By that time, we had drawn as close to the herd as we dared approach by horseback. We dropped into a hollow downwind of our prey and dismounted, tethering our animals to sagebrush clumps, then stealthily ascended the slope on our bellies, slithering through the tall grass at the top like a pack of hungry wolves, until we were within a hundred yards of our prey, a dozen rolling fat young bulls attended by a single old veteran who suddenly threw up his great shaggy head and snorted an alarm. Brass Turtle leapt to his feet, rifle at his shoulder, and fired at almost the same split-second that Micah and Little Mountain rose to their knees and discharged their weapons. Two young bulls dropped to the ground, coughing blood, their lungs shattered. A third fell to his knees, then struggled upright and commenced to weave his way in pursuit of his fleeing fellows. I took careful aim at the only available target and fired, which pitched him forward onto his bearded chin, coughing out his life along with some of his innards.

"Hell, Buck, ye plumb cored 'im out, ye done!" Brass Turtle crowed, a huge grin wreathing his features. "An' ye even clipped off his tail whilst ye war at it! That be some purty shootin'!"

Which remark produced general merriment amongst the others. I shrugged and reloaded my rifle before I started back to the hollow to retrieve our animals. By time I rejoined them, they were all chewing on tender liver sprinkled with gall and I was not a mite behindhand in claiming my share.

We made short work of butchering out the tongues and choice cuts from all three young bulls and loaded the meat into the panniers on our two packmules, who struggled under the weight of it all as we made our way back to camp.

Dureau and Jean-Luc spied us as we approached and came running out to take charge of the mules, chattering cheerfully at the prospect of fresh meat for supper. Cookfires were already blazing, reducing dry aspen branches to glowing coals under copper kettles suspended on steel ramrods, already boiling, awaiting fresh tongue, a prime delicacy. Great gobbets of hump meat and backstrap quickly joined them on the spits, dripping rich fat onto sizzling coals, wafting an enticing aroma throughout the camp that soon got my mouth watering and my belly rumbling in anticipation of the forthcoming feast.

After we hobbled our critters and turned them out, Micah and I headed for the crick to wash off the dried blood from our gory chore. Turtle and Mountain were already there, stripped down to their clouts and splashing in the shallows and evidently trading humorous quips in the Delaware tongue, judging from their bursts of laughter after each verbal sally.

"Thar ye be!" Turtle called out in greeting. "'Bout time ye got the muck off'n ye, afore yer woman makes ye sleep out on the prairie."

I allowed that I needed no such encouragement to rid myself of the sticky mess with which I was plastered and Micah reminded him that neither he nor Mountain had a woman to keep them in line, nor did he reckon that they needed onesuch for that purpose. Which provoked a spate of mutual bantering betwixt the two of them, with Little Mountain injecting his own witticisms whenever the first two chattering magpies paused for breath. I missed out on most of their humorous bickering because I kept ducking my head under the cool crick water, a thoroughly enjoyable experience after a sweaty day in the saddle and a grimy albeit rewarding chore.

🙖 🙖 🙖

After I had eaten a full sufficiency fit for two hungry men and then just somewhat more of the really tasty bits, I retired to the company of the men gathered around a flickering cookfire to smoke a pipeful or two and await my turn at standing horse guard in the meadow. The palaver that evening was livelier, more good-natured and humorous, than usual, reflecting my own contentment at being back amongst our bunch, relieved of the troubling new concerns that had marred the end of the rendezvous, and on our way to new country.

Kathleen had spread our sleeprobes in a secluded grove just inside the treeline and Iris had asked permission to join the other children in spending the night sleeping outdoors in Tallymesko's camp, which we granted. After her strenuous day in the saddle and the other children jouncing aboard travois drags, it was doubtful that any of them could stay awake long enough to get into trouble.

I shared my horse guard stint with Finn McCool, a pleasant companion, always thoughtful and gifted with an antic fancy. Speaking in hardly audible voices, we recalled our California experience. "'Twas a revelation, indade, discoverin' the sweet loife they're after livin' there in their everlastin' sunshine," Finn said dreamily. "'Tis no wonder Don Nicolás calls it a paradise there. 'Tis a home he niver could've realized in the Auld Sod or loikely anywhere else in the intire world."

"Do ye reckon you'll ever return there?" I asked.

"Och, I've thought about it, surely, but 'tisn't bloody loikely I could be makin' a daycent livin' there. The good fortune Don Nicolás experienced isn't loikely to be repeatin' itself. 'Twould be expectin' lightnin' to be strikin' in the same place twice. If I had me medical license in hand, I'd surely be after thinkin' about doin' it someday, but as it is, I'd best be remainin' here amongst good friends in God's country."

🙖 🙖 🙖

When Zeetlah and Half-horse relieved us about midnight, I bade Finn goodnight, shouldered my rifle, and turned my steps toward the grove where Kathleen lay sleeping. It had been a long, hard-working day—the long march a-horseback, constantly chousing errant critters the while, stalking and butchering the buffalo, and finally standing guard in the meadow, constantly alert and straining to identify every alien sound or shadowy movement on the prairie. I should have been dead-tired, ready to close my eyes in slumber. Instead I discovered that my thoughts kept straying persistently to amorous pursuits.

I recalled that I had read somewhere that Napoleon Bonaparte had observed that when he was conducting a military campaign he never had to worry about his infantrymen causing trouble at night, for they were too worn out by their long day's marching. His cavalrymen, to the contrary, according to the Little Corporal, appeared to be stimulated by their long hours in the saddle and required strict surveillance, lest they ravish the womenfolk in towns where they were quartered.

When I neared the grove I took special care to tread lightly, lest I disturb Cat's slumber, for her day had been at least as fatiguing as my own, but when I drew nigh she called out softly in a throaty voice, "Hurry, Tompo! I 'ave missed you!" Something in her tone hastened my response. I laid my weapons on the blanket she had placed near at hand, then frantically fumbled free of my belts and leggin's, but evidently not fast enough for my impatient partner, who wrenched off my moccasins and shoved aside my britchclout, drawing me into a passionate embrace, her steamy breath and murmured endearments clouding whatever judgment I had left, until I regained some shreds of sanity sometime later.

When I drifted back to a few slivers of conscious thought, my mind strayed to my earlier musing about Napoleon's observations about the randy behavior of his hussars and dragoons after a hard day's horsebacking. Now I wondered what the Little Corporal might have had to say about his female troops, if he had possessed any equestrian Gallic amazons.

∾ ∾ ∾

After nearly a fortnight the rolling hills and grassy green meadows gradually flattened and thinned into barren desert where only grey sagebrush and pale cactus and yucca dotted the bleak landscape. Water grew scarce and the noisy children aboard the travois drags mostly ceased their chatter as their rawhide chariots bumped and clattered along a rocky trail, hanging onto the drag poles over particularly rough stretches and, thirsty though they often were, rarely complaining. Iris and little Sean McBride insisted on traveling in their saddles, but they consented to exchange their favorite horses for the surefooted saddle mules that Micah and I provided.

Carson proved to be a reliable pilot over that sterile wasteland. He never failed to deliver us to water by the end of each day's journey, although sometimes the day stretched from dawn almost to dark and the water often amounted to little more than a trickle. Still it was enough to sustain us and our livestock. There was no game in that desolate region, but our women kept us decently fed with stews of dried meat cooked over feeble fires of sagebrush stems and roots, improved more than somewhat with dried mushrooms and turnip-like greens the Shoshone women garnered from some of the cactus plants they knew about.

Our sole luxury in that time of privation was coffee, night and morning, thick and strong and syrupy with sugar.

After the third day in that mostly waterless wilderness, our direction became mostly easterly, until four days later we glimpsed blue mountains in the distance. Patches of scraggy green grass commenced to appear along the trail, gradually growing more abundant until we emerged from a narrow draw in the hills and came upon a clear-running crick flowing through a broad grassy meadow. Our critters smelled the water before we saw it. The free-running stock shoved us riders aside in their haste to get to it and naturally the horses hauling travois tried to keep up with them, which sorely taxed the women fighting to hang onto their leadropes, until several of us men were able to get hold of their halters to hold them back.

Our people were hardly less frenzied than our animals to get at the water, many of them riding into the crick and throwing themselves off, laughing delightedly and splashing their fellows who still remained a-horseback. Even Tuttle baptized himself, flinging himself headlong into the shallows, gleefully rolling about in the cool water, laving off god-only-knows-how-many weeks of sweat and grime, which was a blessing to us all.

Our livestock had suffered more than we had during our weeklong journey through that arid country. Long, hot days without water, hard work, and meager greenery overnight had left them ganted and ribby. Even the usually easy-keeping mules showed the effects of privation. "Thar ain't no need to be killin' ourse'fs ner the critters, neither, gittin' whar we're goin'," Kit opined that evening. "It still be early fer trappin' an' beaver'll still be waitin' when we git thar. We oughta be puttin' up hyar fer a spell, 'til we won't be countin' our critters' ribs no more. What say?" Naturally nobody was inclined to disagree with that suggestion. We stayed there a week.

Lush forage, plenty of fresh water, and unbroken leisure soon restored condition to our animals. Ribs slowly disappeared, ganted bellies commenced filling out, and coats became sleek once again. Although buffalo shunned our paradise during our stay there, deer aplenty roamed the nearby woods and a plenitude of wapiti on the slopes of foothills at the far end of the valley kept our bellies full.

The women and children fanned out in the forest, seeking moist, shady spots in the woods to collect mushrooms and edible roots to enrich their stews and to the prairie, where they robbed the lairs of field mice of their hoard of wild peas that the tiny critters store up for their winter vittles.

The idyllic tranquility of our Eden was marred only once, when Molly and Pretty Horse's Crow wife Nettaqueathy—whom we call Bashful although she long ago ceased to be shy—discovered a grove of ripe plums. A bevy of women and kids immediately headed there, plucking the succulent fruit from the heavily-laden branches, harvesting a quantity for camp and naturally stuffing themselves whilst they were at it, when a fearsome roar froze them where they stood. But not for long. They knew it was a grizzly bear. Mothers snatched up their small children, shooing the bigger kids ahead, and rushed headlong along the path to camp, nearly knocking down Diego and Pablo, who had followed the women to the grove with the intention of gratifying their own sweet tooth.

Our *Californios* are no strangers to grizzly bears. They knew nobody can outrun a bear. They stood their ground and, when Old Ephraim spied them standing in his path and rose upon his hocks and roared, first Pablo, then Diego, fired their new large-caliber percussion rifles and thereby harvested a substantial quantity of fresh bear meat for the camp.

If anybody had harbored doubts about the courage of our recent recruits, their action in the plum grove erased those misgivings. Anyone who can face down a grizzly boar on the prod is easily a match for a war-painted Blackfoot.

Loudest in praise of the *Californios* were, naturally, the women, who pampered them with choice bits from the cookfires and saw to it that the moccasins and other clothing of the two young bachelors stayed in good repair.

❧　❧　❧

Our trail steadily gained elevation and nights grew colder after we entered the mountain range we had seen from the desert. By mid-September several of us had begun setting traps overnight in the streams where we camped, a few of us undertaking to instruct our two newcomers in the skills of our trade, showing them how and where to place the castoreum scent to attract a beaver to their trap, how to skin the critters out, and how to stretch the plew on a willow hoop to cure it in the dry mountain air. They were eager to learn. Both of them soon had a few drying hides clacking and banging on hoops tied onto their pack animals. It was still early in the season and the plews were not yet prime, but it was a start.

Each day, four of us, taking turns amongst the men, rode out ahead of the column to hunt and to make sure that our party was not heading into trouble. Game was plentiful and our daily harvest of wapiti and deer and occasionally a big-horn mountain sheep that strayed within rifle range kept us well-fed. We missed fresh buffalo meat in our diet, but Kit assured us that the privation was only temporary. Bands of buffalo, wandering in from the south, often wintered in the secluded valley where we were headed.

Traveling with the sole intention of putting as many miles as possible behind us each day was a dreary occupation, enlivened, in the main, only by one's own thoughts or occasional palaver with one's companions. We had so far been fortunate in covering a great distance without a challenge by Blackfeet, Bannocks, or any other marauders who would certainly be tempted by our plunder and livestock and encouraged to attack by our few numbers. Such good fortune naturally produced some worry. Good luck has a way of running out.

At length I mentioned my concern to Brass Turtle one day when he and I were riding together in search of game. Instead of chiding me for borrowing trouble, he surprised me by admitting that he, too, had been haunted of late by a sense of impending doom. "Cain't tell ye jist what it be, but it's a kind o' feelin' I've larn't it's wuth payin' some mind to. Like ye say, we been damn lucky an' it ain't likely to be lastin' ferever. Got any idees?"

"Fact is, I do," I replied. "There's just an even score of us men amongst us, besides half a dozen women and a passel o' kids. Half a dozen more guns on our side'd go a ways towards evenin' up the odds if we get into a fight."

"Ye mean to say ye be wantin' to teach the womenfolk to shoot?" Turtle looked incredulous. "Ye cain't be serious!"

"I can be and I am," I assured him. "That's exactly what I mean."

"They'd never put up with it!" he insisted. "Injun women ain't allowed the use o' guns an' sich, Temple! Not even bows an' arrers! Ye oughta know that by now!"

"Our women ain't just Injun women any more, Turtle! They're trappers' wives now! I'm sure you've noticed the diff'rence! Look at the way they dress now and how they act at rendezvous, talkin' to strangers and all, like Injun women in their home village never would! Ner be allowed to. Given half a chance, they'll fight, too—'specially to protect their young'uns!"

I reminded him of Rainbow blowing away the Blackfoot bravo in Iron Bow's village when my daughter was an infant and how, years before, Ned Godey and I had taught Rainbow and Kathleen the use of firearms, in spite of the disapproval of most of the Delawares and Iroquois in our bunch, at the time. "We've got enough extra guns and fixin's amongst our plunder, so I daresay the toughest chore'll be gettin' our Injun men to go along with the idea. I'm sure Cat'll convince the womenfolk 'thout much trouble a-tall."

Turtle's smile was rueful when he replied, "Yep, I reckon Cat wou'n't have no trouble, nohaow, gittin' my Tally, fer one, to go along with yer idee. What ye say 'baout trappers' wimmen thinkin' fer theirownse'fs be the gawddamn truth."

"So ye think it's a good idea, Turtle?" I pressed, although he had said no such thing. "Ye'll talk to Pretty Hoss an' the others 'bout teachin' the women to shoot?" When he still looked uncertain, I added, "Half a dozen extra guns might let us all keep our hair."

"Let me chew it over a spell," he hedged. "I'll let ye know 'fore long."

"Just don't take too long makin' up your mind," I replied, unwilling to let my argument get cold. "There's no tellin' when we might get jumped."

Now that I had actually put my half-baked notion into words, I warmed to the scheme. That night, when Kathleen and I retired to our robes, I proposed the plan to her, relating what I had discussed with Brass Turtle, and suggesting that she talk to the other women to see if they might be receptive to violating all the old taboos concerning women and weapons. Cat laughed aloud when she heard me say that. "Zey weel say why ye takin' so long! Women can fight. Now we fight wiz our knife. We mus' have a knife for doin' woman's work. You learn 'em shootin' guns, zey weel fight wiz guns, too! Yes, I weel tell zem. Zey weel say yes."

I had expected Kathleen to welcome the idea of teaching the other women the use of firearms, but her response was more enthusiastic than I could have hoped for. Iris, always a heavy sleeper, was sleeping even more soundly than usual, completely tuckered out after her long hours a-horseback. Now when I attempted to roll over and go to sleep, I discovered that my lady had something else in mind, something delightful and always welcome.

∾ ∾ ∾

Next morning on the trail, Brass Turtle rode up beside me and declared, "Ye shorely din't waste no time peddlin' yer gawddamn 'cute idee aroun', did ye?"

Startled, I stared at him as I fumbled for a reply. "What d'ye mean?" I said at last.

"Ye mean to say ye din't know yer woman's been talkin' to ever' woman in the bunch about larnin' haow to shoot a rifle gun. Tally jumped me fust thing this mawnin', wantin' to know when she kin start."

I assured Turtle that I had no idea that Kathleen would commence her campaign so quickly, that I had told her that the matter hadn't yet been decided, that it was still only an idea.

"Wal, ye should'a knowed better. Naow thar won't be no livin' with any of 'em 'less'n they git their way."

"Ye say Cat's been talkin' to all o' the women already?" I asked.

"That's what Tally war sayin' an' I reckon she oughta know. Them two are purty thick."

"Well then," I said, feeling halfway smug at making so much progress with so little effort, "I reckon I've done my job. Now it's up to you to be talkin' to Pretty Hoss an' the two Iroquois and gettin' them to go along. I'll talk to Paddy about teachin' Molly."

"Sure," he sneered, "that'll be a hard chore fer ye, won't it?" His laugh dripped with sarcasm. "An' ye be leavin' it to me to talk t'other three out of a thousand years an' more o' he-dog thinkin'! Injuns don't take kindly to changin' their ways, 'speshly whar fambly's consarned." He was still grumbling when he touched spur to his horse's flank and loped off to commence his difficult task.

I reined up beside the trail and let the column pass by whilst I waited for Paddy McBride, who was helping Half-horse drive our loose-running critters, bringing up the rear of our cavalcade. When I broached the matter to Paddy, he favored me with a lopsided grin and replied, "Well, now, sure'n it's taken ye long enough, indade, Temple darlin', to be gittin' 'round to that partic'lar chore. Ye'll be findin' me darlin' Molly's awready a purty fair shot. She has been this long while!"

He chuckled at my surprised expression. "I been teachin' her nearly from the first we met. After she seen your Rainbow woman blow the guts out o' that Blackfoot blaggard, five years past, she was after givin' me no peace 'til I showed 'er the use o' guns. Many a time the two of us snuck off together, out o' camp, fer practicin' her shootin' an', natcherly," here he sniggered lewdly, "fer collectin' me teachin' fee afterwards, as is only right an' proper!"

∾   ∾   ∾

It is a tribute to Brass Turtle's persuasive skills that by mid-afternoon he hailed me with the news that he had been able to wring a grudging consent from our three Indian benedicts. "They ain't none too keen on the idee," he said, "but I war able to git 'em to go along, leastaways fer naow." When I told him what Paddy had revealed, he snorted and replied, "'Tain't surprisin'. You white-eyes got no his'try in sich matters that's gotta be turned upside down."

I bit my tongue and refrained from mentioning that neither did he.

He and I rode to the head of the column and revealed the plan to Kit, who greeted our news with approval. "So fur, so good," he told us, "but we been lucky, so fur. As ye know, ye cain't never tell whar ye mought be runnin' inter Blackfoots, from their stompin' ground up nawth nigh the Aitch-bee-cee, all the way to *Mejico*, anyplace whar they reckon they kin lay their thievin' paws on hosses an' wimmin. Same with Bannocks an' some others, 'ceptin' that kind don't git around so much as Blackfoots do. Extry guns're allus welcome."

We wasted no time putting our plan into action. The women put up their lodges within minutes of our arrival at our overnight camp, placed their small children in the care of older kids, and gathered to commence their training, chattering like magpies amongst themselves, all of them obviously eager to acquire heretofore forbidden skills that might save their lives and those of their young'uns.

Turtle's diplomacy was again called upon when he was required to coax the three reluctant husbands into turning over to their wives their second-best long guns, originally flintlocks that Micah had long before altered into percussion rifles, along with powder horns and other fixin's. Their disapproving stares were reflected in similar expressions on the faces of Little Mountain and Zeetlah, who evidently shared their comrades' displeasure at our flouting of centuries of traditional behavior, blurring the rigid lines between the sexes, threatening their male dominance. I glanced discreetly at Powatawa, who was sitting with young Half-horse. Neither appeared to object to the unaccustomed goings-on.

Cat and Molly were invaluable in interpreting and reinforcing the instructions that Micah and I provided, explaining the importance of keeping weapons clean and dry and well-oiled, then drilling our pupils in loading, making sure the galena ball was firmly seated on the powder charge, lest it explode the gun barrel, fitting the percussion cap securely onto the nipple, and finally shooting at a fixed target, carefully supervised, gently squeezing the trigger, getting used to the muzzle blast and the slight accompanying jolt.

Although their accuracy stood in need of improvement, that first lesson went better than we could have expected. Next evening was devoted to running a supply of rifle balls, each woman melting galena over a small fire and pouring it into her individual bullet mold, so that the caliber of her personal stock of ammunition precisely matched her particular weapon. A lifetime of executing intricate quillwork and similar precise tasks proved a definite advantage in learning that exacting chore, at which our crew of distaff irregulars excelled. Their reward was an extra quarter-hour of target practice, which thoroughly delighted our feminine recruits.

After a week of daily target practice, at which our novices steadily improved, the women, evidently by common consent, appeared one morning with their rifles slung across their back, like us men, as we prepared to mount up. Their husbands appeared to be less upset by their boldness than were our Indian bachelors, who complained about such behavior in public. When I commented on that curious fact to Kathleen, she smiled and replied, "I sink zose married men are more happy now at night zen before. Women know how to make zem happy in zeir robes." She tittered and blushed at her own audacity, but when I suggested that perhaps I, too, should be more domineering, she grinned mischievously and countered, "You know you have no need of zat. Never!" I agreed.

❧   ❧   ❧

Nights grew colder as our trail climbed higher into the sierra. Autumnal chill replaced late-summer warmth. Occasionally we awoke to a dusting of snow over the camp. The few beaver we trapped overnight commenced to improve in quality, the under-fur thicker and deeper. Now and again we crossed broad mesas rich with tall, dry buffalo grass that maintained our critters in good fettle. "This be what Injuns be callin' greazy grass," Tuttle commented approvingly. "Ye kin pratic'ly see 'em pilin' on good hard fat ever' night we git to make camp in it."

Carson did his best to make sure that we were able to benefit from that good graze, sometimes cutting our day shorter in order to camp nigh a meadow lush with belly-high grass. Whenever he was able to do so, he chose campsites that butted against a substantial hill or mountainside, in case we might need to defend against an attack. As good a pilot as Kit was, he naturally hadn't committed that whole trail to memory, but he possessed an almost uncanny ability to find water and decent graze by day's end.

One day, shortly after our nooning halt in a narrow canyon beside a puny little crick, we came out upon another broad meadow, tall yellow grass shimmering like a golden sea under crisp autumn sunshine nigh to the purple hills on its far side. Sharp-eyed Little Mountain suddenly let out a joyful yelp, rising in his stirrups, pointing south'ards and hollering, "Buffler! Thar's buffler out thar! Damn if thar ain't!" Thrilling at his news, I joined several others riding to his side, straining to see what had provoked his outburst. Sure enough, far away across the prairie, I spied the shaggy brown backs of a score or more buffalo grazing in the high grass.

Whooping triumphantly, half a dozen of us left the column and galloped off to harvest buffalo, mouths already watering at the prospect of fresh hump ribs and tongue. Almost equally appealing was the opportunity of running the critters, a sport of which we had been deprived during the rendezvous. Fortunately I was riding Coffee that day. He responded with enthusiasm that matched my own, grateful to be relieved from the plodding gait of the procession, releasing tremendous power as he leapt into pursuit of our prey, head held low, powerful shoulders pumping mightily as he extended his stride into a ground-eating gallop that had my moccasins parting the grass, leaving the others behind.

I checked his speed as we neared the outer flank of the herd, lest I startle and scatter them before my companions caught up. Which was fortunate, for as we topped a low rise in the prairie I beheld a sight that sent my heart plummeting to my moccasins—nigh a double score of mounted Indians riding pell-mell in an easterly direction, Bannocks by the look of them, obviously in pursuit of the buffalo but instantly switching their attention to me, changing course in a wild commotion of rearing horses, waving and pointing, yipping and hoorawing, swinging about and charging through the tall grass.

I skidded Coffee to an abrupt halt, bent him smoothly over my leg, and beat an even faster retreat over our back-trail than we had achieved coming out, yelling and waving my arms when I caught sight of my friends, who wasted no time in pulling up and reversing direction, spurring and quirting their mounts into ever greater speed. When I came up alongside Anse Tolliver, whose long-legged mule was stretched out nearly flat as he raced across the prairie, our Tennessee fiddler glanced up and strangled out, "Thi'shere's a fine howdy-do, Buck! Ye war s'posed to be bringin' back buffler, not Injuns!" In spite of our fearsome circumstances, I burst out laughing as we pounded towards the caravan .

Kit Carson is no slowpoke when it comes to reckoning what needs to be done in a tight spot. We had barely come into clear view of the column before we saw it rapidly reversing direction and heading along its back-trail. By time we covered the remaining distance, they had already reached our nooning place. Women and campkeepers were stripping off packs and piling them into a barrier across the narrow mouth of the canyon. Half-horse and Zeetlah were driving horses and mules into the crick bottom and the rest of the men were rolling big rocks and dragging the trunks of downed trees and driftwood to strengthen the flimsy barricade. Pablo and Diego had retrieved axes from the packs and were felling trees growing along the crick bank. Iris and young Sean had gathered the smaller children into a dry hollow nigh the crick and were doing their best to keep them from straying into trouble. They had tied tethers onto Ben and Turtle's little boy to keep them from crawling off.

I yanked my pistols from my pommel holsters and shoved them into my belt before I led Coffee down the bank and turned him in with the other critters, then hustled to the barricade to lend a hand and prepare for a fight, just in time to greet my fellow hunters come thundering in, bringing their wild-eyed lathered horses to a rearing halt and flinging themselves to the ground, rushing to the barricade, unslinging rifles as they ran, ready to do battle. Powatawa and Paddy shooed the critters into the crick bottom, then trotted to join the rest of us.

Carson appeared to be everywhere, giving orders in a calm, quiet voice, actually grinning as he bustled from one work crew to another. When he mounted the barricade to gain a better vantage point for a look-see, he muttered, "If'n it had to come, we could'na hardly wished fer a better place fer it to happen, Buck. They cain't hardly git a'hind us 'thout doin' a heap o' climbin' an' we got a purty clear shot at 'em when they come up front."

Once, when I took a breather from dragging tree trunks into place, I saw Cat and Molly and Tally hauling packs that contained extra powder and galena and stowing them beneath a heap of fist-size rocks to protect them from a stray shot that might set off the powder. I smiled with pride at my bride's cool forethought at a time when panic might easily be excused.

Meanwhile, the marauders had closed the distance and reined up just out of rifle range, stalled by the sight of our hastily-thrown-together bulwark that likely looked more solid from a distance than it really was. Tuttle and Brass Turtle joined Kit and me on the fort, surveying the enemy, which numbered about forty mounted warriors, most of them armed with long guns, likely mostly muskets, the rest with bows. A few of them squatted on the ground, but most remained a-horseback, milling around, waving their arms and pointing in our direction. Kit brought out a brass spyglass from his belt-poke, which we passed around amongst us. We took note of their dress, which was pretty much unremarkable, dirty calico shirts and faded britchclouts and, here and there, unadorned buckskin shirts and leggin's. Their hair gave them away, short, chopped off at shoulder-length, bound with a dirty rag around the temples. "Yep, they be Gai-bee-shúh fer sure," Turtle pronounced, distaste in his tone. "Bannocks. We might'a knowed."

"Wal," Tuttle declared, "ye kin wager once them bastards got sight of all our critters an' ther packs they be totin', them'ere greedy-guts won't be givin' up on makin' it all their own. They be sp'ilin' fer a fight an' they won't be quittin' 'til we give 'em proper comeuppance!" With that he brought his rifle up and squinted down the barrel. "Let's see if'n they really be out o' range. Thar's one big feller 'mongst 'em what 'pears to be doin' most o' ther talkin'." He raised the muzzle a hair and squeezed off a shot. When the smoke cleared, the big Bannock appeared to be unharmed, but a warrior behind him sagged on his pony's neck, then fell to the ground. "Shee-it!" Tuttle complained. "Thar be more breeze than I calcalated!"

The Bannocks were galvanized by Tuttle's unexpected shot. They quit milling and haranguing and kicked their ponies into a hasty retreat another hundred yards or so out onto the prairie, leaving their fallen comrade where he lay.

Tuttle's shot hadn't provoked a fight that might have been avoided. If anything, it gave us an advantage by riling up the enemy and goading them into making a foolhardy charge. "Git ready!" Kit called out. "They'll be comin' purty quick naow! Don't ever'body be shootin' at oncet. Take yer time! Make 'em count!"

Everybody trotted to his position. Several more men joined us on the log fort. McCool and Powatawa scooted up the hillside behind us and took positions behind large boulders, where they were joined by Diego and Pablo, looking determined, anxious to prove their worth.

We hadn't long to wait. The enemy ranks boiled with activity, their excited horses rearing and cavorting. Their riders, arms waving wildly, seemed more intent on winning a local debate than attacking a common foe. At last they marshaled themselves into a ragged offensive line and kicked their ponies into a frantic gallop, whereupon their offense fragmented as the faster horses quickly outdistanced the slower ponies, reducing the impact of the initial charge, exposing the leaders to our deliberate marksmanship.

My first shot was successful. I took careful aim on the belly of a painted warrior and gently squeezed the trigger when he was about forty yards distant. He threw both hands skyward, his musket flying behind him, and tumbled to the ground. Pleased at that propitious beginning, I stepped down from my perch to reload, spilling powder down the barrel and spitting a rifle ball after it, thumping the butt on the ground to secure the bullet in place, when someone bumped me aside and took my place on the barricade. Occupied with my chore, I took little notice, and proceeded to fit the percussion cap onto the nipple. Ready to resume my place on the rampart, I looked up for the first time and beheld my light-o'-love, rifle at her shoulder, squinting down the barrel, then rocking back on her heels as the charge went off. Her triumphant squawk confirmed that the Bannock I saw flung from his pony had indeed been her target.

She stepped down and grinned at me. "Zat one iss for my friend," she announced, referring to Rainbow, whose name she will never pronounce, who was killed by a Bannock posing as friendly four years before. She stood on tiptoe and kissed me before she scurried off.

When I regained my perch I beheld a scene of chaos. A dozen riderless horses were fleeing across the prairie. At least that many bodies littered the field in front of our defenses, a few writhing in agony, to which Little Mountain and Acorn soon put a merciful end with well-placed arrows to conserve gunpowder. "Odds 'pear to be gittin' a mite evener," Tuttle observed, satisfaction in his tone.

"Anybody hurt amongst us?" I asked, glancing along our firing line.

"Coupl'a scratches," he replied. "Nothin' serious. Mostly chips from off o' them big rocks they used fer puttin' thi'shere fort together."

We enjoyed a brief respite. The enemy retired a safe distance from the long reach of our rifles and were once again milling about a-horseback, gesticulating wildly as they debated their next move. At last they appeared to settle on a plan. Half a dozen riders split off from the main bunch and trotted off out of sight behind the rocky wall that formed the mouth of our canyon retreat.

Kit had kept his spyglass trained on the assembled Bannocks. When he saw their latest action, he climbed onto the barricade and announced, "The bastards are thinkin' on gittin' around us, sure as hell climbin' up thi'shere hill a'hind us an' shootin' down on us from up thar." He jerked his chin skywards in the direction of the canyon wall that protected our right flank, where Powatawa, McCool, and the two *Californios* were already in place halfway up, facing the prairie. "We got time to give 'em a proper welcome up thar, on the top, if'n we git a move on purty quick. Who's game?"

Micah was first to volunteer, followed immediately by Tuttle, which prompted me to hold up my hand, just as Brass Turtle grunted his assent. "That'll do!" Carson called out. "Four o' ye's enough to git 'er done. Ye'd best git to climbin' now, on account o' gittin' thar 'fore they do." He turned to Turtle an' me and added with a grin, "An' don'tcha be frettin' about leavin' us short-handed. Both o' yer wimmen awready counted coup on a coupl'a them dead bastards layin' out yonder. Reckon we kin count on the rest of 'em steppin' up, too, if need be."

At the foot of the hill, Micah scampered on ahead, seeking the best way up, Tuttle close behind him. Turtle and I followed their lead. The lower slope was gentle, then the ascent became more rugged. About halfway up, we halted for a breather. When I caught my breath I turned to Turtle and said, "Sorta reminds me of the first time ye took me to a fight, Turtle, climbin' that hill outside o' their camp, gettin' our critters back from the Crows. Remember?"

He grinned and replied, "I do. All of us war all purty green back then, but ye went an' showed ye had some Injun in ye, even if I din't know it fer sure back then."

I glowed at the compliment. "Neither did I, back then, but thankee for sayin' so."

Micah proved to be a worthy pathfinder. We clambered over the last crag overhanging the canyon wall, without any mishaps, save for skinned knees and suchlike. Down below, our little gathering of defenders was in plain view, easy targets for a gunman shooting from above. When our breathing returned to normal we fanned out and made our way to the far side of the narrow hogback that poked into the surrounding prairie. It was covered with heavy brush that afforded concealment. Bending low, rifles ready, we scuttled through thick undergrowth, straining to see movement ahead, alert to every sound that might betray an enemy.

We emerged on the far side without encountering anything suspicious and scanned the tree-covered hillside below, a gentler slope that stretched much farther out into the plain than the steep incline we had scaled. "That'll make a cornsid'able fu'ther hike fer them than it war fer us gittin' a'top o' thi'shere hogback," Turtle surmised.

"Let's keep lookin' a spell," Micah advised. "All o' those trees'll keep us from seein' 'em unless they stray out in the open."

Both opinions appeared reasonable. I had none of my own, so I held my peace and contented myself with gazing down at the leafy canopy undulating in the breeze that flowed off our hilltop. Once I thought I saw movement, but it turned out to be a wapiti cow ambling along a forest trail.

When at last we spied our quarry they were much closer than we had reckoned. I had been looking in the wrong place. Tuttle spied them first, just below the rim of our slender bench, all six of them together, strolling unconcernedly, confident that that their ascent had not been guessed at, all of them armed with muskets, bows and quivers slung across their backs.

Silently, we crawfished back from the edge. Then, bending low, we faded into the brush and made our way to the footpath they would likely use, a narrow game trail leading to the hilltop. When we neared the place where they would almost certainly appear, we scattered a few yards apart and lay prone, concealed amidst tall weeds, a dozen yards from the edge.

We heard them before we saw them, laughing and joshing one another, already exulting over the havoc they expected to wreak on their white-eyes prey. First one rag-wrapped head, then another poked over the grassy edge, until all six stood on level ground, pausing to get their bearings before heading to the far side of the hogback. The sharp metallic clack of a cocking hammer caused a couple of them to throw up their heads, eyes darting wildly, seeking to locate the sound, but it was too late. Our rifles spoke in a single explosion. Four Bannocks were hurled backwards, arms flung out like rag dolls carelessly discarded, muskets clattering to earth, a couple writhing in agony, the other two lying motionless. The remaining pair stood frozen for an instant, before they swung about and prepared to retreat down the hill. Before they could take the first step, howsomever, I rose to my knees, leveled a pistol at one of them, and sent him off to join his fallen comrades. His companion crumpled at the same instant, drilled by pistol balls from Brass Turtle and Micah.

"Like shootin' fish in a bar'l!"

"Better them than us!"

The entire event occupied no more than a quarter-minute. It was over before it fairly began. I stood and reloaded my rifle whilst I watched Tuttle dispatch the wounded Bannocks with his big butcher knife. As often happens in such situations, my mind went curiously numb for a brief spell, as if it were reluctant to accept what it had just willingly done. Fortunately that feeling lasts hardly any time at all.

"I say," Micah intoned in exaggerated mimicry of Captain William Stewart's cultured British accent, "that was jolly well unsporting of us, gentlemen, wouldn't you agree? They had no time at all to take wing."

Brass Turtle was first to catch on to Micah's playful sally. "Not fer a damn minute," he retorted. "Thar warn't a one of 'em sittin' on his arse when we kilt 'em, so it war fair an' square!"

Which provoked a chorus of laughter from all of us, forestalling any possible regret over the recent bloodletting, which was unlikely anyway. The Bannocks got only what they would have happily dealt out to us.

Micah acquired his vocal skill at impersonation during his servitude as a slave in Chouteau's Saint Louis establishment, learning French and striving to sound like a white American instead of a plantation darkie.

We relieved our fallen foes of their powder horns, bullet pouches, and three of their muskets which were fairly new and in good condition. The others we smashed against a tree trunk. They possessed nothing else worth taking, not even their short-haired scalps. We left the bodies where they lay.

As we trotted back to our starting place we heard the sound of heavy gunfire. "Sure as hell," Turtle opined, "the rest o' them'ere Bannocks must'a heard us shootin' an' reckoned it war their own boys awready shootin' down on us from behind. They prob'ly took it as a sign it war time fer the rest of 'em to hit us from in front."

"Carson'll know what to do," Micah said confidently. "They won't catch him nappin'."

We made our way to the cliffside with all possible haste. Sure enough, looking down from the rim, the camp was boiling with action, men—and women, too—climbing onto the barricade, crouching behind logs for protection, taking aim and firing, before they stepped down to reload, immediately replaced by others waiting their turn.

The plain in front of the barrier was a scene of carnage, littered with dead horses and others writhing in pain, attempting to drag themselves away from the bloodbath, warriors sprawled grotesquely in death or trying to crawl to safety before gunfire arrested their retreat and left them still and unmoving. Bannocks still a-horseback were greatly diminished in number but several still charged as close to the barrier as they dared, firing wildly and loosing arrows at random before they wheeled their mounts and dashed to safety, vaulting over dead horses and trampling the bodies of their lifeless comrades as they fled. Before we were halfway down the cliff face, the gunfire lessened to a few scattered reports, then ceased completely. Half a dozen men remained on the barricade, but most of our people gathered behind it, some of them pointing up at us now, waving a welcome.

Once on the ground, I hastened to see to my loved ones, first to Iris and Ben. She was wide-eyed with excitement but she and Sean were safe in their hidey-hole in the crick bottom, their tiny charges fast asleep, then to Kathleen, her face begrimed with greasy gunsmoke but unscathed, brimming with bloodlust but slowly returning to normal. We embraced, unmindful of others. I kissed her soundly, long and lingering, relieved that this time Bannocks had failed to harm my woman. When at last I turned her loose, she clung to my neck and murmured, "You can be proud, Tempo. I kill two more, I tink." Whereupon I kissed her again.

When Cat trotted off to see to the children, I hunted up Carson to report on our experience atop the hogback, if the others hadn't already done so. I found Kit atop the barrier, its outer surface studded with arrows. It had been reinforced with several big logs since our departure up the hill. His gaze was fixed on the cluster of Bannocks on the prairie, studying them through his little brass spyglass. There appeared to be no more than a dozen horsemen gathered out there. They showed no disposition to resume the attack.

Little Mountain and Half-horse moved amongst the wounded horses, putting those too badly injured out of their misery, leading the few that might be saved inside the fort so that Zeetlah might treat them, administering the *coup de grâce* to the few surviving Bannocks.

At last Carson collapsed his glass and shoved it into his belt-poke, turned to me, and commented bitterly, "'Pears the greedy bastards've got their fill. They be mighty slow l'arners. That's a gawddamn fact!" He smiled then and said, "That war mighty good work yew fellers did up thar. Micah tol' me haow it went. Thankee."

There was nothing I knew to add to what Micah had likely already reported. I asked, "Anybody killed?"

"Nope," he replied with a broad grin. "A few nicks an' scrapes, mostly splinters an' chips flyin' off o' logs an' them big rocks. Nothin' serious. We kep' 'em purty busy out front so's they hadn't hardly no time fer aimin'. Most o' what they tried to throw at us went plumb wild."

He clambered to the ground. I followed, pleased to hear that our people had come through it all with little damage. We parted and I hustled off to join Kathleen and the children. On the way, I stopped with our Frenchy campkeepers. They had gathered driftwood from the crick bottom and were already preparing what appeared to be a stew in a couple of copper kettles suspended over a cookfire.

L'Archévêque had a bloody rag tied around his head, crouching beside the fire, intent on his chore, his musket still slung across his back.

"*Holà!* Jean-Luc!" I greeted him. "*Qu'est-ce que c'est ça, ta blessure sur la tête?* How'd you get that wound?"

He blushed with pride and replied, "*C'est rien!   Eet ees no grande affaire!* I fight *les Indiens*, like ze ozzers!" Always generous, he added, "So deed Yves," nodding towards Dureau, his fellow campkeeper. I complimented them both for their pluck and proceeded on my way.

Cat was spreading blankets for the children in the hollow, along with Molly, who was doing likewise. Paddy was perched on the edge, smoking and dandling young Sean on his lap, smiling proudly whilst he listened to his still-agitated son chattering about the afternoon's events. Iris came running when she spied me, clasping me around my knees and dragging me to a sitting-place. She was still excited, prattling her concern for Cat and me whilst the shooting was going on. Naturally I praised her profusely for protecting her little brother and Brass Turtle's boy, whilst I dug into my poke for a peppermint stick as a reward for her efforts. She broke it in half to share with Sean.

Whilst I smoked with Paddy, letting the afternoon's excitement drain away, Carson came by and announced, "Cain't be sure, natcherly, but it 'pears them'ere Bannocks're pullin' stakes, givin' it up as a bad job. Jist the same, it's best we sit tight fer a spell an' stay tonight whar we be, keepin' watch 'til mawnin', 'fore we git on the way."

Dusk was settling rapidly when we joined the others at the cookfire for a cup of stew, before retiring to our robes in the hollow for some welcome rest. At first I started at every sound, the crack of a twig underfoot, a stone dislodged from the crickbank, but Tuttle had to shake me out of a sound slumber when it came time to join him for our two-hour stint on the barricade.

We relieved Brass Turtle and Tolliver, who reported that their sentry-go had been uneventful. "Reckon them'ere *bandido* sumbitches got theirse'fs a bellyful of our partic'lar style o' horspitality! Mebbe naow they be willin' to leave us be!" was Anse's sour comment.

A gibbous moon cast an eerie glow over the recent battlefield. Dead bodies and horse carcasses still littered the prairie. Tall grass fluttered in the chill autumn breeze where it hadn't been churned up by charging horsemen.

Acorn and Stone Bird, our Iroquois comrades, occupied the far end of the barrier. Now and again we could hear them conversing in low tones in their own tongue, not offering to include Tuttle and me in their palaver, which we minded not at all. We were used to it. We had been together for a dozen years, but our Iroquois, unlike the Delawares, remained mostly aloof from the whites in our bunch. They likely understood English as well as any of us, but they mostly used Brass Turtle or Little Mountain to interpret for them.

Tuttle and I exchanged thoughts on that topic but came no closer to understanding it than we had in the past. "An' them two Eeriequahs ain't likely to git no fonder of yew pers'nally, neither, arter ye went an' taught their wimmenfolk ther use o' shootin' irons. I hear tell them'ere wimmen, Sally an' Mary both, done theirse'fs right proud today, taking their turn agin them Bannock bastards, standin' pat an' throwin' lead with ther best of 'em. Don't know if'n they hit nothin', but thar ain't hardly never no way o' knowin' thet in a fracas like thet'n."

"They were sayin', too, around the fire tonight," I put in, "that Pretty Horse's Nettaqueathy woman wasn't the least bit bashful today, climbin' up atop the fort, like they say she did more'n once, an' takin' careful aim on a

Bannock before somebody'd pull her down. I sure-as-hell never taught her that! She must'a brought that kind o' gumption along with her from the Crows. Good for her!"

I had heard favorable reports, as well, on the steadfast conduct of Molly and Brass Turtle's Shoshone wife Tallymesko in the afternoon's doin's and Carson had gone out of his way to compliment me on Cat's warlike behavior, for which I denied all responsibility, insisting that it was all her own doing.

Our two-hour stretch on the barricade passed without incident. It had been a long, tiring day and we welcomed the arrival of Finn and Paddy to relieve us. Half-horse and Little Mountain greeted us in low tones as we climbed down from our sentry perch. "'Pears ye won't be gittin' no en-joys up thar t'night, Mountain," Tuttle informed the big fellow. "Reckon ye kilt off ther most of 'em awready. What's left turned tail an' run off."

The big Delaware yawned mightily and replied, "Don't mind a-tall, Tuttle. I had enough fun fer one day." If they engaged in further banter, I didn't hear it. Sleeprobes and Cat's warm embrace waiting there had a powerful appeal.

∾   ∾   ∾

Hot coffee and cold meat shortly after daybreak were followed up by a scavenging chore on the battlefield for some of us. Others prepared the pack animals for our journey. Naturally we retrieved all the gunpowder and galena from the fallen Bannocks, along with their muskets. If Micah pronounced a gun to be in decent condition, we kept it for future trading. Guns beyond reasonable repair were smashed against the log fort. A valuable find was two percussion rifles in good condition, with all their fixin's, amongst the lot, doubtless trophies taken from trappers, victims of Bannock predators.

By early forenoon we were on our way, heading across the prairie towards the purple hills we had spied the day before, squinting into the bright autumn sunshine gleaming over the hilltops. Suddenly Half-horse let out a joyful whoop when he caught sight of four riderless Indian ponies, still carrying hair-pad saddles, loping to catch up with our loose horses and mules trailing the column. Wild or tame, horses are social critters, happiest in a herd, needful of the company of their kind. These were evidently runaways from the day before whose riders had perished in our gunfire. Half-horse didn't mess with them. He simply let them mingle with our own animals as we proceeded eastwards.

"I reckon thar be better ways o' gittin' a-holt o' extry guns an' hosses than fightin' fer 'em, like we been doin'," Kit observed wryly, "but leastaways we be showin' a mite o' profit fer all the trouble them sumbitches put us to."

At the nooning halt, Half-horse moved casually amongst his grazing charges, crooning a reassuring sing-song, inspecting the equine recruits. Two of them had shallow bullet wounds, which Zeetlah treated, digging out lead balls whilst Half-horse struggled to hold the frightened critters still, murmuring soothing syllables, slathering the gashes with healing ointment. As soon as they were turned loose, both ponies returned to their grazing, apparently forgetful of their recent ordeal.

Before day's end, two more Bannock ponies joined our cavalcade, both unscathed and eager for the society of their brethren. Besides the possible profit those horses might represent, their joining up with us rather than returning to their home village told us that our assailants had likely been a renegade band roaming far from their home grounds.

We kept our eyes peeled for buffalo as we made our way across the prairie, but nothing stirred on the grassy expanse. In late afternoon we arrived at the range of low hills that bordered the plain. Carson called a halt nigh a sizeable crick that flowed from a shady, tree-lined canyon. "Don'tcha be frettin' fer buffler," he counseled us. "Thar'll be shaggies aplenty purty soon, as I recollect, the closer we git to whar we're goin'. Right naow, wapiti'll do jist fine."

Which was a not-so-subtle hint that some of us should stir ourselves and harvest a couple-three young cows from the surrounding benches. Micah and I, leading a packmule, headed up the narrow side-canyon, our horses carefully picking their way along skinny deer trails and sloshing upstream through the rocky crick bottom when steep paths became too difficult for horses. We hadn't traveled more than a mile when Micah reined up and pointed ahead, barely breathing the words, "White-arses!" his teeth flashing in a broad grin. Sure enough, four young elk cows attended by a hoary old duenna were contentedly cropping grass in a shady glade not thirty yards distant, their creamy hindquarters gleaming in the leafy gloom. My rifle was already at my shoulder when my *grulla* horse Crane emitted a low nicker, which was all it took to make the old cow throw up her head and squeal an alarm, but too late. Micah and I fired only a split-second apart and two fat cows tottered and crumpled whilst their companions scampered into the willows.

Our packmule was having trouble enough finding his footing on the rocky trail down the canyon, burdened as he was by a plenitude of hams and backstraps, shoulders, meaty ribs, tongues, and tender livers swinging in the panniers on his packsaddle, when Micah, riding in the lead, checked his horse and silently pointed upwards to a rocky crag. A curly-horn ewe stood far above in plain view, surveying the countryside. Still mounted, in a single motion, he swung up his rifle and, scarcely taking aim, squeezed off his shot.

The sheep faltered, took half a step forward, then pitched headlong off the crag and into the crick, twenty yards from where we stood.

"I was hopin' she'd do like that," Micah said, a pleased smile on his handsome features. "It's been a long day and I surely din't wish to be climbin' 'way up there after her."

I suspected he was engaging in some sly bragging on his marksmanship. Instead of complimenting him, I demanded, "And how d'ye propose we get that'n back to camp? The mule's overloaded as it is!"

The solution was not what I would have wished. After we butchered out the ewe, we divided the meat into two bundles and loaded them onto our saddles, which required that we hike back to camp afoot, sloshing through the crick most of the way. Tender, tasty curly-horn mutton almost made up for it, howsomever, and I claimed the hide for Kathleen for boot.

-ooo-

The trail wound through low hills, now and again forcing us to backtrack when we followed a blind canyon only to come up against a high, impassable wall, but for the most part Carson's judgment was sound, even when he was mostly guessing which route would get us through. He found water and graze for overnight camps and sometimes even for the nooning halts. Late on the third day, Turtle and Anse came loping back to the column from their scouting chore, broad smiles wreathing their features. "We fine'ly be shut o' thi'shere gawddamn rocky riddle !" Tolliver shouted. "Thar's open country jist ahead!"

"And a galore o' good grass! Likely buffler, too!" Turtle added. "Jist a couple more miles!"

I glanced at Kit and saw that he was stifling a satisfied grin. Nobody was nigh the two of us, so I asked, "Was this where ye reckoned we'd come out?"

His grin broadened. "Sorta. The only other time I come through hyar I war by muh lonesome, so I mostly stuck to the high ground. Thi'shere time, movin' wimmenfolk an' kids and a heap o' plunder on travois drags an' all, took a heap o' guessin', but we made it 'thout losin' nuthin' ner nobody an' that's what counts."

An hour later we emerged onto a vast, rolling tableland covered with yellow buffalo grass, dotted here and there by copses of willows and sweet cottonwoods growing alongside watercourses. Rugged mountains thrust up on three sides of the seemingly endless prairie, their snow-covered upper reaches glistening in dazzling mid-afternoon sunshine, the lower slopes girdled by dense pine forests fingering into the golden plain below.

Approving murmurs rippled from all sides. Even our stolid Iroquois allowed themselves thin smiles. "Wal, thar she be, whar we been headin' fer, this long while," Kit declared in a loud voice, a broad smile splitting his whiskery cheeks. When it sank in that this had been our destination all along, a ragged chorus of whoops and cheers greeted Carson's announcement. "Fer naow, we'd best git to makin' camp nigh one o' them'ere cricks." He waved in the direction of the nearest streams. "An' fer them as has an appertite fer buffler, I wou'n't be a tall bit surrounded if'n ye find some out yonder." He swung his arm in the vague direction of the far mountains.

Ordinarily quiet and unassuming, Kit Carson was enjoying his success at bringing us through unscathed. Nobody begrudged him his moment of glory, which was, howsomever, brief. The gang stampeded to the closest crick bank to set up camp, mouths already watering for buffalo.

I stripped off my saddle and bridle from the horse I had been riding that day and caught up my *grulla* horse Crane. Coffee was still limping from a stone bruise he had acquired a day or two before and I had never put Crane to the exacting test of running buffalo. I was getting increasingly fond of my mouse grey *Californio* gelding, but I still needed to know if he possessed the courage, speed, agility, and judgment that sets a buffalo runner miles apart from workaday horses.

My father and Finn, together with our campkeepers leading packmules, were already waiting when I rode up. We were soon joined by Turtle, Little Mountain, Cesár, and Kit, who announced, "Naow that we got hyar, I'm quittin' the ramroddin' chore. Never liked it in the fust place. You're on yer own agin, like allus."

Even so, Carson led us out of camp and chose our direction over the immense grassy mesa. It was rolling terrain, sliced with swales deep enough to conceal a double score or more of buffalo until a hunter was nearly on top of them.

Which was exactly what happened. Suddenly, as we reached the crest of a low rise, the ground opened up below us and a double dozen fat cows, the harems of a couple herd bulls, grazing at the bottom alongside a measly trickle of a stream, came into view. An old cow threw up her head and squealed an alarm, which set the whole shootin'-match into a mad scramble up the far side of the gully.

We leapt into wild pursuit, skidding down the bank, tails dragging, bounding over the puny crick, scrambling up the far slope, stretched nearly flat, moccasins combing the slippery grass, horses desperately scrabbling for purchase on the crumbling soil until we reached the top. Our quarry had increased its lead considerably whilst we negotiated the gully. Crane strained at the bit. I turned him loose, barely touching him with the spur until he closed the distance to the laggards, then reining him to the left side of a fat cow in the midst of the bunch, checking him slightly to match his speed with hers, reining him outward to avoid her swinging horns.

I jerked a pistol from its saddle holster, took careful aim behind her foreleg, and squeezed the trigger. I heard only the disappointing pop of the percussion cap, no resounding pistol shot. I could have sworn that Crane reproached me with a disgusted grunt as we veered off in the wake of a different cow.

I jammed the useless pistol into its holster and yanked its mate loose, once again closing on our prey, coming up smoothly on her left, slowing behind and just out of reach of the horns, matching her pace precisely, keeping me in position for my shot. This time I felt the reassuring jolt of the pistol bucking in my hand and heard its blast over the hoofbeats of horse and cow. She took no more than a couple-three faltering strides before she crumpled to her knees, shaggy chin ploughing a furrow in the grass, coughing gouts of blood, wild eyes going glassy, then dull, before we whirled away in pursuit of another cow. I holstered the pistol and unslung my rifle, making sure that a percussion cap was firmly fixed on the nipple.

As we overtook a second fat cow, I was much less elated about providing meat for the camp than discovering that my *Californio* horse was a natural buffalo runner. I'm sure it was the latter.

Again, Crane kept me in position to take my shot whilst avoiding the wildly swinging horns of the terrified cow. He matched her speed, adapting smoothly to the change from near side to off, demanded by the use of a rifle instead of a pistol. The rifle butt was tucked firmly to my shoulder, reins dangling loose from my left hand, aiming just behind the right foreleg, when suddenly we spilled into another swale in the prairie, hidden until then. My feet jammed forward in the stirrups prevented my tumbling over Crane's head as we skidded down the slope. The buffalo scrambled to stay upright, tail dragging, hooves churning, huge head bobbing, snorting and blowing snot onto my horse and me. Crane fought to keep his distance from her horns, sliding on his tail in the slick grass, doing his best to keep me in place for my shot, which I took mostly for his sake. Never have I been more surprised than when the cow stumbled, knees collapsing, head sagging, horns ploughing up sod, then cartwheeling in a massive arc before thudding to earth, where she lay coughing out her life onto the bloody grass.

I rolled off the saddle. Crane struggled to stand, took a step towards me as I lay in the grass, then reached out and nuzzled me with his velvety nose, as if to make sure that I was all right.

"How'd'ja manage to teach your critter how to do that, Temple?" a familiar voice called from above. I sat up and beheld Brass Turtle and my father lounging in their saddles at the top of the slope.

"Did you see that?" I demanded. "Did you see what this fool horse just did?"

"Yep," Turtle replied, shaking his head in wonderment. "I saw the whole damn thing and so did your pa, an' we still don't b'lieve it!"

I reckoned I had enough excitement for one day. I headed back to camp, leaving the butchering to the others, stopping only long enough at one of the earlier kills to sample a couple slices of still-steaming liver. Crane, carefully avoiding treading on his trailing reins, browsed on buffalo grass. I wished I possessed a bait of oats to reward him for his remarkable feat, but such luxuries don't exist in the mountains.

Cat had already set up the lodge and stowed our belongings inside, built a fire outdoors with driftwood the children had gathered along the crick bed, and brewed a kettle of strong coffee to welcome me back from the hunt.

Naturally there was general rejoicing when the hunters returned leading packmules staggering under their burden of choice cuts of meat from half a dozen fat buffalo cows. They dumped the bulging panniers in the center of camp and Half-horse and the *Californios* jumped to aid our campkeepers in scooping out a long, shallow trench and filled it with driftwood. Half a dozen men knelt to strike flint and steel into tinder to get a cookfire blazing, whilst others spitted different cuts of buffalo meat on steel ramrods. As soon as the fire burned down sufficiently, the meat was suspended over glowing embers, dripping fat onto hissing coals, bathing the camp in the aroma of roasting meat, pure torture for impatient appetites, until they could wait no longer and commenced slicing off half-raw slivers of juicy buffalo flesh.

Meanwhile, luscious tongues bubbled in copper kettles and coils of plump boudins sizzled and browned in crackling bear fat in sheet-iron spider skillets.

When at last even the most greedy appetite was satisfied, leastaways for a spell, we gathered by the fire to smoke and yarn and congratulate ourselves on our decision to follow Carson to this paradise. "How'd'ja come to find thi'shere place, Kit?" Tuttle queried. "If'n thar's a galore o' beaver hyarabaouts, like ye say, it's as close to heaven as I'll ever git."

"Wal, it warn't percisely by accident," Carson answered. "It begun down south o' hyar in Touse, whar Bill Williams—ol' Solitaire like they call 'im — allus shows up early ever' winter, packin' a galore o' plews, gittin' a head start on his whorin' an' drammin' whilst the rest of us are still bustin' our arse trappin' far an' wide an' countin' ourse'fs lucky to git half as many plews as he allus does.

"Natcherly ol' Bill warn't abaout to be tellin' nobody whar he got his trappin' done. They don't call 'im Ol' Solitaire fer nuthin'.

"So arter a spell, I reckoned it war wuth tryin' to foller 'im to whar he war allus gittin' all o' them plews. I knew it wou'n't be easy—nuthin' wuthwhile ever is—an' it shore-as-hell warn't! Soon's he pulls out o' Touse, ol' Bill gits nervous as a whore in church, peekin' over his shoulder, sometimes draggin' a big ol' leafy branch a'hind his critters, wipin' out their tracks, an' usin' other suchlike tricks. But I war able to stick with 'im an' stay out o' sight 'til we come in on the south end o' thi'shere mesa, passin' through a couple *cañons* ye'd swear war plumb blind 'til ye spy the li'l crack in the wall that's jist big enough to let critters through.

"That's how I come to find ol' Bill's hidey-hole, his pers'nal beaver cache. I ain't never trapped it myownse'f, but I seen a galore o' sign when I war hyar. Fur as I know, ain't no other trappers 'sides Bill an' me ever been in hyar. Likely Injuns know about it, but that don't make no nevermind. Most o' them, down thisaway, don't do no trappin'."

Autumn chill and falling night, after a long eventful day, drove me to my robes and the connubial warmth that awaited there—after just one more visit to the cookfire and one more slice of crispy fat buffalo hump, maybe two.

❦ ❦ ❦

We awakened to a light overnight snowfall, advising us that it was high time to commence trapping in earnest. Half-horse and the *Californios* had set traps in the crick the day before and were rewarded with four plews of much-improved depth and density over any we had taken up 'til that time.

After breaking our fast we met in council and decided to scout a portion of the mesa and approaches to the surrounding mountains to discover the best place to locate our first camp to commence serious trapping. Half a dozen of us set out with Carson to investigate the foothills to the north of us. Coffee still favored his stone-bruised hoof and Crane had earned a day's rest, so I saddled a chunky bay mare I called Polly and rode to join the others.

An hour's brisk trot brought us to the lower slopes, where snow already commenced to accumulate in pine groves and narrow canyons. On the way we discovered fresh-running streams on the prairie that showed beaver sign, promising even greater possibilities for a rich harvest higher in the hills.

The farther we rode across the low hills, from one stream to another, observing a galore of ponds, dams, and lodges, the more encouraged we became at prospects of reaping a bonanza in plews, possibly greater than we had ever taken before. I should mention, howsomever, that such sanguine expectations are common amongst trappers. We prefer to forget years of disappointment and are forever hopeful that this will be the year that gets us out of debt to the Company and lines our pokes with riches. It almost never happens, but hope springs eternal, as Mister Pope tells us, and it keeps us coming back for more. Traders count on it.

We had scattered somewhat as we threaded through thick forest. I had just emerged into a grassy clearing when I heard a snuffling grunt and glimpsed a broad hairy back amidst a tangle of raspberry bushes on the far side. Before I could wheel my Polly mare and retreat, she got a noseful of grizzly stink, let out a terrified snort, and reared over backwards, throwing me to the ground. She scrambled frantically to regain her feet, then charged blindly down our backtrail, crashing through the brush, neighing in panic .

I landed on my back. My rifle, slung across my shoulders, banged my head as I fell, which did nothing helpful to let me save myself from the huge bear I could see through a red haze, shambling on all fours out of the bushes, then rising on his hocks and roaring, bloody red mouth agape, hairy arms outstretched, paws waving. I struggled to sit up, clawing at the rifle sling, fighting to bring my weapon to my shoulder, head reeling and ears ringing from the blow it had received, vision blurred, fumbling to cock the hammer although I could barely see the front sight, when a blast just above my head made me duck, followed by a second gunshot from somewhere behind me.

Old Ephraim faltered, blood gushing from his wide-open mouth, a fearsome roar drowning in a liquid gurgle, paws twitching feebly, slapping at his chest where blood was spurting. Still erect but tottering, he took a single step before he pitched headlong and lay in a quivering heap at my feet.

I slumped forward, forehead on my knees, fear and dizziness slowly draining away, before I heard my father's voice, strained with concern, asking, "You hurt, Seewauseekau?

I tried to shake my head, but a stabbing ache in my temple made me strangle out instead, "No. Don't think so."

The pain in my head lessened slowly. My vision cleared enough to let me make out Powatawa and Brass Turtle shielding me, rifles at the ready in case the grizzly should stir. At length I was able to look up into my father's face and declare, "Well, father, we have come full circle. This is the second time you have saved my life from a bear. This is where you and I began."

Powatawa, looking greatly relieved, chuckled and replied with a roguish grin, "No, Seewauseekau, my son. You and I began many years before that time. Before you can remember anything."

I laughed at his ribald jest in spite of myself, which set my head aching again, but I didn't mind. It was good to be able to feel anything at all, even a headache. Turtle, never slow to appreciate a naughty quip, was laughing, too.

The gunshots had drawn the others, traveling as rapidly through the thick forest as the overgrown game trails permitted. Tuttle arrived leading my mare, the worried look fading from his whiskery features when he saw that I was neither dead nor seriously injured. "Gawddammit, Temple!" he brayed. "I still cain't trust ye goin' out by yer lonesome, 'thout me wetnursin' ye. Haow many times do I gotta tell ye, don'tcha never be playin' wi' no gawddamn grizzle b'ars!"

Naturally all that fresh bear meat was too valuable to waste. Carson, Tuttle, and Micah made short work of the butchering, exclaiming the while over his youth and condition. "Don't reckon this'n be much more'n five-six years," Kit commented. "Young enough to be right tender an' tasty."

"Yep," Micah added, "an' just about ready fer hivernatin', too! Lookee all that purty fat! Must be nigh a foot deep!"

"Shore as hell," Tuttle crowed, "ther Frenchies'll be kissin' ye, Temple, fer findin' thi'shere fat feller fer 'em!"

When the chore was finished, they slung the meat and the hide, wrapped in scraps of sail canvas, from high branches to keep it out of reach of forest critters. "It'll keep safe thar 'til t'morry," Carson said, "when we git back up thisaway fer settin' up camp an' git to trappin'. Naow, let's git Temple on back, whar his woman kin be lookin' arter him."

Tuttle offered to swap horses with me for the ride back, but I refused. It was hard to tell, but the little mare looked downright shamefaced when I picked up her reins and prepared to mount.

❧   ❧   ❧

Back in camp, Cat and Iris came running when the riders up front spread the word about my mishap. Iris led the mare away and Cat fussed over me, trying to lead me off to our lodge so she could attend to my bruise, but I insisted on joining the others at the cookfire. The blow to my head failed to impair my appetite overmuch, although I settled for only three helpings of crispy hump ribs from yesterday's feast and hardly more than a yard of crunchy boudins smoking hot from the skillet.

Just as I reached for my pipe and tobacco pouch, Cat swooped and dragged me to the lodge, where Zeetlah crouched over our little fire, brewing one or more of his medicinal concoctions. At Cat's insistence, I gagged down a cupful of Zeetlah's bitter-tasting tea before she led me to our robes, pulled off my moccasins and tugged off my leggin's, then placed a warm, moist, sweet-smelling poultice wrapped in soft deerskin against my bruised head and neck. Zeetlah's brew, combined with the soothing warmth and fragrance of the poultice and Kathleen's soft crooning as she spooned against my back beneath our robes, carried me off to a roseate land where nothing hurt and everything was beautiful.

❧   ❧   ❧

I awakened at dawn to the aroma of boiling coffee and Ben's insistent chirping, demanding that all else must cease in the universe until his fast was broken. When Iris, rosy-cheeked, magical eyes sparkling, her breath blowing white from outdoor chill, burst through the doorway, snow glistening on her long dark hair and the blanket draped over her shoulders. When she saw that I was awake, she shed the blanket and streaked to my side, throwing her arms around my neck, showering me with kisses, and shrieking, "Oh, Papa, are you hurt still? Did Zeetlah not mend you?" and other such sympathetic nonsense. I assured her that I was fit as Tolliver's fiddle and then I realized that I was indeed as fit as ever I had been.

I reached up and patted, then gently pounded, my jaw and ear and temple and felt nothing more than usual. Cat and our scoundrelly old

Delaware medico had magically wafted away the throbbing pain and ache of the day before.

I bounded from my robes and pounced upon Kathleen huddled over the little fire, stirring and blowing the coals into flame, swept her into my arms, and kissed her soundly. Startled at first, she burst into laughter and returned my kiss most ardently, hugging me to her firm bosom, and murmuring loving Salish nonsense into my newly-restored ear, then gently stroked my face and neck and marveled aloud that yesterday's black bruise had almost entirely disappeared.

Soon after I returned from my morning chore, my nose still in my first cup of steaming coffee, Tuttle came scratching on the lodge cover, allowed that yes, he'd be much obliged for a cup, thankee, and announced that the camp was itching to get a move on up to the new campground.

Fortunately, not much beyond sleep robes and essentials had been unpacked at that temporary camp, so, in less than an hour's time we were making travois tracks in the light snowfall across the prairie, heading for the tree-covered foothills sloping up the mountain towering high above. Ice was commencing to crust along the banks of shallow cricks we passed and crossed on our way, which promised a worthwhile harvest of plews. It was time to get to the trapping chore that had brought us here.

Occupied as I had been with Old Ephraim the day before, I hadn't seen the campground the others had chosen. It was a good one, located betwixt fresh-running cricks on either side of a broad, level, grassy meadow, both of them flanked with willows and stands of sweet cottonwoods for horse feed when deep winter snow would cover the grass. A dense forest of pines and firs on the upper side would provide ample deadwood for fires as well as a welcome break against winter wind sweeping off the mountains.

We hobbled the critters and turned them out to graze. Coffee was no longer favoring his bruised foot, but I left my saddle on Crane and led him to the campground, where Cat and Iris, along with the other women and older children, busied themselves stripping off packsaddles, heaping up plunder, and erecting lodges, whilst the bachelors were occupied with setting up their bowers and tents. We married men were free to commence trapping. Which we did without delay. Brass Turtle, Paddy McBride, and I rode out of camp with a smile on our lips and trapsacks clanging whilst our bachelor brethren doubtless cursed and gnashed and possibly reconsidered their single state.

Our major conundrum was where to commence trapping first. A trapper's dream of desirable watersheds and ponds surrounded us. Several sizeable cricks abounding with beaver sign ran off the mountainside within a quarter-mile of camp. There was no need to scout farther afield. We took turns choosing our territory, letting Paddy go first whilst Turtle and I waited a-horseback, keeping watch, a long-standing practice.

"Ain't seen no Injun sign hyarabaouts since we got hyar," Turtle observed, "but yer run-in yestiddy with that'ere grizzle b'ar's more'n enough to make a feller pay some mind."

The sharp chill of frigid water soaking through my moccasins when I stepped into the pond to place my trap and plant the float-stick behind it was a welcome greeting from a friend long unmet. And the harsh tang of foul-smelling castoreum assaulting my nostrils when I first pulled the stopper from my dope flask to anoint the little come-hither bait-stick brought tears to my eyes that could have been sentimental. They weren't, though. The stuff stinks to high heaven.

Just the same, it was good to be back, practicing the only the trade I know or wish to know.

Crane nickered uncertainly and took half a step away when I attempted to mount, recoiling from the unfamiliar, disagreeable odor of castoreum, but I reassured him by blowing my breath into his nostrils, re-establishing my identity. "If you aim to be a trapper's horse," I told him, "ye'd best get used to it. If Cat can put up with me, you can, too."

❧   ❧   ❧

Cat's quick intake of breath and a fleeting frown greeted my entrance to the lodge, but she hastily recovered and declared with a smile and a throaty chuckle, "So ze trappin' has commence. I almos' forgot. Whew!"

After she dipped out a steaming cup of strong tea for me, she removed my sodden moccasins and stripped off my antelope leather leggin's whilst I lay back on our sleeprobes, happily discovering that she and Iris had greatly improved its comfort with a deep bed of slender pine boughs underneath. Dry winter moccasins and thick Witney blanket leggin's restored my attire and assured my comfort.

Tuttle, Micah, and my father were still readying their bower when I strolled by, heaping chunks of sod around the bottom against the brisk chilly breeze sweeping off the mountain. "How come you're still at it?" I asked.

"Aw, hell," Tuttle replied with a rueful grin, "when we saw y'all ridin' out fer trappin', soon as we got hyar, most o' ther rest of us said ther hell with it an' went off trappin', too. Naow we got to be bustin' our hump ketchin' up afore it gits dark."

Further palaver was stalled by the Frenchies banging on kettles, announcing suppertime, the last of our buffalo bonanza but still more than enough to satisfy a score and more of hardworking appetites.

Next morning's harvest more than made up for the extra labor our bachelors had put in the day before. The camp resounded with laughter and triumphant shouts as our people returned from running their traplines, four or five and sometimes the full half-dozen bloody plews swinging from their saddles. The nearby ponds and streams teemed with inhospitable beavers ready and more than willing to defend their personal fiefs from incursions signaled by the unfamiliar odor of our castoreum dope.

Cat and Iris happily joined me in fleshing the five deep-furred plews I harvested that first morning, then lacing the edges around willow hoops and snugging the well-scraped hides flat and tight to cure in the high dry mountain air. Working together was rather like a ritual, returning to our chosen trade after the long summer layoff—even longer for Iris and Cat— often accompanied by giggles and good-natured laughter prompted by a jest over someone's minor blunder.

Hunting was pretty much suspended during those frenzied early weeks of the plew harvest, except for an occasional target of opportunity, when one of us happened upon a deer or stray wapiti on the way back from running his trapline. We ate mostly fat beaver in stews flavored with wild onions and whatever herbs and tubers our women gathered in the woods and meadows. One time, Tally and Kathleen returned to camp dragging a gutted-out cow wapiti they had shot whilst they were gleaning for mushrooms in the woods. The Iroquois husbands frowned at this incursion into the precincts of traditional male pursuits, but they weren't at all behindhand at stuffing themselves with fresh elk meat at suppertime.

The women did most of the cooking. Our campkeepers were busy from dawn to dark, gathering deadfall, repairing gear, helping trappers fleshing and curing plews, then darting off to the cookfires to tend kettles of bear fat they rendered into precious oil for cooking and keeping moccasins and other leather goods pliable and reasonably waterproof.

The camp was soon cluttered with heaps of cured plews stacked against every available upright. The surrounding trees were festooned with drying plews on willow hoops swaying in the breeze from every reachable limb. Naturally such a successful harvest made it necessary to travel farther out each day to discover fresh trapping, until it became plain that we needed to move camp.

"Best we git to movin' on," Carson observed one evening after supper. "Graze be gittin' measly hyarabaouts an' thar's a heap more good country we ain't touched yet. Mought as well leave some beavers fer seed, 'thout takin' the last one."

"Aye," said Finn McCool, "'tis fast becomin' a hard chore to be findin' a fresh pond without stumblin' upon one of our own. I'm doin' more ridin' than trappin'.'"

So it was decided that we would move eastward after scouting that country for desirable beaver territory and a suitable campground. Naturally beaver must come first. Half a dozen men offered to accompany Kit, but I chose to remain behind and devote some time to hunting buffalo and catching up on my journal. There was plenty to do around camp, chief amongst which was digging a safe and secure cache for our plews.

Tuttle, too, chose to stay in camp, which saddled him with the chore of selecting a suitable spot for the cache and directing its construction, a skill in which he excelled.

The promise of fat hump ribs roasting over coals was too tempting to be put off any longer. Other chores had to wait. Four of us, together with Jean-Luc to tend the critters, set off to harvest supper from the snowy prairie. This time we had no intention of running buffalo. Our mission was serious. Meat was more important than fun. Besides, slippery footing on wet grass greatly increases the peril of what is always a hazardous sport.

The deep swales that sliced the grassland now worked to our advantage. Small bunches of buffalo gathered in those coulees, avoiding the wind, and grazing mostly out of sight, which also hampered their spying our approach or catching our scent. After several unsuccessful attempts to discover a likely bunch, Micah, huddled inside his capote, rifle slung, traveling afoot and bent nearly double as he trotted nigh the lip of a gulch, suddenly dropped to his belly, crawfished backwards until he was safely out of sight of our quarry, and beckoned us to join him. Which we did without delay, leaving our mounts with Jean-Luc and scuttling through frosty buffalo grass on hands and knees, then slithering the last few yards on our bellies.

Nobody spoke, although the brisk breeze in our faces would likely have carried our voices off. There was no need. Down below, no more than twenty yards distant, a massive bull grazed amidst his harem, more than a dozen fat cows. I blinked away tears summoned by the cold, drew a careful bead on a husky young'un, and nodded my readiness. The crash of four rifles firing almost at once rent the air around us, despite the keen wind that moaned overhead. Three cows crumpled to their knees and fell after only a step or two.

A fourth scrambled frantically up the far side of the gully in the wake of her companions, hoofs churning through the snow, until she faltered and slowed, then pitched onto her chin, bright crimson gouts staining the frozen ground before her.

Fresh liver still smoking in the chill wintry air, sharp and pungent with a sprinkle of gall, was our first reward, before we plunged into the butchering chore, carving out meaty hump ribs, generous slabs of rich backstrap and loin, and other prime cuts of tender flesh, preserving yards of boudins that provide much of a trapper's diet of greens, folding it all into the hide, and heaving the lot into canvas panniers slung onto the packmules for our return to camp. Everybody was in high good spirits, congratulating ourselves on our success, anticipating the welcome that awaited us in camp and the forthcoming feast.

"Naow, Temple, ain'tcha glad ye put thet'ere scribblin' book o' your'n aside fer today an' come huntin' 'longside us?" Tuttle demanded, a good-natured smile wreathing his blood-smeared jowls.

I allowed that whatever I might scribble in my ledger would surely keep until another day and harvesting four fat cows made the time well-spent.

"Winter's soon comin' on," McCool observed. "There'll be more'n time enough to be after tendin' to your readin' an' writin' and keepin a journal when the brooks an' meres are frozen tight as a landlord's purse. For now, trappin' an' fillin' our bellies takes precedence."

"Speakin' 'o which," Micah reminded us, "it's high time we quit jawin' an' git to chawin' on all this good meat!"

Which we did.

∾ ∾ ∾

There was no telling how long Carson's scouting crew would be absent on their quest for new trapping grounds. They might return at any time, eager to move on and profit from what was left of the fall harvest. Next day, Tuttle enlisted us in searching for a suitable location for a cache large enough to contain the windfall harvest of plews. Many considerations applied to make it suitable. Not too close to the present camp, but not too far to transport bulky cargo. Nearby natural landmarks to identify its location. High and dry and easily concealed, preferably with a running stream nearby in which to dispose of dirt hollowed out from the cache. Firm, dry soil, with few rocks, for easy digging. Abundant willows nearby for lining the walls and flooring the cache against moisture.

When at last Tuttle was satisfied, we went to work, first carefully removing and preserving enough sod for a bottleneck entrance two feet below ground. Then one man expanded the hole until the underground chamber was large enough to permit two, three, then four men to work together, hollowing out the walls and passing soil out through the narrow entrance at the top before discarding it over a nearby bluff and into a fresh-running stream. When the chamber was of sufficient size to hold all of our plews, we lined the walls and floor with a lattice of willow withes to prevent seepage. We worked in shifts, democratically, giving every man in camp a chance to help. Nobody was neglected. Many hands make light work. The chore was completed early the second day.

Every trapper owns a simple but distinctive mark that identifies his personal plunder, especially his plews, each of which he brands with a smoldering stick from a cookfire. My own brand is the top of a half-circle surmounted by a cross, a rude representation of a temple. No matter how casual a trapper might be about doing his chores, you may be sure that he will be downright religious about marking his plews.

When the cache was completely filled, we covered its contents with scraps of canvas and elk hide, packed the two-foot-wide tunnel entrance solidly with dirt, then carefully replaced the square of sod in its original location. Running livestock over the excavation, scattering snow, and wishing for more snow completed the chore.

~ ~ ~

The scouting party returned after four days, tramping through half a foot of new-fallen snow, red-faced in the chill breeze, and hooting in high spirits over the success of their search. Several of them flaunted fresh plews draped across their saddle bows and cantles, proof of the rich promise of the new-found trapping patch. "It's mebbe even better'n this'n war," Brass Turtle announced, "crawlin' with beavers, thicker'n fleas on a camp dog, ever'whar ye go! Thar's plenty fer ever'body!"

Even usually reserved Carson was enthusiastic about the new location. "It'll be a good winter camp, too," he assured us stay-at-homes. "Wood an' grass aplenty fer naow an' lots o' sweet cottonwoods fer later on. You'll see fer yerownse'fs when we git thar." Kit cautioned against delay in moving to the new digs. "Best we git a move on quittin' hyar, 'fore we git ourse'fs snowed in."

We needed no urging. The scouting party's glowing reports fired everyone's enthusiasm. The prospect of new country always captures a trapper's fancy. First thing next morning, our noisy, colorful procession snaked eastwards across the wintry landscape, hawk bells jingling on women's saddles and apishamores. Fretting, bawling, brawling, grumbling young'uns clinging precariously to travois shafts, jouncing and rattling over the uneven prairie.

Stubborn packmules trudging nose-to-tail through drifting snow, braying never-ending jeremiads. Iris and Paddy's little boy Sean coursing through the column on their horses, chirping and hallooing, now falling behind to assist Half-horse, now riding forward to join the women. Trappers huddled a-horseback in bright-hued blanket *capotes* intoning a monotonous litany of mindless good-natured curses.

"Sir John would feel perfectly at home in this company, wouldn't ye say, Temple?" McCool observed with a wry grin.

"If ye mean Falstaff's ragtag battalion, I can't disagree," I replied. "Still, handsome is as handsome does. One way or t'other, we get the chore done."

The Irishman chuckled and nodded. "Aye, we do indeed! The bloody Bannocks learnt that lesson well, I'm thinkin'!" A gust of frigid breeze made him wince and duck inside the hood of his capote. "Och!" he complained, "California's sunny clime has spoilt me totally. I'll be no good a-tall, come proper winter."

"Do ye ever think of returning there, Finn?"

"I dream of it betimes," he replied seriously, "but it'd be unwise to be arrivin' in those parts lackin' me proper medical certification. Much as I'd hate partin' with all o' ye, howsomever, if I owned me own shingle, I warrant I'd be lettin' no grass growin' beneath me feet!"

The new camp was everything the scouting party had promised and more. Wooded mountain slopes offered an apparently endless lacework of fresh-running streams teeming with beaver and the surrounding forest promised a ready supply of deer and wapiti at a time when our plew-hungry company would be willing to sacrifice time enough to go hunting instead of trapping. Until then, howsomever, beaver stew was the mainstay of our diet. Nobody complained. Every trapper was determined to amass more plews than he had ever done before and our women happified themselves by picturing the gobs of foofurraw they would acquire at next summer's rendezvous.

Only impending winter tarnished our delight with our new-found paradise. Every cold night improved and enriched the plews we were taking, but we regarded with the anxiety of money-grubbing misers the ice forming on the shores of cricks and beaver ponds. Father Frost would soon lock us out of the treasure house. The iron grip of winter would take hold of the land and trapping must cease until springtime.

At last even the greediest trappers had to grant victory to the hoary old Spirit of the North who froze the ponds and sealed the streams and granted respite to the beavers. They retreated to their dams and lodges to wait out the dark days of winter. The last few curing plews stretched on willow hoops rattled and banged on tree limbs in the north wind in noisy testimony to our reluctant surrender.

Now there was time for household chores. The bachelors pitched in to establish a large communal dwelling, digging out a substantial cellar a yard or so below ground and enclosing it within a protective berm to shield against the wind, flooring it with buffalo robes, and roofing it with a collection of elk hides and sail canvas, surrounded by half a dozen fires for warmth and cooking.

The quality of life inside our lodge improved greatly after I stowed my traps for that season. No longer were the lodgepoles festooned with my sodden blanket leggin's and soaking-wet moccasins constantly steaming overhead. And now we were able to reclaim the floor space we had devoted to fleshing and stretching plews on days when snow and biting wind had driven us indoors. Kathleen accepts without complaint her role as a trapper's wife, but the clutter and disorder of trapping chores conducted in the close quarters of the lodge does not sweeten her disposition.

With a score of idle trappers on hand, there was no shortage of meat. A plenitude of black-tail deer and wapiti roamed the lower slopes and meadows of the mountain that loomed behind the camp and big-horn sheep offered a tasty reward for any hunter willing to climb high enough to claim one for a tender prize.

Naturally none of us was willing to go for long without buffalo meat, no matter how plentiful other game might be. Snow was still scant on the prairie when eight of us rode out in search of buffalo, leading that many packmules, accompanied by both campkeepers. Our quarry was elusive that day. We had to ride several miles across the broad mesa before we came upon a band of nearly a score of cows and half-grown young bulls grazing in a deep hollow under the protection of a venerable old patriarch whom prolonged peace and tranquility had made incautious. Little Mountain, trotting ahead on foot, spied them first, dropping to his belly and wriggling back out of their sight before waving the rest of us forward to take up shooting positions.

Eight rifles going off at once creates a thunderous roar, especially if you are in the midst of it. Half a dozen cows wilted onto the snow after stumbling no more than a yard or two. Two more nearly made it to the top of the gully, belching blood onto the whiteness, before lurching onto their bearded chins and lying glassy-eyed and stiff-legged in death.

We wasted no time in getting to the butchering. Our long hike in search of our prey had carried us a considerable distance from camp and we were eager to get back before nightfall, but no man was willing to forego the hunter's first reward. Anse Tolliver cackled his triumph and plunged his lean whiskery jowls into a bloody slab of fresh liver steaming in the wintry air. The rest of us were not far behind, slicing off generous slivers and sprinkling gall, congratulating ourselves on our prowess and good fortune.

Many hands made light work. Soon the packmules were tottering under a burden of prime buffalo flesh—tongues and fat humpmeat, generous backstraps, meaty ribs and roasts, fresh boudins. When each pair of panniers was filled, Jean-Luc led the loaded mule out of the gulch and onto the prairie above, where it was hobbled and left to graze. Resting a moment, I chanced to glance up at our campkeeper. He was standing open-mouthed and trembling with fright. I followed his terrified gaze to the opposite rim of the gully and instantly shared his alarm. A score or more blanket-clad Indians, muskets resting on their knees or bows ready-nocked, sat on their horses, quietly observing us, not threatening attack, but ready to respond to whatever we might do.

Exceeding peace had made our bunch as vulnerable as the old buffalo paterfamilias had been an hour earlier. We had been too long relieved of concern over Indian attack, treating our idyllic mesa as an island of safety, in spite of years of hard experience to the contrary.

"Hold on, fellers!" Carson called out. "They caught us flat-footed! No shootin'! It's time fer talkin'! Nothin' else!"

"Hark!" Tuttle yelled. "Listen to 'im! We be fish in a bar'l if'n they commence shootin'! Hold off!" That sentiment was echoed by a couple others. Nobody offered to fight.

Carson, his rifle still slung across his back, started up the hill towards the horsemen. Brass Turtle caught my sleeve, drawing me along with him, following Carson uphill under the watchful eyes of our strangely-quiet captors.

When we reached level ground we beheld a village of sixty or more lodges coming into view across the prairie. The warriors who had us pinned down in our hidey-hole were doubtless scouts from that village on the move, alerted to our presence when we opened fire on the buffalo. "They be 'Rapahoes," Kit announced. "Which could'a been a helluva lot worse, I'm thinkin'. Hell! they might'a turned out to be Apaches or Comanches!!"

When Carson tried to engage our captors in sign-talk or with his slight acquaintance with their tongue, the leaders signed for him to be patient, the headman would be coming soon. We hadn't long to wait. A few minutes later, half a dozen horsemen riding in advance of the main column approached the spot where we stood. When they reined up in front of us, I was struck by the appearance of one of them. He was the tallest Indian I had ever seen, of middle age, handsome, well-built and muscular, strikingly well-dressed, with a natural commanding air about him. A single golden eagle feather suspended from a quilled browband brushed his broad shoulder, a sure sign, Kit muttered, of his leadership in the Dog-men warrior society.

"Yep," Kit said softly. "They be 'Rapahos fer sure an' that'n's the chief, young as he is, a Dog Society boss-man. That'ere feather says so."

The tall man rested his gaze on us for a brief spell before he left his companions, rode to the edge of the bluff, and looked down into the gully where Little Mountain and the others were continuing to butcher out the buffalo we had killed, most likely simply to soothe their nerves by keeping busy, for the Indians could be expected to claim the meat as their own. He remained there for several minutes, looking down at our people, apparently lost in thought, before he reined about, walked his horse back to the spot where we waited, and resumed his place at the forefront of his assembled sub-chiefs. His manner now appeared somewhat less stern than it had been at first, not precisely friendly but neither was it hostile. He signed the questions, Who are you? Where are you from? and What is your business here? in a single all-purpose gesture.

Carson took half a step forward and addressed his reply only to the tall chief. He stuck to sign-talk, not trusting his fragile grasp on their language, seeking to avoid misunderstandings. None of the sub-chiefs appeared to resent his choice. Carson is not a tall man. Fact is, he is considerably shorter than almost any man I have known in the mountains, but he defers to no man when it comes to his own worth and his dignity. The chief evidently accepted Kit on Carson's own evaluation of himself. We had not rehearsed what we might say to our challengers, but Kit never hesitated in greeting the tall chief warmly and assuring him and all of his people that they were welcome on the mesa. He went on to tell the Arapaho leader that we were trappers and traders from the north country, that we looked forward to making trade with his people, and that we wished to extend our hospitality to the chief and his headmen for supper that very evening in our camp.

Brass Turtle and I were swallowing hard, trying to keep a straight face whilst Kit was spinning his impossible deceits, all the while hoping that the chief would consider our friend to be a lunatic and excuse him on that account.

When at last Carson concluded his sign-talk and folded his arms to indicate that the next move must be the chief's, Turtle and I held our breath, unsure how that surprisingly patient leader might react to Kit's brash proposals, especially his nerve in welcoming the Arapahoes to what was likely their own customary winter hunting grounds. The tall Arapaho responded with a single question. He asked how many people were in our party. When Kit replied with the correct number, thirty, including our women and children, the chief allowed a brief smile to illuminate his features, nodded, and swung his arm in a gesture that told us we were free to go. We were impressed with the authority he exercised, making that important decision without consulting his councilors, a most un-Indian thing to do amongst a people who dearly love to debate every iota of every matter until they have chewed it half to death.

As we turned to go, Carson halted, faced the assembled headmen, and repeated his invitation to supper. Once again, a fleeting twinkle in the leader's eyes assured us of his good will, although he had not actually accepted our offer of hospitality.

Descending the slope, it was difficult to slow our pace to a dignified gait instead of dashing headlong downhill to deliver the news of our liberation. As it was, we used those few moments to express our congratulations to Carson on his success, as well as our lingering disbelief that he had actually pulled it off. "Ye got more cheek than a barrel o' squirrels," I told him. "An' stones that won't fit in a dray-cart!" Turtle commented. "How d'ye walk totin' them big ol' bollocks, anyway?"

"It worked, din't it?" was Kit's only response. "Now, let's git the hell out o' hyar. We got comp'ny comin'."

❧　❧　❧

We did ourselves proud that evening, entertaining a dozen Arapaho headmen in our camp, feasting them with fresh buffalo meat of every description—boiled tongues, roast hump ribs and tender backstrap, boudins simmering in flavorful bear fat—as well as a passel of appetizing stews provided by our women—after first observing the traditional amenities of passing the pipe around the circle of our guests, presided over by Zeetlah, our venerable healer.

The arrival of the Arapaho chiefs provided a dramatic tableau. They roared across the prairie just before sundown, feathers streaming, stirring up a cloud of snow as they coursed back and forth before the camp in mostly military precision on their painted horses, yipping and brandishing feathered lances, bows, and tack-studded muskets, before advancing in a headlong charge and drawing rein in a tail-dragging halt, stepping to the ground in nearly perfect unison. Their clothing was an eye-filling treat, glinting with German silver ornaments, rich fabrics, bright-colored woolen blankets and *capotes*, a rainbow of crusted quills and beadwork covering nearly every inch of leggin's, moccasins, vests, and warshirts. "They be a proper set o' paycocks," McCool observed admiringly. "They make the lot of us look shabby." Which they did, although we had dressed in our go-to-meetin' best to honor our guests.

"Jist as well," Carson commented. "It'll make 'em better customers fer tradin' later on."

We gifted each of them with a carrot of tobacco, a packet of vermilion, a hefty string of blue glass beads, a galena pig, a horn of gunpowder, flint and steel, and a substantial length of scarlet woolen broadcloth, taking care the while to let them understand that our gifts were rendered in friendship as our guests, as equals, and not in tribute coerced by their superior numbers.

Once their initial frostiness wore off, after they filled their bellies a time or two, the Arapahoes proved to be an affable bunch, especially the tall chief called Touches-the-Sky, whose curiosity about us was likely responsible for the success of Carson's fanciful inventions. Although he and I lacked a common spoken language, it was plain to see that Touches-the-Sky possessed uncommon intelligence and judgment, as well as physical attributes that gained him his position of leadership amongst his tribesmen.

Touches-the-Sky engaged several of us in sign-talk, but he appeared to be particularly interested in getting to know our big Delaware Little Mountain, joining him at the cookfire whilst they ate and plying him with questions. The two were close to the same height, both of them nearly a head taller than the rest of us, and equally muscular, although Little Mountain was somewhat more thickset than the Arapaho leader. Seeking an explanation, I supposed that the chief might be more comfortable chatting with someone his own size.

After our guests departed, howsomever, Little Mountain admitted to being puzzled by Touches-the-Sky's insistent interest in his marital status. "Ye don't s'pose he war feelin' whatcha mought be callin' exter-friendly 'bout me, do ye?" he wondered. I replied that such a thing was unlikely, that the chief was merely curious, just trying to learn as much about us as he could. "You'll be seein' him again," I assured him. "Ye can find out then."

The Arapahoes settled in a broad valley less a mile distant from our camp, close enough to come calling in either direction, but far enough apart to prevent conflicts over grazing and hunting. Their village numbered just under seventy lodges, which, together with our scant number, left a vast area of the landlocked mesa unoccupied, plenty of room to hunt buffalo without rubbing elbows with the neighbors.

Naturally our people were curious about our Arapaho neighbors, especially our bachelors. "Thar's got to be some widder wimmen amongst them'ere 'Rapahoes what needs comfortin'," Tuttle declared, "an' thar ain't hardly nobody what pervides comfortin' as good as me."

"Go easy 'til ye git the lay o' the land," Brass Turtle advised, "'til ye see how the 'Rapahoes tolerate ye comin' on to their women. We don't need to be startin' a war."

"Allus do," Tuttle assured him. "Like ye say, it's best to let 'em make the fust move. They know if they want ye. If they do, they'll let ye know soon enough." His voice trailed off as he concentrated on scraping his bristly jowls in anticipation of a romantic foray. When at last he reduced his wiry stubble to a blue-black shadow, he gazed admiringly into a tiny hand-mirror and announced his satisfaction with the result. "I keep fergittin' jest haow purty I kin be!" he declared with a loud horselaugh and dodged a moccasin that Anse flung at him.

"Jist turn loose o' that'ere razor," Tolliver told him. "Yew ain't the onliest one what's goin' callin', Thompson. An' whilst you're abaout it, ye'd best be totin' along a passel o' trade goods fer them widders. Ye ain't near as purty as ye think ye be."

Most of our bachelors were shaving and laving, primping and getting gussied up before trying their luck amongst the Arapaho women. None of them had any idea what their reception might be, nor even what their hoped-for lights-o'-love might look like. So far, we had seen only Arapaho men. Only Kit knew anything about that tribe and he wasn't saying.

As usual in most pleasures, anticipation was a large part of the enjoyment. Tuttle introduced a topic often discussed amongst bachelor trappers. "Did'ja ever gitcherse'f a real-life genuwine virgin amongst all o' ther Injun wimmen ye ever swived at ronnyvoo or anywhars else?" he asked the group assembled in the dugout.

"Nope, never did," Anse replied honestly. "All of 'em war awready broke in. Some more'n others, but never no virgins."

"Me, neither," Tuttle admitted almost wistfully.

"Same here," Finn McCool added. Then, "I daresay she'd need to be a maiden who's remarkably fleet o' foot, indade, if she were able to outrun all o' the young bucks in her band that weren't her kin, for her to be keepin' her maidenhead intact."

Micah, who from his embarrassed expression would have blushed if his complexion had allowed it, admitted reluctantly, "Yes, just once, and I warn't partic'larly proud o' doin' it, neither, but by time I realized she was, it was natcherly too late. She din't 'pear to mind, mind ye, but I felt sorta bad about bein' her first."

Brass Turtle looked thoughtful before he commented, "What ye say, Finn, about not swivin' kinfolk is true amongst all the Injuns I ever come across. Keeps the crazies out of our blood. Somethin' some o' the whites I growed up amongst back in Pennsylvaney could l'arn from us redskins! Least a half o' that'ere crowd's got relatives in their blood!"

The first thing that Kathleen and Tallymesko noticed when we rode into the Arapaho village was that Arapaho lodges are erected using only three poles for the foundation. Flatheads and Shoshones assemble their lodges using a four-pole foundation. I failed to see that it makes much difference, but our sharp-eyed women thought that it does, which provoked a deal of innocent merriment betwixt them and likely stirred some degree of superior tribal pride. Considering that it is always women who erect the lodges, never men, I reckon their authority in such matters is justified.

I was immediately struck by the handsome appearance of the Arapahoes, both men and women, their persons and their clothing. They were, for the most part, fairly tall and well-built, with pleasant, open features, an altogether attractive people. Our bachelor companions evidently agreed.

"Hell, Kit," Tuttle complained to Carson, "ye wou'n't even let on haow purty these hyar 'Rapaho wimmen be! Y'oughta be shamed o' yerse'f, thinkin' on keepin' 'em all to yerownse'f!"

Our first duty was calling on the principal chief, Touches-the-Sky, to obtain permission for us to visit the village. Whilst our women and most of our party waited on the outskirts, a half-dozen of us rode to the center of the village. Because the Arapaho chief had already shown a friendly interest in Little Mountain during their first meeting, he joined our party. The chief and several of his principal headmen were already waiting in the council area by time we rode up. We gifted our hosts with tobacco before requesting permission for our people to enter the village, which was readily granted.

Touches-the-Sky sent one of his men to escort our people into the village, then invited us into his lodge to smoke and share a meal. Young boys led off our horses and we trailed behind our host into the spacious, well-appointed lodge. We took our places on the right, whilst the elders of the band filed down the opposite side and sat facing us on the other side of the fire.

The pipe was passed with customary ritual, each man offering smoke to the four directions, the earth, and the sky, before we commenced to exchange sign-talk. Kit took the lead, but our bunch has always been democratic, never relying on a single leader. Soon, everybody, Arapahoes and our bunch, was having his say. Touches-the-Sky and his people appeared to enjoy thoroughly the free exchange of palaver, even though neither we nor they could understand the others' speech. Hand-talk got our thoughts across. Trade was the gist of the discussion. We informed our hosts that we wished to trade for furs, beaver ideally but also fine furs of every sort, and that we possessed valuable merchandise to pay for them, which offer was received with enthusiasm by our Arapaho hosts.

A scratching on the lodge cover announced the arrival of food. Several women entered bearing bark platters heaped with generous slices of steaming buffalo meat. One of the women immediately caught our attention. She was young and one of the most beautiful women I had ever seen, slim and graceful and as tall as Little Mountain.

She was modest in her demeanor as she carried out her duties but there was no mistaking that she was paying particular attention to Little Mountain. He, in turn, was experiencing extreme difficulty in taking his eyes away from that splendid female. She bore a definite resemblance to the tall chieftain. Even aside from their tall stature, there was hardly any doubt that she was his daughter. Little Mountain tried mightily not to stare at her, lest he offend our host, but without much success. He kept sneaking sidelong glances in spite of his best efforts not to do so. At last he dropped his eyes to his lap and refused to look at her until she departed the lodge with a last lingering look at our Delaware bachelor.

The Arapaho elders continued eating as if they had noticed nothing unusual and filed out of the lodge when they finished their meal, leaving our bunch alone with the chief. Powatawa had engaged the leader in talk about the band's summertime stomping grounds, but it was plain to see that Touches-the-Sky was more interested in keeping an eye on the interplay between Little Mountain and his daughter. For his part, the big Delaware grew remarkably quiet, his customary lively good humor thoroughly squelched.

Even after we made our good-byes, promising to return and inviting the chief to visit our camp, and retrieved our horses, Little Mountain remained uncommonly subdued, riding somewhat apart from the rest of us, apparently lost in thought, now and again glancing back at the chief's lodge until it was out of sight. Brass Turtle tried to tease him into opening up.

"Are ye content, naow, Mountain? Ol' Chief Highpockets ain't in love with ye, like ye war frettin' 'bout mebbe he war, but naow I'll wager it's his girl-child what's workin' up feelin's fer ye. 'Pears that'ere fambly's got plans fer ye, like it or not." His sally produced only a stony stare from the big man.

"She's a looker, Tchewaung," Turtle persisted, using Mountain's familiar nickname in the Lenape tongue. "Ye could do a heap worse'n that'n." The big fellow glared at him for an instant, snorted, touched spur to his horse, and loped out of the village.

"Naow who put a burr under his gawddamn saddle?" Turtle said aloud to nobody in particular.

"You did, for one," I told him. "And I reckon that pretty girl back there helped ye. He's in love!"

∾   ∾   ∾

Winter camp, as usual, provided ample time for leisure pursuits, as well as performing necessary chores such as hunting, gathering firewood, and keeping our livestock fit and healthy. When at last the graze nigh the camp was used up, peeling sweet cottonwood bark for horse feed was a pleasant and useful daily chore for half a dozen or more men sitting in a circle in the bachelors' dugout, palavering whilst we stripped tender bark from the slender boughs. Often men would ask me to read to them from one or another of my books whilst they worked. The works of William Shakespeare and the Bible are always welcome, although none of our people are especially religious. They enjoy the sonorous tone of Biblical text and colorful descriptions in stately classical language, especially the battles in Mister Shakespeare's historical plays.

An English writer, Sir Walter Scott, enjoys universal popularity amongst mountaineers. His lively tales of romance and adventure and derring-do set in the midst of exciting historical scenes of war and conflict fire their imagination and prompt frequent requests for just one more reading of

Ivanhoe, The Talisman, A Legend of Montrose, Quentin Durward, or *Kenilworth.*

Frequent auditors at those readings were my daughter Iris and Paddy McBride's redheaded son Sean, and often Kathleen, whenever she allowed herself leisure time enough to join us. Iris had already devoured every book that I possessed, most of them several times, but she enjoyed listening to the spoken words and I encourage her to improve her English pronunciation whenever possible. Sometimes Finnæus McCool assumed the reading chore and occasionally Padraic McBride volunteered to provide a distinctive Hibernian flavor to our literary gatherings. Paddy was particularly effective whenever he read from the works of Walter Scott, his brogue blending convincingly with descriptions of Scottish events.

Absent from our circle that year was Little Mountain, who in previous winter camps had been one of our most attentive and enthusiastic auditors, when he wasn't wooing one or another maiden from a neighboring Indian village. Now he was either mooning around the outskirts of the Arapaho village, seeking a glimpse of his light-o'-love, or off by himself in the woods above camp, tootling plaintively on Brass Turtle's flute.

He confessed to Turtle that his attempts to seduce the statuesque daughter of the Arapaho chieftain had come to naught. She had flatly informed him that if robe games had been her wish, there was a passel of willing Arapaho bucks who would gladly accommodate her. She demanded a permanent commitment and if onesuch were not forthcoming, she was prepared to wait until it did.

Little Mountain was not accustomed to rejection. Besides his impressive size and strength and athletic skill, his handsome features and generous, easy-going nature had always assured him of willing temporary feminine companionship at rendezvous, winter camp, and during our California sojourn. Many women doubtless regarded his classic size as a delightful challenge, a pleasant attraction akin to a newly-discovered alp still unclimbed. Until he laid eyes on the elegant Arapaho maiden, Tchewaung-Cocheet had been pretty much a stranger to romantic disappointment. Now he was reduced to little more than a lovesick moon-calf, nigh paralyzed with desire, reluctant to surrender his cherished bachelor freedom, yet unable to quench his burning need for the beautiful young woman who had captured his heart.

When Brass Turtle and my father showed up at our lodge one morning, asking me to join them on a visit to the Arapaho village on Little Mountain's behalf, I readily consented. "The big feller's downright pitiful," Turtle declared, "mopin' all by his lonesome up thar on the hill, pinin' fer that'ere 'Rapaho gal, hardly eatin' enough to keep a couple-three ordinary men alive. We gotta do somethin' serious afore he starves hisse'f to death."

On the way to the village, they explained Kit's absence from the delegation. They had asked him along, but he declined, claiming our mission was an Injun chore, not something he knew anything about.

We rode directly to the lodge of Touches-the-Sky and waited in the snow whilst a young lad scratched on the door cover and announced our presence. When at last we were ushered inside we exchanged friendly greetings with the chief, who was seated on his sleeprobes at the far end of the lodge. We presented the customary visitor's gift of tobacco and he called for tea to be brought whilst he prepared the pipe. We looked for the comely daughter, but the tea arrived borne by a fine-looking middle-aged woman. She was somewhat taller than anyone I had seen in the village, although not nearly the stature of either Touches-the-Sky or his daughter.

"That is the girl's mother," my father commented quietly. "A good sign for Mountain if all goes well."

After we smoked, Brass Turtle explained the purpose of our visit. He took special care to perform his hand-signs precisely to avoid misunderstanding. He went directly to the point. He explained that we had come on behalf of our friend, the big fellow whom the chief already knew. Our friend was very much taken with the chief's daughter and we had come to learn what might be needed to be done to get the two of them together.

Touches-the-Sky was obviously impressed by Turtle's straightforwardness, cutting through the circumlocution common amongst Indians. The chief hesitated less than a minute before he launched into a candid description of the situation concerning his daughter. He came straight to the point. His hand-signs gracefully but forcefully conveyed his thoughts. The chief was most eloquent in the use of hand-talk, so I will relate his remarks here as if they had been spoken instead of signed.

"My daughter is too tall, he said flatly. "All of her girlhood friends have been claimed by young men of our village or by men of other bands, but no man has been willing to suffer the ridicule of his fellows for being smaller than his woman. I named my daughter Circling Eagle, but they all call her

Too-tall, when they think that neither she nor I can hear them. But I do hear them and so does she! It wrings my heart to see how such talk injures her."

Here he made a literal twisting gesture with his hands that demonstrated the pain that such derision caused him. I thought of my beloved Iris and how I would hate to have such treatment visited upon her.

"I have eyes," he went on. "I can see with other men's eyes that she is beautiful in her person, more desirable than any woman in this village or any village I have seen. I can judge her not only with the eyes of a father, but as a man, as well. Moreover, she possesses all the useful skills and virtues of a proper woman and wife. She has been honored by membership granted in our Buffalo Women's Society. She is cleanly and hardworking, skilled in her art, modest, of good humor, and prudent in her speech, quick-witted without being bossy or saucy. She wins in all the women's games. She is fearless and she is an excellent trainer of horses."

He halted, eyes downcast, twisting his fingers as he sought to marshal his thoughts and, I daresay, curb his runaway feelings. Whilst we waited for that strong man to collect his thoughts, I observed the several scalplocks that fringed his leggin's. They marked him as a bold, resolute warrior, a man of action, his love for his child likely his only weakness.

I took advantage of his pause to look around the lodge at its rich furnishings, deep-pile buffalo robes and multicolored rugs from the far-off Navajos, his ceremonial robes and headdresses and vivid quilled and painted sashes that proclaimed his leadership in his warrior society—the Dog-men Society, war leaders, as I learned later—and well-made weapons that testified to hard use, lances, bows and quivers of arrows, and tack-studded muskets. Touches-the-Sky was obviously an energetic chief of his band. He returned to his hand-talk.

"Sometimes I blame myself for visiting my own long size upon her, although such things are not left to any man's choosing. It is the doing of the Great Spirit. It is in the nature of things." Once again he grew still, his hands idle on his thighs, studying our faces to see if we had understood his sign-talk. Evidently he was satisfied with what he read in our faces. He smiled then and chuckled softly before he continued.

"Before I say what you wish to know to tell your friend, I will tell you how it is that you are sitting in my lodge today as friends and guests, instead of—" He left off his signing there, his unfinished thought hanging in mid-air.

He resumed his signing. "The day we met on the prairie, the day you killed the buffalo and our scouts heard your gunfire and discovered all of you in the hole in the ground, they first spied on you, then sent word back to our main column describing how many you were and what each of you looked like. It is well-known in our band that I have long sought an acceptable son-in-law. They told me of your big man, as well as the others. When I joined our scouts I saw for myself that he was indeed a big, very tall, young, handsome fellow. I saw, too, that he was not lazy, that he willingly did his share of the work. I thought that it might be wasteful to kill such a man merely for trespassing on our winter hunting grounds."

Here he chuckled amiably again. "When your little man spoke, I learned that you were few in number, that some of you travel with your women, which shows peaceful intent, and that you are traders of valuable goods as well as trappers of beaver. I decided to see what might grow from that seed. That night in your camp, I spoke with your friend and found that he is agreeable and mannerly and unmarried. My daughter could never tolerate the role of second wife. Now you tell me that your friend has strong feelings for my child. I am glad now that I held our young men back when we first met."

Aside from a certain bloodthirsty streak in the chief's idea of good-natured jesting, what he told us was pretty much what we had hoped to hear. What might result from any future commerce betwixt Little Mountain and the beauteous progeny of the Arapaho leader would naturally depend upon the two of them, but it was plain that Touches-the-Sky would do whatever he could to promote romance betwixt the two of them.

Now Powatawa, who possessed, as a former chief of his own band, considerable experience in arranging marriages, inquired about the conditions concerning the purchase price of the bride. My father surprised me by exhibiting a shrewdness that I had not previously observed in him. A lifetime of horse-trading manifested itself when he warned at the outset that although Little Mountain was honest and brave and hard-working, he was not wealthy.

The chief immediately dispelled concern on that score. He signed emphatically that whatever formal purchase price that tradition and the respect due his own position as chief of his band might dictate would be more than made up for by the dowry that Circling Eagle would bring with her into a marriage. With that assurance in place, arrangements with Touches-the-Sky were rapidly concluded and we took our leave.

❧   ❧   ❧

Except for Zeetlah, Brass Turtle was Little Mountain's oldest friend, so he was best qualified to advise him on the best course of action to achieve his heart's desire, once the big fellow was willing to admit, mainly to himself, that he wanted the chief's beautiful daughter more than his treasured bachelor freedom.

"Ye cain't have it both ways," Brass Turtle told him. "She's awready tol' ye that. She's the head man's daughter. Even if she wanted to bed ye jist fer the fun of it, she woun't be likely to. 'Twouldn't look right, her pa bein' chief an' all. Nope. If ye want her, ye'll jist hafta take her fer good an' all. No borryin' jist fer the night." Once Mountain accepted that fact, which didn't come easy, it was possible to prepare him to conduct a proper courtship.

"The good news is, her pa's on yer side," Turtle counseled. "An' from what he war sayin', she's likely ready fer tellin' ye yes, if ye ask her right. If she says she'll have ye, she'll likely make a good woman fer ye. Ye awready know she's a good fit fer ye an' she's a heap better-lookin' than any woman I ever seed ye with. 'Sides, her pa war tellin' 'bout haow good she'll be fer lookin' arter the lodge.

"He war tellin', too, haow them 'Rapaho bucks won't marry no woman what kin look down on 'em, so ye awready got a head-start with her, jist fer bein' bigger'n most. It's gittin' past time fer ye to be settlin' down an' sirin' a coupl'a younkers what'll know what to call ye when they see ye. So naow ye'd best be l'arnin' haow to go courtin' her proper-like." Which instruction mostly involved Brass Turtle teaching Mountain how to play the flute well enough to plight his troth Arapaho-style.

When I told Cat what had transpired with the chief and that Little Mountain had at last consented to surrender his singlehood and go a-courting the tall Arapaho beauty in a fitting manner, she got all enthusiastic, the way women do about such matters, and dug out of our plunder a brand-new six-point Witney woolen blanket from England, so that Mountain could carry along a blanket big enough to cover the two of them if the chief's daughter would consent to share it with him.

Two nights later, Brass Turtle, my father, and I accompanied Little Mountain to the Arapaho village and waited in the shadows whilst our big friend trudged through the snow to the lodge of Touches-the-Sky and commenced tootling on his flute. He was at it for quite a spell before the door-flap swung aside at last and the tall young woman stepped out and faced him, hesitantly at first, whilst he continued to draw the sweetest melody from the flute that a couple days' instruction could provide. At last she turned and folded her shoulder into his, allowing him to sweep the big blanket over her and himself. They stood together quietly for a few minutes before she crept free of the blanket, grasped Mountain's hand, and led him into the lodge.

When I expressed surprise that the young woman would take him to see her father so quickly, Turtle explained that he had called on the chief earlier that day and told him of Little Mountain's impending visit that night. Touches-the-Sky and his wife were discreetly absent from the lodge, so that the young people, who shared no common spoken language, might converse in signs indoors in the firelight.

We stood in the cold a half-hour or more, stamping our moccasins in the snow, until Little Mountain's head poked out the door-flap, retreated inside for a few more minutes, then reappeared. "A good sign," my father commented. "She asked him to return." He stood outside for a minute or two, gazing back at the lodge, before he let out a triumphant whoop and trotted across the snowy common where we waited.

When Mountain joined us, he wrapped Brass Turtle in a bear hug and kissed him noisily on the forehead, whilst Turtle struggled to get loose. "Why'd ye go an' do a fool thang like that, ye big galoot?" he sputtered.

"I war jist tellin' ye thankee fer all ye done an' showin' ye the fust thang I taught my woman 'bout white men's ways," he responded, laughing. "She din't know nuthin' 'bout sich doin's, but she took to it right smart, once she got past bein' frighted."

"Ye mean to say she'll have ye?"

"Yep! Naow I hafta be talkin' to her pa."

They fell into a passel of Delaware palaver that neither Powatawa nor I could understand, but we had already heard what we had hoped for. Our mission was successful.

✷ ✷ ✷

Little Mountain encountered no difficulty with Touches-the-Sky regarding his intended nuptials. The chief dearly loved his only daughter, who, until Mountain showed up, had faced a bleak future of spinsterhood. That pretty much guaranteed the older man's approval. There were, howsomever, certain time-honored Arapaho marriage traditions to be observed, chiefly that of formally purchasing the bride from her father.

When Mountain made the prescribed call on the chief, Touches-the-Sky offered to visit our camp himself and choose the five ponies that custom dictated must be paid as a bride-price. Several of us offered horses to Little Mountain, who lacked that many extra critters in his own *remuda* that he could spare. All of the Bannock horses were placed at his disposal, as well. When the chief inspected the offered livestock he generously selected the least desirable critters amongst those offered, declaring in sign-talk that he already owned many horses and these would satisfy the demands of custom.

It was plain to see the Arapaho leader's mouth fairly watered when he laid eyes on my Coffee horse, but he discreetly looked away and made no comment.

Besides the long-standing affection we all hold for our big Delaware comrade, the generous forbearance of Touches-the-Sky in choosing our least valuable horses as the bride-price earned him the grateful respect of everyone in the bunch. That gratitude resulted in the whole bunch donating an impressive heap of trade plunder to be hauled over to the Arapaho village on Little Mountain's behalf as a token of respect for the chief and his daughter.

Which amply rewarded the leader for his gracious restraint. "Bread cast upon the water returns a hundredfold," Finn quoted piously.

"Yeah," Tuttle commented dryly, "but what kin ye do with a hunnerd loaves o' wet bread?"

∾ ∾ ∾

Drums commenced beating in the Arapaho camp when the first faint streaks of crimson stained the night-time sky over the eastern peaks. Their hollow boom rolling over the snow-covered prairie announced the wedding day of the head man's only daughter. The drumbeat ignited excitement amongst our womenfolk, who had been seething with anticipation for days at the prospect of strutting their finery before their Arapaho sisters. It was bound to be a close contest, howsomever, for our neighbors were among the most beautifully decked-out women I had ever seen in the mountains.

Running the Arapaho belles a close second were their men, who shared their women's keen eye for prairie fashion. Our own bachelors were fast catching up sartorially, howsomever. Many of them quickly took to trading for more than feminine favors, although romantic dalliance was still the primary reason for their visits.

Carson had told us early on that the Arapaho enjoy an impressive reputation in that country as formidable warriors, which in warlike tribes inevitably results in an abundance of widows, which our enterprising bachelors were not behindhand in turning to advantage.

In several cases, howsomever, what had begun as purely carnal arrangements with lonely widows had blossomed into rather more tender liaisons betwixt Arapaho women of marriageable age and disposition and some of our trappers, who, in the leisure of winter camp, lacking the alcoholic diversions of rendezvous, had little else to distract them from the pleasures of robe games. If a deeper affection developed between the two, the women, evidently responding to some mysterious feminine need to prettify their surroundings, no matter how homely, often took to dolling up their rough and tough trapper beaux, arraying them in soft leather shirts and leggin's generously crusted with quills and elaborate beadwork—likely, in many cases, the garments of departed spouses. Our scruffy bachelors bloomed into a pack of gaudy popinjays.

Two of our most pampered and colorful singletons were Micah and our precocious Delaware youngster Half-horse. The Arapaho women were as enchanted as their northern sisters have always been by Micah's swarthy good looks, his slim, muscular frame, and especially his wiry curls that immediately got him dubbed something akin to Buffalo Warrior in their tongue. Half-horse's boyish features proved irresistible to the younger widows, as well as several older ones who should have known better. They both possessed a quiet charm and accommodating nature that assured them friendly companionship whenever they desired it. Zeetlah had given up trying to restrain his handsome young nephew's lubricious behavior. He calls the young fellow Venegus now—Mink, in the Delaware tongue—but Half-horse simply regards it as a compliment. Zeetlah shouldn't have been surprised. It runs in the family.

In the early forenoon a delegation of Arapaho bravos arrived in our camp leading a tall, sturdy, elaborately-painted skewbald gelding and bearing the wedding clothes that Little Mountain was expected to wear to the ceremony, an elegant outfit of butter-soft, elegantly-quilled, ivory-colored bighorn leather—war shirt, leggin's, and moccasins—that decked him out, head to toe, in the pristine hue of purity and innocence.

Which was rather too much for Tuttle Thompson, who had shared a decade of romantic adventures with Little Mountain. Tuttle commenced hooting and jeering and calling out reminders of some of their more notable exploits until Anse and Finn hustled him out of earshot. Mountain blushed and doubtless thanked his stars that his groomsmen couldn't understand his tormentor and tattle on him.

When his attendants finished their primping and painting, they conducted the bridegroom to his richly-caparisoned mount and took him off, signing to the rest of us that we were expected at high noon to attend the ceremony and the feast that would follow.

We married men needed to break our fast that morning at the campkeepers' cookfire. Our women were painting and preening and trying on one outfit after another for themselves and the children, purely terrified that the Arapaho ladies would make them look shabby. By mid-forenoon it was the men's turn to compete with Missus Washington's pet pony.

Cat presented me with a brand-new quilled and beaded war shirt and soft antelope leggin's that she had been working on whenever my back was turned, ever since she first learned that Little Mountain was sweet on the chief's daughter. A new blue blanket-wool britchclout, scarlet woolen broadcloth shirt, and my best pair of go-to-meetin' beaded moccasins completed my outfit. Still Cat fretted that we might not measure up to some sartorial ideal that no male person could possibly comprehend.

When I beheld Cat in her elegant crimson velvet dress that swept gracefully to the ground, silver-spangled woolen leggin's hugging her shapely thighs and calves, a rich Chinese silk scarf draped over her shoulders, long glossy mink-wrapped braids spilling over her delicious bosom, a tasteful fine line of vermilion emphasizing her high cheekbones, I was instantly ready for a honeymoon of our own, but she snorted impatiently, shooed me out of the lodge, and devoted her efforts to beautifying our daughter.

When the women had enough preening and fussing, our gaudy cavalcade assembled at last and we set out for the village. The bachelors and most of our married men were nearly as richly turned out as our women. They were determined not to be outdone, not only in their own appearance, but their men's, as well. We were a colorful crowd of coxcombs that day.

Everybody rode his best horse to the festivities, except, naturally, for Anse Tolliver, who, togged-out in clean new buckskins, straddled his handsomest jack mule, fiddle-case bobbing behind his saddle cantle, a welcome sight, for we had been deprived of his lively tunes since rendezvous.

All six women rode their creamy *palomilla* mares, objects of envy amongst the Arapahoes, who had apparently never seen horses of that color. The foppery extended even to the critters, most of which were painted with multicolored gaudy tribal designs if their color permitted such display. I insisted on riding Coffee, my favorite, much to Cat's disapproval, for his sunburnt-black hide defied such decoration. Her own *palomilla* mare and Iris's were painted with bold, bright-colored Flathead designs and showy ribbons and shiny tinkling hawk bells braided into their forelocks, manes, and tails. The mounts of the other women and most of their men were similarly beautified.

As we came nigh the village, our women reined up and shrugged off their woolen *capotes*, despite the January chill, lest their exotic fabrics and painstaking needlework be obscured from view.

Our women received all the attention they could have wished for. We rode into the Arapaho village precisely when the sun reached its zenith, as we had been bidden. The alleyways between the lodges were thronged with men and women jostling one another for a glimpse of us when we entered the outskirts, chattering and raising a joyful ululation as we passed by, the din nearly drowning out the drumming which had never ceased from early morning. A noisy mob trailed behind our little procession all the way to the center of the village, where we dismounted and turned our horses over to youths who led them off.

As soon as we stepped to the ground, smiling women crowded around us, intent upon a closer look at our women's finery, offering dainties, the bolder ones fingering the luxurious velvets, silks, satins, and broadcloths from faraway Saint Louis, some of them petting our infant children in the manner of maternal women everywhere. Altogether it was a friendly, admiring crowd.

Touches-the-Sky's lodge had been enlarged by attaching at least three other lodges to it, leaving the front raised and open, with several fires to warm it. Seated at the far end, discreetly separate from each other, were Little Mountain, sartorially splendiferous in his snowy duds and relaxed now, grinning broadly, enjoying all the attention, and his beautiful bride Circling Eagle, eyes demurely downcast, her face tastefully painted, dressed head to toe in vivid red, except for a broad elkskin belt richly embroidered with bright yellow quillwork, which we later learned was her ritual garb in the Buffalo

Women's Society. This was to be her final participation in their ceremonial dancing.

The chief and several of his headmen welcomed us and conducted us to our places under the broad canopy formed by the several lodge covers. Several women arrived to offer warm tea from large gourds and a variety of sweetmeats arrayed on bark platters. Meanwhile, Carson and Finn McCool unloaded the panniers slung onto our packmule and presented the gifts from our bunch to the bride's family, which Kit had assured us was the custom. Approving murmurs rose from the assembled tribesmen when they caught sight of shiny tin-lined copper kettles, lengths of trade wool and calico, carrots of tobacco, hanks of multicolored trade beads, a couple shiny pipe-tomahawks, packets of vermilion, amongst a heap of other stuff, and especially the chief's special gift, one of the large-caliber percussion rifles we had retrieved from the Bannocks, its polished brass furniture gleaming in the firelight, with all its fixin's and powder and galena enough to go to war and win it.

When Touches-the-Sky looked askance at the absence of a flint and powder pan, Kit signed that on the morrow he would school him in the use of percussion weapons.

Four drummers took their place on one side of the open space at the center and commenced their performance, joking and jollying one another the while in the manner of Indian drummers everywhere when they are performing at festive occasions. The big drum boomed out a sonorous notice to the entire village that the main event was about to commence.

Circling Eagle rose to her feet when a dozen or so women of various ages, half of them dressed in white, the others in red, filed into the open space in the center. An old woman appeared behind her and placed a rattlesnake headdress adorned with a clutch of owl feathers on her brow and placed in her hand a slender yellow cane about a yard long. The drumbeat quickened and Circling Eagle ran lightly to join the crimson-clad women. They began a shuffling dance past the women in white, who fell into line behind them. The throb of the big drum steadily increased in tempo and volume, pounding out an exciting beat that soon had spectators squirming, stamping their moccasins, apparently yearning to join the dancers, who responded to the quickening rhythm with faster, ever more intricate dance steps and elaborate patterns, passing and falling back, writhing sensuously, interweaving redrobes and white until they all became a harmonious blur, going on and on, the big drum at last reaching an ear-splitting pitch, then halted abruptly with a crash and heart-stopping thump that brought the frenzied dancers to a sudden halt, frozen in place, until a light tickling-tapping on the drumhead stirred them to life and they trooped out of the dance circle single-file, in the manner of buffalo traveling, heads drooping, looking neither right nor left, acknowledging no one, until they disappeared behind the lodge.

Tuttle leaned close and muttered in my ear, "If Li'l Mountain's thinkin' on robe games t'night, he's prob'ly got anuther think comin'. Thet'ere li'l gal's gonna be plumb tuckered arter all thet dancin'! Me, too! Jest watchin' 'em!"

When the Arapaho beauty returned to Little Mountain and her father at the far end of the lodge a few minutes later she appeared as fresh as a newly-blossomed daisy in morning sunshine, beaming with excitement, her step light and graceful, displaying no sign of fatigue. The frumpy crimson dress she had worn for the dancing was gone, replaced by an elegant close-fitting dazzling white sheath that modestly but effectively revealed her supple curves.

With a simple gesture, Touches-the-Sky summoned the two young people to stand before him, placed a hand on the shoulder of each, cast his eyes skyward, and intoned a few words, whilst a much older man draped in a feather cloak flitted behind the pair, brushing their backs with a full eagle's wing with one hand and flinging droplets of water from a gourd hanging at his waist with the other, before he shuffled out of sight behind the lodge. The chief extended his hands outward and gently pushed the bride and smiling groom together so that their shoulders touched, then stepped back and away from the handsome pair.

Carson was standing beside me. "That's it," he said softly. "That's all thar be to it. They're hitched."

Little Mountain had never before looked so handsome and certainly never so well-dressed. At that moment he appeared to be almost worthy of the stunningly beautiful young woman who had just pledged her life to him. Towering above all the people who thronged around them offering good wishes, they were an impressive pair.

The aroma of roasting meat had been wafting over the village during the dancing and the marriage ceremony. My empty stomach was rumbling so loud I feared it might disrupt the proceedings. Skimpy as breakfast had been that morning, I was more than ready for the feast. As I joined the queue heading for the cookfires, an older warrior laid his hand on my arm and earnestly informed me in carefully-delivered sign-talk, "What you have seen today is not the proper ceremony of the Buffalo Women. This was dancing for a different purpose, to celebrate the joining of a woman who is one of their own and the man of her choice. It is meant to depict the activity of the wedding night." Leastaways, that is what I think he meant to tell me. If so, the Arapaho Buffalo Women had successfully got that idea across.

Nobody went hungry that day. Quarters of roasting buffalo hung over the coals of a dozen cookfires scattered around the central council fire area, flanked by bubbling kettles of savory meaty soups and a variety of flavorful stews.

After I had nearly foundered myself by sampling everything in sight, I retreated to a quiet corner of the lodge to smoke a pipeful, admire the Arapahoes' colorful get-ups, and watch one of the several groups of people who had gathered in dance circles to celebrate the occasion, hoping the while that Cat wouldn't discover my whereabouts and drag me into their midst. Suddenly, from all over the village, drummers increased what had been a steady, monotonous beat for dancing into a brief, stormy crescendo that ended in a thundering crash and silence. Dance circles dissolved and warriors and their women and kids streamed like startled minnows to the council fire, where Touches-the-Sky was standing, surrounded by a passel of livestock and heaps of plunder. Little Mountain and Circling Eagle stood nearby.

The chief commenced talking in a loud voice, facing the young couple but addressing the excited crowd as well, gesturing as he spoke towards the bunch of horses that waited nearby, ordering the horse-holders to lead them, one by one, past the young couple. In all, there were eight excellent saddlers, four sturdy geldings, each one at least sixteen hands tall, and not a coarse critter amongst the lot. The remaining four horses, two mares and two geldings, were also tall but finer-boned, clean-limbed, and well-muscled, testimony to their good breeding, obviously meant for his daughter's personal *remuda*. A pair of saddle mules completed the father's equine gift for his daughter's nuptials, a tall, strapping jack and a well-built piebald jenny. It was plain that even Circling Eagle was surprised and impressed by her father's generosity.

When Touches-the-Sky turned to the heap of household plunder, the goods they would need to furnish their lodge, he showed that he possessed a discerning eye. During his visits to our camp he had doubtless observed that our bachelors owned little else besides their saddles, sleeprobes, weapons, and tools. Most of whatever else was required for their survival they owned in common and trusted to the care of our campkeepers.

Now a veritable river of plunder flowed to the newly-married couple— soft-tanned buffalo robes and thick English woolen blankets, willow backrests, copper kettles and other cooking and eating utensils, a heap of brightly-painted *parfleche* rawhide boxes containing all sorts of useful household items, clothing for both of them, a woman's tools such as digging sticks and hide scrapers, elegantly-decorated apishamores, headstalls, breast collars and cruppers, halters, and other horse clothing, together with several packsaddles to transport their possessions.

Little Mountain had married well. He had suddenly become a man of means.

The horses and mules were led off to pasture and a troop of lads commenced hauling the mountain of plunder off to the couple's new lodge, which had been erected at the edge of the village, a discreet distance from its neighbors, where they would spend their first night together. They would join us in our camp the following day.

As soon as Touches-the-Sky turned to leave the council fire, I heard, for the first time in several months, the welcome strains of Anse Tolliver's fiddle launching into a lively Tennessee country tune. The crowd of spectators for the giveaway, who had begun to drift off, halted in their tracks, intrigued by the unfamiliar sound, and turned back to discover its source.

Tolliver, perched atop a heap of firewood stacked up for the council fire, was actually smiling as he sawed away at one spirited hillbilly tune after another, apparently delighted with the sensation he was causing amongst the Arapahoes, who had likely never heard anything like his Tennessee mountain breakdowns. He was soon joined by our Frenchy campkeeper Yves Dureau and his little squeezebox concertina that lent additional depth and volume to Anse's fiddling and further charmed our aboriginal neighbors by contributing to the musical din. Unsophisticated though they were about white-eyes music-making, it took hardly any time at all before they picked up the rhythms of Tolliver's sprightly songs and commenced shuffling their moccasins more or less in time with his music.

When our womenfolk showed up at the edge of the crowd, I retreated in haste, lest Kathleen drag me into the open space before the fire and demand that I dance with her. Our bachelors had long since disappeared with their lights-o'-love, so I hunted up Turtle and Paddy, who had returned to one of the cookfires for just one more helping, which appeared to me to be a first-rate thing to do. We were still stuffing ourselves with crispy bits of hump meat when the women showed up and asked that we return to camp. The children had grown tired and cranky and they themselves had temporarily gratified their need to parade their finery before their Arapaho sisters.

∽   ∽   ∽

Little Mountain and his bride arrived in camp next morning, leading a procession of handsome saddlers, several fully-loaded pack animals, and a couple more hauling travois drags, bearing their new household, their Arapaho helpers assisted by some of our bachelors who had remained in the village overnight. Naturally all of our women turned out to welcome the young woman and help her set up her lodge in an open space next to ours and to lend a hand stowing her plunder in and around it. This was a purely female chore. Men were neither invited nor welcome to participate in it.

Judging by the cheerful look on Mountain's face, the honeymoon night had gone swimmingly. "Whatcha figger on callin' her, Mountain, cornsid'rin' ye don't talk no Rapaho lingo, ner likely be l'arnin' any?" Turtle wanted to know.

"We talked on that last night, oncet when we war restin' up," he replied with an evil chuckle, "— talkin' sign, natcherly—an' we come up with Teholenze Ochqwe in Lenape—Bird Woman fer yew White-eyes," he added for the rest of us—"best I could think of fer sayin' her Rapaho handle that warn't a mouthful nobody'd ever use. She 'peared to like it, so that's what we'll be callin' muh woman from hyar on out."

Within a few days, we heard him calling her Tayho, for short, and that's how the rest of us took to addressing her.

The womenfolk took to the newcomer from the start, showing her how they performed household chores—which likely wasn't much different from what she was used to—and teaching her American words and phrases. She rapidly picked up goddam and sumbitch, the customary foundation for acquiring our tongue.

Tayho hadn't long to yearn for the familiar sound of her native language, howsomever. Little Mountain's example was contagious, especially in a teetotaling dry winter camp with few diversions, located not far from a friendly Indian village teeming with even friendlier young widows. Hardly a fortnight passed after Mountain's wedding before Cesár Pérez and Diego Valenzuela, one of our newly-recruited *Californios*, announced that they, too, intended to marry their Arapaho *queridas*. Their route to the nuptial couch was much less formal and arduous than Mountain's had been, inasmuch as their intended brides were not the daughters of a chief, as Circling Eagle had been, nor were they inexperienced virgins.

Both women were widows of warriors slain in one or another of the constant pony raids and tribal wars that appear to be the favorite recreation of Indians everywhere. A couple middling ponies and an armload of trade goods offered to a father or elder brother for each woman likely sufficed to obtain the blessing of families doubtless relieved to be rid of the burden of providing meat for the lonesome widows.

We weren't invited to the ceremony, if indeed such a rite had occurred. Instead, one morning our two grinning Spaniards rode into camp at the head of a modest procession consisting of their pretty young brides, each woman leading a skimpy *remuda* of spare ponies, their household plunder heaped onto a travois drag.

Once again our womenfolk welcomed the newcomers, fussing over them and helping them set up their lodges, putting them at ease in their new surroundings. Diego called his wife Maria, a popular name amongst Catholic Spaniards. Cesár's *despósada* was remarkably fair-skinned and rosy-cheeked, especially in the January chill, so it wasn't hard for the rest of us to remember that he called her Rosa.

It appeared that nothing would satisfy the womenfolk except our putting on a wedding celebration for the new brides, who had almost certainly attended Tayho's marriage to Mountain but hadn't had one of their own. Cat was particularly adamant in that demand, even when I reminded her that our own joining together, pleasurable as it was, had been notable for its lack of ceremony.

So it was that half a dozen of us set out to harvest buffalo for the belated nuptial feast. When I stopped by to collect Micah for the hunt, he demurred, offering no excuse other than he had other chores to perform.

We returned from the snowy prairie in mid-afternoon with the meat of four fat cows slung onto the packmules, most of which we turned over to the campkeepers for the feast, holding back only a modest portion of fresh liver and a few choice cuts as a treat for hardworking spouses.

Tuttle and I were still draped in the white cloaks that we had been using for cover to hunt buffalo on the snowy prairie. Heavy snows had pushed the critters out of their favorite winter feeding grounds in the deep hollows that laced the prairie, burying grass under deep wind-driven drifts, and forcing them onto open ground where they could still paw through the snow to get a hard-won mouthful. Which naturally made it much more difficult to sneak close enough for a rifle shot, visible as we were—even for buffalo, which have very poor eyesight—in our bright red, blue, or green *capotes* against the snow.

So we begged white petticoats from the womenfolk to make a couple cloaks to cover us up when we went after buffalo. They objected at first at giving up their pretty petticoats, but appetite triumphed over fashion. Their overwhelming preference for buffalo meat over deer and wapiti finally convinced them to surrender several white underskirts.

We hunters changed our tactics. Now we drew straws to select two shooters, each dragging a couple guns, to crawl on our bellies up close to the herd whilst the others waited with the horses and packmules at a sufficient distance to fool weak-eyed buffalo. Two shots were all we got before the critters caught on and made tracks, but four big shaggies sufficed to keep the camp from going hungry.

Jean-Luc and Yves had lighted the main cookfire when they spied our return, still far out on the prairie, so the camp was soon bathed in the appetizing aroma of roasting meat, enhanced by half a dozen fragrances floating from copper kettles bubbling in lodge fires throughout the camp.

Cat had laid out a change of clean clothes and dry moccasins. A kettle of warm water nested in hot coals in the firepit so that I might lave off the blood and grime that always accompanies a successful hunt. I was soon halfway respectable. Leastaways, I didn't smell nearly as bad as I had done.

The rattling of spoons on copper kettles summoned us to the feast. We gathered, out of the weather, in the bachelors shelter to enjoy tender buffalo meat and the several appetizing stews provided by the women. After his third trip to the cookfire, Anse unlimbered his fiddle and entertained us with a clutch of merry tunes from his Tennessee home country, which thoroughly captivated the recent brides, whose previous musical experience had been limited to drums and flutes, rattles and dance bells.

When everybody had stuffed himself to a standstill and the men had gathered to smoke a pipeful, our original six women retired to their lodges and emerged bearing useful gifts for the newcomers, most of them for the Spaniards' new wives, for Tayho was already amply provided with household plunder. When she saw what our women were doing, Tayho trotted off to her lodge and returned with an armload of her own goods, which she divided between the two later arrivals, whose hands kept flying to their mouths in wonderment, lest their spirits fly off at witnessing such prodigies.

When at last our women had exhausted their largesse, Micah stood up and dragged a heavy canvas poke to the open space in front of the Arapaho women. He reached inside and brought out three rifles which he had converted from flintlocks to percussion, freshly oiled, shiny brass furniture gleaming in the firelight. He laid them, one by one, in front of each seated woman. They stared at the weapons, exchanging perplexed looks amongst themselves, not daring to touch them, looking up at Micah, their eyes pleading for an explanation, whilst he added powder horns, bullet pouches, and belt pokes containing the fixin's to each heap. When the sack was empty, he stepped back and signed to Kathleen to come forward and explain the purpose of this final present to the baffled women.

Which I daresay Cat was happy to do, her hands fluttering in rapid finger-talk, a broad smile lighting her face in the fire's glow. She commenced by telling the newcomers that they were trappers' wives now, that the rigid old rules for women no longer applied to them, and that they would be expected to learn new ways and new things, but that she and her sisters would teach them. She went on to reveal that all six original women in the bunch were proficient now in the use of their rifles and she assured them that they, too, could and would learn to defend themselves and their comrades in case of need.

She reminded them that our bunch was few in number, that we could not rely on a band or tribe to defend us if we were attacked. Which naturally led her to the day of triumph that she shared with every woman in our bunch. She described our battle with the Bannocks, Indian-style, relating every jot and tittle of the fight, as warriors do at a scalp dance and at every opportunity thereafter.

As Cat continued her description of the gunfight, my attention shifted first to Little Mountain, who had originally vigorously resisted the idea of arming women. Now he simply looked interested as Kathleen encouraged his new wife and the other two Arapaho women to embrace the heretofore heretical idea of females taking up arms in their own defense. At first Tayho appeared opposed, then merely skeptical of Cat's proposal, which was alien to every feminine rule she had been taught from her cradleboard on up, but it was plain that she was warming to the idea the more she considered its merits, which was an understandable response from the only daughter of a warrior chief. I reckoned that Rosa and Maria would go along with whatever the chief's daughter decided.

Switching my gaze to the Iroquois husbands of Sally and Mary, I saw them exchange a look of resignation followed by a shrug that acknowledged defeat.

Kathleen wisely refrained from demanding immediate acceptance of her proposal regarding the rifles. Later, howsomever, I reckoned that she had been pretty much successful when I saw the two new Arapaho brides pick up Micah's hardware gifts after the feast and tote the guns off to their lodges. More surprising was seeing Little Mountain perform that chore for his beauteous Tayho woman. But then, Little Mountain has always been a fast learner.

∽   ∽   ∽

After that, winter camp life continued pretty much the same as it usually does. The new women blended smoothly into our little band, getting used to our ways and picking up bits and pieces of American lingo, commencing, naturally, with goddam and sumbitch. A plenitude of game thereabouts kept our bellies full and firewood was plentiful, so there was time aplenty to read and re-read my books, add daily scribbles to my journal, and play with my son Ben, who was growing like a proverbial weed and tottering about the lodge in his early attempts to walk.

Attending to Iris's schooling was perhaps my most pleasurable winter camp occupation, almost equaled, howsomever, by the satisfaction I gained from instructing her little redheaded swain, Paddy's son Sean. The elder McBride had tried to teach his son to read, but he lacked both patience and skill for that chore, so he besought me to do the job for him. I was ably assisted by seven-year-old Iris, who had been reading since she was three. Her presence at his lessons guaranteed his rapt attention and determined effort.

Every teacher should have such an aide. I reckon the principal reason why the loutish, half-grown German farm boys in Whynot gained even a shred of literacy was because most of them were in puppy love with my pretty schoolmarm mother.

Story-telling was a popular pastime in winter camp, enjoyed not only by the children, but everyone, Indian or white, male or female, who could understand American English, our common tongue. Powatawa was a treasure house of Shawnee children's How stories, tales that described how the bobcat lost his tail, where the Milky Way came from, how the Man in the Moon got up there in the night sky, and an apparently inexhaustible stock of folklore. And Kathleen would, from time to time, entertain the children with old Séli wintertime fables and legends she had learned as a child. I daresay Zeetlah could have enriched our story-telling sessions with old Lenape lore, but he never did.

Finn McCool and Paddy McBride told from memory in their lilting Irish brogue the cherished myths of Ireland, the ancient exploits of Brian Boru and Cuchulain, Mad Sweeney, and the Voyage of Bran. Tuttle and Anse often delighted us with ballads from the eastern mountain people, such as "Barb'ry Allen" and other musical accounts mostly of unrequited love that ended unhappily for all concerned, Anse sawing sweetly on his fiddle and Tuttle singing the story in his rich baritone.

I took my turn by reading aloud the adventurous tales of King Arthur and his knights of the Round Table from Sir Thomas Malory's *Morte d'Arthur*, a precious book that I had swapped away from my friend Etienne Lebref at rendezvous the previous summer.

Of all the How stories that my father told the children in winter camp, the one they constantly urged him to tell, over and over again, was "How the Bobcat Lost His Tail". I will try to tell it here, without attempting to capture Powatawa's distinctive accent and use of English, a tongue he did not acquire until he was a grown young man.

"One late autumn morning, long ago, in the Moon When Birds Fly South, when Snow-maker had turned all the land white and choked up all the streams with ice every night, although he still continued to let them run free again in the late forenoon. One morning, Bobcat, whom Shawnees call Poo-setha, came out of his den in a hollow tree, shivering with cold and rubbing his empty belly. He was hungry. Game was scarce because of the cold weather. The birds had flown away to the warm southland and most of the forest critters were hiding away from the cold in their caves and holes.

"Now in those days bobcats still had a long, graceful tail of which they were very proud, always switching it around and showing off, like catamounts still do.

"Poo-setha's stomach was rumbling with hunger, but it didn't appear that he would soon find anything to eat. Then he spied an otter trudging along the trail dragging a big mess of catfish. 'Oh-ho!' said Poo-setha, 'there is my breakfast! I'll take those fish away from the otter and maybe I'll eat him, too!' "So he waited behind a tree until the otter came nigh, then leapt out and snarled, 'You have too many fish! I'll take them for my breakfast and, now that I think of it, I will eat you, too!'

"Otter was very affrighted, but they are canny critters. He replied, 'I reckon I can't stop you from taking my fish and eating me for boot, for I can't run fast on land. In the water it would be a different matter. You will eat well today, Poo-setha, but how will you break your fast tomorrow? If you let me go, I can show you how to get a bigger mess of fish than this one every day, the whole year around. You'll never go hungry again.'

"That stopped Poo-setha in his tracks. Hungry though he was, he was even greedier. Food every day, all winter long, was almost too good to be true. How could I do that,' he asked warily. 'I can't swim the way you otters do.'

"'You don't have to,' Otter replied. 'I got these fish in yonder crick. The ice has thawed now. All you need to do is sit beside the crick and hang your beautiful long tail in the water. The fish will get on it and nibble at it. You can tell by how many nibbles you feel just how many fish have snared themselves on it. When you reckon you have caught enough, just draw your tail out of the water very quickly, so they can't jump off, and you'll have a fine mess of fish for your supper.'

"'That's a first-rate plan,' Poo-setha told him. 'All right, you can go.' So without a word of thanks to the otter, he hurried off to the crick, where he sat all day on the bank, dangling his tail in the water and listening to his stomach growling and grumbling with hunger. He felt a passel of nibbles on his tail, but he didn't want to pull it out of the water until he was sure he had a really big mess of catfish on it.

"He stayed on the crickbank all day with his tail in the water, until the sun nearly went to sleep in the west. His tail commenced to hurt, but he was too greedy to pull it out. He wanted a really big mess of catfish for his supper. He told himself, 'I feel more and more nibbles! What a good supper I will eat tonight!'

"The autumn air became ever more chilly as the sun faded into the west. Poo-setha's teeth commenced to chatter and he shivered all the way from his whiskery nose to where his tail entered the water, but he thought only of the huge catfish supper he would have that night.

"At last the aches and pains from the cold water became even greater than his greed. He reckoned it was time to pull his tail out of the crick, very quickly, as the Otter had told him to do. But when he tried to do so, he found that his tail was held fast. He pulled and tugged and yanked. He snarled and growled and howled. But the crick wouldn't let go. The truth commenced to dawn on Poo-setha. His tail was frozen in the ice!

"Poo-setha became very angry then, which never helps anybody's clear thinking, and he gave a mighty heave of his whole body, as if he were pouncing upon a fat doe, which jerked his tail clean off!

"So it was that Poo-setha returned to his den that night, snarling at shadows, even hungrier than he had been that morning, angrier than he had ever been, and nursing a terrible ache where his magnificent tail used to be.

"So that is how Poo-setha lost his beautiful tail and became a bobcat. He still keeps his eyes peeled for that otter."

The way I wrote that is not even remotely like the way Powatawa talks. I got caught up in his oft-told story and wrote it my way. Perhaps I'll try to make it sound more like my father before I turn this manuscript over to Euphemius.

ॐ   ॐ   ॐ

Winter camp provides time, too, to repair worn and broken horse gear and tools, hone my knives, tomahawks, and hatchets, clean and oil and restore to prime condition my rifles, pistols, and my smoothbore fowler, and scrape rust and dirt off my traps, daydreaming the while of springtime and the wealth of plews I will harvest when it comes.

Most of the chores that used to occupy most of my waking hours in winter camp, making and repairing moccasins and clothing and suchlike tasks, had been assumed by Kathleen, not because I asked her to, but because she insists that it is unseemly for a man to perform domestic chores if he has a woman to do them. According to her, it reflects poorly on him and especially his woman if he does. I daresay Little Mountain, Cesár, and Diego were happily adjusting to their new way of life in that regard, as well as not having to sleep alone.

One of the few prices the new husbands had to pay for this connubial felicity, if they still retained any objection to women using firearms, was teaching their spouses how to shoot. Cat wasted no time in marshaling her new recruits each afternoon, together with their husbands, winter weather permitting, and leading them to the edge of camp, where she had set up targets for rifle practice. If the husbands were not available, she dragooned Paddy, Turtle, Micah, or myself into instructing the new brides in loading, aiming, shooting, and cleaning and oiling their weapons afterwards. Like the earlier pupils, they excelled in running a stock of near-perfect rifle balls to refill their bullet pouches.

Of the three women, Tayho took to this once-forbidden pursuit with the most enthusiasm and skill, which was not surprising. This only daughter of a warrior chief had likely yearned for the approbation and comradeship that Touches-the-Sky was required by long-established custom to grant only to a son. No matter how much he might love her, he could not ignore centuries of tradition regarding the respective roles and behavior of the sexes.

In a short time, Tayho's example and encouragement emboldened the other two brides to shed their reluctance to flout Arapaho tradition. They soon became enthusiastic and steadily-improving marksmen.

∿ ∿ ∿

January blustered into February, which blew into March, which warmed its tail end sufficiently to let us commence trapping in early April in the streams that flowed off the surrounding mountains. Our fall harvest had greatly reduced the beaver population nigh our camp, so we had to work farther and farther afield in order to trap the four or five plews a day which my greedy companions and I had come to expect in that beaver-rich valley.

It is a tribute to the comeliness and desirability of Arapaho women that our bachelor comrades conserved enough time and energy to keep on visiting the Arapaho village at night, after they finished running their trap lines during daylight hours. It is a tribute, as well, to those Arapaho widows who were willing to put up with the unfamiliar godawful stink of castoreum bait, which their trapper beaux had been mostly free of during the winter months.

Spring trapping was pretty much the same as the autumn harvest had been, except that the valley's winter cold had enriched the plews to a deep, downy luxuriance that was sure to make a trader's mouth water with greed. Although we needed to ride farther and farther out each day to continue our profitable daily haul of plews, our bachelors were reluctant to move the camp. Even practical Kit Carson voted to remain where we were, seconded by Little Mountain who kept throwing his vote in with the bachelors, likely because his woman preferred a location close to her parents in the Arapaho village. Besides the obvious attraction of a compliant widow somewhere in the village, word was that Kit was powerful sweet on a pretty young girl who had captured his heart.

The argument to move camp diminished, naturally, with the receding snow, so we stayed put throughout much of the springtime, until the Arapaho middens, and our own, became intolerable in the warming weather. We met with Touches-the-Sky to choose the new location for his village and our camp, which happily turned out to be nigh so-far-untouched trapping grounds.

An unusual event, or rather a series of them, helped made the spring harvest in the valley even more memorable. All seven of the pampered *palomilla* mares of our wives and my daughter Iris foaled within the space of a fortnight, producing four fillies and three stud colts, all of the youngsters promising to run true to their creamy *palomilla* color. Most of the extra work of caring for the newborns naturally fell to the women, for hardly anything but a major Blackfoot war can dissuade a trapper from conducting the spring harvest, especially in country swarming with beaver apparently eager to visit our traps.

Constant trading with our neighbors for fine furs—mink, otter, fisher, and marten, which abounded in the valley—as well as the exquisite quillwork and distinctive beaded items their women produced had pretty well exhausted the vast supply of trade goods we had acquired at rendezvous, even at the rock-bottom prices we were paying for them. We were forced, at last, to turn away a galore of furs and craft goods that we would have snapped up in a blink if we had still possessed the wherewithal to buy them.

Even our bachelors found themselves increasingly obliged to rely on their dubious charms to reward their Arapaho lights-o'-love for robe favors.

But even without a ready market at hand, the Arapaho bravos kept on amassing a galore of fine furs and occasional beaver that they clubbed in their dens and their women continued to take advantage of the relative leisure of wintertime to produce more valuable quilled and beaded merchandise—moccasins, fancy shirts and dresses and handsome antelope leggin's, pipe bags, belt pokes, knife sheaths, and suchlike, all of which would bring a pretty penny at rendezvous.

It's impossible to know for sure, but not hard to fathom what made Kit Carson talk Touches-the-Sky into agreeing to call a council with his headmen about taking their band northward along with us to the whiteman's rendezvous at Horse Crick that coming summer. Carson is close-mouthed as a clam about his personal affairs, but his mooning about the Arapaho camp whenever that particular pretty girl showed up purely gave him away. It wasn't that Kit was precisely doing without whilst he was plighting his troth to the maiden of his choice, but most Indian women concede that grown men have their needs and generously overlook temporary dalliances if they themselves are unwilling or unable to satisfy those needs. Tuttle, in spite of how lucky he usually is, teamed up several years before with a Snake woman who refused to tolerate his fornicating ways and threw him out, but she was an exception to the rule. Even her Shoshone family thought she was silly.

We continued trapping well into May of 1835, until warm weather at last called a halt. Snow was nearly gone, even in the woods. The prairie had greened up and critters' ribs were fast disappearing into good hard fat. Shaggy winter coats were growing sleek and shiny once again. Beaver plews had become too measly to bother with.

Heaps of stiff, cured plews cluttered the camp, wherever a forest of drying racks loaded with strips of rich red buffalo meat drying in warm sunshine left any room for them. A festive air prevailed in anticipation of heading for the pleasures of rendezvous. When they weren't busy fleshing and tanning a half-acre of fresh buffalo hides pegged out on the outskirts of camp, our women were bundling into snug bales a wealth of fine furs and valuable craftwork of their own together with the large quantity they had obtained from Arapaho women before we ran out of trade goods.

The bachelors were similarly occupied, though to a lesser extent, since, in most cases, the bulk of their wealth had been spent in pursuit of amatory pleasures.

The Arapaho village was also infected with eager anticipation of a thrilling new experience. Touches-the-Sky's proposal for the band to accompany the white-eyes trappers to their huge gathering in the north country had at last been approved by the council of elders. Although the tall chief exercised considerable influence in his band, his authority was not absolute. Several council members suspected that he was reluctant to bid a final farewell to his daughter and wished to postpone the day of their parting. Which was true. The council, howsomever, was composed of men who had been leading warriors in the band, bold, adventurous men who had gained the esteem and respect of their fellows by their acts of courage and daring. The temptation of counting one more coup was too much resist. After much palavering, they voted to accompany us on the long journey north.

-ooo-

CHAPTER XIII
KAINAHS

I reined Crane off the trail at the mouth of the canyon and halted for a final look back at the lush valley where we had passed our most successful trapping season ever, the most pleasant, as well, and one that had altered the lives of three of our fellows.

"Kinda hate leavin' thi'shere place, even if it's fer headin' up to ronnyvoo," Tuttle opined. He, too, had ridden off the trail and paused beside me to gaze at the broad green prairie, wooded foothills, and towering peaks that had presided over our season in paradise. "Who'd'a thought we could'a been havin' so much fun ther same time we war gittin' richer'n we ever done? Course, had'n'a been fer Sky-toucher showin' up with his widders an' all, ronnyvoo'd be lookin' a whole lot better fer us fellers what ain't packin' our own wimmen along."

"Ye ever think o' tryin' it again, Tuttle?" I asked. "Gettin' married to a good woman, I mean?"

"Oh, hell no!" he replied with considerable heat. "Thet'ere last'n cured me somethin' proper! I'd ruther go without, 'tween times, 'twixt ronnyvoo an' most winter camps, than let m'se'f in fer ther kind o' naggin' an' fightin' thet'ere loony loud-mouth Snake woman put me through fer a whole gawddamn year! No thankee!"

He was so vehement in his resistance to the whole idea of teaming up with a permanent woman that I let it go.

Gazing back across the prairie, I made out the tall figure of Touches-the-Sky, flanked by outriders, in the forefront of a long procession of his people that snaked far behind the leaders until they disappeared in high grass waving lazily in a soft springtime breeze. Apparently the promise of a new adventure that we were taking them on had warmed the band towards us even more than they had been earlier. Even the usually-reserved headmen appeared more cordial now, allowing themselves a fleeting smile and a nod bestowed in our direction, whenever we chanced to encounter them in the village.

By that time the last of our loose horses trailing the column were filing into the narrow canyon mouth in twos and threes, followed by Half-horse and his two helpers, Iris and Sean. The new filly of Iris's *palomilla* mare romped and frolicked at her mother's side, now and again attempting to shove her nose under her belly to avail herself of a teat, which the mare discouraged with a shrug and a halfhearted kick in the filly's direction.

I swung Crane about, brushed him lightly with a spur, and joined them. Tuttle fell in beside me. "I din't mean to bark atcha, pard," he said apologetically. "It's jest thet thet'ere yammerin' bitch gave me a vatchinashun agin hookin' up ever agin thet'll sure-as-hell last longer'n anythin' Doc McCool kin think of to jab me with. Don't take it pers'nal."

I assured him that I didn't. That appeared to please him. A smile replaced his troubled look. Soon he said, "Reckon I'll ride on up front an' see if I kin be of he'p." Which he did at an easy lope, bidding g'mornin' to our comrades as he passed by.

The loose horses and Anse's spare saddle mules brought up the rear of our column. There weren't so many of them this time, mostly our saddlers. Almost every packhorse and mule we owned was either dragging a travois or burdened with a couple packs of plews, soft-tanned robes, vittles, or camp gear. All of the Bannock ponies we had inherited after the battle had been pressed into service.

I commenced to work my way forward in the column, observing that the cranky packmules, fractious from lush graze and their long layoff from regular work, were beginning to abandon their ornery behavior and settle into their chores. In time I came up with the women, riding in a group, the original six all riding their *palomilla* mares in a final showing off to the women of Touches-the-Sky's village. Their colts and fillies frisked and capered nearby, some of them now and then trying to steal a mouthful of mare's milk from mama, only to be met with a nip or a casual gentle kick from their dam. The youngsters were nigh two months old and already weaned on tender new springtime grass. It was past time to give up the teat. Privately I thanked little Ben for his willingness to be weaned the year before, kindly returning those playthings to me.

He was seated behind the pommel of her saddle, chubby legs splayed out, chirping and waving when he caught sight of me. Cat passed him over to me and he and I rode together for a spell, until I spied Carson waiting at one side of the trail, gesturing for me to join him. I handed my boy back to Kathleen while Ben squalled at being parted from me. I leaned out to plant a hasty kiss on his cheek before I spurred Crane into a lope to answer Kit's summons.

Kit swung his mount around, proceeding at a walk towards the head of the column. When I reined up and fell into a walk beside him, he said, "Best ye ride up front with some o' the others fer a spell. Thi'shere narrer canyon, with all o' them'ere big rocks up on the sides makin' it too easy fer hidin' out, is too good a place fer settin' a trap. Keep yer eyes peeled an' yer gun ready 'til we git through it."

His request was one that he would repeat often on our journey back to Horse Crick. Our experience with the Bannocks the year before had made us more cautious than usual. Traveling as I was with my wife and children, I didn't mind a mite being assigned such duty.

∾   ∾   ∾

The next several days were uneventful. We retraced our backtrail through the same country we had traveled the previous autumn. Distance of our daily travel depended on finding enough water for the Arapahoes' numerous band and their huge horse herd, resulting sometimes in remarkably brief days in the saddle, others commencing at daybreak and stretching into dusk.

It had been a thirsty hike since we left winter camp. Our bunch was looking forward to revisiting the valley where we fought the Bannocks. In spite of unpleasant feelings the memory of that encounter might stir in us, its lush prairie and fresh-running streams pretty much erased our ill-feelings about the place.

As we approached the long, narrow, dry, high-walled canyon leading into the grassy, well-watered bowl, Kit called on me again to join a couple others riding out front to keep an eye peeled for possible marauders who might choose such a place for an ambush.

I loped to the head of the column and fell in behind Tuttle and Brass Turtle, who were in the lead, proceeding at a walk, scanning the slopes on either side, alert to any suspicious sight or movement. Our task did not encourage conversation, but there was time for random cogitating.

I wondered how Touches-the-Sky and his people would act amongst the rowdy trappers and drunken Indians they would meet there. Kit had tried to prepare the chief for what they would encounter, but there is no way to describe a trappers' rendezvous, even to someone with whom you share a common tongue. He had explained, too, that tribal enmities are mostly suspended at rendezvous—except for Bannocks, who are slow learners—so the serious business of trading can be conducted peacefully. Fortunately, most of the traditional enemies of the Arapaho reside to the east and south of their home ground, so they would not likely meet up with them at Horse Crick.

Touches-the-Sky and a few of his warriors had already done some trading at Bent's Fort, not far from Taos, that had opened up a couple years earlier, so they had some idea of what to expect from rendezvous traders.

Meanwhile, Kit was doing his damnedest to learn Arapaho lingo so that he could do some serious courting of his intended bride, who was called Wa'a Nibé, Grass Singing. I had caught a glimpse of her once in the Arapaho village. It was easy to see why young Carson had fallen in love with her. Young as she was, she was a sure-enough beautiful woman.

Short in stature though he is, Carson is a natural leader, but he is no Napoleon. Our bunch doesn't cotton to taking orders and Kit doesn't like giving them, but none of us objected to his authority. Young as he is, his quiet manner, thorough knowledge of our trade, grit, and remarkable memory of country he has traveled through, wrapped up with a galore of practical commonsense makes it easy to do what he suggests. He never issues commands. He just suggests.

Whilst I was wool-gathering, while I scanned every rock and bush on the steep, barren hillsides, I wondered, too, how Fitzpatrick and Fontenelle would greet the windfall of plews we were bringing, especially at the premium price Pierre Chouteau and they themselves had agreed to pay us and all the other trappers and Indian bands we had recruited. Although it might represent a negligible amount of money at Saint Louis prices for beaver, it would take a substantial bite out of the new company's rendezvous profits. Maybe Pierre Chouteau would make up the difference for them. Maybe not.

Then, too, another conundrum I couldn't begin to solve was how the new partners proposed to conduct their business this year under the nose of canny Bill Sublette without alerting him to their breach of contract.

From time to time, Kit rode forward, making sure that we didn't follow a wrong trail into a blind canyon. That had happened a few times the last time we came through there and winter snows and spring thaws had mostly washed away our tracks from the year before.

As the day wore on, we began to wish for some of that winter snow. The treeless canyon commenced to heat up in springtime sunshine, much hotter than it had been the previous autumn. My woolen capote went first, then my leather shirt, at last my calico shirt, and I was still sweating.

The trail meandered between high, rocky hills, bereft of water or grass, offering no proper place for nooning, so we kept plodding on, but mindful of the slow-moving caravan behind us, we couldn't speed our pace. At last the trail opened onto a broad grassy basin that stretched out to another range of low hills. "Thar's whar we fit them'ere Bannock bastards las' fall," Tuttle growled, pointing to a notch in the hills, the canyon mouth where we had forted up. He brightened and added, "Thar's buffler hyar thet we never got a chance to git a-holt of! Remember?"

I remembered all too well that right after I first saw buffalo on that prairie, I completely lost interest in them, because the next thing I saw was that band of bloodthirsty Bannocks.

"Fust thangs fust!" Turtle muttered through parched lips. "I be spittin' cotton! Water 'pears a helluva lot better'n buffler hump to my thinkin' right now!"

Crane kept leaning against the bit, swinging his head in the direction of a patch of willows clustered beside the rocky hillside, nickering insistently the while. "There's water nigh those willows!" I called out over my shoulder and turned Crane loose to go find it.

First Turtle, then Tuttle overtook me and left me trailing as they galloped in quest of water, which was flowing knee-deep behind a screen of willows. They burst through the fragile barrier and landed in the midst of a stream a couple-three yards wide. Turtle slung his rifle and fixin's over the pommel and threw himself out of the saddle into the chill water, thrashing and laughing in delight whilst his horse buried his nose in the cool stream up to his eyes.

Tuttle, always careful never to become too familiar with the wet stuff for fear his hide might rust, gigged his mount up the far bank and stepped down before turning him loose to drink his fill, then returned to the crick with his cup.

I followed the Delaware's example, tossing my rifle, horn, and belt onto the far bank before dropping into the water and splashing alongside Turtle, hoping the while that Crane wouldn't roll in the water to cool his sweaty back. Which he kindly refrained from doing.

By time we stepped dripping onto the bank, the main column was emerging from the canyon mouth and heading for the crick, which meandered across the grassy plain.   We caught up our mounts and rode over to join our companions, all of whom were either on their knees along the bank, scooping up handfuls of water to slake their thirst and drenching their fevered heads or squatting in the cool water, doing likewise. Iris and Sean ran full-tilt to the river bank and launched themselves in a spectacular belly-flop, splattering everyone nearby. Nobody minded. Kathleen knelt in the shallow stream, laving cooling water over little Ben, who giggled and chirruped happily as he splashed and kicked in her arms, all previous discomfort forgotten in his delight with his new experience.

Half-horse tried to drive his loose critters downstream to drink, with indifferent success. Most of them broke from the gather, heading for the water even before they saw it. They crowded in amongst the people along the bank, shoving their noses deep underwater, several stepping into the crick and rolling on their backs. Nobody minded them, either.

When everyone had drunk his fill and laved off most of the sweat and grime, we returned to last year's overnight camp under the trees farther up the crick, just in time to vacate the watering patch we had been using, before the Arapaho band with its seventy-odd lodges caught up with us and spread out along the crick until they were lost to view in the tall grass far out on the prairie.

Whilst the women erected lodges and the campkeepers and bigger kids gathered firewood, a dozen of us switched saddles to fresh horses and prepared to harvest a couple brace of buffalo for supper. We didn't need that many hunters, but the possibility of running into hostile Indians again made us cautious.

Crane had righteously earned a night of leisurely grazing and a following day of freedom, running with the loose bunch. I saddled Coffee for the hunt, examining the loads in my rifle and the pistols in my pommel holsters on the way to join the others, making sure that the gunpowder hadn't got wet during our bathing spree. I had already pulled the charges and dried out my belly gun, which had gotten drenched from my plunge in the crick.

When I rode up to the hunting party, Finn was clenching a fistful of grass stems, inviting me to pull one out. I did so and saw it was a long one. I would not be one of the six buffalo runners that day. My job, together with the other five disappointed ones, would be to ride in the wake of the half-dozen shooters, in case they encountered hostiles, and to help with butchering their kills. Our aim was to harvest four young buffalo bulls. Cows were still puny from nursing their calves.

McCool also failed to draw a winning straw. I fell in beside him and he and I moved out from the others, scanning the prairie to the horizon, seeking to detect a mass of brown hides or movement that might prove to be our intended quarry. The earth had pretty much dried out in springtime sun. It was still springy underfoot, but firm enough to permit running our prey without more hazard than that particular sport always presents.

Off to the east, half a mile distant, I caught sight of first one, then two, then three large parties of Arapaho hunters riding onto the prairie from their riverbank encampments. Brass Turtle saw them, too, and waved our party to the west, so that our hunt wouldn't interfere with theirs.

A triumphant halloo from Little Mountain, riding out front on a big deep-chested buckskin gelding, a wedding gift from his father-in-law, set us all—save the two unfortunates who had drawn straws that assigned them to leading packmules to haul the meat back to camp—into a galloping pursuit of a couple dozen buffalo that had suddenly emerged into view from a gully in the gently rolling prairie.

As we drew nigh the bunch, Finn and I and the other long-straws fell back, allowing the hunters to race ahead unimpeded to overtake the buffalo, now in full retreat, gaining speed with every stride. The hunters disappeared inside the mass of critters. Soon we heard the crack of gunshots. First one shaggy brown heap appeared sprawled on the prairie, then another successful kill was exposed as the herd rushed off. Two horsemen appeared, walking back to their kills, reloading as they went. More gunshots in the distance testified to continued success and a guarantee of satisfied appetites in camp.

McCool and I rode forward, passing by Paddy McBride and a grinning Diego Valenzuela already at work with butcher knives on a fat young bull, going after fresh liver. Diego and his *Californio compañero*, Pablo Torres, had become righteous mountaineers in the year since we had released them from Batista's durance vile and adopted them into our bunch.

We continued at a brisk trot, past Micah then Brass Turtle standing nigh their kills awaiting help to commence butchering. We hailed them but kept trotting in the wake of the buffalo bunch, now long gone into the hazy horizon. At last we came upon Little Mountain and, a little farther on, Tuttle Thompson, perched on the flank of a chunky young bull, smoking his pipe and looking glum. "Well, now," I greeted him in a joshing tone, "it certainly took ye long enough to get that'n down."

"Don'tcha be funnin' me 'baout thet, nohaow, Temple Buck!" he replied testily. "I'd'a had muh buffler daown fust off, if ther powder hadn'a got wet in muh rifle-gun in ther crick back thar! I taken this'n daown with muh pistol!"

Mountain had followed us on his handsome buckskin. He, too, was looking somewhat sheepish at taking so long to kill his buffalo. "Dis hoss got a lot o' l'arnin' comin' afore I call 'im a buffler-runner. I war thinkin muh daddy-in-law would'a trained 'im better'n he done! Took more'n a mile 'fore I got 'im runnin' right!"

"All's well that ends well, Mountain," Finn reassured him. "That's all that's countin', lad. Ye got yer buffler, after all. Now ye know what's still to be done with educatin' yer pretty horse. By the look of 'im, once he learns your ways, he'll sarve ye well!"

Remembering our last hunt on that grassy plain, I commenced feeling uncomfortable about so few of us being so far away from the others, We were scattered out over a mile and a half of prairie. "Best we get to butcherin' your bufflers, wouldn't ye say?" I cut in. "There'll be time enough for palaverin' back in camp." Without waiting for a reply, I untied a roll of ship's canvas from behind my saddle cantle and spread it out alongside Tuttle's hefty young bull.

Four of us working at the butchering made short work of it, taking time out only to savor slices of fresh liver. We heaped the choice cuts, hump, tongue, boudins, backstrap, and whatever else we deemed useful onto the canvas, covered it over, and moved on to perform the same task on Little Mountain's bull.

We had nearly completed the job on Mountain's kill when Torres showed up leading two packmules, empty panniers swinging off their packsaddles. We loaded the meat and hides from both bulls in hardly more time than it takes to tell it and headed back to the others, who were ready to return by time we joined them.

❧   ❧   ❧

Several cookfires were already burning down to coals when we dropped the heavy panniers beside them. Jean-Luc and Yves and several women helpers commenced spearing chunks of fat meat onto steel wiping rods, suspending them over the embers, and rinsing boudins in the crick and coiling them in spider skillets generously greased with crackling bear fat. Water was already boiling in a couple-three copper kettles, awaiting the tongues.

I headed upstream and joined the other hunters, washing off blood and dirt from the butchering. Carson came by and pointed out that that we had been too good at our harvesting chore. Four critters were twice too many for our camp, even for carrying along unused cooked meat the next day. The meat from the two extra carcasses would surely spoil, hot as the weather was. Kit recommended that we donate the extra meat to the Arapahoes, which got everybody's approval. No matter how successful their hunters might have been, seventy lodges can always use more meat.

When Carson was out of earshot, Tuttle said in a low voice, "Givin' ol' Sky-Toucher ther extry critters is a damn good idee, natcherly, cornsid'rin' all he's done fer us, but I 'spec ol' Kit's wishin' fer anuther peek at thet'ere li'l gal he's got his heart set on." Which was likely so.

Little Mountain volunteered to accompany Kit on his mission and naturally his Tayho woman insisted on going along to visit her parents, which nobody begrudged her. We loaded the panniers onto a couple packmules and the trio set out for the Arapaho camp.

It required only a fleeting half-second of sympathizing with Kit, whose heart had triumphed over his belly, and Little Mountain, whose concerns were likely centered somewhat lower on his corpus when he chose not to disappoint his beautiful new wife, before I hotfooted to one of the cookfires for slabs of juicy hump meat and a yard of crispy smoking-hot boudins, for a start. Breaking my fast that early morning was, by then, only a distant memory my appetite couldn't recall.

❧ ❧ ❧

We resumed our journey early next morning. Although our critters had been considerably taxed the day before, the trail that day would be gently downsloping and easy and the country would provide abundant graze during the next several days' travel. After that, hungry times for our animals lay ahead and Kit wished to put as many miles behind us each day as conditions permitted. Buffalo grass that had been dry and sere when we last passed through was now springtime green and succulent. Half-horse and his two young apprentices were hard put to keep the loose stock from straying from the column and grazing in the verdant meadows we passed on our way. Once we left Battle Valley, as some of our people had begun to call it, there were few cricks and streams, but Carson, Micah, and a couple Arapaho scouts managed to keep finding enough water to prevent hardship for us and the Arapahoes.

Micah reckoned that Kit was almost as interested in learning the Arapaho tongue from the scouts as he was in seeking their help in locating watering holes. But so was Micah.

This time, Carson was less concerned than he had been the previous fall with locating our night camps in places that might be defended against raiding parties. Touches-the-Sky's populous village camped beside us would discourage all but an army from launching an attack. Horse thieves, howsomever, were another matter. We never failed to hobble our livestock and post horse guards wherever we camped.

As one week slid into the next, the trail continued its downward progress and weather warmed somewhat every day, punctuated now and again with welcome spring showers that cooled our hides and settled the trail dust stirred up by our lengthy caravan. I daresay our Arapaho neighbors greeted gentle rainfall even more enthusiastically than we did, for their cavalcade stretched out of sight and kicked up a dusty cloud when they were on the march.

Buffalo had apparently left that particular stretch of country, but leading the parade, as we were doing, allowed our hunters keep us supplied with enough wapiti and black-tail deer to sustain our small party, conserving our stock of dried meat that we would need when we traversed the barren desert that lay ahead. Sixty-odd lodges of Arapahoes, howsomever, likely wiped the landscape pretty clean of game critters when they passed through behind us.

Long hours in the saddle, seeking each day to put as many miles behind us as possible, with little else to do than chouse up laggard critters and follow my nose, gave me time to spend with my daughter and, inevitably, her constant companion Sean the Redheaded Woodpecker McBride. Iris had grown taller and stronger over the winter we spent in Arapaho Valley, as some of our people were now calling our wintertime retreat. Eden might have been a better name for it. Her horsemanship, for which she had shown a natural talent since she was first able to straddle a critter, had improved greatly during the long daily hikes, which required her to use, each day, several different horses that I had placed in her *remuda*, not only her favorite *palomilla* mare. Paddy, too, had provided his son with three more pint-sized saddlers that he traded from the Arapahoes, so that the youngster might keep up with my daughter.

Filling idle time on what appeared to be a never-ending trail, I took to telling them tales my mother had told to me when I was about their present age, which provided a double pleasure for me, passing along those priceless legends to another generation and conjuring up the image of my mother, as I did my best to recall the words she used to relate the heroic adventures of Cuchulain, Brian Boru, the French Roland, Scottish patriot William Wallace, and King Arthur's knights of the Round Table.

∾ ∾ ∾

After weeks on the trail descending from the eastern sierras, we came to a familiar valley that held pleasant memories for us all, even if it also stirred in us a certain disquiet, for it called to mind what lay immediately beyond. We had come to call it Bear Meadow amongst ourselves, in memory of Pablo and Diego standing fast in the path of a raging grizzly boar and dropping him in his tracks. Our *Californios* had proved their grit that day.

The valley flourished now in springtime splendor, even more delightful than the previous autumn. A riot of colorful flowers sprinkled hock-high grass that carpeted the mile-wide bowl laced with free-flowing streams from the eastern slopes and running off to the south, surrounded on three sides by thick pine forests dotted with green meadows that provided a plenitude of wapiti and deer and, naturally, grizzlies.

Most of the west side of the basin stood in stark contrast to the rest, rising in forbidding, treeless, rocky bluffs that glowered over the fertile vale, stirring memories of the week-long trudge through the barren, mostly waterless country that lay on the other side.

It was profitless, howsomever, to dwell on future privation. We were better served to enjoy our comfortable surroundings whilst we had them at hand. Which we proceeded to do.

Several of us married men headed into the woods to harvest wapiti for the camp whilst our women stowed our baggage and erected lodges beside one of several fresh-running streams flowing off the forested slope. Kids and the campkeepers gathered deadfall for cookfires. Our sweaty, trail-weary critters rolled and romped in belly-high green grass. Bachelors fashioned bowers from willows growing alongside the crick and covered them with hides and sail canvas, for we intended to stay put for a spell.

By time Touches-the-Sky led his band into the valley a couple-three hours later, most of us men were sprawled alongside the cookfire, bellies full, smoking a pipeful of our fast-diminishing tobacco, palavering about how it wouldn't be long now until we got to Horse Crick.

In no time at all five or six dozen lodges sprouted up in the meadow and the hills echoed with musket fire as hunters went in search of supper. Kit saddled a horse and rode over to the Arapaho camp, as a matter of respect and possibly to confer with the chief about what was coming up when we took to the trail again.

I, on the other hand, was obliged to do no such thing. When Kathleen beckoned invitingly from the doorway of our lodge, I jumped to my feet and trotted off to our sleeprobes.

ॐ ॐ ॐ

The next few days were memorable only because nothing occurred to mar our pleasure at doing not much at all. Cat and I took Iris and Sean fishing a quarter-mile downstream. The youngsters ran through the tall grass snatching up grasshoppers for bait whilst I fashioned willow poles and equipped them with English silken line and sharp metal hooks. The sleek, firm-fleshed trout-fish we caught provided great sport and a toothsome variation from our regular diet.

The women scoured the surrounding forest for edible roots and herbs, tender wild onions, and a variety of mushrooms, to season their stews, whilst a couple-three men went along with rifles ready in case of another visit by Old Ephraim, which fortunately did not occur.

Our livestock continued to recruit themselves on the rich graze, relieved of all work except for short hikes under saddle to carry us to the surrounding slopes in quest of deer and elk for our cookfires.

Kit advised Touches-the-Sky to delay leaving the meadow for a couple-three days after our departure to allow the water holes to fill up again after our bunch passed through. We would also be taking along a couple more Arapaho scouts so that they might return to report to their chief what to expect in the way of water and graze, which our experience told us wouldn't be much.

ॐ ॐ ॐ

Early in the morning of the fifth day we dropped our lodges, loaded up our frisky mules and packhorses, and set out through the narrow canyon that led to the Land of Cactus and Misery, as Finnæus so picturesquely described it.

All of our critters were in good fettle after their rich feasting on what Tuttle called the greasy grass, no ribs showing, flanks and thighs bulging with hard fat, hides grown sleek and glossy in springtime warmth, their spirits much improved by the layoff.

I rode Coffee that first morning, impressed as usual with his ability to read my mind before I flicked the rein or touched him with a spur. He understood our chore, helping Half-horse keep the loose-running stock at the end of the column compact and bunched, discouraging renegades from running off into the blind canyons along our route, snaking out his head and nipping deserters on the arse. After nip or two, they usually abandoned their rebellious ways and retreated into the main bunch whenever he came nigh.

Half a day's travel through the rocky canyon brought us out onto the flat, treeless desert we recalled from last year, its only vegetation gray-green sagebrush, wicked low-growing cactus armed with long sharp needles, tall, skinny yuccas bearing pretty white springtime blossoms, and scattered clumps of coarse grass. "'Tis somewhat improved," McCool observed, eyeing the yucca blossoms, "though not nearly as much as I'd be after wishin' for."

As the day wore on, howsomever, Finn appeared to be getting more of his wish granted. Water was a little more plentiful than it had been on our earlier passage through that barren region, likely the scant remainder of wintertime snows that hadn't yet been sucked up by desert heat.

Nooning was a brief affair, consisting of a bait of the previous night's leftover vittles for us and whatever measly forage our critters could snatch from the grudging landscape. Most important, howsomever, was water and, so far, there was enough of it to slake their thirst and our own, if you could ignore how it tasted.

We made good time that day and the next, thanks to a couple of brief, cooling rains that freshened man and beast, although it did little to accumulate water for drinking. Most of it was immediately sucked into the thirsty desert soil. By common consent, we gave up nooning halts in the interest of putting more miles behind us each day. Mothers provided the little ones something to chew on at mid-day as they jounced along on their travois drags and the youngsters complained less this time than they had the year before. I never fathomed why, but we were grateful for it.

At the end of the second day, Kit recommended that we send two of the Arapaho scouts back to the meadow to advise Touches-the-Sky that there appeared to be enough water thereabouts to proceed, even for his populous band and large horse herd. We were glad to hear it. Although we were likely pretty safe from wandering hostiles whilst we were in the desert, once we entered fertile country the likelihood of encountering Blackfoots or Big-bellies greatly increased. Seventy lodges of friendly Arapahoes at our back would make us a much less attractive target for a hostile attack. Blackfoots like the odds long on their side. The sooner the Arapahoes caught up with us, the better.

We slogged through blowing dust and alkali, cursing the heat and the constant west wind that blew in our faces from early morning to nightfall. It was four more days before we saw our first real tree. It wasn't much of a tree, a scraggly jack pine hanging on for dear life in cracked, parched earth, but the Cedars of Lebanon never looked better to the wandering Israelites. Soon after that we came to a measly crick we recalled from the year before.

Men, women, kids, even Tuttle, shouldered our thirsty critters aside and rolled in its shallow depth, exulting in our success in once again crossing that arid, unfriendly, rattler-infested wasteland without losing a single critter or a member of the bunch.

Two more days brought us onto a grassy expanse that rolled westerly to the horizon. When we espied the first bunch of shaggy brown backs in the distance, Carson called a halt and sent half a dozen of us out to discover a suitable spot to establish a camp where we could wait for the Arapahoes to catch up with us. Finn and my father found an ideal site beside a sizeable clear-running stream bordered with cottonwoods and willows, backed up against one of those lone rocky promontories that unaccountably jut up in the midst of the prairie. It was about forty feet high and occupied perhaps half an acre, flanked on one side by a pine copse next to an aspen grove. We moved in without delay.

We were still stripping packs and saddles off our critters when Kit climbed atop a large boulder at the foot of the big rockpile and announced, "I clumb up hyar to tell ye, ye'll be gittin' no more orders from me! I'm shet o' ramroddin' thi'shere outfit er any other! We been thar an' back an' naow ye know that'ere country good as I do! From hyar on, I'm jist along fer the ride!"

Most of us dropped what we were doing and went to thank him for all he had done. Kit hates giving orders, so his offer to guide us had been extremely generous. He brought us through safe and sound and richer than we had ever been.

This time the women put up their lodges rather closer together than usual, mindful that we might be attacked and wishing to use the rocky eminence for protection from the rear. Once the lodges were in place, they arranged the packs in a barricade surrounding the camp. I saw that they placed the packs that contained beaver plews, tools, traps, and the like on the outside. A few bullet holes wouldn't lessen their value, as they certainly would their precious dresses, foofurraw, and trade goods.

As soon as the critters were relieved of their burdens, we hobbled them and turned them out to graze. They had no need to wander far. Grass was plentiful thereabouts and of good quality. They had easy access to water downstream from the camp and a wide place in the deep streambed next to the camp was large enough to hold our livestock out of danger from stray gunfire if a battle were to take place.

Half a dozen men had ridden out to harvest supper from the small bunch of buffalo we had spied when we first came upon the prairie. The campkeepers scooped out a couple-three shallow trenches for their cookfires and gathered deadfall from the aspen grove. Once their lodge-lifting and other household chores had been accomplished, the women departed camp to find a suitable bathing place, upstream from camp, safe from prying eyes. All but the Arapaho brides carried their rifles slung across their backs as they left. They, too, would learn about Blackfoots, I told myself, but hopefully not too soon.

Micah, Finn, Anse, and Turtle lounged on the streambank, smoking and yarning and doing not much else besides, which appeared to be a first-rate way to spend what was left of the afternoon. I joined them in all three occupations.

Naturally rendezvous occupied most of our palaver, mainly speculating on what might transpire betwixt the rivalry of Bill Sublette and the new partnership and what we might expect in either profit or abuse as a result of their competition. Naturally we knew as little at the end of our colloquy as we had at its commencement, for all of us were equally ignorant of what was happening in faraway Saint Louis.

The women came back from their bathe and the hunters returned with packmules overloaded with fresh-killed young bull meat and still we continued to puff on our pipes and pontificate on the future of the fur trade, until the tantalizing fragrance of roasting buffalo, spoons rattling on kettles, and the campkeepers' threats to throw it all to the coyotes called us to supper, which was at last a topic that we actually knew something about.

Next morning, during our bathe in the crick, a luxury long denied during our crossing of the barren waste, Micah asked me along in scouting the country west of our present camp, territory that we would need to pass through on our way to Horse Crick. I immediately agreed. Every man in the bunch knew in his bones an assault was coming, just not when. Women too. We reckoned it was better to provoke an attack rather than being surprised by it.

Yesterday's hunters had come across a couple of recently butchered buffalo carcasses on the prairie. One of them contained two broken Blackfoot arrows. Although it was possible that the arrows had belonged to, say, a Snake who had retrieved them after a skirmish sometime in the past, it was more likely that a Blackfoot raiding party was roaming the neighborhood now.

After breaking our fast, recharging our weapons with fresh loads, and announcing our plans, we saddled our best horses and set out to discover who might be lurking thereabouts. Naturally I chose Coffee for that chore. Micah was mounted on his favorite buffalo runner, a big, handsome buckskin gelding, a gift from Don Nicolás. As we rode out, several of our people were hauling logs out of the pine grove and big rocks and driftwood from the crick bottom to reinforce the barricade.

We hadn't traveled a quarter-mile before we spied Carson overtaking us at a high lope, bringing his horse to a skidding halt, then smoothly matching our jogging gait, whilst hailing us with a cheery, "Thought ye moughtn't mind some extry comp'ny. That so?"

We assured him that he was welcome to come along, which he was. Kit's trailwise smarts and quiet courage make him a valuable asset in any endeavor, especially one that might turn violent.

The pale-green prairie was sprinkled with groves of stunted jack pine and cottonwoods and willows framed the measly streams that meandered across the grassy expanse. We had ridden a couple-three miles in a westerly direction, now and then fording puny watercourses, peering into shadowy pine groves without entering, offering ourselves as bait instead of ferreting out a hidden enemy from the many possible hideaways that existed there—if, in fact, any hostiles prowled that peaceful prairie.

The three of us were spread out, riding more or less abreast, about thirty feet apart, and crossing a little crick with fairly steep banks, when Coffee's lunge up the far side set me back in the saddle just as I heard the whizz of an arrow passing by, close enough to feel the fletching scrape my chin. Naturally I yelped and grabbed for a pistol in its pommel holster, spinning Coffee about on the far bank, just in time to catch sight of a painted Indian nocking a second arrow to his bow not twenty feet away. With no time to think, I swept my hand over the hammer, cocking the pistol as I brought it up, and squeezed the trigger. When the smoke cleared, I saw him drop to his knees, coughing, retching blood, clutching his bare chest, and pitch onto his face.

"Git the hell outa hyar!" Carson yelled, which was excellent advice but completely unnecessary. He and Micah, pistols in hand, had already returned to the other side. This time, Coffee cleared the crickbed in a single bound, legs already stretched into a high lope as I leaned low over his neck, trying to offer as small a target as possible as arrows passed by and overhead, one clanging off my rifle slung across my back. I heard Kit and Micah pounding at our heels, then a pistol shot and Micah's triumphant shout, "Got 'im!" then Carson calling out, "That's two of 'em! Only a couple hunnerd more to go!"

I had to laugh in spite of our situation, which improved somewhat as we left the crickside ambush behind and gained the open prairie, just long enough to let me dump powder down the barrel of my empty pistol, spit a ball after it, pound the butt on the pommel, cap it, and shove it back into its holster. Empty guns save no lives, except your enemy's. Micah was doing likewise as he drew alongside me. Carson, mounted on the sleek, fleet bay buffalo runner he had traded from Touches-the-Sky, pulled slightly ahead, waving and pointing at a pine woods ahead on our left. A couple dozen mounted Blackfoots, likely Kainahs, painted and dressed for war, brandishing lances, bows, and muskets, were spilling onto the prairie, heading straight for us.

I glanced over my shoulder. There was no sensible retreat. At least half a hundred mounted bravos were doing their best to catch up with us.

We did the only thing we could do. We drew abreast, about a fathom apart, drew our pistols, and charged at a full gallop straight at what appeared to be weakest part of the line the enemy had thrown across our path, two warriors waving lances and only one with a musket. We held our fire until we were within thirty feet of their line before taking careful aim and sending our chosen three out onto the Wolf Trail, creating a hole that we passed through whilst the rest lost a couple seconds slowing their headlong charge, skidding to a halt, swinging their ponies about, and setting off in pursuit.

We used those few seconds to advantage, bending low, urging our horses to their utmost speed—leastaways, in my case, until Coffee commenced to pull away from the other two. I checked him slightly until all three of us were again running neck and neck.

Arrows flew overhead and doubtless musket balls, as well. I was trying to shrink myself into a smaller target when I felt a tug on my flapping shirttail, then a searing pain on my neck. Blood spurted onto the pommel. A wave of nausea rose in my throat and clouded my vision, which likely caused me to tighten my legs, jabbing Coffee with my spurs. He bounded forward in a surprising burst of speed that I wouldn't have guessed he still had left, taking us a length or two or more in advance of my companions. My head commenced to clear and I checked his speed enough to allow Kit and Micah to catch up. If the Bloods succeeded in overtaking us, it was vital that we not be separated from one another.

Kit and Micah came up on either side of me, Micah on the left. He spied the blood splattering from my wound and rode closer to my side. "You're hurt!" he informed me unnecessarily, concern twisting his features. "Can ye make it?"

"Reckon so!" I strangled out. "Hell! I better!" Or somesuch response.

"They're fallin' back!" Carson crowed from the other side. "We be outrunnin' 'em! Bastards cain't keep up!"

I took him at his word. It hurt too much to twist my head around and I feared another wave of dizziness might cause me to pitch out of the saddle. It was good news. Even better, the camp came into view just then.

The horses saw it, too. I felt an extra surge of power as Coffee stretched into a ground-eating gallop, belly low to the ground, that had my moccasins mowing a swath through the prairie grass. As we neared, I made out two small figures nigh the crest of our rocky monument, one of them waving a bright red blanket, either welcoming us home or warning those below of the approaching Blackfoots.

I was by then hanging onto the pommel with both hands, the rein bouncing loose on Coffee's neck, letting him take me home. As we neared the camp, he slowed to an easy lope, then a trot, a walk, and halted shivering in the midst of the crowd that poured past the barricade to help me down and to shower Kit and Micah with a noisy greeting. When I tried to dismount, I felt a tug that checked me in mid-descent. My shirttail was pinned to the cantle by a two-foot Blackfoot arrow. Suddenly my neck wound didn't seem so serious.

Somebody yanked the arrow free and helped me down. Several others, Cat amongst them, hustled me past the barricade, into the protection of our makeshift fort. As I stumbled inside, I caught sight of Half-horse stripping off my saddle and pads and leading my sweaty, lathered Coffee horse down the path to safety amongst our other critters in the crickbed below. I felt better, sure that the Delaware lad would take good care of him.

Tuttle and Cat helped me to our lodge where they laid me onto the sleeprobes and Cat clucked and fretted and swabbed away the blood from my wound. Zeetlah shouldered past the doorflap, bearing a big cup of one of his evil-smelling teas that tasted even worse, which he made me drain to the dregs. Then he slathered a soothing salve over the gash on my neck. The half-smile on his lips as the old villain was applying the healing balm prompted me to tell him, before he had a chance to do so, "Yeah, I know. It's a long way from my heart!" It is his favorite joke, possibly his only one.

The rattle of gunfire from the barricade announced the arrival of Blackfoots, come within rifle range. I tried to sit up, but Tuttle caught my shoulder and Kathleen gently pushed me down, muttering comforting words in Salish, her dark eyes moist, betraying her deep concern.

"Ye done enough fer naow, Pard. Best ye letcherse'f rest up fer a spell," Tuttle advised. "We owe ther three o' ye a galore o' thankees fer whatcha went an' done this mawnin'. Better ye stirred ther sumbitches up naow, ruther'n lettin' 'em show up arter dark an' surprisin' us."

Iris burst through the doorflap and threw herself onto me, clasping me close, her eyes wide with wonder and fear as she eyed the ugly gash on my neck, babbling, "Oh, Papa, will you be good again?" and a passel of other sympathetic nonsense which warmed the paternal cockles of my heart, whatever they are. Then she asked, "Did you see me and Sean on our mountain when you came? That was me waving the blanket!" I assured her that I had and that she and the Woodpecker had helped me find my way home. Which pleased her immensely. She nestled against my chest and soon drifted off to slumber.

Zeetlah's evil draught commenced to take effect. I began yawning. My eyelids grew heavy. Kathleen joined us on the sleeprobes and wrapped us both in her arms, straining her lips towards mine for a kiss. Which was the last thing I remembered for a spell.

∾   ∾   ∾

I awakened to the aroma of roasting meat, the sharp crack of rifle fire, the hollow reports of distant muskets, and a Babel of voices in half a dozen tongues. The roasting meat was the most attractive of the three. I discovered that I was possessed of a raging hunger, that my wound hurt hardly at all if I didn't twist my neck, and the cobwebs had been swept clean out of my head. During my snooze, a sweet-smelling poultice had been bandaged in place over the wound to protect it from harm and keep it clean.

Looking through the smokehole, daylight filtered through several rents and holes in the lodge cover from arrows and bullets ripping through, which advised me to stay low whilst I went about my chores.

I had been well taken care of. All that was left for me to do on my own was to attend to my hunger—but only after I clothed my naked body. Cat had stripped off my bloody duds and bathed off the gore whilst I slept, so I needed to dress in the clean shirt, leggin's, and britchclout she had thoughtfully laid out. Which I did without delay, spurred to faster action by the mouthwatering scents wafting in from outdoors and a gnawing in my gut impossible to ignore or delay for long.

Decently attired at last, I buckled on my possibles belt and ducked out of the lodge, taking care to crouch as I headed for the cookfire, lest a stray arrow or musket ball send me back to bed or even farther from the good things in life. As I scampered in quest of vittles, I was greeted warmly by my comrades and several of the women, all of whom were staying low as they awaited their turn on the barricade. Several men and a couple of the women I saw wore bloody bandages. Zeetlah and Little Mountain hustled along the alleyway betwixt the bulwark and the row of lodges, tending to the wounded, still had an arrow in his shoulder. I resolved to take my place amongst them as soon as I satisfied my appetite.

At the cookfire, Yves and Jean-Luc, muskets slung across their back, bounced about on their knees as they tended to their cooking chores. When I complimented Jean-Luc on his devotion to his *métier* and his *devoirs*, he simply shrugged and replied, "*Il faut repousser l'ennemi, naturellement, mais il faut manger, aussi.*" I sliced off a thick slab of smoking-hot hump meat and devoured it on the spot, then hacked off another before I scuttled back to the lodge to retrieve my weapons, munching contentedly all the way.

When I poked my head past the doorflap, Kathleen was just about to depart. Her face was smudged with gunsmoke, dark eyes sparkling with excitement, white, even teeth flashing in a broad smile. "Oh, zere you be, Tompo!" she exclaimed happily. "All good an' bettah now?" I assured her that I never felt better and declared that it was high time that I earn my keep, time to go out and kill a couple Blackfoots.

She remained with me whilst I collected my weapons, regaling me the while with details of the fighting so far, how they had held off a horseback charge and how she had personally shot a much-feathered chief off his horse when he had attempted to leap over the barricade. She sniggered when she expressed her regrets that she hadn't counted coup on his body yet, but she insisted that she would do so later.

She assured me that Iris and Ben were safely ensconced, along with the other children, in a hollow place in the rocky hill behind us, under the care of one of the mothers, which news relieved my mind.

She also told me that none our people had been killed so far. There were a number of wounded, mostly from wood and rock chips and high-arcing arrows that dropped behind the fortress.

Armed now and itching for a fight, I crawled out after Cat and found a place at the barricade where I could safely peer past the logs to survey the field. It was still only late afternoon. Plenty of daylight remained. Skulkers armed with bows and muskets took advantage of the high grass, sneaking close to loose high-flying arrows they hoped would fall just behind our defensive wall or to pop up onto their knees to fire a musket ball before crawfishing to safety. I counted seven bodies littering the ground at likely musket range. Tuttle, awaiting a turn to shoot, joined me about that time, reporting that more than that number had already been dragged off by their brethren.

At least half a hundred horsemen gathered far out on the prairie, safely out of rifle range, racing their ponies in circles, bringing them to a rearing halt, and excitedly waving their arms, doubtless debating various stratagems to oust us from our position. More kept showing up as I watched.

Half a dozen dead horses were strewn in front of the barricade, unfortunate victims of the unsuccessful charge. More than twice that many Kainahs sprawled amongst them, some doubtless victims of the charge, others those of kin and foolhardy friends who tried to retrieve the bodies. Tuttle described fighting off the charge.

As Tuttle told it, the carnage had been prodigious. Naturally the bowmen had to suspend raining arrows on us, lest they injure their own warriors, which let our people, men and women alike, to mount the rampart all at once and level a fusillade at close range, a solid hail of rifle and pistol fire that emptied saddles like a scythe reaping ripe wheat, as Tuttle described the action. He reckoned most of those who managed to hobble off or get dragged to safety were likely *hors de combat*, so badly disabled they could no longer fight. Tuttle didn't use the French words, but that's what he meant. What he did say was, "Thet'ere woman o' your'n be some kind o' hellcat when she gits her dander up! You should'a seed 'er when she shot thet'ere chief off his hoss! I feared she war gonna jump out thar an' chaw up what war left of 'im!" I grinned when I heard that. She is a woman of many virtues. Not all of them gentle.

When Finnæus stepped down and swept his arm in a dramatic gesture of invitation to replace him, I returned an elaborate bow and clambered up to his vantage point, my head protected by a sturdy log studded with arrows on its outside. The arrows provided a handy advantage, for they obscured the shape of one's head when peering between them. I concentrated on one particular shooter, who, time and again, wriggled though the tall grass, rose to his knees, fired his musket, fell flat and crawfished into high grass to reload, then repeated the action a few feet to either side. I waited through a couple-three of his shots before I raised my rifle and took aim where I reckoned he would likely appear. Sure enough, he did, and my ball went true. He flung up his arms and his musket went flying. Tallymesko, Brass Turtle's wife, kneeling beside me, dropped his foolish comrade who tried to retrieve the gun.

We both stepped down, laughing and exchanging compliments on the other's marksmanship whilst we reloaded. We were interrupted by Carson and Brass Turtle, looking solemn. They advised us to be sure to have plenty of powder, ball, and caps in our our horns and pouches.

"'Pears they be gangin' up fer another hossback run at us," Carson said gloomily. "More of 'em than last time. A heap more. Reckon they got their feelin's hurt purty bad tryin' it the fust time. They're itchin' to git even."

"That's Bloods fer ye," Turtle said with a sigh. "Crazier'n greybacks! Bunch o' goddamn loonies'd ruther quit livin' than lettin' their pride git tromped on. Might see more o' their side of it if it warnt fer them allus startin' the whole shebang in the fust place!"

"They been eggin' each other on 'til thar ain't no goin' back 'thout lookin' weak," Kit declared, "an' no Injun I ever seed's gonna 'low anythin' like that! Makin' it wuss, they all got kin er good friends 'mongst them as awready's been kilt. That'll keep 'em fired up!"

I didn't reckon I had anything worthwhile to add to what they had said, so I didn't. As he turned to go, Turtle said, "All we kin do is stand pat an' give 'em hell!" He grinned at me and added, "Mebbe the extry guns ye got fer us'll make the diff'ernce. Thankee fer that." Kit nodded his agreement and they proceeded on their way.

I looked down the firing line, trying to read the faces of the men—and women, too—that I had grown to love as family. Not a one of them showed fear or panic, merely a resolute acceptance of our circumstances. Little Mountain, standing beside his statuesque young woman, merely looked stubborn, but, then, he always looked that way, determined, sure of himself and his ability to deal with whatever came next.

Just beyond them, tetchy Anse Tolliver wore a grim expression, which doubtless reflected another of the harsh judgments our acidulous fiddler constantly visits on anyone who dares to contradict his own humorless views, which amounts to just about everybody most of the time, which the Blackfoots were certainly guilty of right then. Just the same, Anse had stood loyal and unflinching through every scrape we had encountered together for more than a dozen years.

Tuttle, perched on the barricade, his gaze sweeping the prairie, chuckled and grinned as he delivered some humorous quip to a thoughtful but steadfast Finn McCool and my father, whose impassive features rarely reveal his thoughts or feelings and never when he wishes to keep them to himself. Micah is much the same as Powatawa in that regard, mostly keeping his sentiments private, which is likely how he survived his early years of servitude. Paddy McBride, on the other hand, is an open book. Quick to pick up the gauntlet at a challenge or a slight, our sturdy little Mick is a rock to rally 'round in a fight, as he was that warm May afternoon.

Every one of our women, regardless of their tribal origin, having traded their traditional status for a warrior's role, appeared almost impatient for the battle to begin, along with our three Spaniards, who joked and chattered in their native tongue. Our Indians, Delaware and Iroquois alike, had proved their mettle time and again. Now they were plainly eager to draw Kainah blood, even if it meant swapping their own lives to do it.

My heart grew big when I counted myself amongst their number.

I clambered onto the rampart on the side nigh the crick and took my place beside Kathleen. She hardly noticed my presence at first, so intent was she on staring out onto the prairie, where the mounted Kainahs were still milling in a colorful maelstrom of arm-waving warriors and rearing war-painted horses. Some others galloped off only to return a moment later to join what appeared to be heated debate. A few elaborately-befeathered chiefs coursed up and down in front of the scattered ranks, apparently attempting to harangue their independent-minded troops into forming a uniform line for a concerted attack.

Naturally I can't be sure, but it's a fair guess that the bloody defeat of their first horseback assault on our barricade, the withering gunfire that had greeted them, had sapped much of the iron will that forms the Blackfoot character. Despite Kit's assertion that Kainah pride, thirst for revenge, and kinship would carry the day, even the most courageous warrior quails at the prospect of certain suicide. It would require some monumental argufying to overcome that recent memory.

When at last Cat acknowledged my presence at her side, she said, "I sink zey come from many diff'ernt band, zose Kah-ee-nah! Zey don't like takin' orders from ozzer stranger chief. Same like us. We got no chief!"

Before I could reply, I became aware of a ripple of excitement coursing down the line of defenders from the far side of our barricade, where a broad corridor of prairie separated the pine woods from our rocky hilltop. The buzz erupted in a rousing cheer as a line of a dozen painted ponies bearing weapon-waving Arapaho chiefs and warriors in colorful war regalia swept onto the prairie—the unmistakable tall, erect figure of Touches-the-Sky, feathered lance held high, our shiny gift rifle slung onto his back, leading the van—another score of warriors close on their tails, followed by what appeared to be nigh a double score more galloping in pursuit, all of them armed with bows, some few brandishing lances, many with muskets, as well. The entire well-disciplined horde headed straight for the disorganized mounted Kainahs still trying unsuccessfully to form a battle line.

On their way, the Arapahoes flushed concealed Blackfoot bowmen and musket snipers like startled quail as they coursed through the tall prairie grass. The second and third Arapaho ranks loosed a deadly shower of arrows that felled the fleeing enemy, spilling them onto their faces as they attempted to escape afoot. Some, confused and panic-stricken, ran into the oncoming horsemen and were cut down by arrows or trampled. The few who survived the charge were picked off by our riflemen when the horsemen had safely passed on.

As the vanguard of the Arapaho force neared the loosely assembled Blackfoots, the Kainahs tried to rally their number into an organized resistance, but too late. Their scattered fighters, brave and skilled as they might be, were no match for the closely-knit ranks that hit them like a powerful fist, the first dozen horsemen each descending at a full gallop on a single foe, in most cases a man who appeared by his duds and feathers to be a chief of some degree, and attacking with lance, club, or tomahawk, frequently bowling over their victim and his horse by the sheer force of the onslaught.

Even at a distance, the lofty stature of Touches-the-Sky made it possible to follow his movements. At the last moment he swerved his big piebald horse sharply to engage a Kainah chief whose fancy garb and elaborate headdress proclaimed him to be a man of authority, possibly the principal chief, if they had onesuch. The Arapaho's last-moment move caught him off guard and Touches-the-Sky's lance ran him through, the impact ripping the weapon from his hands and sweeping the Kainah chief clean over the tail of his horse onto the earth, the lance sticking straight up like a gory grave-marker.

As soon as they completed their initial attack, which lasted hardly the blink of an eye, the first rank split their force in half and galloped off in a wide arc on either side, returning to the rear of the second rank composed of a score of warriors and joining them in a general attack on Blackfoots who were standing their ground and fighting back. The third, most numerous rank also split in half and pursued enemy horsemen who were attempting to flee the battleground on either side, possibly to prevent their having second thoughts, regrouping, and attempting to start the brawl all over again. More likely, howsomever, the fugitives, retreating singly or in pairs, were easy pickin's and the Arapahoes wanted their horses and weapons.

Although the Bloods outnumbered the attacking Arapahoes, it is unlikely that in the heat of battle and the sheer surprise of the onslaught many of them took account of the inferior numbers of the newcomers. Besides, the Arapahoes' tight discipline in the assault was a tactic almost unheard-of in Indian warfare, where feats of individual courage and daring are prized most highly. The deaths of most of their remaining chiefs in the first encounter further demoralized the already-disorganized Kainahs, depriving them of effective leaders to rally around.

"I never figgered I'd ever see Bloods turnin' tail an' runnin' off like thet," Tuttle said wonderingly from behind us as we watched them doing precisely that. "This'll be one gawddamn fight them sumbitches'll shore-as-hell be leavin' off o' their gawddamn winter-count ner braggin' to their kids abaout, neither!"

The fighting by then had pretty much dwindled to mopping up a few scattered last ditch stands. Most of the Arapahoes were occupied with retrieving their wounded and driving a large herd of captured horses back towards our camp, besides stripping the fallen enemy of weapons, clothing, and anything else they considered worthwhile. Naturally scalps were claimed first.

Far in advance of the horse herd, astride his big piebald, was Touches-the-Sky coming at a high lope to learn of his daughter's well-being.

Arapahoes weren't the only ones claiming fancy Kainah duds for their go-to-meetin' wardrobe. Cat plucked at my sleeve to draw my attention from the prairie and pointed down at Half-horse, Pablo Torres, and Zeetlah busily stripping the handsome clothing off the bodies of the fallen Kainah chiefs sprawled in front of our barricade—much of it I recognized as Crow, likely acquired as trophies taken in previous battles—as well as their weapons and elaborately-quilled horse gear from their dead mounts. Nothing goes to waste in the mountains.

When I turned back to Kathleen to comment on the scavenging, she was gone. When I returned my attention to Half-horse and his companions, I saw my beloved lady slicing the scalp from one of the fallen chiefs, then waving the grisly trophy aloft in triumph, a broad smile lighting her pretty features.

Tuttle, standing at my side, remarked with a snicker, "Thet'ere be one partic'lar special woman ye got thar, Temple. Jest take care ye don't git 'er riled up atcha!"

Meanwhile, Touches-the-Sky had covered the distance from the Kainah battleground, brought his horse to a skidding halt and dropped the reins, leaving him ground-tied, and vaulted our barricade, where his daughter awaited. He didn't hug her, for that would have been an unseemly breach of manners, but his expression showed his love and extreme relief as he surveyed her beautiful face, smudged with gunsmoke though it was. His gaze traveled to the rifle slung across her shoulders. A momentary flicker of disapproval was instantly replaced with a look that bespoke his understanding and acceptance of the necessary measures that accounted for her survival.

He placed his hands on her shoulders then and they spoke rapidly in their tongue, his fingers flexing the while in the closest thing to an embrace that father-daughter etiquette allows in his tradition. The return of his warriors and the arrival of the captured horse herd called him back to duty. He spoke a few more words to Tayho, nodded to Little Mountain and generally to the rest of us, placed one hand on the rampart and easily sprang over it, retrieved his mount, and rode off to join his people. Watching him that day, it was easy to see why he had become leader of his band at such an early age.

❧   ❧   ❧

The Arapahoes set up camp nigh a pine woods betwixt a couple of cricks half a mile distant from ours and turned their horse herd out to recruit their fettle, which they sorely needed after the long, hungry hike over the dry country. Next day they went out after buffalo in bunches of a score or more hunters in each party, in case some slow-learning Bloods were still hanging around in the neighborhood. Which they weren't. Some of us tagged along with them, also just in case, and feasted every night on fresh-killed young bulls, hosting Touches-the-Sky and his headmen a couple of nights in gratitude for their actions in saving our arse.

We learned that the band had suffered the loss of four warriors killed and a dozen or so wounded, which wasn't too bad compared with the dozens of Kainahs who were crowding the Wolf Trail just then, on their way to the Grey Land. The Arapahoes doubtless minded the loss of their men, but they didn't let on.

Next morning, we used our *reatas* to drag the Kainah bodies and dead horses a sufficient distance from camp to avoid the stink that would have occurred if we hadn't. We left the barricade in place, just for luck, but, even hard-headed as they mostly are, the Bloods had learned their lesson this time and kept their distance.

I wondered how the children might feel about their experience during the siege, with all the shooting and yelling and the terrified screams of wounded and dying horses, especially Iris and Sean, who were old enough to understand what was going on, but they took it in stride. I reckon that after the battle with the Bannocks, they accepted it as just the way life is. Tucked away in their hidey-hole, they didn't have to see it, and, after all, an ordinary night at rendezvous can be nearly that noisy.

We remained there for a week, letting our livestock regain their healthy condition, feasting on the plentiful game thereabouts, and allowing our wounds to heal. Nearly everybody in our bunch had suffered some kind of nick or scrape or halfway serious damage, mostly from flying splinters off the barricade logs, but also from falling arrows, fortunately none of it life-threatening. Zeetlah and Little Mountain made daily rounds amongst our number, slathering cuts and gashes with the old Delaware's salves and unguents, hastening healing and guarding against infection. My own arrow scrape mended rapidly, leaving hardly any scar, thanks to one or more of the old man's magical ointments.

Warm, sunny early-June weather allowed young Ben to play outdoors most of the day, usually tethered to a tree to keep him from harm, under the watchful eyes of his big sister, Cat, or sometimes myself when other chores permitted. Always an active youngling, he was walking now, but so far unable to untie knots. Leisure hours let me catch up on my journal, devoting much of my scribbles to everything I could recollect of the recent conflict.

The bachelors resumed their nighttime visits to the Arapaho camp and Kit contrived to put in an appearance there nearly every day on one excuse or another. His courtship of Grass Singing had progressed to a point where he was able to engage her in small-talk, within the limits of his feeble grasp of her native tongue, so long as it occurred outdoors with one of her parents present. Our men had rapidly gained a well-earned reputation amongst the Arapahoes as a good-natured but randy lot.

Pleasant as our circumstances were on the prairie, the lure of rendezvous was too strong to be put off for long. Eight days after the fight, we packed up, along with the Arapahoes, and headed west towards Horse Crick. A week and more on the belly-high rich graze on the prairie had done wonders for our horses and mules. No ribs showing anywhere. They bulged with hard fat and the week-long liberty from labor had completely restored their spirits, which was not desirable in every case, especially our cranky packmules, whose renegade temperament is easily stirred. The morning we set out witnessed a wild melee of kicking and bucking and resisting their heavy loads, the air turned blue with curses and honking complaints. Duty prevailed at last, howsomever. After a desperate tussle, we obtained their grudging surrender, but not without our suffering a passel of nips and kicks. At last the packtrain got underway.

-ooo-

CHAPTER XIV
HOSS CRICK

1835 Rendezvous

The remaining journey to the rendezvous site at Horse Crick was mostly uneventful. Traveling with the large Arapaho village relieved us of our usual concerns about getting jumped by hostiles who often lurk in the neighborhood of the annual gathering to pounce upon small bunches of arriving trappers to rob them of their plews and plunder and collect a few scalps in the bargain. Any Blackfoot war party that dared to challenge our numerous assemblage of well-armed warriors and trappers would need to be extremely bold or, more likely, exceedingly foolhardy. The late June and early July weather was warm and mild with just enough occasional gentle rainfall to keep the greenery fresh and abundant.

Unlike the early stages of the journey, we took to traveling mostly in company with the Arapaho warriors, mingling with them on the trail, picking up bits and pieces of their lingo, and building an even greater respect for them, especially their horsemanship. We took care, howsomever, to keep our cavayard of loose saddle horses separate from theirs. Friendliness is all very well, but fine horseflesh is a powerful temptation for an Indian—and for most trappers, too.

Touches-the-Sky often rode in our midst, usually with his daughter and Little Mountain, sometimes with Carson, who was striving mightily to acquire the Arapaho tongue, which was likely somewhat flattering to the chief. His frequent presence amongst us, as well as his daughter's marriage to one of ours, doubtless convinced most of the Arapahoes that we weren't as bad as some of us smelled.

A couple days out from the place of rendezvous, where Horse Crick meets up with the Seeds-kee-dee, I chanced to be riding up front in the column with Kit when we spied a pair of horsemen waiting in the middle of the trail. They raised their rifles high in the air and fired skywards, a sign amongst mountaineers that their intentions are peaceful. Without reloading, they kicked their mounts into a lope and rode to join us. As they drew nigh I recognized the two as long-time friends, Willard Stringfellow and Gideon Moon, a pair of trappers who had gone to work for Old Baldy Captain Bonneville a couple years earlier. We hadn't seen them since we split away from Joe Walker's brigade in California.

There is no confusing the two of them. Will Stringfellow, a Kentuckian, is loquacious, short and sturdy. Gideon Moon, a Tennesseean, is taller than most, horsewhip lean, tough as smokehole leather, dour in expression, and sparing of his words. Will more than makes up for Gid's reticence. Proof that opposites attract, they have been devoted friends since Andy Henry's time thereabouts.

After the customary horseback hugs and enquiries about the others' trapping success and casualties, Will informed us, "No need fer ye to be hurryin' on to ronnyvoo. Traders ain't showed up yit. T'morra's ther Fourth o' Joo-ly an' thar ain't a dram ner drop o' squeezin's in ther whole gawddamn ronnyvoo fer sellybratin' runnin' ther gawddamn British outa 'Murrica! So ye kin take yer time gittin' thar!"

"Still workin' for Bonneville?" I asked.

"Nope, not no more," Will replied. "Gid an' me, we be goin' back to trappin' free, on our own hook, like allus afore we taken ther shillin' from ol' Baldy."

"How come?"

"Reckon he be runnin' out o' cash thet's been comin' from ol' Jake Astor er ther guv'mint er whoever in hell's been keepin' 'im afloat out hyar. Hot air an' promises don't fill yer poke nohaow, so Gid an' me taken our springtime plews an' made tracks up thisaway to ronnyvoo to sell 'em on our own, but thar ain't hardly nothin' doin' thar yet."

"Well, you're welcome to join us for supper," I told him. I wondered what they were doing a couple days distant from rendezvous without packhorses or camping gear, but there are some questions mountaineers don't ask.

"Don't mind if we do," Will answered for both of them. Then, "Kin ye spare some t'bacca? We're plumb out."

I dug out my tobacco pouch and dumped half of its contents into his outstretched poke, explaining the while, "As ye see, we're runnin' out, too. Nigh half of it's red cedar bark."

"Thankee jest ther same," Will replied. "Mixin' cedar an' t'bacca smokes jest fine." Then, "Best we ride on back an' say howdy to ther others. Ain't seen 'em in more'n a year, since Californy."

Gideon, who had held his peace throughout our exchange, granted us a single "Thankee" and a brief smile as he wheeled his horse and headed down the column. As they passed our Indian wives riding together behind us, I heard Will call out a cheery "Howdy, Ladies!"

∾ ∾ ∾

Next morning, Will and Gideon thanked us for our hospitality and rode off. We never did learn what they were doing so far out of the rendezvous without spare critters, baggage, plews, or camp gear. Naturally we didn't ask and they didn't bother to tell us.

Three days after that, we crossed the Seeds-kee-dee and rode up Horse Creek to reclaim our campground from the year before. This year we had to forego our customary wild entry into rendezvous. With the Arapahoes in tow, a people so far unfamiliar with the rowdy character of mountaineers at rendezvous, we restrained our unruly impulses and conducted our arrival in a manner uncharacteristically sedate. We did, howsomever, dress up in our fancy duds and the Arapahoes, seeing us doing it, did so, too. We made a colorful if quiet entry amongst the few old friends who had arrived so far.

Fortunately nobody had occupied our previous campsite, four miles upstream, so we were able to settle into our old digs, pretty much where they had been along the crickbank. Winter had been severe, as usual in those parts, so there was plenty of deadfall firewood strewn about under the big cottonwoods, sundered by frost from overhanging limbs, which provided welcome shade for our lodges.

It was time to separate from the Arapahoes, but not too distantly. The valley was unoccupied past our camp and pasture, with an abundance of grass for their large horse herd, a fresh-flowing stream that fed Horse Creek, and a lodgepole pine woods flanking one side. Kit rode out with Touches-the-Sky and his headmen to a suitable spot about a half-mile from us that pleased them all—especially Carson, I daresay, who hadn't far to go to conduct his courting of the winsome lass Grass Singing.

We had espied several small bunches of buffalo scattered around the upper end of the valley when we arrived, so several of us married men set out to harvest supper whilst the women erected the lodges and the bachelors gathered willows for their bowers. Mindful of last year's prohibition against running buffalo nigh the rendezvous, we curbed our boisterous impulses once again and sneaked up on a likely bunch of young bulls afoot and, at Little Mountain's signal, dropped half a dozen from a discreet distance. So cautious were we that the bunch took flight only when an old patriarch amongst them smelled blood and gave the alarm.

On the way back to camp, with packmules wobbling under their heavily-loaded panniers, Brass Turtle complained with mock severity, "Thi'sheres gotta stop! Fust we come into thi'shere ronnyvoo quiet-like, like we be goin' churchin', 'stead o' like usual, an' naow we give up runnin' buffler! We be gittin' too damn civerlized!"

When we reached the Arapaho camp, we stopped by and gifted Touches-the-Sky with two of our kills and told him in sign of the rule at rendezvous against running buffalo, lest we scare the herds clean out of the valley. He informed us then that such a rule exists amongst his people when there are large numbers gathered at one place, for the same reason.

When we got back to camp, we turned the packmules over to the campkeepers and distributed the hides and brains amongst the women, most of whom planned to use some of their time at rendezvous to make new lodges. A common casualty of the Kainah battle was the lodges, most of which were badly ripped by arrows and gunfire. They had patched them as best they could in the week we had remained there, but the damage had been considerable.

Skinning our kills had taken more time than usual, for the women had asked that we skin them in a single piece, rather than slicing them down the back, as we mostly did. It was a trifling favor to grant. The real labor would come when the women scraped each hide thin enough to be used in making a lodge cover, not much thicker than heavy canvas. I shuddered at the thought of so much hard work, but Cat was cheerful about it, pointing out that Ben was getting bigger and Iris was growing up, and who could be sure about maybe more children? So we needed a larger lodge, anyway.

An uneventful week went by with no sign of traders, neither Sublette & Campbell, Hudson's Bay, nor any other. Naturally we were still mystified by the question of how Fontenelle & Fitzpatrick intended to do business under the nose of Bill Sublette without his tumbling to it and yelling bloody murder when he got back to Saint Louis. They could do pretty much as they pleased in the mountains, but there are law courts in the settlements.

There was little for us to do besides hunting, repairing gear, and pursuing leisure activities. I spent much of my time reading and bringing my journal up to date, wishing for traders and at least the arrival of Etienne LeBref, so that I might swap some of my less-valued books with him, as he and I had been doing since our earliest days in the mountains. Etienne was trapping with Jim Bridger's brigade, which hadn't yet put in an appearance, nor had Andy Drips, the other major brigade leader of the new partnership. I was getting almost desperate enough for new reading matter to read one of my own books.

I was sitting in the morning sun in front of our lodge, stitching on a new headstall, when Tuttle came by and demanded, "Whatcha got in mind fer the plunder ye got stowed in thet'ere cache we put up two year past?" Before I could reply, he added, "I be near out o' t'bacca an' ther most of it's cedar bark anyways! Same fer ever'body!"

"Me amongst 'em!" I barked at him. "What took ye so long, offerin' to go? If ye weren't so damned busy trollin' for women, we could've lifted that cache a week ago, so don't be blamin' me!"

He was instantly contrite. "Sorry 'baout thet. I jest been payin' my respects to some ol' frien's. Wal, mebbe not so old." He sniggered at his feeble jest. "Anyways, I be ready when yew say so."

I laid aside my task and said, "Now's as good a time as any. Gather up some hands and we'll be on our way." I entered the lodge to get my weapons and let Cat know where I was going, which brought a bright smile to her pretty face. Trading with the Arapahoes had seriously reduced her stock of foofurraw.

Half an hour later Tuttle arrived with half a dozen packmules bearing mostly empty panniers, except for a pick-mattock and a couple of spades. He was accompanied by Finn McCool, Paddy McBride, Little Mountain, Tolliver, and Brass Turtle, more than enough men for the job. I suspect the prospect of a dram or two of the spirits we had cached encouraged them to lend a hand.

Three hours later we arrived at the designated spot upon a high bluff overlooking a stream and breathed a sigh of relief when we discovered the ground undisturbed. Tuttle eyeballed his four landmarks and guessed where a line drawn amongst them would intersect to form the center of an X. It took him only three swipes with the mattock to locate the chimney hole of the cache. Tuttle Thompson is truly gifted in that *métier*.

Our next concern was naturally the condition of the plunder, if the cache had stayed dry for nearly two years. Little Mountain quickly cleared soil out of the chimney hole and Paddy and Turtle stripped away the elk hides and sail canvas that protected the goods in the cave below, Turtle exultantly reporting, "All's dry as muh gizzard down hyar! Whar'dja stow that red-eye?"

An hour's work cleared out the cache, which had survived undamaged, the wall-lining and flooring of willow withes protecting its contents from seepage from the soil. Amongst the last items to be passed up through the chimney in an almost reverential fashion were the curved metal kegs of booze that sloshed invitingly as they were carefully passed up from one man to another. Almost as highly-prized as the spirits was a sheaf of tobacco carrots. They had mostly dried out during their extended storage, but nobody minded.

I was last to be hauled up through the chimney. When I quit squinting in the bright sunlight, I beheld a ring of grinning comrades gathered around me, each with cup in hand, eagerly eyeing the metal kegs. There was no denying their thirst—not if I hoped to return undamaged to rendezvous—and had no wish to do so. My own thirst equaled theirs, except for Tuttle and Anse, Paddy, and likely Finnæus, who is also Irish.

I had marked one particular keg two years before, the one I tapped now. It contained straight grain alcohol generously laced with wild honey. After fermenting for two years, it was bound to produce a powerful wallop.

Tuttle and Paddy hotfooted down the steep bank and returned with kettles brimming with fresh crick water to dilute our libation and make it somewhat less lethal. No wassailing monarch ever felt more magnanimous amongst his knights than I did as I sloshed their cups half-full of booze, filled them with water, and raised my own in a toast to men whom I regard as the brothers I never had, even Anse.

What I might have pledged in that heartfelt toast got lost in the fog that rolled over all of us in short order, after a couple-three cupfuls of that mortal brew. After a teetotaling year with nary a drop or dram, we were ill-prepared for the clout those fiercely potent spirits dealt to our out-of-practice corpuses. I slept where I fell.

∾   ∾   ∾

I awoke with a headache that threatened to split my skull asunder. My fellow-imbibers were in no better condition. After I stumbled back from my morning chore, I rummaged through my bundles in search of roasted coffee beans that I hoped we hadn't used up, whilst Little Mountain struck sparks until he got a fire going. Fortunately we possessed a goodly supply of the precious beans. Mountain crushed a pound-poke of them with his pistol butt whilst I stumbled down to the crick, filled a couple of kettles, and managed to return without spilling them.

The aroma of boiling coffee awakened the most persistent snorer, in that case Tuttle. He sat up rubbing his eyes and exclaiming, "Coffeeberry juice! Damn ef I don't smell coffeeberry juice! Who'd a thought it!" before he collapsed, holding his head and wincing at the pain.

"Y'oughta gitcherse'f a mite o' hair o' the dog what bit ye fer healin' up yerse'f, Tuttle," Anse advised. He had already availed himself of a cupful of strong coffee black as Egypt's night. "Naow that I mention it," he added, "I don't mind if I take a dram er two o' the same fer myownse'f, cornsid'rin' it war my idee in the fust place."

I was still feeling poorly. I reckoned if anybody knew a cure for over-indulgence in squeezin's it would be Tolliver. I splashed a healthy dollop of last night's spirits into each man's cup and my own, which greatly improved my outlook on life. Naturally nobody declined Anse's advice, but in the interest of ever getting back to camp, I resisted all the arguments about not being able to fly on one wing and kept the bungs screwed tight on the kegs.

When the mules were loaded and I prepared to mount my Crane horse for the ride back to camp, I breathed a prayer of thanks to the Great Whoever that I hadn't ridden Coffee on that hike. Even after Anse's cure, I was still not healthy enough to cope with Coffee's high-spirited shenanigans.

∿   ∿   ∿

The rest of July and almost a fortnight of August dragged by without a sign of traders of any stripe. That was not calculated to sweeten the disposition of several hundred trappers and nearly three thousand Indians of many different tribes gathered there, mostly Shoshones, but also Absóraqa, Séli, Kootenai, Nez Percés, Eutaws, and our own contribution to the redskin mix, the Arapahoes. Nobody went hungry, for the fertile valley was a natural retreat for game, especially buffalo, but thirst was another matter entirely. I doled out enough of my spirits to avoid being lynched by my own comrades, but it was hardly enough to provide a spree for a Rocky Mountain trapper. Still, our bunch fared better than most. And we had tobacco, dried out though it was. Most of the others had to make do with kinnikinnick or cedar bark.

After raising the cache, I gifted Kathleen with the foofurraw I had retrieved—woolen, silk, and broadcloth fabrics, sewing items, beads and trinkets, cooking utensils, and the few foodstuffs that remained. Coffee and sugar for sweetening was especially welcome. We had long ago used up the makin's for that delightful beverage.

Naturally Cat shared with the other women in the bunch most of what I had retrieved. She was especially generous to the Arapaho brides of Cesár and Diego, whose meager household possessions and skimpy dowries in no way compared with the largesse that had been showered on Little Mountain's wife Tayho.

Hunting, mostly buffalo, occupied a certain amount of time for us. We ate heartily and frequently donated a buffalo or two to our Arapaho neighbors. We usually harvested more buffalo than we could use, for our women insisted that we provide them with a plenitude of fresh hides for making new lodges.

When I had repaired and refurbished all of my gear, cleaned and oiled my traps, played with Ben, assisted Iris with her schooling, and performed all the chores that Cat deemed acceptable for a man to do, there was little to occupy my abundant leisure time other than reading, which right then meant re-reading the books I had on hand.

One book that I possessed then and still do has been an unfailing source of pleasure, no matter how many times I return to its pages. It is Mister Noah Webster's *An American Dictionary of the English Language*. I am not a religious man, but if I were I would recommend Mister Noah Webster for sainthood or, at the very least, the job of Pope of Rome. Some of my happiest hours have been spent leafing through the pages of Mister Webster's gift to America and civilized people everywhere, even some of us who aren't very civilized.

Another unfailing source of pleasure is Cat, especially when she put aside her digging stick and hide-scraping tools, primped and preened, saddled her horse, and invited me to accompany her on a pleasure ride that usually wound up at our secret grove far up Horse Creek. Playing together in the chill water like a pair of otters, making love as noisily and inventively as we wished, and chatting afterwards in our personal macaroni of Salish and

American talk performed wonders in alleviating the tedium of waiting for a rendezvous that seemed destined never to commence.

Naturally Cat and I took Iris and Ben to pay our respects to Iron Bow and Fast Horse when the Séli band arrived with their forty-or-so lodges and another score of Kootenais, their large herd of horses, and Iron Bow's precious mules. He assured me his mules were the envy of all who set eyes on the progeny of the mammoth jackass I had given him two years before.

We had a lot of catching up to do. After much admiring of young Ben, whom Iron Bow regards as his true grandson, and Iris, who really is his granddaughter, father and son insisted on telling every jot and tittle of the successful battle they had waged against the Pikunis during their buffalo hunt the previous fall.

Naturally we had to describe in equal detail our own encounters with first the Bannocks and then the Kainahs. Telling those histories naturally required that we admit to arming the womenfolk of our bunch, which elicited a frown from the old man, followed by a resigned sigh and a shrug as he conceded that white-eyes trappers and their women, traveling in small, vulnerable bunches as we often do, might possibly be entitled to an altered code of feminine conduct.

We told them, too, about the Arapahoes we had brought with us and promised to arrange a proper meeting with Touches-the-Sky, which we did within the week. There was entirely too much to relate in a single telling, so we stayed overnight in the chief's lodge and finished most of our catching-up the next morning whilst we broke our fast.

When Jim Bridger's brigade arrived at rendezvous, I was able to call on Etienne LeBref and invite my old friend to bring his books over to our camp. I confess that I plied him with my counterfeit metheglin before commencing the trading, which doubtless made him more amenable to the swaps I proposed than he might have been otherwise.

Whilst I was in Bridger's camp, I stopped by to greet Jim, a friend since he and I were green lads coming up the Missouri with Andy Henry in 'twenty-two. Jim was still big and powerful and commanding, in spite of the Blackfoot arrow point that had been lodged in his back for the past three years, which, he told me, never let him forget its presence. "I jist abaout give up on thinkin' somebody mought git that sumbitchin' arrer out o' thar," he said resignedly, his drawn features betraying the constant pain he endured.

Andy Drips brought in his brigade, as well, greatly increased in numbers since the previous fall by French-Canuck trappers he had pirated from the Aitch-bee-cee by promising greater rewards for their plews than the tight-fisted Brits ever see fit to offer, although Andy, like the rest of us, had no idea how Fontenelle & Fitzpatrick would be able to do business without Bill Sublette tumbling to their breaching the contract signed by the AmFur people in New York.

Anxiety grew amongst the trappers as July slid into August and still no packtrain appeared on the eastern hills. It was not surprising that Lucien Fontenelle was late, if, indeed, he would even bother to show up this year. Fontenelle was always tardy, likely too busy with his Saint Louie doxies to tend to business, as Black Harris once surmised, but everybody expected better of Tom Fitzpatrick. Then, too, Bill Sublette was hardly ever as late as this.

Naturally rumors flew like startled quail. The packtrain had been attacked and totally wiped out by Blackfoots, Big Bellies, Pawnees, or Lahcotahs, maybe all four, depending on who you chanced to be talking with. An enormous earthquake somewhere west of Missouri destroyed every man and critter in the supply outfit, wagons too. "Yup," my informant solemnly assured me, "ground jist opened up under 'em, made a hole big as hell, an' swallered up the whole shebang!"

❧   ❧   ❧

Hoofbeats of galloping horses entering camp in the late afternoon and the shouts of Tuttle and McCool announcing the arrival of the supply train propelled me, along with the rest of the bunch, into grabbing up my saddle and flinging it onto my Crane horse, tethered beside the lodge. "They got their sorry arse hyar at last!" Tuttle was shouting. "Half a hunnerd men an' a couple hunnerd critters, loaded fit ter bust 'em!"

"They're settin' up at the mouth of Horse Creek!" Finnæus added in a loud voice. "Fitzpatrick's in charge! No sign of Fontenelle!"

I cinched my saddle on snug, slipped the bridle over Crane's ears, grabbed up my weapons, and leapt aboard. I didn't expect to do any trading and I didn't need a drink, but the long weeks of waiting and wondering and sometimes despairing demanded that I see the elephant for myownself!

As we headed downstream, I espied Carson loping in the direction of the Arapahoes, doubtless to inform them that there really had been a packtrain coming and that it was here at last.

I fell in beside McCool as we rode down to the mouth of Horse Creek. "Tom brought along a couple of parsons," Finn told me. "They say one of 'em's some kind of a doctor, as well." He sounded almost wistful as he added that last part. "That should prove useful, helpin 'im with his preachin' to the Injuns, wouldn't ye say?"

I allowed that it might, if he were any good at it, but not if bleeding and cupping were his stock in trade. I recollected the quack who had weakened my dying mother with such treatment without doing her a mite of good, but I refrained from mentioning it aloud. Don Nicolás had bled some of his older patients at their insistence and I was unsure of Finn's opinion of that procedure.

Instead I voiced a question that was foremost in all our minds. "What d'ye suppose brings Fitz here, settin' up for tradin', as ye say, right out in the open? What about Bill Sublette and the contract?"

McCool shrugged, shook his head, and replied, "I'm as baffled as you. It takes a lot o' cheek to be after floutin' the law an' Billy Sublette in the bargain. I know Fitz for a fighter, but this is one he's not likely to be winnin'!"

"I reckon we'll know soon enough," I said, my thoughts a jumble as I rummaged through all that we had learned the year before.

We soon found ourselves amid a river of horsemen converging on the trader's camp, trappers and mostly Indians anxious to see with their own eyes that the packtrain had come at long last.

When we rode into the clearing where Fitz charged about directing his lackeys where and how to set up his tents and trade tables, I espied Moses Harris lounging under a shade tree, pipe in one hand, a jug in the other, his sedentary posture amid the surrounding hubbub proclaiming that his work ramrodding the packtrain was done and he was at liberty until the return journey.

Black hailed us and raised the jug invitingly for us to join him, which naturally we did. "What took ye so long, Temple?" he demanded by way of greeting. "We been hyar an hour or more. Been lookin' fer ye. Thought mebbe ye'd gone under."

"Sorry to disappoint ye," I replied in the same wry vein, helping myself to a healthy swig and passing the jug to Finn. Its contents were delightfully foreign to the usual raw spirits available in the mountains and I said so.

Black grinned broadly. "Ye damn betcha! Thi'shere be genu-wine honest-to-gawd corn whiskey straight out o' Kaintuck! Brung it up special jist fer meetin' up with yew agin, Temple! An' I war jist funnin' abaout ye goin' under. I asked abaout ye fust off an' some trappers tol' me ye war hyar awready."

Rough and tough as he is and dissolute as he often can be, Moses Harris has a loyal and tender heart. I reckon I blushed at his display of sentiment and quickly changed the subject. "Glad to see ye made it. Any trouble gettin' here?"

"Same as usual," he said matter-of-factly. "Nuthin we couldn't handle. It got a heap better once we got rid o' Fontenelle."

"He go under?" I demanded, surprised at his calm manner.

"Naw, not hardly. We jist dropped 'im off daown thar at Fort Willum an' Fitz took over bringin' the trade plunder up hyar. Had'na been fer Fontenelle, we could'a got hyar a month ago. Shee-it! We din't git out o' Bellevue 'til June war pert'near over! The twenny-second, it war!"

"What held him up?"

"Hell! Don't know fer sartin, but it war likely his drammin' an' gawddamn womanizin'! Shee-it, Temple! Ye know I shore-as-hell ain't no stranger to neither one o' them'ere thangs, but thar's a time an' place fer 'em! We should'a left Missourah a month afore we done! I had the men an' the critters all ready to go, but ol' Lucien warn't, so we jist kep' hangin' on thar in Bellevue 'til he fin'ly got the trade plunder together an' his whores run 'im off!"

"How is it that you're here at all?" Finn demanded earnestly. "Where's Bill Sublette? When is he coming?" I seconded his question.

"Hell! I plumb fergot, nobody up thisaway knows nuthin' abaout what's been happ'nin' in Sain Looie! Billy ain't comin' up this year, ner likely any other! 'Pears Bill an' Bobby Campbell been sellin' out o' ever'thin' they got in the mountains. Fort Willum down on the Laramie, too. Fitz an' Fontenelle are buyin' the whole shootin'-match! Don't know fer sure whar they be gittin' the money fer it, but I reckon ol' Pierre Chouteau ain't no stranger to what's been happ'nin'!"

"When did all this happen, Black?" we both asked at the same time.

"Sometime last winter. Don't know fer sure, but it don't matter. Fur as I know, Fitz an' Fontenelle got it all to theirownse'fs naow. 'Ceptin' mebbe fer Aitch-bee-cee. Course, nobody knows what them sumbitchin' Brits mought be thinkin' on doin'."

I breathed a sigh of relief at the news that Sublette was out of the picture. Selling our plews would not require some complicated sneak. If Fitz, now that he was the only American trader, sought to recoup his earlier losses by pegging what he was willing to pay for plews below their fair mountain value, our bunch had accumulated enough cash on the books from last year's windfall to outfit ourselves for the coming year, which would let us cache this year's harvest until we found a fair-minded buyer.

When that notion entered my head, it felt like a mulekick in the belly to admit that longstanding loyalties had deteriorated into a dog-eat-dog affair amongst friends who once would have given up their lives for one another.

That brought to mind the premium price that Pierre Chouteau had promised in the letter he sent me last year. That letter was pure gold for our bunch and all those whom we had enlisted, trappers and Indians alike.

There was no profit in mentioning Chouteau's scheme to Harris, so I didn't. Instead, I changed the subject and asked about the missionaries that had come along with the packtrain.

"One of 'em, feller name o' Sam Parker's abaout whatcha'd 'spec fer a parson. The same as that'ere Jason Lee feller from last year—stiff-neck know-it-all, hyar to preach an' profit off the Injuns. Anuther'n what don't want to l'arn nuthin'.

'T'other'n, though, name o' Whitman, he's a whole diff'ernt style o' feller. He don't preach at ye er nuthin' like that. Allus askin' good questions, tryin best he kin to l'arn what he kin abaout us an' the Injuns an' the country up thisaway. He's a medico, too, an' damn good at it, too. One o' my hostlers broke his arm—mule kicked 'im. Whitman straightened it out an' put a splint on it, purty as ye please. Nobody asked 'im to, neither. He jist went an' done it. Din't ask fer nuthin' fer his trouble, neither. 'Pears that arm's gonna be good as new by time we head on back!"

"A proper doctor, ye say. Is he now?" Finn's interest was obviously aroused.

"Yep. An' like I war sayin', a damn good 'un!"

We invited Harris to camp to join us for supper. It didn't appear that there would be much in the way of vittles offered in the trader's camp that night. Whilst he went to get his horse I watched Fitzpatrick running about like the proverbial headless chicken, trying to get his trading operation up and running. It would have been easier if Fontenelle had been along to share that chore, but maybe not, if what I had been hearing about Lucien's dramming were true. Fitz was too busy to waste time in social pleasantries, so a wave of the hand sufficed as the three of us rode out.

࿐   ࿐   ࿐

Next morning, after Black rode back to his camp—he slept where he fell the night before—we met to discuss selling our plews. I laid out my thoughts of the day before, about caching our plews if Fitz declined to honor Chouteau's promise from last year. Old loyalties are hard to put aside and we wished Tom success in his new venture, but the bunch agreed to refuse to sell our furs unless he paid the agreed-upon premium. We also agreed that Brass Turtle and I would first meet with Fitz before any new trading took place. Everyone was free, naturally, to use the credit he already had on the books.

After the meeting Turtle and I sorted through our plews and selected a couple dozen of our best springtime beaver to bolster our argument and set Fitzpatrick's mouth a-watering for the rest.

When I returned to our lodge, Cat and Iris had returned from their morning bathe and were getting gussied up in their pretties, long hair braids shining with bear grease, ear bobs and necklaces gleaming, a tasteful streak of vermilion paint on brows and cheekbones. I chuckled when I caught sight of Cat's new leggin's, with three slender coup stripes embroidered in quills, for the enemy warriors she could be certain she had killed. She had earned the right to brag.

When our colorful procession, composed of half our bunch, reached the trade tents, we tethered our horses and left them in the care of a Séli lad we knew. I had taken scarcely a stride towards the trade tents before an old friend, Grover Weed, known as Buzzard, clapped me on the shoulder and croaked, "Howdy, Temple, glad ye ain't gone under! Jist gittin' hyar?" I assured him that it was so. He assumed a conspiratorial look and lowered his voice, lest he be overheard, "Jist wanted to tell ye, Aitch-bee-cee showed up hyar at ronnyvoo jist thi'shere mawnin'. Ye mought want to know 'bout that afore ye do any serious tradin'." I assured him that it was worthwhile to know that information, thanked him heartily, and invited him to supper, which bachelors, especially, appreciate.

When Grover went on his way, Brass Turtle cackled gleefully, "That'ere war truly a slice o' luck! Meetin' Buzzard jist now! Made our chore a whole lot easier! Ol' Fitz'll be a mite quicker to tame with Brits in camp. Nothin' like compertishun to speed up the hagglin'!"

Cat and Iris went off with Tally and the other women. Turtle and I led our packmule off to Fitz's marquee, where we encountered Etienne Provôt, whom I had seen only at a distance the previous day.

"*Bonjour, Temple!*" he greeted me, pronouncing my name in French, "*et M'sieu Tortue,* so good to see you once again!"

"Ye'll be even gladder 'bout seein' us when ye see what we brung along," Turtle replied, reaching casually into one of the mule's panniers and bringing out one of the rich, deep-pile plews and handing it to Provôt. "Thar's a heap more jist like it whar that'n come from."

After a brief exchange of pleasantries, during which Provôt fingered the sample plew admiringly, I advised him, "Before ye git too enamored of our furs, Etienne, ye'd best get Fitzpatrick over here. There's a few details we need to be talkin' over before we do any tradin'."

Either my tone or expression alerted Provôt that something serious might be afoot. Replying only, "*Attendez, s'il vous plait,*" he hotfooted off in the direction of the trade tents.

"He knows somethin's up," Turtle surmised. "Jist as well. Fitz'll come ready to talk straighter'n usual fer the tradin'."

When Tom Fitzpatrick arrived, he greeted us warmly and invited us into the marquee, whilst Provôt tethered our packmule to a picket pin beside the doorway. Inside, Fitz poured tin cups of French cognac all around, waved us to a couple of wooden benches beside a deal table, and said, "Now what's got our Frenchy friend in such an all-fired lather?"

"Mebbe it's his conscience," Brass Turtle responded, favoring Etienne with a grin and a broad wink. Provôt looked confused.

"We've come to trade, Tom," I cut in, not sure what prank Turtle might have in mind. "First, I reckon you'll be wishin' to see what we've got to offer."

"Indade I would," Fitz replied. "Provôt tells me ye be packin' prime fur."

Turtle and I set our cups aside, stepped outdoors, and returned bearing a couple armloads of plews which we dumped onto the table. Fitzpatrick ran his fingers through the deep under-fur of one plew after another, obvious approval sneaking past the blank look he was striving unsuccessfully to maintain.

"'Tis sartinly prime fur ye be off'rin'," he said at last. "If it's all as good as this, we'll take the lot" and he named a fair price per pound.

"That'll be jist fer startin'," Brass Turtle cut in, seeing me already reaching into my belt poke for Chouteau's letter. "Thar be more to the tradin' this time, Fitz, as' ye know."

Fitzpatrick sighed and replied, "Yes, I know full well what you're after referrin' to, but that was a year past. Circumstances have altered consid'rably since that toime. Sublette's no longer in the picture, as ye surely know. The offer contained in the letter Mister Chouteau sent ye, Buck, no longer applies."

"No longer applies, ye say!" Turtle exploded. "Tell that to the trappers an' all the Injuns we talked into backin' yew an' Fontenelle this year!"

"Ye read his letter last year, Tom," I told the red-faced Fitzpatrick, who was struggling to frame a suitable argument, "and ye didn't tell me no. I knew ye didn't like what Cadet was offerin', for damn sure, but ye never said ye wouldn't go along with it."

"We backed ye, Fitz, an' now it's us what're on the hook for keepin' your word to pay extry money fer plews this year," Turtle insisted. "That'ere extry money comes to half agin fer our bunch, includin' Kit Carson, an' a quarter more fer all the trappers an' Injuns we got to side with ye. We know who did an' who din't, so thar won't be no cheatin' ye."

A heated debate dragged on for at least half an hour, threatening at times to become personal betwixt Tom and the two of us—always in the shadow of an unspoken threat of our going over to trade with Aitch-bee-cee and taking a passel of trappers and Indians with us, just for spite. At last Fitzpatrick threw up his hands in defeat and acknowledged his new company's obligation to honor Chouteau's commitment from the previous year, rash as it might have been. He insisted, howsomever, that at the end of rendezvous I must write a letter to Pierre Chouteau, Cadet verifying the amount of extra value in trade goods or credit that Fontenelle & Fitzpatrick was required to pay out in order to live up to the offer made by Cadet in his1834 letter to me. Which I agreed to do.

Once the affair was settled, Fitz shoved out his hand and Turtle and I shook it in renewed friendship, the pledge pleasantly reinforced by another round of cognac sloshed brimful in the tin cups.

❧   ❧   ❧

After we opened the packs and every man claimed his own plews, fine furs, and other tradeable plunder, they were able to take them to trade for whatever they wished or to receive credit in F&F's ledgers for future commerce. Except for Brass Turtle, all of our Indians and our two *Californios* were illiterate. One of us who was able to read accompanied each of them to the fur buyers to make sure they received correct payment for their plews, plus the premium, and that proper amounts of credit were entered in the company's books. Once each man learned the total of what he had coming, no wily clerk could cheat him. Basic ciphering, addition and subtraction, appears to be an inborn skill, unlike reading, which must be taught.

Often, one or another of our Indians asked me to accompany him to the fur buyers' tables to witness ledger entries for their peltry, which took me to the trade area more than I otherwise might have done. Which is likely why I chanced to be present the morning that the missionary doctor Marcus Whitman removed the Blackfoot arrow point that plagued Jim Bridger for more than three painful years. McCool and I had gone along that day with Zeetlah and Little Mountain to sell some of their plews. Our transaction was almost completed when Buzzard trotted past and called out, "Ye'd best wind up yer bizness thar, Buck! Time ye get a move on! C'mon an' see ther ellerphunt!" He continued on with no further explanation. Trappers and Indians alike were gathering in an open space amid the cluster of trade tents. Our business concluded and curiosity aroused, the four of us followed along.

At first we could see nothing. A sizeable crowd already ringed the area, blocking our view. Zeetlah chattered something in the Delaware tongue to Little Mountain and the big fellow obligingly shouldered his way through the press of onlookers. Zeetlah, Finn, and I followed in his wake until we stood in the front rank. There in the bright August morning sunshine we beheld a shirtless Jim Bridger on his knees, spread-eagled over a large stump, chin resting on its top, big-muscled arms clasping its girth, whilst a fair-skinned man stood over him, a small knife in hand, then bent down and traced a line on Bridger's bare back with the knife.

Blood welled up from the wound. One of Harris's hostlers standing by reached out with a clout and swabbed it away while the surgeon probed deeper with his knife, laying the flesh aside as he sought to expose the iron arrowhead that Jim had carried between his shoulder blades since the battle with the same Blackfoots that had cost Vanderburgh his life, more than three years before. Finn and Zeetlah had tried to remove it and failed. So had

Doctor Harrison, who, one hopes, was reasonably sober when he made the attempt.

Even at a distance I could see sweat glistening on Bridger's brow as the surgeon dug deeper, probing ever deeper into the flesh as he tried to loosen the broad arrow point from its deep bed in the muscle. Jim clamped his whiskery jaws but released hardly a moan as the doctor forced his little knife, as we learned later, all the way to the shoulder bone and twisted it about in an effort to release the embedded arrowhead. A river of sweat mingled with involuntary tears. Bridger grunted past the willow twig he now clenched in his teeth as Whitman sliced carefully at the muscle that held that wicked point fast.

At last the surgeon stood erect, bent down and fumbled in the black bag at his feet. His hand emerged gripping a pair of shiny pliers, which he plunged into the gaping, bleeding wound. He commenced twisting, wiggling, tugging gently, then with greater force, while Jim grunted, squeezed his eyes tight shut, clamped his teeth ever tighter on the willow twig until it snapped, just as Whitman released a triumphant yelp and raised the three-inch black arrowhead high above his head.

A mingled gasp and ragged cheer went up from the whites gathered there. Even Indians, trained from birth to be stoical, clapped hands over their mouth to keep their soul from flying off at the sight of such a prodigy.

Bridger gripped the stump, powerful shoulders quivering, grunting through clenched teeth, as Whitman laved the gaping wound with something liquid and proceeded to sew the tortured flesh together.

I glanced at old Zeetlah, whose deeply-lined face remained impassive, then at Finnæus, who remained rooted to the spot, a look of awe flooding his features, as if he had seen a miracle, or perhaps a revelation.

When Jim attempted to lift his head from the stump, Joe Meek darted from the crowd and shoved a kettle under his chin, then held it steady as Bridger craned his neck and buried his nose in it. A moment later, he raised his head and grinned before slumping down again.

Now that the show was over, the crowd broke up. Most of the trappers and Indians wandered off. We stayed put, watching the missionary doctor finishing his chore before he examined the broad black arrow point. We moved closer whilst he held it up. It was a full three inches long, the point curled back where it had struck bone, bent back, and become a barb, defying all previous efforts to extract it from the tough muscle that had grown around it.

Bridger commenced to rouse. He lifted his head, squinted at what was left of the spectators, and growled, "Whar the hell's Meek an' his gawddamn kettle?" before sagging onto the stump again before Joe could offer his particular kind of comfort. Jim stirred a couple minutes later, took a sip of Joe's nourishment, and scrambled to a seat on the stump. Whitman showed him the bloody black arrowhead and said, "You say you carried this terrible thing in your back for three whole years? I'm amazed that you didn't die of infection!"

Bridger chuckled deep in his throat, grinned weakly, and replied, "Hell, Doc, meat don't spile in the mountains!"

In a foolhardy moment, flush with the profit of an exceptional beaver harvest and the generous premium promised by Cadet, I told Kathleen to buy anything and everything she wished from F&F's trade tables. Which proved to be a serious blunder. I began to fear that we lacked enough pack animals to carry all of her plunder when we moved on from rendezvous, if, indeed, our lodge could hold it all beforehand.

Much of Cat's trading was with her own goods, most of it fine furs and quillwork obtained from the Arapaho women the previous winter. She was not alone. Most of the wives engaged in such commerce when they weren't wheedling the wherewithal from their menfolk to buy fine fabrics, foofurraw, cookware, and tools from the traders at F&F and the Aitch-bee-cee.

After several forays into Fitzpatrick's Halls of Mammon, Cat insisted on visiting the Hudson's Bay Company establishment. As always, I had held back several prime plews from my initial trading. Furs are the coins and banknotes of the mountains. Kathleen still retained most of her trade items.

As we approached the HBC trading tents, I espied the distinctive red marquee of Captain William Drummond Stewart, somewhat faded now from a couple years' exposure to the elements but still a colorful testament to its owner's flamboyant personality. It was set in the midst of the weathered white canvas living quarters of the *bourgeois* and his chief assistants.

We tethered our horses and the packmule and entered one of the trade tents, where I was struck by the fine quality of the merchandise the Brits offered for trade. Large, thick Witney woolen blankets caught Kathleen's fancy and she traded for two of them, informing me they were destined to be new *capotes*, the white one for herself, bright green for me. Later, at another table in a different tent, I discovered a small, collapsible, shiny brass spyglass like Carson's, which I added to my poke.

As we turned to depart, I spied a dainty, ornately-chased, double-barreled percussion pistol, which, small as it was overall, fired 40-caliber balls. It was nested in an inlaid rosewood chest that also contained its ball mold and gun tools. What especially caught my interest was a delicate inscription etched on one of its stubby barrels, Jos'h Manton, together with a tiny engraving of a tiger. Word was that Joseph Manton had gone bankrupt several years before. Although he had also made dueling pistols, besides rifles and fowlers, I had never seen or even heard of his belly guns. I wondered if this sturdy little weapon might have been made for Joe's own wife.

The sharp-eyed trader detected my delight at discovering the little gun and soaked me three of the prime plews I had brought with me.

Outdoors, heading for our mounts, we encountered the Hero of Waterloo and Antoine Clement making their way through the press of trappers and Indians thronging the alleyways that threaded amongst HBC's various trade tents. I would have preferred to escape unnoticed, but Stewart hailed me with a cheery, "Halloo, Mister Buck! So good to see you again!"

I returned his greeting, less cheerily but civilly, and prepared to continue on our way, but apparently the Scotsman was feeling unusually democratic that day. He planted himself before us and declared, "I've been meaning to come to Tom Fitzpatrick's establishment since we arrived from Nat Wyeth's new trading fort he's calling Fort Hall, but one thing and another . . ." He trailed off uncertainly, then brightened when he espied another gentleman approaching. "Have ye met Mister Ermatinger, Mister Buck?" I confessed that I hadn't. "Well, now, we must remedy that omission forthwith!"

He called out to the other fellow, whom I recalled as the Hudson's Bay partisan at Nat Wyeth's trade tent the year before. Francis Ermatinger was a well-set-up man, perhaps a few years older than myself, but not many, dressed in well-worn but gentlemanly attire, shod in quilled and beaded moccasins. His most striking feature was his large, red, bulbous nose, a veritable beacon amid his otherwise handsome features. I learned later that his nose had earned him the good-natured nickname of Bardolph amongst his Aitch-bee-cee colleagues, a reference to Mister Shakespeare's comedic tosspot in *Henry V*.

Just then, Ermatinger was occupied with trading affairs, instructing a couple of his *engagés* in some matter or other. I heard him rattle off a volley of fluent French in response to their report in that tongue, before he left them to join us. "Frank, I'd like you to meet Mister Temple Buck," Stewart started off, "an American free trapper, one of my earliest friends in the mountains." I was surprised to learn that I had been promoted to the rank of friend by the aristocratic captain.

"Pleased to meet ye, I'm sure," Ermatinger said with a genuine smile, in a hearty voice strongly flavored with Cockney that betrayed not a trace of French accent. He shoved out a work-toughened hand that I dutifully shook.

"Oh, yes, Frank, Mister Buck has been in the mountains nearly as long as you yourself," Stewart nattered on, "one of the first Americans to enter the fur trade." Impatient as I was to depart, I lost interest in the rest of my biography as the Scotsman related it, picking up only bits and pieces concerning our meeting on Stewart's first journey to the mountains, his first buffalo kill, a mention of my California trip, and not much else.

I noticed Antoine Clement waiting patiently, standing respectfully behind his haughty benefactor, completely ignored. I felt unaccountably sorry for the handsome redheaded French-Cree trapper who had traded his independence for whatever largesse he received from his high-handed patron. I nodded hello to Antoine, who returned my greeting with an eager grin.

Equally ignored up to then had been Kathleen. I resolved that she would suffer the like of Antoine's isolation no longer. "It's a pleasure to meet you, sir," I said to the HBC partisan, "may I present my wife Kathleen?" whilst I nudged Cat forward. My spouse nodded and smiled broadly, saying nothing but sticking out her hand for a handshake, which Ermatinger grasped with a good-natured chuckle, followed by a most surprising remark. In his Cockney-accented English he asked, "Of the Séli people are ye, milady?'"

Cat's eyes widened in surprise and her hand flew to her mouth, but she replied, "I am Séli."

Ermatinger responded gallantly. "Of course you are, beautiful as ye be." Then, "And, I confess, I also recognized the handsome quillwork designs on your dress and moccasins as those of your people."

Someone summoned him just then in an urgent French voice. He turned and called out that he would be coming *tout de suite*, before apologizing to us for the interruption, followed by his sincere-sounding invitation that we call on him another time, "when ye can meet me own missus." Upon which he hustled off to attend to business.

We pried loose from Stewart as soon as we could decently do so. Surprisingly, the captain's torrent of genial blather contained no mention of William Sublette, his long-time friend and original host in the mountains. In parting he said, "And please do assure Tom Fitzpatrick that I will visit soon. It'll be jolly to reminisce together, eh?" I assured him that I would do so, wondering the while how jolly would be their reminiscences of losing their horses and plunder to the Crows.

Riding back to camp, musing on the events just past, I reckoned that now I had a rather better understanding of the rock that Nat Wyeth promised last year to roll into Fitz's garden and who might be helping him push it along.

On the way, our path took us through a couple of wooded areas. I reined up in one of them and dismounted and Kathleen did likewise, her look questioning my intention. I assured her that my purpose, leastaways right then, was not romantic. Whilst she tethered our critters, I stood several stout deadwood limbs on end in the moist soil, walked back half a dozen paces and toed a line on the ground. Then I retrieved the pretty rosewood box from the mule's pannier and removed the elegant little belly-gun from its velvet nest, loaded powder and ball from its modest stock, and fitted caps on the nipples. Cat closely observed my every action, the idea rapidly taking shape that the diminutive firearm was not intended for my larger hands, but for her own.

I stepped to the line, swung up my hand, cocked a hammer, took aim, and gently squeezed the tiny trigger. The little pistol shuddered rather than bucked. Splinters flew from the stob as it was yanked from the earth and knocked flat. Small as the weapon is, its 40-caliber ball packs a deadly wallop.

Naturally Cat insisted that the next shot must be hers. I guided her through the loading procedure, cautioning against using too much powder in the little gun, then turned her loose to practice. Which she did until she used up all but two of her pistol balls and splintered most of the targets.

Riding home, I suggested that she carry her new pacifier in the poke that hangs from her sash, which was a waste of breath. She won't likely let the pretty little pistol stray far from her hand.

~ ~ ~

A day or so later Kit Carson asked if I would accompany him to Fitzpatrick's trade tents. He needed plunder and, being unable to read, he wanted someone along to make sure the clerks didn't cheat him. I was pleased to help out, after all the good fortune we had received at Kit's hands. Cat, never at a loss for an excuse to visit the traders, came along, as well.

On the way Cat enquired how his courtship of Grass Singing was going. Kit is an extremely private person, but that morning he allowed that his suit was on a successful track with the young Arapaho woman. Then he revealed his mission that day was to purchase trade plunder to swap for enough horses to convince her parents to give their consent to the union.

The trading went well enough, Kit leading the clerk from one tent to another, one table to another, amassing a heap of trade goods—tobacco, yard goods, cookware, tools, knives, gunpowder and galena, a couple-three muskets, horse clothing, bits and spurs, gobs of foofurraw, and I don't know what-all. Kit had already parted with most of his plews to F&F, so it was necessary only to tot up the total cost and deduct it from Carson's account. Whilst Kit went to retrieve his packmule to haul his plunder back to camp, I made sure the arithmetic was accurate and recorded in ink.

One curious thing about the transaction was the clerk's headgear, a smooth, shiny top hat perched jauntily atop his noggin. Neither Carson nor I had seen the like of it before. Old, shaggy, well-worn beaver toppers were fairly commonplace amongst clerks and greenhorns come up from the settlements, but that glossy stovepipe was something altogether new. When one of us commented on his hat, the clerk grinned proudly, tapped the narrow brim, and said, "Newest thing in French fashion! Catchin' on with Brits, too, I hear. Handsome, ain't it? Made o' silk, it is. Light as a feather. Don't do too good in the rain, o' course, but they be a heap cheaper'n beaver. Purty soon, ever'body'll be wearin' 'em! Beaver'll be dyin' out."

"Not gawddamn likely," Carson spat. "Beaver toppers been around ferever! That thang you're wearin'll never shine!" I was inclined to agree with him, but a nagging recollection from Chouteau's letter the year before came to mind, his warning that something could change the world as we knew it.

Further contemplation was interrupted by Kathleen entering the tent in a hurry, a disturbed look on her face. "Come, Temple!" she cried in an agitated tone. "You, too!" she added, addressing Carson. "Ver' big bad man makin' hell! Hurtin' men! Grabbin' women!" She swept out of the tent, heading for the open space amongF&F's cluster of trade tents. I trotted in her wake whilst Kit hurried his to secure his packmule.

I heard him before I spied him, a big, mean-mouthed French-Canuck bully, name of Chouinard, that Andy Dripps had brought to rendezvous, one of several Frenchies pirated from the Aitch-bee-cee with a promise of better wages. Most Americans called him Shunar and gave him wide berth when he was in his cups, which was most of the time. Now the dark-bearded giant stalked belligerently around the circle of booze tents where trappers lined up to fill their kettles. He roared curses in French and American and challenges to one and all, bragging at the top of his voice that he could whip any Frenchman, American, Spaniard, or Dutchman, punctuating his tirade now and then by punching one or another of the French-Cree trappers and knocking them flat.

At one point he yanked up his greasy leather sleeve, exposing a hairy arm and crowing, "*Regardez*! No Injun blood in me! Pure *Français, moi! Grâce à Dieu!* I 'ave no trouble to flog *les Français*! Now I weel take a switch an' flog *les Américains* like schoolboys!"

A growl and sharp movement at my side announced Carson's return from the picket line. "Somebody's gotta settle that'n purty quick," he snarled in a low voice but he stayed put.

Cat darted from my side just then and raced across the open space to join half a dozen young Arapaho girls who had wandered into the clearing, evidently attracted by the crowd and the hubbub, not realizing the peril posed by the drunken loud-mouth braggart. I recognized one of the girls as young Grass Singing, Carson's intended bride. Cat gathered the girls around her and, her hands a blur, making sign describing what was happening, urging them to depart.

Kathleen's sudden dash to join the girls first caught Shunar's attention, then the bouquet of tender young prairie flowers clustered around Cat awakened his drunken lust. He covered the distance to them in half a dozen strides, shoved Kathleen roughly aside, and grabbed Grass Singing, who yelped with pain as his strong fingers dug into her shoulders.

Everything happened at once. I saw Cat's hand plunge into her belt poke as I raced to her side, yanking my pistol from my sash as I ran. Before I could close the distance, Carson was there before me, butcher knife in hand, pricking the giant bully in the back. Close up, Shunar was even bigger than he had appeared before. Kit could have walked under the bully's outstretched arm.

Shunar let go of the girl and spun about to confront his attacker, black eyes burning with rage, clenching his huge ham-like fists, mouth falling slightly open when he spied the diminutive Carson, wicked-looking knife in hand, crouched and ready to fling himself into combat. Kit retreated not an inch. "Listen hyar!" he yelled, "Ye gawddamn overgrown heap o' stinkin' Frog-shit! Ye keep yer gawddamn dirty paws offa my woman an' yer rotten garbage mouth off us Amurricans! Heah me? I be the worst Amurrican in thi'shere camp! If ye don't do like I'm sayin', I'll rip yer stinkin' guts!"

Instead of flinging his huge bulk onto Carson, which would naturally have included falling onto Kit's big knife, the big bully fell back a step, the features showing above his bristling black beard contorted with fury, beet-red with rage, staring wide-eyed, unbelieving at the unlikely little man who had dared to call his bluff. Without uttering a single word he spun on his heel and ran for his horse and his rifle.

Carson watched him go. When he understood that Shunar meant to make a duel of it, he ran to get his horse off the picket line. "Li'l feller's runnin' off!" some idiot trapper called out. "Big 'un's got 'im buffaloed!"

"Like hell he is!" I yelled back. "That's Kit Carson! He don't run from nothin'!"

A moment later, Kit returned at a high lope, pistol dangling in his hand. He skidded his saddler to a halt in front of the big Frenchman, the horses' noses nearly touching each other, the riders face to face. "Is it me ye be aimin' to kill? Do ye?" Carson shouted.

"No," Shunar yelled back, at the same time bringing his rifle up to fire. The two charges exploded in a single blast. Carson's hat flew out of the gunsmoke. When the smoke blew away I spied a lock of his hair lying on his shoulder and a red stripe of powder burn on his cheek. He was grinning.

Shunar's rifle lay on the ground, the big Frenchman slumped over his horse's neck, face buried in the mane, right arm hanging limp, spewing blood, the fight clearly drained out of him.

"Finish 'im off, Kit!" "Kill the big sumbitch off, oncet an' fer all!" "Bastard begun it! Yew finish it fer 'im, Carson!" "*Tuez le sale bravache! Tuez lui!*"

Carson got a heap of such free advice about then, but he made no move to administer the *coup de grâce*. He was offered a dozen pistols, mine amongst them, but he just shook his head and proceeded to reload his own. Shunar, groggy with shock and pain, lifted his head at last and begged for his life amid the jeers of the mountaineers, those of the Frenchy trappers loudest amongst them. "Naw, I ain't gonna kill 'im," Kit announced. "I reckon he's pert'near lost his itchin' to go pickin' on folks. That'ere busted arm'll likely remind 'im he dassn't even try."

He reined his horse about, returned to the picket line, retrieved his packmule, and rode off in the direction of camp.

That night, Finn McCool, who had been sticking close as a shadow to Doctor Whitman since Jim Bridger's surgery, told us the aftermath of the horseback duel. Andy Dripps hunted down the missionary doctor and pleaded with him to treat the wounded French-Canuck, which the young parson agreed to do. McCool went along to help. There wasn't much that Whitman could do for the loud-mouth bully. Kit's bullet had smashed Shunar's hand, came out at the wrist, re-entered the forearm, which it tore up until it destroyed his elbow, and came out somewhere above it. Kit's prediction will likely remain true. The bullying career of *le grand bravache Français* is likely a thing of the past.

McCool also told us that Whitman had performed a second operation much like Bridger's, removing a large iron arrow point from the back of a trapper called Simon Ball, who had carried his unwelcome burden almost as long as Gabe had done.

Next morning, when Carson strolled by our lodge, Kathleen invited him in for flapjacks slathered with honey. She sweetened her invite even more when she told Kit that, the day before, during his duel, his Arapaho sweetheart Grass Singing had sharply reproved one of her young friends who expressed her admiration of the brave young American, telling her, in sign, "Keep your hands off him. He's mine!" Which happified Kit in no small measure.

Each of the next two days Carson returned to camp leading three horses he had purchased for marriage gifts to the parents of Grass Singing. Each day his critters included a tall, splashily-spotted piebald, a color highly-prized by all plains Indians, not only for their eye-catching appearance, but also for their near-invisibility at a distance. Their blotchy hide breaks up their outline, blending into their surroundings.

On the third day Kit asked me to go along with him to the traders to purchase some eleventh-hour items to complete the generous dowry he meant to offer for her hand and whatever else that might be included in that delicious parcel. It was high time he got whatever he reckoned he needed. Fitzpatrick had already struck a couple trade tents, a sign he was commencing to pack up.

"Ye'd best be gettin' a move on with your proposin', Kit," I advised, "before ol' Touches-the-Sky takes the whole shebang back east—and your girl in the bargain."

He allowed that he had been cutting it pretty fine, but today he intended to sew up the deal. "Besides," he confided, "Touches-the-Sky tol' me he's on my side. Sez he'll he'p me whar he kin."

Naturally Cat and Iris came along, sporting brand-new duds and showing off their *palomilla* mares bedecked in equine foofurraw that rivaled their own outfits. They abandoned us when we reached the F&F tents and scurried off in search of more settlement treasures. Whilst I tethered Coffee to a picket line I espied Will Stringfellow and Gideon Moon, whom I hadn't seen since our chance encounter on the trail to rendezvous. Which isn't surprising amid a mob of more than three hundred trappers and a couple thousand Indians. Will hailed me and I told Kit to go on ahead, that I would catch up later.

After a friendly hello and an offered swig from their kettle, which would have been rude to turn down, the tough little Kentuckian said, "I reckon ye wondered what in hell Gid an' me war doin' out thar all by our lonesome on ther trail, when ye come by with all o' yer Injuns. Din'tcha?"

I allowed that the thought had crossed my mind.

"Wal, thankee fer not askin' at ther time. Truth to tell, me an' Gid an' a coupla other fellers war sorta cachin' ourse'fs in ther woods nigh whar we met ye, lest ol' Bonnyville mought be comin' up thisaway lookin' fer ther plews we taken along, claimin' 'em fer his'n, an' makin' a stink abaout us runnin' off with 'em. 'Twar only later we come to find out ol' Baldy's quittin' ther fur bizness fer good an' all, anyways. He's prob'ly halfway to Sain' Looie by naow an' thar ain't no need fer worryin'. 'Sides, we awready traded off all o' them'ere plews an' got ourse'fs set an' ready fer nex' season." Gideon nodded affirmation of Will's confession, if that's what it was. It sounded more like bragging.

After another nip or two, we parted ways and I trotted off to join Carson in the trade tent.

☙   ☙   ☙

Later that day, Kit showed up at our lodge and asked me to accompany him to the Arapaho village, where he intended to present his formal marriage proposal to the parents of Grass Singing. She had already let him know that she returned his affection. From there on, the transaction was merely a matter of commerce with her folks. He had also asked Brass Turtle and Tuttle to join him on his mission. Naturally I went along.

I had never seen Carson look as dandified as he did that day—freshly bathed, cheeks shining, bereft of every whisker, his fair hair neatly brushed and falling past his shoulders—the empty patch where Shunar's rifle ball had chopped off a lock plainly visible, a badge of honor—his quilled and beaded war shirt, leggin's, britchclout, and moccasins all brand-spankin' clean and new and of Arapaho design. Kit meant to impress his prospective in-laws.

Naturally Kathleen insisted that I, too, get gussied up. She dug out some of my handsomest togs—to show respect, as she put it. Meanwhile Iris groomed Coffee to gleaming ebony, even decorating his rump with a checkerboard design, using a fragment of comb on the wet hair.

I rode out to the pasture in time to see Half-horse and the others performing a final grooming of the handsome gift horses and a packmule loaded with panniers stuffed with presents. I picked up the lead ropes of two horses and fell in behind Kit, who also led a handsome pair. Brass Turtle led two more, and Tuttle, freshly-shaved and resplendent in a bright red shirt and clean leggin's, brought up the rear with the packmule in tow.

"All o' these purty hosses an' thi'shere heap o' plunder oughta git Carson a whole lodgeful o' wimmen, like one o' them'ere Chinee nabobs, 'stid o' jist ther one li'l gal he's been courtin'," Tuttle commented as we rode the short distance to the Arapaho camp.

"Cain't afford to be hagglin' with her folks, Tuttle," Kit sang out. "Time's runnin' out. 'Sides, Wa'a Nibé be wuth ever' crumb of it an' more!"

It took hardly any time to cover the half-mile to the Indian village, but somewhat more was required to reach the lodge of Grass Singing's parents at the far end of camp. By time we got there we had acquired a noisy crowd trotting in our wake, eager to witness Carson's generous giveaway for the toothsome Wa'a Nibé. The good-looking gift horses we were leading had already prompted murmurs of approval and the heavy panniers swaying on the packmule provoked wild speculation as to the treasures they contained.

As it turned out, our mission that day amounted to primitive theatre, acting out a foregone conclusion. When we arrived at the lodge of Wa'a Nibé's parents, Kit dismounted and, still leading his two horses, scratched on the lodge cover. Her father emerged first, clad in what was likely his best go-to-meetin' get-up, certainly not his everyday attire. Carson handed him the two halter-shanks and commenced signing his wish to marry the girl, first beckoning Turtle, then me, to come forward with our critters and hand over our lead-ropes, until Daddy, a good-looking middle-aged warrior, found himself hanging onto more horses than one man could conveniently handle. He growled something through the doorway and two young men came out and relieved him.

Then it was time for Tuttle to bring the packmule forward, but before Kit could start hauling out his plunder, Daddy again spoke through the doorflap and Mama came out to join him. She, too, was much too handsomely outfitted for our visit to have been unexpected. Her crimson woolen dress bedecked with elk ivories, crusted with elaborate quillwork, was not an ordinary work dress. Mama was even lovelier than her outfit, provoking Tuttle to blurt out, "Thet'ere be one purty female, begawd! Ther dotter's lucky to have that'n in her blood! So's Carson!" Fortunately nobody thereabouts understood American.

Then Carson commenced spilling out a cornucopia of precious trade goods—a nest of copper kettles, porcelain cups, skillets and spiders, sugar and English tea and roasted coffee beans, yards of woolen and calico trade cloth, hanks of shiny glass beads, thread, needles, packets of vermilion and other paints and dyes, carrots of tobacco, pipe tomahawks, firesteels, two muskets, gunflints, powder and galena, traps, brass tacks, manila rope, butcher knives, headstalls, bits and spurs, awls, files, a hand-axe, a draw-knife for skinning lodgepoles, a seemingly unending river of settlement merchandise, a king's ransom that in most circumstances would have purchased a harem of Indian maidens.

At last the canvas panniers hung limp on the mule's flanks and Kit faced his intended father-in-law, staring into his eyes, hands at his side, saying nothing. The warrior and his wife had fought to keep a straight face, struggled to keep their hands from darting to their mouths in wonder as Carson revealed one treasure after another. Now the father placed his hands on Kit's shoulders as a gesture of acceptance. His comely wife appeared transfixed, unable to tear her eyes away from the heap of unimagined wealth.

Now the father called into the lodge and Grass Singing scooted out the doorflap, dark eyes dancing, a shy smile wreathing her pretty features. Her father reached out his arms to push the young people close together, shoulders touching. Then he put her hand in Kit's and stepped back, his broad smile announcing his approval of their union.

Riding back to camp afterwards, Tuttle enquired, "Thet mean ye be married naow, Kit?"

"Nope, not yet," the prospective bridegroom replied. "That'll happen t'morry. Her folks gotta have time to git their side of it together. I awready done my part. Now it's their turn."

ર્જ્   ર્જ્   ર્જ્

Our womenfolk would have been severely disappointed if yesterday's gifting had been all there was to Kit's getting hitched to Grass Singing. That would have deprived them of a prime opportunity to flaunt their foofurraw. As it was, their only distress at the actual event next day was that the Arapaho women rivaled them now in showy apparel and feminine gimcrackery acquired at F&F's trade tables. Beribboned bonnets, lacy parasols, and other un-Indian fashions abounded amongst our hostesses, as if those dusky beauties had cause to shun the mid-day August sunshine to protect their complexions.

The men, too, strutted in calico shirts and colorful woolen britchclouts. Their proudest new possessions, howsomever, were gleaming new muskets slung on their shoulders and shiny butcher knives and pipe-tomahawks tucked into showy French-Canuck sashes.

Buffalo roasting over a score of cookfires provided a mouthwatering welcome to the Arapaho village, a delicious redolence wafting on a gentle western breeze far out onto the prairie, stirring the appetite of our mountaineer crew, always eager for a feast. The sun was at its zenith, the appointed time of our arrival, when we rode into the village, our nine women in the vanguard, and headed for the council fire.

Most of the village had already assembled, awaiting the bridegroom, anxious to see what Wa'a Nibé would bring to the marriage in her dowry. Kit was likely already shuddering at the thought of hauling along a passel of household plunder when time came for trapping after rendezvous.

The wedding wasn't nearly as elaborate as that of Circling Eagle had been. There was no dancing by a women's society. Grass Singing was too young for membership. The drumming, which had commenced at dawn for Tayho's rites, was confined to immediately before the marriage ceremony and a brief spell afterward. Carson, who avoids drawing attention to himself, was doubtless relieved at that.

Wa'a Nibé's father joined the two young people in marriage in the formal ritual and Touches-the-Sky pretty much repeated that gesture immediately afterwards, which, Brass Turtle opined, was a sign that the chief regarded Kit as his adopted son. That appeared to be even moreso when Touches-the-Sky added two fine horses to the four good critters that Grass Singing's father presented to the couple.

Centerpiece of the giveaway was naturally the handsome lodge that the bride's parents provided, along with much fine-looking clothing for both bride and groom, a welter of soft-tanned buffalo robes, elk hides, and deerskins, new woolen blankets, a handsome riding saddle for Wa'a Nibé and a heap of packsaddles and pads, a pair of ornate apishamores crusted with quills and jingling with hawk bells and brass thimbles, an otterskin pipe bag, quilled and beaded belt-pokes and knife sheaths, backrests, digging sticks, fleshing tools, brightly-painted *parflêche* boxes stuffed with dried buffalo meat and pemmican, woven baskets filled with dried plums and berries, prairie turnips and such, painted gourds, and I don't know what-all. But it was surely a generous gifting.

After the feasting, whilst we were riding back to our camp, where another giveaway to the new couple would take place, Brass Turtle observed, "Them two, her pa an' that awful purty mother o' hers must'a been purty damn sure, early on, that ol' Kit war plumb serious about teamin' up with their li'l gal. A good-lookin' lodge like that'n they gave 'em takes a heap o' hides an' time an' hard work to git itse'f done."

∾   ∾   ∾

Next day a procession of travois drags and horses and a passel of Arapaho women arrived to deliver the plunder Kit and Grass Singing had acquired from her kin and friends and to set up still another lodge with a three-pole foundation in our camp. We now had four Arapaho brides in our midst, leastaways for a spell, but Kit had expressed his intention to join up with Jim Bridger's brigade for the fall hunt. Like almost always, our bunch was still undecided about what we would do.

That afternoon, we had our own celebration of the couple's nuptials. Anse Tolliver rounded up Harry Harpoon and Cap'n Billy and a couple other fiddlers to join him in making music for Kit Carson's jumpin' the broom, as Anse called it. Tuttle saw to it that they stayed well-oiled, along with the rest of us. Yves and Jean-Luc scurried amongst half-a-dozen cookfires, frantically turning spits sagging under great chunks of fat buffalo meat sizzling and sputtering over the fires, whilst our bunch, our women and kids, as well as a host of trappers and their wives and temporary sweethearts drawn by the music and appetizing aromas wafting over the valley, helped ourselves to slabs of tender flesh carved from the massive roasts suspended over hissing coals.

Paddy McBride led off the dancing by flinging himself into a high-kicking Irish jig when Harry and an Irish fiddler launched into a spirited reel, which inspired our well-lubricated guests to spring into frenzied action, each according to his or her custom and impulse, prancing and twirling, hopping, gamboling, skipping and frolicking, madly cavorting, lurching into their fellows, stamping moccasined feet on the prairie sod more or less in time with the music, voices raised in a good-natured lunatic chorus of hoarse shouts, high-pitched Indian trills, and snatches of half-remembered song.

Tom Fitzpatrick and Black Harris showed up leading a packmule bearing a couple kegs of sugary honey-mead metheglin, which gained them instant popularity, especially amongst the womenfolk. About the same time, Joe Meek and Umentucken rode in with a crowd from Bridger's brigade. The Mountain Lamb, obviously enceinte, was as pretty as ever, laughing and waving to our women, who raced to welcome her and help her down from her horse.

Bridger looked to be more cheerful and relaxed than I had seen him for years, thanks to the skill of the missionary doctor Marcus Whitman, who had arrived with Jim's party, along with his sour-faced sidekick. The Reverend Samuel Parker spent most of his visit clucking his disapproval of drunken trappers frolicking with tipsy Indian girls, especially whenever one of them led his giggling light-o'-love into the shadows. The acerbic parson briefly suspended his censure, howsomever, each time he visited a cookfire to help himself to another juicy slice of buffalo.

When Jim and I found a few minutes to chat, he mentioned that he had taken a wife for the first time. "That be her, over thar by your lodge, palavering with your woman. I call her Cora," he said, pointing her out. "She be Flathead, too," he added, "daughter o' Chief Insala, what brung his band to ronnyvoo his year an' set up nigh your Iron Bow." I followed his pointing finger and beheld a pretty young girl engaged in animated conversation with Cat, the two of them dissolving into laughter from time to time.

Then Jim asked, "What d'ye reckon your bunch'll be doin', come time fer the fall hunt?" I replied that, as usual, that decision was still up in the air. "Wal, I know haow all o' ye hate j'inin' up with a brigade, takin' orders an' sich. Even so, ye kin tell the others that ye'll be welcome to tag along with us—trappin' free, mind ye, on yer own hook, like ye allus done." I thanked him for that generous offer, which provoked a snort and the laughing reply, "Hell, it ain't charity, Temple. We kin allus use an extry score o' plumb-shootin' guns when Blackfoots come callin'! 'Sides, judgin' by the raft o' plews yew boys been haulin' in these past couple years, mebbe ye'll rub some o' that'ere luck off on the rest of us!"

We let it go at that. I assured Jim that I would pass his offer along to the others, next time we met to decide on our course for the autumn harvest.

‽ ‽ ‽

Naturally Tayho, Rosa, and Maria, the Arapaho wives of Little Mountain, Cesár, and Diego were first to pitch in to help the new bride settle in, making her feel at home, but our other womenfolk weren't far behind. Whatever shyness Wa'a Nibé maintained during Kit's courtship quickly wore off in our camp. In just a few days, she was happily gawddamning and sumbitching along with the rest of them—with not the faintest idea of the meaning of those oaths.

My father had mostly been elsewhere during this rendezvous. I attributed his absence to his paying court to the Nez Percé woman who made the beautiful quilled garments and moccasins in which he dressed at rendezvous. He showed up for Kit's gifting in our camp and told me, afterwards, that he was plumb exasperated with the Shahaptins. They had invited the Reverend Mister Parker to set up shop amongst them on their home stomping grounds when the rendezvous came to its end. Even worse news, the Reverend Doctor Whitman intended to return to the East in order to recruit more Christian Bible-thumpers that he would bring back with him next year.

In spite of Powatawa's impassioned arguments against swapping their time-honored religious beliefs for a hike to hell on the Jesus Road, the Nez Percés turned a deaf ear to his fervent warnings about tribe after Eastern tribe who had converted to the whiteman's religious teachings and lost their will and their skill to fight for their traditional way of life and their land, only to be overrun, dispossessed, and murdered by land-greedy white-eyes who despised all redmen. In vain he encouraged them to acquire white-eyes plunder by trapping furs and swapping buffalo robes for the things they desired, as they were already doing. The Shahaptin religious leaders were convinced that the Christian god who showered his magical blessings of guns, steel knives, woolen blankets, and copper kettles upon the white-eyes would immediately do likewise for the Nez Percé people, if only they would learn to rattle off the teachings contained in the whiteman's Talking Leaves.

Most of the Shahaptin elders liked Powatawa well enough—they even offered to adopt him into the tribe—but they were adamant in their resistance to his warnings of future dangers posed by the preachings of missionaries. After all, they insisted, when had their own gods ever provided guns and copper kettles? Clearly, my father must be mistaken.

Even Iron Bow's Flathead band was not immune to the Christian contagion. Although the old chief himself remained unconvinced that the bearded white-eyes Jesus would obligingly open a cloud and shower the Séli people with a never-ending deluge of trade goods if only they would kneel before His Book, there were many in his band who believed that He would do precisely that.

Finn McCool, who had stuck to Marcus Whitman like a cockleburr ever since he witnessed Bridger's surgery, observed, "If these missionaries are even half as slick-tongued as their Romish counterparts in me own priest-ridden Ireland, 'tis a lost cause for our innocent red brethren. They be lambs eager for their own bloody slaughter. Much as I admire Whitman for his medical skill, I shudder whiniver I hear him preachin'."

᠃   ᠃   ᠃

When Fitzpatrick sent word asking me to come over to write the promised letter to Chouteau regarding payment of the premium on plews for our bunch and the others we had recruited on his behalf, it was a signal that rendezvous was fast drawing to a close. I asked Brass Turtle to come along with me to the F&F trade tents.

Fitz invited us into his marquee, where paper, pens, and ink were already present on the raw plank table, ready for my chore. He filled three cups with good Kentucky whiskey, passed ours to us, and lifted his own in a toast.

"Drink up in good health, me good friends," he said in a solemn tone, his tired features almost without expression, "to what is perhaps the last good rendezvous we'll ever see."

All three of us downed a healthy swig before Turtle said, "I'll keep on drinkin' these hyar good squeezin's as long as ye keep on pourin', Tom, but how come ye be sayin' what ye jist did?"

Fitz, without replying to Turtle's question, reached under the table and brought out a tall leather hat box and set it on the table. "What's in this box," he said, "will be after destroyin' our intire way o' livin', that's what!" He flipped open the clasp and brought out a silk top hat identical with the one Kit and I had seen perched atop the counter-jumper's balding pate. He handed it to Turtle and declared, "There's the bloody culprit! That's what'll likely be turnin' the likes o' you an' me into bloody greyback farmers!"

Brass Turtle looked confused, a rare occurrence for my quick-minded friend. Fitzpatrick enlightened him. "That's a silk topper, Turtle. 'Tis all the rage amongst the dandies in Paree an' London-town, I'm hearin', and even some in New York. They tell me the fashion's changin'! Word is, beaver's goin' out an' silk toppers'll soon be the style fer all the city fops!"

Turtle bounced the hat from one hand to the other, exclaiming the while, "Thar's nuthin' to it, Fitz! It don't weigh hardly nuthin' a-tall! An' what'll they do when it rains? This'n sure-as-hell won't hold up in the wet!"

Fitzpatrick shrugged. "It's likely they don't care. Most of 'em rarely ever see the sunshine, anyway! And if they do, they'll just get themselves another. Silk's a heap cheaper'n beaver, by a long chalk!"

"Whar they gittin' it? Silk, I mean. Whar's it come from, anyways?"

"Silk's a thread the Chinee get from little worms that spin their nests out of it, like spiders makin' their webs."

"Ye mean to be tellin' these hyar newfangled toppers be made outa worm shit?" Turtle demanded, incredulous, twirling the hat on a fingertip, marveling at the revelation.

"That's what ye could be callin' it," Fitzpatrick replied, cracking a half-smile for the first time.

"An' worm shit's gonna put beavers outa biz'ness?" Turtle looked stricken. "That's what you're tellin'?"

"Prob'ly not right off. It'll likely take a spell, p'raps as long as a couple years. Can't say for sure." Fitz picked up the earthen jug and refilled our cups, then raised his own in a salute. "Anyway, we've had a good run of it. Let's drink to the good times we've enjoyed together!"

The whiskey didn't taste nearly as good as it had the first time around, but we drank it down anyway.

Fitz showed me his account books and Turtle inspected them, too. His figures appeared reasonable, so I penned a letter to Pierre Chouteau, Cadet, stating the total amount, reminding him of his promise the year before, and recommending that he reimburse Fontenelle, Fitzpatrick & Company for the extra monies paid to our bunch and those whom we had recruited at his request. The letter appeared to satisfy Fitzpatrick, so we bade him good luck and godspeed and returned to camp in a mood considerably more glum than when we left it earlier that day.

On the way back, Turtle and I agreed to keep mum about what Fitz had said about silk toppers possibly wrecking the fur trade. Rumors were already flying amongst the trappers about the matter, usually greeted with derisive hoots from men unwilling to entertain such a heretical notion. We didn't wish to add fuel to that fire.

~o ~o ~o

Fitzpatrick's impending departure for the settlements and the breakup of rendezvous pushed our bunch into making up our mind about what we would do about trapping in the coming year. The usual objections to joining a company brigade were mostly overcome by Bridger's offer to let us "tag along," trapping on our own hook, not subject to a booshway's absolute authority or required to sell our peltry to his company. This last consideration was hardly worth mentioning, for now there was no other trading outfit, save HBC, to buy our plews.

The winnowing out of traders was a significant factor in our decision. Wyeth and Bonneville were out of the running now and most of the rag-tag traders operating on the fringes of rendezvous had pretty much given up trying to compete. Fontenelle & Fitzpatrick and the HBC now had it all pretty much to themselves, which eliminated most opportunities for free trappers to play off a particular trader against the others.

What we heard about increased hostility from Blackfoots and Grovants also greatly influenced our final decision. Half of the men in our bunch now had a wife and most had children or one on the way, which saps a married man's confidence in his invincibility. Anse's arguments about safety in numbers acquired added weight with each new birth.

Our friendship for Jim Bridger and our respect for his judgment were also powerful factors. Jim has learned his wilderness lessons well. His personal courage is unquestioned, but it's not foolhardy. He makes prudent decisions and mostly keeps his people alive and healthy, unlike some leaders whose arrogance and thirst for profit outweighed their concern for the welfare of the men in their brigades.

When Bridger rode into camp to announce that he intended to commence fall trapping in the neighborhood of Pierre's Hole, resistance to our going along melted. We signed up on the spot.

-oOo-

CHAPTER XV
HUNGRY DOIN'S

Preparations for quitting rendezvous didn't require much time or effort this time. The scaffolds supporting our drying meat had sagged under a constant heavy burden since we first arrived, thanks to the women's demand for buffalo hides to make new lodges or to replace portions of others damaged in our battle with the Kainahs. Of all the supplies we require to commence each year's hunt, dried meat is among the most important, along with gunpowder, galena, caps, and tobacco. Jerked meat lets us survive when weather or scarcity of game critters would otherwise starve us.

Our livestock was healthy, fat, and well-rested after their long summer layoff. Even the womenfolk were not reluctant to leave rendezvous this time. Our rich harvests of the past couple years had provided more than enough profit. Even the most acquisitive amongst them were sated with foofurraw and settlement wares and groceries.

If I entertained any regret about quitting rendezvous it was because trapping would curtail the time I could spend with my children, assisting Iris with her studies and rambling in the woods with her, and playing with little Ben. His favorite occupation was sitting spraddle-legged before me in the saddle, chirping and crowing as we rode one of my lively saddlers through the camps.

Cat and I paid a final visit to our leafy hideaway on Horse Creek, swimming naked in its chill waters and making noisy love on its grassy banks. The children were getting older now, so cold weather lovemaking in the lodge must be more quiet and discreet.

For the women, the most painful part of breaking camp was, naturally, bidding farewell to parents, brothers and sisters, and childhood friends when the bands of Absóraqa, Shoshone, and Séli made ready to depart. This year our four new Arapaho brides underwent that experience for the first time, but there were no tears. They were Indian women, raised from the cradleboard to keep their feelings inside. Tears are for serious occasions, such as the death of a loved one. Only the solemn expression on their faces betrayed what the three young Arapaho women were likely feeling when they embraced family and friends returning to their home hunting grounds with Touches-the-Sky.

All of us were sorry to say goodbye to Touches-the-Sky. He had proved to be a generous friend to our bunch. It was with regret that we wished the Arapaho band Godspeed on their long eastern journey.

Our bachelors would miss the Arapahoes most of all. They had grown accustomed to the attentions of their friendly widows, who had looked after their domestic chores and provided loving comfort in the robes for more than half a year.

Saying farewell to Iron Bow and Fast Horse is never pleasant. They renewed their invitation that I join their band and settle on their home ground. I politely declined, assuring them that I value their friendship and someday I might accept their generous offer, but not yet.

The other Séli chieftain, Insala, had agreed to accompany the band of Nez Percés who would guide the Reverend Parker west to their home country. He did his best to convince Iron Bow to join them, but my old friend begged off. The wily old fellow told me that he was having trouble enough keeping some of his own people from embarking on the Jesus Road without exposing them to the blandishments of Insala's Christian zealots.

Bridger's brigade left camp on Friday, August 21st, 1835. Our departure from rendezvous was the usual gay occasion. Our women were attired in their most splendiferous settlement garb and rode their showiest horses accoutered with gleaming bridles bespangled with shiny coins, their burnished Mexican saddles glittering with tinkling hawk bells and brass thimbles, resting atop bead-encrusted apishamores shimmering in summer sunshine. We men provided a no less dandified pageant, togged out as most of us were in brand-new calico shirts spilling over new-made leggin's and moccasins embroidered with multihued quillwork, girt with bright sashes, flaunting colorful garters.

We waved at old friends and called out farewells as we passed through the remaining camps on our way to Bridger's meeting place nigh the mouth of Horse Creek. As our procession passed by Fitzpatrick's trade tents, I saw that he was still preparing for departure. Although most of his trade tents had been taken down, the number of individual bowers and canvas shelters had greatly increased, together with the saddlers and pack animals grazing in his pasture.

I commented on this to Finn McCool, who was riding near me. "Oh, yes," said he, "Fitz'll be leadin' many more men out of here than he brought up with him. He told me yesterday that nigh two-score men have signed to go along with him to Fort William and beyond, besides the half a hundred teamsters, counter-jumpers, clarks, an' sich he brought up from Saint Looie in the first place."

With so many men leaving the mountains, it was clear why Bridger had been anxious for our bunch to go along with his brigade that year.

Frapp and Jean Gervais were standing beside one of Fitz's remaining trade tents, smiling, waving, and wishing bon voyage to our bunch. Neither appeared to be going anywhere. They certainly didn't appear ready to join Bridger today—certainly not Andy Drips, who had departed two days before. "Do ye see that, Finn?" I demanded. "What d'ye suppose those two are doin', standin' idle when Jim's about to put his brigade on the trail?"

"Oh, they won't be goin' with us this toime. Fitz is takin' 'em both to Fort William an' makin' sure the two of 'em accompany Fontenelle an' the peltries to Saint Looie. Lucien's drinkin' has got completely out o' hand, Tom tells me, and Fitz is not about to risk losin' a couple hundred packs an' more o' prime beaver to his tosspot partner!"

∾   ∾   ∾

Our first day's journey covered a scant three miles, to a broad grassy meadow where Horse Creek spills into the Seeds-kee-dee, which is the common practice. It allows the brigade to send back to the rendezvous to retrieve equipment that was overlooked and left behind and to allow free trappers indulging in a final drunken spree to catch up overnight.

The meadow was already filling up with the lodges and horse herds of the Nez Percé and Flathead bands, as well as Bridger's men and their critters. We headed for the riverside to set up our overnight camp.

The weather was warm and pleasant. Cat decided not to put up the lodge, spreading our sleeprobes instead on the grassy bank before she joined the other women helping the campkeepers with supper chores. It was still early, so I cut willow poles and took Iris and Paddy's son Sean fishing. Whilst the youngsters romped in the meadow catching grasshoppers for bait, I tethered lively little Ben to a tree to prevent his falling into the river before I sat in its shade to catch up on my journal.

We caught a dozen large, firm-fleshed trout-fish and turned them over to Yves and Jean-Luc to provide variety to their usual offering of roast buffalo. Most valuable, howsomever, was the time I spent with my children.

We returned to camp in time to witness the arrival of the Reverend Samuel Parker, accompanied by Doctor Whitman, who had come along to see his colleague on his way. McCool invited the affable medico to join us for supper, even though his gesture saddled us with the tetchy company of Whitman's crabby companion.

Throughout the meal, Parker glared whenever Finn stole away Whitman's attention with a medical question—whenever, that is, the prickly parson wasn't casting disapproving glances at his young Colleague of the Cloth for his rude table manners, which were no worse than the rest of us. He ate with his knife and he often talked with his mouth full, which the fastidious Parker considered atrocious behavior.

The rivalry for Whitman's attention continued into nightfall. McCool followed the clergymen into the darkness, still asking a string of medical questions. His importunities likely caused him no further loss of Parker's affection. The Presbyterian preacher had doubtless marked Finn for a Papist from the start.

I was snugging the cinch on the last packsaddle when a dozen or more riders appeared through the morning mist and reined up in camp. Our rowdy companions had remained in camp for a final spree or the attentions of a complaisant prairie flower, or both. Most of them scattered to their own messes, except for Tuttle and Anse, along with Cap'n Billy and Harry Yeats, all blear-eyed and crapulous. They stepped shakily to the ground and chorused, "Still got coffee?"

I waved them to the cookfire, where Cat had kept a kettle warming, accustomed as she was to the vagaries of trappers reluctant to part with the seldom pleasures of rendezvous. They tottered to the fire, removing cups from their belts as they stumbled along, and plunged them into the thick, black, sugary brew, then sank to their haunches croaking paeans to Kathleen's generosity.

They hadn't much time to recover their health. A brassy blast from Gabe Bridger's old bugle announced our imminent departure, a summons as imperious as any issued by his namesake angel. A collective groan rose from our guests, but they dutifully gulped the healing potion, filled their cups a final time, struggled to their feet, nodded their thankees, and staggered off to retrieve their waiting critters.

We traveled twenty miles or so that day, much of which Anse and Tuttle spent sound asleep on their mounts, hunched over, feet braced in the stirrups, snoring, their pack animals running free with Half-horse's loose horses and mules, rousing only briefly at the nooning halt, then falling into the arms of Morpheus once we got on our way again.

Bridger called a halt in Jackson's Little Hole, one of Davey's favorite retreats, where water, graze, and firewood were plentiful. A few trappers scattered out to set traps in nearby streams, but it was still only August, too early and warm for decent plews. After supper and a couple pipefuls, most of us retired to our sleeprobes, until it was time to take our turn at horse guard. That neighborhood, not far from Pierre's Hole, is a favorite stomping ground for horse-thieving Grovants.

~o   ~o   ~o

Next day was Sunday. Bridger, in consideration of his ecclesiastical guest, announced an extra day's delay to observe the Sabbath. Which Kathleen observed by cooking up a batch of flapjacks slathered with bear butter and sorghum, a treat certain to attract half a dozen hungry bachelors to wish us good morning.

After we stuffed ourselves enough to founder ordinary human beings, we retired to the shade of an aspen grove to smoke and palaver. A half-remembered sound intruded on my ear, raising my hackles, setting my teeth on edge—the cracked, quavering tenor of Parson Parker raised in one of the Sabbath hymns I recalled from my boyhood, when the bootlegging, skirt-chasing, Bible-pounding scoundrel who thought he was my Pap led his Sabbath congregation in pious psalms and harangued them with threats of hellfire. I beheld in a nearby clearing a crowd of Indians gathered around the Reverend Mister Parker, intoning a ragged response to the words he was trying to teach them.

Tuttle was already on his feet, advising, "Let's get ther hell out o' hyar, afore I lose thet'ere good bait o' flannel cakes I jest et!"

Which we did—that is, removed ourselves out of earshot.

Later that day, Powatawa, curious about the missionary's proselytizing style, invited me to accompany him to Bridger's camp to hear Parker's Sabbath-day sermon. I find it difficult to refuse his rare requests, so I agreed to do so. Several of our companions, having nothing better to do, rode along with us.

A sizeable throng of Nez Percés and Flatheads had already gathered under the trees, along with a surprising number of trappers who were likely as bored as we were. We found a place on the fringe of the trapper crowd, nigh Joe Meek, Doc Newell, and Harry Yeats, who were trading irreverent quips, in contrast with the solemn expressions on the faces of the Indians waiting to hear the Holy Word that would make them wealthy beyond all previous imagining.

After a brief benediction, the Reverend Parker launched into his sermon, which consisted mostly of a depressing string of thou-shalt-nots, such as killing, even in warfare, divorcing or the taking of more than one wife at a time, without bothering to explain what was to be done with one's current wife if a man remarries the wife he divorced, or what to with the extra wife if has two of them now, amongst similar omissions. Several of the commandments he spoke of hardly apply to these particular tribes. Flatheads and Shahaptins honor and care for their parents more than most Christian whites ever do. Stealing and lying are rare amongst them and are severely punished when they do occur.

As we listened and watched, howsomever, we realized that what the parson was bellowing about hardly mattered. Parker delivered his sermon in English, the only language he knew, relying on his Nez Percé interpreter to translate his words into the tongues his converts could comprehend. The interpreter naturally accompanied his speech with hand-signs, as all Indians—and trappers—almost always do.

Powatawa, who by that time had acquired a considerable grasp of the Shahaptin tongue, nudged me and whispered, "Watch his hands. He tells them little of what the black-suit says. He tells them what they wish to hear." It was true. As I paid closer attention to the interpreter's gestures, I had to admit that the young Nez Percé was himself quite a sermonizer, spellbinding his audience with grandiloquent promises of material wealth to be gained if only they would follow the instructions of his black-suited boss.

My father and I weren't the only ones to catch on to the fraud. The white, Delaware, and Shawnee trappers, all of them adept in sign-talk, commenced to snort and snicker, now and then breaking into hoots and guffaws, drawing disapproving glares from the Reverend Mister Parker. Before he could deliver a stern reproof for our disrespectful behavior, howsomever, somebody hollered out from beyond the crowd, "Buffler! Buffler! Jist look at 'em!"

All of us spun about to behold the prairie behind us black with buffalo and even more of them pouring into the valley. Quick as scat, every man leapt into the saddle if he had brought his horse with him or ran to get one. I scrambled aboard my Coffee horse and raced off in pursuit of the double pleasure of fresh buffalo meat and the long-delayed fun of running them a-horseback.

As we galloped to overtake Tuttle and Brass Turtle, I slung my rifle across my back and checked the loads in my pistols, thrilling the while in the delight of the chase. I caught a hint of what British nabobs must experience when they pursue an inedible fox or hare over country gates, even if they never reap the reward of smoking hot fresh liver or fat hump ribs.

The field was already alive with a double score of hunters, both trappers and our Indian companions, coursing through the herd, dropping their prey with arrows and rifle shots. I chose a young cow rolling fat with late-summer flesh and gave Coffee his head to come up behind, then beside her, smoothly following her leap across a narrow stream, keeping safely out of reach of her horns, matching her furious pace, letting me swing my pistol out and fire a fatal ball that brought her coughing and stumbling to her knees, belching blood, to lie stiff-legged in death on the prairie.

I checked Coffee's rush, reckoning that one fat cow, together with what my comrades would garner, would suffice for our bunch. As I stepped to the ground, I espied Half-horse riding towards me, leading half-a-dozen packmules at a high lope. He threw a halter-shank to me and kept on running to catch up with our companions and their kills.

Butchering and loading the mule's panniers with the tongue, hump ribs, boudins, backstrap, and other choice cuts didn't take long. By time I finished laving blood from my cheeks and arms in a nearby stream, several other hunters came straggling back across the prairie, leading mules loaded with sagging panniers. Jim Bridger was amongst them. He drew rein and grinned down at me. "See ye got one fer yer bunch, Temple. We got a plenty, too.

Why'n't ye send yer mule back with the boy an' jine us fer supper? Yew an' all yer pards're more'n welcome."

"Much obliged," I told him. "I'll do that." Jim rode on and I extended his invite to the others who hadn't already heard it, handed the mule's halter-shank to Half-horse, and told him to join us in Bridger's camp after he turned the meat over to Yves and Jean-Luc and the women.

❧   ❧   ❧

Merriment reigned in Bridger's camp, as ye might expect after a successful buffalo hunt enhanced with the fun of running the critters instead of sneak-shooting them. What had been a dreary afternoon had been transformed into a rousing break from routine. High spirits sparked generosity. Trappers who had brought along a final jug of spirits produced them now and shared a tipple all around.

Bridger's men had killed a score or more prime cows. Great chunks of fat meat sizzled over a dozen cookfires, filling the air with a delicious fragrance. Anse rode over from our camp, fiddle case jouncing behind his saddle. Soon Cap'n Billy and Harry Yeats' *guitarra* joined him, infusing lively melody into the mouth-watering atmosphere.

The happiness was general but not universal. I was standing with a knot of trappers chuckling at one of Joe Meek's ribald yarns when Doc Newell poked me with an elbow and jerked his chin in the direction of the black-coated Mister Parker. The reverend gentleman did not appear pleased with our jollity. Quite the contrary. He glowered and clucked his displeasure as his icy gaze swept our roistering brethren, sucking in his skinny cheeks in near-apopletic indignation, resting his snapping blue eyes at last on our merry *musicos*, who, as each of them became aware of his disapproving scowl, dwindled discordantly into silence. Which the outraged preacher evidently took as his cue to launch into a fierce tirade against our sinful ways, damning us as heretical Sabbath-breakers for chasing after buffalo on the Christian Day of Rest and Reverence, scolding and berating our manifold iniquities until he quite ran out of breath and stood open-mouthed and glaring, unable to continue his rant.

If the parson had wished to discourage our frivolity, he succeeded— leastaways for half a minute, while the assembled trappers regarded him in surprised silence, seeking to fathom what the unfriendly gentleman in the rusty black coat might have in mind with his judgmental words and frosty stare, until one trapper loosed a loud, guffawing horselaugh, which triggered a wave of good-natured laughter. Gaiety was restored. The *musicos* returned to their instruments. Bantering chatter and horseplay resumed and the puritanical Parson Parker was henceforth ignored.

He was ignored, that is, only as long as he was able to resist the tempting aroma of juicy buffalo hump roasting over the cookfires, dripping tasty fat onto the coals, wafting tantalizing clouds of delicious fragrance throughout the camp. At last even Parker's iron will was bested. Looking neither right nor left, he stalked deliberately to a firepit and sliced off a heaping plateful of juicy hump meat from a huge gobbet suspended on a spit, then trod resolutely back to his seat on a stump and proceeded to consume it.

The trappers' disapproval was immediate and unanimous. Not a single man in our fraternity failed to observe and condemn the preacher's cupidity. "The partaker is as bad as the thief" was the universal verdict. His appetite had destroyed forever his sanctimonious claim to the moral high ground. "Hell!" Joe Meek declared, "He ain't nawthin' but a pious humbug!"

❧   ❧   ❧

Our westward hike from Jackson's Little Hole was mostly uneventful and unproductive. The large company of trappers and friendly Indians discouraged roving bands of Blackfoots from attacking and attempts at stealing horses were usually detected and swiftly dealt with.

Late summer produces poor-quality plews, which likely prompted Bridger to use that unprofitable time to deliver his missionary charge as soon as possible to Nat Wyeth's new trading post he called Fort Hall, from which point the Indian converts would guide Mister Parker to their home country farther west.

Once we were no longer encumbered by our charges, the brigade, numbering now some sixty mountaineers and a score of Flathead trappers who had joined up with us, headed for the streams that feed Henry's Fork of the Snake. We arrived in that neighborhood the first week of September in an unseasonably heavy snowstorm. It soon melted and we struck out in small parties of a dozen or so trappers to commence the autumn harvest in earnest. Women and children remained with the main encampment on Henry's Lake.

Tuttle and I, along with my father, Micah, Turtle, and Little Mountain, teamed up with Meek, Newell, Harpoon Harry, Carson, and a few other trappers, and headed east to Madison Fork, trapping as we went, expecting the brigade to join us there. We had fairly good luck, although plews were pretty measly that early in the season.

Trapping down the Madison, we came upon a party of a dozen people, half of them campkeepers, trapping out of Wyeth's Fort Hall establishment. They were camped in a narrow valley with high tree-covered bluffs on either side—not the best choice if an attack should come. They were an affable crew, so we accepted their invite to stop with them overnight.

We passed a pleasant evening feasting on wapiti and sheep meat and regaling our hosts, who were mostly newcomers to the mountains, with Joe Meek's and Tuttle's tall yarns, which occasionally possessed a tinge of truth. I renewed acquaintance with one of them, young Osborne Russell, who had been clerking for Wyeth at rendezvous the year before. He, in particular, appeared to relish the story-telling, politely urging them to tell just one more.

Next morning, Micah and Little Mountain rode out with some of Meek's men to set traps. They returned in less than an hour at a high lope, pursued by some fourscore Blackfoots out for blood and plunder.

The enemy immediately took the high ground on the timbered bluffs on either side, hiding amongst the trees and pouring musketfire into the camp, whilst we retreated to the dense thickets surrounding it. Their muskets at that long range were mostly ineffective, except for killing and injuring some of our hosts' penned-up horses, which the greedy Blackfoots must have regretted doing. They soon ceased their random firing. Some of them tried, instead, to creep down the slopes to gain more accuracy with their smoothbore muskets. Which we promptly discouraged by picking off a couple-three of their more foolhardy warriors. Except for that, lacking visible targets, we held our fire and waited.

After a couple hours of trying unsuccessfully to rouse us to action, they set fire to the dry grass and tree trash that surrounded us, even though it would cost them our horses and plunder. A brisk breeze soon fanned the blaze into an inferno that encircled the camp and united above us, promising certain death.

Shielded from sight by the flames, Brass Turtle leapt into the clearing, yelling, "Turn it back on 'em! Give 'em back their gawddamn hell!" He scooped up an armload of dry grass and fallen tree bark, grabbed a fiery brand, and set fire to it. All of us rushed from our hideaways and joined him, scraping the ground free of anything that could burn and flinging it into the surrounding blaze, creating a backfire that within several minutes had passed around us and now threatened the Blackfoots themselves.

Several warriors scampered to safety up the slopes. The musketfire dwindled, then ceased. After a few minutes we caught sight of a tall Indian, likely their chief, standing on a big rock high up the hill, grasping his robe by the corners and striking it to the ground three times, a signal for their retreat. Then all was silent.

Except for smoke-blackened faces and singed hair and beards, we had escaped unharmed. Wyeth's men had lost two horses killed and a few more wounded in their pen. We had dragged our own critters into the thickets with us, fortunately avoiding damage to them.

No one wished to tarry there any longer than it took to saddle up and load the pack animals, which was accomplished with remarkable dispatch. Before we left, howsomever, Little Mountain clambered up the hillside to ascertain the identity of our attackers. He returned swinging a bloody scalp and a pair of beaded moccasins, announcing, "Goddamn Síksikah!" Not that it mattered. Blackfoots are Blackfoots.

A large party of hostiles roaming the neighborhood convinced us to rejoin the brigade as fast as possible and the Wyeth men expressed a desire to come along with us. Russell and I rode together most of the way to Bridger's encampment on the Madison, passing time mostly with his account of his first year in the mountains. He told me the leader of their trapping crew was named Joseph Gale and that his tyrannical disposition and ignorance of mountain lore had cost him the confidence and respect of his men. They now numbered fewer than half of their original group, due mainly to desertions, and they had lost most of their horses, as well. Russell and most of the others intended to resign from Wyeth's employ as soon as they fulfilled their contract with him, which was due to expire soon. Which spoke well for their code of conduct.

My original favorable impression of young Russell was reinforced during that ride. He is intelligent, well-spoken, inquisitive and open-minded, well-set-up and physically fit, and possessed of an even temperament and a willing nature, an altogether ideal candidate for the mountain life we have chosen. I suggested that he speak to Jim Bridger when we got to camp and volunteer his services to the brigade when his obligation to Wyeth was fulfilled. Which he agreed to do.

The ride to the encampment was happily uneventful and the warm greeting I received from Kathleen was even more welcome than usual. All of us save Micah received a deal of chaffing for our smoke-smudged faces. Anxious as we had been to put the Síksikahs far behind us, nobody had wished to linger thereabouts to perform his toilet.

The prairie thereabouts was black with buffalo. Cookfires throughout the camp were sending up clouds of mouth-watering aroma, an invitation not to be ignored by men famished from hard labor and lack of food since the night before. We fell to with great gusto, stuffing ourselves like French geese, postponing the niceties of hygiene until we removed our stomachs from the vicinity of our backbone. Only then was I willing to scrub off most of the soot and grime in a nearby crick and let Kathleen drag off my filthy duds before I fell onto the sleeprobes and into deep, dreamless slumber.

≈   ≈   ≈

We continued to trap the cricks and streams that feed the upper Madison until we pretty much used up the beaver thereabouts. Trappers are always jealous of where they plant their beaver sets, never revealing where they intend to trap, always sneaking off to conduct their business, but too few beaver for too many trappers soon created friction. "If I'd'a wanted to be rubbin' elbows," Tuttle declared disgustedly, "I'd'a hung on at ronnyvoo, whar ther elbows war attached to purtier folk than these hairy bastards!" His illogical sentiment was nonetheless heartfelt.

Some of our bunch argued for pulling out and going on our own hook, as had usually been our custom, but the increasing number of roaming bands of Blackfeet of every stripe—Síksikah, Káinah, and Píkuni, and their greedy Grovant allies—discouraged that impulse, especially amongst those of us with women and kids. We were backed up by the crabby bachelor Anse Tolliver, who preached, "Thar's safety in numbers. Stick with the brigade!"

Too many empty traps convinced Bridger to move the brigade south and west to the streams along Henry's Fork and the Snake, with indifferent success. What was apparently successful was the Aitch-bee-cee's policy of creating a "beaver desert" in that whole swatch of country, doing their best to wipe out the entire beaver population, to discourage Americans from coming in. That strategy dated as far back as our first encounter with Peter Skene Ogden, a decade before, where we first heard of it. We laughed about it then. Now it didn't appear so comical.

We had to compete for the remaining plews with friendly Shoshone bands who had developed an active interest and considerable skill in trapping on their own, a development not overlooked by the HBC's Mister Ermatinger, whose agents snapped up nearly every plew as soon as they were out of the water.

Russell and his companions from Wyeth's outfit trapped along with us. But as year's-end approached, signaling the end of his enlistment with the crotchety Yankee, Russell took his leave from the brigade, promising to rejoin us in winter camp, and dutifully returned to Fort Hall. The others remained with us.

Even though trapping was unsatisfactory that autumn, we ate very well. The prairie fairly swarmed with fat cows. We feasted on fresh tongue and juicy hump ribs nearly every night. Trappers, disappointed with their meager harvest of plews, took to running buffalo as much for amusement as for meat. Some of the older Flatheads trapping with us cautioned against such wasteful behavior, warning that the wild sport would run the herds clean out of the neighborhood. Nobody listened. Even Bridger couldn't control the free trappers in his brigade. They argued that the buffalo were limitless, an unending supply, impossible to use up. And so it seemed. I confess that we, too, ran our share of fat cows more than once.

Our women showed more good sense than we did. They insisted that we return with more than only the choice cuts for supper, so that extra meat and marrow and such might be dried and stored against the hard, lean days of winter, which weren't far off.

Sure enough, by time cold weather set in, freezing the cricks and streams, blanketing the land with heavy snow, and driving us into winter camp along Blackfoot Creek, there was hardly a buffalo cow left in the entire valley. Our self-indulgent sprees had scared the herds and pushed them over the mountains. Deep snowdrifts prevented their return until the springtime thaw. Only mature bachelor bulls remained, driven out of the herds by belligerent patriarchs jealous of their harems.

∾   ∾   ∾

Winter camp that year was a dreary affair and a hungry one for most, as well. It was especially dull for the bachelors, for no friendly Indian bands cared to join us in our dismal surroundings. True, we possessed water, abundant firewood, and adequate sweet cottonwood bark to feed our horses and mules, but fat cows were but a bittersweet memory in those parts. Our livestock ate better than most of us did.

Nobody starved. There was a plenitude of poor buffalo bulls roaming the valley, but the meat was blue and tough as rawhide. Most mountaineers maintain a stiff-necked pride about living day-to-day off the land, rarely putting anything aside, taking their chances that something good will turn up. If it doesn't, they go hungry, or worse.

Many a time, strolling through that winter camp, I have witnessed one or another brigade campkeeper digging out an enormous bull's ham from a heap of smoldering ashes and beating it halfway clean with a stout club, making it bound a yard or two in the air with each blow, like a huge ball of gum elastic. After repeating this action several times in a vain hope of making it tender, he draws his butcher knife and calls to the men of his mess, "Come now! It's ready as it ever will be! Won't ye take a lunch of Simon?" When those hivernants who are hungry enough to try once again to commence sawing and hacking thick slices from the leathery mountain of bull meat, one of them will often observe that although "this be tough eatin', it's a heap tougher when thar ain't none a-tall!" Then they all promise to make the fat cows suffer before the year rolls around.

Married men naturally made out much better than their single comrades. Times were lean in our lodges, too, but skinny times were nothing new to our Indian women. Feast and famine are the red man's calendar, but millennia of living in the wilderness have taught his women how to prepare for times of want and privation and how to survive them. They harvest plums, berries, and chokecherries in summer and fall and dry them for use in pemmican and stews. The same for camas, prairie turnips, and other edible roots. Most important is dried meat, preferably buffalo, but mountain sheep mutton and wapiti and deer meat are welcome to the mix, providing flavor and vigor in wintertime stews.

We ate well enough, mainly thick soups and stews, bolstered with dried camas and turnips, unrecognizable tubers, and jerked buffalo meat simmered almost tender, as well as a surprisingly tasty cake made of minced dried meat, plums, and choke cherries mixed with buffalo marrow. Lucullus might have sneered at our repasts, but they were infinitely superior to bull hams.

Naturally our married households extended hospitality to our single brethren, especially at suppertime and often all three meals when harsh weather made cooking in their open lean-to's difficult and sometimes impossible. My father, Tuttle, Micah, and Finnæus were our most frequent guests, often crowding in to sleep, as well, during severe blizzards. Married men now outnumbered the bachelors in our bunch, so there was always a place at the cookfire or a warm corner in somebody's lodge for our stubborn singletons.

Osborne Russell arrived at the Blackfoot Creek winter encampment about the middle of February. He and fifteen of his messmates had obtained their proper discharge from Wyeth's employ just before Christmas and had retreated to winter quarters on Mutton Hill on the Portneuf, where they lived warm and well-fed on fat mutton until deep snow and bitter cold drove them off. He bade *adieu* to his friends then and joined Bridger's brigade, as he had earlier pledged to do. Russell told us that Yankee Nat had anticipated their defection and had thoughtfully replaced them with a crew of sailors and Kanakas from the Sandwich Islands that he had recruited at Fort Vancouver, where he spent much of his time nowadays.

Although Russell established quarters amongst Bridger's brigade, he was a welcome guest in our lodge. His keen mind and good manners endeared him to both Cat and myself and he, in turn, enjoyed our company and spirited discussions, borrowing my books, which he read voraciously, playing with the children, and happily joining us at suppertime. He got along well with all of our bunch. He especially enjoyed talks with my father and he was an enthusiastic recruit to our Rocky Mountain College sessions, displaying a remarkable range and understanding of literature.

Russell kept an admirably detailed journal which exceeded my own in its attention to the geography of his Rocky Mountain travels and his terse comments on the inept, bullying leader he had recently escaped provoked many a chuckle.

Besides our own bunch, the young fellow gained easy acceptance amongst the tight circle of Bridger's cronies. They even paid him the extraordinary compliment of christening him with a handle whilst still in winter camp. Gabe Bridger, Major Meek, Squire Ebberts, and Cotton Mansfield now called him Judge Russell for whatever obscure reason, but it was a signal mark of their approval and acceptance, especially for a newcomer.

≈   ≈   ≈

March of 1836 was nearly over before Father Frost loosed his icy grip on the land. The brigade departed winter camp on March 28 without a shred of regret and headed north to Lewis Fork, which feeds the Snake, then ascended it as far as the mouth of Muddy Creek, arriving there some ten days later. Melting snow and high water discouraged most attempts at trapping during that hike, so we made good time if not much profit.

Bridger sent a dozen men to trap the headwaters of Grey's and Blackfoot Creeks, which were high enough in the mountains to let us avoid most of the heavy spring runoff of snowmelt that had hindered our earlier trapping efforts. We decided to tag along after them. Besides, an extra dozen rifles nearby would not be amiss in the event of a hostile attack.

By time we crossed the mountain, springtime weather had warmed considerably, increasing the snowmelt so much that the larger cricks and streams were often too swollen to permit trapping. We made the best of it, howsomever, taking care to stay out of the way of Bridger's men, traveling higher on the mountain, and trapping the many small watercourses that feed the Grey, which proved to be halfway successful.

After a week or so, the entire party moved on about 40 miles southwest, trapping as we went, feeding on wapiti and blacktail deer and occasional mountain sheep, for that high, broken country doesn't attract buffalo. We crossed a low mountain and reached the Blackfoot, which we ascended for a couple days before we set up camp and spread out, trapping the many feeder streams in that neighborhood with a fair amount of luck, until the first week of May. Three Company trappers, out running their traplines early one morning, were jumped by a couple dozen Blackfoots in a narrow draw. One fellow was slightly wounded by a musket ball in the side, but all three got away and hightailed it back to camp, where Zeetlah tended to the trapper's injury.

That was our first scrape with hostiles that season. That afternoon, all of our womenfolk insisted on bringing out their guns for target practice, which caused considerable consternation amongst some of the Bridger men, particularly the ones who had a woman along. As Brass Turtle put it, "Now them fellers be afeared their own women'll be wantin' guns, too, an' there ain't hardly nuthin' what'll make a man mind his manners more'n a woman what's got a gun." Which is likely so. Lodgepoling a defenseless woman loses its charm if she owns a gun and knows how to use it.

I daresay the consternation extended well beyond the camp. Doubtless the Blackfoot spies, alerted by an hours-long fusillade of rifle fire, discouraged their companions from attacking such a well-armed camp. Seeing nine women doing the shooting must have distressed them no end. We retrieved our traps in parties of half a dozen men and suffered no further attempts on life, limb, and plunder, leastaways not thereabouts.

We struck camp on the Blackfoot at first light a couple days later and crossed the mountain, heading southwest through a dense forest and deep snow, which seriously slowed our passage, especially the several travois in our column. Naturally Iris insisted on riding, but I made her switch her saddle onto my sure-footed saddle mule Sugarfoot. Paddy provided likewise for his son Sean, the faithful Woodpecker, who stuck to Iris like a devoted cocklebur.

Just at nightfall we descended into the valley on Bear River. We camped about 25 miles above Soda Springs—not far from where a young Jim Bridger launched his bullboat on his memorable voyage down the Bear to what he was sure was the Pacific Ocean.

Next day we traveled up Bear River to Thomas Fork, where we found Bridger's main camp, as well as Andy Drips' brigade, which numbered some sixty whites and nigh that many Delawares and French-Canucks, nearly twice as many trappers as Bridger's. The two brigades were camped beside some 400 lodges of Snakes and Bannocks mixed together, along with another hundred or so lodges of Nez Percés and Flatheads. The grassy plain alongside Bear River, all the way to Smith's Fork, was a colorful moving tableau, mottled with the shiny hides of the Indians' vast horse herds.

While the women were erecting the lodges, Micah and I rode out leading a couple packmules, past trapper camps and Indian villages, past the mouth of Smith's Fork, onto grassy prairieland devoid of human presence, heading east towards Ham's Fork, enjoying the solitude and quiet after weeks of living and working cheek by jowl with Bridger's people and our own, saying nothing until Micah muttered softly, "Buffler!"

Screened from view by a stand of aspens until then, perhaps a score of buffalo bulls grazed in a clearing about 500 yards ahead. We slipped to the ground, tethered our critters to sagebrush clumps, and removed the unadorned buffalo hide apishamores tied behind our saddles, which we threw over our shoulders. Then, bent over double, rifles cradled, a faint breeze in our faces, we stealthily closed on the bunch, pausing now and then to dispel alarm at our advance, if indeed the buffaloes' poor vision at that distance permitted their seeing us at all.

A shallow swale in the prairie about sixty yards distant from the grazing bunch offered the best concealment. We dropped onto our bellies and selected our targets, a brace of yearling bulls grown rolling fat on abundant springtime graze. At Micah's nod, we fired in a single stuttering report. Micah's bull keeled over as if from a giant hammer blow. Mine dropped onto his knees, then struggled up and staggered after his fleeing comrades for about twenty yards before he collapsed, coughing out his life, then lying stiff-legged and glassy-eyed.

"Just look at 'em," Micah crowed, "tender enough fer eatin' ri'chere! Neither of 'em more'n a year off from feedin' off their mammy!"

I nodded my agreement and started back to bring up the critters, whilst Micah commenced the butchering.

Riding back in high spirits, content with a chore well done, we talked about the forthcoming rendezvous at Horse Creek. Aside from chatting about anticipated pleasures, the both of us admitted a mild concern about what we might learn there regarding the market for beaver and what it might portend for our way of life. In the manner of mountaineers, howsomever, we soon abandoned that dismal topic, preferring the here and now. The future takes care of itself. Fretting about it makes no meat.

∾ ∾ ∾

It was by now mid-May, the weather much too warm for continued worthwhile trapping. After a couple more days on the plain beside Bear River, the entire company, Bridger, Drips' brigade, and all the Indians removed to Ham's Fork, except for Andy Drips, who took a small party with him to Black's Fork on the Seeds-kee-dee to lift a cache of furs and other plunder that he had left there after his autumn hunt.

Thankfully, soon after we got to Ham's Fork, most of the Indians left us. They scattered off in different directions, seeking fresh graze for their large herds, promising to gather at Horse Creek about the first of July, when the packtrain from the settlements was expected to arrive.

After a spell, even without the Indian bands and their numerous horses, Ham's Fork grew too crowded for us. Game grew scarce in that neighborhood and the men in Andy Drip's brigade, lacking his presence and authority, insisted on running the few buffalo that remained nearby, which drove them elsewhere. Sometime in the first week of June, we packed up and moved to our old Horse Creek campground before somebody else occupied it. "Leastaways we'll be eatin' better," Tuttle opined, "an' I never did hanker fer thet much comp'ny anyways."

We arrived at Horse Creek about a fortnight later after an unhurried journey north along the Seeds-kee-dee. Few trappers had showed up by then and we were able to reclaim our old camp area, setting up about a quarter-mile higher on the stream, where there was deadfall firewood aplenty along its wooded banks. The valley had rebounded from last year's occupation with belly-high grass, which quickly restored our jaded horses and mules and guaranteed a nearby supply of buffalo. Cows were still nursing their calves, but a plenitude of fat young bulls kept our cookfires sizzling and our company well-fed and contented.

Comfortable as we were in our familiar summer surroundings, the palaver amongst our people developed a tart, vinegary flavor, most likely due to the slender returns we had garnered for two hard seasons of trapping. "Mebbe we been spiled by the old days," Brass Turtle declared, summing up the general feeling, "but it don't 'pear to be hardly wuth all the hard work— an' dodgin' Blackfoots atop of it, whilst we war doin' it—fer what we got out of it this year!"

"Too gawddamn many trappers, that's what!" Tolliver chimed in. "Thar's Snakes an' Flatheads an' Napercys ever'whar ye look, 'sides a galore o' Comp'ny trappers allus crawlin' up yer arse, the lot of 'em all totin' traps!"

"Not just them," Finn added. "Even Blackfoots are trappin' now, usin' traps they get from the Aitch-bee-cee."

"Ye be right, all o' ye," Tuttle agreed. "Thar be too many trappers an' thar ain't enough beaver to go around. But what do ye figger on doin' abaout it?"

Nobody had an answer to that, least of all myself.

I chose not to ponder a solution to that conundrum. I devoted myself, instead, to what I could accomplish more or less successfully, namely being a proper father of my children and a loving partner with Kathleen, a good provider for them and my companions, and their protector to the best of my ability.

Rendezvous provided nearly unlimited leisure to pursue my favorite recreations. I passed many pleasant hours attending to Iris's schooling, roaming in the woods with her, and just palavering aimlessly with her, marveling the while at my daughter's imagination and how much knowledge she had extracted from my books, from my companions, and from the several Indian tribes that made up the society that was our bunch. I realized that she was fluent not only in English and French, but also *Español* from Diego and Pablo, as well as all the Indian tongues spoken by my comrades and their wives—Séli, naturally, but also Shoshone, Absóraqa, Arapaho, Lenni Lenapee, Shawnee, and whatever Iroquois tongue Acorn and Stone Bird spoke privately and in their lodges. And naturally she was adept at finger-talk, with which she unconsciously accompanied her speech in whatever language.

Ben had grown like a weed over the winter. He was more active than ever, prattling incessantly in Salish mixed up with fragments of English whenever I came nigh. A favorite recreation of his was straddling the saddle bow, pretending to be in charge, whenever he and I toured the trapper camps a-horseback. Iris and I often took him along on our rambles in the woods and on the prairie, where his curiosity and attention to every new discovery assured me that he possessed an equally sound mind to match his remarkably sturdy body, in the best classical Greek tradition.

Warm June weather and leisure time allowed Cat and me to revisit our sylvan retreat far up Horse Creek, where we swam naked together and made wild then tender love on the grassy bank, where I never failed to marvel at my great good fortune at being joined with this beautiful woman possessed of such variety.

🙖 🙖 🙖

As June drew to a close various bands of Indians commenced to show up. Most welcome were Iron Bow's Sélis and my father's Nez Percés, setting up on the far side of Horse Creek, where broad pastures accommodated their large horse herds and in Iron Bow's case, his growing cavvy of well-bred mules. The old man was still in charge but Fast Horse had inherited much of his father's authority. It was plain that he would one day succeed to leadership of the band. The young men Micah and I had trained in the use of rifles, now prominent amongst the principal young warriors, were ardently loyal to him.

Bands of Snakes, Crows, Bannocks on good behavior, Kootenais, Pend Oreilles, and even a small band of Coeur d'Alènes come down from the North showed up and scattered along the grasslands bordering the stream. Naturally our bachelors welcomed the supply of eligible young widows these new arrivals brought with them, the inevitable product of traditional intertribal warfare.

Bridger's brigade drifted in from their camps along the Seeds-kee-dee, where they had been biding their time, along with Andy Drips's people, settling in close to the mouth of Horse Creek.

As always, an air of anxious anticipation pervaded the various camps and villages, whites and Indians alike, as June slipped into July, wondering when the packtrain would get there or if some misfortune had befallen it. Naturally, as in every year, wild rumors flew, reporting fantastic catastrophes that must have sorely taxed the imagination of the pranksters who dreamed them up but which were nonetheless widely believed at the time.

On the sixth day of July, Tuttle, who had been hanging around Bridger's camp, gambling with some of his cronies there, came galloping into our camp, his horse all lathered and blowing, shouting, "Gitcherse'fs onter yer hosses an' c'mon! Packtrain's a-comin' naow! An' yew ain't gonna b'lieve whatcher gonna be seein' thar! It's a gawddamn prodigy fer damn sure!"

-oOo-

1836 Rendezvous

As we galloped past Bridger's camp we picked up a score or more trappers and twice or thrice that many Indians, all heading out to welcome the packtrain. Early on, I lost track of Tuttle in the pell-mell rush of the greeting party, so I remained ignorant of what he meant when he promised a special surprise when we laid eyes on the travelers from the settlements. Some three miles past Bridger's camp, howsomever, we caught sight of the advance guard fording a crick and a seemingly endless caravan snaking out behind them with a couple-three mule-drawn wagons lurching amongst the column of pack animals. Our company reined up inside a grove of aspens to plan our advance, lest the people in the packtrain open fire on us, thinking they were being attacked.

Joe Meek solved the problem. He whipped off the yard-square white head-clout he often wears to disguise his coal-black hair against the skyline and tied it onto his rifle barrel, then rode out in plain sight and fired into the air as he kicked his horse into a wild charge towards the packtrain, which signaled the rest of us to join him, whooping and yelling, firing off our guns, providing a joyful welcome for the trail-weary travelers.

Tom Fitzpatrick had by then joined his scouts at the head of the column. He raised his rifle over his head, pointed it skyward, and fired, a sign to the rest of his people that we were friendly fools, not Blackfoots bent on inflicting a massacre. They responded by loosing a ragged volley along the long line of packmules and horses swaying under their heavy loads as we swept past the leaders and coursed alongside the plodding column, causing any number of wrecks amongst startled pack animals and earning fervent curses from their drovers. I snatched a fleeting glimpse of Black Harris as we raced by, then Captain Stewart, but, caught up in the frenzied rush of trappers and Indians, I was unable to slow up to greet them, let alone halt.

Hooting and hollering our heads off, the Indians howling their glee, we sped along both sides of what appeared to be a never-ending procession of pack animals, in the midst of which I spied Milton Sublette perched on a mule-drawn dearborn, until we came nigh the end of the column. Bringing up the rear was a couple of big wagons and some loose horses and mules, a number of milch cows, a young bull, and a few calves, except for a couple-three guards trailing behind to protect them.

As we thundered past one of the wagons, I thought I saw a pale-faced woman seated on the box, but immediately dismissed that notion as ridiculous. We skidded to a halt in a maelstrom of wild-eyed, snorting, lathered horses, wheeled about, and retraced our path in a somewhat more orderly fashion. That is, some of us did. Half of the trappers and all of the Indians persisted in their madcap antics, showing off their horseback skills with vaults and drags and other such exhibitions of equestrian prowess, appearing to concentrate their efforts in the vicinity of one of the wagons at the tail-end of the column.

I put Crane into a brisk walk, fast enough to overtake the plodding four-mule team hauling the wagon, and came up beside it. Out of habit, I proceeded to reload my rifle, but just as I came in sight of the driver and his passenger, I nearly dropped my gun. Seated beside Doctor Marcus Whitman was a beautiful copper-haired white woman! I gasped and rubbed my eyes, but she was still there, a sure-enough, real-life white woman in the midst of the Rocky Mountains!

I checked Crane into a walk to match the mules' pace and gawped at her like the veriest hick, until she noticed me staring and favored me with a tired smile that, even through the trail dust, lighted her soft features like a halo. I felt my cheeks burning, flashed an embarrassed smile at her, touched spur to Crane, and galloped off, confused and unbelieving and feeling unaccountably guilty at having somehow betrayed Kathleen.

I slowed Crane as I came nigh Milt's dearborn rattling over the rough trail. I hailed him and he returned my greeting with a broad smile, expressing his delight to be once more in the mountains and amongst old friends. He explained his present mode of travel by rapping his leg with his knuckles, eliciting a hollow sound. "It's cork," he told me. "They fin'ly had to take the old 'un off 'fore it went an' kilt me, so Bobby Campbell's brother sent me this'n out o' Phillydelphy. Natcherly it ain't the same, but leastaways it's lettin' me git up thisaway one more time." I wanted to say something like there would be many more times for him, but I'm not good at such talk. We chatted for a spell about the old days and promised to talk more at rendezvous, before I moved up the column to find Black and Fitz.

As I rode I wondered how Milton and Joe Meek would resolve the matter of Umentucken, now that Milt had unexpectedly made it to the mountains. Until now, the dictum 'Out of sight, out of mind' had sufficed. Now his presence posed a conundrum that only the two of them could solve.

Captain Stewart, astride a tall, showy chestnut gelding, greeted me with surprising warmth. His Rocky Mountain experience had evidently smoothed off some of the jagged edges of his highborn manner. He was convinced as ever of his inherited superiority, but he had learned to wear his rank like a comfortable coat. Although still far from a democrat, nowadays the Scottish lord was not nearly the aristocratic snob I had first encountered. He appeared to take pleasure in reminiscing over his original western journey. He surprised me by quoting some of the remarks I had made to him during his earliest days in the mountains. As I prepared to take my leave, he insisted that I visit him in camp. He waved to a light two-horse freight wagon and a string of pack animals conducted by his servants. "I promise to entertain you with the choicest European food and drink, Mister Buck, dainty sweetmeats and delicious libations unknown in the mountains. And do bring with you your beautiful charming lady!"

As I rode forward to find Moses Harris I marveled at the changes his few years in the mountains had wrought in the pompous nobleman. His physical stamina and oft-demonstrated courage had gained him acceptance amongst our rough-hewn fraternity, grudging at first, but now universally granted. "Ol' Stewart's shore-as-hell got the ha'r o' the b'ar in 'im!" was the unanimous verdict. He was no longer simply a gentleman sportsman out on a lark. Years of rubbing elbows with our unwashed brotherhood, sharing our hardships and perils and joyful celebrations, had instilled changes in him that with any luck he would carry home with him when his wilderness sojourn was at an end. His countrymen could not fail to profit from it.

I mentioned it to Harris when I caught with him. "Yeah," he agreed, "I seen it, too. He's still got that stuck-up stick up his arse, but naow he don't mind rollin' in the muck with the rest of us. Fact is, he plumb enjoys it!"

Black and I swapped whatever news we thought the other might be interested in. When he spoke of the doin's in Saint Louis, except as they might apply to Pierre Chouteau and the fur trade, it seemed to me like a world apart. When I mentioned the absence of Fontenelle in the packtrain, Harris sniggered. "Yep, an' ye won't likely be seein' ol' Lucien hyarabaouts no more. Ol' John Barleycorn's got a-holt o' him somethin' fierce. They had to let 'im go. It's all restin' on Fitz naow, 'ceptin' fer Drips an' Bridger up thisaway." He glanced around, making sure no one else was within earshot, before he added in a lower voice, "Fact is, the whole shebang's feelin' sorta shaky naowadays." Then he asked, "Did ye 'spy Josh Pilcher when ye come bustin' past?"

I said that I hadn't. "Wal, that ain't s'prisin'," Harris said with a laugh. "He's up front somewhar's, but ol' Josh don't look much like he useta. He's gone an' let hisse'f git old!" Then, "Glad that ain't happenin' to yew an' me!" he added with a wink.

I have known Joshua Pilcher for a courageous, generous gentleman since 'twenty-three, when he recruited an army of Lahcotahs to punish the Rees for their massacre of Ashley's people on the Missouri, and again a year later when he gifted our bunch with powder and lead and a welcome sip or two, when his Missouri Fur brigade ran across us in the woods. The last time I saw him, at Snake Lake in 'twenty-eight, Missouri Fur was on its last legs after a passel of ill luck, but even then, Josh Pilcher was fair and honorable in his dealings with me.

"Word is," Black confided, "Pilcher's come over from Fort Pierre on the Missourah tryin' to buy out Fitz an' t'others fer Amurrican Fur an' Fitz ain't havin' none of it. He wou'n't even let Josh buy fresh hosses down at Fort Willum fer comin' on to thi'shere ronnyvoo, but Pilcher got hisse'f up hyar anyways, hosses or no. Ol' Cadet wants this outfit fer Amurrican Fur an' Josh ain't takin' no fer an answer. Fort Willum's been eatin' cornsid'rable into the Injun trade, crowdin' Fort Union purty bad, so Chouteau wants it all fer hisownse'f, him an' Pratte."

We were by then approaching the outskirts of the rendezvous and Harris was needed at the head of the column to oversee the fording of Horse Creek. We promised to get together once he was relieved of his duties and I rode off to impart the wondrous news of white women in the Rockies to our people back in camp. They would likely call me a liar until they saw for themselves.

~ ~ ~

Next day, although it was three days overdue, trappers paid their proper respects to America's Day of Independence with a wild shindy well-lubricated with equally overdue trader's booze. Fiddles sawed lively airs morning and night and Irish Harpoon Harry Yeats strummed and sang himself hoarse celebrating our country's freedom from the Sassenach yoke. Even Captain Stewart had his people brew a tub of sweet metheglin in honor of our nation's birthday, generously serving every trapper who dropped by his crimson marquee. Stewart's recognition of that particular American holiday naturally earned him the disapproving glares of John McLeod and Thomas McKay, the Hudson's Bay traders who had arrived from Fort Hall two days earlier.

Traveling with the Aitch-bee-cee partisans was Nathaniel Wyeth, on his way back to the States after concluding the sale of his Fort Hall trading post to the Hudson's Bay Company. No matter how much money Wyeth received from the deal, I daresay the spiteful Yankee's greatest satisfaction came from making good his threat to roll a stone of serious competition into the American fur traders' garden, as he had sworn to do two years before.

McLeod and McKay lacked the easy-going charm of Francis Ermatinger, the HBC partisan we had met the year before. They were a humorless brace of hard-eyed, tight-fisted Scots, loyal Company-men who regarded American trappers with ill-concealed dislike and contempt, which naturally eroded most of the profit they might have realized from our trade. Their Indian customers, howsomever, cared nothing either for their affection or lack of it, only the excellent quality of the trade goods on their counters, so they conducted a brisk business with our redskinned brethren.

The principal attraction provided by the newcomers, for whites and Indians alike, were the missionaries' wives, two of them, Narcissa Whitman, whom I had seen seated beside her husband on the wagon coming into camp, and Eliza Spaulding, an older woman who was ailing from the rigors of the westward journey. After a day's rest and a bathe, Narcissa bloomed with good health and enthusiasm for her new surroundings. She generously held court daily for an unending stream of visitors, especially Indian women, a few of whom insisting on touching her fair skin, all of them marveling at her blue eyes and coppery-golden locks, several fingering the fabric of her costume before running off to find its like on a trade table. Narcissa Whitman was indeed a beautiful woman by any standard, gifted with buoyant good health and possessed of a kind and generous nature imposed on a resilient core that let her respond to new experience and hardship with easy grace and equanimity.

Her female companion was a rather different article. Eliza Spaulding was somewhat older, spare of frame and sallow-complexioned, dark hair and eyes, with a habitually-strained expression and querulous manner. She hadn't traveled well. Jolting a thousand miles and more over rough trails in a freight wagon, sleeping on the ground after a lifetime spent on featherbeds, and living on a diet of fresh buffalo meat three times a day and little else were not calculated to improve either the health or disposition of an eastern lady. Narcissa was an exception. She thrived on it. Eliza barely survived it.

Competing with the Indian women for Narcissa's favor and attention was a constant stream of white men come to pay her court, some who fancied themselves to be gentlemen, as well as several trappers togged out in their most colorful quilled and beaded best, Joe Meek foremost amongst them. Chief amongst her gentleman admirers were the gallant Captain Stewart, who had enjoyed her society since Missouri, and Nathaniel Wyeth, who managed to put aside his customary crusty manner, leastaways in her presence, and an aging but still handsome Josiah Pilcher, spruced up and presentable in a well-brushed topper and creamy buckskins.

Most trappers were content to admire Narcissa from afar, clad in their Sunday-best duds, respectfully touching their caps in a courteous salute as they paraded before her tent at a respectful distance. Not so the bumptious Joe Meek, who wasted no time before thrusting himself into her company with wondrous tales of his b'ar-wrasslin' and Injun-fightin' exploits, some of which bore a faint trace of truth, and found that he was welcome there. Joe, too, was dandified top-to-toe in quilled and beaded buckskins, certainly the product of months of skilled effort by his cherished Umentucken.

"Jist look at 'im," Brass Turtle commented with a wry grin. "Ol' Joe don't hardly never own a whole clout to cover his nekkid arse an' naow he could be headin' up a Blackfoot war party!"

Joe wasn't trying to seduce the fair Narcissa, nor was she encouraging anything of the sort. It was simply that the handsome, black-haired, smooth-talking Virginian is never satisfied to play second fiddle. Although he shuns leadership, he strives to be the best at anything he puts his hand to and he usually succeeds.

Although Narcissa outshone Eliza Spaulding with the men, she definitely took second place with the Nez Percé and Flathead women, whose nurturing nature responded to the frailty of the pale invalid. They fussed over her toilette, assisting as much as she would allow in dressing and grooming her, and they vied in preparing tasty dishes for her meals, seeking to tempt her finicky appetite and restore a semblance of health to her pasty, sunken cheeks.

Kathleen chose not to include herself amongst the missionary wives' ladies-in-waiting, but her natural curiosity demanded that she visit their camp and see for herself what all the hullabaloo was about. And naturally she insisted on dressing herself and Iris in their most elaborate native clothing when they paid their call. They wore no settlement fabrics this time, only their softest-tanned creamy mountain sheep leather dresses adorned with a galore of dyed quillwork. A thin line of vermilion emphasized her high cheekbones and the aristocratic planes of her cheeks and her long, glossy plaits were wrapped in rich mink fur, altogether a stunning portrait of native nobility. Narcissa must have thought so, as well, for she shrieked delightedly, caught Kathleen by both hands and led her to Eliza's chair to be admired. The unsmiling invalid merely regarded Cat with a dull stare for a moment, then turned away. Which diminished Kathleen's pleasure not a whit. She knew which of the two women provoked all the excitement amongst the menfolk.

You may wonder where the good Doctor Whitman was when all that attention was being paid to his comely wife. Almost from the moment of his arrival in camp he was kept busy attending to Indians and trappers suffering from a variety of illnesses and injuries. Good-natured and dedicated as he is, he could not refuse to assist them. He rode out from his camp early each morning, his medical satchel swinging from the pommel post, and rarely returned until dusk.

Finn McCool attached himself to Whitman immediately upon his arrival, assisting the medico whenever he was asked to do so, otherwise carefully observing the doctor's every ministration. Zeetlah often accompanied them. He lent a hand when needed, interpreted for Indian patients, and sometimes offered his own medical concoctions, which Whitman gratefully accepted and often applied.

The Reverend Henry Spaulding and the Reverend William Gray were a much different sort from Doctor Whitman. Those two were cut from the same somber cloth as the two missionaries who had preceded them and their medical colleague. Their attire, like the earlier bearers of the Word, proclaimed their calling. Whitman, always willing to learn new things and adopt practical solutions, was clad in buckskins now, like the rest of us, although he wore leather britches, not a clout. Spaulding and Gray clung to their rusty black tailcoats and threadbare trousers, morning and night, as a badge of their profession, like their predecessors Jackson and Parker had done.

And like Parker the year before, it was plain to see that Spaulding did not approve of Whitman's unparsonlike demeanor, his casual table manners, his easy-going acceptance of the trappers' mostly irreverent, often bawdy behavior, and his preference to spread his Christian faith by his own worthy example and good works rather than by grim sermonizing that is mostly laughed off by our impious crew, anyway. It is a difficult chore to stir up much fear of hellfire and brimstone amongst a breed of men who are unfazed by a daily diet of grizzly bears and rattlesnakes, starvation and deadly thirst in boiling summers and freezing winters, and hostile Blackfoots who may be lurking at the next bend in the trail.

Henry Spaulding was a fitting spouse for Eliza, her exact male counterpart, of middling age, spare of build and balding, his features pinched from a lifetime of disapproving judgments, icy blue eyes in which there was no love, graceless, and ill-mannered towards anyone he deemed inferior to himself, which was nearly everybody.

William Gray was a younger man, but it was plain to see that with a little study and effort he would become another Spaulding.

₭ ₭ ₭

Something ominous seemed to be hanging over that summer's rendezvous. I couldn't precisely put my finger on it, but our customary good times lacked their usual galloping gait, sort of like a favorite horse favoring a leg just before he goes completely lame. The missionary crew didn't help matters. Even good-natured, obliging Marcus Whitman and the presence of the beauteous and vivacious Narcissa couldn't remedy the chilling influence of their ecclesiastical colleagues, whose pursed lips and cold, disapproving stares dampened the spirits of all but the most drunken trappers who wandered nigh their camp, which the trappers had irreverently dubbed Jerusalem.

"Damn if thet'ere pair o' black crows an' thet scrawny woman with 'em ain't puttin' a dreadful hitch in my good-time gitalong!" Tuttle complained. "Ever' time I'm shufflin' cards or takin' a swaller, I look up an' see one of 'em staring a gawddamn hole plumb through my en-joys! 'Tain't right! 'Tain't Christian, begawd!"

The parsons' condemnation wasn't reserved only for the sinful excesses of our beaver-trapping brethren. They visited their vinegary censure on Indians and their native customs, as well. When the Snakes, Flatheads, and Nez Percés conducted a four-hour scalp dance in honor of the missionaries, with a couple-three hundred colorfully-clad warriors stomping the ground and waving weapons and war-trophies, at the doorstep of Jerusalem, the humorless clerics greeted that well-intended tribute with sour faces and disapproving cluckings of the tongue. "Do these people have no training or understanding before they come out here," Finn McCool wondered, "about what they might be expectin' to find amongst the people they've come to convert?" Apparently not.

It wasn't only the missionaries who cast a pall over our usually festive holiday from the rigors of the trapping trade. Something was amiss at the trading tents, as well, even more than that year's sharp spike in prices for settlement merchandise. Beaver brought four or five dollars the pound, but trade goods was marked up well over a thousand percent over Saint Louis prices, pretty much wiping out a whole year's hard work just to get outfitted for another year. "Never thought I'd be drinkin' up a whole beaver plew in jest half a swaller!" Tuttle lamented when he paid four dollars a pint for watered-down trader's booze.

The gloom was universal. Trade clerks were sullen or briskly businesslike at best, as if they could already hear bad news coming. The dark cloud hung especially low over Tom Fitzpatrick's marquee, where he and Josiah Pilcher spent many hours sequestered in discussions that the rest of us could only guess at. Whatever they talked about could not have been pleasing to the ear of our Irish friend, judging by his expression whenever he emerged. "What d'ye reckon ol' Pilcher's tellin' Fitz in thar?" Brass Turtle wondered. "Tom's got a face long enough to trip a goat ever' time he sticks his head out o' thar."

I had a pretty fair idea of what they might be haggling about, but I held my peace. I reckoned we would find out soon enough.

Kathleen showed admirable restraint at Fitzpatrick's trade tables, explaining that she had acquired quite enough fabrics and foofurraw the year before. Most of her purchases were confined to replenishing groceries and replacing tools and utensils that had worn out, broken, or strayed. She was aware that we had experienced a lean beaver harvest that year and I refrained from telling her that even with the sharply higher prices my credit was virtually unlimited. Such was not the case with my comrades and I had no wish to provoke comparisons.

On one of our visits to the traders, Captain Stewart hailed us and renewed his invitation to visit him at his marquee, insisting that we come along with him right then and join him for "high tea," as he called it. When we entered the grove beside Stewart's camp we discovered several other trappers and their womenfolk, Jim Bridger and Joe Meek amongst them, already there. Cat immediately joined her good friend Umentucken and Bridger's wife Cora, a young Séli woman with whom she had become friends over the past trapping season. I looked around for Milt Sublette, but he wasn't there.

"Sitcherse'f daown an' gitcherse'f around some o' these hyar good vittles, Temple!" Joe insisted. "I warrant y'ain't never et ther like o' what ther Cap'n's sarvin' up hyar! It's furriner food fer damn sure an' I ain't sure haow ye be callin' ther most of it, but it's mighty good eatin'!"

"Hyar ye be, Temple," Bridger said affably, offering a bottle labeled Spanish brandy. "Best ye wet yer whistle afore ye pitch in to the vittles." He sloshed my cup mostly full, then did the same for Kathleen. The brandy possessed a fiery flavor that warmed my innards, stronger than French cognac, but pleasantly piquant.

Stewart's people emerged from the marquee bearing platters of food and headed our way to serve us. Both Jim and Joe surprised me by waving them off and directing them to serve our women first—a most unIndian and untrapperlike thing to do, but a gesture I approved.

When it was our turn, I could hardly believe the quality and variety of the comestibles they offered, most of it imported from Europe, several items I had never encountered before, even in Lucette's lavish establishment— bottles of rich Guinness stout and delicious Polish ham, served up with fancy English bread slathered with butter, preserves, and jams of several flavors, gobs of steaming corned beef brisket, goose liver paste from France smeared on a peck of crumbly Scottish biscuits, tiny fish in tasty oil and smoky little oysters from a tin, washed down with French champagne, upon which Meek pronounced his verdict: "I reckon it'll do fer drinkin' when you're eatin', but fer serious gittin' drunk, I'd hafta say it's more'n jest a trifle thin."

After we stuffed ourselves nigh to foundering, we retreated to a shady part of the grove, propped our backs against aspen trees, and lit our pipes.

"Yer bunch made up yer mind 'bout whar ye'll do yer trappin', come fall?" Bridger asked. I replied that the matter hadn't come up yet. "Wal, when it does, ye kin tell 'em my outfit'll be headin nawth up to Yellerstone country an' they be welcome to come taggin' along, like last year."

"Yer bunch been thinkin' on trappin' on yer own?" Joe wanted to know. "If ye do, ye'd best keep yer eyes peeled fer Blackfoots day an' night. They be swarmin' naowadays more'n ever. Ever'body's been sayin' so." I repeated that no decision had even been discussed, let alone decided.

"Wal, when ye git 'em together, ye mought let 'em know we'll be pullin' out purty soon," Jim added. "It's a fur piece gittin' up thataway an' thi'shere ronnyvoo ain't hardly wuth hangin' around fer long—this year, anyways."

I nodded my accord with that last sentiment, although I still couldn't say precisely why I felt that way.

Joe Meek was not nearly so uncertain. "Them'ere black-hats're sure-as-hell gonna ruin ever'thin' good abaout ronnyvoo if we let 'em! Allus lookin' daown their gawddamn noses at us mountaineers, allus givin' us ther bad-eye, scoldin' us fer drinkin' an' gamblin', an' tellin' all ther Injun gals to be keepin' their distance from us white-eyes! 'Tain't right!" He cast a quick glance at Umentucken, but she was engaged in talk with Cat, which obviously relieved Joe.

"I'm s'prised ye be thinkin' thataway, Joe," Bridger said with a sly grin, "cornsid'rin' haow ye been courtin' the doc's yeller-hair woman since she come up hyar, gittin' yerse'f all gussied up like Miz Washin'ton's pet pony ever' day fer doin' yer sweet-talkin'. Hell! I figgered ye meant to git 'er to move in with ye!"

Joe looked shocked. "Not fer a gawddamn minute!" he sputtered. "I wou'n't swap my Umentucken fer a dozen yeller-hair wimmen like that'n an' yew know thet fer a gawddamn fact! I war jest tryin' to make 'er feel more t'home up thisaway, 'stid o' hankerin' fer ther settlements."

Joe took a final swallow from his bottle of Guinness and laid it aside before he added, "If you're lookin' fer somebody what's got a mortal hankerin' fer Narcissa, ye'd best look to thet'ere skinny Parson Spauldin'. Thet Bible-thumpin' humbug'd ditch ol' 'Liza in a gawddamn blink an' run off with ther doc's wife if he could jest figger haow to git 'er done!"

Then Joe said something I had heard from many white trappers since the white women had arrived in camp. "'Course Narcissa's pow'ful easy on ther eyes, but then ye cain't help lookin' at her friend Eliza an' rememb'rin' jest haow most o' ther white wimmen back in ther States really are! It don't take long to 'preciate haow good we got it up hyar with ther Injun wimmen we awready got!" Once again, I realized that rough and tough-talking Joe Meek is an acute observer and a serious thinker.

☙   ☙   ☙

There was hardly any discussion and no serious opposition when I conveyed Bridger's offer to have us come along with his brigade when they headed north to the Yellowstone. Even contrary Anse Tolliver offered no objection. His only comment was, "Jist so's we keep out o' Aitch-bee-cee's gawddamn dooryard, spesh'ly naow that Yankee Nat's sold out to McLeod! That'ere cold-eye Scotchman'll scrape ever' beaver thar be clean out o' that whole country, jist fer keepin' us out o' thar!"

Our decision to go along with Bridger came only a day before we received the news that Tom Fitzpatrick had lost his battle with Josiah Pilcher. Fontenelle & Fitzpatrick was no more. Henceforth the Company would be Pratte, Chouteau et Cie., which was really the western arm of American Fur. From that day on it would be the only American trader at rendezvous. The deal also transferred ownership of Fort William to Pratte, Chouteau, thereby relieving Cadet's Fort Union of a troublesome gadfly to its otherwise exclusive Indian trade.

It was a dark day and every trapper knew it. No longer would we be able to play one trader off against the others. Now le Cadet owned it all. Nothing would ever be the same as we had known it.

Fitz and Fontenelle had been playing a losing hand all the way. Chouteau's money had financed F&F's operation from the first giddyap, so it should have been no surprise when Cadet called in their IOU's. Why Chouteau had chosen to back their outfit in the first place, instead of taking over directly from Bill Sublette two years before, is a mystery I am not equipped to solve.

Heeding all the talk of an even more numerous than usual Blackfoot presence this year, I paid a final visit to the trade tent, where I bought a plenitude of gunpowder and galena and another gallon of percussion caps, most of which I gifted to my fellows and the women upon my return to camp.

The tender care and nourishing vittles of the Nez Percé women had quite restored the always-delicate health of Eliza Spaulding, so the missionary party was preparing to continue its journey to Oregon. Doctor Whitman agreed to abandon his large freight wagon for the trip over rough mountain trails, but he insisted on keeping his light wagon, even though he was warned that even with the most strenuous effort he would not be able to take it beyond Fort Hall.

Captain Stewart would accompany the party as far as Fort Hall and, if he followed his customary pattern, would likely winter with the HBC's Doctor McLoughlin in Vancouver. He, too, had abandoned his freight wagon, which was likely empty, anyway, after his open-handed hospitality in camp.

Whitman would likely have plenty of help getting his wagon over gullies and steep hills, for both the Nez Percé band and Insala's Flatheads would attend the missionaries all the way to their homeland.

The light wagon was doubtless for the use of Eliza Spaulding. Narcissa would be mounted a-horseback for the rest of the journey, perched precariously upon her sidesaddle, a contraption which earned her much amused attention from Indians and trappers alike. "If it weren't for Miz Spaulding," Finn McCool surmised, "I daresay the doctor's missus would be ridin' astride by now, like every other woman hereabouts." He was likely right, for feeble as she was, Eliza exercised an iron will in matters of decorum.

McLeod and his HBC crew agreed to shepherd the missionaries on the way to Fort Hall and possibly some of his people would accompany the pilgrims all the way to Oregon. The belligerent Scot lectured the parsons against encouraging American trappers to settle in that new land, as several mountaineers, discouraged with the diminishing beaver harvests of the past couple years, had expressed an interest in doing. McLeod warned the newcomers against assisting American trappers to put down roots in Oregon or even accepting their help in establishing their missions, claiming our people would surely cause trouble, especially amongst the Indians. Strong-minded Narcissa paid no heed to McLeod's scare talk, howsomever. She promised her help and the doctor's for any trapper who wished to settle in their future neighborhood.

We witnessed with mixed feelings the departure of the missionary party for their new homes. Most of us were glad to be relieved of the scolding sermons, the clucking tongues and judgmental stares, and the icy superiority most of them claimed, but even so, many of us felt sympathy for those naïve newcomers who could have no idea of the hardships that lay ahead in their adventure into a harsh and unforgiving wilderness, especially for the doctor and his generous wife, both so willing and eager to learn. I feared the lessons might prove to be too severe, even for them.

Fitzpatrick closed up shop as soon as his missionary guests departed. Moses Harris rode over to our camp for a farewell drink together and informed us that the packtrain would be returning to Fort William after passing barely a fortnight at Horse Creek. "I reckon Fitz ain't feelin' much like hangin' around fer a party after what he run into hyarabaouts," Black explained. "If he decides he wants one, looks like we'll have plenty o' comp'ny all the way to Sain' Looie. Nigh a score o' trappers 'pear to be hangin' up their traps, quittin' the life fer good, comin' along with us. Ol' Pilcher won't be one of 'em, though. He's been keepin' his distance, naow he's got what he come fer. Leastaways naow he's got hisse'f some decent hosses fer ridin' back to Fort Willum, 'stid o' the worn-out nags he rode in hyar on."

Our women and the campkeepers had busied themselves throughout the rendezvous drying buffalo meat in preparation against the lean days of winter, as well as storing up substantial stocks of pemmican, rendering bear fat and preserving marrow, and drying plums, chokecherries, berries, and vegetable truck from the forest and prairie. When word came that we would be leaving in a couple days, they were ready. Although our bachelors had been no more helpful than us married men in the work of putting up foodstuffs for winter, they had pitched in with us to harvest a plenitude of buffalo, wapiti, curly-horns, and deer, as well as a couple grizzlies that unwisely challenged our right to be in the woods.

When Doc Newell rode over from Bridger's camp to let us know that the brigade would be pulling out on the morrow, we were ready.

-oOo-

CHAPTER XVII
YELLOWSTONE COUNTRY

eparture from the rendezvous camp on July 16 was the usual colorful procession of women, although most of the Indian bands, including Iron Bow's, had already headed out for their home grounds. Fitz had packed up and left the day before. Just the same, the women insisted on a final opportunity to strut their prettiest duds before donning their workaday attire for the coming year of trapping. As usual, we rode only the few miles to the overnight stop nigh the mouth of Horse Creek to make sure nothing important had been left behind and to allow the laggards to catch up by morning. Little Ben rode on my saddle bow, squirming about and calling out farewells to the few remaining camps. It was plain that he would be riding on his own by the following spring, which Cat would surely welcome. We had already taught him to swim in a shallow backwater of Horse Creek that summer.

When Bridger's brigade assembled next morning it amounted to about sixty white trappers, which was most of the Americans still left, half that many Flatheads, Nez Percés, and Snakes, their families, and a couple dozen campkeepers.

The common term "white trappers" includes Delawares and Shawnees, not only white-eyes. We were headed north to country infested with Blackfoots, so Bridger welcomed our bunch.

Andy Drips had left a couple days before, headed south, leading a large brigade made up mostly of Snake and Flathead trappers and naturally their wives and kids.

I reckon that this might be a good place to describe a more or less typical trapping season of a brigade, fall and spring, in sparing detail, without much description of our personal lives or quoting my comrades, as I am wont to do. Fact is, Mister Hobbes has cautioned me that this manuscript is getting perilously close to becoming two books.

Bridger split his brigade into sizeable trapping parties and our bunch started off in the same direction as the year before, up Grovant Fork to Jackson's Little Hole, then Davey's Big Hole, then to Jackson's Lake, where fishing is good and game is plentiful in the marshy areas, but so are horse flies and mosquitoes, a dreadful nuisance to man and beast during daylight hours. Fortunately, chill air sweeping down the flanks of the snow-capped *Trois Tetons* looming ominously above us drives them off at dusk to shelter amongst tree leaves and grass.

We trapped thereabouts with some small success and, happily, no trouble with Grovants, until the first week or so of August, when we packed up and headed for Yellowstone Lake, trapping ice-cold streams as we went through the mountains. We crossed the Divide, where snowmelt flowing from a high snowy peak on the prairie divides into two streams, one flowing east to the Atlantic, the other west to the Pacific, where a foot-long trout can cross the mountains in safety. We followed the eastern branch down to where it enters the Yellowstone River, which we forded in belly-high water, then followed the river north through marshes and swamps to Yellowstone Lake. We trapped the streams that feed the lake until mid-August, when Bridger arrived with the main party and moved down the east shore to a beautiful grassy plain surrounded by pine groves that provided a plenitude of wapiti and deer that retreat into their shade to escape the mid-day heat.

Not far from the brigade's encampment were several boiling hot springs hissing and whistling constantly, sending up noisy plumes of water and steam that can be heard five miles away. Our original bunch had seen and heard those wonders many years before, when Blackfoots chased us into that neighborhood, but those who joined us later, along with our wives and children, had to be reassured that they were a harmless curiosity.

It became difficult to hang onto that conviction when Bridger once again split up his brigade and our bunch headed easterly to trap several streams that feed the Yellowstone. After an hour or so on the trail we entered a tract that resembled the roof of hell, a netherworld boiling far below the surface, steam and hot water hissing and belching skyward through holes in a milky limestone crust as we threaded single-file afoot across its expanse on a half-mile-long elk trail, leading our critters, whose hoofs thumped and echoed and sometimes broke through the crusty surface, bathing them in hot water.

Once across that infernal zone, we entered a grassy draw nestled betwixt high forested ridges, a small clear-running stream tumbling merrily down its center. The sudden contrast prompted Finn McCool to pronounce it an Eden. "Sure'n who'd'a thought the Good Lord would'a located His darlin' Paradise next door to Satan's Hell, consid'rin', mind ye, how much real estate He had to choose from?"

Children scattered to the hillsides gathering firewood whilst the women set up camp. Several of us went in search of supper, bringing in three fat wapiti that were soon dripping succulent grease on the coals, its fragrance floating on the air further providing the notion of Eden.

After supper, bellies full to bursting, smoking a pipeful, we lazed about and listened to Anse Tolliver coaxing sentimental melodies from his fiddle, a pleasant departure from the lively tunes he produced at rendezvous, until dusk commenced to settle. One by one, we retreated to our robes for a night of welcome slumber.

∾ ∾ ∾

We continued on our way for a few more days, spreading out each afternoon to set our traps and retrieving the harvest each morning, before moving on to another likely spot. On the fourth day we crossed a high, rugged mountain and descended into a beautiful valley about eight miles long and roughly half as wide, surrounded by high, thickly-forested mountains, making our way beside a rushing stream that widened and gentled by time it reached the valley floor, its low banks bordered by cottonwood groves.

As we entered the valley we spied a dozen or so men and women herding about that many children up a hillside, fleeing our approach. A few of us followed them on foot and convinced them of our peaceful intentions, using gestures and antique fragments of the Snake tongue. They were a cleanly people, small in stature and neatly-dressed in well-tanned sheep and deer hides. They immediately warmed to us when they saw that we had women and children in our company, inviting us to set up our camp nearby their own dwellings. These were the Sheepeaters we had heard about from other trappers but never encountered until now. Which wasn't surprising, considering that small bands of them lived in secluded mountain valleys, avoiding contact with other Indians lest they be plundered and killed for sport.

Although they were well-provided with Nature's bounty, plentiful game animals and abundant forest produce, they possessed hardly any manufactured goods past a couple steel knives worn to slivers from years of sharpening, a battered iron kettle or two, and a couple of ancient fusees which were useless for lack of ammunition. They had no horses, but a couple dozen dogs carried their scant belongings on hunting trips and camp moves. They were expert with their excellent bows, made from sheep, buffalo, and elk horn, wrapped with sinew, artfully decorated with quills, and measured about a yard long. Their strong, straight arrows were tipped with obsidian.

What began as a merely friendly gesture when Cat and Talley gifted the Sheepeater women with a couple new butcher knives turned into a trade fair when the grateful Sheepeaters responded by throwing a heap of soft-tanned sheep and deer skins at their feet. Soon a stack of copper kettles, awls, hand-axes, firesteels, tobacco, gunpowder and galena, worn but serviceable woolen blankets, and I'm not sure what-all was more than matched by soft-tanned sheep, elk, and deer hides, along with several large catamount skins tanned to velvety perfection. There was no haggling. The Sheepeaters simply tossed the skins at our feet, saying, "Give us what you wish in return. It will be enough. We can get many skins, but we rarely see Tee-boo-boes (Sun People)." They told us that there used to be a galore of beaver in the surrounding streams, but they had pretty much wiped them out for food, singeing off the fur in cookfires, not aware of its value.

We had to teach them the use of firesteels and flints, for they made fire by rapidly twirling a stick on soft wood with two hands until it first smoked, then burst into flame.

We stayed with them for several days, hunting wapiti and blacktails with them in the nearby woods and climbing after curly-horns on the surrounding cliffs. Time to meet up with Bridger at Gardner's Hole was drawing near, howsomever, so we reluctantly took our leave. An older man offered to draw a map of the surrounding country on a white elkskin with a burnt stick, showing the route we had already traversed and the land that lay between us and our destination. His drawing of the early part of our journey was so accurate that it inspired our confidence in his depiction of the remainder.

Our parting gift to those kind and open-handed people was three serviceable muskets and their fixin's we had retrieved from our battle with the Bannocks on our eastward trip, along with a few extra horns of gunpowder, galena, and a flask of whale oil to resist rusting.

I daresay I wasn't the only one who felt a tinge of regret at leaving that peaceful valley and its gentle, generous residents.

∾ ∾ ∾

Two days' westerly travel brought us to Gardner's Hole and Bridger's main camp, where we tarried only a couple days before striking out once more in quest of plews, which were steadily improving with crisp, sunshiny days and chill nights. A single day's ride brought the whole brigade to the Yellowstone. Next day the entire party followed the river another dozen miles onto the Yellowstone Plain, where trappers scattered out in small parties of half-a-dozen or so each and Jim Bridger and his campkeepers headed slowly down the river.

Our bunch generally tries to stick together, women and kids and all, so we traveled down the Yellowstone about forty miles, then headed north up a branch called 25-yard River for another twenty-five miles or so before establishing camp. Fortune smiled in that location. First, the high, rolling country and belly-high grass attracted immense herds of buffalo, which we hadn't seen since Horse Creek, as well as large bands of prairie goats, a plenitude of deer and wapiti, and no shortage of grizzly bears to prey on them. The cricks and streams spilling off the surrounding hills provided more beaver than we had seen in more than a year, which helped make up for the slim pickin's of last year and so far that season.

Naturally our first chore was harvesting a couple-three fat cows. It was mid-September by then and they were no longer nursing their calves. Each time we went after buffalo, the women insisted that we bring back prairie goats, as well, not so much for the meat but for the hides, which make the thinnest, softest, toughest leggin's of any leather. Problem is, unlike near-sighted buffalo, pronghorn prairie goats are sharp-eyed and skittish. Only their unfailing curiosity lets you get close enough for a shot by waving a red rag on a stick, which draws them in to investigate.

Newcomers mostly call them antelopes, but most of those Johnny-come-latelies are also calling the Seeds-kee-dee the Green River nowadays. It's hard for us old-timers to know what they are talking about.

The abundance of plums and cherries and other wild fruits in that neighborhood attract an unusual number of grizzly bears fattening up for the coming winter. Several times whilst riding out to run my trapline in the morning, I spied half a dozen and more grizzlies standing on their hind legs, scooping cherries off the bushes with remarkable skill. They paid little attention to my presence, according me a mere glance before returning to their breakfast. Approaching winter prompted our women to insist that we harvest a couple of the portliest bruins for their fat, which naturally we did.

After a week or so, we joined the brigade on Rocky Fork, where we learned of the death of a French trapper called Bodah. He was waylaid whilst running his traps by Blackfoots, whose attentions we had been spared until then. Several war parties had been seen in that neighborhood but Bodah was the first casualty.

Our women were still setting up the lodges when Joe Meek and a trapper called Dave Crow arrived in a hurry. Meek's tall grey horse had dried blood staining his neck. Naturally everybody demanded to know what news he brought. "News? I'll tell ye ther news!" Meek exploded. "Me an' Dave hyar war runnin' our traps over on Pryor's Fork when we come onter a bunch o' Bug's Boys stuffin' theirse'fs with plums off ther trees thar. Natcherly they commenced shootin' an' shot muh horse, ol' Two Sherbit hyar, in ther neck an' sent us heels over head in a heap, but we raised up a-runnin' an' got ther hell out o' thar!" He turned to Dave Crow and asked, "Thet abaout haow it war, Dave?" and Crow, a quiet man, a first-rate hunter and trapper who had been with us since Andy Henry's days, smiled and nodded his assent.

Next day the brigade moved camp downstream to where Rocky Fork joins up with Clark's Fork, about three miles off the Yellowstone. Next morning a trapper name of Howell and another fellow went out to set their traps, when a war party of threescore Blackfoots jumped them, drove them into the river, and shot after them as they swam their horses across. Howell was shot in the chest by two fusee balls. The other trapper escaped unhurt.

Howell, a hardy trapper who had come out with Nat Wyeth's first outfit, rode within half a mile of camp before he fell from his horse. We brought him in on a litter. Both Finn and Zeetlah tended to him before admitting that his wounds were beyond their skill. Howell lived about twenty hours in extreme pain but remained resolute, even amazingly cheerful. Tuttle stayed by Howell's side until the end. When it was over, he said admiringly, "Ol' Howell war one brave sumbitch! I jest hope I kin show as much sand as he done ef it ever comes to thet kind o' dyin' fer me."

We buried him that day under a big cottonwood beside the camp. From then on we called that spot Howell's Encampment in his memory, a tribute to his hardihood.

After Howell was first brought into camp, about a score of us rode out to scour the brush along Rocky Fork, looking for Blackfoots, thirsting for revenge. When we found them, they turned tail and ran, although they outnumbered us three-to-one. Píkunis aren't much for fighting face-to-face. They much prefer ambushing their enemies. It's safer.

They retreated to a small island in the crick to make their stand. We hunkered down in hidey-holes scattered along the bank, firing whenever a Blackfoot raised up to shoot. The battle lasted until dark, when we backed off, retrieved our horses, and returned to camp, bearing the body of a Nez Percé trapper. One white-eyes trapper suffered a fusee ball in the shoulder, which Zeetlah dug out and patched up, doubtless assuring him the while that it was "a long vay from yer heart"—the old man's favorite and possibly only joke.

Next morning, the island was deserted. Bloody evidence of severe Píkuni losses was everywhere, but they had secreted their dead and dragged off their wounded, hopefully somewhat wiser about messing with white-eyes.

The day after that, a dozen of us rode over to Pryor's Fork to retrieve Meek's and Crow's traps and to find out if Joe's brag about the size and sweetness of the plums growing thereabouts was true. It was. We gorged ourselves on ripe plums for half a day, then tightened our belts and loaded our shirts, front and back, with the succulent fruit to carry back to our wives and kids.

A few days later, the middle of September, it snowed 15 inches, which kept most of us indoors for a couple days, except for guard duty, which provided time to catch up on my journal, play with Ben, and help Iris and Sean with their studies.

When the snow disappeared, eight of us—my father, Turtle, Little Mountain, Tuttle, Finn, young Russell, and a long-time trapper name of Tom Hoare—left camp and rode up Rocky Fork about 25 miles and set our traps in streams nigh the mountain, keeping pretty much together the while. After we had been there about a week, a party of about fifty Absóraqas came by, on their way to steal horses from a Blackfoot village nigh the Three Forks of the Missouri. They offered no harm, stayed with us overnight, and moved on at daybreak. We had pretty well used up the beaver thereabouts, so we headed back that day to the brigade at Howell's Encampment, lest the Crows' horse raid, proving unsuccessful, they might try to make up for their loss of profit by raiding us.

About the first of October the brigade moved west to the Rosebud, where we scattered out to trap its many beaver-rich feeder streams until about the tenth, when a sudden cold snap froze the cricks nearly solid overnight and brought trapping to an abrupt halt. Bridger had moved the main camp down to the Yellowstone where he had decided to pass the winter. Since trapping was suspended, leastaways for the time being, there was naught else to do but follow him there. It proved to be a most pleasant respite. The prairie teemed with thousands of fat buffalo and we had little else to occupy us but running the big woolies every day and filling our bellies to bursting on fresh tongue and fat hump, night after night, for a fortnight, until the weather warmed in the last week of October and summoned us back to our trade.

Our bunch first set up on the east branch of Pryor's Fork, where we remained about a week, before moving northeast across about a dozen miles of broken country and coming onto a stream called Bovey's Fork that runs northeast into the Big Horn. Trapping was good and we stayed there ten days. The country thereabouts is hilly and slashed with gullies and deep swales. It abounds with buffalo, wapiti, deer, and grizzly bears, lured there by miles of succulent belly-high prairie grass, as well as thousands of acres of high-quality hops whose vines entangle the trees and low-growing shrubbery along every crick and stream. Anse Tolliver's mouth fairly watered at the sight of such a profusion of hops vines. "If I war livin' hyarabouts an' not huntin' beaver no more," he said dreamily, "I reckon I'd be mostly brewin' beer, 'stid o' jist stillin' mountain dew! Jist look at all them purty hops out thar!"

The second week of November, weather turned bone-chilling cold again and cricks froze nearly solid. We packed up and headed back to the brigade, which we found on Clark's Fork, about a mile from Howell's Encampment. We remained there until Christmas, before moving down about four miles onto the Yellowstone. Fortunately the bottoms along the river are thick with sweet cottonwoods, providing rich vittles for our critters. Buffalo had eaten nearly all the graze thereabouts, but the nourishing bark kept our stock fat and healthy.

Two large bands of Flatheads had joined our winter camp on Clark's Fork—which naturally pleased the bachelors—and both bands followed after us when we moved down to the Yellowstone. There was little else to do there besides stripping sweet cottonwood bark to feed our mules and horses, hunting buffalo and living high on fat hump and fresh tongue, and entertaining one another in our Rocky Mountain College sessions, often swapping yarns for entertainment, but also sharing useful knowledge and unexpected wisdom possessed by our remarkably diverse assortment of men from different origins and previous occupations before they came west to get rich by trapping beaver.

An extra benefit of traveling with a brigade is being relieved of nighttime horse guard duty. Bridger's campkeepers were responsible for cooking, gathering wood and keeping fires burning, and guarding livestock. Our bunch looked after our own cooking chores, but not having to rouse out of our sleeprobes to shiver in the midnight chill was a welcome benefit.

Fiddlers are always popular amongst trappers, especially in winter camp, and Anse and Irish Harry Yeats were often pleasantly well-oiled when the rest of us only wished we were. Tolliver had long ago become adept at wheedling booze from mountaineers whose hunger for music exceeded their thirst for the spirits they had squirreled away. That Anse was willing to share with Harry, or anybody, was almost a miracle.

Near the end of January 1837, buffalo were getting scarce nigh the camp, so a half dozen or so of our bunch and about that many other brigade trappers decided to ride out in search of another herd, taking along a mule or two for each man to pack our robes and carry home the meat we expected to harvest. Snow was light, only four inches deep. We traveled up Clark's Fork about a dozen miles, killed a cow for supper, and camped. Next morning, we set off towards Rocky Fork across a level plain that gradually rises to a range of hills that separates those two watercourses.

I confess that we had grown careless, myself included, rifles resting loose on our thighs, chatting as we rode along, when we came upon a narrow gulch. Suddenly the earth appeared to sprout a hundred feathered Kainahs, war cries and an ear-splitting volley of musket fire, and a shower of fusee balls. The Blackfoots were likely caught almost as much by surprise as we were, inasmuch as most of them took no time to aim.

A Company trapper name of Isaac Rose howled with pain and dropped his rifle when a musket ball shattered his elbow. A half-naked Kainah brave darted from the ravine, scooped up the weapon, fired a shot at us, and fled to safety before we could stop him, occupied as we were with wheeling our rearing mounts about and yanking wild-eyed mules into a headlong retreat, out of range of their muskets.

As we returned to camp we sorted out what we had collectively observed—about fourscore Kainah warriors had hidden themselves in that deep gully and waited until we rode within fifteen feet of them before rearing up and opening fire. A few Company hotheads, grieved that a man had been seriously wounded, maybe crippled for life, and that a rifle had been lost to the enemy, wanted to ride back and get revenge. Cooler heads prevailed, howsomever.

"Yew ain't no madder'n me, gawddammit!" Brass Turtle told them, "but I ain't abaout to be takin' on them 'ere partic'lar Blackfoots what's got us outnumbered mebbe six or seven-to-one!"

"An' neither are yew, oncet ye think on it!" Tuttle added heatedly. "We'd best be gittin' on back to camp with a whole hide, whar we kin study on haow we kin be givin' them bastards some gawddamn proper comeuppance fer what they done today!" Which we did.

Three days later, a hunter espied a party of about twenty Kainahs crossing the open plain along the Yellowstone about six miles distant from us. About a score of us, half Company men, mounted up and got there just as the enemy rode into the timber. The odds, this time, were about even. The Blackfoots had no wish to fight. They retreated into a collection of rotten old forts made of slender poles slanted into conical shapes to make their stand.

We scattered around their flimsy fortress, taking cover behind downed timber and low hillocks, and poured a withering fire into their rickety redoubts until darkness fell and increasing cold advised us to retire. One Company man received a fusee ball through the hip, which fortunately missed the bone, and a Delaware trapper called Manhead was struck in the leg by a ball which lodged under his kneecap. We didn't know at that time that the ball was poisoned. Manhead died four days afterward in great pain and was mourned by us all, especially Joe Meek and Doc, who had shared many an adventure with him.

We returned next morning to a deserted battleground and discovered a charnel house of blood and brains littering the inside of the fragile forts. Every shot we fired had whistled through the flimsy walls of rotten sticks. Half a dozen warriors were killed on the spot and had been hidden under the river ice. Another seven or eight, too badly wounded to ride or walk, had been dragged off on travois by their fellows.

It is written that revenge is sweet, but Manhead's agony and death left a bitter taste.

∾ ∾ ∾

By the fourth week of February we had moved winter camp to a high bluff overlooking the Yellowstone and the broad plains on either side of the river.

It was an excellent location from which to keep an eye on the surrounding country. Which Bridger never failed to do.

It was Gabe's custom to climb to the top of a high bluff nigh the camp each morning "so's to keep an eye out fer squalls," scanning the terrain in every direction with his spyglass. One chilly morning he came trotting back from his lofty perch looking flustered. "Time we git a move on an' commence fortin' up thi'shere camp!" he roared out. "Thar's Injuns comin' 'til hell won't have it! Comin' onter the prairie 'longside the river. They be mebbe ten mile off. Cain't tell yet jist haow many. Looks to be mebbe a thousand of 'em, mebbe more!"

The bottoms along the base of the range of steep bluffs on which we were camped were heavily timbered with large cottonwoods and not much underbrush. The steep slopes leading up from the broad plain below and the forested bottoms were bordered by rough broken hills and slashed by deep ravines and snow-filled gulches. We were well-situated for defense, but word of a thousand bloodthirsty Blackfoots on the prod spurred every man and woman to immediate action, forting up our encampment. Within minutes the ring of axes felling large trees blended with shouts and good-natured curses of trappers and high-pitched yelling of the Flatheads striving to build a breastwork around the encampment.

By time darkness fell on a bitter cold night, a six-foot-high barricade built of heavy logs and brush, surrounding an enclosure about 250 feet square was complete. Big as it was, the fort was barely able to contain the brigade, our women and kids, lodges and livestock, as well as the Flatheads and all of their people and critters, but somehow everybody doubled up and crowded inside its protective walls.

A double guard was mounted at sunset. The air turned freezing cold. Tree limbs popped like pistol shots in the arctic chill. Brass Turtle, Tuttle, and I, swathed to the ears in fur hats, *capotes*, and woolen mufflers, moccasins stuffed with buffalo hair, belching clouds of frozen breath, went on sentry duty at nine o'clock, wondering if we would be frozen solid by time our relief arrived at midnight. The sky was clear as crystal, velvety blackness harboring not so much as a wisp of cloud, stars shining with a flawless brilliance.

"Betcher glad ye din't bring yer brass monkey along wi' ye thi'shere time," Tuttle muttered through chattering teeth to nobody in particular. "This'd freeze his gawddamn bollocks off, fer damn sure!"

"Ye kin worry 'baout yer gawddamn monkey, if ye like," Turtle rejoined. "I'm jist worried abaout my own!"

I was thinking that it would take a mighty dedicated Blackfoot to be crawling up the hill through a foot of snow to get at us on a night like this, but I said nothing. Ye can never tell about Blackfoots.

About an hour into our sentry-go, the sky over the river plain suddenly lit up. Particolored lights darted and flashed in the firmament, streaming across the darkness. Finn McCool came trotting through the snow, craning his neck skyward as he shuffled toward us, his face mostly obscured in frozen breath as he exclaimed, "Ah, 'tis the aurora borealis, to be sure! What a marvelous sight it is, surely! 'Tis a gift from the Almighty Himself!"

"What say?" Tuttle demanded. "Thet'ere, up thar, be what folks be callin' ther north'ren lights hyarabaouts! Purty, ain't they?"

We stared transfixed, the bitter cold forgotten as we drank in the celestial display, red and greenish-white and pale blue beams whizzing and glimmering, sparkling, then disappearing into still another radiant spectacle. The colorful shooting and flashing slowly commenced to fade, sliding into a blood-red canopy that occupied half the sky, ending directly over the river plain below us, where the Blackfoots and their allies had been assembling all that day. Over us, the sky remained completely black, adorned with twinkling diamonds.

The crimson canopy hung over the river plain for nearly two hours, then slowly faded into blackness, by which time our relief arrived and we retreated on numbed feet to our lodges and the warm comfort of our women.

Next day we returned to our labor, strengthening our fortress on the inside with big logs propped against the previous day's barricade. "Sure'n that'll keep the bloody savages out," Paddy McBride assured anyone within earshot, "unless the haythen bastards bring up some cannons!"

When I returned to our lodge for dinner, I discovered Cat and several of our women cleaning and oiling their rifles and running a stock of rifle balls in the little cookfire in our lodge. She informed me that the others were engaged in similar occupations.

In mid-afternoon Jim Bridger and half-a-dozen men rode in from a scouting mission to announce that the enemy was camped on the river about three miles below us, a large number of them afoot, but our scouts hadn't observed any signs of an immediate attack.

"Faith an' d'ye mean to be tellin' us, after all our bloody hard work, we're to be deproived o' killin' Blackfoots," Paddy complained, "an' takin' scalps that should be our rightful reward!"   Paddy's sentiment was echoed by most of us, keyed up as we were by that time and itching for a fight.

Another uneventful night passed until dawn, when a single gunshot brought us rolling out of our robes, grabbing up *capotes* and weapons and rushing to the barricade, only to learn that a single Blackfoot bravo had crept up the mountainside and fired at Jim Bridger's Negro cook from 200 yards away and missed. The would-be assassin ran off and the cook continued his wood-gathering outside the fort.

Bridger was naturally concerned about the enemy getting that close to us. He sent a Spaniard name of Maselino up to his lookout post. As the Spaniard drew nigh Jim's aerie, another Blackfoot popped up. Maselino turned a backward somersault and leapt onto a fifty-foot slide down the snowy bluff. The Blackfoot's fusee ball nicked his heel just as he jumped, but he was otherwise unhurt.

About half-an-hour later, word came that Blackfoots were approaching on the river ice, long, closely-packed columns of them. They came within about 400 yards of us before they turned onto the plain and halted. A chief wrapped in a white blanket stepped forward and signed that he would not fight that day in that place and that he would return to his village now. They turned away then and headed off in a northwesterly direction towards the Three Forks of the Missouri. We watched them go—about eleven hundred of them—a vast collection of Káinahs, Píkunis, and Síksikas, with a healthy sprinkling of their hangers-on Big-belly Atsínas amongst them. We viewed their departure with mixed feelings, relieved that our wives and children, critters and plunder would now be safe, yet assailed by a gnawing regret that all of our hard labor building the fort had been for naught. Most of us felt that we had been cheated out of a well-deserved fight.

Naturally all the cookfire palaver that day and night concerned why the Blackfoots had gone off without offering to fight. Some maintained that the strength of our fortifications had convinced them that an assault would be too costly, but those of us who had been in those parts long enough to learn a little something about Indian thinking reckoned that the startling events in the heavens two nights before had persuaded the chief and his counselors that their attack had been cursed with bad medicine. The red sky on their side betokened blood and sure defeat of their forces, while the clear sky on ours assured the white-eyes and our allies of victory at little cost to us. Even their two sneak attacks had come to nothing, which was likely regarded as another omen of our divine protection.

About a week later, on the last day of February, the brigade packed up and started for the Big Horn through six inches of snow, which somewhat slowed our progress. We arrived at the mouth of Bovey's Fork eight days later, about 15 miles below the lower Big Horn Mountain, where a multitude of buffalo congregated, providing us with a wealth of meat and easy living, much more meat than we could consume. Drying racks in every camp and trappers' mess sagged under loads of fat buffalo flesh.

Weather had warmed and we enjoyed a plenitude of leisure time for playing outdoor ball games, running foot races, wrestling matches, and joining in on Indian winter games. Harry Yeats, the Irish harpooner, delighted in teaching our own youngsters and a platoon of Indian kids from the Flathead camps how to throw a lance through a hoop rolling across the snowy prairie, conducting contests, and rewarding the winners with foofurraw.

Our idyllic wintertime holiday from care came to an abrupt halt after only a week. Our scouts reported a Crow village moving down the Big Horn in our direction. Games halted immediately. A well-armed mounted group rode out to meet them and a large work party proceeded to fortify the camp. We had entered country the Absóraqas consider their own and it is always best to be cautious and well-prepared when dealing with that nation. Crow hospitality blows hot and cold. It is unwise to bet your life on last week's friendship with them.

"Best we be puttin' on our war-faces if it's Crows a-comin'," Brass Turtle advised. "Ye know haow they be, struttin' an' pushin' ye 'round if they think they kin git away with it."

"Yep, an' crawlin' an' kissin' yer arse, oncet ye show 'em who's boss," Tuttle added, "pervidin' ye got guns enough to back it up!"

When our scouting party returned they were accompanied by several Crow chiefs and an American Fur Company trader named James Kipp. After they smoked and parleyed with Bridger and took a good look around our encampment, sizing up our defenses and our well-armed numbers, they returned to their own village about three miles upriver.

Next morning they moved into our neighborhood, about 300 yards off, some 200 lodges and about that many warriors. The village was called Longhair's band, after their principal chief, an old man of eighty winters, whose hair is nearly twelve feet long, done up in a huge queue nigh two feet long and six inches thick. He would have been the idol of my old enemy Pretty-on-top. The old man was afflicted with dropsy, an ailment rarely seen amongst plains Indians, which severely bloated his body and limbs.

Fortunately there were more than enough buffalo thereabouts to satisfy the needs of both the Crows and our brigade, so we avoided friction on that score. Naturally we doubled and sometimes tripled our nighttime horse guard, for Absóraqas are accomplished horse thieves. All mountain Indians steal horses, of course, but Crows take particular pride in their skill and daring in that activity.

I got to know the AmFur trader Kipp halfway well during Longhair's stay nearby. He was an affable chap, originally from Canada, who had been sent to Fort William after Josh Pilcher's successful hard-bargaining the previous summer. Kipp's current mission was drumming up Absóraqa business in plews and robes for AmFur's new outpost, saving the Crows the much longer hike to Fort Union.

Longhair's people stayed with us about ten days before moving six miles downriver. We pulled out a week later, on April first, to commence our spring hunt, starting some ten miles up Bovey's Fork, then moving another twenty miles farther upstream a few days later, delighting the while in the rich, deep-furred plews that the severe winter had bestowed.

One morning, after they ran their traplines, Little Mountain, my father, Pretty Horse, and Half-horse set out in search of buffalo in the surrounding hills, where they were attacked by a dozen Blackfoots who lay in wait for them, thinking they were easy prey because they were riding with their rifles slung across their back. When the enemy rose up and commenced to take aim with their muskets, all four of our people yanked out their pistols and opened fire, killing one Síksika on the spot and wounding three more. The rest, rattled at the unexpected response, fired at random and took to their heels while our bunch unslung their rifles and winged a few more of the fleeing assassins. The only damage our side sustained was a packhorse slightly wounded in the neck. Little Mountain claimed the scalp.

❧   ❧   ❧

A week or so after that we returned to Howell's Encampment at the mouth of Rocky Fork, where we received a pleasant surprise. That whole country was crowded with buffalo driven in that direction by Longhair's Crow village. Next day we raised a cache of plews and plunder we had hidden the previous November, before scattering out to trap the surrounding streams. One good-sized crew of a dozen Company trappers and two campkeepers crossed the Yellowstone to trap the cricks that feed the Musselshell, while the rest of us headed out in all directions from the brigade's main camp.

Our bunch ascended Rocky Fork about twenty miles but discovered too much snow and ice thereabouts to allow trapping until it thawed. We contented ourselves the next several days with feasting on the mobs of buffalo that roamed that neighborhood. We never did get to trap that place, for a week later Bridger's whole brigade camp moved in and our bunch retreated another dozen miles upstream to resume trapping.

Beaver were plentiful in that neighborhood, but so were Blackfoots. Hardly a day passed by without one or another of us espying a war party passing through. One day Tuttle and I were hiking through the trees and heavy brush that bordered the crick in which we had set our traps when we came upon two conical forts of the Blackfoot sort, smoke rising from their peaks. We tarried a spell in silence. When nobody stirred, we entered and found the owners had departed no more than half an hour before. "Blackfoots're gittin' too gawddamn common hyarabaouts," Tuttle opined. "Wouldn't be s'prisin' ef'n find one hidin' in muh britchclout, next time I look!"

The trapping party from the Musselshell straggled back to the brigade at the end of April, much the worse for wear. One trapper had been killed and several seriously wounded. They had lost most of their horses and traps to the Blackfoots, as well as most of their plews.

When the enemy wasn't trying to ambush individual trappers running their traplines, they dogged our camps in darkness to steal horses that had gotten loose from their pickets or hobbles. An oft-heard homily was "It's better to be countin' ribs than tracks," meaning that it is preferable that your horse goes hungry, if need be, than trying to track him after an Indian steals him.

The brigade left Howell's Encampment on the first of May and commenced to trap our way south past Clark's Fork, Stinking River, and the Grey Bull Fork of the Big Horn, then along the Medicine Lodge before ascending to the top of Big Horn Mountain, where we ate well, thanks to the great number of curly-horn sheep that abide there. Much of that country is broken by spurs off the mountains and slashed by deep gullies bare of timber except along the watercourses.

The brigade descended Big Horn Mountain on its south side in mid-May and camped on a small branch of Wind River, which was running high in the spring runoff, as were most of the streams thereabouts, which made all trapping difficult and often impossible. In the fourth week of May, Russell and Tom Hoare returned to the main camp in a most undignified hurry, reporting that a war party of eighty Blackfeet had chased them back to the safety of the brigade.

Next day we moved to the North Fork of the Popo Azhieh, then to the Middle Fork a day later, and to the oil spring the day after that, where a gallon of pure coal oil bubbles out of the ground every hour and puddles in a shallow ditch before it runs some 30 feet into the South Fork, lending a rainbow hue to the water.

Anse Tolliver swears that imbibing coal oil is a first-rate cure for rheumatism. I was tempted to try Anse's nostrum, for I had lately occasionally been afflicted in my movements by that ailment, especially early in the day. Rheumatism is an all-too-common complaint amongst trappers, who spend the cold half of the year wading up to our hips in icy cricks and ponds. A single sip of that vile-tasting liquid, howsomever, convinced me to put up with my aches and pains.

That is beautiful country, lush with tall-growing grass lavishly sprinkled with colorful spring flowers. Far out in the west the Wind River Mountains rise abruptly from a low range of foothills, ascending to snowcapped peaks rising high above garlands of rosy cloud in the soft mid-day sunshine. Looking eastwards, the fertile Wind River plain rolls out seemingly forever until it blends into a low range of hills betwixt Wind River and the Powder.

The brigade stayed at the oil spring eight days, through the end of May, enjoying warm spring weather and a plentiful supply of game critters. Plews were measly by then, not worth taking, so we made the most of our leisure. Bunches of fat young buffalo bulls roamed the prairie in all directions, an attractive invitation to mountaineers to run some of them after months of tending to our proper trade. It was a temptation too alluring to resist.

Half a dozen of our bunch headed out to indulge in our favorite sport, too long postponed. I was riding Coffee, my preferred buffalo runner, although my *grulla* gelding Crane is almost equally swift and just as reliable in the chase. Tuttle and Brass Turtle rode on either side of me, carrying on their customary banter, trading quips and mild insults intended to provoke the other into a humorous exchange of ever more outrageous jibes and retorts. "Take care ye don't fall off your hoss, Tuttle," Turtle counseled with mock concern. "Ye know it's been a spell since ye been runnin' buffler an' ye likely forgot haow by naow."

"Hmmph!" my Kentucky friend retorted. "I reckon I'll be gittin' my own buffler fust, like allus, an' be pickin' yew up off'n ther ground on ther way back, also like allus!"

Their harmless mockery continued in that vein until we came in sight of a likely bunch of two-year-old bulls herded along by a hulking old seed bull that had been driven off his harem by a younger, stronger patriarch. "See that old bull, Tuttle?" Brass Turtle said with a smirk, reining up and pointing. "That'll be you purty soon, Kaintuck, all alone an' runnin' with young boys, if ye don't quit yer whorin' an' settle on jist one woman an' gitcherse'f a lodge o' yer own."

Tuttle snorted with disdain. "Hell! I ain't near so selfish as ther two o' yew! Ye'd have me deprivin' all o' them'ere prairie flowers o' what I got to offer an' givin' it all to jest one woman what cou'n't handle thet much ef'n I did!"

Their teasing was interrupted by Little Mountain, McCool, and Half-horse riding up to join us. Jean-Luc followed behind, the halter-shanks of half-a-dozen packmules in hand. We were downwind of the bunch we had settled on to run. Hampered as buffalo are with poor eyesight, they hadn't yet identified us. They continued grazing undisturbed.

Bunched up and picking our way across the prairie at a slow walk, lest we spook the buffalo by rapid movement, we steadily closed the distance. The terrain was becoming increasingly broken, sliced here and there by deep swales and steep-sided coulees. As we drew near the bunch I saw that we had chosen well. The young bulls were sleek and rolling fat from abundant springtime graze. The old bull, his hide scarred from a hundred old battles defending his harem and patchy with half-discarded wintertime hair, suddenly threw up his massive head and screeched out a warning, then threw himself into a lumbering run to safety. Unlike cows that tend to run more or less bunched up, the young bulls scattered but ran in the same general direction.

I chose my quarry, touched Coffee lightly with a spur and turned him loose, guiding him only lightly with the rein until he fixed upon my intended prey. Coffee appeared to thrill as much as I, springing into the chase. He required no urging. He stretched his powerful muscles into a ground-eating gallop that had my moccasins scraping the ground as he flattened his stride in pursuit of the stout young bull.

We soon outdistanced my companions, whose mounts were unable to match Coffee's speed, but they trailed behind on the same general course. As we closed on my bull, my rifle slung across my back, I pulled a pistol from my saddle holster and prepared to draw alongside for my shot, when suddenly the bull simply disappeared. Before I could check him, Coffee spilled into a deep coulee, falling all topsy-turvy, belly skywards, legs flailing, loosing a terrified scream as he plummeted downwards, flinging me from the saddle when he crashed onto the dazed young buffalo sprawled in the narrow coulee, thereby breaking his fall.

I landed heavily on my back, slumped against the bank, gasping for breath, a red haze fogging my vision, the pistol knocked from my grasp. My main concern was for my horse scrabbling in the narrow gully to regain his feet, when I saw an Indian run up and grab his bridle as he struggled upright. I lunged for my pistol lying a yard away, when I felt a white-hot burning across my shoulder, nigh my neck, and saw a second Blackfoot, closer to me, pointing a smoking musket at me, white teeth flashing a wicked grin in his black-and-red-painted face. He dropped his musket and dived for the pistol, snatching it away just as my fingertips brushed it.

He fumbled with the hammer on the unfamiliar percussion weapon. I heaved myself at him, only to be knocked back with a stinging blow to the temple when he swung the long barrel at my head. Groggy, my back against the steep bank, fingers clawing for my belly gun, I dimly saw him cock the pistol and swing it up to aim, when the Blackfoot suddenly disappeared in a tangle of thrashing arms and legs. It all happened in a blink—bodies struggling in the cramped confines of the gulch, a surprised howl mingling with Christian curses, a pistol shot, then another, the bodies sagging, twitching, coming to rest, followed by the sharp crack of a rifle, then two more. Then silence.

I fought to regain my feet, succeeding just as Brass Turtle slid down the steep slope and joined me. He bestowed a cursory glance on my bleeding wound, grunted, and turned to the bodies laced in combat, both unmoving now. He bent to lift the one on top and exclaimed, "He's alive! Tuttle's breathin'! He ain't dead!"

I dropped to my knees and helped drag Tuttle off the lifeless Blackfoot. Tuttle's pistol shot had entered under the chin and shattered the pate, totally destroying the scalp. We hauled Tuttle free and propped him against the sloping bank, trying in vain to stem the blood pumping from the smoke-blackened wound in his chest and a much larger one in back.

Little Mountain and McCool joined us in the coulee. Half-horse remained with Jean-Luc above, lest we be surprised by still more Blackfoots.

"No more Pée-koo-nee sumbitches 'round hyar no more," Little Mountain announced. "See?" He elaborated his report by swinging a fistful of three fresh scalps in our direction, sprinkling blood drops as he did so.

Finn hastily examined Tuttle's wound, shook his head somberly, then clambered up the bank to obtain whatever medical supplies he carried in his saddlebags. As he departed, Tuttle's eyelids fluttered, then opened. His gaze swept the faces of the three of us hovered over him before he wheezed, "Purty bad, ain't it?" Nobody answered. "Thought so, hurts like hell," he said huskily, a trickle of blood dribbling from the corner of his mouth. Then, "Whar's Finn?"

"Gone up fer somethin' to bind up yer gunshot hole," Turtle answered. "He'll be back purty quick."

"Good," Tuttle muttered through a liquid gurgle. "Quick naow, afore he gits back. Don't want no thankees. Whar's Temple?" He moved his head enough to see me. "Ol' pard, git out paper an' ther pencil ye allus got in yer poke. Quick naow! Thar's sum'pin' needs signin'. I ain't got much time."

I was already digging in my belt-poke for a pencil and the couple sheets of foolscap I always carry with me. I waved the paper in front of him and asked, "What d'ye need this for, Tuttle?"

"I need to be writin' muh name on it, naow, while I still kin. Then I'll tell ye."

Brass Turtle sputtered something in Delaware and Mountain squatted in front of Tuttle, offering his broad back as a writing table. Turtle braced Tuttle upright and I placed the pencil in his trembling hand and held the paper steady, pointing at the bottom of the sheet where he should sign. Which he did, inscribing his name, Tuttle Thompson, in shaky but legible letters. When he completed the final letter, he dropped the pencil, slumped against the bank, grinning at me past bloody teeth, murmuring, "Thar naow, thet's done!

Ain'tcha glad ye larnt me readin' an' writin'?" I nodded and grinned back at him. I was unable to speak. He spat out a mouthful of blood, then, "No time to waste. Thet'ere's muh will an' I'm leavin' it all to Finn McCool, ever' scrap of it. Ye kin write it up proper-like when ye kin. Finn wants to go to doctorin' school, like Whitman. Thar oughta be enough 'mongst muh possibles an' 'speshly with Chouteau in Sain' Looie fer payin' his way." He commenced coughing and spat out another gob of clotted blood. He grinned again and said, "Thar's a fair nest egg thar. With what I made gamblin', I hardly never spent much o' muh trappin' money."

McCool returned just then and Tuttle pursed his lips, as if to tell us not to inform Finn of his good fortune until later. The Irishman busied himself doing what he could to stanch the blood leaking from the chest wound and the much larger hole in his back. Tuttle, growing weaker, looked around at our grieving faces and said, "Don'tcha be frettin' none 'baout me goin' under. Reckon it's time. What'd a trapper like me be doin' back in Kaintuck or Missourah when thar ain't no beaver left fer trappin' hyarabaouts? It's time. Gittin' dark naow." His gaze fixed on me. "S'long, Pard. We had ther best of it." He closed his eyes and the best friend I will ever have was gone.

∾ ∾ ∾

We rode separately back to camp, keeping apart, each man wrapped in his own thoughts. It isn't seemly for men to show tears. Only Jean-Luc let his tears flow, unabashed in his grief, but Frenchmen aren't afflicted with our phony stoicism. There is no profit in describing here what I was feeling on that ride back. If the reader can't imagine what I felt at the loss of the man who had been my protector, mentor, champion, guide from boyhood into manhood, and the elder brother I had never had, then he hasn't been paying attention throughout these four books.

It wasn't until we got back in camp that I was able to learn what my companions had observed on the prairie when a buffalo, my horse, and I apparently disappeared into thin air. "Fust thing we know," Brass Turtle related, "Temple and the whole shebang—his hoss an' the buffler, too—jist ain't thar no more! One minute he's out thar, runnin' like hell in front o' the rest of us, an' then he ain't! None of 'em! Natcherly we pull up, tryin' to figger out what's happened, when we hear a shot.

"We ride like hell up to thi'shere big gulch ye cain't see 'til you're almost in it an' jump off the hosses an' run up to the edge an' look daown, whar we see Temple layin' on his back an' a Blackfoot aimin' a pistol at 'im an' a coupl'a more Blackfoots runnin' up to git into it theirownse'fs. Tuttle must'a figgered thar warn't no time fer waitin'—an' thar warn't! He grabs up his pistol an' jumps off the top—ten-'leven feet, mebbe more—an' lands plumb on top o' that'ere Blackfoot what's set on killin' Temple. That'ere Blackfoot war tougher'n most, an' Tuttle fallin' on 'im don't kill 'im right off, so they roll abaout fightin' a spell afore both their guns go off. Arter that, nobody war movin' much a-tall.

"Meantime, the rest of us war runnin' up an' daown that'ere ditch, shootin' daown at t'other Injuns still daown thar. Thar war only three more of 'em still hidin' out an' we got 'em all."

Turtle went on to describe Tuttle's last few minutes, which I won't repeat here. He didn't mention the will and McCool's inheritance, which was nobody's affair but Finn's. I will resume his account after Tuttle's death.

"Natcherly, arter we kilt them Píkunis an' took ever'thin' wuth takin' off 'em, we still had to git Temple's purty hoss out o' thar, so we run along that'ere ditch 'til it run daown to a shaller place, whar we come onto four more hosses what use'ta b'long to them'ere Píkunis, what don't need 'em no more, natcherly, so we took 'em along, too."

Starved as mountaineers are for amusement in the wilderness, even an account of the death of a comrade is welcome entertainment if it's well-told. Brass Turtle made the most of it and I enjoyed his narrative along with the rest of the brigade.

Turtle, Finn, Little Mountain, and I buried Tuttle deep in the woods near the oil spring, clad in his favorite red shirt and wrapped in his best capote. I placed his greasy deck of cards in his bosom as a final gesture. Brass Turtle nodded his approval and predicted, "Them cards'll likely keep ol' Tuttle out o' hell, if he kin talk Sain' Peter into a game of Ol' Sledge fer decidin' whar he oughta send 'im."

Finn volunteered to read some words from the Bible over the grave, but Turtle and I blocked the Irishman's well-meant intention. Tuttle would have scorned such ceremonies. We reckoned it was up to us to protect him from rituals he had disdained in life.

Tuttle's belt-poke and his possibles had yielded a surprising cache of gold and silver coin, finger-rings, jeweled cravat pins, and the like, convincing testimony to my old comrade's consummate skill at the hand game and cards and the gullibility of greenhorn hostlers and newcomers to the trade. Seasoned trappers knew better.

Brass Turtle and I handed the treasure over to McCool at the gravesite, along with Tuttle's will witnessed by the two of us, and we told him what Tuttle's last wishes had been, which left our usually talkative Irishman totally speechless, as ye might imagine such news would do.

∾ ∾ ∾

Jim Bridger ordered the brigade onto the trail next day, which especially pleased our bunch. We had no wish to remain in that neighborhood. Naturally somebody set fire to the oil spring as we rode out of camp, sending a dense cloud of black smoke skywards. McCool swiveled in the saddle and looked back. "'Tis a fitting farewell to Tuttle," he said solemnly, brushing a hand across his eyes, "rather loike the auld Vikings burnin' a galley fer a chief an' sendin' 'im out to sea."

It was by then the third day of June 1837, too warm for trapping, time to head for Horse Creek on the Seeds-kee-dee and rendezvous.

∾ ∾ ∾

Two days travel brought us to the first apparently deserted Blackfoot lodge that we encountered on the trail. It turned out to contain the bodies of nine Pikunis, men, women, and two children. Finn McCool determined that they had died of smallpox. He and Zeetlah put their heads together for a spell before they called a council amongst our bunch, men and women both, and advised that all of our people who hadn't been vaccinated in California immediately do so now. Such decisions are not easily come by amongst folks who are generally healthy, but their deathly fear of smallpox was a powerful persuader. That so many of us, whites and Delawares alike, had already been vaccinated with no ill effects was a potent argument. Even our always-suspicious Iroquois let Finn and Zeetlah scratch their arms with the mysterious concoction they brewed from serum obtained from the dead Pikunis.

The procedure delayed our travel by a full day, so we hastened in pursuit of the rest of the brigade, which had proceeded without us. On the way, we came across several deserted lodges that contained Blackfoot bodies, all felled by smallpox. On the second day, we caught up with the brigade, which had tarried on its way in order for some hotheads to attack a Blackfoot village, most of its people stricken with smallpox.

To their credit, Jim Bridger, Joe Meek, Carson, and Russell, along with a few other old hands, chose to sit out that one-sided battle.

-oOo-

CHAPTER XVIII
DECISIONS

1837 Rendezvous

During the ten days it took to travel to Horse Creek, the sun failed to shine with summery golden warmth, prairies lacked their brilliant verdure, spring flowers faded from their vibrant hues, the laughter of my fellows rang hollow in my ears, even Cat and my children were beyond my reach. By time we reached New Fork, a day before our arrival on the Seeds-kee-dee, I had taken to spending most of my free time with my horses, doctoring imaginary hurts I kept discovering, first on Coffee as a result of his spectacular plunge into the coulee, then on my other critters whenever I required a further excuse to absent myself from the society of my comrades.

Brass Turtle rode over to the pasture where I was treating Crane for a stone bruise that didn't really exist. He stepped down from his horse and squatted beside me before he challenged, "Haow long d'ye figger on hidin' inside yerse'f afore ye really b'lieve that Tuttle's gone an' ain't never comin' back?"

Naturally I declared that I didn't know what in hell he was talking about, but it did no good.

"Ye know damn well what I'm sayin'! Ye ride by yer lonesome most o' the day an' then ye hide amongst yer critters ever' night, mopin' 'til dark, 'til it's time to go to yer robes, so ye won't hafta talk to nobody! It's hurtin' yer woman an' yer young'uns don't hardly know ye nowadays!"

I mumbled something about not doing anything of the sort, but the words stuck in my throat.

He said a lot more in the same vein before he demanded, "What makes ye think behavin' like thi'shere's gonna change what happened? Tuttle's gone an' it hurts like hell, but hurtin' yerse'f an' ever'body around ye ain't never gonna bring 'im back! Nothin' will!"

Something he said made something break inside. "Goddammit, Turtle, he died savin' me!" Suddenly hot tears commenced to flow. I turned away, ashamed to let another man see me crying.

Turtle refused to quit. "An' yew would'a done the same fer him! Ye know ye would! Ever'body knows ye would'a t'run yer life away fer Tuttle, jist like he done fer yew. Tuttle knew it, too! So ask yerse'f this—War it wuth Tuttle dyin' jist so yew could mope yerse'f to death grievin' over him, 'stead o' keepin' on livin' the kind o' life yew an' him war so good at? He gave ye that! Use it!"

Still turned away, hiding my wet face, I heard him stand up, swing onto his horse, and ride off without another word.

I have no idea how long I stayed in the pasture, pondering Turtle's words, probing my own thoughts and feelings until I used them up, letting tears come until I had none left to cry, until I felt strangely lighter, even younger. The sun had disappeared. I found my way to the crick bank, where I bathed my face and swollen eyes in the spring-chilled water before I trotted back to the lodge, eager to feel Cat's warmth, to inhale her fragrance, to blend her strength with my own. She welcomed me into our robes silently, for there was nothing to say, only to feel, only to share.

~   ~   ~

When I returned from my morning bathe with Micah and our Indians, I saw that Cat had laid out my most festive garments to wear for our entry into rendezvous, an appropriate match for her own splendid outfit and that of Iris. Even young Ben was togged out in new clothes, fringed leggin's and britchclout surmounted by a fancy beaded war shirt that reached past his knees. He looked so grown-up that I resolved to teach him to ride his own horse before rendezvous was over.

Breaking our fast that morning was a celebratory affair with strong sweet coffee and flapjacks made from the last of the coffee beans, sugar, and flour that Kathleen had jealously hoarded from last year's rendezvous, slathered with wild honey that Half-horse had gathered at a cost of numerous bee-stings. The children chirped and chattered in high good spirits that had been too long absent from our lodge and Cat hummed quietly as she went about her chores. It felt as if I were being welcomed back from a long journey. Which was pretty much the case.

Our bunch possessed a holiday air as we rode the final few miles beside the Seeds-kee-dee to the mouth of Horse Creek. The women vied to outshine one another with their colorful costumes and horse trappings. Most of our men were togged out in their go-to-meetin' best. Cat and Iris rode their freshly-groomed *palomilla* mares decked out with elaborate quilled apishamores jingling with shiny hawk bells and brass thimbles, bridles and breast-collars decorated with sparkling silver coins and gleaming silver-plated bridle bits, creamy manes flowing in the fresh morning breeze.

My Coffee horse, fully recovered from his horrendous tumble into the coulee, got caught up in the spirit of the occasion, our grand entrance into rendezvous, reflected in his arched neck and sprightly gait as we passed by the camps of trappers and Indian bands who had arrived before us.

The trapper camps contained a generous sampling of humanity—white-eyes Americans, Delawares and Shawnees, and Canadian French-Crees, lavishly sprinkled with Irish, Scots, Dutch, German, and English, alongside villages of full-blood Indians of nearly every Rocky Mountain tribe and nation. Whilst their women went about their chores, the men, white and Indian alike, amused themselves with cards, dice, or the Indian hand game, horse racing, shooting at a mark, or gathered in small groups for gossip or spinning tall tales.

In a way I regretted that our bunch no longer entered rendezvous in a joyous hell-for-leather stampede, as we used to do in our early days, but I had to admit that such an entrance would be ill-advised nowadays with our several trundling travois loaded with yammering youngsters.

We separated from Bridger's brigade at the mouth of Horse Creek, where Jim established camp to await the arrival of supplies from the settlements. We continued a few miles upstream to our previous campground, which, we were pleased to find, was still unoccupied. Circumstance conspired to make our welcome complete. As we approached the old camp we spied, far up the valley, a small herd of buffalo grazing on belly-high grass, which deep winter snows and generous springtime rainfall had bestowed on the land.

Whilst the women and the campkeepers unloaded the pack animals and children scattered out to gather firewood under the cottonwoods that bordered the crick, a half-dozen of us led packmules up the valley to harvest young bulls. It was too early for cows, still scrawny from nursing springtime calves, but nobody disdained tender young bull, especially after dining mostly on jerkmeat stews on the trail for the previous fortnight.

❧   ❧   ❧

It was still only mid-June, too early to expect the packtrain from Missouri, although there is never a sure way to predict when the traders will show up. This year and likely in future there would be only one American trader, American Fur, now the property of Pierre Chouteau, Cadet and his French Creole partners in Saint Louis. Its only competition was the Hudson's Bay Company, whose minions harbor no love for American trappers and show it. The Indian trade is their main interest and the superior quality of their English-made goods assure them of most of the redman's custom.

Early July was the soonest that we could sensibly expect the arrival of supplies from the States. Naturally every American hoped it would occur before Independence Day, in order to celebrate our nation's freedom from British tyranny with a mind-numbing drunken spree.

I lost no time in keeping my promise to teach young Ben to ride, which effort Kathleen warmly applauded. Our son had grown too big and was entirely too active for her to be carrying him all day long upon her saddle bow. Half-horse shared my chore. He combed through the large herd of Iron Bow and Fast Horse until he found a suitable eight-year-old piebald gelding endowed with commonsense and a gentle disposition, a bare hand taller than pony-size. Whilst the young Delaware was working out whatever behavior kinks the new horse might still possess, I traded for a small Spaniard saddle from a trapper whose son had outgrown it, then adapted it so that Ben's short legs would fit comfortably and solidly in the stirrups, the key to establishing in a new rider a firm and balanced seat for the rest of his lifetime. I was determined to start Ben off correctly. It had worked with Iris and she makes me proud every time I see her a-horseback.

Ben was absolutely giddy with excitement when he first saw his splashy-hided piebald and realized that the critter would be his own. For the first week or so, he named the animal something different every day, sometimes several times a day, finally settling on a Salish word that means something like "Rags" or "Tatters," which seems appropriate for a high-colored piebald.

My headstrong young son surprised me with the attention he devoted to his riding lessons, curbing his customary madcap impulses and striving mightily to follow my instructions regarding his posture, weight in the stirrups, adapting to the horse's gait, and suchlike. Cat and I both had let him hold the reins when he rode with us. Now I discovered that he had little to learn in that regard. He was both firm and gentle in his commands. "The lad surely has Irish hands," Finn pronounced approvingly. My rash and reckless three-year-old had been paying attention all along.

It was a pleasure now to take Ben along when I visited other camps, having him riding by my side, proudly perched atop his little Spaniard saddle, feet firmly planted in the stirrups, carefully neck-reining Rags around sagebrush clumps and such, although I still kept hold of a lead-rope attached to his horse's halter, just in case.

Fortunately I chose to forego the pleasure of Ben's company the day Kathleen and I visited Bridger's brigade to learn if there had been any news of the supply train. Cat had busied herself with domestic chores since our arrival. She deserved a holiday and an opportunity to gossip with Meek's beautiful Shoshone wife Umentucken. They had bonded even closer than before over the last two winter hunts, their friendship clinched forever by Cat's assisting Umentucken in the birth of Joe's daughter, now nearly two years old.

Ben objected hardly at all at being left behind. When he wasn't tagging at my heels, he became Half-horse's pint-size shadow as the young Delaware went about his horse-training doin's, his second-favorite recreation.

Our pleasant horseback stroll in summer sunshine was punctuated harshly by a hornets' nest of angry commotion in Bridger's camp. I tethered our mounts whilst Kathleen joined the Mountain Lamb at the edge of a crowd of boiling-mad white and Indian trappers. When I returned I caught Doc Newell by the arm and asked what the hullabaloo was all about.

"Gawddamn Bannocks agin, that's what!" he replied heatedly. "Stinkin' sumbitches allus makin' trouble! Naow they be at it agin! Stealin' hosses, like allus! This time they stole a passel of 'em off o' some of our Napercy trappers, thinkin' they kin git away with it! Cain't tolerate sich doin's, nohow!" He stomped off, fuming.

Just then I spied a cluster of our own men on the far side of the crowded alleyway that ran between the tents and lodges. I elbowed my way through the noisy throng and plucked at Finn McCool's sleeve to get his attention. "What's goin' on, Finn?" I demanded. "What's happ'nin'?"

"Ah, Temple," he replied with a broad smile, "ye've come just in toime fer gainin' some pers'nal satisfaction, I do b'lieve." When I shook my head in puzzlement, he went on. "'Tis the bloody Bannocks again. Sixty lodges of 'em showed up three days past an' set up about three miles off." He waved in the direction of the Seeds-kee-dee. "Then, first thing the blaggards do is steal a dozen good horses off some o' Bridger's Nez Percé trappers an' dared 'em to try takin' 'em back. Gabe told the trappers he'd protect 'em if they could recover their property. Which they did, early this mornin', whilst the Bannocks were out chasin' buffler."

Finn pointed past the crowd of trappers. I saw half a dozen Nez Percés holding a dozen or so horses by lead-ropes and *reatas*. Several of the critters appeared to be first-rate animals, one tall white horse in particular. McCool continued his account. "Now, we're hearin', the Bannocks are on their way here, armed to the teeth, makin' threats, demandin' their bloody property be returned to 'em!" He grinned, but it contained no mirth. "But ye don't see anyone hereabouts runnin' off, now do ye?"

Whilst Finn was informing me of the situation, Jim Bridger stepped out of his lodge, followed by Jim, his Negro cook. Both of them were armed, as were the rest of us. A trapper is rarely without his rifle close at hand. When the Nez Percé trappers saw Gabe, they came forward leading the horses. The trapper leading the tall white horse handed the *reata* to Bridger and signed that they were turning over all of the horses for safe-keeping, but that special animal was a personal gift to Gabe, then stepped back amongst his fellows.

Just then we were treated to the spectacle of thirty or more painted Bannock warriors thundering into camp a-horseback, flourishing muskets, bows, and lances and brandishing war clubs, screaming threats, crowding their mounts through the press of trappers standing nigh the booshway's lodge. I doubt the Bannocks expected to be greeted by so many armed trappers, but they tried to bluff their way through.

Their chief, an ugly, pockmarked ruffian, forced his painted pony past the assembled mountaineers, heading for Bridger, who stood calmly, his rifle slung, holding his white horse by the *reata*, a half-smile on his lips. The chief gigged his mount forward, trampling the *reata*, leaned down, and jerked the rope out of Bridger's hand. Which was the last thing that savage ever did on this earth. Jim the cook swung up his rifle and shot him through the breast. As the chief tumbled backwards off his pony, two more galena pills thudded into him. The astonished Bannocks fired off a volley of musketry aimed in no particular direction and loosed a shower of arrows from their bows, most of which rattled harmlessly to earth.

One arrow, howsomever, struck Umentucken in the breast, where she stood alongside Kathleen, piercing her heart and killing her instantly. An anguished blood-chilling oath roared out in a mighty voice over the crowded alleyway as she fell, freezing mountaineers and Bannocks alike in their tracks for a split-second. Joe Meek raced through the crowd like a charging bull, sending men sprawling in his haste to reach his woman. He shouldered Kathleen aside as he knelt to take the limp form in his arms and bent to kiss the still features, only to lift his face an instant later and loose a murderous howl that promised bloody revenge.

Panic overtook the Bannocks. A dozen of their number toppled from their saddles in a hailstorm of rifle fire. The rest struggled to wheel their horses amid the surging mob of trappers, half of whom were trying to take aim at the fleeing enemy, whilst the other half ran for their critters in order to pursue them. I joined the pursuers, leaping onto Crane and spurring him into a gallop almost from a standstill, images of a dying Rainbow and Mountain Lamb and a grinning Bannock killer from years before swirling in my head.

My powerful *grulla* horse loosed his tremendous strength, glorying in the thrill of the chase, soon leaving the trappers behind and rapidly closing on the fleeing Bannocks. As we drew nigh a trailing warrior in the fleeing horde, drumming his heels on his pony's ribs, furiously lashing him with a rawhide *cuarta*, I unslung my rifle, dropped the rein on Crane's neck, leaned out to shove the muzzle under my enemy's flailing arm, and literally blew him out of the saddle.

He turned a cartwheel in the air, arms and legs thrashing wildly, landed on his head, and lay in a crumpled heap. I slowed Crane's pounding gallop, swung him in a wide arc, and brought him to a halt in order to reload, regretting the while that I had left my pistols in camp. As the mob of mountaineers swept past, I glimpsed a wild-eyed Joe Meek flogging his lathered mule in a desperate attempt to overtake the enemy. He was flanked by Brass Turtle and Little Mountain with Doc Newell, McCool, and Judge Russell galloping close behind. I fell in with the pursuing company, which by that time numbered more than a triple score of trappers and campkeepers.

Our pell-mell pace soon consumed the scant three miles to the Bannock village, where the miscreants attempted to mount a resistance, but in vain. Our superior force of well-armed men goaded by outrage at the senseless death of Umentucken and the insult offered by the arrogant Bannocks soon overwhelmed their flimsy defenses. They retreated to a small island in the Seeds-kee-dee, which wasn't the wisest strategy they might have employed. While half of our force plundered the village, the rest of us surrounded the island from the banks on either side of the river and proceeded to pick off any chop-haired Bannock who dared lift his head into view. Even nightfall granted them no relief. A full moon cast a warm yellow glow on the river's surface, so that it was an easy matter to espy an enemy warrior attempting to swim to safety and send him to a watery grave. "Sorta like shootin' fish in a bar'l, only more satisfyin', all things considered," was how Brass Turtle described it.

By time morning came, the shooting had just about ceased for lack of suitable targets. An ancient crone hobbled over from the village bearing a ceremonial pipe in her gnarled hands and announced in a rasping croak, "You have killed all our warriors, every one of them. Now do you wish to kill the women, too? If you wish to smoke, I have brought the pipe."

As the old woman said, we had used up the warriors and nobody wished to shoot the women or smoke with them, either. We all looked to Joe Meek, his eyes bloodshot and features drawn with grief. Joe simply shrugged and turned away. We took that for assent and went to retrieve our horses.

A few days after that, three white trappers on their way to rendezvous, ignorant of what had recently occurred, stopped by that same Bannock village and were treated in a most courteous manner. Their hosts explained the scarcity of warriors by claiming recent battles with Blackfoots.

℮   ℮   ℮

Kathleen was desolated by the death of her friend. For several days she went about her chores as if in a trance. At first I feared she might chop off her hair or tear her face with her nails as an act of mourning, but apparently there exist certain conventions concerning one's precise relationship to the deceased that prevented such extreme manifestations of grief.

Cat had immediately volunteered to care for Umentucken's two children, the four-year-old that Milton Sublette had fathered and Joe's nearly-two-year-old daughter, but the Shoshone wives in Bridger's brigade and Umentucken's kin in the Snake village attending the rendezvous claimed that responsibility. Naturally I didn't let on that I breathed a sigh of relief when Kathleen's generous gesture was declined.

Ben and I took to riding over to Iron Bow's village, showing off my youngster's horseback prowess to his adoptive uncle and grandfather. The old chief and Fast Horse convinced me as never before how sincere the Séli are whenever they declare an individual to be their adoptive kin. Their pride in my son's accomplishments could not have been greater if their bloodline had truly been flowing in young Ben's veins. The same was true of Kathleen. Iron Bow adopted her the day that Cat and I announced our union. He told me then that I could become a member of his band whenever I might choose to do so, but I had always been careful not to remind him of that offer.

June drifted into July and Independence Day came and went with no sign of supplies from the east. Our national holiday was notable only because the mountaineers grumbled even louder at the tardiness of the packtrain. Andy Drips' brigade showed up in time to increase the volume of the general discontent with our unslaked patriotic thirst.

The Reverend Gray arrived from his western missionary outpost on his way back east to recruit more of his Christian brethren. He had traveled to Horse Creek with McLeod and McKay, the unfriendly partisans of the HBC's Fort Hall trading post, but the Canucks intended to go no farther east, so Mister Gray was forced to remain in our profane midst until the packtrain returned to the settlements with the furs. The Aitch-bee-cee deprived itself of a tidy haul of peltries by its teetotaling policy banning spirituous liquors in trade. American trappers would have put aside their patriotic loyalties for the sake of a day-long drunk, but no such remedy was available.

∾ ∾ ∾

Nearly three weeks of July dragged by before a dust cloud on the eastern horizon signaled the arrival of the caravan from Fort William. It rolled into rendezvous in the late forenoon of July 18th, accompanied by 45 men, most of them hostlers, and twenty mule-drawn carts loaded with supplies. Our Delaware Pretty Horse galloped into our camp three miles up Horse Creek to herald the news and grab up a bundle of plews to trade. Several of our people rode back with him, but I lingered until Kathleen got herself suitably gussied up to go parading in public, consoling myself by reckoning it would likely take a couple hours for the traders to water down the booze, flavor it with tobacco, molasses, hot peppers, and possibly rattlesnake heads, and otherwise prepare it for sale.

When we arrived at American Fur's trade tents in mid-afternoon, Cat scurried off to feast her eyes on the trade goods still being unpacked. I wandered in the direction of the booze tent, but I despaired of ever getting a cupful. The mob surrounding that mecca of the alcoholic faithful was half a dozen deep with impatient trappers and jostling Indians. A long-absent but familiar voice roused me from my distress. "Ye don't want to be curin' yer thirst fust-off with that'ere rotgut, anyways, Temple! Gitcherse'f over hyar an' gitcherse'f a proper snort!" It was my old *compañero* Moses Harris reclining in the shade of an up-ended empty cart, waving a jug in my direction. I hustled over to where he was sprawled, threw myself down, and reached for the jug. The delicious Kentucky squeezin's burned all the way to my belly. I gulped a second mouthful before I said, "Took ye long enough gettin' here!"

"Came as quick as I could," he replied with a frown. "Ye kin blame ol' Fontenelle when ye see 'im."

"He's here?" I demanded. "How come? I thought they fired his drunken arse."

"Me, too, but I reckon he snuck back into Chouteau's good graces, one way or t'other. Ye know haow them Sain' Louie Frenchies allus hang together. Thick as m'lasses, they be! We picked 'im up daown at Fort William, whar he's been runnin' the tradin', but he'll be stayin' up hyar fer trappin' naow!"

"Fontenelle ramrodded the packtrain this time, ye say?" I asked, surprised.

"Nope. Fitzpatrick war in charge out o' Independence an' fer comin' up hyar, but I'm wagerin' this'll be the last time fer Fitz. Don't know fer sure, but I'm thinkin' he's plumb fed up with the whole shebang."

"How long did it take ye?"

"Three weeks, this time. Pulled out o' Fort William the last week o' June with forty-five hostlers an' twenny carts o' goods, with Fitz an' Lucien an' Etienne Provôt an' that'ere Englishman Stewart, what's brung along that redheaded Antoine Clement, as ye mought expec', and a artist-feller fer drawin' pitchers o' trappers an' Injuns an' bufflers an' sich-like—tryin' to git it all daown on paper afore it's plumb gone, like the two of 'em been sayin'."

"Where's it goin'?"

"Beats the hell out o' me, but Stewart's afeared it's all goin' somewhars an' he wants to git hisse'f a passel o' pitchers of it afore it does."

"What do ye hear in Saint Looie concernin' the price of beaver nowadays?" I asked, recalling Fitzpatrick's pessimistic prediction the year before, along with an image of the silk topper he had shown us.

"Still mostly holdin' up, but some say it's gittin' sorta spongy. Ever'thin' is, 'count o' trouble with the banks. Cain't explain it, 'cause I don't unnerstan' what it's all abaout. Nobody does. Leastaways nobody I know. Folks say the whole country's goin' to hell, but Sain' Looie's still holdin' up purty good."

Further palaver just then was cut short by the arrival of a couple hostlers with some sort of problem. Harris handed me the jug for a final swig and promised to ride out to our camp for supper that evening. As I stood up to go, Black said, "Almost fergot to tell ye. Speakin' o' old trappers goin' under, Milt Sublette died last spring daown at Fort William. April Fools Day, they said it war. Cornsid'rin' haow Milt's been suff'rin' with that laig o' his, all o' these years, it's abaout time, don'tcha think?" I nodded my agreement and decided I'd wait to tell Black about Tuttle and Umentucken when I saw him at suppertime.

As I set out to rescue Cat from the temptations of Mammon, my thoughts returned to William Drummond Stewart and what Black had said about the captain's concerns for our future. For all his aristocratic snobbery and elegant affectations, the Hero of Waterloo harbors a genuine love for the life we lead in the Rocky Mountains and the men who wrest their living and their freedom from the harsh wilderness. Something keeps drawing him back, year after year, testing his undeniable courage and fortitude, sharing our perils and privations, when he might at any time return to the life of ease and luxury to which he was born. What might have begun as mere curiosity and a dilettantish taste for adventure when I first encountered him four years earlier had become for him a way of life that he was apparently reluctant to surrender. Although Stewart's circumstances and my own are worlds apart, we share a deep and abiding love for this untamed mountain land and a stubborn unwillingness ever to let it go.

Next morning I was forced to make do for breakfast with plentiful scraps from supper the night before. Kathleen and Iris were busy prettifying themselves and Ben and their *palomilla* mares for their favorite excursion of the entire year—their first foray into the trade tents of the rendezvous. My own sartorial excellence was not neglected. When I returned from my morning bathe in the crick, my fanciest garments and moccasins were neatly laid out on the sleep robes and, soon afterwards, Half-horse led my freshly-groomed Coffee horse and Ben's painted piebald up from the pasture and tethered them to nearby trees. Then Iris darted out of the lodge, lightly anointed Coffee's hindquarters with bear grease, and inscribed a checkerboard pattern with a fragment of comb, a most attractive equine decoration in lieu of paint, which doesn't show up on his sunburnt black hide.

Riding out of camp on our way to the traders, my heart was big in my breast as I filled my eyes with the sight of my beautiful woman, my daughter growing into lovely womanhood, and my vigorous three-year-old son riding his own horse between them, all of them proudly erect and graceful aboard their lively mounts, all richly clad in the height of prairie fashion, the genuine nobility of our mountain wilderness.

As we came within sight of the American Fur tents, Kathleen reined up and waited for me to overtake them. She deems it unseemly for a woman to ride in advance of her man, a breach of Indian etiquette. When we were properly aligned we proceeded at a stately trot until we reached the outskirts of the camp, then slowed to a dignified walk.

As we approached the center of camp we came upon a colorful assemblage of horsemen, whites and Indians alike, milling nigh the crimson marquee of Captain Stewart. As I commenced to turn away from the group, Stewart himself, resplendent in quilled and beaded buckskins, mounted on a magnificent tall, white Kentucky horse, broke free of his companions and reined up in our path, a broad smile on his smooth features, approval in his expression as he surveyed the elegant attire of my handsome family. "Mister Buck," he called out in a hearty voice, "how very fortunate it is that you should arrive just now, just in time to join us in our review of the Snake parade. My old friend Chief Mah-wo-mah has sent word that he will arrive shortly with several hundred warriors for a grand parade on their way to their camping ground. I shall be most honored if you and your charming family will join us."

I found myself in a quandary. I really didn't wish to be a spectacle, an ornament in Stewart's reviewing group. I would have preferred to melt into the throng of mountaineers, but when I glanced at the smiling faces of Cat and Iris, who had heard every word of Stewart's invitation, I realized that my popularity at home would be greatly damaged if I should decline it. I heard myself mumbling that we would join him, which produced even broader smiles on my womenfolk.

As we fell into line behind Stewart, who led the way to the edge of camp, where we would review the passing parade of Mah-wo-mah and his warriors, I saw that our select company included Tom Fitzpatrick and Lucien Fontenelle, along with Jim Bridger and his Séli wife. Andy Drips was accompanied by both of his wives, all of them clad in their go-to-meetin'-best togs. Antoine Clement, Stewart's half-Cree constant companion, rode beside a well-set-up young man in his mid-twenties whom I guessed was the artist Harris had spoken of. I was sure of it later, when he dug a sketch pad and pencils out of his saddle bags to record the parade of Snake warriors.

When we halted and commenced to form a line to review the approaching Snakes, Stewart gestured for me and my family to ride up beside him, on his immediate left, with Fitz, Fontenelle, Bridger, and Drips on his other side. The others arranged themselves beside Kathleen. As we waited for the Snakes to arrive in procession, I was at last too overcome with curiosity to hold my tongue any longer. I leaned toward him and whispered, "Why me?"

The Hero of Waterloo stared straight ahead, a faint smile wrinkling the corner of his mouth, beneath his close-cropped moustache, and replied in a low voice, "Because you were my first friend in these mountains. I value that, Mister Buck."

There was neither time nor need for further palaver. The Shoshone horde had arrived. They were led by Chief Wah-wo-mah himself, easily as tall as Bridger and nobly handsome, astride a tall white horse that rivaled Stewart's own, his height enhanced by an eagle-feather warbonnet, a necklace of grizzly claws around his neck, his quilled leggin's fringed with scalps.

Riding directly behind him was his son, Si-roc-u An-tua, powerfully-built, in his early twenties, his grizzly-claw necklace proclaiming that he, too, had taken scalps. Square-cut bangs covered his brow and his hair was plaited in a thick queue that would have reached his knees had he been afoot.

Following the chief and his son came the Shoshone host, 250 finely-dressed painted warriors, mounted on excellent horses, presenting their shields and eight-foot lances, plumes and scalps fluttering, most with a musket slung across their backs, all of them armed with a bow and quiver, as well, some smiling with the honor accorded them, others scowling in an effort to appear warlike, which was for the most part successful, muscles rippling on smooth bronzed torsos, as they passed in a grand salute to Stewart, flaunting their pride in their prowess and appearance not only to the captain and his few retainers, but also the mob of admiring mountaineers and Indians from half-a-dozen other tribes and nations that had gathered to applaud those truly impressive men of war.

I had questioned in my mind the wisdom of including three-year-old Ben in our reviewing company, lest he disturb the decorum of that solemn occasion by fidgeting or, worse, howling his displeasure at some real or imagined affront. My boy did me proud. He observed the entire spectacle with open-mouthed wonder, fascinated by the vivid panoply presented by the Snake warriors, their weapons, and accoutrements. He broke his solemn demeanor only when the last of the fighting men had passed in review, followed by a marching company of medicine men shaking rattles and beating hand-drums and brandishing a variety of sacred objects meant to drive off evil spirits. Ben stayed put in his saddle as they passed and evidently his crowing and hand-clapping didn't bother them, if they were even aware of him through their own noisy performance.

Much more of a distraction to the ceremonies than Ben's appreciative gestures were the actions of Stewart's young artist on the far side of Kathleen, scribbling feverishly with pencils and charcoal sticks, excitedly ripping out pages of his sketchbooks and stuffing them in his saddlebags, seeking heroically but in vain to capture every lively moment and vibrant image of the flamboyant procession

After the medicine men had passed by, the rest of the band followed on their way to the Shoshone campground a short distance up Horse Creek, a vast, seemingly endless procession of old men, yelling women, yapping dogs, pack animals, and travois loaded with screaming children perched atop towering heaps of lodge covers and household gear. Riding in their wake, young boys drove the immense horse herd of the band to the pasture nigh the Snake village.

When the chief and his retinue disappeared from view, Stewart signaled us to follow him and led the way to his marquee, where we dismounted and gathered around a large wooden box that his servants dragged out and proceeded to open. When the last board was pried loose, Stewart asked Jim Bridger to step forward before he reached in and brought forth a shiny steel cuirass, which he proceeded to buckle around Gabe's bulging chest, before he plopped a polished steel helmet topped with a flowing white horsehair plume atop Bridger's unshorn locks.

Finn McCool had wormed his way to my side through the press of mountaineers and Indians surrounding us. "Damn me," he muttered unbelievingly, "if Stewart hasn't got hold of the armor of the Sassenach king's own Life Guards for his prank today! 'Tis surely a triumph of Rocky Mountain horseplay!"

Bridger, startled at first, quickly picked up the jest, rapping his knuckles on the steel cuirass, strutting around the circle of spectators, nodding vigorously to make the horsehair plume flutter wildly, then stepped onto his tall white horse and paraded through the cheering crowd, before crossing a shallow stream that feeds Horse Creek to let even more spectators in on Stewart's grand jest. Dogging Jim's heels was Stewart's young artist, trotting after Gabe's horse, scribbling madly, unwilling to miss a single image or dramatic gesture.

When Gabe completed his comical tour, Stewart invited us to join him for luncheon in a shady grove beside his marquee. This year's comestibles were even more delicious and elaborate than those that Cat and I had enjoyed the year before. My daughter's eyes were round with wonder as she gazed at the tempting array of corned beef briskets, Polish hams, and tinned smoked oysters, pickled vegetables, and all manner of rolls and shortbreads slathered with butter from Fort William and a variety of fruit preserves. I encouraged her to try everything, explaining that this was another aspect of her education, which Iris accepted as a happy fact and did her healthy best to comply.

Ben stuffed himself on all the sugary treats that Kathleen allowed him to get hold of, until his eyelids commenced to grow heavy. He nestled against her bosom and at last fell asleep, possibly dreaming of a sugar-plum fairy or whatever wilderness equivalent he might have conjured up.

I continued to sample the tinned and salted meats, as well as a variety of sweetmeats and exotic spirits, when my gourmandizing was interrupted by Stewart's smooth-cheeked young artist. He seated himself on the grass beside me and announced, "We haven't met. I am Alfred Jacob Miller, formerly of Baltimore, now of New Orleans. And you?" Although I was amused that he had used his full name and professional title, I approved his straightforwardness. Besides, Stewart's French cognac had mellowed my mood. I told him my name, as he had asked, and waved my hand vaguely towards the mountains, as if to say that I was now from thereabouts. Miller caught my jest and chuckled, then plunged into the purpose of his visit. "I have been observing you and your handsome family, Mister Buck." he declared earnestly. "I request your permission to make some sketches of all of you, especially your wife. She possesses most striking features . . . ." He trailed off, a stricken look betraying his fear that his admiring words, innocently meant, might have offended me.

I smiled at his discomfort. "Don't worry, Mister Miller," I assured him. "I think she does, too. You have my permission to make your sketches."

The young fellow looked relieved, thanked me profusely, promised that he would be discreet and not intrude on our privacy, and made haste to depart, lest I change my mind.

We took our leave soon afterwards, thanking Captain Stewart for his hospitality and the opportunity to view the Shoshone procession from that excellent vantage point. I was especially impressed with the Old World courtesy that the Scotsman had accorded my wife and daughter throughout the day, not a whit less than he might have displayed before an English gentlewoman of his own rank.

Our original intention abandoned, we headed back to our camp, Ben still fast asleep, spraddled on Cat's saddle bow. I rode in front, Ben's piebald in tow, thinking over the events of the day, especially Iris's innocent wonderment at the miracles displayed at Stewart's sumptuous picnic spread.

∿   ∿   ∿

Kathleen refused to delay any further her visit to the trade tents. By time I returned from my morning bathe, my horse had been saddled, my clothes laid out, and my breakfast was warming by the lodge fire. Cat and Iris, freshly dressed and discreetly painted with tasteful touches of vermilion, observed my own preparations with ill-concealed impatience. Only when we were at last a-horseback, on our way out of camp, was I granted an approving smile.

At first I was pleased to learn that beaver was bringing four or five dollars a pound, depending on quality, until it became clear that the price of trade goods, even the most essential supplies for trappers, had been increased to as much as two thousand percent over their cost in Saint Louis. Although no reasonable man disputes that the workman is worthy of his hire, that the trader is entitled to earn a reasonable profit for enduring the perils, hardships, and expense of hauling merchandise a thousand miles and more through a hostile wilderness, such murderous gouging of the men who make the fur trade possible is likely to kill the entire enterprise. And now that American Fur enjoys a monopoly—except for the HBC, which is even less generous—there is nowhere else for a trapper to trade.

Most of us realized that the five-dollar price for prime beaver was merely a cynical attempt to convince gullible trappers that the fur market was still firm, but the sudden sky-high increase in merchandise prices gave the lie to that feeble ploy. Mountaineers understood all too well that their hard-won peltries were becoming next to worthless, in spite of their noisy insistence that "Beaver'll shine agin!"

I ran into Grover Weed nigh the booze tent. My old friend Buzzard lamented, "'Tain't hardly wuth it no more, Temple! Sperrits sellin' fer five bucks the pint an' mostly water at that! Hell! 'Tain't Christian!"

Amid widespread grumbling about the ruinous high prices for goods that trappers cannot do without came unpleasant news of a different sort. Men lately returned from trapping up north, nigh the three forks of the Missouri, brought word that smallpox was rampant amongst the Blackfeet and all the tribes that ranged along the Missouri. "It's killin' 'em off like gawddamn flies, begawd! Thar ain't hardly a Mandan or a Hidatsu left up thataway!" was the sinister message. "Blackfoots are runnin' fer cover like skeered rabbits nowadays! Din't hardly see a one o' them murd'rin' bastards since late spring!"

Trappers, like everybody else, draw their conclusions from what they know, which in our case isn't much in the way of reliable knowledge of recent happenings. So it was hardly surprising to hear a number of men soon blaming Jim Beckwith for starting the smallpox epidemic, although there was no earthly reason to suppose that Jim had anything to do with it, except that word was he had moved into those parts and they didn't like him in the first place.

Kathleen was shocked and indignant at the sharp increase in prices since the previous year, but I told her to buy whatever she wished. I reckoned that the growing fortune I had stored up with Chouteau over the years wasn't likely to be dented by her splurging at the trade tables. Besides, I had been looking forward to breaking my fast with a feast of her delicious flapjacks and I refused to be deprived.

∾   ∾   ∾

Next day I led two packmules to American Fur, panniers bulging with the plews I had taken over the past year, and went on a buying spree of my own, purchasing large quantities of galena, gunpowder, and percussion caps, half a dozen pretty good rifles and fixin's, butcher knives, woolen blankets, tobacco, coffee, sugar, molasses and the like, and a galore of Indian trade goods.

As I rode out of the trading area, Tom Fitzpatrick hailed me and invited me into his marquee, where he sloshed Kentucky whiskey into our cups, swigged a healthy mouthful, and smiled for the first time. "Drink up, Temple darlin'," he said affably. "'Tis likely this'll be the final toime the two of us'll be bending elbows together. This is a farewell toast to all the good days we've known these past fourteen years in these darlin' mountains." I sipped and shivered with pleasure as the whiskey made its fiery way down my gullet, whilst I watched Tom's thin smile slide into the weary frown that had become his customary expression in recent years.

"A farewell toast, ye say. How come?" I asked, although I had pretty fair idea what was coming.

"This'll be me last trip to rendezvous. I'm after givin' it up, Temple, all of it." He spat disgustedly before he added, "What's left of it!"

There was no need to pursue the matter, so I didn't. Fitz and I both knew that the glory days of the mountain life we had known and loved throughout our youth and into approaching middle age were fast coming to an end. Trying to hang on to them as they had been must end only in bitter disappointment.

"What'll ye do, Tom?" I asked. "Any plans?"

"None to be speakin' of," he replied with a shrug. "Nothin' sartin, mind ye. Gin'ral Clark tells me not to be worryin' meself overmuch, but he's after keepin' a tight lip fer details." He filled my cup again and asked, "And you? What'll you be doin', Temple Buck?

"I'm not sure," I told him honestly. "Still trying to work matters out."

Fitz laughed aloud and this time it had a sincere ring to it. "You'll succeed, no matter what! Ye've always been after leadin' a charmed loife, Temple! All the lads've always said so!"

I was startled by his remark. I had never supposed that anyone outside our bunch had ever paid much attention to me. "I hope you're right" was all I could think of to say.

≈   ≈   ≈

Now that half a plan had commenced to build in my mind, I needed answers to a few important questions. Instead of returning to our camp, I rode directly to Iron Bow's village, where a lad came running to take charge of my horse and my heavily-loaded packmules. Observing etiquette, I waited outside the chief's lodge until I was invited to enter, which didn't take long. I was an old friend and a frequent visitor, so the old man dispensed with much of the ceremony that might have been required for a less familiar caller. Whilst I waited, passers-by nodded and smiled, which is always a welcome sign in an Indian village, where attitudes toward strangers can be as changeable as summer breezes.

When at last the chief's smiling eldest wife bade me enter, I dodged past the doorflap into the dim interior and paused a moment to let my eyes adjust from the bright sunshine outdoors. Iron Bow sat alone at the far end of the lodge, clad in casual everyday clothes, leaning against a willow backrest, flanked by his pipe stand and the tripod bearing his ceremonial shield and lance and various accoutrements of his office. I saw with satisfaction that the fine Hawken rifle I had given him, well-oiled, its polished brass fittings gleaming, was included with his other prized weapons. He smiled and beckoned me to come forward, at the same time calling out to his woman to bring food for their guest.

After the usual preliminaries and my assuring him that all was well with Kathleen and the children, I told him that I wished to speak to him of a very important matter, but that the presence of his son Fast Horse was needed before I did so. Iron Bow's expression became suddenly grave, but he merely nodded and called out a summons for his son. Whilst we waited, he filled his pipe, deftly fished a coal out of the fire with calloused fingers, and lit it. He offered it to the sky, the four directions, and the earth before he passed it to me, indicating that he took me at my word that my message would be of serious import.

When Fast Horse arrived, still sweaty from the horse pasture, I attempted to relieve his concerned look by assuring them both that what I wished to say, while serious, might be beneficial to all concerned. Then I plunged into the matter, relying not only on my knowledge of the Salish tongue, which had improved during my years with both Rainbow and Cat, but also the sign talk, the constant companion of Plains Indian speech, with which I felt much more comfortable and confident.

I explained that after the fifteen winters I had spent pursuing the trapper's trade, my *métier* was dying out. Beaver were growing scarce and there was a lessening demand for their plews. Soon there might be no demand at all. I told them what they already knew. Traders were growing ever more greedy. Soon they might stop coming to the mountains from the faraway white settlements. Then I said honestly that I had no wish to live in those parts ever again. The mountains were the only home I desired.

When Iron Bow saw me hesitate before I attempted to put into Salish words and sign the next thing I wished to convey, that wise old man read my thought. He raised his hand to forestall my request and renewed his invitation for me to join his Séli band, naturally together with Kathleen—he used her Salish name Sin-gel-eh Sim, Coyote Woman—and our children. As his father spoke and signed, Fast Horse smiled and nodded his agreement. Naturally I was greatly relieved, not so much at his repeated invitation to join his band, which I had been reasonably confident would be forthcoming, but mainly because now I didn't need to struggle with the formal Salish words and expressions appropriate to that weighty matter.

My reprieve was only temporary, howsomever, for now I wished to propose a much more serious request to them. I asked them to recall that in the nine years that we had known each other I had always acted honorably in my dealings. Then I declared my loyalty to my comrades and said that I could not turn my back on them. I asked that Iron Bow and his council accept all those in our bunch, their wives and children, who wished to join his band, accepting his authority in tribal matters, and defending the band as they would their own lives.

It was a tall order. Iron Bow and his son, who would likely become the next leader, looked grave, unsmiling, deeply thoughtful. My request was not one that could be granted offhand, nor solely by themselves. After a spate of rapid palaver betwixt the two of them, Iron Bow declared that the council of elders would need to decide the matter. Fast Horse left the lodge to summon the council and the old man called out to his unseen wives that it was time now to bring the vittles.

Whilst we ate boiled fresh buffalo tongue and steaming slices of hump meat, Iron Bow assured me that both he and Fast Horse were of a mind to grant my request, but such a drastic decision needed to be made by the entire council, which surprised me not at all.

Most of the elders were not old men. The council was mainly composed of still-vigorous seasoned warriors who had earned the respect of the band by their prowess in battle and the prudent judgment they exercised in the conduct of daily affairs in the band. Although two of them were well past fighting age, neither one was behindhand in debating every aspect of the proposition put before them now. The harangue went on for an hour or more. Each man had his say, often heatedly, in a torrent of words usually too swift for me to comprehend, but at last Fast Horse turned to me and told me with a smile that my request had been granted, providing that my people would pitch our lodges together, discreetly separate from their Séli neighbors, until the council could judge if their behavior was acceptable. They had observed too many years of trappers' wild antics at rendezvous. Which was all that I could have wished in the first place.

As soon as the council departed, I asked Iron Bow to have the plunder on my packmules brought into the lodge. When it was heaped up, I told him that it was his to distribute as he saw fit and immediately took my leave. The gift showed my gratitude, but, taking place after the council made its decision, it could not be construed as a bribe.

Riding back to our camp, I withheld my self-congratulating. Now would come the hardest part of my plan that was only starting to take shape.

∾   ∾   ∾

I decided to wait until the morrow before I announced to my companions my own decision to quit the trapping trade, let alone broaching the matter of those who also might be willing to do so possibly joining up with Iron Bow's Flathead band on a year-round basis. Such weighty decisions should be addressed with clear-headed thinking and sober judgment, qualities that are rarely available at rendezvous, especially late in the day.

My first daunting chore would be to convince Kathleen that the life of boundless freedom that she and I have lived and loved as a free trapper and his woman was fast drawing to a close. Our livelihood has depended on just two things —beaver, which are getting scarce, and a gentlemen's fickle fashion, which, like it or not, has altered drastically. It will soon be impossible for my mountaineer comrades and me to thumb our nose at the civilized settlements from which we obtain the essential supplies without which we cannot continue to live in the mountains. Without gunpowder, galena, and percussion caps even our rifles would be useless. Even Indians are unwilling to return to a life bereft of woolens, copper kettles, guns and steel knives and a hundred other manufactured articles that have become essential to them, once they discovered that such things exist.

As much as my white and Delaware comrades value the unlimited freedom we have known in the mountains, I think that our women cherish even more than we do the freedom we have known in the mountains, their liberation from millennia of male domination dictated by tribal custom. Even rude, rough-handed trappers are often regarded as preferable mates.

Before I entered our lodge, I turned the packmules out to graze, asked Half-horse to saddle Cat's *palomilla* mare, her favorite, and tethered my

Crane horse nearby. Kathleen must have read something in my look that portended a matter of importance. When I invited her to ride out with me, she rose without a word and followed me out.

Once clear of the camp, we let our horses out in a gallop, clearing the cobwebs from my brain, refreshing my spirit in the cool late-afternoon breeze, borrowing strength from Crane's deep well of power. When we neared our favorite grove beside the stream, I checked our speed and swung onto the narrow trail that led to our trysting place.

So far, she and I had not exchanged a single word. When I stepped down and turned Crane loose to graze, Kathleen favored me with a quizzical gaze and a half-smile as she joined me on the grassy bank. I chuckled self-consciously and assured her that this time my intention in bringing her there was not amorous, only to assure us of privacy, which she greeted with a mischievous look of mock disappointment. Cat's quick mind and puckish, often ribald sense of humor is one of the qualities that first endeared her to me.

I wasted no time before I attacked what I feared would be a painful chore, telling her first of my talk with Fitzpatrick and describing my growing certainty that our way of life stands in imminent danger of being rubbed out, that soon beaver plews will be all but worthless and traders will cease coming from the settlements, depriving all of us of the goods we can't live without.

Cat listened intently, her eyes fixed on mine, her expression grave but not despairing, missing not a word, until I ran out of words. She gently placed her finger on my lips and said, "I know. I see what you tell of now. I hear men talking. This is no good time for us." Then she made my heart big in my breast. With a look of childlike innocence and absolute faith in me, she asked, "What will you do, Tempo?" As if she were confident that I would conjure up a solution.

I told her then of my visit to Iron Bow and the favorable result, quickly adding, when I saw her face fall, that living with the Séli band could be only a temporary measure, which greatly restored her spirits. Then I took a deep breath and uttered the words that I had feared to say aloud. "I must leave you and the children with Iron Bow —" Her sudden sharp intake of breath made me hasten to finish my thought "— only 'til spring! I must go to Saint Louis to make my plan work. It's the only way I know for us to live our life here!"

She studied my eyes with solemn attention for what felt like eternity, until her look of distress slowly faded into an expression of trust and faith in my love for her and our children. When I was able to bring myself to speak again I reminded her that I had gone to the settlements once before and returned to make her my woman. For once in my life I wished that I might swear on the Bible or something like it to bolster my pledge, but here, my word would have to suffice. Then Cat spoke for the first time. "If you say it, Tempo, I know it is so. It is enough." Relieved, I took her in my arms and held her close, profoundly grateful for her faith in me.

After a time I released her from my embrace and rose to my feet, but she looked up at me with that mischievous smile and patted the grass beside her as she said, "Why go so soon, Tempo?" Then I knew for sure that her faith in me was absolute. We lingered there until dusk.

๛   ๛   ๛

Next day, even before my morning bathe, I made the rounds of all the lodges and bowers in our camp, asking my companions to meet in the mid-forenoon. Most of them readily assented, expecting that we would decide where to trap that fall. Fontenelle, with Bridger as pilot, was already getting a brigade together to trap the area around the Three Forks headwaters of the Missouri, now that word was that Blackfoots, terrified of the smallpox, were fleeing northwards. I included our campkeepers in the meeting, as well. They had been with us from the get-go and deserved to be heard in the matter at hand.

When all eighteen men in the bunch had gathered, I got to my feet and let my gaze rove over the faces of my comrades, several of whom I had known since our earliest days coming up the Missouri. All of the carefully-rehearsed arguments I had spent most of the previous night putting together simply evaporated.

I have rarely taken the lead in arriving at decisions for the bunch, preferring instead to cast my vote for someone else's proposal. Now I stood dumb and awkward, reaching for the right words to explain the only proposition that I believed might let us continue living our life in the mountains. At last I strangled out, "I mean to quit trappin' beaver for a livin', right now, from here on—before it quits me, leavin' me and all of us high an' dry an' starvin' on our own here in the mountains!"

It wasn't much of a speech, but I couldn't have got their attention any better if I had lit the fuse on a keg of gunpowder and tossed it in their midst. My stumbling words were greeted with a roar of disapproval mixed with doubt that I could possibly mean what I had said. "Ye cain't be meanin' it, Temple!" "Yew gotta be funnin' us!" "Tain't funny nohow!" "Whatcha got in mind fer real, Temple?" and similar disbelieving comments.

Oddly enough, the hubbub served to help me compose my thinking enough to let them know what I had in mind. When they grew quiet enough to let me make myself heard, I yelled out, "The shinin' times ain't comin' back! All of us know it's so! Plews are gettin' scarce an' the beaver market's fallin' apart, anyway! Pretty soon, traders'll quit comin' up an', like I said, we'll be left high an' dry an' starvin', unless we do somethin' on our own hook."

The first storm of objections was mild compared with the response my words received this time. Cries of "Beaver'll shine agin!" rang out from several men, along with several others questioning my sobriety or my sanity for expressing such heretical sentiments.

I despaired of convincing my fellows or even getting them to listen to what I wished to propose. Then Brass Turtle rose to his feet and raised his arms for quiet, calling out, "Thar ain't a man hyar what don't know what Temple hyar's been sayin' ain't nothin' but the gawddamn truth! The good life we been livin' up thisaway is gone beaver! That's a gawddamn fact! Beaver's nearly gone! The market in Sain Looie's goin' fast! An' purty soon all of us'll be gone, too, 'less we git a'hold o' some smarts an' do somethin' abaout it! Let's give a listen to what Temple's got to say. He ain't never steered us wrong yet!"

Brass Turtle is a natural-born leader, which I am not, nor ever wish to be. Whilst he was speaking, I sank to my haunches and listened. He turned to me and waved me to my feet, encouraging me to describe my plan.

Which I did. First, I repeated much the same things I had told Cat the day before, things that every trapper already knew in his gut but preferred to ignore or disbelieve, how beaver were running out and how, try as we might, getting a pack or two was well-nigh impossible for a man to amass in a whole season, and even if we could, traders' prices for goods were going sky-high and would likely keep climbing, until we would soon be unable to outfit ourselves for the next year's trapping.

I told them, too, what Fitz had foretold about the crashing market for beaver in Saint Louis and that he himself was quitting the business, leaving the mountains forever. If an old, experienced hand like Fitzpatrick was giving up on the beaver trade, I predicted that it wouldn't be long—a couple-three years at most—until the rest of the traders ceased making their long, dangerous, expensive journey through South Pass for the measly profits they might realize when the market for beaver collapsed entirely. The end of rendezvous would mean the end of the mountaineer.

Then I declared that I myself was unwilling to give up the mountain life if I could possibly hang on to it, which produced a rumble of assent and a sprinkle of skeptical queries about what I might have in mind.

What I told them next was the most difficult part for me to say aloud. I have always been reticent about mentioning my own good fortune, especially how much of it has depended on the good will of Pierre Chouteau, Cadet. If I hoped to convince my comrades to go along with my plan, howsomever, it was necessary to explain it all.

I reminded them of our meeting the previous spring with American Fur's agent James Kipp, when he was traveling with Long Hair's Absóraqa band, seeking their trade in robes and furs for the Company. He told me then about AmFur's Fort McKenzie, located nigh the Marias River on the Missouri, as high up on the Muddy as steamboats are able to travel. Which got me to thinking that it might prove worthwhile for a trading outfit to use that Fort McKenzie as a depot for trade goods to deal with the Indian tribes northwest of there for buffalo robes, fine furs, and beaver that they now carry south all the way to rendezvous on the Seeds-kee-dee. The fort is close enough to the home grounds of the Flatheads, Kootenais, Nez Percés, and Pend d'Oreilles to make transporting trade goods in one direction and robes and furs in the other a profitable venture. Moreover, the good relations the people in our bunch have established with those tribes make us the ideal people to do it.

Then I swallowed hard and admitted that Chouteau had coaxed me for a decade or more to join his company in just such a venture. I didn't brag on it. I just told the truth.

After that I told them of the arrangements I had made with Iron Bow and his Séli band for as many of our bunch as wished to do so to travel north and spend the winter with them, while I travel down the Missouri on a steamboat to make arrangements with Chouteau and return next spring with a supply of trade goods.

Brass Turtle stepped in then. "Ye don't hafta make up yer mind right naow. Think it over an' bring yer questions to Temple if ye got any. He'll be glad to tell ye ever'thin' he knows abaout it. We'll git together t'morra mawnin' fer decidin' what ye want to do."

The meeting dispersed after that, men wandering off in twos and threes, talking over what they had heard. It was plain that our bunch would be breaking up. Independent thinking is a large part of what makes a mountaineer. It would have been foolhardy to suppose that my arguments could convince them all.

☙　☙　☙

Turtle walked back to my lodge with me, at first saying nothing, then asking, "Haow long have ye been thinkin' abaout thi'shere scheme o' yours?"

"Depends on whether ye mean some of it or all of it," I hedged. "I've been doin' some serious thinkin' about it for a year or more, ever since Fitz showed us that silk topper and what he said about beaver plews goin' to hell. Then, havin' just one American trader comin' up to rendezvous wasn't exactly good news, either. I've been chewin' on that all winter. But the high prices they're chargin' this year an' hearin' Fitz tell me what he did about the beaver market nowadays and how he's quittin' the whole shebang for good tied it up for me, good an' proper. The whole thing sort of came together in my mind right then and I pretty much worked it out from there.

"When I heard Tom say what he did, I reckoned it was time to run for cover, 'stead o' waitin' to get picked off like a dumb greenhorn. Tradin' for robes an' such won't be the same as trappin', nothin' will, but it's better than goin' back to the settlements. How about you?"

I reckon Turtle hadn't expected me to ask him that direct question so soon. His head snapped up and he glared at me before he replied with a laugh, "Aw hell! I been thinkin' purty much the same thing as you come up with fer a year naow. If ye think ye kin pull it off like ye say, I reckon it's wuth a try." He looked thoughtful for half a minute before he added, "Course, I'll hafta be sweet-talkin' Tally into it, but I reckon she'll go along."

"I reckon Tallymesko will," I said with a laugh, reflecting that her proper name, Tallymesko, means 'I'll go' in the Delaware tongue.

Finn McCool was waiting outside my lodge. "Ah," said he, "'Tis jist as well the two of ye came along now. It'll save me sayin' the same difficult thing twice. But I suppose ye might already be guessin' what it is I'm after tellin' ye. Whin ye take your trip down the river to Saint Looie, Temple, I'd loike to be trav'lin' along wi' ye. 'Tis not an aisy thing to be sayin', but 'tis toime that I be after pursuin' me medical studies, now that I can, thanks to Tuttle's gin'rous bequest." He paused to take a breath. That whole speech had been delivered in an embarrassed rush.

Neither Turtle nor I were surprised at Finn's announcement. We had expected our Irish friend to return to Missouri with the trading caravan at the end of rendezvous. Now it made more sense for him to go by steamboat down the river when I went.

"We'll miss ye, Finn," we told him. "You've been a good *compañero*."

"Do ye know where you'll go for your studies," I asked.

"I do indade," he responded with a broad smile, evidently pleased that we were accepting the news of his departure with good grace. "I'll be applyin' to the Fairchild Medical College in the State of New York, the same institution where darlin' Doctor Whitman earned his own medical license. He wrote me a handsome letter introducin' me to that school before he and his missus went up north last year, but I niver thought I'd be after usin' it so soon—" He quit in mid-sentence, reddening, lest he dishonor Tuttle's memory by his joy in being able to complete his education at the cost of our friend's death.

Before I could speak, Turtle reassured him, "Don'tcha fret, Finn. Tuttle'd be proud to see ye goin' off to doctorin' school. It's what he wanted fer ye!"

"What'll ye do once ye get your license?" I enquired. "Still mean to go back to California?"

"I will indade," he replied, smiling. "I niver quit dreamin' of the warm sunshine an' charmin' *señoritas* an' rivers o' Spaniard poteen callin' me back! It'll be worth iv'ry shiver and icicle on me nose, sailin' around bloody Cape Horn, to be gittin' back to that darlin' land agin!"

We parted then and I entered the lodge, only to discover my father waiting for me, my children and Paddy's redheaded Sean gathered at his knees, fascinated by one of his well-told stories. We nodded hello but he went on with his tale to its conclusion, before Kathleen, sensing that Powatawa had come on serious business, sent the children out of doors. She handed us both a cup of hot tea and retreated discreetly to a corner of the lodge, where Ben was stirring from his mid-morning nap.

Although my father looked serious enough, he did not look unhappy about what he intended to tell me. Quite the contrary. As he commenced to speak, his expression lightened to one of good-humored warmth. A merry twinkle appeared in his eyes as he said, "Seewauseekau, my son, I will not be going with you when you travel with Iron Bow to the Séli country when we leave this place."

I had half-expected as much. I had reckoned my father's frequent absences were likely attributable to attentions he had been paying his mysterious woman in the Nez Percé village for the past couple years. What I hadn't expected was what he told me next.

"What I must do now is remain with my woman and your small sister. She was born this last Moon of Budding Trees. I will be needed there. The Shahaptin have made me welcome in their village and in their council."

If he said anything more just then, I didn't hear it. My mind was reeling with his almost casual remark that I had a sister newly-born that past spring. When he imparted that startling news, Cat exploded with a smothered shriek of glee and my phiz must have expressed dismay. Powatawa greeted our surprise calmly and continued explaining why he was needed in the Nez Percé band. I was speechless. Fortunately, Ben had fully awakened and ran to throw himself into his grandfather's arms, babbling his pleasure at seeing him again, giving me time to recover my wits.

I had always known that Powatawa was reserved, residing in his natural dignity, sparing of expressing emotion except with children, but his reticence regarding his newfound connubial felicity was remarkable even for him.

He concluded his visit by inviting us to call on him and his bride on the morrow, which we promised to do. I saw him to his horse and stood gazing after him as he rode off, erect in the saddle and lithe as a youth, marveling again at my good fortune in having been sired by such a man.

❮ ❮ ❮

I lingered over my breakfast coffee next day, revisiting with Kathleen the events of the previous day, especially what my father had revealed to us. Cat accepted the news with her usual levelheaded calm, commenting, "The Shahaptin woman must be ver' happy to keep him in her lodge. I am no surprise her people wish him to stay with them. He is wise an' strong and a brave war-maker. He will be a good father for his girl, same like for you, Tempo."

I had no doubt that all she said was true, but learning that your father has just gifted you with an infant sister when you are already thirty-three years old takes some getting used to. Still, recalling how pleased he was with his reclaimed role of paterfamilias, I chided myself for harboring a mite of childish selfishness for no longer having him all to myself.

Further reflection was curtailed by Ben exploding past the doorflap, loudly insisting that Cat and I come with him to the pasture "to see the secret!" He tugged me to my feet and dragged Cat and me along, jabbering the while about Half-horse and Rags and "the secret" we were about to see.

Except for briefly performing my morning chore, that was my first real use of my legs that day. The rheumatic ache I felt as we trudged across the pasture provided yet another argument in favor of the course I had proposed to my companions the day before. Fifteen years of wading up to my hips in icy beaver ponds for half the year had commenced to exact a toll. Swapping my *métier* as a trapper for a trader's occupation was becoming increasingly attractive with every step.

A smiling Half-horse was waiting in the meadow, Ben's small piebald horse Rags in hand, already saddled and bridled, standing quietly, occasionally craning his neck to snatch a mouthful of grass. Ben turned loose my hand and raced to the horse's side, his head barely reaching to the little animal's belly. It was always necessary to lift him into the saddle.

As Ben neared, Half-horse tossed the reins over Rags' head but kept hold of the headstall. As soon as he reached the horse's side, Ben reached out and delivered a smart clap with his right hand on Rags' hind leg, just above the hock. Immediately the little critter sank his hindquarters, shoving his hind legs under his belly, until his tail dragged the ground. Whereupon Ben, with a triumphant shriek, scrambled onto the saddle, picked up the reins, and slapped the little horse on the neck, signaling him to rise to his full height. Crowing his coup to the high heavens, Ben flailed his short legs, heels drumming on Rags' shoulders, and ran off in an easy lope, circling around us a time or two before he brought the little piebald to a halt in front of us. Kathleen was flushed with pride and I confess that I dabbed at my eyes once or twice, likely because of the bright sunshine, naturally.

When I reached out to lift Ben from the saddle, he waved me off and poked Rags sharply on the neck with stiffened fingers, causing the critter to sag his rump once more, allowing the youngster to slide to the ground unaided, laughing and puffed up with pride at his newfound prowess.

It was an excellent start for what promised to be a trying day, attempting to convince my hard-headed *compañeros* to accept my proposal. I thanked Half-horse and resolved to reward him with the best thing I could find at the traders, no matter the cost.

∾   ∾   ∾

Brass Turtle proved to be a powerful ally in realizing my plan. His Tallymesko woman had agreed to accompany the Flatheads to their home country, rather than returning to live amongst her own people, the Snakes. When Tally was safely out of earshot, Turtle told me, "Thisaway, we won't have the lodge allus full of her kinfolk, spongin' off me an' runnin' her to death, fetchin an' totin' an' feedin' 'em. 'Sides, Tally's pow'ful fond o' Cat."

Little Mountain went along with Turtle, which I might have guessed he would do, but he insisted, "Awright, we gonna stay 'longside o' Flatheads fer a spell, like ye say, but jist 'til ye git back from the settlements. Then we gonna have our own camp agin, like ye been sayin'. That so?" I assured him that that's how it appeared to me. I hastened to add that I did not intend to ramrod the new outfit, that we would make decisions together, like always.

Zeetlah and Half-horse nodded and signed their willingness to go along with Turtle and Mountain, which was also predictable.

Cesár Pérez shrugged and expressed his assent, as well. Later he told me that there would have been no living with his Arapaho wife Rosa if he had tried to separate her from Mountain's Arapaho princess Tayho.

Diego Valenzuela was in much the same situation with his Arapaho wife Maria, so he consented to join the new venture. Pablo Torres, still a bachelor, was unwilling to part with his Spanish-speaking *compañeros*, so he, too, agreed to come along.

Anse Tolliver unwound his long, lean frame and stood up to deliver his decision. A fleeting smile came and went across his craggy, usually sour features before he commenced to speak. "Don't reckon I'm cut out fer what y'all 'pear to be thinkin' on, takin' up the drummer's trade, swappin' trade goods with Injuns fer buffler robes an' fine peltries an' sich. I got m'se'f a trade o' my own, one I l'arn't from my pappy, gittin' good an' gittin' better at it, man an' boy, 'fore I come out thisaway. If ye mean to be makin' yer livin' offa them'ere Injuns, ye'll be needin' whiskey fer tradin' an' thar ain't nobody this side o' 'Tinnessee what knows haow to make better squeezin's than me. That's what I'm aimin' to do, over on the Muddy, buyin' corn from frien'ly Injuns thar an' 'stillin' better booze'n most of ye ever drunk.

"I'll come along wi' ye to Sain' Looie, so's I kin buy the 'quipment I'll be needin' an' then I'll be comin' back up the river fer settin' up my bizness. Natcherly ye'll be welcome to buy what I'll be makin'." He dropped onto his lean hams and propped against an aspen at his back, a satisfied grin wreathing his bony cheeks.

As the import of Anse's pronouncement sank in, I realized that his decision to set up as a bootlegger was a stroke of good fortune for our intended enterprise. As he said, Indians—as well as our own crew— would demand whiskey along with our other trade goods. What better source of potent spirits than Tolliver, operating his still practically in our dooryard, safe from the revenuer's reach? I shuddered at the thought of putting up with his acid tongue all the way to Saint Louis, but it would be worth the discomfort.

When it came time for Micah to say how the stick floated, he chuckled and said, "You an' me, we've come this far together, Temple, an' ye've never done me wrong. Reckon I'll stick with ye. Just so I never lay eyes on Sain' Looie ever again!" Which I greeted with relief. Micah's years of experience working in Chouteau's Indian trade—a side of the business I knew little about—would be essential to achieving success in our new venture.

Our two Iroquois trappers, Acorn and Stone Bird, and the Delaware Pretty Horse had drawn Brass Turtle aside and engaged him in earnest palaver, accompanied by much hand-signing that often extended to excited arm-waving. At last Turtle stepped into the circle of men and announced, "These hyar three fellers ain't ready to quit on trappin'. They reckon beaver's gonna shine agin', like some're sayin' it will, an' they don't mean to give up on what they been doin' all these years. All three of 'em awready signed up with Fontenelle an' Gabe fer headin' up nawth to the Forks, along with their wimmen an' kids. I told 'em whar we'll be next year, in case they change their mind."

I hated losing good-natured Pretty Horse and his no longer bashful Crow wife Nettaqueathy from our number, but it was neither surprising nor very regrettable to me that the two surly Iroquois had chosen to sever ties with us after fifteen years together.

Paddy McBride appeared still to be conflicted over reaching a decision. "'Tis true," he began, "our darlin' beaver-trappin' days are limpin' to the end of the road. 'Tis toime to be thinkin' o' what's next fer all of us. As ye surely know, a great many trappers are after goin' off to Oregon"—he pronounced it O'Reagan—"an' takin' up land there fer farmin' an' the loike. An' I, too, have been thinkin' o' doin' somethin' loike—ownin' me own piece o' ground, which I niver could've even dreamed of back in the Auld Sod. 'Twas a plaisin' idea, it surely was, until I thought o' what I'd hafta be doin' there fer makin' some kind o' livin' fer meself an' me woman an' kids. Then it come to me mind that the only bloody thing I know how to do besides trappin' castors is spadin' bloody 'taties, which is why I said farewell an' niver agin to darlin' auld Ireland in the first place. P'raps I kin learn tradin' fer buffler robes wi' the rest o' ye. Ye kin count me in."

Later, Paddy told me privately, "'Sides, there'd be no livin' wid me darlin' Molly if I took her off from gossipin' wid yer Kathleen woman, 'speshly whin we have the chance o' stayin' nigh Iron Bow's people. An' Sean, me young spalpeen'd niver forgive me fer partin' 'im from yer Iris lass, as ye well know."

I had wondered how our French-Canuck campkeepers would fit into our plan, but they relieved me of concern when they announced their intention to return to Quebec. We had paid them generously for their loyal service to our bunch over the years. Now they reckoned it was time for the two of them to go home to Quebec and start raising families, while they were still able to do so.

That left ten of us still together, enough hard-working, experienced men to conduct the business I had in mind. If more were needed later on, I had no doubt that diminishing returns from the vanishing *métier* we had loved and practiced from our youth to impending middle age would provide enough seasoned recruits to get the job done properly.

❧   ❧   ❧

By time I got back to our lodge, all four of our showiest saddle horses were tethered nearby, well-groomed and painted and saddled with their handsomest apishamores, their polished silver and brass decorations gleaming in mid-day sunshine. The packmule standing with them bore panniers bulging with what were doubtless wedding gifts for Powatawa's bride.

Inside, Kathleen fretted over her own appearance and Iris's and strove to keep Ben from rumpling his clothing before we set out for the Nez Percé encampment, always a losing battle with my boisterous son. My own elaborate outfit was already laid out and Cat fussed over my grooming as she oiled and braided my hair anew, whilst she worried aloud that we would somehow fail to pass muster in the eyes of my father's new woman. Any uncertainties of my own at meeting my new stepmother were drowned in Kathleen's anxiety.

At last we mounted up with me in the lead on Coffee, followed by the two women riding their creamy *palomillas*, and Ben, who had insisted on leading the packmule, bringing up the rear on his colorful piebald Rags. The two-mile hike to the Nez Percé village was uneventful, except for admiring stares we garnered along the way, mostly from women, a tribute to Kathleen's sartorial skill.

When he saw us approaching, Powatawa detached himself from a circle of men with whom he was smoking in a shady grove and strode toward us, a welcoming smile on his handsome features. He led the way to a large, well-cared-for lodge and helped us tether our critters. When he stretched out his arms to lift Ben to the ground, my son insisted on poking Rags' neck and sliding off on his own when the little horse sagged his hindquarters. My father was genuinely impressed and praised the lad, who generously informed his grandfather that the credit really belonged to Half-horse, which pleased me even more than his acquiring his new skill.

Powatawa called ahead, announcing our arrival, then led us inside. I am not sure what I expected to see, but when my eyes adjusted to the dim interior, I was shocked to behold a smiling, beautiful woman not much older than Cat, if at all, holding an elaborately-quilled cradleboard from which a dark-eyed, chubby-cheeked infant peered out and gurgled a welcome.

When I was able to tear my eyes away from the real-life Madonna and child, I saw that the lodge was spotlessly clean and well-ordered, furnished with willow backrests, artfully-painted *parfleche* storage chests, gleaming copper cookware around the lodge firepit, a multi-hued array of woolen blankets strewn atop the buffalo sleeprobes, a pipestand for my father, and the traditional tripod for his weapons. It was plain to see that this had been Powatawa's rendezvous residence for several years past.

When next I looked towards the young woman who had become my stepmother, I saw that she was engaged in animated palaver with Kathleen and Iris was holding the cradleboard, cooing at the infant girl and gently jiggling her to keep her amused. Naturally I was relieved that Cat's fears had come to naught and pleased that my father had chosen a woman who willingly welcomed my family into her lodge. It wasn't surprising that the women got along well, for the Shahaptin and Séli have maintained a longstanding friendship between their peoples, built largely on mutual defense against their foes as well as trade. Frequent intermarriage between the two tribes has further strengthened those bonds.

The women commenced preparations for a meal and Ben commenced coaxing my father to observe his horseback prowess. We stepped outside to chat and smoke and watch Ben show off his newfound skills. When the boy rode into the horse pasture, I broached a matter that had occupied my mind. "Father," I asked, "what will you do when you leave here with the Shahaptin?"

He shot me a quizzical look, surprised at the question, then paused to consider his answer. "I will do the same as all able-bodied men of this band are expected to do. I will hunt with them to fill our bellies and I will defend these people against their enemies. Too, I have been invited to sit in their councils and share with them what little wisdom I have been able to store up in my lifetime." He fell silent, then added with a wry grin, "I am sure you have guessed, Seewauseekau, I will do what I can to keep their moccasins from treading the Jesus Road that, for Indians, leads to the Whiteman's Hell."

"But will you also work with me and the others, next year, in our trading outfit?" I described then the outcome of that morning's meeting—who decided to continue trapping and who chose to work with me. "Ten of us remain. I ask you to join us."

He looked pained but resolved to stand by his decision. "I have told you that my path lies now with my woman—Welethee Wapethee in Shawnee, Pretty Swan in English—and my girl-child, your sister. I will not desert them. I have neglected my woman for too long, as it is."

"Good!" I replied. "I would never ask you to do that, any more than I could turn my back on Kathleen and my own children. I ask only that you stay with the Shahaptin and provide them with the goods we will supply in trade for their buffalo robes, fine furs, and whatever else they wish to trade. The home ground of this band and Iron Bow's are not far apart. We could see each other often."

He looked skeptical but intrigued by this new possibility. "You have often said, Father," I went on, "that the elders in your band think the Whiteman's god will shower them with white-eyes goods if they walk the Jesus Road. You and I know that won't ever happen, but if you can provide them with all the settlement wares they could wish for and still let them stick to the old ways, it will certainly strengthen your arguments."

He was still not convinced, but he looked thoughtful. "Come, let us eat," he said. "I will think about it and give you my answer."

That was the best I could have hoped for right then. While we waited for Ben to finish his lope around the pasture, I thought about my father's age. Although he is still a strong, vital man, a skilled hunter and warrior, simple arithmetic tells me that he must be in his fifties now. When age at last overtakes him, his position as factor for our trading outfit would guarantee him a long, respectable career amongst the Nez Percés.

I hardly tasted the well-cooked meal that Pretty Swan and Cat served up that day, so enchanted was I with the new member of my family. Once she got over her initial shyness around me, she proved to possess more than enough intelligence and good nature to match her loveliness in form and feature. I tried to keep in mind that this graceful young woman was now my stepmother, although she was no more than a year or two older than Kathleen. Silently I complimented my father for his taste and prowess, although I would never have dared express it in words.

After we finished eating too much and exchanging too many gifts on both sides, Powatawa came with me to retrieve our horses. Whilst I snugged up saddle girths, he came nigh and said in a low voice, "I have thought about what you said. I will do as you ask for a time. I named you Seewauseekau, A Door Opened. Perhaps this is how you will live up to that name, creating trust through honest trading, treating Indians fairly, showing good example to create understanding between redmen and white."

I'm not sure that he said it precisely like that, but that is pretty much what I remember that he meant to say. I am also not sure that I will ever know how to achieve what my father desires, peace and understanding between Indians and whites. But I will be an honest trader and hope for the best.

I did, howsomever, succeed in getting Powatawa to agree to take on the trading chore with his Nez Percé band. Once trade is established with that one village, the other Shahaptin bands will come to him to trade. If he is willing to stay with it, my father's old age will be secure—and in light of his new family, a happy one.

Riding back to camp, Kathleen chattered about her newfound friend, when we weren't trying to explain to Iris that the baby girl on the cradleboard was, in fact, my sister and, therefore, her aunt, which failure wasn't surprising. I am still having trouble getting used to it.

ʠ ʠ ʠ

July was drawing to its end. Iron Bow's people were commencing to pack up their plunder for their northern journey. Pretty Horse and our two Iroquois moved their families into Fontenelle's camp in preparation for the fall hunt. He and Bridger already had more than a hundred trappers willing to go with them into Blackfoot country.

"Most of 'em are countin' on what they been hearin' 'baout haow thar ain't hardly no Blackfoots left up thataway arter the pox mostly wiped 'em out," Black Harris surmised. "Mebbe so. Then agin, mebbe not. Only the good die young an' Blackfoots don't qualify."

Naturally I informed Harris of our plans, which he greeted with a mixture of approval and disappointment. "Reckon it's a good move fer those o' ye what ain't wantin' to come back to the settlements, but, gawddammit! I hate to see all this goin' to hell an' never comin' back!" He waved vaguely at trappers' tents and surrounding Indian encampments.

We talked about Tom Fitzpatrick's decision to quit. "What about you?" I asked. "You quittin', too?"

"Aw, hell no! Reckon I'll hang on as long as they keep payin' me to keep 'em from gittin' lost. An' if they quit havin' ronnyvoos, I kin allus show pilgrim farmers the way to Oregon, much as I hate the thought o' doin it!"

"If you don't, there's a heap of others that will," I reassured him.

"Reckon so. Leastaways I'll git 'em thar, wagons, cows, kids, an' all."

"When'll ye be pullin' out?" I asked. "Any idea?"

"Nope. Not fer sure. Leastaways not 'til Fitz an t'others git back from their huntin' trip over t' the Wind River range with Stewart an' his artist feller an' Antoine, an' natcherly his two sarvints, a cook, an' a couple hostlers fer campkeepers. Drips an' Provôt went along, too, figgerin' a taste o' the high life with the Cap'n war too good to pass up. Stewart's got a fav'rite lake over thataway he's allus ravin' abaout an' the huntin's good thar, too.

"Reckon we'll be hittin' the trail back to Missourah soon's they git back. Fitz's traders awready scraped up nigh all the plews an' robes an' sich hyarabaouts, so thar'll be nothin' holdin' us hyar."

We parted then, promising to get together in Saint Louis.

~ ~ ~

The evening before Fontenelle and Bridger put their brigade on the northward trail, I received a visit from two Irishmen, Finn McCool and Harry

Yeats. An extra saddler and two packhorses loaded with Harry's plunder stood nigh McCool's bower. Harry asked if he might join our party on the journey to Iron Bow's home ground and then the river trip to Saint Louis. Naturally I assured him that he was welcome to come along with us as far as he wished. "So you're quittin' the fur trade, are ye, Harry?" I asked. "How come?"

"Och, fer much the same reason that you yerownself are doin' the loike," he replied. "Castors are gettin' scarcer iv'ry year, as ye well know, an' prices fer goods are gettin' higher in turn, 'til it won't be long before I'd be owin' me very soul to the traders. The lads've been after keepin' me swimmin' in poteen these sev'ral years past, thankin' me fer the tunes I've provided an' savin' me the cost of it, so I've put enough coin away on the Comp'ny books to pay me way to Boston town an' from there to board ship fer Californy."

"And what'll ye do when ye get there, Harry?

"Ah, there's the fun of it, Temple! I mean to build me a proper boat to go huntin' them darlin' sea otters, the hide of a single one of 'em worth half a pack o' beaver plews, an' the briny thereabouts purely swarmin' with 'em, jist pinin' fer Harry Yeats an' his trusty harpoon to come along an' harvest a bloody fortune! An' if a great bloody whale chances to come swimmin' close by to shore—as ye've seen they sometimes do—I'll not be behindhand in harvestin' thim, too."

"And ye won't be getting' seasick?" I asked, trying not to smile.

Harry's color rose a mite, but he plunged on. "Divil a bit of it! I'll not be goin' far out to sea, jist stayin' close to shore, where the otters are. Whiniver it starts to blow, I'll be rowin' me handsome Hibernian arse to land an' waitin' it out an' keepin' me breakfast where I put it."

Micah and Fast Horse rode in advance of the column, leading the way across open prairie, engaged in earnest palaver, swapping languages as they went , perfecting fluency in the other's tongue, Micah with an eye toward future commerce with the Séli bands, Fast Horse in preparation for one day succeeding to his father's leadership position. Soon, ability to speak American will prove valuable in dealing with white settlers coming in the wake of missionaries. Unlike mountaineers, most of whom first learn sign-talk, then native tongues from their Indian women, few pilgrims from the settlements will bother to acquire native languages or learn the customs. The

Indian who learns American is certain to gain stature in his band and tribe. Fast Horse was born and raised in his father's political shadow. Gaining advantage in the tribal power game is second nature in him.

I trailed behind them, training Sunshine, my *palomilla* stud horse. Centuries of selective breeding bestowed a gentle, cooperative nature on *palomillas* that let lets a rider channel the fire and courage natural to stallions into useful qualities in war and other violent occupations, such as running buffalo. Sunshine is a good-natured critter, powerful, quick to learn, and fearless without being foolish.

It was the second day of August. We were by then three days on the northward trail. Rendezvous had been breaking up and the old chief was anxious to get to his customary buffalo hunting grounds before returning for the winter to his home country. Which had been welcome news to me. I was eager to get to Fort McKenzie, high up on the Missouri, before the river froze up and put an end to steamboat traffic until spring.

I regretted not being able to bid farewell to Captain Stewart and his young artist friend. They were still absent on their hunting trip in the Wind River Mountains. My opinion of the British lord had altered considerably since I realized that his love of our Rocky Mountains and our way of life hardly differs from my own. Regarding Miller, I wished I could have seen his sketches of Kathleen, made when he lurked nigh our camp or spied on us when we went to trade.

As for old friends, it was just as well to depart Indian-style, without awkward goodbyes and promises that would likely never be kept. Joe Meek, still numbed by grief over Umentucken's death and the river of booze he drank to forget it, waved vaguely in our direction as we filed out of camp.

❧   ❧   ❧

We made good time for so large a company, Iron Bow's band of eighty-odd lodges and our own bunch besides, sometimes as much as thirty miles a day. At night we camped off to one side of the Séli, as the elders had requested, but we were rarely separate. Whenever Tolliver and Harry unlimbered fiddle and *guitarra* and commenced to play, goodnatured Flatheads, especially the younger ones, were drawn to our camp, at first shuffling their moccasins in time to the lively tunes, then breaking into spirited dancing.

A welcome benefit was Flathead boys standing horse guard for us at night, which we repaid with buffalo harvested along the way, as well as wapiti and grizzlies our scouts picked off on the prairie. We kept a sharp eye out for Blackfoot war parties, but the size of our company evidently discouraged them. "Natcherly thar ain't no tellin' fer sure," Turtle surmised, "but I'm thinkin' mebbe what some war sayin' back at ronnyvoo abaout the pox drivin' 'em to ground up nawth mought be so. We shoulda run into some of 'em by naow, don'tcha think?"

Nobody disagreed, but we kept our eyes peeled for hostile sign. Old habits are good because they work.

∾   ∾   ∾

One week slid into the next as we plodded north, taking advantage   of the good campgrounds the Séli had discovered in the several years they had traveled that same route to rendezvous, leafy groves with abundant firewood and nearby streams.

Naturally an attractive place to camp doesn't remain anybody's private property. One late afternoon, Little Mountain, Diego Valenzuela, and a couple of Séli warriors scouting ahead came galloping back to the column, concern on their faces as they neared. "Bettah we don't stay that same place fer camp tonight!" Mountain exclaimed. "It war a Síksikah camp, but not no more! All dead! All of 'em! Pox kilt 'em!" The two Sélis, anxious to carry the news to the leaders, barely slowed their mounts as they raced past.

Fast Horse, riding betwixt Micah and Finn McCool, commenced jabbering excitedly to his companions, then signaled a halt to the column and loped to the rear. I gigged Sunshine forward to join Finn and Micah, who read the question on my face. "Finn's been tellin' Fast Horse how he an' Zeetlah vaccinated our bunch against the pox," Micah announced. "Now Fast Horse wants them to do likewise for the whole Séli band. What d'ye think?"

This was serious, not a step to be taken lightly. Certainly not one that I wished to decide by myself. Somehow, ever since most of the bunch agreed to quit trapping that year and join in the trading venture, they had begun to defer to my judgment, a role that I had avoided throughout my life, as all of them were aware.

"Let's get together with Turtle an' Zeetlah and anybody else who wants in on it an' decide," I responded at last. "If somethin' goes wrong, we could wipe out Iron Bow's whole band!"

Whilst Diego rode back to collect the others, I asked McCool, "How d'ye know, Finn, if your vaccinatin' really works?

"I don't," he replied simply. "All I know for sure is what we've been doin' hasn't harmed any of us and not a one of us has come down with the pox. The good Doctor Den came up with the procedure fer extractin' the serum an' preparin' it an' Zeetlah added one or more of his secret yarbs an' took over the cookin' of it. Like I say, nobody we've vaccinated has got the smallpox so far. But that's all I can be sure of."

When the others joined us, Finn repeated what he had told me, after which we voted to comply with Fast Horse's wishes in the matter, provided that Iron Bow and the other members of the council granted permission. Whilst we waited for the council's decision, McCool, Zeetlah, and Little Mountain rode to the Síksikah camp to collect serum from some of the dead bodies there and commence preparing a quantity of the vaccination material. They would need a lot of it. Eighty-odd lodges amounted to some three hundred people, counting children.

At last Fast Horse rode up and announced that the elders had agreed to allow those who would consent to be vaccinated to do so. It was plain to see that the youngest member of the council was exasperated at the delay in reaching a decision, but he had at last succeeded in getting his way.

On our way to an overnight campground, safely higher up the stream from the Síksikah camp, we passed within sight of a dozen small lodges of the Blackfoots, which identified them as a war party of fifty or so warriors. "Thar's allus some good fer somebody, even when it's somebody else's bad luck," Brass Turtle observed wryly, jerking his chin towards the silent camp. "Thar's likely half a hunnert muskets an' sich in thar, free fer the takin', once these hyar Flatheads git theirse'fs vaccinated, an' prob'ly twice that many hosses runnin' free hyarabaouts." He was silent a moment before he added, "Best be leavin' clothes an' sich be, howsomever, an' be takin' jist the hardware. Cain't tell haow long the pox'll be hangin' around on clothes an' the like."

His musing was interrupted by Micah pointing out to the prairie and yelping, "Buffler!" Suiting action to the word, he touched spur to flank and set off in pursuit with Turtle and me close behind, followed by Tolliver, Diego, Paddy, and Harry, and a dozen Flatheads streaming out of the column.

Sunshine, grateful to be released from the plodding gait of the column, fairly leaped into a pounding gallop across the grassy prairie, head outstretched, leaning into the bit, low to the ground, dragging my moccasins through belly-high grass, thrilling me with his power and willing response to command when I collected him slightly and directed him to a fat cow running in the open. This would be his first buffalo. Each time we had come upon a herd, I happened to be riding either Coffee or Crane. Now was his chance to show if he could be a proper buffalo runner.

As we closed on the cow, coming up on her near side, I pulled a pistol from its saddle holster, the rein in my left hand, ready to check him if he got too close to the wide-swinging head—which he did, narrowly dodging a vicious swipe of her horns, which threw him off his stride, letting the cow gain a length or two. I brushed him with a spur and guided him back in pursuit, closing the gap until we came up beside her, Sunshine's chin now safely even with her hump. A twitch of the rein settled his onward rush into a flat gallop, smoothly matching her pace. I swung my pistol out at arm's length, aimed just above and behind the churning front leg, and squeezed off my shot.

The cow continued for a stride and a half, maybe two, before her knees buckled and she slid on her bearded chin, belching blood from shattered lungs, and lay still, wide-open eyes glassy, unseeing, outstretched legs already stiffening.

I swung Sunshine in a wide arc, slowing his pace to gentle lope, patting his neck the while and crooning compliments, and surveyed the field. Nigh a score of hunters ranged over the prairie, a few still in pursuit, most of them already afoot, in twos and threes, commencing the butchering chore. Women and kids leading pack animals were riding out from the column to claim the kills and carry the meat to camp.

I stepped to the ground nigh the cow, led Sunshine several paces upwind from the fresh-spilled blood, and dropped the reins to ground-tie him and let him graze. When I returned to the cow, Brass Turtle rode up. "Give ye a hand?" he offered, which I happily accepted, promising to trade the favor afterward. "Reckon ye be purty pleased with your yeller stud hoss," Turtle commented as we set to work on the butchering. "I seen haow he jist natcherly took to runnin' thi'shere cow, once he caught on to what ye war askin' of 'im. Ye kin be proud o' that'n, fer damn sure—an' fer trainin' 'im, too."

"I can't claim all the credit," I told him. "Half-horse deserves most o' your praise. That lad thinks more like a horse than anybody I've ever known."

"Sure does," Turtle replied with a smirk. "An' a stud hoss at that!"

I had to agree. "Yep, that, too."

∾   ∾   ∾

The aroma of roasting meat from a couple score cookfires throughout the encampment, coupled with full bellies, put everybody in a good mood that night. Anse and Harry brought out their instruments and soon our camp was crowded with smiling young Sélis shuffling and prancing more or less in time to sprightly Celtic tunes. "Hyar's hopin' thi'shere happifyin' feelin' hangs on 'til t'morra mawnin', when time comes fer gittin' their arms scratched," Turtle observed.

"Speakin' o' which," I asked, "have ye seen anything of Finn an' Zeetlah an' Mountain?"

"Yep. Me an' Half-hoss took 'em a bait o' supper, down at the Blackfoot camp. All three of 'em are cookin' up a mess o' that'ere medicine, what Finn's callin' the smallpox vaccine. Finn told me Zeetlah's fin'ly lettin' 'im in on what kind o' yarbs an' sich he's been puttin' in the mix an' haow an' haow long he cooks it an' sich, naow that Finn's quittin' the mountains an' headin' back East an' ain't never comin' back. He wou'n't tell 'im afore naow. Zeetlah don't care none fer compertishun, even from his frien's."

"Let's hope they get it right," I said fervently. "It'd be one helluva way to repay Iron Bow for all he's done for us."

∾   ∾   ∾

Fast Horse had been making his rounds through the Séli camp since dawn, haranguing the people about protecting themselves against the dread disease that wiped out the Blackfoot war party and would certainly spread to them unless they trusted him and the new medicine. Cat and Molly did what they could to bolster his arguments, showing their vaccination scars and speaking in their native Salish to convince their kin and former neighbors that the treatment wouldn't harm them. Even so, when it came time to gather to receive the vaccination, some three-score members of the band hung back and refused to come out of their lodges.

Fast Horse was first to bare his arm, choosing Finn to administer the vaccine, demonstrating his confidence in what the tribesmen were calling the White-eyes medicine. Next was Iron Bow, his stolid features inscrutable, as they almost always are, no matter the situation, good or bad. He was followed by the elders of the council, most of them looking somewhat less confident than their chief but unwilling to show fear. Each time Finn scratched an arm and dabbed on the thick fluid, a sharp intake of breath rippled among the assembled tribespeople, until at last they appeared to accept that their leaders would not keel over and die. Fast Horse's closest adherents, the young men we had trained in the use of rifles, jostled one another to be first in line to prove their worthiness, which encouraged several other warriors to gather behind them. Zeetlah and Little Mountain, seeking to profit from that apparent approval, stepped forward then and joined McCool in applying the vaccine.

Our three medicos worked as fast as they could, unwilling to pause for rest, lest they break the spell that steadily captured the crowd, nervous titters and giggles amongst women and youngsters notwithstanding. Warriors, unwilling to appear daunted before their fellows, shoved forward to present their upper arms for the medicinal scratch, then hauled up their wives and children to receive the life-saving treatment.

At last the crowd dwindled to nothing, except for the sixty-or-so tribespeople still leery of the White-eyes medicine, fearful that it would infect them with the dreaded pox. Which wasn't a far-fetched notion. I myself would have been a lot less willing to let myself be vaccinated in California if I hadn't already had the cowpox as a youngster. Rocky Mountain Indians don't milk cows.

Still, sixty-odd people, most of them women and children, could not be allowed to die a horrible death because of fear born of ignorance. It was likely that most of them were being dominated by a few hard-headed loudmouths. Such was the palaver amongst our bunch when we gathered for dinner, after the morning's chore was ended. "We cain't jist let 'em die, even if some of 'em are gawddamn blockheads!" Brass Turtle complained aloud, but nobody came up with a solution to the problem.

"If Fast Hoss cain't change their minds, ye kin be damn sure none of us kin tell 'em nothin' they'll be b'lievin'," Tolliver declared. "Reckon we jist gotta let 'em die. That'll larn 'em!"

It was a stupid remark, typical of Anse, who is always ready to give the rough side of his tongue to anybody who disagrees with him. Nobody paid it much nevermind, except for Zeetlah. The old healer jerked up his head, stared at Tolliver for half a minute, then growled something in Delaware to Little Mountain and rose to his feet. Without another word, the two of them caught up their horses and rode off in the direction of the Blackfoot camp.

"Now what do ye s'pose them two are after now?" Paddy wondered aloud. "Is there some'at ye left behind in that Blackfoot pest-hole, Finnæus?" he asked, addressing McCool.

"Not that I know of, Padraic," Finn replied, "but I've learned niver to question that darlin' auld man. His ways are often mysterious, but he wastes no time on foolishness."

I looked to Brass Turtle for an explanation, but he merely shrugged.

Half an hour later the two Delawares returned and went in search of Fast Horse, who obligingly rounded up his recalcitrant tribesmen and told them to get their horses and follow our old healer, which a couple dozen of them, mostly warriors, did. When they passed by our camp, most of us put aside our pipes and mounted up, eager to learn what Zeetlah might have up his sleeve.

We fell in at the tail end of the column, beside Fast Horse, who appeared to be as mystified as the rest of us. When we arrived at the Blackfoot camp, only Zeetlah dismounted, signing to the rest to remain on their horses at a distance from a lodge cover spread out on the prairie grass. Zeetlah commenced signing then, for it is doubtful that he knows much of the Salish tongue, explaining that he brought them here to let them see for themselves the likely consequence of their decision to forego vaccination. Lacking a formal sign for the procedure, he pulled up his sleeve and scratched at his shoulder cap.

Then he stooped, snatched up a corner of the lodge cover, and dragged it after him as he trotted to its far end, revealing half a dozen rotting bodies ravaged by smallpox, barely recognizable as the strong young men they had been before the scourge claimed them, faces deeply pitted and caved in, cheekbones exposed, some with eyes still staring blindly at the horror that had overtaken them.

Horses recoiled at the sudden stench that rose up from the corpses. Their riders were no less appalled at the odor and the sight of horrible death. Hands flew to their mouths in shock and disgust. Several leaned over to vomit. Others covered their eyes, until Zeetlah called aloud for their attention, then launched into signing a stern lecture on the fate that awaited each one of them who dared believe that he could avoid the plague that was loose in the land. He pointed out that he and all of our bunch were safe from the disease and now so were their fellow tribesmen who had received the scratches that morning, but agony and a ghastly death awaited those whose pride and willfulness kept them from saving themselves and those who looked to them for protection.

He told them all that and more without uttering a single syllable aloud, relentless in his denunciation of prideful men who doomed their families to ugly, painful death for the sake of their own petty vanity. It was plain that Zeetlah was achieving his aim, going after self-important bullies. Warriors who had ridden out from the camp with a flaunting, arrogant demeanor now drooped in their saddles, shamed by our tough old healer and his eloquent hands. Satisfied that he had made his point, he quit his rant, turned on his heel, and stalked to his horse, while Little Mountain hastened to pull the lodge cover over the bodies to discourage the buzzards circling overhead.

Brass Turtle and I raced back to camp ahead of the others. Sweeping into camp, Turtle called out to McCool, "Ye'd best git some o' yer potion ready, Finn! Reckon ye got more customers comin' by!"

Which he did. When the rest arrived, the Sélis scattered to their lodges and soon came trooping to our camp, women and children in tow, cowed and willing, even anxious, to receive the White-eyes medicine that might save them from what they had just witnessed.

When Jean-Luc trotted by later, announcing suppertime, I reckoned I'd as lief pass on the vittles that particular night.

❧ ❧ ❧

We remained two more days in that camp to give the Sélis time to round up Blackfoot horses that had scattered over that neighborhood. Meanwhile, our bunch salvaged muskets, bows and sheaves of arrows, and other weapons and useful hardware from the death camp, laying it all out on the prairie for the Sélis to retrieve, before setting fire to the lodges, cremating the ghastly remains of their tenants. A huge cloud of black smoke bloomed up from the fatal grove and hung overhead like a funeral pall for an hour or more, a grim reminder of the death we had averted.

"'Tis a fittin' farewell to that bloody mob o' rapparees," Paddy pronounced solemnly. "Better'n they desarve, I'm thinkin'."

❧ ❧ ❧

The remainder of our northward journey was happily uneventful, with no more than the customary number of minor catastrophes you might expect in a caravan of three hundred or more people dragging travois overloaded with plunder and kids, driving pack animals, and herding a thousand horses. Our bunch kept pretty much to ourselves on the trail, usually keeping near the head of the column, which gave us an early crack at game encountered along the way, providing vittles for ourselves and extra meat to share with our hosts.

Iron Bow's band had always been friendly enough, but after our brush with the smallpox, they warmed up more than ever before. After the first few days passed with no more discomfort than arms itching from vaccinations, doubt about our intentions transformed into gratitude for saving them from a hideous death. Our singletons profited most directly from this increasing good feeling. Nocturnal visits by Séli widows to bachelor bowers became commonplace. Young Half-horse went about with a perpetual smile pasted on his handsome mug.

Ben insisted on riding his little piebald Rags every day, although many Séli children his age still rode with their mother or jolted along the rugged trail clinging to a travois. When he wasn't riding alongside Turtle's son Otter, his closest friend, or tagging after Iris, Ben often rode beside me, chattering incessantly, demanding to know the English name of every bird, critter, flower, plant, and landmark along the way and repeating it back to me until he got it right. He did the same with Kathleen and Iris in Salish, which greatly reduced the amount of trouble his active mind and restless body would have got him into otherwise.

Iris often joined me on the trail, almost always accompanied by her redheaded shadow, Paddy's son Sean. The two of them, Sean equally with Iris, insisted that I tell them stories drawn from my memories of the heroic tales my mother had related to me of Persian princes and Spanish grandees, bloodthirsty Mongols, Crusaders in the Holy Land, and Irish and Scottish heroes fighting for their freedom from English tyranny. When memory failed, I often invented characters and incidents to fill in the gaps, but they appeared to enjoy it, anyway.

The long hours in the saddle that our children happily endured each day provided a pleasant benefit for Kathleen and me. By time the youngsters finished their supper, their eyelids drooped and they headed for their robes, which afforded uninterrupted opportunities for Cat and me to do pretty much as we pleased.

∾ ∾ ∾

The merry mood of the Flatheads grew less carefree as we drew nigh the vast prairies that lie east of the Sélis' home country, their traditional buffalo hunting grounds. Each year, returning from rendezvous, Iron Bow's band interrupts its homeward journey to conduct their annual harvest of buffalo to carry them through the hungry winter months in their mountain homeland.

Warriors grew watchful, constantly alert, bracing for Blackfoot attacks that have forever been an accepted price they pay for hunting on the boundless sea of grass the Blackfoot nation claims as its rightful fiefdom. All but Káinah, Píkuni, and Síksikah tribesmen are regarded as trespassers. Even Big-bellies hunt there at their peril.

Even so, Séli, Kootenai, and Pend d'Oreille bands have little choice except to risk Blackfoot wrath. Appetite is a powerful persuader. Battle is the better choice when famine is the alternative.

That year Iron Bow was in a better condition than usual to assert his right to hunt. The windfall of Blackfoot muskets and ammunition from the pestcamp greatly increased the firepower of his band and the presence of our bunch of fighters who harbor no love for bullying Blackfoots would do much to even the odds if Blackfoots came a-calling.

It was by then the last week of August. Weather was sunny and mild and buffalo cows were rolling fat, the best time for harvesting a winter meat supply. The band camped alongside a sizeable crick bordered with cottonwoods and scattered aspen groves. Good graze, dry, level ground, plenty of firewood, and clean water is all an Indian or a mountaineer asks for his camping comfort.

Hunting commenced the day we arrived. Whilst the women erected lodges and meat-drying racks, men headed for the prairie, where small herds of a hundred or fewer animals grazed. We rode out a-horseback to get to our prey, but hunting would be conducted afoot and at a distance. This was a meat hunt, serious business, no time for sport. Running buffalo would scatter the herds and drive them off, requiring long daily hikes to find the critters and to carry meat back to the drying racks in camp. It would also make hunters and meat-haulers more vulnerable to attack by dispersing them over a wide territory in pursuit of fleeing herds. Gunshots startle and cause buffalo to run off a distance, but if nobody's chasing them, they soon settle down and go back to grazing.

Micah and I, accompanied by Cesár and the two *Californios*, Diego and Pablo, set out the first afternoon with Jean-Luc leading a couple brace of packmules. Within a mile of camp, we came upon a small herd, consisting of a double score of young cows, heifers, and half-grown bull calves lorded over by a couple-three seed bulls and a few canny old cows. Giving them wide berth, we circled far around them, until we could feel the soft western breeze on our face, then rode slowly towards them, picking our way through the broken ground, imitating grazing critters, trading on their poor eyesight.

When we came to a broad swale in the prairie, deep enough to conceal our livestock from the herd, we slipped to the ground and turned the horses over to Jean-Luc, who remained there whilst we crawled up the far side on hands and knees through high grass, a couple yards apart, rifles slung, pausing every minute or so, lest constant movement alarm our prey, until we were within a hundred yards. Lying on my belly, I wriggled free of my rifle sling, eased the hammer to half-cock, and slipped a cap onto the nipple whilst I chose the stout young cow that would be mine.

All eyes were on Cesár, who would give the final nod. When he did, one-by-one we eased our rifles to full-cock, but Pablo's hammer sounded a harsh squeak and metallic clack. Even at that distance, one shaggy old cow threw up her head and loosed a warning squeal, which threw the whole bunch into confusion. Instead of the single fusillade we had intended, each man adjusted his aim and took the best shot he could. My cow stumbled and sprawled, tumbled over and lay still. Two more fell in their tracks as they sought to follow their fleeing sisters. Another was limping badly as she disappeared into the high grass with the others.

Cesár showered Spaniard curses on Pablo, who blushed under his leathery tan, blaming him for spoiling our ambush. Micah came to the young fellow's rescue. "Aw, hell! Cesár, let it go!" he yelled. "Three out o' five ain't bad. Thar's a heap o' meat out thar! Ain't nobody goin' hungry!" Then he addressed something in Spanish to Pablo, likely promising to fix his rifle when we returned to camp.

We stood to reload, scanning the prairie, lest our rifle fire had drawn unwelcome attention, but nothing stirred. I trotted back to Jean-Luc to help bring our saddlers and packmules forward. By time I returned, my companions were indulging in the hunter's reward, chomping on fresh liver. Typically, hot-tempered Cesár's ire had vanished. He was swapping Spaniard jibes with Pablo, who was apparently giving as good as he got.

Even with our abbreviated kill that day, the packmules staggered under their burden of meat when we returned to camp. We harvested much more each day than we normally would have done. The main purpose of this hunt was preserving meat and fat and marrow for the wintertime needs of the Sélis, as well as our own.

We stuffed ourselves every night and morning on boiled and roasted tongue and boudins and prime cuts, but the abundant supply of buffalo on that vast grassy ocean provided far more provender than we could possibly use up. The lodgepole racks in our camp sagged under their daily load of red meat strips drying in the high, dry mountain air and smoky fires burning underneath to hasten the process. Most of the meat we harvested went to the Séli band, which further cemented the already good feeling betwixt them and us.

Each day increased a sense of impending doom, threatening a Blackfoot attack whose presence was almost palpable. "I'll be gawddamned if I kin figger what in hell them'ere Blackfoots be waitin' on," Brass Turtle complained. "I'm almost wishin' them sumbitches'd jump us an' git a proper fight started, 'stead o' teasin' us thisaway, keepin' us hangin', makin' us wonder when an' whar it's gonna happen, 'cause it shore-as-hell will!

"Fast Hoss says he's been comin' hyar with his pa fer more'n thutty years, man an' boy, huntin' buffler, an' they ain't never got off 'thout a fight with Blackfoots! Whar-in-hell do ye s'pose they be?"

"If I had to say," McCool opined, "I'd be after supposin' 'tis the smallpox. Either it has already hit them and wiped out the most of 'em or it's got 'em sufficiently frightened that they've high-tailed it up north, keepin' a distance 'twixt themsel's and all others who might be after infectin' 'em."

Nobody had a better idea. Just the same, we kept our head on a swivel, ready for an eruption of scalp-hunting Blackfoots. But it never came.

After a fortnight of hunting and drying meat, even the most cautious Séli elder conceded that nobody was likely to go hungry in the coming winter. It was time to go. The free-running herds of loose horses were greatly reduced in size as many of them were pressed into service as pack animals loaded with bundles of dried meat, pemmican, and such.

Fast Horse returned the horses I had left with him in previous years, so that our bunch might possess enough animals to lug our own large stock of wintertime provisions. My family and friends would be well-fed when the snows came.

I was even more relieved to be on our way. It was already September and I feared that river traffic on the Missouri might be suspended before I could reach Fort McKenzie to obtain passage on a steamboat to Saint Louis.

-ooo-

CHAPTER XIX
CHANGING TIMES

nother week brought us to Iron Bow's home ground, south and west of the large lake trappers call the Flathead, well-forested mountain country dotted with grassy prairies and watered by many cricks and streams that flow into the large forks that feed the lake. Naturally, next spring, when I return, the band won't likely be where I left it, but I expect I'll be able to find them.

Settling in for the winter required not much more time than an overnight stop would demand. A Rocky Mountain Indian village is always speedily portable, ready to pick up and move on for whatever reason.

This time the lodges ringed the forepart of a high, rocky hill with huge rocks and boulders scattered around its base and up its craggy sides, with a fresh-running crick running past one side, a natural fortress in case of attack. By that time our customary location on the outer fringe of the Séli camp was well-established, so no one disputed our convenient position nigh the water.

Finn, Harry, and Anse were as anxious as I to get on our way to Fort McKenzie on the Missouri. Problem was, none of us had ever traveled the route we needed to follow to reach the Great Falls of the Missouri. We knew the fort lay somewhere below that natural barrier, but all we were reasonably sure of was the likely direction, nothing more. Valuable time that we couldn't afford would be consumed in trying to find our way through the rugged mountains, forests, and prairies that lay betwixt us and our goal.

Iron Bow came to our rescue. When we explained our predicament, he nodded and said nothing. He merely looked solemn and thoughtful, which is how he almost always looks, anyway. An hour later, howsomever, three men showed up in our camp, two well-set-up warriors about my own age and a weathered-looking man past his middle years but sturdy enough. Fast Horse accompanied them. "We comin' 'longside you for goin' Big River, awright?" he informed us, then pointed to the older man and said, "Crowfoot awready been dere. He know road to big-water-fallin'-down. No gittin' lost. You neider." Naturally Fast Horse accompanied his words with hand-signs, which Crowfoot observed and confirmed with his own.

We couldn't have wished for better. Indians may talk big or blow smoke at a whiteman, but if he declares to a fellow tribesman that he knows or has done a certain thing, you can wager on it. We agreed, on the spot, to depart the following morning.

I had already laid out what I would need, as well as the animals I would take. My three favorites, Coffee, Crane, and Sunshine would remain with Kathleen. I chose two sturdy, well-gaited saddlers and a stout, easy-going saddle mule for myself, as well as a packmule to carry my plunder.

I had seen that the three Séli guides carried muskets of uncertain vintage and dubious condition, so I hunted up Micah and obtained three decent large-caliber flintlock rifles he had converted to percussion and their fixin's, freshly oiled, brasswork gleaming, a gift sure to earn a warrior's thankees. Fast Horse already owned the fine Hawken rifle I had given him years before.

Cat had already packed up extra workaday clothes and sturdy moccasins for the trail, as well as a couple fancy outfits for me, my sleeprobes, capote, extra blankets, dried food for lean days, Indian trade goods, and such. I took little else besides a generous stock of gunpowder, galena pigs, and caps, extra knives and camp tools, and my journals, securely wrapped in oilskin.

ta   ta   ta

Our guides set a brisk pace from the outset, warning that we would soon be entering a heavily-forested area, followed by increasingly high mountains and difficult trails that would surely slow our progress. Fast Horse had made it clear to them that we needed to reach the big river before cold weather caused it to freeze. Naturally, none of them, including Fast Horse, had ever seen a steamboat or anything larger than a bullboat, so they likely accepted our wish for haste as an example of white-eyes whimsy but did their best to comply.

Two days out from Iron Bow's village, after skirting the south end of the lake then heading mostly due east, we came to the forest and the trail assumed a steady upgrade. Crowfoot's younger cronies, Eagle Ribs and The Moon, now demonstrated valuable skill, coursing ahead through thick woods, sometimes a-horseback, mostly afoot, discovering the best trail for us to follow, the most direct and least obstructed by fallen trees and deep ravines. Traveling alone, frequently on foot, they provided most of our vittles, as well.

Although we mostly followed deer and elk trails through the forest, our numerous mounted company spooked most of the game we might have harvested if we had been fewer in number.

In spite of Crowfoot's knowledge of the country and the wise choices of his helpers, avoiding the several high peaks that jutted into the clouds along the way, it was still slow going through the heavily-timbered terrain. The ring of axes clearing a path past fallen trees provided a constant refrain during daylight hours and the rasp of files sharpening tools around the cookfire at night took the place of most palaver before we fell exhausted into our sleeprobes.

McCool and I had each been making a map of the country we were traversing, comparing our efforts every night at suppertime and making corrections and adjustments, in anticipation of our bunch making that journey each year to transport trade goods from the Great Falls to Flathead country. Harry Yeats and the campkeepers assisted our effort by helping us enlarge the tomahawk gashes our Séli guides left on trees along the way to keep us on the right track as we proceeded through the seemingly endless forest.

When we crossed a broad but shallow river that ran northwards, Crowfoot cracked one of his rare smiles and announced that we had now completed half of our woodland journey. If he had expected us to be jubilant at the news, he was mistaken. "Only halfway, is it now?" Harry groaned. "Does he mean to be sayin' we have all that to be doin' over again?"

"He be tellin' now comes hard part," Fast Horse told him with a grin. "Harder, higher, colder."

He didn't lie. We continued to climb and nights became chillier. I dug out three thick English woolen blankets from my packs and gifted them to our guides, who, typically, were traveling too lightly-equipped for the harsh conditions, leastaways to my mind. We couldn't afford to lose a one of them.

Graze became sparse at our nighttime halts and our critters snatched at any greenery they encountered along the way. We continued eastward, threading through narrow passes we never could have found on our own, until we headed up the broad shoulder of a towering peak. When we reached the crest, our guide jumped from his horse, laughing out loud, flapping his arms, and executing several intricate dance steps. "That ol' man gone an' taken leave o' his gawddamn senses?" Anse enquired tartly, always one to see the dark side of every situation. "If he has, we be plumb swived, the lot of us!"

"Crowfoot be tellin' we be standin' on backbone o' the world," Fast Horse told him, smiling with satisfaction. "He say we almos' thar!"

Which wasn't precisely so, but the hardest part of the journey was pretty nearly over. Two more days of downhill travel through thinning timber brought us out onto what looked like an endless grassy prairie the summer sun had parched to a waving yellow sea. Our critters, woefully ganted by meager rations, especially the horses, perked up when they beheld all that luscious graze, increasing their lagging gait to a jog-trot, and straining to close the distance to a long-awaited suppertime.

We human travelers were no less anxious to reach the valley floor. From our vantage point on the slope, we had espied a couple small bunches of buffalo grazing on the lush forage. We had been too long deprived of our favorite vittles. Deer and wapiti and curlyhorn meat will do when there is no better to be had, but nothing else pleases like buffalo.

Whilst the others pitched camp nigh a stream running off the slope and turned the critters out to graze, Moon, Eagle Ribs, and I rode out to harvest our supper. Which we did, sneaking on our bellies through the tall yellow grass and dropping a pair of fat young cows, butchering out the prime cuts in short order, yipping in triumph the while, and grinning through blood-smeared cheeks.

ã€€ã€€ã€€ã€€

We lingered there for two days, letting our tired livestock recruit condition on lush graze and gorging ourselves on fat meat, congratulating ourselves on completing that arduous passage without serious mishap or loss of any of our critters. We had seen not a single human being during the entire trip through the forest.

After the rugged country we had traversed, the remainder of our journey appeared to be, from what we could tell, an agreeable romp across mostly level prairie, provided with good graze and plenty of buffalo.

Except for running into Blackfoot war parties, which would likely grow more numerous as we drew closer to the Great Falls of the Missouri. Anse and I recalled our early days at the mouth of the Musselshell in 'twenty-three, when Andrew Henry lost nearly half his men and almost all of his horses and plunder to Blackfoots when he attempted to trap the Great Falls neighborhood. There was no reason to suppose that the Píkuni were feeling any more hospitable to outsiders nowadays. A party of only ten men and thirty critters would appear to be easy pickin's.

At suppertime on the second day, Crowfoot announced, through Fast Horse—although all of us understood his sign-talk—that it was time to resume our journey. A gibbous moon would cast enough light on the prairie to let us find our way to our next destination, he told us, after which we could travel by day with relative safety. We packed up and set out at dusk, just as a humpbacked moon was rising, casting a shimmering silvery glow on the tall dry grass waving in a gentle evening breeze.

Crowfoot set a steady pace in a northeasterly direction across the broad expanse, mostly at an easy lope, rarely slower than a high trot, halting only briefly to refresh the critters at one of the numerous streams that water the prairie. Eagle Ribs and Moon rode far in advance of the main body, flung out on either side, scouting for possible trouble. After seemingly endless days of plodding on forest trails or rocky mountain tracks, happy to gain yet another step forward, loping now on a fresh horse through belly-high grass bestowed a marvelous sense of careless abandon and well-being on both man and beast.

Not everyone in our party experienced the same feeling of reckless joy that I did, loping across the prairie in moonlight. Our campkeepers, spurring and belting their cranky mules in order to keep up, filled the air with a cloud of *sacrés* and *merdes*.

After a dozen miles, our guide called a brief halt at a crick to let us switch saddles to our spare mounts and stretch our legs. After a spell, Fast Horse called out, "Crowfoot say we come halfway now. Bettah we go now!" From the darkness I heard a sputter of French profanity at the word "halfway."

As much pleasure as I drew from our rapid ride across the open prairie, I would have enjoyed it much more if I had been mounted on any one of my favorite horses, preferably all of them in turn. In a trapper's workaday life there is seldom an opportunity to ride free and unfettered for long distances. Even the pell-mell pursuit of buffalo, as much fun as it is, must be of short duration.

At last Crowfoot reined up and signed that we had arrived at our overnight resting place. We had covered a distance of twenty-five miles or so. No one had challenged us and the scouts had discovered no threats on the way. Even as fatigued as many of our party and all of our critters were, if

Crowfoot's prediction about the rest of the journey proved true, it had been worth the effort.

⁊   ⁊   ⁊

I was awakened by a buzz of excited palaver flavored with expressions of disbelief. "Who'd'a thought sich a thang?" "'Tis truly a wonderment!" "Surely the eighth wonder o' the world, indade!" and suchlike, which brought me bounding from my robes, snatching up my rifle as I did so, purely out of habit.

"Ye won't be needin' your gun, Temple," McCool advised. "Whatever they are, or were, they're long dead."

I looked past him and beheld a huge skeleton, bigger than a dozen buffaloes put together—maybe a couple-three dozen—half-buried in the soil of the coulee where we were camped. Where the head should have been, only a couple of long bones, or maybe tusks, protruded from the earth.

"I've allus heared fellers talkin' 'baout haow they seen the ellerphunt," Anse said, wonder in his voice, "braggin' on haow much they been around, but I allus reckoned they meant, mebbe, haow they'd gone an' seen a ellerphunt in a circus somewhars. Ye reckon mebbe they war talkin' 'baout seein' somethin' like that'ere thang out thar?"

I didn't even try to come up with an answer. Looking farther down the coulee, I saw another huge skeleton, even larger than the first one.

Just then I caught a whiff of morning coffee and followed my nose to the cookfire, where I discovered Yves Dureau dividing his efforts between breakfast chores and trying to comfort Jean-Luc, who was huddled on his hams, head betwixt his knees, shivering in fear.

"*Qu'est-ce que c'est ça?*" I enquired of Yves, jerking my chin at Jean-Luc whilst I filled my cup.

Yves shrugged and laughed self-consciously. "*Il pense que le grand truc là-bas est peut-être les os d'un grand carcagne et peut-être il y a des autres carcagnes près d'ici qui mangeront lui.*" Yves shrugged again and spread his hands in a helpless gesture. "*Je crois que non, mais Jean-Luc n'écoute pas!*"

What Dureau told me was that Jean-Luc feared that the skeleton in the coulee was the bones of a dreaded *carcagne*—Americans call it a Carcane—a huge mythological beast with the head of a wolf, a grizzly bear's body, the clawed feet and tail of a catamount, and a nasty disposition. Jean-Luc, who is good-hearted but gullible, believed there might other carcagnes in the neighborhood who might eat him. Yves didn't believe that was likely, but, as he said, Jean-Luc never listens.

I reckoned if his good friend Dureau couldn't reassure L'Archévesque, he certainly wouldn't listen to me. I moved on to learn what and when our next move might be. Our Séli guides and Fast Horse were squatting on their rolled-up sleeprobes, coffee cups in hand, plotting our course. When the others joined us, Crowfoot explained that although we had ridden somewhat out of our way the night before, the ancient boneyard in which we were camped was sure to keep us safe from Blackfoots, who shunned those precincts as the abode of evil spirits, the worst kind of bad medicine. There were several such deposits along the way, he said, and our route to our southward destination would require hopscotching from one to the next to avoid war parties, which would hopefully give wide berth to the whole area.

Whilst we saddled and loaded our pack animals, Anse and I regaled the Irishmen with our experience on the Yellowstone, a dozen years before, when bad medicine saved our collective arse from Blackfoots who refused to pursue our bunch into a neighborhood of spouting geysers and boiling, evil-smelling sulphurous springs. "Shee-it!" Anse cackled, "That'ere whole shebang war a-belchin' an' a-fartin' sulphur smoke wuss'n Pappy bilin' mash in the still an' them'ere Blackfoots wou'n't come nowhars nigh whar we war hid out from 'em. Critters tharabaouts war plumb used to it an' we war livin' high on the hawg on ever' kind o' meat ye kin think of, bilin' it in them'ere hot springs, 'til them sumbitches plumb give up on us an' went on abaout their bizness!"

I include that passage because it was the only time in that entire journey that I recall Anse Tolliver ever expressing pleasure about anything.

As we rode down the coulee past what we could see of those big skeletons mostly buried in sand and soil, I thought the shape of some of them looked sort of like giant lizards, but naturally no lizard could ever get to be anything like that big.

We passed that day and a couple-three days afterwards darting across the open plain from one coulee to another, in a southeasterly direction, unchallenged all the way, hardly believing our good fortune but thanking our lucky stars for it. Now and then we risked the sound of a rifle shot to harvest a buffalo, of which we consumed all but the hide and horns and hoofs, but even that failed to alert an enemy. At last we came in sight of the Great Falls of the Missouri River, a colossal cascade of white water forever tumbling over its rocky ramparts. Crowfoot allowed himself a satisfied grin as he stared down at the swirling eddies at its base. He had brought us unscathed through difficult, dangerous country and it was still September.

༂ ༂ ༂

Although we had thought of our destination as the Great Falls, we still had a way to go downriver before we reached Fort McKenzie, which was located in the Píkuni stomping ground for trading purposes. We would be more vulnerable than ever until we got there. Kipp, the AmFur trader, had told me the fort was located at the mouth of the Marias River, where it spills into the Missouri. We couldn't miss it. Except for maybe running into the whole Blackfoot Nation on our way there.

Before starting out we held a parley in which I explained that we no longer required guides. All we needed to do was to follow the river, so the Sélis were welcome to return home if they wished to do so. To a man and without hesitation they all declared they would stay with us until we reached the fort. I didn't query their reasons, but I suppose Fast Horse had told them that after the fort we would be completing our journey on a big boat, which meant abandoning our critters at the fort. Which was true. They reckoned a few more days on the trail would be a trifling price to pay for all that livestock. And who could blame them?

Besides, the prospect of seeing the "fireboat" we had described, mostly in signs, was too much for the Sélis to pass up. Being able to brag to their fellows of having laid eyes on such a prodigy would be a coup that would last a lifetime.

Three more days of travel through mostly wooded country bordering the banks and bluffs of the Missouri brought us in sight of Fort McKenzie. Although we encountered no challenges on the way, it was plain that there had been a fair amount of human traffic there in the past.

༂ ༂ ༂

Kenneth McKenzie had done himself proud with his namesake fort. It was a substantial affair with high wooden palisades, watchtowers at the corners, and a wide double-doored gate, built on a high knoll overlooking the river, not nearly as large or impressive as Fort Union, but imposing enough in the wilderness.

The gates were closed when we rode across the clearing that surrounded the fort. A sentry called down from a watchtower demanding to know our business. Lacking anything else to tell him, I called out, "Temple Buck and party, on our way to Saint Louis to meet with Pierre Chouteau, Cadet!" Apparently the boss-man's name is magical thereabouts, for after a few minutes, one of the big doors swung open to permit our passage inside.

As we filed inside, I spied a buckskin-clad man trotting across the courtyard to greet us. As he neared I recognized him as Charles Larpenteur, the eager young fellow who had joined Bobby Campbell's packtrain to the mountains in 'thirty-three. "Ah, M'sieu Buck, *bienvenue!*" he shouted. "So good to see you 'ere! Welcome!"

"Good seein' you, Charlie," I greeted him in turn, then, anxious to learn if our arduous journey had been in vain, I demanded, "Tell me, Charlie, has the last steamer come yet?"

"No, not yet," he replied with a broad smile. "You're in luck. Any day now."

Greatly relieved, I rattled off the names of Fast Horse and my trapper companions by way of introduction.

"Charlie," I asked, overcome by curiosity and unwilling to wait longer, "how come we haven't run across a single Indian all the way from Flathead country? Even here, nigh their trading post?"

Larpenteur looked distressed and nodded. "*Vous avez raison. Ni peau ni poil ici aussi!*" Then hastily correcting himself, he repeated, "You're right. We haven't seen hide nor hair of a Pikuni for a fortnight or more. It's the pox. They're terrified. Many have died. Horribly! They've all run off up north to escape it. I wish them *bon voyage et bon chance!*" Then, always the loyal Company man, he added, "It is very bad for business." Remembering his manners, he smiled and insisted, "Come then, please come down from your horses. I will show you to your quarters. It is not a palace, but it is clean and dry."

We dismounted and stripped off our saddles and packs, which several Métis *engagés* lugged off to a long, low building built into a wall of the fort. A couple more led our critters to a large pen at the far end of the broad courtyard. When they attempted to provide a similar service for Crowfoot and his Séli companions, howsomever, they were met with a firm refusal to turn loose either their possessions or their animals.

Larpenteur, evidently accustomed to such behavior by Indians, shrugged and instructed his *engagés* to show our guides to an open hay shed next to the horse pen, where they might bed down and still keep an eye on our critters. Fast Horse looked skeptical when he eyed the wooden building where he was expected to sleep, but, chief's son that he is, he was not about to compromise his dignity by accepting quarters inferior to those of his white-eyes companions.

Whilst Larpenteur showed us to our spartan accommodations, I learned that he was not in charge of the fort, but second-in-command to one Alexander Harvey, who, Charlie warned, is a gentleman of uncertain disposition, capable of sudden rages and implacable grudges, but generally fair and forthright in his dealings. I hoped that Mister Harvey had some experience of mountaineers, who have no patience with self-important bullies and will not tolerate slighting treatment by any man.

Charlie was as good as his word. The rooms were bare, separated by seven-foot partitions, enclosed by a canvas drape for a door, but they were clean and dry. We spread our sleeprobes on the wooden floor and counted ourselves lucky that the roof didn't leak.

It was by then late in the afternoon, getting on to suppertime. Larpenteur escorted us to the dining hall, which also served as the trade room, where we spied a tall, clean-shaven, well-built man seated at the head of a long table lined on either side with benches, much as I recalled seeing at Fort Union when I stayed there in 'thirty-two, except here the table was of rough-hewn planks, unlike Kenneth McKenzie's polished mahogany and snow-white napery.

As we entered, Larpenteur called out, "Alexander, I have brought our guests. They will stay with us 'til the *Piegan* arrives to carry them to Fort Union, then on to Saint Louis." Harvey was just finishing his meal and barely looked up as we took our seats on either side of the table. Larpenteur looked somewhat discomfited but plunged ahead, commencing to introduce us, beginning with me, until his boss waved him off and growled, "I don't give a damn who ye be. Jist mind yer manners so long as you're hereabouts an' cause no trouble an' we"ll git along jist fine!" With that he rose to his feet and stalked from the room.

Just as he reached the door, in what sounded like a single voice, McCool and Harry shouted out, "An' ye be bloody welcome!" I shuddered and braced for a brawl.

Harvey skidded to a halt, cast a venomous look back at us, then shrugged and continued out the doorway.

Supper was brought in by a couple of *engagés* wearing stained aprons, supervised by the cook, a tall, one-eyed, unbelievably skinny French Canuck. He looked none too clean himself but he produced remarkably tasty vittles, especially a savory buffalo stew which we wolfed down to the accompaniment of loud praises, which almost brought a smile to his grim features.

After supper we retired to the stoop that ran along the front of our quarters to smoke and trade palaver. After a spell, McCool suggested that music might make a successful day perfect. Harry rarely needs urging and Anse, after insisting that he wasn't sure he was able to play, dry as he was, consented at last to get his fiddle. Before long Fort McKenzie's courtyard echoed with Anse's Tennessee fiddle and Harry's Celtic *guitarra*, with Yves' battered and oft-patched squeezebox inserting a Gallic tang here and there.

Métis *engagés* drifted into the courtyard to listen, their appreciative murmurs punctuating every tune. Teetotaling Charlie Larpenteur at last minded his manners and came trotting with a jug of fiery trade booze, apologizing for its tardiness. It was raw and nigh blistered the gullet as it went down, but nonetheless welcome after our prolonged abstinence. Ardent spirits, primitive and brutal as that batch was, enlivened our musicians even more and the fort rang with their melodies.

I was roused from my reverie by Finn poking me gently in the ribs and nodding in the direction of the dining hall. I espied the tall, lean figure of Alexander Harvey striding purposefully across the courtyard, a big jug in hand. When the *musicos* caught sight of him, the music trailed off in disorderly squeaks and twangs, but as he neared he called out, "Don't quit! Keep on playin'! Ever'body's lovin' it!" When he spied Charlie's jug of trade booze he roared, "Ach, put that'ere rotgut aside! Ain't hardly fit fer Injuns!" He swung up his earthen jug and set it in our midst. "Here's some proper drinkin' likker fer wettin' yer whistle! Jist keep on playin'! There's more where that'n come from!"

Everybody, even Fast Horse, took a swig of mellow, well-made squeezin's and the musicians picked up their instruments and launched into a lively Irish reel. Harvey moved off a dozen feet and sat, propped against a roof post, his eyes closed, smiling, drinking in the melody.

"Who'd'a thought?" McCool muttered. "'Tis said, music hath charms to soothe the savage beast. I daresay the poet was after knowin' his business."

I nodded my agreement and refrained from telling Finn that the poet said "savage breast." In this case, it was closer to correct the way he said it.

ॐ   ॐ   ॐ

The next several days at the fort presented a sharp contrast with our initial experience of Alexander Harvey. He wasn't exactly charming, but he was civil and even helpful when it didn't interfere with his routine. I was able to explain the purpose of my visit to Saint Louis. When I mentioned Pierre Chouteau, his interest perked up and remained reasonably keen thereafter. I daresay he saw that using the fort as a supply depot for the Flathead, Kootenai, and Nez Percé robe trade might help to assure his future employment.

Likely of greater significance to him, howsomever, was Anse Tolliver's intended project, which, if successful, would provide the fort with a nearby source of reliable grain alcohol that wouldn't poison his Blackfoot customers. He advised Anse on where and how he might obtain a supply of corn for his still, if smallpox hadn't completely wiped out the corn-growing downriver Mandan, Hidatsa, and Arikara tribes, as well as where a bootlegger might locate his enterprise in order to escape the notice of the Army and government revenue agents.

We repaid the fort's hospitality by keeping them supplied with fresh buffalo meat every day and enough extra to dry for future use in the coming winter. Thanks to the Blackfoot exodus from that neighborhood, we didn't need to ride out far in order to harvest all they could use.

Larpenteur invited me to his quarters, which he shared with a pretty little Hidatsa woman, who retreated as soon as she caught sight of me. Charlie's digs were modest, except for his well-stocked library, where I spent most of my time at the fort when I wasn't needed elsewhere. He possessed a remarkable collection of classic and modern writers in both English and French, but the one book that captivated my interest was written by a Greek soldier, Xenophon, three or four hundred years before Christ. It is titled *On Horsemanship* and it contains not a single bit of advice on the care and training of horses that is not just as true and complete today as when Alexander the Great rode off on Bucephalus to conquer the world. I devoured it, page by page, trying to memorize every word, so that I might repeat them exactly whenever I teach Iris and Ben.

ॐ   ॐ   ॐ

Life at the fort was pleasant enough, but I commenced to chafe at the delay after a week. Larpenteur assured me that the steamer would not fail to arrive, for it would be bringing much-needed supplies from Union and picking up Fort McKenzie's valuable cargo of robes and furs to be transported to Saint Louis. Still, I continued to fret, recalling how treacherous the Missouri can be, fraught with ever-shifting shoals and sand bars, vicious snags and sawyers, and a thousand other perils.

When at last I was jolted by a deafening blast of a steam horn and caught a first glimpse of the *Piegan* rounding the river bend below the fort, its smokestack belching clouds of black smoke and glowing sparks, no faithful Christian confident of his Eternal Salvation, upon hearing Gabriel's trumpet announcing Judgment Day, could have been happier than I was at that moment.

Not everyone greeted that apparition with the same enthusiasm that I did. Horses reared, screaming in terror, eyes rolling, hoofs flailing air, some of them falling down in fright. Our Frenchy campkeepers and our Indians, including the usually resolute Fast Horse, stumbled backwards, hands clapping open mouths lest their souls fly off, eyes popping with shock and horror at the fire-breathing monster come to devour them.

Only when the steamer swung neatly in the stream and came to rest against the dock and they saw a gang of Métis *engagés* racing to grab ropes to secure it against the current did they gradually cease to mistrust it. They gained a little more confidence when they saw me start to walk down to the wharf. They commenced to follow hesitantly behind, until the boat's engineer shut down his boiler and released the pent-up steam pressure with an ear-splitting scream that sent Flatheads and Frenchies tumbling over one another in frantic retreat helter-skelter through the open gate of the fort.

I proceeded to the dock, where I introduced myself to the captain, a fresh-faced young man named Ellis Carpenter, explaining my mission and those of my companions, offering to pay for our passage to Saint Louis.

"Oh, we won't be goin' to Sain' Looie," he told me, "only to Union. That's as far as we go." When he saw my face fall, he hastened to add, "From Union on down ye'll go aboard the Yellastone, Cap'n Joe LaBarge commandin'."

My sigh of relief likely rivaled the steam boiler. Carpenter explained that his vessel, the *Piegan*, possesses a shallower draft than the much larger Yellowstone and most other steamboats that ply the lower Missouri, which enables his boat to service American Fur's trading forts located higher up the river than Fort Union. "I hope you an' your friends are ready to leave now," the young captain cautioned. "We're leavin' first thing in the mornin', soon as cargo's stowed." I assured him that we were indeed ready to go, the sooner the better.

As I returned to the fort, three crews of *engagés* were already hard at work, one hauling supplies into the fort, a second stowing bales of buffalo robes and furs and whatnot in the steamer's hold, and a firewood detail replenishing fuel for the steam engine's boiler.

Suppertime that evening came as close to festive as such occasions ever get at Fort McKenzie. The arrival of the supply boat undamaged and reasonably on time is always cause for celebration. The cadaverous, one-eyed French cook, resupplied with fresh groceries, outdid himself in regaling the steamboat captain, engineer, and crewmen with a feast worthy of Saint Louis' finest restaurant—delicious buffalo tongue, succulent roasts, spicy meat pies, and an array of luscious baked desserts. I wondered what felony had driven such a culinary genius to that remote wilderness.

Right after supper we gifted all of our horses and mules to our Flathead guides, as much in gratitude for their loyalty as in payment for their services. Larpenteur had assured me that I would be able to purchase saddlers and pack animals from the fort for my return to the Flathead when I came back in the spring.

Alexander Harvey, seeking to capture one more tuneful evening, plied our *musicos* with his best liquor and kept them playing until he himself fell asleep, a victim of his own jug.

~ ~ ~

The staccato chirp of the steam whistle signaled time to board the *Piegan* for our downriver journey. A black cloud was already thrusting skyward from the smokestack as the boiler built up a head of steam to propel the big paddlewheel on the stern. A crew of *engagés* insisted on hoisting our plunder onto their backs and trotted down to the dock with it. Anse and Harry hung onto their instrument cases, unwilling to entrust them to anyone.

Fast Horse and his Flatheads had parted with us at first light, preferring to avoid a second catastrophe like the day before. As Eagle Ribs had told me that morning, they and their critters would be safely many miles upriver before the ill-mannered steamboat emitted its first evil-smelling fart.

Just as I was about to step onto the wharf, Charlie Larpenteur came running up and thrust a book into my hands. It was his copy of Xenophon's treatise *On Horsemanship*, beautifully-bound and obviously expensive. I tried to refuse, but Charlie insisted. "No, Temple, you must have this book. For you, horses are everything. For men such as me, a mule is only somewhat faster and much less comfortable than walking. Bon voyage, mon ami. Until next springtime."

Another tootle of the steam whistle summoned us aboard. We hustled up the broad plank resting on the dock just before the crewmen hauled it onto the *Piegan*'s deck. *Engagés* cast loose the mooring lines and tossed them aboard. The current caught the prow and swung the craft into midstream, when the engine thundered into action, the boat horn blasted a final salute, and the huge paddlewheel commenced churning, turning green Missouri waters into a foamy white wake.

∽   ∽   ∽

Plentiful late-summer and early-autumn rains upstream on the Missouri helped speed our voyage through a beautiful passage of the river the *Piegan*'s crewmen called the Missouri Breaks. Towering rocky palisades overlooking the river resembled feudal castles and the walled cities of Spanish Moors, evoking fantasies of medieval adventures and feats of derring-do.

The *Piegan* was underweigh every day at first light or if morning mist lay thick and heavy on the water's surface, as soon as it lifted enough for the steersman to see a clear channel through the many obstacles that cluttered the riverbed—floating trees, snags and sandbars, occasional dead buffaloes drifting in the current, and countless other hazards. Only nightfall or stopping onshore long enough to take on a load of firewood provided by AmFur woodcutters halted our downstream passage. Depending on the terrain where dusk chanced to overtake us, sometimes we slept on shore, grateful to be relieved of the constant vibration of the engine and the shuddering paddlewheel. Once the noisy machinery shut down and if enough daylight remained, we often repaid the captain and crew with fresh meat, harvesting a buffalo or wapiti wandering nigh the riverbank.

"There was a time, before the pox, when we would'n'a dared sleep ashore," Captain Carpenter told us, "lest Injuns come fer scalpin' us an' raidin' the boat. Nowadays, 'ceptin' fer a coupl'a friendly Hidatsa villages, I don't hardly never see a redskin along the river or if I do, he's likely hightailin' it north'ards, gittin' clear of us fer fear o' the pox."

Yves and Jean-Luc helped out the *Piegan*'s cook in his cramped galley and Finn patched up the inevitable cuts and abrasions suffered by the crewmen. Anse and Harry provided musical entertainment almost every night. Except for story-telling, the best ones borrowed from Black Harris, I was pretty useless, but nobody appeared to mind.

Carpenter and his engineer, a serious-minded, grease-bedaubed gentleman named Ferguson, took particular pride in putting as many miles of river behind us as possible each day, crowing in triumph if they achieved a "hunnerd-miler." Which was truly an admirable feat, considering the hazardous clutter through which they navigated in the Missouri riverbed.

A dozen days and nights aboard the *Piegan* brought us in sight of the impressive palisades of Fort Union, perched on the forested spit of land betwixt the Missouri and where the Yellowstone spills into it. Anse Tolliver stood beside me at the rail as we approached the shore, his expression unbelieving as he surveyed the large fort itself, the scores of workshops and dwellings that surrounded it, and the Indian encampments that stretched beyond them all the way to the far-off woods. "Shee-it, Temple!" he exclaimed, "An' we thought we war some punkins back when we built ol' Andy's li'l backhouse whar that'n stands naow! It's 'most as big as Sain' Looie, ain't it?"

"Ye been gone fifteen years, Anse," I told him. "Times change. Not necessarily for the better, but there's no stoppin' it."

"Aw, hell!" he muttered, regaining his composure. "No matter how big they git, they're gonna git thirsty an' I'm gonna git rich, begawd!"

Captain Carpenter expertly swung his vessel in the Missouri current and brought it neatly to rest against the wharf with hardly a perceptible thump.

As the *Piegan* snugged close to the dock, crewmen lashed it fast, and the engineer released steam from his boiler with a banshee scream that drained into a querulous hiss, Captain Carpenter descended from his pilot house, a satisfied grin on his boyish features. "Shaved nigh a day and a half off our best time afore this," he announced proudly, "an' hardly a bump an' nary a bruise on the hull doin' it!" Recalling the litter of snags and sawyers and sandbars through which he had threaded on his downriver passage, I reckoned his satisfaction had been well-earned. Just then his attention was claimed by a couple of people emerging from the fort and strolling down the path to the jetty. "Look sharp!" he called out to his crewmen. "Here comes the boss an' his lady!"

A tall man clad in unadorned buckskins and a well-dressed Indian woman were approaching. As they drew nigh, I saw that he was somewhat younger than I and she was strikingly beautiful. "That'ere's Mister Alexander Culbertson, the chief factor," the captain informed us, "an' that's his woman alongside o' him. Ye don't hardly never see 'im without 'er." Whilst they were still out of earshot, he hastened to add, "'Course, if I had a woman purty as that'n, I reckon I'd be keepin' 'er handy, too. She's sure-'nough quality amongst her own people, too, some kind o' Blackfoot princess. Her daddy's ol' Two Suns, a chief amongst the Bloods. Her name's Napawista-Siksina—means somethin' like Holy Snake in her Blackfoot lingo."

The hands had thrown out and secured the gangway planking just as the factor and his wife stepped onto the dock. Mister Culbertson hailed the captain with a smiling welcome and a genial compliment on his speedy upriver journey, which Carpenter modestly acknowledged was the result mainly of good fortune and the skill of his crew. Then, "I'd best be interducin' Mister Buck here. He's on his way to Sain' Looie fer settin' up Injun trade we ain't never had afore now."

It was a clumsy introduction, but it provided an opportunity to identify myself and my companions and briefly describe the purpose of my journey. A single mention of the name Pierre Chouteau, Cadet was enough to capture the attention of Fort Union's chief factor, although I was careful not to presume any favor from that powerful gentleman. The factor and I were both aware, howsomever, that if my plan succeeded, Mister Culbertson and I would be conducting considerable commerce together. He offered us quarters in the fort until the arrival of the Yellowstone and very graciously invited us to dinner that evening, a most welcome gesture after a fortnight of the *Piegan*'s spartan fare.

Our quarters, if not luxurious, were clean and warm and dry. Warm water and a big oaken tub were available in the bath house for whoever desired such affectations, which turned out to be me alone.

I wore my best outfit at supper that evening, which earned Kathleen generous praise for her elaborate quillwork from the factor's wife, who speaks very good English and uses it in a refreshingly direct manner, unhampered by a false modesty too often affected by native women in deference to the fragile pride of their spouses. Seated beside her husband at table, she displayed a lively interest in whatever conversation that occurred, often pursuing a topic with queries intended to expand her knowledge of peoples and events. She appeared to be particularly interested in learning about the Flatheads, Nez Percés, Kootenais, and Pend d'Oreilles and I was more than happy to tell her whatever I knew. It was easy to see that her lifelong position as the daughter of an important tribal chief had equipped her with a rare and refreshing self-confidence fortunately rooted in a vigorous intellect.

Culbertson had gathered his guests that evening at the head of the long dining table amongst his senior clerks. Lesser ranks occupied places farther down the board, below the salt, as the expression used to be. My table companion was an old acquaintance, Mister Hamilton, a very formal English gentleman of advanced years, who had been Kenneth McKenzie's principal clerk and major-domo when I had last visited Fort Union and who apparently still occupies that position. It was likely the old gentleman who informed Alexander Culbertson of the friendship I enjoy with Pierre Chouteau, as he had observed when le Cadet and I had visited Union in 'thirty-two.

We were a congenial company at table, consisting of our people, Captain Carpenter, Mister Ferguson, and a dozen or so Company clerks of varying ranks. Culbertson wears his authority comfortably, in pleasant contrast with what I recalled of his imperious predecessor, Kenneth McKenzie, who had ruled Fort Union with an iron fist. The easy-going banter that prevailed at the long refectory table that evening would have been hushed and restrained and timidly respectful if McKenzie had still been in charge.

The food served that evening was well-prepared and substantial, but it hardly compared with the Lucullan banquets that McKenzie had laid on for his honored guest Pierre Chouteau five years before. This time, watered rum sufficed in place of imported wines, but there was enough of it to loosen our tongues and lubricate goodfellowship. After supper, Captain Carpenter and Mister Ferguson called upon Anse and Harry for musical entertainment and those two worthies, who rarely require much coaxing, willingly complied. The rafters of the dining hall rang with Tolliver's lively fiddle and Harry's full-throated baritone accompanied by the rich strains of his Spanish *guitarra*. The music trebled the friendly warmth that had prevailed throughout suppertime, increasing good feeling and stimulating the flow of palaver.

During a break in the music, the prevailing friendly mood and likely half a bottle of Madeira wine prompted the usually reserved Mister Hamilton to relate to me the circumstances of Kenneth McKenzie's departure from Fort Union, where he had reigned as the all-powerful King of the Missouri. Like many others who have incurred the spiteful wrath of Nathaniel Wyeth, McKenzie lived to rue the day in 1834 that he earned Nat's enmity by treating the Yankee with his customary high-handed insolence and disdain when Wyeth stopped at Fort Union on his way to Saint Louis. Never one to let a slight or an injury go unpunished—as Fitz and Bridger can testify—Nat got even. During his brief stay at Union, the inquisitive Yankee discovered that McKenzie had installed his own distillery at the fort, which is against American law in Indian country. So when Wyeth got to Saint Louis, he assuaged his injured pride by tattling to the authorities, all the way to Washington. Even John Jacob Astor and Pierre Chouteau couldn't save McKenzie. He was sacked and sent packing.

Mr. Hamilton's most attentive listener was Anse Tolliver, who was fairly licking his chops by time the old gentleman finished his tale. "An' what d'ye s'pose happened to ol' McKenzie's 'stillin' hardware arter that?" he queried.

"Oh, I daresay it is stored somewhere around the fort. There will be a record. We keep very precise inventories," he replied with a hint of pride.

When Anse picked up his fiddle again his humor was much improved, downright sprightly, in fact.

῾ ῾ ῾

Next day at dinnertime Anse announced that he wouldn't be traveling with us to Saint Louis. "No need fer it no more," he declared. "I kin git ever'thin' I'm needin' ri'chere in Union an' likely better'n what I mought be findin' in Sain' Looie. This mawnin' ol' Hamilton showed me all that'ere fust-rate 'stillin' hardware what their old boss McKenzie war usin' fer cookin' mash an' I could'na wished fer nuthin' better, no matter whar I might'a done muh lookin'.

"Natcherly the ol' feller warn't 'lowed to sell nuthin' to me on his own hook, so I had to go see the boss-man, Culbertson, abaout buyin' it. At fust he warn't willin' to part with none of it, seein' what happened to McKenzie, but I tol' 'im I mean to take the whole shootin'-match 'way upriver, no whar nigh Fort Union, so's thar ain't no way he kin git hisse'f blamed fer anythang I'll be doin'. Wal, we dickered a spell, 'til he fin'ly come 'round an' lowed that he'd jist as lief git the whole shebang out o' hyar, anyhaow, whar it's doin' nobody no good an' likely to cause 'im trouble someday, like it awready done fer ol' McKenzie.

"Comin' to a price war the easiest part. Once he made up his mind to git rid o' the 'quipment, he named a figger an' I met 'im halfway an' we settled 'baout halfway 'twixt the two. Naow all I got to do is git myself a whole new outfit an' a passel o' trade goods hyar at Union an' hitch a passage on the *Piegan* back up the river to one o' them frien'ly Hidatser villages whar they grow corn an' I kin settle in an' commence cookin' mash."

He looked at me appraisingly and added, "Time ye git back from Sain' Looie next spring an' commence yer tradin' up on the Flathead, I'll have a passel o' good drinkin' likker ready fer ye, Temple." It was plain to see that Anse Tolliver was eager as a schoolboy to resume his original profession, his first love, bootlegging unlawful spirits.

❧   ❧   ❧

At first, time hung heavy on my hands, waiting for the *Yellowstone*, anxious as I was to get to Saint Louis. I daresay that my companions felt the same. The usual distractions of Fort Union were greatly reduced because of the smallpox scare. The various Indian encampments surrounding the fort were nearly deserted, their usual occupants abbreviating their trading visits to a day or so, just long enough to swap furs and robes for settlement wares before making tracks to the relative safety of the wilderness.

Lessened commerce provided Mister Culbertson with additional leisure to spend more time with his guests. Finn McCool and I were able to see more of him and his lady than we otherwise might have done. The factor, an intelligent, well-schooled young man endowed with a broad-ranging curiosity, was intrigued by my Irish friend's intention to return to the East to pursue his medical studies after a decade spent trapping beaver. Finnæus, when he is amongst appropriate company, reverts to the genteel speech and manners in which he was reared and educated, which recommended him to the Culbertsons. Evidently they found my behavior and conversation acceptable enough to include me in their society, as well.

Of particular interest to Culbertson was Finn's varied medical history, first attending formal medical school in Dublin, then adding a decade of practical experience in the Rockies, patching up gunshot wounds and splinting broken bones, as well as learning all he could of native cures and preventions from our old Delaware healer. The factor's curiosity has a practical side. Every sensible man living in the wilderness acquires whatever he can of medical knowledge, especially if he is responsible for other people.

Medical doctors are few and far between and good ones are rarely encountered.

Whilst Finn regaled Mister Culbertson with medical reminiscences—notably Bridger's arrowhead—his lady mined my memory for knowledge of tribal customs amongst the Séli, Shahaptín, Absóraqa, Shoshone, Arapaho and whatever other native peoples of whom I had any experience. As usual at such times, I regretted how little useful knowledge I had acquired in fifteen years, but she appeared to value what I was able to relate.

In the course of the several talks I had with Alexander Culbertson and his wife Napawista, I came to learn that the grilling I received, especially from her, had a practical intent. It is their aim to promote peace and cooperation through trade, wherever possible, amongst the various tribes over which they have some degree of influence. Making war on neighboring tribes is the favorite recreation of most Rocky Mountain Indians, sometimes for traditional reasons obscured in the mists of imperfectly-understood and half-forgotten lore, sometimes for a fancied affront, sometimes for profit, which is rarely realized, and usually at a loss of young men and horses and hard-to-come-by merchandise. However much fun killing and scalping the neighbors might be, it is mostly an expensive, profitless pastime. The Culbertsons would like to replace it with trade and education.

It was Culbertson who established Fort McKenzie, American Fur's trading post amongst the Píkuni. He intends to expand the trade in furs and robes amongst all the Blackfeet, as well as other tribes along the Missouri and as far west as he can reach, demonstrating the while that profitable trade with the whites and not warfare will bring prosperity to the redman. As he spoke of the vision that he shared with his beautiful wife, Culbertson's voice became infused with an almost evangelical enthusiasm, describing what he called a Pax Americana, a universal peace amongst the tribes and with the whites throughout the Rocky Mountain wilderness.

He is, howsomever, no starry-eyed idealist, but rather a knowledgeable businessman, who expects to achieve his aim only one band and tribe at a time and who is prepared to experience setbacks on the way. He encouraged me in the venture I described to him and assured me of his enthusiastic support in future if Pierre Chouteau should agree with my proposal.

We spoke every day during the week that we remained at Fort Union. When at last the *Yellowstone* chugged up the river and moored at the quay, I felt a twinge of disappointment that I would now be deprived of the society of Alexander Culbertson and especially that of his charming and talented wife.

ॐ   ॐ   ॐ

The long voyage down the Missouri from the *Yellowstone* seemed even longer and more tedious than it actually was because of my impatience to get to Saint Louis and learn if Pierre Chouteau would be agreeable to the proposition I intended to present. I had too much time to worry, too much time for self-doubt and second-guessing, and too little to occupy my hands and my mind. I have spent my entire adult life responding to circumstance, doing the next thing with little time for reflection before action was demanded. Now I had too much leisure, too much time to worry and reconsider, rather like the centipede, who lay distracted in a ditch, wondering which leg comes after which.

It had been fifteen years since I had first embarked on a voyage up the Missouri River on Andrew Henry's keelboat, the Saint Pierre, rowing and poling that clumsy ark through the stubborn current, too often a score and more of men dragging it through the shallows on a *cordelle*, shoulders rubbed raw, stumbling for footing on the muddy bottom, laughing and cursing and joking and straining to haul it just one more foot upstream in what seemed to be an endless nightmare of aching muscles and mindless effort, until the journey itself became the only reality, impossible to imagine ever arriving at a destination or knowing any other existence, condemned to a grinding eternity of tugging and towing that ungainly hulk forever westward.

With a few exceptions, that ordeal, tough as it was, welded Andy Henry's company of seventy-odd recruits from all over America and most of Europe into a loyal and spirited unit capable of meeting the challenges of life in a raw and unforgiving wilderness. Over the years since that first summer on the Missouri, the men who made that original journey share a kinship rooted in pride and mutual respect.

Much as I despised that ugly old scow at the time, I am proud to count myself amongst that fraternity.

ॐ   ॐ   ॐ

As the steamboat Yellowstone scudded through the Missouri's muddy depths I marveled at the skill of our pilot, Captain Joseph LaBarge, who possesses an almost uncanny sense where the widest and deepest channel might lie in that constantly changing murky river, as he guides his big side-wheeler through a menacing gauntlet of snags and sawyers and sandbars, meanwhile putting as much as a hundred miles a day behind us, steaming from first light until dusk every day.

This was my second voyage with Captain LaBarge aboard the *Yellowstone*. My first had been five years before, in 1832, when Pierre Chouteau had accompanied his new steamship on her maiden voyage to Fort Union. Unlike the *Piegan*, the modest, shallow-draft steamer we had traveled aboard from Fort McKenzie to Fort Union, the *S.S.Yellowstone* is a large side-wheeler, 120 feet in length and 20 feet wide, with three decks, an altogether impressive vessel.

Naturally we lent a hand as required, according to our various skills. Jean-Luc and Yves helped the cook with his chores in the galley. Finn stayed busy binding up cuts and scrapes and anointing healing unguents onto the constant scalds and burns suffered in the engine room. Harry Yeats' Spanish *guitarra* and rich baritone booming out old sea chanteys and a peck of naughty ditties was always welcomed by a captain and crew hungry for diversion. I provided what entertainment I could by retelling Black Harris whoppers in the evenings, after the *Yellowstone* was forced to anchor or tie up to the bank.

The *Yellowstone* stopped at each of American Fur's trading posts along the river, picking up packs of furs, castoreum, bales of buffalo robes, and whatever other merchandise the company deems valuable. We usually spent those nights aboard, for the steamboat provides more comfortable quarters than the rude accommodations available ashore.

On days when LaBarge shut down his boiler while enough daylight remained, Finn and Harry and I would go ashore and harvest a buffalo cow or wapiti, glad to stretch our legs on dry land and get away from the constant shuddering thumping of the paddlewheel. Fresh meat for a dozen crewmen was always welcome.

Where resident woodhawks were not in attendance, accumulating a supply of firewood for the vessel's constantly-hungry firebox, we usually joined the crew on their wood-gathering chores, a frequent requirement. The *Yellowstone* burns as much as ten cords of firewood every day.

We lost most of two separate days of travel because of huge herds of buffalo swimming across the river, a vast shaggy brown avalanche of massive heads and hairy backs clogging the river, shore to shore, filling the air with their mournful bawling, paying no mind to our impatient steam whistle and blaring boat horn, stalling the steamer's progress until the last little heifer waggled her impudent arse up the far bank.

As the *Yellowstone* passed the mouths of the rivers that feed the Missouri, I revisited in memory many of the scenes of my youth. When we came opposite the Little Missouri, I felt a stab of personal loss from fifteen years before, when a vainglorious scamp called Luther Pike cost Andy Henry four dozen good horses, lost to a bunch of Assiniboine horse thieves for no good reason, simply because Pike couldn't bear to have his authority questioned. I am still bitter over losing those horses, even if I didn't own them.

The Mandan village at the mouth of Knife River is still there with its mud-and-thatch beehive houses, far-stretching cornfields, and vast herds of horses, where we drove hard bargains for horses with good-natured Mandans and Buffalo Calf's Hidatsas—for all the good it did us, as it turned out.

As we steamed past Grand River I saw that the Rees had rebuilt their two fortified villages after Josh Pilcher burned their stockades to the ground in 'twenty-three for killing a dozen or more of Ashley's men.

Coming in sight of Cheyenne River stirred good memories of the first buffaloes that Tuttle and I shot, the biggest critters he or I had ever seen. As Hamish Davidson had counseled at the time, after tasting my first mouthful of buffalo I never savored deer meat again.

When the *Yellowstone* neared Bad River, where I had first laid eyes on real wild Indians fifteen years before, Captain LaBarge advised Harry and Finn and me to keep our rifles handy. "Can't never be sure," he cautioned, "but there's no tellin' with the Teton Sioux if they'll be remainin' peaceable or go back to their piratin' ways. It's best to be ready." Fortunately we were not challenged that time and we slipped on by without incident.

Nearly every river that we passed conjured up a fragment of reminiscence for me. The slow progress of keelboat travel had provided plenty of time to experience and commit new things to memory. Everything had been fresh and unfamiliar in my life at that time. Even the names of the rivers had been exciting in the ears of an untried lad not yet twenty years old—the Chariton, Grand, Kaw, Osage, Kansas, Platte, Niobrara, Little Sioux, Floyd's River, Big Sioux, the James, the White, and Bad River.

Naturally some of those watercourses possess more significance for me than others do. Above the Kaw, just below where the Osage flows into the Missouri, is the site of Mike Fink's infamous destruction of Ashley and Henry's keelboat, the *Bonhomme*, fairly early in the expedition. Tuttle and I had been hunting game all day and were returning to our own keelboat, the Saint Pierre, our skiff loaded with deer and fat geese, when we spied a red-faced Mike Fink aboard the *Bonhomme*, brawling with the tillerman, waving his arms and blustering, making threatening gestures, at last walloping the Frenchy *batelier*, knocking him to the deck, releasing the tiller, letting it spin free in the fast-running current, whirling the big keelboat like a matchbox and smashing the *Bonhomme* against a huge tree in mid-stream. Half a hundred screaming men leapt into the boiling river and we spent the rest of the day and half the night fishing them out of the muddy water. The *Bonhomme* and all it held was lost. I never did understand why Ashley and Henry never turned Fink loose and made him walk back to Saint Louis, but they didn't.

૨૦ ૨૦ ૨૦

It was inevitable that sooner or later I would connect the Culbertsons' dream of achieving a Pax Americana amongst Indian tribes and the whites with my father's wish that I might live up to the name he bestowed on me at my birth, Seewauseekau, A-door-opened, that somehow I might in my lifetime help achieve peaceful understanding and mutual acceptance between red man and white. I confess that I had never believed that there was much possibility of success in achieving that aim, unless an immediate mutual profit could somehow be assured. Trade appears to provide the only practical means to let that happen. Honest commerce will likely establish more effective and lasting peace than government peace commissions ever will.

Ancient tribal enmities are set aside, even if not forgotten, and peace, however uneasy at times, prevails at rendezvous so that commerce may be conducted without trouble amongst the various tribes.

Only the itinerant trader is guaranteed safe-passage in hostile Indian country, his scalp and his merchandise more or less inviolate simply because the promise of his future services is regarded as more valuable than the immediate profit and satisfaction of seizing his goods and collecting his topknot. If you rob him or kill him, he'll never return.

Thinking about the Culbertsons and their idealistic wish to establish a universal peace along the Missouri and in the mountains, it came to me that Kathleen and Turtle's Shoshone wife Tallymesko, together with the other wives, with their knowledge of languages and customs, will prove valuable in conducting trade. Alexander Culbertson doubtless credits Napawista with much of his success in establishing Fort McKenzie amongst the Blackfeet.

I doubt that I myself will ever see a change in the Blackfeet's bellicose behavior—cherished old habits are hard to put aside and making war is fun— but perhaps the Indian trade we conduct will help to make Powatawa's dream come true someday.

∾ ∾ ∾

By time the *Yellowstone* passed through Pawnee country the crew talked of little else but the pleasures of Saint Louis. Naturally Finn and Harry expressed a healthy interest in visiting the fleshpots the boatmen talked about. I, on the other hand, anticipated my first meeting with Lucette with something akin to mild terror, reluctant to injure the feelings of my long-time lover but unwilling to betray Kathleen's trust in my fidelity, if in fact she believed that I would remain celibate for half a year or more. The matter hadn't come up before my departure for Saint Louis, unlike the eve before I left for California, when Cat generously gave me leave to indulge in fleshly pleasures, assuring me at the time that she understood how men must be. That, of course, was before we married.

Signs of settlers commenced to appear along the riverbank, lone cabins in clearings and raggedy white people staring wistfully over the broad expanse of the river as the big side-wheeler chugged past, followed here and there by a scatteration of rude buildings, lean-tos and cabins and occasionally more ambitious structures, that amounted to rude settlements, until at last we swept around a broad bend in the muddy stream and the town of Independence came in sight.

A mighty blast of the boat horn and the scream of the steam whistle announced our arrival at the dock, trumpeting our return from another adventure in the wilderness of the Upper Missouri, but unlike the reception I recalled from my first voyage on the *Yellowstone* five years before, when brass bands and the well-dressed cream of local society turned out to greet us, this time our appearance at the quay caused hardly a ripple of interest amongst the townsfolk of Independence, Missouri.

When I commented on that lack of excitement to Mister Stubbs, the mate, he sighed and shrugged and replied, "It's how folks be nowadays. Nuthin' much holds their 'tention fer long. Allus somethin' new required to keep 'em int'rested."

The *Yellowstone* wasn't alone on the river for the remaining voyage down the Missouri. Several other steamers plied the lower reaches of the river, sounding their steam whistles and boat horns in comradely greeting when we hove into view, saluted in turn by our own.

At last we came in sight of the broad, brown Mississippi boiling with cross-currents and eddies, steadily picking up speed as the Missouri gathered itself for a final slingshot punch that sent the big *Yellowstone* arrowing into the larger stream as if it were a flimsy skiff, while LaBarge and Stubbs and the helmsman fought for control. Once out on the broad back of the Mississippi, I caught a glimpse of the Illinois shore where, fifteen years before, a bedraggled, rain-soaked bunch of pilgrims spent their first night of the great adventure that became the American Rocky Mountain fur trade.

-oOo-

arry and Finn joined me at the rail as the helmsman swung the big steamer expertly to rest against the broad wharf in front of Berthold et Chouteau's mercantile. The throaty bray of the boat horn and the shrill scream of the steam whistle, together with a gentle thump of the hull against the sturdy planks announced the successful completion of an 1,800-mile voyage through some of the most hazardous waters on earth in just twenty-six days—not quite a record, the mate told me, but nevertheless respectable. "Would'a made it a coupl'a days sooner," Mister Stubbs complained, "hadn'a been fer them goddamn bufflers cloggin' up ever'thin' upriver."

The *Yellowstone's* crew heaved half-a-dozen sturdy hawsers onto the dock, where they were eagerly snatched up and made fast by people from the mercantile come to assist us, a cheerful crowd of warehouse workers, mostly black slaves, laughing and joshing one another as they snugged the big steamer securely to the jetty and prepared to empty its cargo holds . Hastening after the good-natured throng was an individual I recognized from many years past, Gaston, Chouteau's sour, skinny, sallow-cheeked chief clerk. The arrival of the *Yellowstone* had summoned him directly from his inkpots and ledgers. He was still stripping the bombazine sleeves from his rusty black tailcoat as he trotted after the workmen.

When the crewmen secured the gangplank in place, Gaston came aboard and proceeded directly to the wheelhouse, where he stiffly informed Captain LaBarge that le Cadet was occupied elsewhere that day. He, Gaston, would certify the kind and quantities of merchandise stored in the *Yellowstone's* cargo holds. Evidently LaBarge had long ago learned to despise Gaston's officious strutting. The skipper merely frowned and nodded brusquely and summoned Mister Stubbs to deal with Chouteau's fussy clerk, turned his back, and declined further commerce with Cadet's humorless counter-jumper.

Gaston looked me full in the face as he passed by, but there was no more than a hint of recognition in his eyes and only a curt nod as he hurried on to address LaBarge. That was not surprising. There was no good reason that he should remember me after my four-year absence from those parts.

Learning that Chouteau was absent from his office that day let me postpone my meeting with him until the morrow. On one hand, I burned to learn his decision regarding my proposal, but at the same time I dreaded hearing him turn it down. I chided myself for such cowardice, but I was nonetheless relieved that I could put off discovering my fate until morning.

My apprehension regarding Cadet's possible response was not without good reason. Although my long-time benefactor had persistently invited me to accept employment in his business for the past dozen years, current circumstances in the volatile beaver trade nowadays might have already erased that opportunity for me and my comrades. The recent example of our friends in Rocky Mountain Fur seeing their hopes and dreams and long years of dangerous hard work come to naught in the changeable *métier* that the fur trade had become was a lesson I could not ignore.

We bade farewell to Captain LaBarge and his crew, thanking them for a safe and speedy voyage down the treacherous Missouri, surprised and gratified at their warm response when they expressed their gratitude for our willingness to lend a hand with their daily chores. "Glad to have ye along on thi'shere last trip o' the season. Most o' the swells we haul on the river need a wet-nurse," Mister Stubbs told me. "You trapper fellas pitched right in from the git-go, helpin' out wherever ye could. Yer bunch earnt yerse'fs a passel o' thankees."

None of my companions was familiar with Saint Louis, so it fell to me to see to our lodgings. When we stepped out on the dock lugging our belongings, we were hailed by half a dozen draymen offering to carry us to a lodging-house, an eating-house, or a brothel, or all three. Fortunately I recalled the name and general location of the comfortable establishment in which Chouteau had installed me several years before. I provided instructions to the teamster and the five of us clambered aboard his wagon in high spirits, content to be treading dry land once more, relieved of the *Yellowstone's* noxious smokestack and shuddering paddlewheel.

A couple of stops at dramshops we passed on the way greatly improved the journey, inspiring Yves to unlimber his concertina, which prompted Harry to bring out his *guitarra* and break into song, joined by Finn and our

Irish drayman, whose tenor voice improved with every additional sip I imbibed.

The pasty-faced little concierge looked shocked when our rowdy crew trooped into the foyer of his sedate establishment, noisy, long-haired and clad in stained and sweaty buckskins redolent of castoreum, bristling with an armory of rifles, pistols, and cutlery, but his look of alarm was quickly replaced with a broad smile when he recognized me and recalled the generous gratuities I had bestowed on him and his fellow *hôteliers* when I had last been a guest there. He clapped his pudgy white palms together and positively purred a welcome as he assured me that I "and all of ze *monseigneurs des montagnes* weel be mos' *confortable* een zis *établissement* . Whatever you may weesh, M'sieu, we weel 'appily provide."

I was glad that my companions, occupied with their joshing, didn't hear that last assurance from the concierge, after their two-month drouth of feminine companionship during the long hike from the Flathead. They would soon be leaving town, but I expected to stay there until spring. I preferred that my quarters not be overrun by a bevy of Saint Louis trollops accustomed to catering to my comrades' baser impulses

Whilst the concierge showed us to our quarters, a spacious apartment provided with four bedchambers and a number of curtained alcoves for an additional degree of privacy, I instructed him to lay on a proper supper worthy of his city's reputation for fine cuisine. Which he did, admirably.

Although each bedchamber was furnished with a bed and a scatteration of chairs and little tables, not surprisingly my companions ignored such affectations and spread their sleeprobes on the floor, then squatted, hams resting on heels, to smoke fresh tobacco and drink and palaver until the arrival of supper. I did likewise.

Michel the *concierge* guaranteed himself a handsome lagniappe when a platoon of smiling waiters trooped into our common room bearing trays of smoking-hot vittles smothered in exotic aromatic sauces—a mountain of baked ham and tender beef and pork cutlets braised to flavorful perfection, whole young chickens stuffed with a dressing of chestnuts and piquant *écrevisses*, hearty roasted canvasback ducks and delicate breasts of carrier pigeons, terrapins boiled in rich bouillon, omelet's containing oysters and only-the-chef-knew-what-else, crispy filets of trout and breaded catfish, an impressive array of fresh vegetables of which I remember the asparagus best of all, towering mounds of fluffy white-bread rolls and slabs of sweet yellow butter, pickles and jams and jellies and preserves, tubs of wine and beer bottles chilling amid chunks of ice, followed by an astonishing array of éclairs and other pastries for which French Saint Louis is famous, assisted to contented digestion by whiskey and cognac. Only buffalo meat was missing, but nobody appeared to mind.

When every man had stuffed himself to a contented torpor, we lay about and smoked and sipped and palavered and nibbled at the remnants of the vittles, until Harry enquired with a sly wink, "And what delights have ye in mind for our further amusement this foine evenin', Temple darlin'? So far, ye've done yerse'f proud, indade, but the night is young."

I was unsure if the Irish harpooner was speaking in jest or if he meant his question seriously, but I took him at his word. I preferred, if possible, to keep my quarters to myself, undisturbed by doxies peddling their wares, after the departure of my friends for their eastern destinations. It was only a matter of time until one of them would enlist Michel to recruit feminine companionship for them and the tubby little entrepreneur would be only too happy to oblige.

Although I had passed considerable time in Saint Louis awaiting the departure of packtrains, my knowledge of its seedier pleasures was limited. I knew of only two establishments where the carnal appetites of my comrades might be satisfied. Lucette's was out of the question, even if, in fact, my rough-and-tough, unwashed, leather-clad companions would even be allowed inside that refined gentlemen's retreat. The other was the bordello of Madame Mathilde in the Vide Poche, Tuttle's former favorite hideaway and still the preferred sanctuary of fleshly pleasures for Moses Harris.

Five well-armed men tramping through the narrow byways of the Vide Poche had little to fear from the toughs and footpads who infest that villainous neighborhood. Vide Poche translates to Empty Pocket, which is the common characteristic of its mostly penniless residents and the almost certain result of an unwise and unwary visit to its precincts. It is an area of docks and warehouses sprawled along the riverfront, teeming with grogshops, gambling dens, and cathouses, shoddy lodgings, pawnbrokers' shops, and cheap eatinghouses, a lodestone for riverboatmen, trappers on holiday from the mountains, visiting farmers seeking adventure, and a variety of brutes and thugs lurking in its dark alleys who are eager to provide it.

Our number and the pistols, tomahawks and other hardware we displayed discouraged thuggery and guaranteed our safe passage through the narrow thoroughfares of the Vide Poche. Our only encounters were with sauntering prostitutes, single or in pairs, trolling the dimly-lighted lanes in hopes of being first to offer their merchandise to customers seeking a cathouse.

Fiddle music screeched out of open doorways and echoed off the close-packed buildings that lined the narrow streets as we made our way from one patch of yellow lamplight spilling onto the cobbles to the next as I tried to recall the route. At last my footsteps slowed and halted, my progress arrested by a faintly familiar façade, certainty growing and jelling. We had arrived.

Inside the open door a large Negro clad in a bottle-green tailcoat, a tall beaver topper perched atop his head nearly scraping the low ceiling, presided behind a high desk, his size and forbidding mien discouraging frivolity, demanding one's respect and attention.

"Temple Buck to see Madame Mathilde," I announced, lacking anything else to say. He made no reply, continuing only to favor me with a stony glare. Then I added, "Tell her Tuttle Thompson."

He frowned but he nodded and left his post, returning half a minute later trailed by Madame Mathilde. She was even larger now than I recalled, preceded by an enormous bosom straining her crimson satin gown, its bare powdered surface bedecked with an acre of shiny necklaces and gaudy pendants, high-piled hair dyed the hue of a raven's wing, rivaled by her eyes, black and hard as obsidian, sunk amid doughy powdered cheeks. Her gaze swept over me. She was not enchanted with what she saw. "Tootle?" she demanded in a cracked, anxious voice. "You tol' 'im Tootle, *n'est-ce pas?*"

"I did," I admitted hastily, "so you would come out here. And ye did."

"Tootle is not 'ere," she persisted. "'E is coming soon, *peut-etre?*"

As quickly and briefly as I was able I explained that Tuttle Thompson would never again be coming there or anywhere else. Evidently she read the grief on my face and in my voice. Then that rawhide-tough old whorehouse madam did a most remarkable thing. She reached out her flabby arms and hugged me into that monumental bosom, burying my face in the fleshy canyon betwixt those colossal udders, and held me there whilst she rocked on her heels and sobbed. Yet, when at last she turned me loose, her painted eyes and powdered cheeks were dry and undamaged.

She swung about on the heels of her satin slippers, snapped her fingers, and called out, "*Venez! Bienvenue!* You 'ave of ze *monnaie, je crois.* You may entair!" conducting us past the formidable Negro doorman and into the brightly-lighted main room. Painted women of varying ages, sizes, and shapes, clothed in flimsy, revealing garments, shuffled amongst the tables, serving drinks and chatting up the mostly working-class customers, here and there leading one by the hand up the broad staircase to the upper storey. A skinny Negro was pounding out a lively, foot-stomping tune on a tinny-sounding upright piano, accompanied by a pair of fiddlers, which immediately captured Harry's attention. Naturally he had slung his *guitarra* on his shoulder as we departed for a night on the town. Mathilde led us to a large table in the crowded saloon, shooing off a trio of scruffily-dressed townsmen nursing mostly-empty glasses, and seating us, snapping her fingers and calling out for serving women to attend us as she did so.

A bevy of scantily-clad doxies descended on our table bearing a couple-three bottles and a dozen glasses and plopped themselves in our midst, scattering amongst us, taking care to display their bosoms invitingly as they leaned on the table, chattering in French and English, according to their reckoning of the origin of their chosen prey. Yves and Jean-Luc beamed with delight at such attention. Harry and Finn, both of them more urbanized in their former lives than our campkeepers had been, looked less impressed but were obviously enjoying the female companionship. Even a couple-three whiskeys failed to improve the charms of the snapper who had selected me as her quarry. Painted lips and eyes, plucked eyebrows, and bleached-blonde hair and layers of crusted white powder on her face and bare shoulders and blue-veined breasts lent her all the natural charm and sexual allure of a puppet-show Judy.

In no time at all a well-oiled Harry succumbed to the musical lure of the tinny piano and fiddle tunes and commenced strumming on his *guitarra*, lending his big voice to the lyrics and introducing some of his own. Naturally Yves produced his concertina. Soon our whole table was invited to move next to the musicians, where liquor flowed like crick-water to our *musicos* and the rest of us.

My female companion was growing more insistent. I pressed a couple of silver dollars into her eager palm to encourage her to remove it from beneath my britchclout, stood up, and took my leave. My bleary-eyed friends hardly noticed. On my way out, I stopped with Mathilde and handed her a gold *Louis* from my much-diminished poke, declaring, "That should take care of *l'addition* for *mes amis*, no matter how horny they get tonight." Her hard black eyes sparkled at the sight of the coin. She bit it, grinned at the mark it left, and called out a blessing as I fled before she could hug me again.

൙   ൙   ൙

I awakened with a clear head and a bellyful of katydids. This would be my day of reckoning. The confidence that had borne me along from the high prairie and down the Missouri had been fragmenting the closer I got to Saint Louis. Now my resolve crumbled like dry driftwood in a cookfire. I am a trapper, not a trader. My proposal rang hollow in my ears. Pierre Cadet would laugh me out of his office.

No matter. Chores, no matter how difficult or unpleasant, had best be done promptly. Putting them off only makes them harder.

I rummaged through my warbag for clean clothes and moccasins, selecting the handsomest of the garments that Kathleen had sent along with me—a quill-encrusted warshirt of nearly-white, soft, linen-thin bighorn leather and brand-new fringed and beaded and belled antelope leggin's, and a new blue woolen shirt that reached to my knees, mostly covering a fresh crimson britchclout, the outfit completed with a new pair of quilled and beaded moccasins—all of which I carefully folded, tucked under my arm, then buckled on my pistol belt and pouches, slung my horn, and headed for the door. My companions had not yet returned from the brothel, but I was confident that that the gold *Louis* I had given Mathilde had guaranteed them generous treatment and probably breakfast in her bordel.

I stopped long enough to drink a *café-au-lait* laced with a *soupçon* of cognac with the ever-present Michel at his desk before stepping into the narrow alleyway and making my way to the sign that proclaimed the services of a *chirurgien-barbier*. Fortunately I had returned through Vide Poche unscathed, so I required only the tonsorial attentions of the barber and his bath-house, his leeches and plasters happily unneeded.

Half an hour up to my chin in a deep tub of gloriously warm water refreshed both body and spirit, after which a close shave and a modest trimming of my shoulder-length hair completed my ablutions. Freshly-appareled in my Sunday-best, I set off for the riverfront through the still-sleepy streets of Saint Louis, marveling at the growth that had occurred there since my departure four years before. Many of the vast empty fields and city lots that I recalled were now crowded with houses and still-shuttered commercial shops and businesses. Towering stacks of bricks and fresh, green, newly-milled lumber promised still more construction. Drays rumbling over the cobbles in the early-morning mist and platoons of drowsy workmen in faded blue blouses shuffling off to another day's labor ensured that Saint Louis town will continue to flourish.

Autumn chill hugged the morning river mist close to the water, but I was able to make out a couple small steamboats thumping their way to the Illinois shore, scattering fishermen's skiffs as they churned past them through the Mississippi sea of *café-au-lait*.

At last I could drag my feet no longer, putting off a confrontation that I dreaded as much as I desired it. It was time to "screw your courage to the sticking-place," as Lady MacBeth advised her husband. I walked to the modest doorway that displayed beside it a small polished brass plaque that identified the premises of **Pratte, Chouteau et Cie.**, nothing more, and entered the gloomy interior, where rows of tall desks half-concealed the bobbing heads of a battalion of clerks on high stools bent over their account books and ledgers, scribbling the fortunes of Pratte, Chouteau et Cie., and to a small degree, myself.

One elevated desk stood out in front of the others, occupied by the chief clerk Gaston, on duty in his shabby tailcoat and bombazine sleeve-guards. He delivered a chilly greeting from his high stool with formal courtesy, craning over a thick ledger to call out in a flat, frosty voice, "*Bonjour*, M'sieu Bock, *bienvenue à Saint Louis. Je crois que* you weesh to meet wiz M'sieu Chouteau. Eef you weel wait 'ere, I weel inform eem of your *arrivée*." Without waiting for a reply, he descended from his perch and trotted down the corridor and gently rapped on Cadet's office door. After a moment, he poked his head inside without entering, soon withdrew it, and hurried back to where I waited.

Wasting no more than a shrug inviting me to follow him, he led me to Chouteau's door, spun on his heel, and returned to his desk. Cadet rose from behind his uncluttered work table, beaming, when I stepped past the heavy oak door. "*Bonjour*, M'sieu Bock, so good to see you once more een *Saint Louis!* Eet 'as been *trop longtemps* zat you 'ave stayed een ze *montagnes* zis time. *Quelle agréable* surprise to see you 'ere!" He waved me to a chair beside his table and pulled on a bell cord behind him, calling out, "*Café-complet, tout de suite!*" as he did so, then turned to me to ask, "An' what ees it zat breengs you 'ere to *Saint Louis, Temple*?" pronouncing my name in French. "*Naturellement*, you are always mos' welcome 'ere," he added with a broad smile.

I mumbled something about wishing to present a business proposition, but he held up his hand, stalling me, "*Les affaires* weel wait! *D'abord, nôtre café-complet et la causerie, la gossip!*" From here he switched out of his quaint English and remained there. Chouteau knows that I understand his Creole French well enough. I reckon he uses his English with me as matter of courtesy and for practice for his business dealings with Americans.

First, he enquired where I was staying. When I told him, he said, "Then you know that our Lucette has married again." I was instantly relieved, but only mildly surprised, for it is not in the ardent nature of that fiery female to remain celibate for long. I told him no, that I was not aware of that event. "Yes," he said with an urbane sigh. "She longs for respectability, but again she has married a wealthy older gentleman of an old French family here, who will likely leave her a widow once again. This time, fortunately, she has restrained her impetuosity and retained ownership of her *maison*, which she oversees and manages from afar, so she will be able to resume her customary responsibilities when the time comes, which it inevitably will do.

"You will doubtless receive a discreet visit from her, before long." I was pretty sure that I would do so.

A servant arrived just then with a large tray loaded with a couple of steaming coffee pots and heaps of flaky *croissants* and delicious light but substantial *brioches*, sweet butter and thick cream, a generous array of jams, conserves, and jellies, the delicious clutter surrounding a small carafe of cognac. The good news concerning Lucette stimulated my appetite and I pitched in with great gusto, slathering *croissants* and *brioches* with butter and sweet cream and conserves and washing them down with great draughts of *café-au lait*, a rare treat for me, for milk and butter and breadstuffs are never met with in the mountains.

Chouteau nearly matched my enthusiasm in consuming breakfast. He is a man of keen appetites, in business, social situations of every sort, and at table. I reckon he must be nearing the half-century mark, but he looks and acts more than a decade younger, active and agile, slim-waisted and muscular, tall and straight, a competent, comfortable horseman, hawkishly handsome, clean-shaven and impeccably barbered, lightning-quick   in movement and response to every new idea. He is as vigorous as a mountaineer. I recollected then that he had been a trader amongst the Osages when he was only sixteen, which might make him even more amenable to my proposition.

When at last we reduced the generous *café-complet* to crumbs, we lighted slim cheroots, leaned back in our chairs, and Cadet fixed with me a friendly but businesslike gaze. "You said that you have business to propose," he said in a level tone. "What is it?"

I wished for a moment then that I hadn't indulged my appetite so liberally, but I plunged headlong into my proposal, rattling uncertainly at first but warming to my subject as I got further into it, perceiving no strong objections, only interest, on Cadet's face and especially in his piercing grey eyes.

I started off saying that I and the rest of the bunch are well-aware that beaver have gone bust, leastaways from what we have been used to, but fine furs and beaver will always be valuable. We are also aware that soft-tanned buffalo robes will soon exceed furs in importance in trade. I told him most trappers can see the day, not far off, when rendezvous will come to an end, that it has been dwindling in profit and importance, hardly worth the effort and expense of the long journey from Missouri. Our bunch wishes to establish a different method of getting robes and furs to market, at first from Flathead country, starting with the Séli, Kootenai, Pend d'Oreilles, Kalispells, and my father's newly-adopted people, the Nez Percé and Palouse. Once word gets around, and it won't take long, other tribes farther out, Coeur d'Alènes, Umatilla, Cayuse, and Yakimas, will find their way to our traders. They won't have many buffalo robes, but they'll trade other profitable goods, such as furs, dried salmon, and such. In time, even farther-away Shoshone, Bonnack, and Crows to the south will come to us or we'll go to them. I refrained from telling him what he already knew, that Indians had become as dependent upon settlement wares as American trappers are, that they cannot live nowadays without guns and gunpowder, cloth and metalware.

Starting with Micah, whom Cadet knows well and values highly, I described each of the dozen men remaining in our bunch, most of them veterans of Andy Henry's original expedition, all of them honest, reliable, hardworking, and experienced in dealing with Indians of every tribe and disposition. In particular I extolled the extraordinary virtues of Brass Turtle as a man who is as qualified as I to run the proposed enterprise, likely moreso.

Recalling my thoughts aboard the *Yellowstone*, I mentioned Culbertson's admirable Blackfoot wife Napawista, reminding him of her likely influence in getting her people to allow the construction of Fort McKenzie, then pointing out the importance of our Indian wives in developing and maintaining good relations with our Indian trading partners.

Now and again Chouteau interrupted me with an incisive query or request for additional information, but for the most part he let me run on.

At last I brought out the crude map Finn and I had drawn, tracing the pack-animal route we had blazed through the forests and mountains betwixt the Flathead and the prairieland nigh Fort McKenzie on the Missouri, confirming the practicality of transporting trade goods to the mountains from a warehouse at McKenzie and bringing back valuable wilderness produce to the Fort and steamboats to transport it to Saint Louis.

I finished by pledging to invest all that I possess, joining with his capital and expertise, in the venture, convinced as I am of its practicality and its all but certain success.

Cadet asked few questions as I exposed my plan. At last I pretty much ran out of breath and fell silent. He, too, sat unspeaking, heavy-lidded eyes downcast, evidently deep in thought, his face expressionless, before he straightened, smiled, and fixed a steady gaze upon me, demanding , "Why, Temple Buck, do you wish to engage in this enterprise? You know that you possess enough money so that you need never turn your hand at work of any sort for the rest of your life. Why, then, do you propose to abandon the comforts of a civilized existence and risk your life and your fortune in a hard, dangerous, uncertain, risky career that could very well leave you a pauper or dead at an early age?"

He caught me flat-footed, unprepared for such an incisive question. I had rehearsed this interview for weeks and months, but I had not anticipated his thrusting straight to the bone like that. I felt my face go crimson. I choked, then blurted without thinking, "Because I must! You have your *métier*! I have mine!" You have your Saint Louis and the world. I have all I need or will ever want in my mountains! You know your business better than any other merchant in America, maybe the whole world. Could you give it up? Retire? I know my trade and my people in the wilderness. There can never be a life or living elsewhere for me!" I likely didn't get it said precisely like that, but that's the gist of it. Embarrassed at my outburst, I settled in my chair and stared at him. He remained impassive, unsmiling, apparently deep in thought for a spell.

"*D'accord!*" he barked, slamming his fist on the polished table. "You shall have your wish!" He hesitated a moment before he added with a thin smile, "After we work out a few particulars, naturally."

My heart grew big. I felt my cheeks stretch in a broad grin.

"Naturally there are many details to resolve and many things for you to learn," he said, "but you will be here throughout the winter. There is time enough." He swept a neat stack of papers closer to him and commenced to riffle through them. It was time to depart. I had succeeded. As Tuttle used to say, "Quit when you're ahead." Now was no time to dally.

As I got to my feet, Chouteau looked up at me with a friendly gaze and a warm smile. "This, Temple, is what I have wished for a long time, with you in my company, from your first return from the mountains with Fink's fortune in your hand, ten years ago, as I believe you have been aware. We will make this a success."

Gaston hailed me as I passed his desk on my way to the door, leaning down from his perch to hand me a heavy leather poke. "M'sieu Chouteau 'as instructed me to provide you wiz zis *monnaie d'or et argent*," he informed me in his stilted English, his tone formal and remote. I heard the dull clink of gold and the bright ring of silver as he dropped the bag into my hands. Its weight was considerable. I nodded my thanks and tied it onto my pistol belt. Then I asked Gaston to total up the accounts of my four companions as well as that of Tuttle Thompson. They would be withdrawing their savings from Pratte, Chouteau et Compagnie later that day and traveling aboard the next steamboat bound for Cincinnati or river ports east of there on the Ohio. He consulted a gazette on his desk and informed me that the *Pride of Cincinnati* was scheduled to depart Saint Louis at four o'clock that day. I told him to book passage on it for all four of them and deduct the cost from my account, a final gift for my companions.

My moccasins hardly touched the cobbles as I sped back to the lodging-house, where I discovered my bleary-eyed comrades lately returned from

Mathilde's. They cheered when I told them of Chouteau's acceptance of my proposal, but the response was less enthusiastic when I announced that they would be leaving town on another steamboat that very afternoon. "An' jist when I was gittin' me shore legs back agin," Harry lamented. "Oh well, the sooner I git to Boston town, the closer Californy'll be fer me."

Gathering their plunder took little time and Michel had a dray waiting at the door. We stopped on the way at an eating-house renowned for its chef and especially its elaborate cocktails, stuffing ourselves with the fine cuisine of Saint Louis and saluting one another with the talented barman's mysterious concoctions of flavorful spiritous liquors and exotic ingredients, pledging lifelong friendship although we would likely never see each other again,   celebrating our camaraderie a glassful at a time. When I addressed Finnæus with one of Paddy's favorite well-wishing toasts, "May the road rise up to meet ye!" Finn ruefully confessed that the cobblestones in Vide Poche had done exactly that on the way back to our lodgings earlier that day and he had the bruises to prove it.

Reviewing accounts at the mercantile and cashing out their savings accumulated over their several years in the mountains turned out to be a joyous occasion. Chouteau belied his tight-fisted reputation. He had been generous with the interest their monies had earned. Yves and Jean-Luc were round-eyed with wonder at the pile of hard money that rose up before each of them, chattering excitedly of what such fortunes would buy in Quebec. Gaston scratched and scribbled and rattled his abacus as he tallied the accounts of Harry Yeats and Finnæus McCool. Cadet accepted without question their receipts for the furs they had turned over to American Fur at rendezvous. Neither of them could quit grinning when the totals were reckoned at last.

Finn's greatest surprise came with the reading of Tuttle's simple last will and testament, in which he bequeathed all his worldly goods and wealth to his Irish friend, signed in Tuttle's shaky scrawl as he fought to stay alive long enough to get it done and witnessed by Brass Turtle and myself. Naturally Cadet presided over that matter, his solemn expression reflecting Finn's and my own. When the final reckoning was reached, McCool visibly paled under his deep suntan and windburn. It amounted to nearly all the profit Tuttle Thompson had realized during fifteen years of beaver-trapping and trading, as he had told Turtle and me with his dying breath. His sharp eyes and dazzling dexterity at the Indian hand game and his greasy deck of cards had kept him in booze and his modest need of merchandise at rendezvous, so his trapping profits and winnings in plews kept piling up. I doubt Tuttle ever reckoned how much, nor cared if he did.

"Saints presarve us!" Finn choked out when Gaston slid the paper bearing the total figure before him. "This'll be after lettin' me get a surgeon's shingle, as well as me physician's license, at the medical school in New York.

His remark caught Cadet's attention and he questioned McCool further about his plans to attend medical school. It was a subject dear to Finn's heart, especially now that Tuttle's bequest assured its success. He described his history and his disappointment at being unable to complete his medical studies in Ireland and his brief association with Doctor Marcus Whitman, producing from his pouch Whitman's glowing letter of introduction to the Fairchild Medical School in upstate New York. Chouteau read the letter carefully, nodding his approval as he did so. Then he advised Finn and Harry to accept most of their new-found wealth in the form of a *lettre de crédit*, lest they be robbed along the way, and provided them with the addresses of his correspondents in Boston and one in the neighborhood of the Fairchild School in New York state, who would convert those letters of credit into cash money, which they agreed to do.

He refrained from offering that safeguard to Jean-Luc and Yves, who would never have accepted anything less than hard money that jingled in their pokes.

We made two more stops on our way to the dock where the *Pride of Cincinnati* awaited, first at Hawken's gun shop, where, mindful of Cadet's mention of robbery, I had Jake provide each of them with a double-barreled belly gun and fixin's, then a mercantile, where Harry and Finn purchased settlement clothing more suitable to civilized climes than their clouts and greasy buckskins. Yves and Jean-Luc disdained such affectation, declaring that their *Quebeçois* friends and relations would run them out of town if they showed up looking like *gentilhommes anglais!*

There was little time for farewells by time we got to the dock where the *Pride of Cincinnati* was already splashing and chugging and belching spark-filled black smoke, straining at its hawsers. Crewmen were rattling the gangplank, preparing to haul it aboard. A brief *abrazo* all around and muttered well-wishes sufficed for leave-takings of men who had shared hardships and dangers as well as joyous celebrations, but that made it no less heartfelt and indelible in my memory and I daresay in theirs.

I watched the steamer disappear in the late-afternoon mist on the Mississippi, sentimental Jean-Luc still standing at the rail waving farewell to the great adventure that will doubtless found the lore of his future clan in faraway Quebec.

I turned my steps toward my lodging-house, stopping only at a stationer's shop to purchase a ream of foolscap, steel pens and ink blocks, a couple handfuls of wooden lead pencils, and rubber erasers. I had already resolved to write this final chapter in the history of the American Rocky Mountain fur trade and the men who made it happen, although at that time I had no idea that it would require so many words scribbled on so many heaps of foolscap or cause so much distress for my editor, Mister Euphemius Hobbes, who frets about its great length and the difficulty of publishing it in a single volume. Mister Hobbes usually worries about my plain honest talk offending the sensibilities of well-brought-up young women, so this gives him a suitable diversion from that concern.

I lugged my purchases back to the lodging-house, where Michel exchanged my present apartment for comfortable quarters of roughly half that size, took my supper in my rooms, then set to work that very night on this history, revisiting the people, places, and events that have made up my life during these past four years.

એ એ એ

It should come as no surprise to a thoughtful reader that nothing very exciting occurs in a writer's life when he is practicing that craft, nothing much, that is, that happens outside his own mind. But once he conquers his fear of a blank sheet of foolscap and surrenders to memory, it is possible to return to and relive real-life experiences on paper, good and bad, frightening and humorous, tender and brutal. Naturally keeping a journal is a tremendous aid to recollection.

There is little to record here of my activities during the next several months. I pretty much lived the life of a hermit, keeping to my rooms, taking most of my meals there, and scribbling this final installment of the history of my life and that of my comrades in the fur trade, fulfilling my promise to my mother, burning gallons of whale oil in the lamps on my writing table and covering acres of foolscap with my personal account of that time in our lives.

Soon after I took up residence in my lodging-house I paid a visit to Mister Euphemius Hobbes at the *Missouri Republican*, where he is employed in an editorial capacity, and engaged his services to prepare my new manuscript for the printer. He presented me with a copy of *Shinin' Times!*, the narrative of my life in the mountains in the years 1828 to 1833. Although Hobbes and I are engaged in constant warfare over what I write about and how I describe it, he keeps his word not to alter my manuscript further than correcting my grammar and spelling. Hobbes is a puritanical prude, a self-appointed guardian of America's literary reputation and especially the sensibilities of the fair sex and the morals of unmarried virgins in particular, but once he agrees, however reluctantly, to render my text as I write it, he does so.

A few days after that I was summoned by a loud rapping on my chamber door, delivered by Israel, Lucette's long-time Negro major-domo. Israel hasn't changed much since I first beheld his imposing presence fifteen years ago, still straight-backed and gigantic, imposing in his gravity, commanding respect for his mistress and himself. The principal difference nowadays is his wardrobe, no longer the bright reds and grass-greens and electric blue frock coats and yellow breeches of yore, but now a butler's formal black tailcoat and trousers, the only concession to his former flamboyance a colorful floral waistcoat discreetly peeking past his lapels. He nodded briefly in a wordless greeting, barely changing his sober expression, and inclined his head to one side, where Lucette waited just out of sight.

She brushed past him then and swept through the doorway, grasping my hands in hers as she did so and holding me at arm's length, gazing into my eyes and exclaiming, "Oh, *cheri*, you 'ave not change! Still *mon beau garçon! Les montagnes* 'ave been kind to you!" and a spate of similar flattering nonsense.

Her compliments were better applied to herself. Lucette appeared not a day older nor a whit different from the day we bade farewell four years before, still fashionably attired, her *café-au-lait* complexion flawless and unlined, bubbling and vivacious, dark eyes dancing, chattering with lively good humor, except that she continued to hold me distant, unlike former times when she would have long since melted into my arms, until she whirled with a flutter of swirling silken skirts and petticoats and sank onto one of my fragile chairs, turning loose my hands as she retreated.

It was plain to see that my long-time lover was nervous, concerned that I might seek to renew our amorous relationship. I hastened to relieve her fears. "Cadet has informed me of your marriage," I told her in as formal French as I could muster. "I wish you and your husband every happiness and I respect that gentleman's honor and your own completely."

Her relief was immediately apparent. The strained look faded and her good humor became genuine. I launched into a recitation of my own good marital fortune, which met with somewhat less enthusiasm than my own, but I should have expected that cool response from a former lover. I rattled on about Kathleen, Iris, and especially young Ben, using those anecdotes as logs in a barricade, lest she and I be tempted to breach our spousal vows. Lucette is a beautiful, desirable woman and my own resolve might prove too fragile to refuse an invitation. I was glad that Israel lurked just outside my door.

She told me about her present life and her newfound respectability, describing her new husband, his old New Orleans and Saint Louis family connections and social position, and his business activities, but she avoided mention of his age, as well as her continuing arm's-length supervision of her *maison*. Naturally I refrained from enquiring into either matter.

After a pleasant hour-long chat, she took her leave, promising to return soon, bestowing a chaste peck on my cheek and a friendly squeeze of my hand, nothing more, as she departed.

At suppertime that day, a lavish evening meal replete with champagne wine from France and a bottle of cognac arrived in my rooms, not from the cuisine of my lodging-house but from one of the finest restaurants of Saint Louis, served by two liveried waiters accompanied by Michel, who informed me that my elaborate repast had been provided by my guest of the morning.

I have not seen Lucette since that day. Perhaps it is just as well that way.

∾ ∾ ∾

Chouteau had warned me that I would need to learn the Company's customary methods of record-keeping—accounts, requisitions, inventories, and such—which is my least favorite interruption of my preferred activity, which is writing this history. My instructor in that dull discipline is the imperious Gaston, whose unforgiving world consists solely of inflexible numbers, in which there is no humor or humanity, sentiment or supposition, or allowance for the unforeseen occurrences and accidents that beset daily life, especially in the wilderness. For Gaston, if it doesn't add up, it is unacceptable. Any error or deviation, no matter how slight, is a mortal sin. There are no venial sins in his catechism.

To my credit, I put up with that petty tyrant through seemingly endless training sessions, learning the rudiments of the Company's double-entry accounting and a host of other arcane clerkish procedures, even to haughty Gaston's grudging acceptance, all the while without thrashing that overbearing bully even once.

Much more pleasant are my meetings with Cadet—usually conducted in French, for his comfort and, he explains, my instruction—which frequently take place over dinner at a restaurant in town. He enlightens me about the world of commerce in America and Europe and even the Orient, where he deals in the raw materials we supply from the wilderness and obtains the manufactured wares we use in trade, ideally extracting profit from both transactions.

Sometimes we simply enjoy each other's company, often chatting about my life in the mountains. Chouteau possesses tremendous curiosity about Indians, their customs and habits, likes and dislikes, their needs and wants.

Not long ago he startled me when he said, "I have enjoyed reading your books, all three of them, once I learned how to interpret the speech of your comrades and the other trappers. It is not precisely the English language they employ, is it?" He paused, obviously curious about the shocked expression that must have occupied my phiz. "You didn't know that I have read your work, Temple? I bought your books from your M'sieu Hobbes a couple of years ago. Doubtless he was short of funds, as he often is. I employ him now and then, writing business letters in English for me and correcting some of my own.

"No matter. I have enjoyed learning of your adventures and the daily life of a trapper in the mountains. I assume that you will be writing another installment of your history during your stay in Saint Louis this winter. I look forward to reading it." My mind was racing over the oceans of words I had scribbled, wondering if I had written anything that might offend him, when he must have read my mind. "Don't be troubled, Temple. You have been more than generous in your remarks about me in your books." He chuckled and added with a wry smile, "Much kinder than most people are when they talk about my business dealings."

~ ~ ~

So that is how I embarked on a new and different career, that of a trader dealing in buffalo robes, furs, and whatever else of commercial value the

Indians bring to swap for the settlement wares on which they have become as dependent as their white-eyes brethren are. It hurts to think that my trapping days are over, leastaways mostly, that I will never again set out to explore some unknown yonder where only Indians have trod before, but I console myself with the knowledge that I have already seen a few of those and, besides, not many such places still exist. My fraternity of mountaineers likely numbered no more than a thousand men over the fifteen years since the first of us came up the Missouri, but we have thoroughly combed the mountains, the prairies, and the deserts in our unremitting quest for beaver, never enough to satisfy a trapper, no matter how many he harvests.

Greed is what brought most men to the mountains, but few have gotten rich from trapping. Getting outfitted for another season, replacing lost, broken, or stolen gear, and a two-week drunken spree at rendezvous leaves most trappers broke or in debt to the traders, who are the only ones amassing wealth. What mainly keeps a free trapper in the wilderness, with all its privations and perils, is the absolute, limitless freedom of his life in the mountains. He calls no man boss. He knows no authority past the natural forces that govern the world. If he is tough enough, smart enough, and lucky and plucky enough to survive hostile Indians, ferocious grizzlies, hungry catamounts, rattlesnakes, and wolf packs, scorching summers and freezing winters, starving times and waterless deserts, when a broken leg can mean your death, he can know total, unrestricted freedom such as no man in any human society with its manners, rules, and laws has ever known. It's not for everyone, but once you've tasted such freedom, it is almost impossible to settle for less.

Naturally it is not possible to exercise absolute freedom at, say, rendezvous, wild and rowdy though such gatherings are, where everybody is armed with all sorts of weapons, so the free trapper stows his need for unrestrained liberty in his poke while he's slaking his thirst and replenishing supplies. He can give it free rein once he's off alone and on his own.

Naturally, once a mountaineer takes an Indian wife and sires children, he gives up a certain amount of that freedom. How much depends on him and her. If it's worth it depends mainly on her.

Freedom is only a part of what draws me back to the mountains. The sheer natural splendor of rugged, snow-covered peaks towering into the clouds, their pine-clad shoulders sloping into green and golden prairies stretching out of sight into a blue haze on the horizon, after all these years, still makes me catch my breath in wonder and admiration. Being one with such natural beauty at every turn is a powerful incentive never to leave it.

It is now early May 1838. I will soon board a steamboat to travel up the Missouri to Fort Union, then to Fort McKenzie, where I will store the trade goods for our enterprise, then retrace the trail we blazed back to the Flathead to rejoin my comrades and especially my beloved Kathleen and my children.

Mister Hobbes will doubtless breathe a sigh of relief when he bids me *adieu*, for he keeps cautioning that this account of the final years of the American Rocky Mountain fur trade has run overlong. Even so, I have fulfilled the promise I made to my mother before her death in Whynot, Ohio, thirteen years ago. She made me promise that I would record my fur trade experiences on paper. Now I have done so. There will be no more books after this one.

I wish that my mother could have read the four books I have written at her behest. I doubt that she would have blushed overmuch, if at all, at some of the earthier accounts I have included. She was an eminently sensible woman with a clear-eyed view of the world she lived in. She understood that its imperfections are what makes it perfect.

FINIS

ABOUT THE AUTHOR

Edward Louis Henry (a.k.a. Poredevil) has been a working cowhand, rodeo contestant and Wild West performer, WWII infantry sergeant (Pacific), newspaper reporter, U.S. Foreign Service officer, and executive speechwriter, plus thirty years in advertising. A lifelong horseman and outdoorsman, Henry is active in mountain man rendezvous. Western history is his abiding passion. Henry, a member of Western Writers of America, is the author of *Poredevil's Beaver Tales* and the Temple Buck Quartet: *Backbone of the World, Free Men, Shinin' Times!* and *Glory Days Gone Under*.

<u>Other Books by Edward Louis Henry</u>

THE TEMPLE BUCK QUARTET
A Rocky Mountain Odyssey
1822-1837

Volume I: Backbone of the World, 1822-1824 is a coming-of-age story of the first two years of the Rocky Mountain fur trade, 1822-24. It is told in his own words by Temple Buck, an Ohio-born lad whose rollicking tale begins with growing up in the Ohio wilderness, how he is kidnapped aboard evil Mike Fink's keelboat, is rescued by a beautiful St. Louis madam, and finally enlists in Ashley and Henry's
first expedition up the Missouri River to the beaver-rich Rockies and a wealth of adventure and undreamed-of new experiences. This painstakingly researched tale blends historical and fictional characters in a colorful tapestry of actual events spiced with bloody battles, Indian customs and characters, homespun humor, and earthy romance. If you've ever wished for absolute freedom and hair-raising adventure in the early Old West, come along with Temple and his trapper companions and breathe the free, pure air of the Rocky Mountains!

Volume II: Free Men, 1824-1826 chronicles the exploits of Temple Buck and his rowdy trapper companions in the American Rocky Mountain fur trade from 1824-1826. In this, the second volume of the Temple Buck Quartet, they push ever farther west in their quest for beaver pelts, exploring new country and encountering fresh adventures, some of them welcome, others not at all. This well-researched tale, told in Temple's own words, blends historical and fictional characters against a colorful backdrop of actual events, pungently flavored with gory battles with hostile Indians, homespun humor, and earthy romance, culminating in Temple's disappointing return to his Ohio birthplace.

Volume III: Shinin' Times!, 1828 – 1833 Temple Buck returns to the

Rockies, rejoining his trapping bunch and picking up the free, unfettered life of the American free trapper where he left off in 1826. He and the other members of his trapping bunch explore uncharted new country and gain new and different experience in a changing and expanding fur trade. Their personal lives change, as well, as they take on new responsibilities while continuing to enjoy the happy-go-lucky life of the Rocky Mountain free trapper, its rich flavor much improved now by their wider knowledge, deeper experience, and greater appreciation of everything that living in the American wilderness can provide for men who possess the savvy and smarts and courage to survive on Nature's bosom.

Volume IV: Glory Days Gone Under, 1834-1837, is the fourth and final volume of the Temple Buck Quartet. All things, good and bad, come to an end. Fashions change and human greed injures even all-bountiful Nature. Faraway factors in Europe and the American East destroyed the market for beaver pelts, which occurred just when beaver were growing scarce in the mountains. Without a market, pelts were worthless. The mountaineer's income was wiped out. White settlers, following trails blazed by the early trappers, were moving west, bringing with them families, farming, civilized customs, laws, and missionaries, all of which the trappers despised, corrupting the Indians and crowding them off their ancestral lands, all in the name of a Manifest Destiny that mountaineers, tough, resourceful, and courageous as they were, were powerless to resist.

Poredevil's Beaver Tales You can almost hear the voice of a tough, experienced early 19th century mountain man in this collection of 24 humorous mountain man tall stories and poems narrated in a loose sort of verse. All of the stories contain glimpses of the difficult and dangerous life of that rowdy breed of men who challenged America's uncharted wilderness and who survived and triumphed because of their courage, fortitude and unquenchable laughter in the face of hardship and peril.

http//:christophermatthewspub.com